LIFE AS A
LITERARY
DEVICE

*A Writer's Manual
of Survival*

LIFE AS A LITERARY DEVICE

A Writer's Manual of Survival

VITALI VITALIEV

Beautiful
Books

www.beautiful-books.co.uk

Beautiful Books Limited
36-38 Glasshouse Street
London W1B 5DL

ISBN 9781905636440

9 8 7 6 5 4 3 2 1

Cover design by Ian Pickard.
Typesetting by Peter Ward.
Printed and bound in the UK by CPI Mackays, Chatham ME5 8TD

In fond memory of my mother,
Rimma Mikhailovna Rapoport.

and

To 'Natasha Anne Webster, Australian artist'.

'The lives of writers are a legitimate subject of inquiry; and the truth should not be skimped. It may well be, in fact, that a full account of a writer's life might in the end be more a work of literature and more illuminating . . . than the writer's books.'

V.S. NAIPAUL

'. . . But the acts have been ordained,
Irreversible the journey's end.
I'm alone. The Pharisees swamp all.
Living is no country stroll.'

BORIS PASTERNAK, *Hamlet*

'A bird sings because it has a song, not because it has an answer.'

A Chinese proverb

Nothing short of death can stop me from telling this story.

Unwritten books

Books get unwritten for different reasons . . . Like human foetuses, they either survive and get born or die in the womb.

They can also be aborted.

A giant television screen above the bar was dispassionately blank. Its emptiness was unnerving and yet somehow reassuring, for we were not looking forward to what we knew we were going to see. The barman—a typically Dutch young man, with prominent features and a waterfall-like mane of straight blond hair, was fiddling with the controls trying to galvanise the TV set into action; all in vain.

Amsterdam wakes up late. At midday, it often feels like London does at 7 a.m. Apart from the barman, my eldest son Mitya and I were the only people in the seedy pub off Nieuwmarkt at this pre-lunch hour on Tuesday, 11th September, 2001—Mitya's twenty-first birthday. We dashed into it at random after checking our emails at an Internet café next door. It was there that Mitya received a call from one of his mates in Melbourne on his mobile phone. It was late evening in Australia, and lots of people were watching television before going to sleep.

'A plane has just hit one of the Twin Towers in New York,' Mitya's friend said. 'Switch on your telly immediately!'

There was no 'telly' at the café. Instead, we tried to access first the CNN, then the BBC websites. In both cases, access was denied: apparently too many people were trying to log on to them at the same time.

We ran out of the café and popped into the nearest pub. 'Have you got a telly? ' Mitya asked the barman. 'Allegedly, a plane has just crashed into the Twin Towers . . .'
We had to try three different pubs until we found one where a TV set was actually working. Several worried patrons, mostly tourists, were already huddled around it.
With utter disbelief, we watched the second plane hitting the South Tower, next to the North one, already ablaze, still trying to fight away a painful realisation that our world and our lives would never be the same again.

'Damn it!' Mitya muttered through clenched teeth. 'You shouldn't have come here, Dad.'

I understood him immediately. His remark had nothing to do with not wanting to see me. We had always been very close, even after my separation from his mum (or rather her separation from me), with me living in London and him in Australia, and I was overjoyed, when at the age of twenty and without any pressure from myself, he interrupted his university course in Melbourne and came to Amsterdam. He found a job and a flat overlooking a canal, and we started seeing each other often. Having missed several of his previous birthdays, I was particularly looking forward to his twenty-first.

Mitya was simply reminding me of what had happened during one of my previous visits to Amsterdam ten years before, in August 1991. My KLM flight Melbourne-London (I was going to London from Australia, where I lived then, to promote my second book *Dateline Freedom*) included a free stopover in Amsterdam which I decided to use walking off my jet-lag and preparing for numerous publicity functions in the UK.

For the first two days I was staggering along the canals as if drunk, overwhelmed by the half-forgotten smells of a European summer and by the peculiar Amsterdam fragrance of canal water and tulips mixed with a faint whiff of cannabis smoke. On the second night I went—alone!—on a candle-lit dinner cruise along the canals. Surrounded by snogging homo- and hetero-couples, I wouldn't have been surprised to discover that going on such a 'romantic' cruise on one's own constituted a minor offence in Holland. But I didn't mind my loneliness in the least. The boat was sliding noiselessly under the bridges, and the reflections of burning candles were wriggling in the water like some restless fiery serpents. I remember feeling such indescribable happiness at being back in Europe after many months down under, at being reunited with the smells and sounds of my childhood that I couldn't help thinking: this simply cannot last. From experience, I knew that one could only feel such bliss on the eve of a disaster.

The following morning, the military coup took place in Moscow, where my mother was still living. Barred from returning to the Soviet Union as a recent defector, I spent the next several days trying—in vain—to get through to her by phone, from Amsterdam, from Brussels, and then from London, but was only able to speak to her after the putsch was defeated. Having given up smoking six months earlier, I lit up again on the first day of the coup and had now been unable to quit for over seventeen years.

Curiously, I experienced a similar near-blissful feeling on the night of 10th September, 2001, when Mitya and a bunch of his cosmopolitan Amsterdam mates dragged me into a disco—the first disco I had visited in my entire life. I tried to resist, saying I was too old for it, but they persevered, and, fuelled by a couple of

Amstels, I soon found myself twitching and shaking next to my son in the middle of a crowded hall. Contrary to my expectations, I was enjoying everything: the music, the open and civilised faces of my fellow dancers of whom— I was pleased to note— I was far from the oldest, the fact that everyone in the disco was bouncing strictly within his or her imaginary little square, never trespassing into someone else's. At some point, a young Dutch woman came up to Mitya and whispered something in his ear pointing at me. 'What did she say?' I yelled trying to outcry the deafening techno beat. 'Have I done something wrong?' 'No!' my son screamed back. 'She told me that looking at the two of us she had guessed we were father and son and that it was very nice to see us dancing together . . .'

Dancing in an Amsterdam disco with my own grown-up son . . . I had never thought I would live to see this happen.

It was then that I felt the same creeping feeling of foreboding I had had ten years before. On the way back from the disco, I shared it with Mitya. It was already early morning of 11th September, 2001.

I had never seen my boy's face look as serious and adult as when we were watching the first reports from New York that afternoon.

Still in denial, I couldn't help noticing that on the TV screen the two mutilated Towers did look like an open book, skewered and shredded by some giant barbaric scissors, as if the planes had indeed just flown through the pages of my unwritten book on the United States, the product of the three-year-long painstaking research that took me to thirty-nine states of the Union.

After what was now happening in front of my eyes, I realised very clearly I could not carry on with it.

This realisation was mixed with guilt and shame for having such trivial thoughts in the face of an enormous human disaster. But I am being totally honest here: my American book—an

4

ironic, poetic and at times satirical look at American life and culture—was the first thing on my shocked mind then. You don't poke fun at someone who has just been stabbed in the back and is bleeding profusely—even if the vitriol is perfectly justified, and even if this 'someone' is a powerful athlete and a world boxing champion. The stab wound may heal with time, and the athlete might be fit enough to compete again, but the dull gnawing pain will never go away completely.

As it was put one year later by Martin Amis, who must have experienced a similar writer's shock at the sight of the collapsing Twin Towers, 'the so-called work-in-progress had been reduced, overnight, to a blue streak of pitiable babble.'

Fear came later. For the poor people trapped inside the towers. For my beloved son, whose birthday was ruined forever. For my other children. For everyone else on the face of the earth.

I couldn't help feeling that it was not just the Twin Towers that had collapsed in front of my eyes, but that some very important and seemingly impregnable bastion of my own existence had gone down with them—the feeling that, I am sure, was shared by so many powerless onlookers on that horrible autumn day . . .

It was only a few months before that I had been in New York on the last leg of my research. They put me up at the Marriott Financial Centre—a skyscraper hotel a stone's throw from the Twin Towers and part of the same World Trade Centre complex. My room on the 32nd floor had a stunning view of Manhattan and the Hudson River, especially at night.

Of an evening, I would pop out for a takeaway meal from a small Chinese supermarket in Church Street around the corner. It was small by American standards, but massive by any other. Manned by one elderly Chinese man in snow-white overalls, it was open twenty-four hours and offered more or less everything: from light bulbs and basic medicines to over a hundred(!) hot and ready-to-go meals of all imaginable cuisines—an archetypal American establishment.

Always a sole customer at the store, I remember wondering what the Chinese man, who had come to recognise me after my first visit, did with all the unsold food at the end of the day (or night)—dumped it in 'garbage' bins or gave it to a charity?

My New York hosts supplied me with a free pass for two to the top of the Twin Towers—a pass I never had a chance to use. On checking out, I left it in my room with a note inviting my invisible chambermaid to use it or to give it to her friends, if she so wished.

I hope she didn't do so on the morning of 11th September, 2001.

A couple of months after the terrorist attacks, I received a letter from the New York City Convention and Visitors Bureau, advising me about the damage suffered by the buildings within and directly outside the World Trade Centre area. Whereas the media attention was mostly focused on the Towers themselves, it was not common knowledge that several dozen other structures had either gone down completely or had been substantially damaged in the blasts.

'Your hotel has collapsed,' my New York friend told me in a phone conversation shortly after the attack.

But I could not visualise the full extent of what had actually happened to it until I looked at a thoroughly drawn diagram enclosed in the NYC letter: what remained of 'my' Marriott was a pitiful eight-storey-high broken 'tooth', all the floors above it had vanished—literally—into thin air.

For several nights after receiving the letter I was unable to sleep. I lay in my bed thinking about the Chinese man from the store in Church Street. Was he alive? Was he still presiding silently over his gargantuan set of ever-steaming food containers? Or had the 'eternal' fire that kept them warm been put out by clouds of dust and falling rubble?

I thought of what had actually happened to the guests in 'my' 32nd-floor room. What were they doing, when death struck?

Having a room-service 'American breakfast', with a more than adequate supply of warm puffy muffins and waffles in maple syrup? Taking a shower? Making love? Or still sleeping and experiencing some particularly vivid morning dreams?

And a terrifying afterthought: it could easily have been me!

I had had a similar brush with death once before—in late 1995 while making a travel documentary in Tasmania. With a Channel 4 film crew we lunched in a tacky touristy café in Port Arthur, on the site of the horrendous historic gaol, where we were filming.

Two and a half months later, Martin Bryant, a schizophrenic killer, stumbled into this very café at lunchtime to brutally murder every single customer in what was the start of the worst ever massacre in Australian history. Hearing about it in London, I was able to visualise that moment with such clarity that I could almost feel the smell of gunpowder mixing with those of barbecued sausages and sticky Tasmanian 'national pies'.

Then, on 11th September, 2001, I could have been forgiven for feeling relief and even joy at having 'missed' both fatal dates by several dozen days each, but instead I felt helplessness and angst at the fact that my life and the lives of many others were so fragile and could end up unbeknownst to us, being at the mercy of terrorists and deranged killer-maniacs.

Being in the wrong place at the wrong time.

It was like the National Lottery in reverse: those who got the numbers (dates) wrong were the winners.

Overnight America became a different country, and to write a book about it I had to start it again, from scratch . . .

Flowers by candlelight

In the UK, there is a Library of Unwritten Books, founded by

Caroline Jupp and Sam Brown in 2002. Inspired by a fictional book repository in *The Abortion: An Historical Romance 1966* by American writer Richard Brautigan (the main protagonist of the novella is a librarian who catalogues and shelves titles of unpublished books, such as *Growing Flowers by Candlelight in Hotel Rooms* or *The Culinary Dostoevsky*), they collect book ideas through random encounters in parks, streets, community centres and so on.

Richard Brautigan, who committed suicide in 1984, is often referred to as 'a cult writer', which makes me wonder what it takes to be branded as such as opposed to 'a famous writer' or simply 'a writer'?

Can it be that becoming 'a cult writer' involves taking one's own life?

Back to unwritten books though—these 'flowers grown by candlelight in hotel rooms'.

Caroline and Sam desktop-publish some of the ideas, making them into small differently coloured pamphlets, the size and format of a ('Welcome to an Idea!') greeting card, and give each of them a number: Book No. 576: *Save Our Squirrels*, or Book No. 712: *My Secret Marbles*. One copy always goes to the 'author', the rest end up in a special unwritten books archive.

Among over 800 'titles'/ideas they've catalogued so far are *Life without Dreams* and *The Man who was Addicted to Seeing* (the latter, to my mind, is a fine euphemism for 'writer').

It is probably not such a bad thing that most of those books will never get written. A beautiful one-liner can—literally—speak volumes.

The Gentle Art of Tramping—the title of a (written and published!) book by Stephen Graham—an early 20th-century British travel writer and a homeless vagabond by conviction—has always sounded to me so capacious, poetic, melodious and alluring (on top of being beautifully, almost hypnotically, onomatopoeic) that it almost makes the rest of this singularly fascinating little volume (from the 'golden shelf' of my favourite books of all time) superfluous . . . It is not only the beginning of a good book that, according to one modern British writer, contains the entire book. At times, it is just its title.

They say there is probably a book in every single person. This may be true, yet very few take it further—to actually writing it. The reason for that is simple: writing a book, i.e. creating one's own new world out of nothing, is one of the hardest tasks a human being can face. It is like climbing up a steep and forbidding mountain without any mountaineering equipment—using just your bare hands and feet.

It takes a true writer to undertake this decisive ascent from an idea to a book.

'These are the penalties paid for writing books. Who ever is devoted to an art must be content to deliver himself wholly up to it, and to find his recompense in it,' wrote Charles Dickens

But what is it that makes a 'true' (and not necessarily a 'cult') writer?

'A writer needs two things: luck and industry,' Alan Sillitoe, the doyen of British letters, told the audience of Cambridge Wordfest in March 2008.

I do agree with that, if only up to a point. By 'industry' the famous writer must have meant 'self-discipline'. I would narrow it down to what I call overcoming the fear of a clean sheet of paper.

Clean sheet of paper

A writer should enter (read start) a book like a Muslim entering a mosque—having taken off his shoes first.

The writer's shoes are tight and stick to his feet as if glued to them.

9

As an old nonsense rhyme goes: *'It was a dark and rainy night. A man stood in the street. His bleary eyes were full of tears, and his shoes were full of feet . . .'*

The man must have been a writer.

Every single scribe suffers from the impossibility-of-starting syndrome.

The best opening sentence I can think of comes from the novel *Jealousy* by a 1930s Russian writer, Yuri Olesha: 'He sings on the toilet of a morning.'

Another excellent one opens Joseph Heller's autobiographical novel *Now and Then*: 'The gold ring on the carousels was made of brass.'

Both of them are examples of an ancient literary device: *in medias res*—'in the middle of things'—the expression first coined by Horace commenting on the works of Homer. In my creative writing seminars I advise students to take a plunge into the narrative, begin with the climax (if any), and then, if appropriate, revert to the chronological order. It is indeed like a decisive dive into ice-cold water: your whole self is rebelling against it, and the sooner you take the plunge, the better.

The classic case of *in medias res* is the proverbial 'When he woke up, the dinosaur was no longer there . . .'

'The boat overturned in the middle of the river' as the first sentence of a book or a chapter is a good example of 'taking a plunge'. In more than one sense, in this particular case.[1]

1   As for the best ending of a book, a good example can be drawn from John Motley's *The Rise of the Dutch Republic*: '. . . and when he died the little children cried in the streets'. That was how Motley concluded his description of William of Orange on the last—900th!—page of the 1883 edition of his superb (and weighty) monograph.

I applied the *in medias res* approach in a substantial chapter on Mount Athos (the unique self-governing monastic mini-state on the Halkidhiki peninsula in Northern Greece) of my book *Little is the Light*, the first paragraph of which was as follows:

. . . The mountain path was steep and narrow. Strewn with rough shapeless rocks and mule droppings, it wound mercilessly uphill along the edge of an abyss, and it seemed endless. Cicadas chirred deafeningly, as if they were laughing at me. The white-hot disc of the midday sun with several fluffy clouds around it—like a giant freshly cooked portion of bacon-and-eggs—glared from the blue sizzling frying pan of the Hellenic sky. Puffing like an early steam engine, I trudged higher and higher up the track, scaring tiny agile lizards from under my trainers. My feet felt alien, as if I was walking on stilts, and streams of hot, salty sweat were pouring down my forehead . . .

I did it again in my unwritten book on America, *The Land of Plastic Fossils*:

. . . She was sitting on the pavement (or, as they say in America, 'sidewalk'), next to a 'Paws for Coffee' coffee-shop for dogs, in a wind-swept suburb of Anchorage, Alaska's biggest city . . .

This sentence opens a chapter on one of my life's most amazing discoveries, made in Alaska. An unwritten book inside an unwritten book?

The difficulty of starting is in direct proportion to the amount of work that lies ahead: it is pretty hard to begin a column, yet it is almost impossible to force yourself into typing the very first line of a long book. And the handy compact paperback *Meditation for Writers* urging you on every page to start writing TODAY doesn't always help. Nor does endless staring at a shelf full of your previous books.

'You have done it before—you can do it now.' 'Yes, but that was a long time ago. I was younger and stronger then . . .' It took me almost two months of exhausting internal arguments, loitering, guilt and self-hatred before I was able to squeeze out the first line of my latest book. And, believe me, it doesn't get easier with time, no matter how many books you have published already.

'The main thing for a writer is to learn not to recoil from a clean sheet of paper,' said Ivan Bunin, a Nobel Prize-winning Russian novelist and poet.

The paradox is that the moment you stop having panic attacks at the sight of a 'clean sheet of paper', or—in modern terms—a blank computer screen, the moment you stop struggling with your internal 'little devil' urging you to sit on your hands for yet another day, yet another hour—you lose an essential chunk of your creativity.

Being a writer is one of the hardest professions on earth. John Steinbeck rightly called it 'the hell of a job' and Thomas Mann assured us that 'a writer is someone for whom writing is harder than it is for other people'. It is very important therefore to understand that while you are trying to force yourself to sit down at your desk, while you keep looking for and coming up with countless excuses for NOT working (emails, phone calls, cups of coffee, newspapers, walks in the park 'to freshen up your head' etc.) you are ALREADY deep in the process of writing. This struggle is part of it, and an essential part at that, for as you struggle with yourself, your subconscious mind is already WORKING on the book. Sitting down and putting words on paper (or on screen) is the last link in the long and torturous chain of the creative process.

The last axiom was very well expressed by James Thurber in his 1955 interview for the *Paris Review*:

'I never quite know when I'm not writing. Sometimes my wife comes up to me at a party and says, "Dammit, Thurber, stop writing." She usually catches me in the middle of a paragraph. Or my daughter will look up from the dinner table and ask, "Is he sick?" "No," my wife says, "he is writing something.'"

I have lost count of the times when I've found myself in trouble with my wives/girlfriends and simply friends for suddenly—without any visible reason or warning—switching off, getting carried away in the middle of a conversation while turning over the words of a poem, a story or an article in progress in my mind, i.e. writing without putting words on paper. 'Oh, look at him: he is miles away,' is the most frequent comment. It can be embarrassing, for in most cases you don't mean to be 'miles away'—it happens against your will and you can't do anything about it.

It should never be easy to create SOMETHING worthwhile out of NOTHING—and this is exactly what writers do.

Thank God for deadlines! Without them, very few books would ever have seen the light.

I recently heard how a well-known writer suffering from a chronic impossible-to-start syndrome was cured by an inventive psychotherapist who forced her to walk upstairs to her study and write down one sentence the moment she woke up—while still in her pyjamas. What exactly the sentence was about did not matter—it could be a total abracadabra—yet the writer dis-covered that it helped her overcome the proverbial fear of the 'clean sheet of paper' when she returned to her desk later in the day.

Difficult?

Yes. Enormously so. 'Life is not meant to be easy, my child,' said George Bernard Shaw. So why should good writing, aimed at portraying life as it is, be?

In early April 2008, I was astounded to learn about the collective decision (or was it a threat?) by members of the Society of Authors (I once belonged to that organisation myself) to put down their pens and stop writing, simply because their incomes were in decline due to the growth of self-publishing and the Internet and now averaged no more than four thousand pounds a year. They sounded like obstreperous children trying to frighten their parents into submission by throwing a tantrum. The best 'parental' response to this behaviour would be to ignore the manipulating little brats. You want to stop writing? Do us the honour. Real scribes, who know how to savour 'the joy and privilege of the one who had an urgent message for the world' (George Gissing), who are prepared to open their veins and write with blood when they run out of ink (in the words of a nineteenth century Russian literary critic Vissarion Belinsky) would only benefit from that.

Was it them that George Bernard Shaw was trying to reach from his jolly grave: 'Life is not meant to be easy, my child'?

The good thing, as I have just realised, is that I have already STARTED this book and am well into it by now.

Tiree

At a time of uncertainty and anxiety, it is good to know that there is still a place in the world where a policeman walks his dogs among the stars of a night.

This is also the place where a postman enters unlocked houses without knocking and leaves the mail on kitchen tables;

- where people sing psalms to seals resting on the rocks;
- where low-built thatched cottages squint at you playfully with their deep-set little windows;
- where a local remedy for blisters is cotton dipped in whisky;
- where in the morning you wake up not from noises, but from silence so deep and deafening that it almost makes your teeth ache . . .

I am talking about Tiree, the outermost island of the Inner Hebrides archipelago, where I spent several relaxing days in the wake of the horrendous 9/11 events in the USA, when the whole world held its breath in grief and fear.

Not that the terrorist attacks had no effect on the islands. On Mull, the most populous and the closest to the mainland, the already high real-estate prices began to rocket.

On Tiree, the carriage of mail by the service plane had been suspended, and the locals who normally receive morning newspapers in the early afternoon had to wait for the arrival of a late-evening ferry.

A local guest-house owner, who had gone on a transatlantic cruise, got stranded in Boston.

And John Brady, the editor of *An Tirisdeach*, the island's fortnightly newsletter, has been showered with questions about the well-being of his North Carolina-based son.

'I cannot look at these planes now,' Charles MacLeash, a pensioner, told me, pointing to a silvery dot of a Boeing flying high over the island: Tiree lies on the path of Transatlantic flights to and from the UK, and the mosque-shaped white dome of the radar station, locally known as the 'golf-ball', is its main man-made landmark.

And yet my time on the Hebrides could be best compared to a three-day-long exposure to the 'relaxation tape' which I bought shortly after the tragic September events.

While still in London, I tried to beat the stress by listening to a deep-voiced shrink (ironically, he had an American accent) urging me to imagine myself in an idyllic place—lying supine in the tall grass and staring into the blue sky, or walking along an empty beach towards the surf.

The Hebrides in autumn were a 'relaxation tape' that came to life.

Mull's checked forest-covered mountains, touched by contrasting shades of yellow, red and brown, made me think of Scottish Tartan, the very pattern of which had probably been prompted by the Highlands in autumn.

Autumn in the Hebrides is the time when quiet and stillness reign supreme, when most tourists are gone and the strong winter gales that are known to have lifted schoolkids off the ground have not yet arrived. It is the season of crisp sunny mornings, of vast all-embracing skies mixing with granite-coloured sea, of stunning schizophrenic sunsets—exorbitant and over-the-top for a solitary viewer having no one to share them with—and of cool whisky-tinted nights, when a lonely island policeman walks his dogs through the large pimple-like stars.

The dog-walking policeman is neither a metaphor nor a figment of my writer's imagination. He was a real person, whose name was PC Daniel Apsley—the only guardian of law and order for the islands of Coll and Tiree. He took charge of me the moment I stepped onto Tiree soil after the almost four-hour ferry crossing from Oban. Because of a Scottish Bank Holiday, all my local contacts were out of reach and their phones were dead. I stood in a red public phone cabin on the pier listening to long dispassionate ringtones until a uniformed policeman knocked on the glass and asked whether he could help.

'Don't you have answerphones on Tiree?' I asked him sardonically.
'No, we don't,' he replied. 'There's no need. People are likely to bump into each other the moment they leave their houses.'
He offered me a lift to my guest-house, about eight miles away.

All roads on Tiree, an island ten miles long and one to six miles wide, are single-track, and the rare passing vehicles waited patiently in special road pockets for our police van to go by. Daniel waved to each of the drivers, and they waved back. It looked as if he knew all 720 residents of the island personally—and, in actual fact, he did. As we rode, he would often roll down his window to enquire about their health and families. At some point, a boy in his late teens caught up with us on a bike. On his way to take his driving test, he wanted Daniel to certify his photo. The formality was completed in the nearest road pocket.

'Bicycle is the best means of transport for Tiree,' the policeman remarked as we continued our unhurried progress. 'If you wish, you can hire one from Mr McLane who lives in the croft over there...'

Two minutes later, my freshly hired bike was rattling amicably in the back of the police van, where drunks and offenders are routinely carried on the mainland—an observation that I shared with Daniel.

'Crime on the island is virtually non-existent, and houses and cars are normally left unlocked,' he said.

I thought that his job was probably the world's second-best police sinecure, the best being on the Maltese island of Comino, with two policemen for the population of three.

My guest-house, the Glassary, stood in an open field overlooking a rocky bay. As soon as Daniel left to continue his leisurely island beat, I jumped onto the saddle and cycled off 'to where my eyes looked', as we used to say in Russia, along Tiree's only paved road.

The day was surprisingly warm and sunny, and I was ready to believe that, due to the proximity of the Gulf Stream, Tiree indeed held the UK's sunshine record, although I had heard the same claim in several other places.

Coincidentally, my last bike ride had been in Amsterdam, where I had to veer among cars, trams and absent-minded tourists.

Cycling on Tiree was very different. I rode past grazing sheep and stern-looking cows, who gave me (or was it my red sweater?) heavy disapproving stares.

Tiree's answer to Amsterdam canals was numerous little lochs, from where flocks of wild geese would take off noisily on my approach.

And instead of gable-topped Amsterdam houses, I was whooshing past Tiree's traditional thatch-covered cottages, their neatly combed roofs held down by large round pebbles on ropes—a detail that gave the huts a slightly hip-hop modern look, as if they were wearing bandanas. With their chimneys canted outwards and away from the roof—to minimise any collapse in a storm and to divert sparks from the thatch—they also looked like some daredevil Russian Cossacks in their sheepskin hats.

I dismounted near a detached parish church, built of local pink granite. On its gate, there was a plaque commemorating a Tiree family who emigrated to Canada in 1893—a time when the population of the island was in the region of seven thousand. It has been declining ever since . . .

'There is not a single tree/on the island of Tiree.'

I was humming this unsophisticated doggerel of my own making (variant: *'Life is totally stress-free/on the island of Tiree'*), to the accompaniment of the wind whistling in my ears like a hooligan, all the way back to the guest-house. Indeed, not counting three smallish hillocks, Tiree is flat and totally treeless, due to the tireless winter winds ranging between point 8 ('Fresh gale') and point 12 ('Hurricane') on the Beaufort Scale.

'Tiree', 'treeless', 'tireless'—I was savouring the melodious alliterations of Tiree which in Scots Gaelic, a nice-sounding and laconic tongue with just 18 letters in the alphabet, means 'Land of Corn'.

Agitated seagulls were screaming something in Gaelic that evening as I sat in the conservatory of the Glassary's small restaurant. The last tinges of red were lingering in the dark sky like the taste of malt whisky on my palate. On the plate in front of me, one could observe the fourth 'natural' landmark of Tiree—a hillock of haggis, topped with a sharp-edged carrot rash. The whisky was excellent, and I came to understand why many islanders had flushed faces. 'Whisky helps us to beat the wind,' a local woman told me. So the fact that their faces, particularly noses, often resembled badly printed maps of the London Underground was probably the result of combined effects of whisky and the winds it was supposed to beat.

'It takes time to adjust to the slow pace of the island's life,' Daniel, the policeman, was saying to me next morning from behind the wheel of his private 'civilian' car (it was his day off). A compulsive traveller spending every holiday overseas, he had been on the verge of leaving Tiree several times. But each time he eventually changed his mind. 'As I exercise my two dogs on the beach every night I look at the stars—so bright and near you feel you can walk through them How can one leave a place like this?'

Instead of moving to the mainland, Daniel bought himself a 'summer cottage' on Tiree—a semi-ruin in a secluded part of the island on the very edge of the ocean.

At Daniel's 'main' Tiree house doubling as . . . the police station, we were eating a sumptuous lunch, cooked by his wife Liz. The tiny police office, complete with a standard detention cell, was next to the family kitchen. 'When Daniel locks someone up, I cook for the detainee too,' Liz said with a smile. 'Luckily, this doesn't happen often.'

I asked Daniel if he had a weapon. 'I do have a truncheon, but I've never used it and never will. If I use it even once on Tiree—it will mean I have lost the battle.'

He told me that the island's elderly, who live alone, trust him with spare keys to their houses in case something happens to them. 'If a single person has a stroke, there is no danger that it will go undetected and he or she will die as is often the case on the mainland. Within minutes the alarm will be raised.'

I thought that was probably why the residents of Tiree routinely lived well into their nineties.

I spent the whole of my return journey on the ferry deck

watching yet another glorious sunset.

I knew what I would do first thing on returning to London—chuck out my 'relaxation tape'. There was no longer any need to imagine an idyllic place where all my worries would disappear as if by magic. Instead, I could simply remember my thirty stress-free hours on the real-life island of Tiree.

When darkness fell and the piercingly bright stars popped out above the sea, I looked up: there, between the Great Bear and the blinking little light of the international space station, was my new friend, the Tiree policeman, walking his dogs along the Milky Way.

A writer's life

In February 2004, when I reached the lowest point of my protracted, nearly ten-year-long, personal crisis—the worst and the deepest in my entire life—I blew my very last twenty pounds on *Where There's a Will*, John Mortimer's quirky autobiography.

I opened it at random in the semi-darkness of the permanently empty Waterstones bookshop in Folkestone, Kent—the place of my enforced solitary exile:

'A writer not only has to write, he has to live in order to have something to write about. And of the two occupations, living is much the hardest.'

I remember that bleak February day so well. Grey tearful skies above the harbour. Piercing, almost childlike (I was missing my kids enormously) screams of seagulls. I was puffing up the hill to my desolate rented cottage with the hardback under my jacket to shelter it from the drizzle.

On my way, I went past the 'Old High Street Books' second-hand bookshop that had a display of my books in its window (as it turned out later, when I regained enough confidence to enter the shop and introduce myself, Nick, the owner, was a long-time fan of mine, and we eventually became very good friends).

I never bothered to look at them for that smiling and self-assured 'Vitali Vitaliev' on their covers had very little in common with my Folkestone 'I'—lonely, lost and desperate.

This time, however, I paused at the window and grinned uneasily at my former cheerful self . . .

With every step up the road, I felt a little better—as if I was indeed slowly but surely escaping from the seemingly bottomless pit of solitude and depression. I no longer felt alone, as if a good friend had put his hand on my shoulder and said: 'It will be OK, mate.'

'And of the two occupations: writing and living—living is much the hardest.'

I was a writer and therefore everything in my life at any given moment—like the annoying drizzle, and the screaming seagulls and the satin sky above my head, and my ancient Honda jalopy outside the cottage, with its screen-wipers bent and almost tied into knots by local vandals the other night, and the drab 'local', the Richmond Tavern, in my street, where I once saw a funeral: the dead man in a black suit lying in state on top of the bar—all of that was part of the yet unwritten book of my life, and life itself was but a never-ending *research* for that main PERMANENTLY UNWRITTEN book that can never be completed.

It occurred to me then that, alongside metaphors, allegories, similes and synecdoches, a writer's life was but another LITERARY DEVICE to be incorporated into his work (albeit at that particular point, my own life resembled one large and fairly meaningless oxymoron).

Professional survivor

'Hello,
Relax about tomorrow and just see it as gathering information

for your survivor's guide. What would George Orwell make of such an opportunity? Down but not quite out in . . .' (from a friend's email)

Having reached the cottage on that grim February afternoon, I took out a new notebook (I had always found starting a 'fresh' notebook therapeutic) and compiled a list of near-death points in my life. There were twenty-four of them—from stupidly biting through a mercury-filled thermometer at the age of five (I am still puzzled at how a tiny drop of the deadly substance did not end up inside my mouth) to being targeted by neo-Nazis and the Soviet Mafia during my journalistic investigations in Russia—all of those before defecting to the West from under the nose of the KGB.

I was also nearly stabbed to death—twice: by some drunken hoodlums in the central Russian town of Velikiye Luki where we were on holiday with Mum when I was fifteen (they mistook me for another—much older—guy who was 'interfering with their girls') and by totally smashed anti-Semitic bandits during a boozy outing with my schoolmates in Ukraine.

'It is good that you left: we would have killed you otherwise,' a former Moscow 'colleague' with KGB connections confided to me sombrely in Australia a couple of years after my defection. He was visiting Melbourne as part of a Soviet military dele-gation, and we met for a beer at a 'hotel' (they call pubs 'hotels' in Oz) near the offices of the *Age* newspaper where I worked.

I wasn't then able to include the incident that happened a year and a half after Folkestone, in 2005, when I was living in Dublin and visited the North–South border town of Newry while researching my book *Vitali's Ireland*.

I was then saved by the severe cold that I had brought with me from Dublin.

Having dropped my bag at my Canal Court Hotel, I briefly

contemplated the idea of having a pint in a nearby pub, but, due to my constantly running (God knows where to) nose, rejected it and decided to visit a pharmacy instead. That may have been a life-saving decision, but I didn't know it then.

It was 7.30 p.m. While I was talking to a friendly pharmacist at 'Felix McNally's Drug-Store', a gunman, wearing a cheap Halloween mask, stumbled into the crowded McSwiggan's pub in Water Street (a couple of hundred yards from the pharmacy) and—paramilitary-style—shot several people sitting at the bar before escaping.

I only learned about the incident from the following day's papers.

It has to be said, however, that in the West, the near-death experiences grew less numerous, yet each of them was debilitating and long-lasting: several times I went from 'rich and famous' to penniless and lonely, but every time somehow managed to bounce back.

I was like a hero in one of the novels of Douglas Kennedy, a brilliant writer whose protagonists are all survivors par excellence. 'To Vitali who is definitely a survivor and a friend,' he wrote on the title page of his book A Special Relationship.

The date under the dedication is 21.08.03, the place Edinburgh, where I lived then, having reached—simultaneously—the lowest and the highest points of my life and career.

Having lost my home and my job (my successful weekly column for the Glasgow Herald was stopped as a result of the paper's sudden takeover by an American conglomerate—a rather common occurrence in the cruel world of journalism), I had just returned from London where I'd recorded a 'Desert Island Discs' style programme for Radio 4, and my solo appearance at the Edinburgh Book Festival was due the following day.

After days of trying to suppress the shame I felt, I visited Edinburgh Council's Advice Shop and explained my situation to a sympathetic Scottish lady who happened to be familiar with my work.

'We'll put you up at a B&B first and will soon find you a nice flat, where the children could visit you,' she said. 'Here in Scotland we have lots of resources to help the homeless . . .'

'But I am not really homeless,' I tried to protest meekly.

'Yes, Vitali, you are. You have nowhere to live and the sooner you face it, the better. There's nothing shameful about it—it can happen to anyone . . .'

The incongruity of these events happening at the same time defied belief (and still does). That was probably why few of my friends were inclined to take my downfall seriously. And, in my heart of hearts, neither did I—a fact that probably helped me get over the impasse in the (very) long term.

> That is my first **Survival Tip (ST)**: when in crisis, try to detach yourself from reality and refer to yourself in the third person—as 'he' or 'she'.

In a way, each of my 'Western' crises was of my own making, as if someone or something inside my head (my writer's self?) kept goading me to make a *faux pas* every time I reached a certain level of stability.

Like junk food, instability can be addictive. For someone who grew up in a permanently volatile environment, it can even become a sort of a comfort zone—in the same way a prison cell can be mildly and perversely comforting for an inmate who has spent most of his life there.

'How are you going to cope with stability, Vitali?' my former editor demanded one day when I was recovering (or so it seemed) from yet another of life's dreadful blows.

By the time I ended up in Folkestone, I already knew that the visible 'external' enemies whom I had to confront in the Soviet Union were much less devious and easier to deal with than the so-called 'foes from within'.

'If you are given a lemon, make lemonade,' an omniscient friend, himself a veteran hack, advised. And so I tried:

Survivor's Diary

PROPOSAL

A quirky column/series of features on how a man in his late forties, a writer with a reasonably high public profile, is coping with a massive crisis, involving, sadly, young kids too?

A fighter and survivor by nature (as proved many times in his past), he is determined to make it again this time. Somehow. And he knows he will. He is getting lots of moral support from all over the globe, but the danger is there, and it is real. In many ways, it is worse than the KGB, which he successfully confronted (more than once) back in the USSR. 'Famous and homeless', as a friend of his put it . . . Also— 'famous and jobless', 'famous and penniless', etc.

This would ring a bell with so many other people in a similar situation, and he has no qualms about basing his writing on his own personal experience, because his life and his books/films/columns, etc. have always been inseparable. One is the continuation of the other.

It can be a moving, instructive and inspiring story.

What do you do? How do you cope on a daily basis? What responses do you get? Mood swings. A 'litmus test' for real friends. Panic attacks. Balancing on the brink of depression. Drawing on your past experiences. Thinking you might be 'programmed' for a constant crisis.

And carrying on . . . No matter what.

Something like that . . . And it can also be funny—in a dark sort of way, of course.

It didn't quite work out. I think I know why . . . Just as to produce a good book about a country, one has to leave it first (*pace* Vissarion Belinsky and Andrei Makine), to be able to write about a personal crisis, one first has to get over it.

My friends used to say (these are actual, word-for-word quotes):

'How do you deal with all this? In your shoes, I'd have gone mad several times over . . .'

'If I were you, I'd lie on the floor and scream . . .'

'You seem to be constantly departing without ever arriving anywhere . . .'

'Dad, you remind me of the Middle East: constantly in crisis . . .' (my eldest son).

That latest crisis did seem terminal. I very nearly lost myself.

But here I am: writing about it, which means I have survived again.

How?

That is what this book is about (among other things, of course).

A born survivor? Quite possible. Having attended a series of Christmas lectures on 'The Science of Survival' at the Royal Institute in London in 2007, I learned that the reason for one particular person's survival in an extreme situation that would destroy all of his/her better-trained and better-equipped fellow-sufferers, could well be the so-called 'survival gene' or genes inherited from his/her ancestors. If there's such a gene (or genes) in reality, I've definitely got it (them) too.

Looking back at my life, I can see very clearly that if I do possess any know-how at all, it would be that of surviving all sorts of crises: social, political and personal.

Thirty-five years in the USSR, where survival was part of everyday life (albeit we didn't think about it in the same terms) must have made me into a fighter, and survival tips are the only bits of advice, the only specialist 'know-how', I can offer my fellow humans, both writers and 'normal' people, each of whom is bound to meet with an upheaval at some point of his or her existence.

In short, I think I have reasons (and credentials) to regard myself as a professional survivor.

Or a survival coach, if you wish.

Having spent thirty-five years of my life in a grotesque and cruel totalitarian country, I am now going through my Second Life (not to be confused with the eponymous virtual reality website)—in a thoroughly different environment: new society, new friends, new culture, new values. I write, think and often dream in English, which I call 'my second mother tongue'.

That is probably why I love rereading my favourite Russian books in English translation, particularly when feeling low. Savouring the familiar plot lines, characters and images, expressed in my 'second mother tongue', adds some coveted balance and logic to an otherwise unbalanced and utterly illogical life.

Writers (including yours truly) are often criticised for being obsessed with their past. I have always thought such criticism was unfair: the past is the writer's working material, and telling him off for being engrossed in it is like criticising a wood carver for being obsessed with wood.

'Whatever you write about—write about yourselves,' Konstantin Paustovsky, one of my literary mentors, used to advise aspiring writers.

'Writing about oneself' is not just solipsism and does not mean having a huge ego. Rather, it implies having something to say, i.e. plenty of life experience. Or else: 'living like a writer'.

John Mortimer, whom I met only once—at a 'Gala Literary Lunch' in Manchester in September 1994 (and will never meet again because he died in early 2009)—was spot on. Neither self-consciousness, nor self-admiration, but an increased SELF-

AWARENESS is essential for a writer. In that sense, every writer IS a solipsist, and so am I.

'Faith is the refusal to give up.' These words by Jonathan Sachs, Britain's Chief Rabbi, once overheard on Radio 4, became my life's main mantra. I typed them in large print on a frighteningly white sheet of A4 paper, pinned up on the wall above my desk. As I am writing these lines, I look up and squint at them from time to time.

Among the multiple readers' responses to one of my previous books, *Dreams on Hitler's Couch*, there was an email from Montreal, Canada. A poet, who earned his living by working at a bookshop (for, alas, you can't make a decent living from writing, let alone poetry, these days), told me how my book had helped him overcome writer's block and a major personal crisis.

I was pleasantly surprised: my impressionistic and largely autobiographical book, after all, did not contain any survival tips as such. It was, however, reassuring that the story of my life and work (and I always treated those as synonyms) could be instructive, possibly even inspiring, for other people—and not only writers.

Dreams first came out over ten years ago, its publication coinciding almost to the day with the start of my latest, longest and last (I am sure of that and am saying it without having my fingers crossed) downfall. It appears as if a whole life (yet another—third—one?) has elapsed since then.

'His next book should be a novel,' an omniscient *Financial Times* literary critic wrote in his review of *Dreams*. In a way, I did produce a novel, a real-life drama with myself as a protagonist, without putting it on paper just yet . . . And why is it that real literature for many is just fiction?

'Vitaliev transcends his genre, producing a new travel writing of the soul. A journey with lessons about what really matters in life. That makes it literature,' Dennis Sewell wrote in the *Literary Review* in his preview of *Dreams on Hitler's Couch*.

I was lucky (still am) to have had an extremely interesting, eventful and fulfilling life, so why should I strive for fabrication?

As Yuri Olesha, one of my favourite Russian/Soviet writers (the one who gave us that beautiful example of *in medias res*— see above), remarked in his *Book of Farewells* (which was, incidentally, banned in the Soviet Union and was first published in the early 1990s, thirty odd years after the writer's death), 'I hate fiction . . . I started with poetry . . then proceeded to prose, but in my literary essence I always remained a poet, i.e. a lyricist—a processor and 'expressor' of myself. Plots about some invented strangers' lives are not my cup of tea . . .'

And although I do occasionally write fiction, as someone who also started his literary life as a poet, I could put my name under these words.

Olesha did remain a poet, for it takes one to say about a platan tree (of which there were plenty in his native Odessa): 'The world's most beautiful tree—platan. It can be called the antelope of the plants. This tree has a crotch. It is powerful and indecent.'

SURVIVAL TIP (ST): When everything goes wrong, look at your life as a novel in progress. Don't rush to put it on paper, though: to appraise a crisis one has to come out of it first.

Life as a Literary Device therefore picks up at the point where *Dreams on Hitler's Couch* is interrupted. It can be seen as yet another chapter in that ever-**unwritten** book of the writer's existence.

Entering the lake

I want *Life as a Literary Device* to have a number of different layers incorporating all yet unwritten works of mine, including *The Land of Plastic Fossils*, the permanently unfinished pre-9/11 book on the USA, and *Life as a Literary Device* itself.

Why was the would-be book on the States called *The Land of Plastic Fossils*? Here's an explanation:

I arrived in Badlands National Park at the end of my American travels, so tired that I didn't feel like getting off the bus. It was scorching outside and, having visited several canyons and national parks during the previous couple of weeks, I thought I could hardly get excited by the sight of yet another moose or curiously shaped rock. The numerous 'Scenic Turn Off' highway signs had suddenly acquired a negative second meaning: to my exhausted self, American canyons were like lap dancers—no matter how stunning, if you've seen one, you've seen them all.

The ground in the Badlands was barren, bumpy and hard to walk on, which led me to understand why the Dakota Indians referred to the area as *mako sica*, meaning 'land bad', and early French–Canadian trappers termed it *les mauvaises terres à traverser*—'bad lands to travel across'.

In the end, I was glad to have made the effort. Thanks to a couple of knowledgeable and straightforward rangers, I have learnt a lot about this ancient natural reserve, which used to be the bottom of a giant sea and—later—a breeding ground for such prehistoric creatures as three-toed horses, sabre-toothed cats and ruminating pigs(!), whose politically correct scientific name was Oreodonts. These (and other) animals' remains gradually turned into millions of fossils that—due to the unique nature of the soil—would have stood a good chance of remaining in the Badlands forever, had it not been for fossil-hunters who started carrying away wagonloads of petrified remains to be sold to museums, scientists and private collectors, or just for souvenirs. With such methodical embezzlement of fossils going on for over a hundred years (since the late nineteenth century), no wonder that by the end of the twentieth century there were none of them left in the Badlands. What could be done about it? Anywhere else, plenty, but in America, probably nothing. And the Badlands—for better or worse—WERE in America.

In the early 1990s, it was decided to make a number of replica fossils out of . . . plastic and scatter them around the park. This done, the pseudo-fossils kept disappearing even faster than the real ones, probably because—to a dilettante collector's eye— they did look exactly like the real ones, probably even slightly better, who knows. There is no force that can stop an average American from pocketing a nice natural 'souvenir', particularly if it is free, for his general hands-on approach to nature can be best characterised by the notorious quote from Ivan Michurin, a Stalinist Soviet biologist: 'We must not expect gifts from Mother Nature—we must forcibly take them away from her!'

In the end, they collected all remaining plastic fossils and put them under glass cases displayed along the footpaths. That is where they are now, and I had a chance to stare at them for as long as I wanted (about ten seconds at a time) They did look authentic, even slightly dusty (with the carefully replicated dust of history?)—but the fact remained: unbeknownst to most visitors, the Badlands fossils were made of plastic! Their real place was not under museum-style glass domes but on the shelves of the nearby Wall Drug shopping mall specialising in kitsch of all shapes and sizes under the dubious logo 'A Blast from the Past'. . .

'Plastic fossils' therefore came to symbolise a certain super-ficiality and brashness of modern American culture: its oxymoronic, at times simply moronic, manifestations—the sort of criticism my editors wanted to hush in the aftermath of 9/11. I don't blame them.

Like my unwritten book on America, this one—*Life as a Literary Device*—has neither beginning nor end; nor does it fit in with any existing literary genre: partly a memoir, partly a novel, partly a meditation, partly a poem, partly a diary, partly a dream, partly a survival kit, partly an extended metaphor for the writer's life, i.e. indeed a 'literary device'. I am destined never to finish this book (not for as long as I live), yet everything I've ever written and am still going to write can be included in it.

I will certainly keep looking back at my life: at the places I visited, the pieces I wrote and the people I met—using another favourite literary device of mine, flashback.

Memory is like a scrapbook—a cut-and-paste job.

Yet the hero, or anti-hero if you wish, of the book is not necessarily me, Vitali Vitaliev. 'I' (my literary ego) can assume different personalities—real and fictional: of my late Mum; of artist Edward Bawden; of Adam Grigor'yevich Nadin, a retired accountant and a football fan; possibly even of Ebenezer Howard, a traveller, a dreamer and the founder of the world's first Garden City (where I now live), and many, many others.

From the 'closed town' near Moscow, where my parents worked at a top-secret military facility and where I spent the first three years of my life, to the world's first 'Utopian' Garden City. Via Britain, Australia, America and Ireland. A jumpy trajectory of my existence.

At times, the 'I' will transform itself into 'inanimate' objects, like Chekhov's writing table, or a declining, as if deeply depressed, town, like Fraserburgh in Scotland. Or into my favourite writers—alive or dead, like Valentin Kataev, the inventor of *mauvism*: 'I had discovered in myself the ability to become reincarnated not only in all manner of people, but also in animals, plants, stones, household objects, and even in abstract concepts, such as subtraction . . .'

I want 'I' and 'he' in the book to be conventional and mutually interchangeable, but 'he' will most often kick in when describing a crisis: again, it is much easier to cope with one when you detach yourself from what's going on by switching over to a third-person narrative (see a **Survival Tip** above).

At some point, I may even introduce an alter ego called Victor R.

Why 'Victor R'?

Many of my childhood friends preferred to call me 'Vitya'—a diminutive of 'Victor'—rather than the somewhat alien-sounding (for a Russian-speaker) 'Vitali'. I published my first poem under the pen-name 'Victor Rapoport' ('Rapoport' being my mum's maiden name) that seemed to me so roaringly poetic.

Or perhaps I ('he'?) will sometimes be called Vin which means 'he' in Ukrainian—the language of my motherland. Or simply 'VV'?

And all the women in my life, except for the Loved One, can then be monikered 'Ona' ('she' in Russian) which echoes so many female names: Spanish Donna, Slovak Dana, Russian Nonna, Ukrainian Hanna, Irish Oonagh and so on—and sounds rather feminine to me.[2]

For, after all, *'What's in a name? That which we call a rose/By any other name would smell as sweet.'*

Each of the unwritten books that constitute *Life as a Literary Device* exists on its own. It neither complements nor diminishes the mainnarrative, simply because there isn't any. Likewise, it is impossible to put them in any numerical order: book number one, three, four, or flashback number seventeen, say. The words I am typing now are not a belated Introduction, but can just as well be placed in the middle of the book or on its last (but never final!) pages.

I want the narrative to resemble a pet cat walking next to its owner (the reader) and being simultaneously ahead of him and

2   I also recently learned that 'onna' is Japanese for 'woman'.

behind—as only cats can.

This book is therefore not a river, which, if we believe Confucius, one can only enter once, but rather a lake into which the reader can immerse himself repeatedly—in any place and at any time (albeit I don't exclude the possibility that one underwater spring feeding that lake can occasionally give rise to another).

Yet, on the very last page of the volume (not of the book, which, as we have agreed, doesn't have an end or a beginning), I want all those different springs to leave the lake and to arrange themselves into a stream that will carry on flowing ahead on its own—like two small rivers that merge at the Meeting of the Waters: that scenic spot in Ireland's beautiful Valley of Avoca.

Will I be able to do it all? I don't know. But I'll give it a try anyway. Rather than just writing this book, I am going to live through it. Like every human life, it is totally unpredictable. This means I have no idea of what exactly will follow after I finish this sentence.

For all I know at the moment, it could be the last one.

Rainbow in the night

The pain comes out of the blue as he reads reclining on a sofa after a nice al fresco dinner with the Loved One.

It is actually worse than pain. It feels like being suffocated from inside, as if some red-hot foreign object with sharp protruding edges is being hammered deeper and deeper into his chest.

'Angina' (an-ghee-na) in Russian means 'flu'—a classic 'false friend' for an inexperienced translator.

The accepted Russian medical term for angina as a heart disease is 'grudnaya zhaba', or literally 'chest toad'. Wherever this bizarre phrase comes from, it strikes him as precise and morbidly poetic as he wriggles on the sofa covered in cold sweat. Without any logical connection, he recalls that the word for cancer in Russian is 'rak', the same as 'crayfish'.

Chest toad . . . Is this it? Is this how it feels? There is no fear. If there's nothing at all after death, how can one be afraid of 'nothing'?

Curiosity? Maybe . . . He remembers a puzzled half-smile on the face of his Dad as his coffin was sliding slowly towards the opening doors of a crematorium oven, as if he was curious to see how it all worked.

With the Loved One, they've had a lovely Sunday exploring the countryside around their new abode—Letchworth Garden City. In a tiny old pub in the village of Barley, a free Sunday roast was on offer. They then drove on to Saffron Walden and walked hand in hand in its beautiful and near-deserted Victorian gardens.

In a small art gallery at the edge of the gardens, there was an exhibition of paintings by Edward Bawden, an official war artist during World War II who had spent a long time in the Middle East. In a special glass case, some of the artist's letters and personal possessions were displayed.

In a letter to his kids from Arabia, he wrote about a rainbow he saw in the desert at midnight.

Dear Joanna & Richard,

One dark night a week ago I saw a rainbow. The Moon was full and very bright, the rainbow was not over or around the Moon but facing it, that is, I had to turn my head to the Moon to see the rainbow. It was not brightly coloured as rainbows are in the daytime when the sun is shining, and the bow is seen against the black sheet of a cloud or rain-storm, but very pale & silvery. Rainbows at night are very rare, many people never see one, &

that was the first I have seen myself, but I am told that if you go to the great Victoria Falls which Mummy will show you on the map—you will often see a rainbow at night by the light of the Moon . . .

The letter was written from somewhere near Baghdad.

Shortly afterwards, Bawden experienced a drama. After two years abroad, he set sail for home from Cape Town. The ship was torpedoed six hundred miles from Lagos; survivors were picked up after five days in a lifeboat by a Vichy warship and interned in Casablanca. When rescued by Americans, he was taken to Virginia, eventually arriving back home in 1943.

Contrary to what many would think, seeing a rainbow in the night, as it turned out, does not necessarily imply impending happiness. Maybe this one had been a sinister omen of approaching disaster.

VV was nevertheless touched by the story. Partly because the book on Ireland that he had just finished writing ended with a rainbow—not a midnight one, but with a no-less-unlikely multicoloured heavenly arc that he saw on the North–South border in mid-December.

'I pull over at a currency exchange outlet marking the unmarked North–South divide and come out of the car.

The rain has stopped.

A huge juicy rainbow, with one end in Ireland, and the other, resting on the other Ireland, is effortlessly bridging together two parts of the same small nation, dissected by the non-existing frontier.'

Unlike *Life as a Literary Device*, the book on Ireland did have a beginning and an end (see above) too.

Or could it be that a thoroughly untoward midnight rainbow signifies an unexpected turn of events rather than happiness?

As the frightened Loved One drives him to hospital, the chest toad's frantic leaps under his ribs become less frequent. Could it be that he has conjured it up himself?

In a conversation with his publisher several days before, he had stressed the necessity of a new experience to bring *Life as a Literary Device* up to date. He said he needed a fresh angle, a new bit of 'research' as the book was in progress, and was seriously contemplating a journey. Where to? It really didn't matter as long as the place evoked some memories that could provide a link between past and present.

He thought of travelling to Turkmenistan, a sparsely populated Central Asian country on the southern fringe of the old Soviet empire, to find his old friend Bairam Zhutdiev, an accomplished Turkmen poet, whom he met while on a journalistic assignment in Ashkhabad in the mid-1980s. Bairam's poems appealed to him so much that he translated many of them into Russian and had them published.

> *When your stallion jingling his harness finishes the race last, don't you hit him in the face for he is very much like a human. He will suffer with guilt for having lagged behind everyone else. He will shed tears from the large tea bowls of his eyes. The day will come when the same stallion will race forward like lightning. The whirlwind will start, the fire will flash, the mountains will swirl around in a horror dance. And the hippodrome, rotating like a tornado will drown in the rattling of hooves. And the stallion will fly—laughing—along the endlessness of circles. But if your stallion jingling his harness finishes the race last, don't you hit him in the face. Be human, you, human being!*

'. . . along the endlessness of circles'. He was quite proud of this metaphor of his, not to be found in the original.

With Bairam, he had spent hours drinking *chal* (a warm and mildly alcoholic drink made out of camel's milk) and talking about poetry, literature and politics. He knew he could trust Bairam: he had such an intelligent open face, and the poet's views—just like his own—were unorthodox and iconoclastic (for which read anti-Soviet).

They were mocking the tongue-tied stupidity of Brezhnev's and Andropov's public speeches.

Many years later, having just returned to London from Australia, he wrote a column for *The European* newspaper on the cruel and bizarre personality cult that had gripped the newly independent Turkmenistan and was suffocating the country from inside.

Like a 'chest toad'?

A former Soviet Communist Party apparatchik, Saparmurad Niyazov, had proclaimed himself the lifelong president and prime minister, 'First Hero of Turkmenistan' and 'Turkmenbashi'—'the father of all Turkmens'. He made his own birthday a national holiday, changed the names of calendar months and days of the week (calling them after himself and his relatives), banned ballet as 'pornographic and unnecessary' and erected a hundred-metre-tall rotating statue of himself made of pure gold. Thousands of factories, schools and stadiums in Turkmenistan bore his name. Totally devoid of a sense of irony, Turkmenbashi also ordered a pig-breeding farm to be named after . . . his mother.

Any criticism of Niyazov was, of course, strictly banned. 'Only he who writes about me positively, without criticism, can be called a truly honest person,' he announced in one of his speeches.

The unquestioning adoration of the humourless and ruthless 'great leader' was guaranteed by Niyazov's secret police, mercilessly suppressing any smallest sign of dissent.

It was shortly afterwards that, having accidentally tuned in to a Russian-language propaganda broadcast of the Turkmenistan State Radio, VV heard the name of his friend Bairam Zhutdiev. He had been worried for Bairam and thought he must have become one of Turkmenistan's political prisoners. It was with consternation therefore that he listened to his friend's hooray-patriotic poem glorifying Niyazov and calling him 'greater than Allah'! The poem was read by a Turkmenistan radio presenter with intonations so euphoric that, had it not been for his impeccable Russian (ethnic Russians constitute half of the country's population), he could easily have been mistaken for an ever-orgiastic announcer of North Korea's Radio Pyongyang International.

VV could hardly believe his ears. What had they done to his intelligent, independently minded friend? Or had Bairam simply gone mad?

Having thought about it all for some time, he decided that, knowing Turkmenbashi's total lack of self-doubt and sense of humour (remember the pig-breeding farm named after his Mum?), Bairam had proclaimed him 'greater than Allah' ironically. He could not have been serious . . . Or could he? Was he forced to write the eulogy by threats or torture?

It was only Bairam himself who could resolve these doubts, and VV immediately applied for a Turkmenistan visa. And immediately got a point-blank refusal: his column for *The European* must have had its time-bomb effect.

He had to forget about his quest, but remembered it again— over ten years later—when Niyazov died in December 2006 and a factotum of his was appointed to succeed him.

His second application for a Turkmen visa at the end of 2007, however, was rejected almost as quickly as the first one. 'Your presence in Turkmenistan is undesirable,' stated an embassy official.

He printed out the refusal and was thinking of framing it— like an honorary diploma or a certificate of knighthood. If one is not welcome in a dictatorship, it means he must have done something right.

Another unwritten book?

Having failed with Turkmenistan, he started making

arrangements for a trip to the Baltics, the small post-Soviet countries he had always had an affection for. These tiny long-suffering nations were survivors par excellence and visiting them from time to time throughout his life had been essential to recharge his own 'survivor batteries'.

It was at that point that the 'chest toad' leapt into his life, having given him a research opportunity of a totally different nature.

Sleepless in his hospital bed, he was recalling his trip to the Baltics several years before. A vicarious journey of the type he had become so used to as an armchair buccaneer little boy in the cage of the former USSR.

What a curious substance, human memory! It can be compared to an overflowing rubbish bin, which our brain, the amnesiac dustman, chronically forgets to empty. Having forgotten many useful addresses, I still remember this one from 1966, when our family was spending its summer holiday in the Tallinn suburb of Pirita: 12, Sakala Street. At the age of twelve, I was already a keen amateur photographer and kept snapping right and left, especially on vacations, with my crude 'Smena' camera. When it started malfunctioning—due to over-exploitation, I assume—my mother and I had to have it repaired.

It took us hours to find the place. Tallinn passers-by, whom we repeatedly stopped for guidance (due to an inexplicable Soviet paranoia, city maps were non-existent), would politely direct us elsewhere. We ended up criss-crossing the whole town before accidentally stumbling upon the blasted shop.

Unbeknownst to us, we had found ourselves on the receiving end of the so-called 'passive protest'—the only way the natives of the Baltic republics of the USSR (Lithuania, Latvia and Estonia) could voice their angst at what they rightly perceived as the Soviet occupation: the three republics were forcibly 'annexed' by the Soviet Union in 1940 in the wake of the treacherous Molotov–Ribbentropp Pact.

Apart from sending visitors to the opposite end of town when asked for directions in Russian, the locals practised another form of the 'passive protest' by totally ignoring Russian speakers at a public place, be it a restaurant or a morgue. The staff would simply look through you as if you were an empty space, which once made my granddad, an old Bolshevik and Civil War veteran, lose his temper. 'Russians and dogs are not welcome here, are they?!' he exploded in the face of a dispassionate doorman at a Pirita restaurant who had staunchly refused to take any notice of us.

Despite this obvious downside to holidaying in the Baltics, we used to do so often. It was the closest one could come to the West, still firmly out of our reach. In defiance of blatant 'russification', the three small nations were desperately clinging to their national identities, languages and culture and kept surprising visitors from elsewhere in the USSR with the higher living standards, civility and style they had somehow managed to preserve.

It was in Estonia, in the late sixties, that I had my first experience of a self-service 'supermarket'—an establishment unheard of in the rest of the Soviet Empire. The thing that baffled me most was that there was a special shopping basket for every customer. 'How come the baskets don't get stolen?' I kept wondering.

Among a few 'Western-looking' products, they sold jam in tubes. And although the jam, when squeezed (or, in my case, sucked) out, had a distinct taste of lead, I could not have enough of it and kept walking around with the tube protruding from my mouth cigar-like—as once captured on film by my mother, when I inadvertently allowed her to hold my faithful 'Smena'.

All black-and-white snapshots of my childhood have been lost for good, yet many of them are so firmly imprinted in my memory that it only takes closing my eyes to bring them back to life. This is probably why I couldn't help the constant feeling of recognition during my trip to Tallinn and Riga, my first experience of Estonia and Latvia as independent states.

Tallinn, the capital of Estonia, to which I returned after thirty odd years of absence, was covered with melting snow, and thawed patches of black earth were showing through the white slush here and there. Like in my childhood photos, the city was all black-and-white!

And not just in terms of colour. Whereas Russian signs, cars and monuments had disappeared completely, it was Russian that most people in the streets were fearlessly speaking.

The 'passive protest' had gone. In a free market society, ruled not by dogma, but by Mammon, it was unnecessary. Money speaks no languages, except for the language of profit—its own internationally accepted Esperanto. It has no prejudice, except for that of a class.

The predominance of Russian speech in the streets of Tallinn, where only about 40 per cent of the population were officially Russian-speaking, could be explained by the fact that Estonians are generally taciturn and, like their neighbours the Finns, prefer meaningful silence to idle verbal exchanges. No wonder, if we remember that Estonian, a tongue-breaking Finno-Ugric language, has fourteen case endings; two different infinitives, yet just one word for 'he' and 'she'; no future tense, and, to cap it all, something called 'the partitive plural'. Not to mention the ubiquitous double vowels and consonants, as if the alphabet itself suffers from a chronic stutter.

Tallinn's Old Town, where my five-star Schossle Hotel was located (it was skilfully built into the robust frame of a thirteenth-century mansion), remained one of the best-preserved in Europe. And one of the cosiest too. There were amazingly few cars, and parking was hardly a problem.

With the proliferation of well stocked shops and brand-new restaurants of all imaginable cuisines and with prices four to five times lower than in London, modern Tallinn had few visible signs of the poverty endemic in most European capitals. Crumbling and neglected in Soviet times, it was now a secret tourist paradise, a living proof of the creative might of capitalism.

In this all-embracing and somewhat idealistic world, a place had been found for The House of Russian Culture'—a grim 'Stalin Gothic' structure in Mere Street. Inside, one could spot the Soviet national emblem—the last remaining in Estonia—and the sullen-faced patrons still addressing each other as 'Comrade'.

'Undress! Are you deaf, or what?! Undress immediately!!!' Piotr Nikolayevich, the old, ruddy-faced doorman of the 'Ostap' restaurant, bellowed (in Russian of course) at an unsuspecting Estonian, who was trying to sneak inside in his overcoat ('*razdet'sya*' 'to undress' in Russian means both 'to strip naked' and 'to take off one's coat'—the doorman obviously meant the latter). I thought that his manners and appearance betrayed an ex-Soviet serviceman, possibly a KGB officer, and I was right.

'We were sent here in 1946,' he said, having finally dragged the coat off the recalcitrant Estonian's shoulders. 'Stalin told us: stay here and serve our Motherland—and that's what we did: stayed and served for fifty-odd years . . .'

For patrons of 'Ostap', irrespective of their nationality, there was no danger of being ignored by this vigilant doorman, for whom every deposited coat meant a tip.

Standing on Toompea Hill, I was looking down at Tallinn's impressive panorama, mentally comparing it with my long-lost photo, taken from the same spot thirty-five years before.

At the first glance, little had changed, and the main landmarks: tiled Gothic roofs; church-spires; the guard towers Fat Margaret and Kik in de Kok (Peep into the Kitchen); the medieval Town Hall, topped with the weather-vane figure of Vaana Toomas (Old Toomas), Tallinn's main mascot, were still in place—as was the Soviet-style railway station (railway stations all over the world are resistant to change).

Yet something was definitely missing. I recalled that my old photo had been largely ruined by three tall ugly masts sticking out of the ground and spoiling the view. Those were special jamming towers built by the KGB to interfere with 'corruptive' radio and TV broadcasts from neighbouring Finland—just eight miles away across the gulf (the fourth one was hidden inside the spire of the magnificent twelfth-century St. Olaf's Church!). The town's tallest structures, they were eyesores in more than one sense: the over-intensive round-the-clock jamming was also affecting the quality of reception of the politically correct programmes from Moscow, and the picture on the locals' TV screens was constantly blurred and jumpy.

The towers had gone, and the vision and sound on all twenty odd TV channels (a couple of Estonian, a dozen German and only one Russian) in my hotel room were crystal-clear, although at times I wished they were not. Estonian news featured such ground-breaking stories as:

– The Tallinn Mayor's (unofficial) visit to a well-known striptease bar, also housing an underground brothel. 'But there was no show there that day,' he said when confronted.
– The Estonian Prime Minister using the photograph of the opposition leader as his target during a shooting exercise. Unlike the hapless Mayor, the Prime Minister admitted the misdeed and publicly apologised.

And so on. In despair, I flicked over to the Russian channel, on which a professorial bespectacled weatherman was delivering a forecast: 'Tomorrow the temperature will fluctuate between five and zero degrees, snowfall is not excluded, but if a woman becomes pregnant she can rely on *Pregnavit!*'

It took me a while to realise that they had turned the weather forecast into a commercial, at which point I felt a momentary pang of nostalgia for the jamming towers of yesteryear . . .!

They kept him at the hospital overnight, did numerous tests and let him go in the morning—with a bagful of medicines and a nitroglycerin spray in his pocket.

The chest toad, however, was not in a hurry to leave him alone. He had another nasty attack a week later, while on business in London. This time the doctor's verdict was firm—an angiogram, with a possible angioplasty to follow.

'PTCA—*often called angioplasty—is a procedure to treat coronary artery disease. It involves flattening the fatty material (atheroma) that can build up inside the walls of the main blood vessels (arteries) to the heart causing them to narrow. During angioplasty, a catheter is threaded through an artery in the groin or arm to reach the coronary arteries of the heart.*' From an online medical directory

'. . . but what am I going to do with the fallen yellow leaves in the park . . . ?'

The poignant refrain of a song, performed by a Russian busker, was echoing in the freshly painted Art Nouveau facades of Riga's Old Town.

It was a late afternoon in March. Stray cats were copulating frantically on time-beaten cobbles. A plush Volvo of the latest make was crawling up a narrow lane, squeezing itself into the gap between houses like a gleaming dagger into a tight sheath.

The sedan's owner must have been wealthy enough to afford the charge of five lats (£5.50) per hour for entering the Old Town. He obviously did not belong to the Russian busker's metaphoric 'fallen leaves'—those bypassed by Latvia's post-Communist boom.

Or could it be that by 'yellow leaves' the busker meant his

numerous fellow Russians (60 per cent of Riga's population were officially Russian-speaking)? Indeed, Russians in Riga had been turned into an overwhelming ethnic minority.

Even menus in Russian restaurants were printed exclusively in Latvian, the republic's only official tongue, I found. Russian schools were being closed down at an alarming rate, and a respected Riga publishing house had launched a students' competition for the best project on the Russians' deportation.

Such nationalistic excesses could be partly explained by the fact that out of the three Baltic republics of the USSR, Latvia had suffered most from 'russification'.

By the 1980s, the Latvian language and culture were on the verge of extinction, and some drastic measures were needed to galvanise them after independence.

Latvian nationalism was like a forcefully depressed spring: the tighter you press it (and the longer you hold it) the higher it will jump when released.

My old photos of Riga were much clearer in my memory than those of Tallinn.

I often came to Riga on holidays and on journalistic assignments in the 1980s.

During one of those assignments I met Borya, a Riga-born satirist of Jewish origins, who became one of my best friends.

The hotel where I was put up had no water (hot or cold), and Borya kindly invited me to stay in his flat, located in an exclusive apartment block for party functionaries in Lenin Street. Not a functionary himself, he lived there courtesy of his mother-in-law, who worked for Latvia's Communist Party Central Committee.

Ironically, this building was now the equivalent of a council estate, inhabited by the poor.

Its smelly littered courtyard was the only place in Riga where I spotted a dozen rusty Ladas.

As for Borya, he lived in Israel with his family (including his once influential mother-in-law).

Lenin Street had been renamed Liberty Street, and 'Shalom', a small Jewish restaurant, was doing brisk trade in the basement of the house next to Borya's—a little Israel on his former doorstep.

Unlike Borya, his elder brother Sasha still lived in Riga and had the official status and passport of a 'non-citizen', due to the fact that his parents 'only' came to Riga after World War II. His whole salary went on rent, and he had to rely on his wife's casual earnings to survive. A 'fallen leaf' in the blooming park of capitalism, Sasha still spoke about 'us' and 'the West', not realising that 'the West', with all its pros and cons, had returned to Latvia after fifty years of exile, and he had found himself there without emigrating.

Jauniela, a quiet and unremarkable Art Nouveau street in Riga, used to be Soviet Latvia's most photographed site (I remember using a whole roll of film in it once). The reason was simple: the hard-currency-starved Soviet cinema industry chose it as a natural film location for movies set in the 'decaying' West. It was there that Sherlock Holmes's Baker Street flat from the popular Soviet TV serial was located. And it was there that the Geneva- and Berlin-set scenes of *Seventeen Moments of Spring*, a Soviet blockbuster spy-thriller, were shot by the inventive Moscow film-makers.

All it took was removing the 'Let's Pull Together' slogans from the facades, sweeping the pavement, and bingo—'the West' was there, with all its seductively un-Soviet neatness.

These days, the most photographed Riga attraction was the Freedom Monument, also known as Milda—Latvia's own Statue of Liberty. Built in 1935, it had survived untouched all fifty years of Soviet domination, even if those who ventured to lay flowers before it were whisked away to the near-by KGB headquarters.

The Monument was undergoing a face-lift and was covered with scaffolding. Looking at the solid wooden box hiding bashful Milda from public view, and trying to remember what she looked like, I had to summon up in memory another old photo of mine which featured the statue of a graceful Latvian girl, holding three stars, representing three provinces of Latvia, high above her head.

I was hoping that Milda would emerge from under the scaffolding in all her unscathed beauty—as she once appeared on one of my black-and-white holiday photos.

Except that, after revisiting the Baltics, I no longer saw these photos as black-and-white: they had gained colours—the dazzling and often conflicting colours of the free world.

Connections

How do parts of this book link up to each other?

Seemingly disjointed snippets of real life, they connect by association alone—like random pieces of coloured glass that form themselves into a pattern if viewed through that wonderful children's toy, the kaleidoscope.

Example:

During a Sunday afternoon walk in Letchworth Garden City, I spot a 'No Footpath Ahead' road sign. It features a black silhouette of a man holding a little boy by the hand.

In my mind, I immediately see myself walking along a forest path with my eldest son, Mitya, then aged seven, heading for our small dacha outside Moscow. I am holding his hand, and we are both singing: 'Only we are not scared/ There are two of us—father and son/ We are both soldiers/ We are both heroes!'

Many years on, I walk hand in hand with my younger boy, Andrei, along an Edinburgh street during one of my frequent visits to see my 'estranged' (I hate this word) 'new' children (him and his younger sisters: Anya and Alina). My plane back to London leaves in less than two hours, and it is time to catch a bus to the airport. Andrei is clinging to me desperately, not wanting to let go of my hand, while I am trying to pacify him by saying that we are going to be together again soon . . . If only my grip could be strong enough to delay (or altogether prevent) the mutually hurtful separation.

I then see myself as a little boy holding my Mum and Dad's hands while walking in Sumskaya Street in Kharkov. They are taking me home from the kindergarten. I am happy and keep jumping up in the air and swinging, while grasping my parents' hands, as little boys (and girls) do.

It is important for children to be able to hold their parents' hands. A hand thus becomes a replacement for an umbilical cord—a warm and living link to their sense of belonging, of blood connection and connectivity. Letting go therefore feels like a little vivisection—almost physically painful for everyone involved . . .

When both of your parents die, no matter how young or old you are, your hands are destined to flail in the emptiness forever—until you get reunited with them, either in an anxious dream or in that mysterious dimension sometimes referred to as 'the other world'.

One never feels as safe, secure and balanced as when walking hand in hand with one's parents.

I recall and repeat in my mind Longfellow's poignant poem 'The Open Window' which many years ago, when I had no children of my own, moved me to such an extent (especially its last stanza) that I translated it into Russian:

'The old house by the lindens Stood silent in the shade, And on the gravelled pathway The light and shadow played. I saw the nursery windows Wide open to the air; But the faces of the children, They were no longer there. The large Newfoundland house-dog Was

49

standing by the door; He looked for his little playmates, Who
would return no more. They walked not under the lindens, They
played not in the hall; But shadow, and silence, and sadness
Were hanging over all. The birds sang in the branches, With
sweet, familiar tone; But the voices of the children Will be heard
in dreams alone! And the boy that walked beside me, He could not
understand Why closer in mine,—ah! closer,— I pressed his warm,
soft hand!'

I regard the publication of my translations from Longfellow by
Moscow's prestigious *Literary Gazette* in 1981 as one of my biggest
achievements as a writer so far. Incidentally, that was the last
work of mine that my father saw published before his sudden
death from a heart attack at the age of fifty-six a couple of weeks
later.

And so on, and so on . . .

No one was able to express this connectivity of everything
better than Daniil Kharms, a Russian absurdist writer and
children's poet, who died of starvation in his prison cell in
February 1942, at the age of thirty-seven, while incarcerated 'on
suspicion of anti-Soviet activities', i.e. his own totally harmless,
yet unorthodox and tongue-in-cheek (and hence clearly 'anti-
Soviet'), writings:

The Connection

'Philosopher!

1. I am writing to you in reply to your letter, which you are
   intending to write to me in reply to my letter which I
   wrote to you.
2. A certain violinist bought himself a magnet and was taking
   it home. On the way some hooligans attacked the violinist
   and knocked his cap off. The wind caught his cap and
   carried it along the street.

3. The violinist put his magnet down and ran off after his cap. The cap landed in a puddle of nitric acid, where it decomposed.

4. And the hooligans had, by that time, grabbed the magnet and made off.

5. The violinist returned home without his coat and without his cap, because the cap had decomposed in the nitric acid and the violinist, distressed by the loss of his cap, had forgotten his coat on the tram.

6. The conductor of the tram in question took the coat to a second-hand shop and there he exchanged it for some sour cream, grain and tomatoes.

7. The conductor's father-in-law stuffed himself on the tomatoes and died. The conductor's father-in-law's body was placed in the morgue, but then things got mixed up and, instead of the conductor's father-in-law, they buried some old woman.

8. On the old woman's grave they placed a white post with the inscription: 'Anton Sergeyevich Kondrat'ev'.

9. Eleven years later, this post fell down, eaten through by worms. And the cemetery watchman sawed the post into four pieces and burned it in his stove. And the cemetery watchman's wife cooked cauliflower soup over this fire.

10. But, when the soup was just ready, the clock fell off the wall right into the saucepan full of soup. They got the clock out of the soup, but there had been bedbugs in the clock and now they were in the soup. They gave the soup to Timofey the beggar.

11. Timofey the beggar ate the soup, bugs and all, and told Nikolay the beggar of the cemetery watchman's generosity.

12. The next day Nikolay the beggar went to the cemetery watchman and started asking him for alms. But the cemetery watchman didn't give Nikolay the beggar anything and chased him away.

13. Nikolay the beggar took this very badly and burned down the house of the cemetery watchman.

14. The fire went from the house to the church and the church burned down.
15. A lengthy investigation took place, but the cause of the fire could not be established.
16. On the spot where the church had stood they built a club and on the club's opening day a concert was arranged at which performed the violinist who, fourteen years before, had lost his coat.
17. And amid the audience there sat the son of one of those hooligans who, fourteen years before, had knocked the cap off this violinist.
18. After the concert they travelled home in the same tram. But, in the tram which was following theirs, the tram-driver was that very conductor who had once sold the violinist's coat at the second-hand shop.
19. And so there they are, travelling across the city in the late evening: in front are the violinist and the hooligan's son, and behind them the tram-driver and former conductor.
20. They travel on and are not aware of what the connection is between them and this they will never learn until their dying day.'

This beautiful and funny vignette was written by Daniil Kharms in 1937—at the height of the Stalinist purges, of which he became a victim.

Kharms's work (unsurprisingly, banned in the Soviet Union) carries a trace of yet another amazing connection: between the writer and his fate. In the same year of the Great Purge, 1937, when millions of innocent people were arrested and subsequently murdered on the orders of the paranoid Soviet dictator, he wrote the following poem:

A man had left his home one day with bag in hand and metal bar,
and off he went, and off he went, a stroll that took him very far.
He walked on straight and forward and always looked ahead,
he never slept, he never drank, he never stopped to eat and

> drink nor even rest his head. And once upon a morning dawn,
> in darker woods he fared, and from this time, and from this time,
> he vanished in thin air. But if perhaps your path with his just
> happens to be crossed, then quick as you can, then quick as you
> can, run quickly telling us.'

On a fine August morning of 1941, Kharms left his home. In a Leningrad street, he was picked up by the NKVD (a forerunner of the KGB)—'And from this time, And from this time, He vanished in thin air . . .'

From Letchworth Garden City to Leningrad via Moscow and Edinburgh. From Henry Wadsworth Longfellow to Daniil Kharms—a seemingly endless chain of memories and associations unleashed by a simple road sign, randomly spotted on a routine Sunday stroll . . . That was probably what Chekhov meant when he famously claimed he could write a novel about anything, even an ashtray.

Art and literature rest on associations, on invisible and often impalpable connections between everything and everyone in this world.

'A beautiful illness'

> **ST:** When in crisis, reread the familiar books of your childhood and youth. Reading them is calming—like looking at the quiet sea.

I often take my little kids for holidays to a cottage on a farm near Berwick-upon-Tweed, a town I adore for its all-permeating English/Scottish dichotomy.

All my younger children (now aged six, eight and ten) are great readers and love books.

Exploring the area, we like to visit 'Barter Books' in the

nearby Northumbrian town of Alnwick—an enormous second-hand bookshop, claiming to be the largest in the UK.

The bookshop occupies the Victorian building of a former railway station. It was there that, in November 2007, I stumbled upon a small shelf of Russian books: about a dozen totally random titles altogether.

Among them, squeezed between the 1956 Guide to the USSR Exhibition of Economic Achievements and a trashy hooray-patriotic novel *Cement* by Fyodor Gladkov, I saw a tattered 1986 paperback, *The Dry Estuary*—a selection of 'mauvistic' novels and short stories by Valentin Kataev. 'Moscow, Soviet Writer Publishers, 1986' was printed on the title page. In Russian, of course . . . The price—'£3.20'—was scribbled in pencil in the top right-hand corner.

I immediately bought the book.

1986. The onset of glasnost. I am already a well-known Moscow journalist, a staff special correspondent for *Krokodil*—a popular satirical magazine selling over six million copies all over the USSR.

We journalists rejoice at the timid changes. Suddenly it is possible to write about serious social phenomena, not simply carry on exposing the peccadilloes of petty officials and small-time swindlers.

I write about crime, high-level corruption, hard-currency prostitution which officially never existed in the 'world's first state of workers and peasants', and what's even more amazing—my stories do get published, with only minor 'corrections' by our resident *Glavlit* representative (official government censor).

I get showered with readers' letters and even win awards.

We are all slightly drunk with glasnost, which never equalled freedom: the amount of truth allowed into print was strictly measured and controlled, whereas freedom as such is a volatile substance that cannot be rationed or cut into pieces—it is either there or not there . . . The disappointment that followed several years later was bitter.

But then, in 1986, as a perk of glasnost I was magnanimously allocated a tiny dacha (summer retreat) outside Moscow—one room in a shabby log cabin that I had to share with several of my colleagues and their families. The village was idiotically called *Zaveti Il'yicha*—'Lenin's Bequests' (it still carries this name at the moment of writing).

We loved our tiny country retreat, where we could chill out after a working day in scorching polluted Moscow.
I enjoyed my frequent trips to the well with two squeaky aluminium buckets (the cabin had no running water).
In the evenings, we baked potatoes on bonfires, drank vodka and had endless discussions about the country's future, mulling over that eternal Russian question: what's to be done?

Later, in 1993, already living in London, I chose the dacha as an abode for Peter Baranov—an intellectual, an art historian and a devious criminal—the protagonist (very much an anti-hero) of my thriller novel *The Third Trinity*. And whereas Baranov himself was fictitious, the village where he (and I) lived was a hundred per cent real:

'The Moscow train's loudspeaker system crackled uncertainly into life: 'Zaveti Ilyicha station.' As he stepped out onto the platform, the soft country air enveloped him. Forty minutes out on the railway line from the Yaroslavski station was this other world of silver birch trees, well tended plots and dachas. Outside the station a miniature market had come mysteriously and rapidly into existence and would melt away once the few arrivals had disappeared about their business. Old country women in white kerchiefs offered cherries and strawberries in thick glass tumblers at a rouble a glass . . .
Here and there on either side of the road, which wound its way haphazardly through a wood of birch, fir and poplar, stood the dachas—country houses masquerading as log cabins in a kind of compromise between the rural

simplicities of the past and the sparse luxuries . . .

Round a bend in the road he came up to the house he was looking for, a structure much like the others, save that an extension had been built onto its side, clearly at a later date.'

The familiar commute that neither 'he' nor 'I' will ever make again.

The chances of finding one of my favourite books of all time—in Russian!—in a small town in the North of England were close to zero. But there it was: staring at me from the shelf as a clear sign of **something** I couldn't grasp on the spot.

The realisation came several hours later, when, having opened the book at random, I read: 'Chronology, to my mind, only harms art, and time is the artist's main enemy . . .'

And below: 'It appears that mauvism is a literary device consisting of the complete negation of all literary devices . . .'

For someone who had been perceiving his own life as a literary device it was an amazing revelation. It simply meant that a writer's life was 'mauvism'—whatever that word stood for, and—vice versa—mauvism was life itself.

It was on that day that I decided it was time to start putting down on paper my own *Life as a Literary Device*.

Let me introduce you to a magician.

Listen to this: '. . . Or, perhaps, they were small sound detectors, intently probing the regions of space for a source of frequencies inaudible to the human ear . . .'

The first sentence of *The Grass of Oblivion* by Valentin Kataev (1897-1986), or 'Kataich', as he was known among the Moscow literati.

He is talking about the flower called 'bignonia'.

And here's the last paragraph of his autobiography *A Mosaic of Life* describing the eclipse of the sun in 1914:

'And then I suddenly noticed a slight roughness. blurring its edge, then a black spot that gradually became transformed into an oval, as though it had been squeezed with tongs, and finally the dazzlingly white disc of the sun turned into a half-moon. A whiff of ice-cold air from high up in the heavens seemed to ruffle my hair as the shadow of the moon raced across the battlefields.'

I can feel that distant cold 'ruffle' all over my face every time I re- read these truly magnificent words.

A Mosaic of Life was called *Broken Life, or The Magic Horn of Oberon* in its Russian original, with 'broken' implying not 'ruined' but rather 'deconstructed' or 'taken apart, bit by bit' like a completed giant jigsaw puzzle before being put back into the box.

In a letter to his granddaughter at the beginning of the book, Kataev wrote:

'I will try to concentrate on my memories in exactly the way that Tolstoy advised: in no particular order, just as they come, as I remember them, never forgetting, however, that art does not tolerate self-consciousness. From now on, may I be inspired by imagination and feeling.'

A Mosaic of Life was Kataev's third book written in the style of mauvism he himself invented in the mid 1960s (the first two were *The Holy Well* and *The Grass of Oblivion*—see above). It was like a breath of fresh air in the stale, stuffy and windowless room of 'socialist realism'.[3]

---

3   The best known tongue-in-cheek definition of 'socialist realism', the USSR's only permissible artistic trend, was as follows: if an impressionist artist draws what he sees and an expressionist artist paints what he feels, a socialist realist draws (or writes) what he hears.

A well known 'Soviet' writer, author of a number of popular children's books and founder of the Yunost' ('Youth') literary monthly, he could get away with being innovative—unlike Daniil Kharms.

Besides, Khruschev's 'thaw' of the early 1960s was in relative terms much more 'liberal' than 1937.

The writer himself refused to be tied down to defining his new approach seriously, but his English translator, Robert Daglish, insisted that mauvism was about creating 'a stereoscopic picture of life' in no chronological order. 'These works can be read from the middle, from the beginning or from the end. They are like life itself,' echoed a prominent Russian poet, Andrei Voznesensky.

Why 'mauvism' then (for *'mauvais'*, as we know, means 'bad' in French)? As Kataev himself once jokingly commented: 'I am the founder of the latest literary school, the *mauvistes*, from the French *mauvais*—bad—the essence of which is that since everyone nowadays writes very well, you must write badly, as badly as possible, and then you will attract attention.'

One must be totally dumb not to grasp the irony in these words of the ageing maître.

As a handful of Western scholars studying Kataev's work (there are a couple in the USA) profoundly observed, his mauvism, or 'writing badly' was a reaction to (I would even call it a protest against) Soviet political and cultural restrictions. In the topsy-turvy world of the USSR, where 'white' was officially perceived as 'black' (and vice versa) and which claimed, among other non-existent achievements, the world's best literature and writing, 'bad' inevitably meant 'different' and therefore something 'not bad at all'!

In his book *The Art of Writing Badly: Valentin Kataev's Mauvism and the Rebirth of Russian Modernism*, the only existing Western monograph on the subject, Richard C. Borden even asserts that

Kataev's 'bad writing' is 'among the best art to emerge from contemporary Russian culture'.

And a fellow 'Western' literary critic praises Kataev as 'one of the most brilliant writers of modern Russia' and adds: 'Of the authors writing in Russian, only Nabokov could be considered a worthy rival in his ability to convey with almost cinematic precision the images of visually perceived reality.'

Broken Life was first shown to me by my mother, an avid reader and a connoisseur of literature, who assiduously followed all new literary trends (not that there were too many in the USSR of the 1970s). The autobiographical novel was published in the country's only 'liberal' (again, in very relative Soviet terms) *Noviy Mir* ('The New World') magazine.

I was transfixed by it. As if indeed a whole 'new world', full of air, colours and smells, opened up to me as I was magically teleported to early twentieth century Odessa where Kataev (or was it I?) was growing up.

> 'I was walking with Mama, holding her hand, along a part of the street that I already knew well . . . The part of the street running from our garden gate to the corner seemed to me very wide and long, but my small watchful eyes took in all its details, or, rather, since my eye-level was that of a small three-year-old child, all those on a low plane: the round, well-fitting cobbles of the roadway, the hard granite of the kerbs, the cast-iron grilles over the sewers in which old rags and pieces of rubbish had stuck, the sidewalk composed of three parallel rows of bluish lava slabs so easy to step on in my new shoes with straps and pompoms, the lower part of tree trunks, surrounded by railings, on which were hung at regular intervals small bowls of water for the dogs to prevent them from going mad with thirst . . .'

'Can that boy really be me as well?'—so starts *Kubik*, Kataev's other mauvistic memoir.

His first-ever boat trip with his parents:

'Papa in his pince-nez and a black felt hat with a wide
brim, mama in her pince-nez and a jacket with narrow
sleeves, a veil, and a hat with an eagle's feather tossed about
by a fresh, rather angry sea breeze, sat on the deck on a
slatted bench; behind them, with a vertiginous uniformity,
dark waves with crests of foam and lacy white horses rolled
back after gushing out from beneath the wooden paddle-
wheels of the steamship. Smoke poured in thick clouds from
the two black funnels and soot flew obliquely across the
deck, disappearing into the dark green water, now almost
black from the approaching storm.
Papa and Mama, shivering quite cheerfully, thrust their
cold hands into their sleeves. Sitting between them, I tried
to do the same, but discovered that I had grown out of my
sailor coat with its golden buttons and could no longer insert
my arms into the sleeves, which had become too short and
narrow.
The sea continued to flow past us, angry and heaving,
stretching out to the farthest horizon as a whirling column
emerged from the low-flying clouds and another, farther
ahead, rose to meet it; finally the two merged and a lead-
blue tornado coursed along the horizon . . .'

In the enchanting world of mauvism, or 'self-fiction', as Kataev
himself once called it, every minute detail, on which the writer
focused his unfaltering attention, became a sparkling gem:

'. . . Papa's pince-nez, with their steel frame, cork pads that
clamped them to the bridge of his nose, and black cord
looped to the top button of his waistcoat. Such pince-nez are
now called old-fashioned or even Chekhovian, and you can
only see them on stage, when the wearer is supposed to
represent a pre-revolutionary member of the intelligentsia. I
can see Papa putting on and taking off his pince-nez, or
discarding them with a light twitch of his fingers, so that the

shining oval lenses swung for a moment like a pendulum at the end of the cord and the coral marks on the bridge of Papa's nose became visible, somehow making his bearded face particularly dear and disarmingly helpless.

Mama also wore pince-nez on a cord, but hers were in a black frame. I didn't like it when she put them on, for in my eyes she immediately became a stern lady and not my mama at all . . .'

Deconstructing the lightning

'Jodie Page, Director of First Impressions' was printed on a business card I once saw at a real estate solicitor's office in a Melbourne suburb.

I had always thought that, among other things, a writer should be his own 'director of first impressions' which, although often misleading, are invariably most memorable and revealing.

In his thoroughly impressionistic 'self-fiction', however, Kataev heavily relied on his own pioneering concept of 'pre-first impressions'.

'Imagine: a flash of lightning,' he wrote in his essay *Renovating Prose*. 'One could break down this phenomenon into its constituent parts, try to narrate in all its nuances what sticks in one's memory, and to the first perception add a subsequent one—one, as it were, "deeper" . . . I aspire to trust not even the first impressions, but . . . the 'pre-first". The lightning has not yet flashed, but you already know it, have sensed its presence, detected and understood its character. It's this seizing the moment of illumination to make artistic truth that is the very first task of artistic creation!'

Forty years after the essay was written, in a 2008 issue of *New Scientist* magazine I read about the latest human brain scans revealing that a corresponding part of the brain 'lights up'

seconds before we make a conscious decision or utter a sound. The latter phenomenon is called the subvocal speech process. Small button-sized sensors on the neck are able to capture electro-myographic (EMG) signals before the actual words are spoken.

A scientific proof of Kataev's 'pre-first impressions' theory! (Remember Oscar Wilde: 'Poets, you know, are always ahead of science'?)

Milan Kundera once noted that a man is separated from his past by two forces: 'the force of forgetting (which erases) and the force of memory (which transforms)'.

Mauvism, to my mind, is very much about that second, transforming, force.

It is also:
- a search for lost time
- a significant (or sophisticated) mess, like London or New Orleans
- a Fellini film in prose
- a succession of dreams
- a smooth roller-coaster of memory
- a literary equivalent of Moscow's St Basil's Cathedral (famous for its eclectic and asymmetrical beauty)
- fossils-strewn
- 'les mauvaises terres'—the Badlands—of literature

And many more. Memory, after all, cannot always be squeezed into the frames of time and space. It exists in its own, fourth, dimension with no metric or chronological parameters. In this respect, mauvism is not dissimilar to the Internet, where one website routinely carries links to many others. You open a link in a story that you are reading—and it takes you away to another story (loosely connected to the first one yet years and/ or miles away from it); you then close the link (if you wish) and return to the story you were reading in the first place. Or click on another link that takes you further away from it. . . Mauvism as a precursor of the Internet? Why not? . .

From Kataev's letter to a granddaughter: 'What is so extra-ordinary is that that boy was no-one else than myself, your ageing, ancient grandfather, with his dry hands, covered in brown, so-called "buckwheat" spots . . .'

If there is such a thing as immortality, Kataev has definitely achieved it (with the help of mauvism), having turned the dates of his earthly life, with a scary short dash in the middle: 1897–1986—into meaningless numbers.

Reading his words, we can still see him as an Odessa boy, walking along Deribassovskaya Street, holding his parents' hands, jumping up in the air and swinging, as little boys (and girls) do.

The street has neither beginning nor end, and nor has the walk . . .

This immortality has spread to Kataev's characters, the people whom he described, including his beloved 'Mama' who died very young, while giving birth to his younger brother Zhenia—the future renowned writer Evgeny Petrov (his *nom de plume*), who, in tandem with another Odessan, Ilya Ilf, was destined to co-author two of the best satirical Russian novels of the twentieth century: *The Twelve Chairs* (the idea of which was suggested to his brother by Kataev!) and *The Little Golden Calf*, and to perish, aged thirty-nine, while working as a military correspondent during World War II.

Speaking about connections . . .

Like a child who inherits some character traits of his parents and grandparents, a writer is the product of influences from his favourite authors (or mentors, as I prefer to call them) that merge together to give him his own unique style and voice.

My dream has always been to write a book in which I would be **guided** by mauvism: thoughts, observations and memories 'in no particular order', just as they come; poems written down like prose, in one line; gaps between paragraphs and even sentences, like the brief stops of a marathon runner to regain his breath.

A book not constrained by the limitations of either time or distance, the narrative fluctuating with ease between London and Australia, between Ukraine and the Falklands—just like in cyberspace.

A book with a number of my writer's 'alter egos'—like Kataev's Rurik Pchelkin, an ex-army officer and a young poet, who appears in several of his mauvistic novels.

Kataev himself served in the Russian army during World War I and was awarded the Order of St George—Russia's highest token of bravery, equivalent to the Victoria Cross—while always remaining a 'young poet' at heart.

You may have noticed that I have started carrying out this dream already: trying 'to concentrate on my memories in no particular order . . . as I remember them, never forgetting, however, that art does not tolerate self-consciousness'.

'The man who was addicted to seeing', Kataev once referred to his solipsistic mauvism as 'a beautiful illness'.

As probably one of the world's last remaining mauvists, I am also infected with this free-flowing stream of consciousness (not **self**-consciousness!), fed by the springs of memory and self-awareness.

One of those internal 'springs' was activated in my mind by the sight of the dog-eared Russian paperback on the bookshelf in Alnwick.

A blue notebook

In Melbourne—after a particularly hot spell preceding an abrupt temperature drop, when layers of hot and cool air collide due to a rapid fall in the atmospheric pressure—one can sometimes hear a loud whining sound coming, it seems, from above as well as from below, as if a thousand Hounds of the Baskervilles were howling in chorus on some invisible celestial moor . . .

He only heard that blood-chilling sound once, and later saw it as the precursor of what seemed to be a bout of depression. The Hounds of the Baskervilles metaphor was probably prompted by a biography of Churchill he had read on the plane from London. One of the things he had learned from that weighty (to match the lengthiness of the flight) volume was that Britain's war-time prime minister used to refer to his recurrent depression as a 'black dog'.

Despite his turbulent, peripatetic life, Vin was an optimist by nature. Having lived in Russia for many (too many) years, he came to hate the proverbial Russian gloom-and-doom and the monopoly on suffering willingly usurped by that country, whose history, art and literature had always encouraged its people not just to suffer, but to do it with gusto. He never embraced that particular Russian streak, and his favourite literary device had been irony—rather than Gogol's notorious 'laughter through tears'. He was sure he was immune to depression and did not quite believe his numerous Western friends who claimed to be suffering from it.

The moment he bought a small notebook, with its hope-inspiring aquamarine cover featuring seals, dolphins and starfish—'Cover design by Australian artist Natasha Anne Webster'—from a newsagent in Glenferry Road, he knew he was going to get better soon.

It was the first meaningful thing he had done in two months— since being hit by what was later (somewhat reassuringly) diagnosed as a 'post-traumatic stress disorder'.

For over two months he had lain supine on a small sofa bed in the permanent semi-darkness of his ageing Mum's tiny bedsit, where the window curtains were always drawn to block the pitiless burning rays of the Melbourne sun: his mother could not stand the heat, and neither could he.

Despite all the precautions, the scorching sun was bursting mercilessly through the tiniest gaps between the curtains and the walls. Looking at those slits from the sofa made his eyes hurt . . . He tried not to move, for even the slightest motion, like stirring his finger or lifting his head, caused unbearable pain—not a physical ache, but something much worse: a gnawing realisation of being caught irretrievably and inescapably between two ultimate nightmares—the one that had happened already and the one that was yet to come.

His Mum had never left his bedside, but he was too ill to talk to her and could only hold on to her frail withering hand—his wrinkled and semi-deflated lifebelt that kept him from sinking deeper and deeper into darkness.

Once, about a month into the stupor, he tried to open a newspaper, but having read just a couple of lines, felt so exhausted that he had to give up, his forehead covered with sweat.

He was sure he would never be able to write again.

It took many days of his Mum's devoted hand-holding vigil and litres of her famous thin chicken soup to put him back on his feet, and many more days before he dragged himself out for a first faltering walk up the sun-drenched suburban street.

It was then that he spotted the blue notebook in the opaque dusty window of the newsagent's.

He stumbled in, picked up the notebook from the shelf and opened it, squinting guiltily at the blindingly white pages—all blank, except for the eight words printed on the flap: 'Cover design by Australian artist Natasha Anne Webster'—the first line of text he had been able to read since the failed newspaper endeavour.

He remembered that he was in Australia. That 'Natasha' was the name of his wife, from whom he was now divorced but remained friends. 'Anne' was an anglicised version of his long-deceased granny's first name ('Anna')—as well as that of his one-time blue-eyed Siberian girlfriend ('Anya'). And 'Webster', well, wasn't he the author of the comprehensive dictionary that Vin himself consulted at times when writing?

Yes, Vin used to be a writer too. Albeit in a different genre. Compiling dictionaries was probably easier and more fun than trying to put together the never-ending compendium of a life, where new entries keep popping up every second in a totally unalphabetical and thoroughly unchronological order . . .

He thought that were he ever to write another book, he would dedicate it to Natasha Anne Webster, the 'Australian artist', who, unbeknownst to herself, had put him on the way to recovery—not so much with her 'art' but with her name alone.

He started recording his dreams.

– I am getting ready for a sky-dive and am about to board a small plane. Somehow I know for sure that my parachute won't open, but keep walking towards the aircraft, as if in a trance, when my way is suddenly blocked by a little Chinese man who pushes me backwards with his small, yet surprisingly strong, hands . . .

– I am inside a windowless van, having just been released from prison. I have no idea where I am being driven, but am happy to be out of jail. After a long bumpy ride, the van comes to a stop, the back door opens and I take my first timid steps towards freedom. Only what is it? Instead of being set free, I am grabbed by the guards and frogmarched to another prison-like building with barred windows. The only difference from the one I've just escaped is that the staff are all wearing white gowns. I realise with horror that it is a psychiatric prison of the Soviet type. They used to lock up dissidents in such prisons camouflaged as high-security hospitals. I visited a couple of those as a journalist while researching an article on Soviet punitive psychiatry. One thing I know for sure is that there's no escape from such an establishment . . .

– I return to my hotel room in a town and country the names of which I cannot remember and find it in total disarray, my few possessions scattered all over the floor . . .

– I am in the wintry park of my childhood strewn with broken wooden chairs. With Mum, I am picking the chairs up from the snow—one by one—and putting them upright. But there's no way we can clear up the whole snow-ridden mess . . .

Vin's mother took him to see a homeopath who examined his eyes with a small magnifying glass. It took a very long time, or so it seemed.

'I've never seen anything like this,' she said afterwards. 'Your adrenalin glands are completely empty. Your batteries are dead and need recharging . . . No wonder: after all you've gone through even the strongest person in the world would be in a terrible state . . .'

He duly recorded her words in his blue notebook.

His Mum's GP, whom he saw too, advised complete rest and wrote out a prescription.

The first purple capsule, taken next morning, knocked him off his feet like a glass of the pure alcohol he used to drink in his student days. Or rather, like a powerful flying kick from a karate fighter.

He found it hard to believe that only a few months before he himself had won a red belt in taekwondo.

For the rest of the day, he slept fitfully in his Mum's room to the loud chirping of merry Australian birds behind the curtained window.

'Read Kataev', a sympathetic Russian friend advised, when Vin's reading ability returned. And he did. With great difficulty in the beginning, yet gradually getting immersed in and carried away by the magic and timeless flow of mauvism:

'As we drove home [from the theatre] that night in a cab
. . . Papa was unable to fit my dead mother's small theatre
glasses back into their case, and I stared in terror at the
gas street lamps as they appeared at regular intervals with
such chaos in my heart, such despair, and such a definite,
unconquerable fear of death as I had never felt before. The
fear of death, the terror of its inevitability was—I do not
know why—connected with the lazy clatter of hooves
along the granite paving of our town, lit by the green
sinister gaslight; connected with the shadow of our cab and
its wretched bony horse, which became more and more
elongated as we retreated from a lamp-post, or began to
shrink, disappeared for a moment somewhere underneath
us and the wheels, then came to life again like a new moon
on the other side, as we approached the next lantern,
and stretched out mysteriously as before, attached to the
slumped figure of our driver and two other shadows—
father's and mine—as though emerging from another world
. . .The sharp shadows of the horse's legs, moving as though
on hinges, of the turning wheels and of ourselves—three
people travelling in the silence of the sleeping town—
seemed to be death itself . . .'

Mauvism became his medicine, his anaesthetic for the constant, yet slowly subsiding, pain.

More entries appeared in his new notebook, chronicling his recovery like a devoted duty nurse in a blue hospital gown:
  – Reading Dovlatov[4]: 'I look back and the only thing

4   A Russian émigré writer who died of alcoholism in New York in the
early 1990s.

I can see is ruins. A person who deals with words doesn't agree well with possessions.' And more: 'Debts are the only connection of a writer to "normal" people.' And: 'The most horrible thing in life, worse than hopelessness, is chaos . . .'
– The Club of Victoria's Society for the Blind is called 'Vision' . . .
– Brodsky quoting Akutagava Runoske: 'I have no principles, all I've got is nerves'.
And I've got dreams instead . . .
– If moving house is indeed a cleansing experience, then I should be transparent by now . . .
– A book on sale in a St Kilda bookshop: *Paedophiles and Sex Offenders of Australia* (sounds a bit like the *Trees & Shrubs of Britain & Europe* directory I have in London). On the bright yellow cover—a drawing of a teddy bear . . .

Somewhere at the back of his mind Vin had a vague recollection of the fact that his next book was about to come out in London, yet he deliberately tried to dissociate himself from these thoughts, bound to unleash a chain-reaction of memories and emotions he was not yet ready to face up to.

One day the same Russian friend who'd advised him to read Kataev came to visit. Under his arm, he was carrying a roll of white paper. 'This fax has arrived for you from London,' announced he. The Russian friend's fax number was the only contact option he had left with his London publisher before leaving for Australia.

It was a copy of the preview of his book from Auberon Waugh's *Literary Review.*

Vin knew Bron and had been a member of the Academy Club in Beak Street, round the corner from 'the heart of swinging London' (another name for Carnaby Street). With just two small rooms and a handful of eccentric literati members, the Club had its own 'dress code', written by Bron himself: 'Dress is informal, but shoes must be worn.'

Vin always perceived the Academy as a fragment of Sixties Carnaby Street that he had missed through no fault of his own.

The club had come to an end one Saturday afternoon (a couple of months prior to his departure for Australia) after a stray lorry drove into its ground floor lounge. Luckily, the lounge was empty.

The preview was written by another Academy member whom he didn't recall ever meeting or talking to:

'Readers of *Literary Review* who were members of the Academy club may remember him. He was the roly-poly Russian in the scruffy suit who told improbable stories: the one who disappeared for three months, fell in love, gave up drink, shed three stones and ten years, returning kitted out in Jaeger. But don't get the wrong idea: this book isn't just a memoir of passing interest—"one Russian's personal account of coming to terms with life in the West"—the writer transcends his genre, producing a new travel-writing of the soul, a journey with lessons about what really matters in life. That makes it literature. Perhaps now the Academy's door is shut, a new door will open and Chekhov or Dostoevsky will emerge, embrace him in the Russian fashion and say "Welcome to the club." . . .'

Vin did not immediately grasp that it was all written about HIM.

It was time to go back to London to restart his life. The doctors said he was not ready yet, but he decided to go anyway.

London was calling again.

London as a state of mind

. . . A nineteenth-century Russian literary critic once remarked that to write a good book about Russia, one had to leave it first.

I think this can be applied not just to Russia, but to any place one had felt attached to before having to leave it.

I have left London again—for the umpteenth time—despite my friends' advice to the contrary. Again, I have ignored Sydney Smith's pronouncement that any life led out of London is a mistake—bigger or smaller, but still a mistake. I know it is, but keep leaving London, walking out on it like on an unfaithful woman, whom I still love, only to miss it (her?) almost to tears and then—against all odds—to come back again.

Indeed, there is something distinctly feminine about London (at least, to me there definitely is). No wonder the English, while talking or writing about London, sometimes use the pronoun 'she'.

And not just the English. Didn't I myself once compare London in summer to a curvaceous bikini-clad blonde who has wandered by mistake into a drab male-only Pall Mall club?

Never before, it seems, have I missed London as much as now—after my latest 'walkout' on it (on her?). Perhaps the time has come to do a book about it? About London as a state of mind, as a chameleon city, effortlessly adjusting to my changing moods: grieving and rejoicing with me—like no other place in the world. About the city, constantly opening up new horizons, offering hope and snatching it away the moment you succumb to its (her?) treacherous charms.

Karl Baedeker once called Paris 'the temptress of a city'. If so, London is probably the bitch of a city.   An expensive and devious, yet totally irresistible, whore. A dangerous liaison for a writer . . .

'Having become a Westerner, better, a Londoner . . .'—this is a snippet from a *Financial Times* review of one of my books. I like this ostentatious and somewhat cocky 'better, a Londoner' and tend to regard it as the highest praise I have ever received. The reviewer, whose name I cannot recall, was right, for 'Londoner' is not just a definition of residence, but rather an honorary title (like knighthood, perhaps?), bestowed on those who—whether they realise it or not—have won the main prize in the lottery of life; a title that is awarded for good and—like a 'final and unchangeable' Soviet-style court verdict—cannot be altered or annulled.

What was it that dragged him towards London with such tremendous force?

Was it London's reputation as a literary Mecca? The attraction so beautifully described by one of his favourite English writers, H.V. Morton, who could have been a mauvist, had mauvism been invented in his lifetime:

> 'London has always shone like a promised land in the eyes of those ambitious to make a name in English literature. Some, such as Lamb, have been Londoners; others have been drawn to London, like Shakespeare, who journeyed up from dreamy Stratford-on-Avon to try his fortunes in the great city, so typical of that hope which has, century after century, dazzled the writer or the artist with the promise that some day he might keep a tryst with Fame in the shadow of St. Paul's. Some of them—as the long line of great thinkers proves—realised their ambition; some found sadness, neglect, and poverty; some harshness in this life and fame at the hands of another generation.'

Or was it something much more personal—something that, miraculously, went back to his own Soviet childhood in the dusty Ukrainian city of Kharkov?

. . . At the age of seven, I (together with three other boys of the same age) was cajoled into learning English. The name of the private teacher hired by our persistent parents was Grigoriy

Alexandrovich Polonsky. He was a tall, sturdy old man, with a loud voice and droopy Cossack-style moustache. In his youth, he had studied at a pre-revolutionary grammar school, from which he graduated in the memorable year of 1917 (when the Bolshevik *coup d'état* took place), having mastered—alongside all his classmates, no doubt—three living and two dead (Latin and Ancient Greek) tongues.

Grigoriy Alexandrovich resided in the distant and obscure— like the Brahmaputra River—Kharkov suburb of Kholodnaya Gora ('Cold Mountain'). I can still see his lanky snow-covered frame (it must have snowed constantly in 'Cold Mountain'), energetically entering—almost falling into—our flat.

In his battered capacious briefcase our teacher carried— among other things—some faded postcards with coloured views of London. They came from a hard-to-obtain 'Cities of the Capitalist Inferno' (or something of that sort) postcard set, shoddily printed by our local 'Red Proletarian' publishing house. These postcards were given out to us—one at a time—as prizes for diligence in our studies of the English language. As 'moral stimuli', so to speak . . . For three 'fives' (the highest mark in Russia and Ukraine) in a row we would be entitled to a bleak Piccadilly Circus postcard, for five, to the Buckingham Palace one, for ten, to something more politically significant, like, say, the grave of Karl Marx in Highgate Cemetery, featuring Marx's cartoon-like bust, with its disproportionately huge head and bulging eyes, staring at the world with wild cretinous rage.

We were very proud of those postcards, gained in unfair battles with English irregular verbs. To please our parents, we even glued them into special albums. I remember a badly drawn 'British worker', hastily printed into my Piccadilly Circus picture—probably on the orders of a vigilant postcard censor— to add a proper political balance to the otherwise rather decadent 'capitalist' view, with no tractors or red banners in sight. With a Soviet-style flat cap on his head, the 'worker' stood on the stairs next to the Eros statue holding a poster that ran simply: '1st of Mey' (the spelling mistake here is not mine, for even at the tender age of seven I already knew how to write the names of the months correctly).

This 'Mey' poster added a feline touch to the picture. At least in our still largely Russian-speaking little boys' eyes it did ('МЯУ' in Russian equals English 'meow'.) Even now, crossing Piccadilly Circus, I cannot help looking down so as not to stumble over one of the numerous cats that, as we used to imagine, must be swarming all over the square.

To earn enough 'fives' for the 'Piccadilly', let alone 'Karl Marl', as we irreverently nicknamed the founder of Marxism, was not easy. And not just because of the fact that at the beginning of each lesson we had to recite from memory—in English!—'The Solemn Oath of the Young Pioneer'[5]: 'I, a young pioneer of the Soviet Union, solemnly promise before my comrades to love my Soviet Motherland dearly, to live, learn and fight [sic: VV] as the great Lenin bequeathed to us, as the Communist party teaches us!' Not that Grigoriy Alexandrovich was so hooray-patriotic, but being a teacher, even if private, he had to play by the rules, so to speak. No, the main difficulty lay in our Pestalozzi's rather unorthodox teaching methods. These days they would probably have been branded 'forceful immersion into a foreign-language environment', or something like that.

The whole truth was that, due to the total absence of that very 'foreign-language environment' in our industrial Ukrainian city, 'closed' for all foreigners, except for a few ever-tipsy Bulgarians, he had to invent it for us. That was why—as a way of introducing the verb 'to pinch', for example—he would squeeze our cheeks with his stiff pre-revolutionary fingers and wouldn't let go until the victims wailed in English 'Stop pinching!!'

By modern politically correct standards, he could have easily

5 'Young Pioneers' – a state-run communist organisation for young children (between 9 and 14), membership of which was compulsory.

been labelled a sadist, or even a paedophile, yet in reality, he was neither. On the contrary, he was an excellent teacher, and, thanks to his learn-as-you-play approach, alien-sounding foreign words were firmly imprinted in our submissive brains.

Yes, at times, on our cheeks, too . . .

One day, Grigoriy Alexandrovich left his glasses behind in our flat. A couple of days later, his wife called to cancel our next lesson (and all the following ones, too), because our playful teacher had died suddenly of a heart attack.

His glasses were still lying on our table, and I remember being amazed and somewhat puzzled by their sudden and rather scary good-for-nothing-ness.

At least, he could now practise his two dead languages in peace, or so I thought.

The teacher passed away, but our trophies—the postcards—remained. I looked at them for hours, and, notwithstanding the awful quality of the print, could not help admiring London's unique colour pattern: red buses and red pillar boxes against the background of white Portland stone houses. That was probably how I became an Anglophile. Or rather—a Londonophile, if there's such a word at all (I don't see why there shouldn't be, by the way).

When—many, many years later—I came to London for the first time, my immediate impression was how much it resembled the fuzzy postcards of my childhood! Even the ridiculous 'worker' was still stuck near Eros, only his poster ran not '1st of Mey', but 'The End of the World is Nigh,' which—as I already knew—was rubbish, because MY real world was only just beginning.

I realised with sudden clarity that for all those years I had resided in an alien country and had only now found my true spiritual home . . .

In the years to come, I would often ask myself:

Does London actually exist?

To anyone from, say, America or the Continent, this may seem an absurd question. It only acquires a meaning if we look at London from within. As writer Duncan Fallowell once observed, 'London doesn't have straight lines. Its space, like that of the universe, is curved. But, as with the universe, you can only be inside London. There is no way of standing outside it.'

If London does exist, then what is it: a city, a region with not one but many centres, 'a nation, not a city' (Disraeli, 1870), 'a thousand villages' (Ian Nairn, 1966), or just 'an endless addition of littleness to littleness, extending itself over a great tract of land' (Edmund Burke, 1792)? And where are its boundaries?

To try and find an answer to all those questions, let us look at the concept of 'London identity'.

In my travel writing, I have always liked to personalise places. I once compared Venice to an ageing, yet still graceful, lady suffering from insomnia and shuffling around the house in her loose and worn-out slippers in the night. And living down under, I visualised Australia as a freckled and angular, albeit sporty, teenager. There's little doubt that towns, cities, villages and countries—just like people—clearly have identities of their own.

So what (or who) is London?

There is no consensus as to the great city's nature, character or even 'gender'. When London is depicted as a human being in British literary sources, it is almost always as a woman ('she'). However, London's significant parts are often represented by male figures, as is 'Old Father Thames'.

Interestingly, in Russian, the word 'London' is masculine

('*on*'—'he'), and a female Russian friend told me repeatedly that for her London was definitely a '*muzhchina*' ('a man')—an attitude shared, surprisingly, by renowned English travel writer H.V. Morton, who regarded London as 'the most masculine city in the world'.

Peter Ackroyd in his *London. The Biography* sees London as 'a human body': 'The byways of the city resemble thin veins and its parks are like lungs. In the mist and rain of an urban autumn, the shining stones and cobbles of the older thoroughfares look as if they are bleeding.' Likewise, H.V. Morton was convinced that London had a 'heart'. On the other hand, the late Ian Nairn, one of the most brilliant architectural commentators of modern times, once noted authoritatively that 'London as a single personality simply does not exist.'

Personality or not, London has always been able to evoke purely human emotions. T.E. Lawrence missed it (him? her?) so much when in Arabia, that on his return, he was ready 'to eat the pavement of the Strand'. And according to the confession of Charles Lamb in 1801, 'The wonder of these [London] sights impels me into night walks about the crowded streets, and I often shed tears in the motley Strand from fullness of joy at so much life . . .' What is it about the Strand in particular that seems to provoke such passion in writers? It would take a separate article, or a book, to muse over . . .

In return, writers have always been happy to ascribe to London some purely human qualities and character traits. W.S. Campbell, in his book *The 'Passer By' in London* (1908) called the city 'a true democrat', and Jan Morris has diagnosed it as 'manic depressive'— 'on top of the world one day, all despondency the next'.

One could speculate endlessly about London's qualities. I personally tend to agree with James Bone, *The London Perambulator* (1925), who observed: 'The character of London is its bulk and multitude, and the quality of London is its accidentalness. It never seems to have set out to be or to look like a capital.'

To me personally, London has always been a chameleon city—the only place in the world that is somehow capable of adjusting itself to my changing moods: bright and jolly when I am happy, dull and depressing when I am down. And I am not alone here: 'London appears beautiful or ugly, according to one's turn of mind,' A.R. Hope Moncrieff wrote in 1910.

As you can see, London's identity (if any) is rather blurred and resides 'in the eyes of the beholder', i.e. very much a question of outward appearance.

So does London actually exist?
The truth is I don't know. But I will keep searching . . .

As often happens, one glowing preview of his forthcoming book triggered more of the same.

Vin's Russian friend's fax machine kept working hard during Melbourne's long autumn nights, when it was the height of a working day in London. He got an offer to write a weekly column for a London-based national broadsheet. He was invited for interviews and talks. One radio station sent him a 'quirky' questionnaire to fill in:

Q: What are the two best sentences you ever wrote?
A: 1. Freedom of sausage comes first, freedom of speech follows. 2. You can redecorate the interior of a room and rearrange furniture, but you can't alter the view from its window.

Q: What flatters you?
A: Hearing that my books make people laugh and cry.

Q: What gives you hope?

A: The sound of a moving train: it signifies that, even in the most horrible situation, there's always an escape, a way out . . .

Q: Your philosophical *bête noire*?
A: 'No one is irreplaceable.' (Stalin)

Q: What risks would you never run?
A: 1. Bungee jumping- 2. Driving in central London.
   3. Flying Air Mauritius, the airline whose official logo is 'Go Straight to Heaven!'

He ended up flying not Air Mauritius, but Cathay Pacific.

He had initially booked the Emirates, but at the last moment, when, accompanied by his faithful Mum and hunched under the load of medicines weighing down his backpack, he arrived at the airport, he found out that his flight had been cancelled and the passengers were being transferred to other airlines.

The difference between his intended Emirates flight and the Cathay Pacific one he now had to take was that the latter was a non-smoking one.

An unexpected hurdle he was not ready for.

He had smoked a lot during his illness. With coffee and alcohol strictly banned, smoking was his only remaining prop. 'You can smoke to your heart's content,' his doctor told him. Now, that last prop was about to be taken away from him too.

Halfway through the flight, he had a massive panic attack. Suddenly, he was enveloped in thick blackness and the only way to shake it off was to jump off the plane—or so it felt. Or, at least, to have a cigarette . . .

He called the stewardess—a tiny Chinese woman looking like a girl in her early teens.

'Look,' he said to her. 'I don't want to break any rules, but I need a cigarette. Surely, there must be a place somewhere where I could have one . . .'

He showed her the doctor's certificate to the effect that he was recovering from PTSD.

The girl-woman studied it and said: 'This can only be done by special permission from the Captain.'

'Could you please go and ask him?' he pleaded.

And so she did. Allegedly.

'It won't be possible, sir,' she mumbled apologetically several minutes later.

In her tiny hands she was holding a tray with lemon slices.

Vin was about to explode, to start screaming that he was a well-known writer and that having one cigarette was not going to blow up the plane . . .

'Please, have some lemon, sir,' the stewardess chirped.

He stretched his hand towards the tray, but felt he could not decide which slice to choose. He was physically unable to do so. The realisation was so scary that he broke out in a cold sweat.

He sat there sweating, his palm hovering above the tray like a confused (or frightened) butterfly above an open fire, but was still unable to mobilise enough willpower to make a choice . . .

'OM-216-ST-2' . . . He could see these seemingly meaningless letters and numbers in front of his eyes. The coded name of a psychiatric prison for dissidents he visited in the Soviet Union as part of his pioneering journalistic investigation into punitive psychiatry in the late 1980s. A burly orderly told him how they fed handfuls of potent psychiatric drugs to 'politicals' to paralyse their will. That was what was happening to him now: his willpower was affected by the cocktail of medicines he had been taking.

'Could you please pick one up for me?' he asked the air hostess.

And she did. The bitter astringent taste of lemon pierced his whole being like a pang of sharp toothache, momentarily numbing and driving away all other senses, including his craving for a fag.

'. . . a wavering, red-hot line, beginning at the spot of the exposed nerve, surrounding the jaw, rising along the temple bone and exploding somewhere in the depth of the hearing area . . .'

The best description of toothache he had ever come across. From Kataev's *Broken Life*.

Another miniature stewardess soon joined the first one in trying to pacify him. Like a couple of exotic 'kolibri' humming-birds (he had seen these tiny, bumblebee-sized birds on a Great Barrier Reef island off the coast of Western Australia), they had been humming above him cheerfully, asking questions about his life and feeding him lemon slices for a couple of hours—until his craving and his anxieties subsided and he was able to doze off.

Before surrendering to coveted slumber, he remembered with sudden clarity his dream of several weeks before: a Chinese man stopping him from boarding a doomed flight.

The dream turned out to be prophetic. Even if, instead of an old Chinese man, the rescue was provided by two minuscule air hostesses.

He was on the way back to London, where no one was waiting for him any longer.

No one except for Ona . . .

ST: When in crisis, buy a new notebook (preferably

blue or yellow—the colours of calm and hope) and start recording your feelings, thoughts and dreams. The painful reality then ends up 'packaged' in a small memo pad that can be carried in your pocket. It can be opened or closed at will, or even chucked out, if necessary. By doing so, you dissociate yourself from your suffering and put things into a proper perspective.

Fear of phone calls

It all started with a phone call on a hot and humid February morning when the scorching northern wind from the Nullarbor Desert had driven Melbourne to the point of suffocation.

Shaving in front of a bathroom mirror, Vin was singing to himself. The day after next he was returning to London, having recorded eight travel programmes on Australia for BBC Radio 4's 'Breakaway'—an assignment that had taken him all across the country, from Melbourne, Adelaide and Kangaroo Island to Perth and the peculiar Western Australian town of Nea Norcia (New Norcia), populated and owned by Benedictine monks who came there from Spain in 1835.
Spanish colonial-style churches among gum trees. He had wished he was making a film instead.

Vin had every reason to be pleased: on top of completing the recordings, he had caught up with his mother and with his son, whom he was even able to take with him on his journeys across Australia.

While in Perth, he had finally persuaded himself to start the triple antibiotic treatment for his stomach ulcer—developed, coincidentally, by a Perth doctor (Barry Marshall, who proved that stomach ulcers were caused not by stress or by poor diet, but by a bacteria known as h pylori)—and prescribed to him in London by Prof. Epstein at the Royal Free Hospital.

It was Ona who had insisted he saw the elusive and omni-potent Professor Epstein, the appointment with whom was granted after six months of waiting and on condition that medical students would be present during the consultation. And they were—making VV feel like a live learning aid (which, incidentally, he was!).

He left the hospital carrying a weighty box of pills, but did not start taking them until several months later. While in Perth, he was popping handfuls of them daily for a week, but when the pill box was emptied, the duodenal ulcer, his inseparable internal companion for over twenty years—a souvenir of student years in the USSR and his first encounters with the KGB—had disappeared without a trace.

The massive dose of antibiotics made him feel pickled. He thought he could easily be cut up and operated upon without an anaesthetic.

It was in Perth that he started missing Ona; they had—rather typically—quarrelled before his departure for Australia and had not communicated since.

From Perth, he sent her a postcard saying that, unlike other places in Australia, the city was dynamic, bubbly and vivacious and that, as such, it resembled her in a way.

Ona was probably missing him too, for shortly after his return to Melbourne she rang and told him to come home soon.

His flight booked for the day after next, he was shaving in front of the bathroom mirror when the phone rang.

He dashed to the lounge dropping foam flakes on to the floor as he ran.

It was Ona calling *from London*.

'I have something important to tell you,' she said.

'Wait a sec, I have to turn off the tap . . .'
He ran back to the bathroom . . .

In his countless recollections of that moment for many years to come, he will be savouring that ten-second delay. In his memory, he liked to play it back in slow motion: floating above the floor on the way to the bathroom, slowly replacing the razor and turning off the tap before sliding back to the sunlit lounge room unhurriedly—as if skiing without skis.

The last ten seconds of quiet before the storm . . .

Like Bob Slocum, the paranoid protagonist of the novel *Something Happened* by Joseph Heller (whom he was destined to befriend a couple of years later), he had been suffering from the fear of things unexpected, particularly phone calls.

That long-lasting phobia was probably triggered by a bizarre childhood episode when a large and thoroughly secured Christmas tree (or 'New Year tree', as they were supposed to call it in the atheistic USSR), bought and delivered to the fifth floor (without a lift) of their apartment block by his ailing grandfather, whom he adored, mysteriously collapsed in his room at the very moment his granddad died at a hospital several days later and many miles away.

It happened during the night when he was fast asleep in his old-fashioned narrow bed with polished nickel-plated legs. The phone call from the hospital woke him up in the morning.

Sparkling pieces of Christmas (New Year?) toys, made of glass, were mixed with the fragments of his shattered Christmas (New Year?) dreams and scattered all over the parquet floor.

It was 31 December 1968, the day when his childhood came to an end.

Or maybe it all started much, much earlier, when his Dad gave him a bulky children's book, *Telephone* by Kornei Chukovsky, as a birthday gift?

How old was he then? Three? Or, possibly, four?

One of his very first memories

The door bell rings, his father comes in (due to the permanent Soviet housing crisis, his parents were then living separately), his coat and hat of cheap rabbit's fur sprinkled with snow. He lifts little Vitya and throws him up in the air—up to the very ceiling—before giving him the book.

> *'A telephone rings in my room.*
> *'Who is calling?'*
> *'Elephant!'*
> *'Where are you calling from?'*
> *'From Camel's place.'*
> *'And what do you want?'*
> *'Chocolate!'*

It was a lovely nonsense poem, and the fact that in Russian it rhymed nicely made it sound less nonsensical, albeit a bit scary.

He was wary of answering the huge black telephone that had just been installed in their flat and hearing the Elephant's ear-piercing trumpet-like voice demanding chocolate.

That wasn't his first-ever memory though.

The very first one was from Zagorsk, near Moscow, where he had spent the first three years of his life.

A sunny winter day, snow is lying everywhere (nearly all his childhood memories are covered with snow). He is playing in the courtyard of their block of flats. A little boy, only slightly older than VV, approaches him. The boy is wearing a brown fur coat and a round 'girlish' fur hat with ear flaps tied under his chin. In his hands he is holding a beautiful blue carafe. The carafe is empty, yet VV is fascinated by the bluish shadow it throws onto the nearest snowdrift. Suddenly, without any provocation, the girlish boy hits him on the head with the carafe's lid and runs away.

Vitya (Vin, VV, he) is left on his own. He stands there, in the middle of the empty courtyard, his tears burning little dark wormholes in the snow.

Very first impressions of the world

The Nobel-prize winning Russian émigré writer Ivan Bunin claimed (in his autobiographical novel *The Life of Arseniev*) that he could recall the very first flash of light shortly after his birth:

'I call to mind a large room lit by the sun of a late summer's day, spreading its parching glow over the sloping hill-side seen through the window facing south . . . And that is all—only one single instant!'

He also remembers seeing his Mum for the first time and thinking how beautiful she was.

Were those really his very first memories, or had they been generated much later by the extraordinarily rich imagination of this brilliant writer and poet? Like Lika, his fictionalized autobiography's main heroine and the writer's first love, who, as Bunin himself once confessed 'was a total and complete fabrication'?

Like Arseniev, the novel's main protagonist and Bunin's alleged alter ego, himself?

Where does reality end and fiction/imagination begin? I've already posed this rhetorical question in this book and will keep doing so.

Like Bunin's Lika, my Ona is largely fictional. Although, in reality, I did have a girlfriend called Lika in my late teens. It is a rather uncommon name in Russia, and as a young poet and a huge fan of Bunin I simply could not help falling in love with that girl. Or rather, with her name.

Bunin, incidentally, was the main literary mentor of Kataev, the founder of mauvism. One of Valentin Kataev's first mauvistic novels, *The Grass of Oblivion*, is very much a book about Bunin.

Kataev met him in 1914, in Odessa, where the great writer had his dacha (holiday house). One day, Valentin, then still an Odessa schoolboy and an aspiring romantic poet, gained enough courage to show his youthful poems to the maître.

'And on the threshold of the verandah, buttoning on his foreign braces, there appeared Academician Bunin himself. He gave us a quick glance and at once disappeared, but a minute later re-emerged in quite a different rhythm and fully dressed.
   Many people have described Bunin's appearance. I think the most successful was Andrei Bely: the profile of a condor, tear-washed eyes, and so on. I have forgotten the rest.'

Having forgotten the rest, Kataev remembered the main, most striking, detail: 'tear-washed eyes'.
   A number of great Russian writers, including Chekhov and Bulgakov, have 'tear-washed eyes' in their few photo portraits too (Bulgakov's are also burning with hatred of the Soviet regime which was making him suffer and eventually killed him).
Was it because they had all embraced one of Russian literature's main dictums formulated by Gogol—'laughter through tears'?

Bunin gave a couple of Kataev's poems his cautious approval and gradually became Kataev's literary mentor.

One of my favourite episodes:

In *The Grass of Oblivion*, Kataev recalls showing the Master his poem that ended with:

> "'A vase of blossoms that in autumn flower, saved by the
> poet from early blight, last survivors of beauty's bower,
> living in dreams of lost delight."
> Bunin winced as though from toothache.
> "What were you actually trying to say here?" he asked. "It
> sounds like Fyodorov's studio upstairs at his villa, where he
> paints his still-lifes. Is that it? In that case it would have been
> better to put it like this."
> Bunin crossed out the last verse with his pencil and wrote in
> the margin:
> "Autumn flowers upon the table, saved by the poet from
> early death."
> He thought for a moment, then ended firmly: "Sketch-boxes.
> Crumpled canvases. And someone's hat upon the easel."
> I was astonished at the accuracy, the brevity, the
> substantiality with which Bunin's three strokes of the brush
> amid my vague general lines had suddenly brought to life
> his friend Fyodorov's studio by selecting its essential details
> . . . With amazing clarity I saw the heavy, roughly built,
> paint-splashed easel and hanging from it the velvet hat, its
> brim artistically bent in Tyrolean style, which so perfectly
> conveyed Fyodorov's character with his elegant dilettantism
> and his innocent attempts to appear Bohemian.'

In short, Bunin took Kataev under his wing, so to speak.

Many, many years later Peter Ustinov did the same to me.

I have no doubts whatsoever that Kataev's mauvism was heavily influenced by *The Life of Arseniev*, Bunin's 'pseudo-autobiography', in the words of Andrew Wachtel, a scholar from Northwestern University in Evanston, Illinois

Arseniev himself therefore becomes a 'surrogate Bunin'—not a twin, yet definitely a literary sibling of the writer—just like

Rurik Pchelkin was for Kataev, or like Vin, VV and Victor R are for me.

> 'Bunin's narrator—a professional writer,' [continues Andrew Wachtel in his Introduction to *Life of Arseniev*] 'weaves large portions of his text around other works of literature [sic: VV]. This technique of subtext . . . places the narrative in a tradition and, most importantly, enforces the narrator's unspoken desire to show that the literature of emigration is the true continuation of Russian literature. Similar techniques are used by other émigré writers (particularly Nabokov) in order to emphasise their rightful place in the national literature which, in their homeland, had no use for them.'

I am not sure I can agree with the respected scholar's last conclusion. It is rather lucrative, of course, to justify a 'pseudo-autobiography' by a writer's gnawing nostalgia for his 'ungrateful' motherland. It is a well known fact that Bunin profoundly detested Soviet Russia and kept staunchly (and wisely) refusing all invitations (one was from Kataev himself!) to come back even for a short visit. Was he nostalgic for the place? Hardly. But he was definitely pining for his bygone childhood and youth and grieving over his impending demise: he had always had an extremely acute awareness of his own mortality:

> 'We lack a sense of our beginning and end. And it is a great pity that I was told exactly when I was born. Had I not been told, I would have no idea of my age ... and would therefore be spared the absurd thought that I must supposedly die in ten or twenty years' time.'

Nostalgia? Yes. For the years and months and days that are gone and cannot be repeated. That and the cruel absurdity of inevitable death—as well as the no less absurd, yet a hundred per cent natural, desire to cheat it in a peculiar writer's way—are, to my mind, the underlying motifs of both Bunin's 'pseudo-autobiography', with a surrogate writer as protagonist, and

Kataev's mauvism.

All Kataev's mauvistic novels are 'pseudo-autobiographies' of sorts . . .

Incidentally, Kataev's close writer friend (they rented a flat together in 1920s Moscow) and a fellow Odessan, Yuri Olesha, who—without realising it—came very close to mauvism (many years before Kataev himself invented it) in his 'pseudo-autobiographical' novel No Day Without a Line and whose own first-ever memory (according to the same novel) was: 'I am eating watermelon under a table, and I am wearing a girl's dress. The red slices of watermelon . . .' summed up both Bunin's 'nostalgia' and Kataev's intrinsic fear (or was it the other way around?) in the following passage (again, from No Day Without a Line):

> 'Sometimes the notion enters my head that the fear of death is perhaps nothing more than a recollection of the fear of birth. And indeed there was a moment when, rending my mouth in a scream, I became separated from some kind of integument and, slipping into surroundings unfamiliar to me, fell into the palm of someone's hand . . . How could that not have been terrifying?'

A strong and timeless—umbilical-cord-like?—connection of the teacher, the pupil and the pupil's friend . . .

The opening sentence of The Life of Arseniev: 'Such things and deeds as are not written down are covered in darkness and given over to the sepulchre of oblivion, while those that are written down are like unto animate ones . . .'

Now, back to VV's umpteenth unveiling crisis, his fear of phone calls and hence—to the third-person narrative.

Incidentally, the end of the whole of his previous, Soviet, existence was also heralded by a phone call.

It happened shortly after he addressed a rare gathering of

foreign and Soviet journalists in Moscow in October 1989. This was how one of the former described it in his newspaper report:

> 'Vitaliev spoke about his work, undertaken on his own
> initiative, investigating corrupt and criminal social webs . . .
> As a result of his publications, which threw a strong light
> even on connections in the political sphere, he was able to
> report 138 arrests and, what is more, a new existence for
> himself which compels him to take on certain anonymity
> and to constantly change his telephone number . . . Vitaliev
> drew attention to the fact that Soviet journalists are not
> protected in such a case by any laws and that he often
> lacks the simplest technical resources for carrying out his
> investigations. How welcome such daring press people are
> in the Soviet Union was the dubious question posed by a
> Swedish editor and answered by no one.'

From Vin's diary:

. . . They called me the next evening. 'Vitali Vladimirovich?' a velvety voice inquired. 'This is the State Security Committee. Please excuse the late call. We know how busy you are, but could you spare a moment to come and see us some time next week, perhaps?'

He realised that he wasn't being conned: only KGB agents themselves never abbreviated the name of their organisation and talked about 'us' instead of 'me' . . .

The meeting that followed was but a clumsy attempt at recruiting him—an offer that he refused with a mixture of disdain and disbelief.

After that, the harassment started. Much of it was done over the phone.

His and his wife's phone conversations were often interrupted in mid-sentence by threats and rude comments. The characteristic crackling noise in the receiver was a clear indication of the phone being permanently bugged.

His letters were routinely intercepted and then sent on in a rumpled concertina-ed state—a sure sign of having been steam-opened.

He was constantly followed in the street.

All those things were aimed at undermining him psychologically, at making him capitulate and accept the initial offer of collaboration.

Instead, they succeeded in forcing him to defect.

. . . January 30, morning. I stopped answering telephone calls at home . . . Only two days for me to hold out, though I am trying not to think about it. Two burly men in fur hats are standing outside my window and I am sure I saw one of them in the Underground yesterday . .

January 31. Three hours before departure my mother and my in-laws came. We had an impromptu farewell dinner . . . The unplugged telephone was staring at us silently from my desk—but the desk, the flat, the city, the country, they were not mine any longer . . .

ST: Having made an important life-changing decision, switch off all your phones (both real and metaphorical, i.e. receptiveness to other people's advice) until you start translating this resolution into reality.

No wonder that, already in the West, he had been resisting owning a mobile phone for many, many years until finally accepting it as a gift from the Loved One, with whom he didn't want to lose touch under any circumstances . . .

What did Ona say to him on that fateful Melbourne morning?

Does it really matter? Moreover, that Ona ('she' in Russian)—as we have agreed—is but a collective moniker for many women in his life.

Let us just assume that Ona's 'news'—something she did in Vin's absence—was perceived by him as the end of his world.

It was perhaps an exaggeration. But he was tired. Exhausted. Completely shattered. By three years of their tempestuous relationship. By nearly seven years of living between Melbourne and London without being able to settle down in either and resorting instead to long-haul intercontinental commuting. By forty-odd flights to and from Australia to see his son, sometimes for only one week at a time. By six years of almost non-stop globe-trotting, in the course of which seven books, five films and thousands of articles and columns (all in English—his 'second mother tongue', as he liked to call it) had been produced.

And the massive, even if largely positive, shock of his defection had not quite petered out yet . . .

Ona's news therefore, unpleasant and unexpected as it was, became that proverbial straw that breaks the no less proverbial camel's back.

It didn't hit him immediately.

Having put down the phone, he finished shaving and went out into the scorching Melbourne summer day.

He needed to see his Mum.

On the way he popped into an off-licence (a 'bottle shop', as they say in Australia) and bought a flask of vodka.

He was supposed to be distressed, he was thinking in an almost detached fashion, and when one is distressed, he is expected to drink vodka. He didn't particularly feel like drinking, but kept swigging absent-mindedly from the bottle as he walked, and by the time he reached his mother's tiny bedsit, the flask was nearly empty.

He shared the news with his Mum, and together they went out for a stroll, during which he finished the flask.

The rest of the day went by as if in a haze.

The shock (or whatever it was) caught up with him the

94

following morning when he realised with horror that he was unable—and unwilling—to get out of bed.

He spent five days and five nights lying supine on the sofa and staring at the ceiling—not bothering to shave or even to wash.

On the sixth morning, a worried friend had him dressed and dragged him to see a psychiatrist, who prescribed some pills (that made him feel even worse), banned him from drinking alcohol and coffee, but—on the positive side—said he was welcome to smoke as much as he wanted to.

There were still a couple of months to go before he would feel strong enough to come out and buy the Blue Notebook . . .

Why is it that bad news has always been conveyed by telephone rather than by letters, telegrams and (later) emails?

When I was a little boy in Kharkov, we were among the first in our street to get a telephone. Probably due to the fact that my granddad was an Old Bolshevik who had fought in the Revolution and the Civil War of 1918–21 and had even lived through the Great Purges of 1937, although as my Mum used to recall, the fear of a random arrest was such that he used to faint at a knock on the door after dark. A telephone was probably a sort of reward to those who had survived all the above and were still able (and willing) to talk.

An antediluvian black contraption—heavy and unappealing—was placed on a special wooden shelf, next to the KVN TV set (which had a powerful water-filled lens attached to its matchbox-sized screen to make it appear larger).

To me, the telephone always looked disturbing, even scary, as if I could somehow foretell its gruesome New Year's Eve ring of eight years later.

We had a facetious relative who would call us up of an evening (he was Chief Engineer of a large factory, and as such another proud telephone owner) and bark in a disguised voice:

'Hello, this is a telephone exchange warning. A thunderstorm is approaching, so please make sure your apparatus is covered with a wet rag, lest it explode!'

And we did—just to be on the safe side—who knows: what if, indeed, it did explode . . .

Strangely, I can still remember the number: 3-39-22. You can dial this number endlessly now without reaching anyone, for all the subscribers, except for me, are dead and do not need a telephone any more.

Significantly, the death of each of them (starting with my granddad) was announced to me via the telephone—as most modern tragedies are, I presume.

That piercing Sunday telephone call in Moscow . . . I had just had lunch (or dinner, as the midday meal is known in Russia) and was putting two-year-old Mitya to bed for his afternoon nap.

My mother was calling from Kharkov.
'Papa oomer.' (Your father has just died).
These cruel and meaningless sounds: 'Papa oomer.' Thank God one only gets to hear them once in a lifetime.

I don't envy my kids who are still in for the experience.

With Mum herself, it was a bit different. I had just returned to the UK from Australia where I was visiting her in hospital. She was in the final stages of Alzheimer's.

At the age of seventy-two, her mind, adversely affected by years of exposure to toxic chemicals (she used to work as a chemical engineer in the Soviet Union), began to give in. She had to be taken to a psychiatric hospital, where she fell over one night, broke her hip and after that was confined to a wheelchair. Her eyesight had all but gone, too.

Moved from one hospital to another, she—an intelligent, well-educated lady, a connoisseur of music, art and literature, who, during several years in Australia, had learned English from scratch by reading my books with a dictionary, to the extent that she was able to write in it and to get her stories published!—spent her days sobbing and wailing like a baby.

Her rare moments of lucidity were often harder to take than her moans. One day she suddenly recalled how I drove her and 11-year-old Mitya to Mount Buller in northern Victoria shortly after her arrival from Moscow.

'I heard about the Blue Mountains in New South Wales,' she said, with her faded unseeing eyes coming back to life and shining with her former intelligence. 'But until we went to Mount Buller, I could not imagine that a mountain could be truly blue—aquamarine, like in Nikolai Rerikh's paintings . . .'

I held my breath, hoping against hope (an old Russian bad habit) that her condition had been miraculously reversed, but my hopes were short-lived.

'I also remember you being a naughty boy there,' she added with a smile. 'You didn't want to get into the car to go back home—just wanted to keep playing in the snow . . .' I was thirty-seven at the time of the trip, and she must have confused me with her grandson.

One most disturbing sign was that she started addressing me as, 'Vitali,' not as 'Vitya' or 'Vitiusha' (my childhood monikers) as she had always done in the past.

I kept 'seeing' Mum trudging through the sun-soaked streets of Melbourne in the beige mackintosh that I had bought for her in Paris.

I would often bump into her on a tram on the way to the hospital, but she would look straight through me and wouldn't communicate.

A friend explained that these hallucinations were the start of my grieving. At times, you do grieve for a person while he or she is still physically alive.

About a year earlier, Mum had been transferred to Namarra—a specialised psycho-geriatric nursing home at Melbourne's Caulfield General Medical Centre. Her dementia was progressing, for that was the only possible course of the debilitating disease—it invariably got worse with time.

My first glimpse of Namarra was heartbreaking. The residents wandered aimlessly along the corridors, bumping into walls, mumbling and calling out. Some lay in armchairs in fetal positions, with their eyes closed, only twitching slightly every now and then.

It took me several days to get used to them. From the staff, I learned their life stories—no less tumultuous and inspiring than my Mum's—and was able to see their true human selves behind the misleading and often scary facades of their illness.

It was a painful reversal of looking at a baby and trying to fathom what it was going to be like as an adult.

Who said that getting old is like being constantly punished for a crime one hasn't committed? Yet, unless we die young, we are all destined to receive this punishment—in one form or another. Looking after my Mum, I couldn't help parallels with my then one-and-a-half-year-old daughter in Edinburgh: same 'pushchair' (only heavier), same paper tissues sticking out of every pocket of mine, and, sadly, more often than not, same level of communication.

I took her out in her bulky wheelchair every day. We went out for coffees, we listened to music in her room, and I read out her favourite poems. The rare moments of clarity she experienced were my best reward. They were precious.

What sort of life did she have?

In the USA's National Atomic Museum in Albuquerque, New Mexico, which I visited while researching *The Land of Plastic Fossils*, my unwritten book on America, I saw a map of Soviet 'secret cities'.

Collectively, these secret cities were known as *zakrytye administrativno-territorial'nye obrazovaniia* (ZATO), or 'post-boxes', and many were built by slave labour from the Soviet Gulag. During the Cold War many of Russia's towns and cities, including some of its largest, were 'closed'. Anyone with a foreign passport was forbidden to enter, and many were out of bounds even to Soviet citizens. These closed cities provided the technical foundation for Soviet military technology including chemical, biological and nuclear weapons research and manufacturing, enrichment of plutonium, space research, and military intelligence work. Large numbers of highly qualified scientists and researchers were concentrated in these geographical areas, developing new technologies but isolated from the global research community. Such 'secret cities' were known only by a postal code, identified with a name and a number.

To me, the map seemed incomplete, for one simple reason: I spent the first three years of my life in one of the 'secret cities' near Moscow, to which my parents, young scientists (Mum a chemical engineer, Dad a nuclear physicist) and newly-married graduates of Kharkov University, were dispatched in the early 1950s to work at a top-secret Soviet government facility, developing nuclear and hydrogen bombs. The town of 40,000 people—both unmapped and unnamed (it was referred to as 'Military Unit BA/48764', or something similar)—was definitely not on the map.

I approached the Atomic Museum's Director and told him about the omission. He became very curious and asked me how I could prove 'my' secret town's existence.

Of course, I didn't remember much from those distant years; I was too young. But strangely enough I could recall some smells, vague impressions and feelings. I remember the chiming of church bells (the nearby town of Zagorsk was the centre of Russia's Orthodox Church—then heavily corrupted and KGB-controlled), black-robed priests, holy-water springs in which the area abounded, and brand-new portraits of Stalin (who died one year before I was born), displayed in the windows of log cabins next to faded icons of the Virgin Mary.

I can clearly evoke a walk in the wintry forest when I—for the first time in my life—saw a wild hare jumping away from us across the snow.

We lived in a so-called 'communal flat' having to share bathroom and kitchen with several other families.

One of our neighbours—an engineer who worked at my parents' laboratory—used to keep his motorbike in the corridor (our apartment was on the fifth floor of a standard block of flats, and there was no lift, so the motorbike owner had to drag his vehicle up the stairs every evening). That mechanical monster once fell on top of me as I was playing in the communal corridor. My screams must have been heard all over the town.

Because my parents were at work all day, they had to hire a child-minder to look after me. She was an ancient woman ('babushka') in a kerchief and looked very much like Baba Yaga—the long-nosed witch from Russian folk tales who lives in a hut standing on chicken's legs.

Once, coming home from the laboratory, my parents saw the Baba Yaga with me in a bundle, standing near the church and asking for alms to feed 'the poor little orphan' that was me. It must have been the 'orphan' bit of her whining mantra that offended my parents the most (I don't blame them), and the begging Baba Yaga was sacked the same day.

I visited the town with my mother shortly before my defection from the USSR—in late 1989, after thirty-three years of absence.

The devilish 'facility' was still there, and still located in the grounds of the old monastery: only instead of crosses, the factory buildings had faded metallic red stars mounted on the onion domes.

The town was still surrounded by a thick concrete wall topped with barbed wire. You could only get in through a couple of checkpoints and provided you had an invitation from someone living inside the compound.

A young military guard having carefully scrutinised our credentials, gave us a one-day pass into my childhood and Mum's youth—equally constrained and repressed.

We were invited by a woman who had worked with my parents many years before. She was the only person still alive out of those who had worked with my father. The treacherous effects of radiation, dormant for many years, had finally come to the surface and destroyed them all (including my Dad) one by one. And the woman herself? Yes, she was alive, but was no more than a skeleton covered with skin. In her late fifties, she looked at least eighty years old. Her hands trembled incessantly, and her skull was practically bald. What a far cry from the smiling plump laboratory assistant of a girl in the old yellowish photo my mother had shown me. And God, what a miserable life she led. Alone in the whole world, without any relatives or friends, she inhabited a tiny bedsit. Books were piled everywhere: on the bedstead and under the table. Among them not a single romance or thriller, nothing that could pass as pulp or easy reading—they were almost exclusively art, history or philosophy. She offered us tea and produced a small packet from the drawer, saying it was her monthly ration. Having wasted her whole life for the sake of the system, what did she get in return? A seventy-five-rouble pension, a tiny hole of a flat and one packet of tea a month!

But she said she was happy. 'I have lots of books and lots of memories—what else do I need?'

'The place hasn't changed a bit,' my mother noted sadly on

the way back.

The early 1950s were tough. Stalin wanted to develop nuclear weapons by hook or by crook to achieve military parity with the West and then, ultimately, superiority over it. My parents had to work for twelve hours a day and there was practically no protection against the excessive radiation. My mother recalled how skin peeled off her palms when she was pregnant with me (so I must have got my share of the stuff too). According to her, some of her colleagues literally expired in front of her eyes from overdoses, and my father was particularly affected, since he dealt directly with radioactive substances and often used to travel to 'Lemonia'—a secret nuclear weapons testing range in Kazakhstan. He died of a heart attack at the age of fifty-six. None of his co-workers had lived to see his or her sixtieth birthday.

How could I prove it?

I said to the Atomic Museum Director that I'd ask my mother to pen her memories of the place and post them to him.

My Mum was then already living in Australia. She agreed to write some notes on the 'secret city' of her youth and started working on them.

Shortly after that she fell ill and had to be moved to a hospital.

Sorting out her papers in her miniature Melbourne bedsit which I knew she had left forever, I found several notebooks filled with her characteristic scribbles. Some of them were the Notes she had written for the Atomic Museum.

I've translated them into English:

Zagorsk, 1951

Winter. Early morning. I open the door to my laboratory. The room is lit up with some strange fluorescent light. Where is it coming from? The lead-lined fume cupboard holds retorts containing radioactive substances, and it is these that emanate the weird light. My first thought is: 'How beautiful!' A colleague arrives, and together we admire the sight, not realising immediately that those fluorescent solutions carry colossal radioactivity doses. They were sent to us for research purposes from a range in Kazakhstan, where nuclear bombs are being tested. This highly radioactive glow accompanies us on most of our working days. The only 'protection' we have is a pair of rubber gloves.

Midday. We are staring at Geiger counters showing the quantity of radioactive particles in the substances that we analyse. Suddenly, all the counters go into 'red' models indicating a massive radiation dose Where did it come from? People from other laboratories complain in the corridors that their counters show the same picture, and everyone is concerned about the source. At this point, at the end of the corridor there appears Major Gramolin, a young and capable scientist, a recent graduate of Moscow Chemical Defence Academy. He is short, muscular and has a noble 'aristocratic' face like a hussar in Pushkin's time. He is dressed in a protective suit that he wore while working in the contaminated (or 'dirty', as we used to call it) zone of increased radioactivity. It was the radioactivity of his suit that has made our Geiger counters go crazy—despite the 'special' decontamination shower he had to take before leaving that horrible zone.

His suit had to be incinerated. As for Gramolin himself, he died suddenly of a heart attack in his early 40s.

Olya and Raya—two girls from Ukraine—worked as our laboratory assistants. They were sent to us straight from a Poltava comprehensive school. Olya was a tall green-eyed blonde, and Raya a plump, short and brown-eyed joker. They both worked in a Drinking Water Decontamination Laboratory. Radioactive water was decontaminated with the help of a chromatographic column, and that was why they always kept three separate vessels with normal drinking water, radioactive water and water decontaminated in the column. Once—in a rush to get to the factory's canteen during a lunch break—the girls mixed up the vessels and drank some radioactive water. It was tragic. They were soon diagnosed with radiation sickness. Hospitals, disability and slow painful deaths followed.

I will never forget it, never!

A young colleague of ours, with whom we shared a communal flat, once brought home a Geiger counter to measure the radiation background. It transpired that all our personal belongings: clothes in wardrobes, cushions, blankets, even handkerchiefs were radioactive—a fact that, however, did not worry us in the least. We were young and naive, despite being scientists. Besides, what was the point of worrying when we lacked effective means of protection; our clothes and bodies were not properly decontaminated after work. Protection of the staff was never the authorities' concern: the only thing that mattered was the order of 'our great leader and teacher Comrade Stalin' to come up with the Bomb as soon as possible. After that, several of our co-workers, having armed themselves with dosimeters, measured radioactivity levels in the forest outside the factory (formerly the monastery) walls. All the trees, the grass, the flowers and the ground were emitting the invisible deathly rays. It was the same in the residential part of the town only half a kilometre away . . .

I would call Mum from London almost every day, although it was not always possible to talk to her: she was increasingly not up to it.

Shortly after returning from Australia in July 2006, I went on a two-day assignment to Liverpool.

I called Mum prior to leaving London. Several days earlier she had fallen out of her wheelchair (was thrown out of it by another demented patient), damaged her skull and had to be taken to hospital where her wound was stitched up. She was in a fairly lucid state—an increasingly rare occurrence, but had no recollection of either the fall or the operation.

'Have you found yourself a good woman from the North?' she asked me.

This needs explaining. My Mum was a great fan of the Russian North to which she had often travelled for work: its lakes, its forests, its wooden buildings and its gentle and kind blue-eyed people (at least that was how she used to perceive them). From my late teens, I remember her telling me that she would very much like me to meet 'a genuine and unspoiled girl from the North'. She was a bit of an idealist of course, my Mum. Yet, amazingly enough, my best-ever Ona (before meeting the Loved One) was from the northern Russian town of Vologda, and the Loved One herself comes from Sunderland—also 'from the North', albeit of England, not of Russia.

I said that I hadn't yet and suddenly added: 'I love you very much, Mum!'

We didn't often exchange assurances of love, and I am still at a loss why I felt an intuitive urge to utter these words then.

'I know that you love me,' she said.

Those were the very last words of hers that I was destined to hear. Not counting our frequent conversations in my subsequent dreams . . .

On my first evening in Liverpool, I went out to buy a take-away meal.

It was coming up to 8 p.m. The city centre was dead, if you didn't count several drunks and a couple of bored teenagers kicking a football across the road.

The only catering outlet that was open was a solitary kebab shop, with its floor and counters in desperate need of cleaning. None of this quite agreed with Liverpool's PR-generated image as the following year's 'European City of Culture'.

Having ordered a kebab, I thought I'd call Mum from a public phone (I still didn't own a mobile). Nearly all of them were out of order. It took me a while to find one that worked. The inside of the phone booth stank of urine.

It was coming up to 7.30 a.m. in Melbourne. They got up early in the nursing home and went to bed early too: by 7 p.m. all the patients were supposed to be asleep—indeed, like babies.

I knew all the nurses by name, but this time the voice of the woman who answered the phone was unfamiliar. 'Your Mum passed away last night. We tried to call you in London . . .'

She had to be buried the following day. There was no way I could be in Melbourne in time for her funeral.
She wouldn't have approved of such an impossible and futile rush anyway.

I had interviews fixed for the following morning.
Mum, my closest friend and biggest fan, wouldn't have wanted me to abandon them.

At least she died knowing that she was loved.

And here I am ready to repeat after Bunin, my Mum's favourite writer of all time (a dog-eared biography of Bunin was the very last book she was reading—or rather rereading—when her illness struck):
'Mother was to me, among all the rest, quite a special being, inseparable from my own, and I probably noticed and felt her at the same time as myself . . .'

My biggest regret is that she had never met the Loved One—my 'woman from the North'.

Poems in prose

Mum's sketches—or poems in prose—were written in her simple, beginner's English and published (alongside her other lyrical haiku-like vignettes on Leningrad, on Moscow, on London) in *Anthology of International Women Writers*, Melbourne, 2000:

'A scorching summer day in Melbourne.

On a summer Melbourne afternoon at the end of February the temperature reaches 40 degrees.
I stay in my friend's big house looking out of the wide window. The bright yellow sun in the blue sky reminds me of a burning ball. There are no clouds, no wind—the nature looks so quiet, like a theatre set.
But I feel something sinister in this calm. Soon, very soon, will be the big change. Like a disaster—the fire, or the earthquake, or the end of the world . . .
The hot dry wind comes suddenly, howling loudly, taking water from the air, soil, trees, plants and human bodies. The sun burns out, colouring everything around in gloomy grey-brown.
The branches of the trees, bushes in the garden begin to rock. The flowers bend and fall on the ground—as if begging: "Please save us! Save us! Give us a little water, we are dying! You have shelter and water. We don't!"
Poor trees, poor plants. poor people. We are all alive. We are all part of nature. And we are all suffering on this scorching Melbourne day. When heavens send us rain in the evening, we experience life together . . .'

She was suffering from heat and loneliness in Australia.

I arranged for her to join me there in December 1991. It was difficult. Several times, the Soviet authorities had rejected her application to emigrate: 'Your son is a defector, and we don't allow them to be reunited with their families.'

Now well known in Australia, I used all my influence and contacts (and those included the Foreign Minister and the Prime Minister) to get Mum out, but it was only in 1991, when the USSR was on its last legs, that she was finally allowed to leave.

Eight months after her arrival in Australia, however, I got a job offer from *The European* and left for the UK. And just like two years earlier in Moscow, when confronted with my decision to defect (which, by existing Soviet terms, meant never seeing each other again), she was distraught at first but quickly composed herself and said: ' I am going to miss you terribly but you have to do what's best for you. I give you my motherly blessings . . .'

And there she was, left on her own again—face to face with her memories:

'A little town outside Moscow.

After the university, I came to live in a little town near
Moscow, to where my husband was sent to work as a nuclear
physicist in a secret factory.
It seems the time passed quickly, because my memories are
very clear.
The little old town outside Moscow with small wooden
houses and narrow streets, the beautiful northern forest
with springs and lakes.
A big cathedral stands in the town centre. The domes are
the colour of blue sky with gold stars decorating them.
Even under Stalin's Soviet system, when religion was
actually forbidden, the bells of the cathedral were rung.
I remember our factory housed in the building of a former
cloister where on the gates the crosses and five-point Soviet
red stars were together.
The winter forest coloured white with snow . . .
The silence . . .
The Place . . .
Two young and happy skiers skiing along the track . . .'

A great admirer of Kataev, Mum was probably a mauvist at heart too . . .

These 'two young and happy skiers' are my parents of course.

After twenty-four years of waiting (the gap between my Dad's and Mum's deaths), they are now together—this is how I see them in my dreams—always together, waiting for me— sliding along the endless ski track dividing the world into two identical snow-ridden parts and leading into eternity.

A map with a scale

Another horrible phone call pierced my life in March 2004.

It was from BBC Radio 5 Live.

'Can you comment on Sir Peter Ustinov's death? You were friends, weren't you?'

Learning about his death from Radio 5 **Live** . . . Ustinov would have cackled at this.

I had known it was coming: Piotr Ionovich, as I had been politely addressing him Russian-style: by first name and patronymic (his father was called 'Iona') since our first meeting in 1990, was approaching eighty-three. Yet the news still came as a shock.

I remembered him telling me in Melbourne in 1992: 'I've just received a new passport that expires in 2002, so my aim now is not to expire before my passport . . .'

He had succeeded. He always did.

It was hard to imagine that he would never call me again and, pretending he was Mikhail Gorbachev or President Bush Senior, ask me to come and see him at his favourite London hotel—the Berkeley—or to have lunch.

Having lunch with him was like sharing a meal with a whole crowd of people—actors, drunks, priests, politicians—whom he mimicked tirelessly and relentlessly. While our food was served, he would impersonate the waiter.

He was also in the habit of mimicking my accent, and would address me in heavily accented Russian as 'Comrade Colonel'.

His biggest reward was people's laughter. 'I was irrevocably betrothed to laughter, the sound of which has always seemed to me the most civilised music in the universe,' he wrote in his best-selling autobiography *Dear Me*.

At times, it felt as if he was afraid of ceasing to perform even for a second, because for him that would be on a par with no longer breathing. And the size of his audience—be it the Barbican, the Royal Festival Hall or just one person, whom he had met in the street—did not matter.

Once, having come to see Piotr Ionovich in the Berkeley Hotel, I found him alone in his suite, piled with clothes, books, letters, manuscripts and whatnots. He waved me in without stopping his phone conversation and offered me a vodka.

Reclining in a leather armchair, so deep and soft that it negatively affected the sitter's self-esteem, I couldn't help overhearing his words. He was obviously being interviewed—and, as always, he was brilliant: wise, quick, funny and irreverent.

'Who is it on the other end of the line?' I was musing an hour later downing my fifth shot. 'The *Guardian* or, maybe, the *New York Times*?'

'Who was the interview for?' I asked Ustinov when he finally (and rather reluctantly, it has to be said) got off the phone. 'Oh, it was some little university newspaper from Essex,' he replied.

One of his most beautiful human qualities was his complete lack of arrogance or pomposity—traits that could easily have been forgiven in a winner of two Oscars and the only foreign member of the French Academy of Arts.

He was extremely—almost excessively—accessible and, despite being terribly busy with all his shows, plays, films, books, columns, charities and so on, found it hard to refuse favours to anyone.

'Friends are not necessarily the people you love most—they are simply the ones who got there first,' joked he.

Needless to say, people often used him for self-promotion, but he had no regrets (except, of course, for *House of Regrets*—the West End play that he wrote and starred in at the age of twenty-one!). 'If you do good things, then good things will come to you,' he said to Terence Stamp, his co-star in *Billy Budd*—the film that Piotr Ionovich also produced and directed. And they did. Frank Muir was right when he called Ustinov 'one of the best-loved people in the world.'

Ustinov's friendship changed my life.

I often wondered why he singled me out of thousands of people he had come across and 'took me under his wing'.

Was it because we both had Russian names (although by then I had defected from Russia, and Ustinov himself was only conceived in St Petersburg and born in London, to which he 'defected' inside his mother's womb), yet in actual fact combined lots of ethnicities ('Ethnically, I am filthy,' he liked to repeat)?

His French wife Hélène once confided in me that I reminded Peter of the way he himself used to be (and to look) in his younger days.

'For Vitali—Brother, Nephew, Son—in Spirit, in Laughter, in Rotundity, and in a tranquil earnestness of purpose'—he wrote on the dedication page of his book *My Russia*.

Was 'Rotundity' the main reason for singling me out, I sometimes wondered uneasily?

In mid-November 2004, I flew to London from Dublin (where I was then temporarily based) for my last meeting with Piotr Ionovich.

In fact, I was invited to two of his 'memorial services': at the University of Durham, of which he had been Chancellor from 1992 ('Can you believe it, Vitali, I've only just been appointed Chancellor of Durham University and have already received a letter, addressed to 'Dear Mr Rectum'?') and in London—at the Church of St Martin-in-the-Fields. Due to my very busy schedule, I was only able to attend one—in London.

I felt considerable guilt at having to refuse an invitation from my 'Brother, Uncle, Father', even if deceased. One thing I was sure about, however, was that he himself would have taken his own demise in his stride.

'Life without death is like a map without a scale,' he once observed.

Piotr Ionovich was with me constantly during this trip. He squeezed his bulk into the seat next to mine (no chair was ever big enough for him—in more than one sense) on my Aer Lingus flight.

In reality, he had ended up sitting next to me on a trip once before—inside my brand-new Mazda 121.

'What a lovely little car you've got there! I have never seen a car like that before!' he exclaimed on spotting it in front of my Melbourne house in early 1991. Like a perennial teenager refusing to grow up (his face always struck me as not that of an elderly man, but rather of a long-suffering youngster, and the mane of grey hair—paradoxically—made it look even younger) he had a great passion for cars and even collected them. I knew he also had a personal jet, but was not sure whether he collected planes too.

'I'd like to have a ride in your car!' he insisted.

I could not share Ustinov's enthusiasm. It was only one day before that I had got my first driving licence, and my recent collision with an unsuspecting street fire hydrant, the memories of which were still fresh, did not bode well for my driving future. Besides, I had never driven the car on my own, without an instructor.

'I want you to drive me to the restaurant in this lovely car of yours!' he repeated.

We were supposed to have dinner in one of Melbourne's Russian restaurants.

I tried to talk Ustinov out of it by explaining what an awful tyro driver I was. I told him about the tragic fate of the fire hydrant, but he stayed firm.

He pushed himself inside my 'droplet' of a Mazda, knees first, and the tiny car sagged under his weight. I climbed onto the driver's seat (remember: a 'brother . . . in rotundity'?)—and the Mazda's metallic underbelly touched the ground. Off we drove, striking sparks from the asphalt . . .

I sat behind the wheel trembling like an aspen leaf. If something happens, I'll go down in history as the man who killed Peter Ustinov, I was thinking obsessively. The thought in itself was not conducive to safe driving.

By the time we reached the restaurant, I was covered in cold sweat and had totally lost my appetite.

'Your driving was perfect!' Ustinov reassured me as he slowly levered himself out of the car. He had survived the experience, and his genius had been preserved for humankind. It was spared by the then world's worst driver (myself), to allow us many more meetings—in Melbourne, Sydney, London, Paris, Rome, Manchester—for thirteen more years to come.

As I flashed my passport in the poker face of an immigration officer at Heathrow, I recalled Peter Ustinov's innate dislike of borders and immigration controls.

A compulsive traveller, he was puzzled and offended by the old immigration forms he had to fill in on entering Australia ('One of the questions was "when was the last time you had indigestion?" and the next "whether or not you are insane?"') and the USA ('In the space for "Your Skin Colour" I always write "pink"'). A true internationalist, he took pride in having Italian,

French, Russian, Swiss, German and even Ethiopian blood in him, but—contrary to what many people thought—not a drop of English. When he directed an opera at the Bolshoi Theatre in 1998, one Russian newspaper printed an article headlined 'Englishman Saves the Bolshoi', which prompted him to say: 'I've never been accused of being English before.'

Kofi Annan, who knew Ustinov well as a roving UNICEF goodwill ambassador for over twenty years, once remarked that Piotr Ionovich could easily 'double as permanent representative of all the UN member states'.

I thought Ustinov would have been pleased to see me waving my *European* passport. And although we first met when I lived in Australia, he always said (not in a didactic but rather in an avuncular manner) that my place was in Europe.

I was having dinner with Piotr Ionovich and Hélène in Rome on a hot summer evening in 1992. Earlier in the day we had all had an audience with the Pope, and, of course, afterwards Piotr Ionovich started mimicking the Pontiff too.

At the restaurant, Ustinov was drawing caricatures on serviettes (a brilliant cartoonist was one of his less known multiple incarnations). He was joking with the waiter in fluent Italian ('How many languages do you speak?' I asked him. 'I make mistakes in eight,' he replied.) Halfway through the meal, Hélène told me it was the twentieth anniversary of their marriage. I was extremely touched and rushed out to buy flowers for her.

'Listen, Vitali, it is time for you to move back to Europe,' Ustinov said when I returned. 'The editor of The *European*, for which I write a weekly column, knows your work. Why don't you go and talk to him?'

We ended up writing for the same newspaper, and our respective columns often appeared on the same page, next to each other.

Ustinov adored writing his *European* column and was very proud of it. He once opted out of taking part in a top-rated BBC chat show, saying he had his column to write. Having published over twenty books, he still felt he was undervalued as a writer, particularly in Britain, where he thought they perceived him only as a funny fat man, or a 'dancing bear'. The political views he expressed in his columns were sometimes naive (great artists seldom make good politicians), but always honest, well written and highly humanitarian. He was extremely saddened when The *European* had to wrap up in 1997.

The bells of St Martin-in-the-Fields were tolling cheerfully, not mournfully, above Trafalgar Square. The day was as dark and chilly as only London can be in mid-November. Street lights were still burning well into the morning, and in their treacherous light the rain-soaked air looked like a condensed yellow ganglion suspended from the sky. One could almost scoop it by handfuls and cut it into pieces.

A line of black-clad people, hiding under umbrellas, was snaking into the church for Peter Ustinov's last performance. Yes, it did feel more like a performance than a 'memorial'. The church entrance was besieged by paparazzi and autograph-hunters who had come here to spot a royal or a celebrity. Even after his death Ustinov didn't stop attracting crowds.

Young boys and girls in sailors' uniforms, the so-called 'London Sea Cadets', guarded the church entrance. I thought that was moving and somehow conveyed two very prominent streaks in Piotr Ionovich's character—childishness and romanticism. Yes, he was an unlikely modern celebrity—too sensitive, too kind and too approachable. He was a dreamer—a lucky dreamer who had managed to have almost every dream of his realised.

Looking at the kids, I had a flashback to my own Ukrainian childhood, when I wanted to become an engine driver, and a sailor, too, no doubt. Playing truant, I used to hide in a small cinema, round the corner from my school. It was there that I first saw Stanley Kubrick's *Spartacus*, where Ustinov played a character called Batiatus—the role for which he won one of his Oscars. I had watched that movie over a dozen times . . .

Inside the church, one could indeed observe a curious mixture of celebrities, royalty (like, say Prince Michael of Kent—a relative and complete look-alike of the unfortunate last Russian tsar Nicholas II) and 'ordinary people' like me. Many of the latter, like young actor Nick Atkinson, had been 'singled out', helped and advised by Ustinov—just like I was.

I sat next to an empty space with the name tag 'Countess Madeleine Douglas'. Ustinov would have loved that and would have immediately come up with a joke. I remembered how much he laughed when I told him the story of a German woman, who wrote for The *European* and had 'Countess Tatiana von Dunhoff' printed on her . . . credit card. She was probably indeed a countess: there are plenty of them in Germany.

Ustinov disliked hereditary and other 'titles' and regarded his own belated knighthood with a good deal of irony. I could never seriously think of him as 'Sir Peter Ustinov, OBE' (apart from his natural and rather charming OBEsity that is).

It was a highly unusual church service, with lots of laughter, theatre and music. Piotr Ionovich adored classical music, particularly Mozart, whom he prized for 'his most profound superficiality'. He could imitate the sounds of most musical instruments and one evening, for a bet (as recalled at the service by his American friend Theodore Steinway Chapin), wrote down from memory the names of forty (!) Swiss (!!) composers.

He had extraordinary brainpower, and once, having spotted some dictionaries on a shelf in my Melbourne study, noted: 'Vitali, you are the last person who needs dictionaries. Writers don't need dictionaries. Get rid of them.' And I did.

Piotr Ionovich did come up with a surprise for me during the service, the 'script' of which, as I was told, he had written himself. It happened when his daughter, actress Tamara Ustinov, and

Malcolm Rennie came to the altar (I nearly wrote 'on stage') to perform a short extract from his play *The Love of Four Colonels*.

'It was raining in Kharkov last Sunday,' were the words of Malcolm Rennie's character, the Russian Colonel'.

Out of all Ustinov's huge literary heritage, this one sentence, mentioning my native Ukrainian city (he knew I grew up there), was read out in the church on that day! It was also a gentle reminder of his humorous way of addressing me as 'Comrade Colonel'.

Spasibo, Piotr Ionovich . . . I've heard your greeting . . .

I was sure each friend of his in the 'audience' had received his or her own greeting, too.

After all, we didn't turn up there 'to pay our last respects', as London newspapers reported the following morning. We came to express our ongoing love for 'one of the best-loved people in the world'—a friend, an actor, a writer, a columnist, a dramatist, a wit, a mimic, a cartoonist, a raconteur, a film-maker, a director, a producer, a musicologist, a satirist, a playwright, a polyglot, a peacemaker, a goodwill ambassador and, first and foremost, a wonderful human being whose name WAS, IS and WILL ALWAYS BE 'Peter Ustinov'.

Until love, joy and laughter die out completely on this small and lonely planet of ours. . .

Back in Dublin, I called my childhood friend in Kharkov and asked him whether it had rained there the previous Sunday.

He confirmed that it had.

Chasing ghosts

A quote from Joseph Heller's *Something Happened*, a scathingly hilarious literary catalogue of modern complexes and anxieties: 'I hate funerals—I hate funerals passionately because there is always something morbid about them—and I do my best to avoid going to any (especially my own, ha, ha).'

I always found this 'ha, ha' a bit spooky. A dead man's chuckle from the grave . . .

I first met Joseph Heller only a few months before his death, in summer 1999, at a lunch given by Simon & Schuster in his honour. His latest (and last as it turned out) autobiographical book *Now and Then* was about to be released in the UK, and he was in London to promote it.

I was invited to this lunch because two of my books: *Borders Up!* and *Dreams on Hitler's Couch*—were coming out simultaneously with his as part of the launch list of Simon & Schuster's new imprint 'Scribner UK'.

As always, I turned up early and settled down to wait on a bench near the restaurant's entrance.

I was soon joined by a tired-looking old man whose sallow face looked vaguely familiar.

His younger self—smiley, curly-haired and known to the whole world from the back cover of his masterpiece *Catch 22* (I read the smuggled paperback of it while still a student in Kharkov)—was showing through the badly fitting camouflage of ailment and age. He was suffering from an incurable debilitating illness that had left him partially paralysed only a couple of years before and was to kill him by the end of the year.

But I didn't know it then. And neither did he.

'You must be Joseph Heller,' I said.

We shook hands. His movements were slow and appeared forced, as if his every small gesture or a slight turn of his head were painful. They probably were. Yet his warm brown eyes were lively and full of youthful glimmer.

The eyes of an eternal Coney Island teenager who grew up in the shadow of a ferris wheel—curious, mischievous and hungry for adventures.

He asked me a lot of questions about my life in the Soviet Union and was nodding knowingly as I answered.

He had a peculiar squint that made him look as if he knew everything about you.

I told him I was about to start researching a book on America and was very interested in Coney Island, where knish and hot dog were invented and part of which was now known as 'Little Odessa', for 150,000 Soviet emigrants, mostly former inhabitants of Odessa, had settled there in the last twenty-five years.

I heard they had radically altered the face of that 'old world' New York neighbourhood, nicknamed 'a retired poor man's Miami Beach' in the 1930s, where Joseph Heller was born and grew up.

Our next meeting was a couple of months later, at the Cheltenham Festival of Literature. But prior to that, I started researching my American book with a ten-day-long trip to New England.

It was like chasing a ghost.

The ghost-hunting feeling was enhanced by schizophrenic pre-Halloween displays of grinning carved pumpkins and plastic skeletons on the porches of clapboard country houses along the highway—as if they were smirking disdainfully at the sheer futility of my quest.

I was trying to find the former abode of Alexander Solzhenitsyn, last century's greatest Russian writer, near the town of Cavendish, tucked away among the hills of Vermont— the place where he had spent seventeen nostalgic and highly prolific years of exile before returning to Russia in 1994.

I had always wanted to see that house. Why?

The answer can probably be found in the spirit of mystery

and mass hysteria which surrounded Solzhenitsyn's name in the Soviet Union of my youth. All his books were confiscated from shops and public libraries, and one could easily end up in prison for simply possessing (let alone reading) any of his works.

Bans and fatwas have always been the best publicity for writers, and I shall never forget the peculiar ticklish feeling of danger I experienced while reading a tattered copy of *One Day in the Life of Ivan Denisovich*, aged sixteen.

Hiding the book under the blanket in my bed, I read (or rather devoured) it in one sleepless night (next morning I had to pass it on to the next person in line) by the treacherous light of a small torch. My full awareness of all the dangers involved only added to the joy of reading.

The book described one routine day of a prisoner in Stalin's Gulag, where Solzhenitsyn himself had served a stretch. And while heroic Soviet workers and peasants all joined in the well-rehearsed propaganda chorus of 'unanimous condemnation' ('We haven't read his books, but we furiously reject Solzhenitsyn's views . . .'), I treasured an old copy of *Novi Mir* magazine, with one of the writer's early short stories, which they 'forgot' to confiscate from our school library.

Later we learnt that, 'in accordance with the Soviet people's demands', Solzhenitsyn was 'thrown out' of the country and, after a spell in Switzerland, settled in Vermont, USA, where he, allegedly, lived the life of a reclusive O'Reilly, penning his 'anti-Soviet drivel' in a palace, surrounded with barbed wire.

And here I was in autumn-charged Vermont, on my way to that mysterious 'palace', whose famous dweller, then eighty and still alive, was no longer there.

He was back in his ungrateful motherland, where his prophet-like beard and his laughable attempts at teaching the Russian people 'how they should rebuild' their country became subjects of bitter comments and open ridicule. 'There's no prophet in one's own fatherland,' goes an old Russian proverb. Solzhenitsyn should have known better . . .

It was with sadness that I spotted a copy of *One Day in the Life of Ivan Denisovich* on sale at a street kiosk in Kiev in 1994 for one tenth the price of a can of Coke!

And nobody was in a hurry to buy it . . .

After the village of Plymouth, birthplace of America's mediocre president Calvin Coolidge, the road wound through desolate countryside, dotted here and there with broken agricultural machinery, left to rust in the field, and forlorn uninhabited houses in different stages of disrepair—as if I had left prosperous New England and was driving through some dreary time-frozen landscape, only slightly brightened up by the exquisite palette of autumn forests.

It was not long before I spotted the first weather-beaten 'Cavendish' sign, and shortly the town itself came into view.

To call Cavendish a town was a typically American over-statement: by European standards, it was but a medium-size village stretching for a couple of miles along the track.

Walking in its deserted main (and only) street was like going back seventy odd years, to the times of the Great Depression. Nearly half of the houses were abandoned. Shabby wooden sheds signposted 'The Black River Medical Centre' and the 'Mammoth Hobbies Full Line Hobby Store' looked permanently closed down. The only town service that seemed to be still running (at least, its sign had a phone number) was 'Chimney Care'.

In the town square, next to a firmly locked hut designated 'town hall', I spotted a granite obelisk, which—from a distance—could be mistaken for a regulation countryside war memorial.

It was indeed a memorial, not to the fallen of Cavendish (the town lost only nine men in all the wars of the twentieth century), but to a nineteeth-century local railway foreman called Phineas Gage, who, as it transpired from the carved inscription, once had his tamping iron accidentally blown through his skull and out the top of his head—and survived.

I later learned that the Phineas Gage Historic Festival and Anniversary Commemoration, to mark 150 years from the day when poor Phineas's head underwent its historic piercing, was held there in 1998. The events of this Rod-Through-the-Head Commemoration Festival included a 'BBQ chicken lunch, hosted by the American Legion Post'! The sad irony of commemorating the piercing of Phineas Gage with a barbecue was lost on the proud natives of Cavendish, who now wanted to make the Festival (and the barbecue, no doubt) an annual occasion.

My first port of call was Joe Allan's general store, made world-famous by the hand-written sign 'No Directions to the Solzhenitsyns' that used to adorn one of its walls. In accordance with New Englanders' traditional respect for other people's privacy, the locals had been unconditionally protective of their own eminent exile and stayed mum about his whereabouts, although few of them were able to comprehend who exactly he was and from whom he was hiding in Cavendish.

The sign was no more, and a stocky blonde woman, unhurriedly frying burgers behind the counter, initially claimed complete ignorance not only of Solzhenitsyn, but of Joe Allan, too. It took her half-a-dozen burgers to recall that the latter had sold the shop a couple of years before and had moved out of town. Well, the first pancake is always a lump, as they say in Russia (I am not so sure about the first burger).

Apart from the store, the only other Cavendish establishment which wasn't shut down on that Saturday morning was a small bungalow, insisting on the title of Cavendish Fletcher Community Library. There I had a sudden stroke of luck.

Joyce Fuller, the librarian, not exactly inundated with customers and whiling away her time in the company of a fashion magazine, was genuinely happy to see a fellow human. She pointed to a near-empty shelf with thirteen Solzhenitsyn volumes in English translation, presented to the library by the writer himself shortly before his departure. The glossy hardbacks were neatly spread out along the shelf to give the impression of abundance.

She confessed to having been present at both of Solzhenitsyn's public appearances before the townsfolk: in February, 1977—to say hello and to apologise for the fence (a sacrilege, by Vermont standards) that he had to build around his property to protect himself from 'the reporters and idle types'; and in February, 1994—to thank the people of Cavendish for their 'kindness and hospitality' and to bid farewell. She then kindly offered to photocopy the text of both addresses for just ten cents each, with a pamphlet on the extraordinary survival of Phineas Gage thrown in.

'Are there any plans to commemorate Solzhenitsyn's seventeen years in Cavendish?' I asked her. She was not sure and suggested I call up Rich Speck, the town clerk, which I did without leaving the library.

The town clerk sounded suspicious, as if Solzhenitsyn was still there and needed to be protected. He assured me that there were no plans for a Solzhenitsyn memorial and added that the writer's presence 'had no day-to-day impact on the Cavendish community'. Unlike that of Phineas Gage, no doubt . . .

According to Mr Speck, Solzhenitsyn's house was now owned by his two sons, but he was not sure whether they were in town.

Using a sophisticated, almost spy-like, map drawn by Joyce Fuller, the librarian, on the margins of the hapless Phineas Gage brochure, I set out in search of the old Hoffman house and farm, bought by Solzhenitsyn in 1976 for $150,000.

From the reminiscences of those few 'reporters and idle types' who did manage to worm themselves on to the 50-acre property,

I knew that it consisted of a two-storey main house; a library-cum-study, where Solzhenitsyn wrote from 8 a.m. to 9–10 p.m. every day (without a single holiday in seventeen years!) standing at a lectern; a guest house; a small pond; a vegetable garden, and a tennis court, where he would 'gracefully but slowly and inexpertly' (to quote one of his biographers) hit the ball during rare intervals in his writing.

Whoever Solzhenitsyn was hiding from, he couldn't have hidden better.

I turned off the paved road onto a dirt-track, snaking through the thick forest alongside a bubbly creek. After an umpteenth zigzag, I finally saw it. Not the house itself, but the notorious fence and the gate with an imposing 'No Trespassing. Police Take Notice' sign. Several closed circuit security cameras were staring at me blankly from nearby trees. The rusty intercom button got stuck in its socket when pressed, and there was no reply. It was evident that no one was inside the compound.

Three polythene-covered parcels of books lay on the ground, on the other side of the gate. They were addressed to Ignat Solzhenitsyn, the writer's elder son, a one-time child-prodigy musician.

For a while, I stood in front of the locked gate, listening to the jolly chatter of the creek and to the soft rustling of falling leaves, as if nature itself was shedding the leafy baggage of the crazy epoch when authors were either imprisoned or had to encage themselves behind fences and security cameras, only because they wanted to keep writing the truth.

But, somehow, there was no finality about the scene. A leaf-carpeted path led from the gate towards Solzhenitsyn's house, which could not be seen from where I stood. The path climbed up the hill before disappearing from view. That was probably why—just like my quest—it seemed incomplete, as if cut off in the middle. But it also implied continuation.

What was going to happen next? The Vermont forest was offering no answers. Only the fallen leaves slowly pirouetted in the air, as if trying to delay the ultimate moment of dying. And the snow-white trunks of 'Russian' birches were bursting through the red-brown sylvan setting—like piercing screams of discord through the harmonious symphony of autumn.

As it turned out, that was not the last writer's ghost I was destined to chase that year.

In the Cheltenham Festival Programme (in November of the same year), our photos—Joseph Heller's and mine—were printed on the same page, next to each other.

Our talks were to be given on the same day, at precisely the same time, but at different Festival venues.

We stayed at the same hotel and agreed to meet up for breakfast one morning, before our respective book-signing sessions.

'I hate book signings,' Heller muttered, sipping his tea. He then told me how he was once invited to sign some books in the Mall of America.

'There were three people at my table. And next to me, the lady from 'The Wheel of Fortune' who never says a word in the programme—just rotates the wheel—was signing copies of her autobiography. And you know, Vitali: the queue to her table stretched for over a mile!'

With *Catch 22* as his very first book, he became a living legend who had been trying to catch up (no pun intended) with its resounding success for the rest of his writing career.

'You know what, come to New York and I'll show you my Coney Island,' he said when we were saying goodbye in the lobby. He gave me his phone number and asked me to call him several days in advance. 'I'll have to come over from Long Island where I now live,' he explained almost apologetically.

With his publicist in tow, he then went off to sign his books.

I was not destined to see him ever again.

Several weeks later, having agreed with the *Daily Telegraph* to do a feature on Joseph Heller's Coney Island, I was about to fly to New York and called him at home.

The phone rang for what seemed an eternity, and as I was about to replace it, he finally answered.

In a semi-whisper he said he was not feeling very well, but didn't cancel our 'excursion' and asked me to call him again from New York.

I did. We agreed to meet inside the Grand Central Station in the morning of 13th December.

On the afternoon of December 12, I was on a Subway train when a man next to me opened an early edition of The *New York Post*.

Joseph Heller's haggard face was on the front page.

The man hardly looked at it and flicked over to the Sports section.

I got off at the next station and bought the paper, although I already knew what must have happened.

You can see a photo of a writer, even of a great American writer, on the front page of a US tabloid on two occasions: if he wins the Nobel Prize for Literature or if he dies.

I knew that the 1999 Nobel Prize for Literature had been awarded to Gunter Grass. Therefore . . .

A later edition of The *New York Post* for the same day had Joseph Heller's obituary moved from page one to page twenty-six.

I kept our 'appointment' inside the Grand Central next morning hoping against reason, that he would somehow turn up . . . At times, it felt I could almost see his light-grey (nearly white) curly hairstyle and his stooping frame in the crowd.

And then I decided to go to Coney Island on my own.

Brighton Beach, the part of Coney Island to which I decided to travel first, was one of the most idiosyncratic places in New York, if not in the whole of the USA. Going there was not just about catching up with Joseph Heller's childhood and youth. It was an opportunity to visit the country of my own birth, the Union of Soviet Socialist Republics that didn't exist any more.

I knew that spiritually, linguistically and psychologically, Brighton Beach was not part of the USA.

'We don't go to America. We have nothing to do there,' its residents liked to say.

On that gruesome and wet winter morning, when Manhattan resembled a post-modernist version of Venice and the shoe-cleaners near the Grand Central Station were earning more in one hour than during the whole of July, I left the United States and boarded a B-line Subway train to Brighton Beach.

My wobbly and unkempt carriage resembled an Aeroflot plane of the 1980s. After crawling through Chinatown, decked in spider-like hieroglyphic graffiti, the train rattled across Manhattan Bridge and entered Brooklyn, whose ugly littered streets and battered red-brick houses were full of unspeakable Soviet-style despair.

Having heard a lot about the dangerous types riding the Subway during the day, I looked around nervously and kept my hands in my pockets (which were empty anyway).

Soon, I concluded that I was the most dangerous type on the train, simply because for most of the trip I was alone in my carriage: no one in his right mind—not even beggars or muggers—would think of going to the Soviet Union by New York Subway in the middle of a working day.

Nearly two hours later, I got off the train in Coney Island Avenue—Brighton Beach's own 'Broadway'. It was raining, and the strong wind from the ocean immediately grabbed my umbrella, like a street bully, trying to break it in two. Nestling in the shadow of the Elevated, the whole neighbourhood looked like the interior of a huge neglected house with a leaking roof.

Suddenly I was surrounded by semi-forgotten and painfully familiar smells and sounds. The air reeked of borscht and fried *'pirozhki'* (meat-pies). In front of me, a fat angry-faced lady was telling off a young woman with a pram: 'Button up your baby, mother, or you will freeze it to death!'

Almost all signs were in Russian: 'Michael Kozhin—American Dentist', 'Footwear from Italy', 'Best Goods' (it was a one-dollar shop selling hats, toys, suitcases and tacky postcards), 'Cheap Goods from Russia' (this shop was Chinese-owned), 'We Accept Foodstamps' and 'Bella Works Here'.

Having resisted the temptation to see the mysterious (and obviously famous) Bella at work, I wandered off to the nearest *Gastronom* (food shop).

Inside, there was a queue for cut-price concentrated orange juice. Just like in the Soviet Union, one had to queue at the cash desk first, and then at the counter, behind which a busty peroxide blonde in a grubby apron was unhurriedly handing over the coveted cartons of juice to the customers. 'Are you buying it or not, woman?' she shouted at a little old lady, whose decrepit shopping trolley squeaked like a Moscow tram turning the corner. The queue was regularly jumped by rough-looking men buying packets of Marlboro—without a whisper of protest from the queuers.

The whole scene struck me as utterly un-American, for in the USA, according to *'The Americans. A Study in National Character'* by Geoffrey Gorer, even 'the smallest purchase should be accompanied by a smile, and the implied assurance that the vendor is delighted and privileged to serve you . . .'

The people did not smile in the *Gastronom*, where the facial expressions fluctuated between the uncomplaining indifference of the customers and 'the implied assurance' of the vendor that she had a personal vendetta against everyone in the queue.

I couldn't tear my gaze from the display of *'vatrushki'* cheese pies—like the ones I used to have for my school lunches; from fat-oozing *'salo'*—a pure pork lard that can be sliced and eaten with bread, with each slice containing more kilojoules than all the dishes from Delia Smith's 'Complete Cookery Course' put together; from dusty bottles of 'Troika *kvas'*—a mildly alcoholic drink, made of yeast and rye bread, and from other culinary delights of my previous Soviet life.

'Can I have a cabbage pie, please?' I asked the salesgirl politely, when my turn came.

'Are you flirting with me, or what?' she snarled back. She must not have heard the word 'please' since childhood.

There were no self-service food stores in Brighton Beach, where, despite the over-abundance of food, shopping for it remained a masochistic Soviet experience, featuring totally superfluous cash desks, rude salesgirls and queues to be jumped.

Not so in the numerous music stores, where I was allowed to browse on my own, having deposited my shoulder-bag with a blue-faced attendant in exchange for a *'nomerok'*—a soiled piece of cardboard with a number.

For some reason, the biggest sections in many of these stores were reserved for *'Blatnaya Muzika'*, or 'Thieves' Cant'.

'We've got plenty of Russian criminal folklore,' an attendant told me proudly, inviting me to look at the stand with hundreds of tapes and CDs.

'Do I look like an underworld type?' I was wondering.

I ventured into *'Parikmakherskaya'*, a barber's shop run by Syoma, an old Jew from Minsk and a former 'Soviet activist' (in his own words). Cutting my hair and squinting to ensure he didn't chop off my ears, he complained of his life in Brighton Beach:

'We are besieged by home-grown gangsters here. The other

day they killed a jeweller round the corner. Burst into his shop and shot him in broad daylight. And took the jewellery. Shame our Jews . . .'

'The Mafia? Which Mafia?' Liova, a leading Brighton Beach businessman, raised his bushy eyebrows in response to my question. 'All this Russian Mafia bull was invented by New York City fathers, who hate us for being so entrepreneurial and successful. . .'

He proceeded to tell me how they were slowly but surely pushing out Africans and Puerto Ricans from the area, and I suddenly realised why music of the underworld was in such great demand in Brighton Beach. The people, who—for generations—had to cheat the Soviet system to survive, were finding it hard, if not impossible, to change their way of thinking in the West. Some of the scams originating from Brighton Beach, like the one which involved selling water-diluted petrol to hundreds of gas stations across America, stunned the whole country by their crafty simplicity.

Talking of the so-called Russian Mafia, a NYPD spokesman once noted: 'It is much easier to deal with a criminal who breaks the law than with a person who doesn't know that the law exists.'

By mid-afternoon, the rain had stopped, and pairs of elderly immigrants, carrying the indelible 'I-am-waiting-to-be-hurt' expression on their faces, could be seen strolling along the wet timbered boardwalk. From time to time, they would stop and stare at the ocean, as if trying to discern the outlines of their native Odessa on the horizon.

Some of them would later flock to the 'Odessa' Restaurant, where local bard Willie Tokarev performed his poignant nostalgic songs. In one, he called Brighton Beach 'a gypsy encampment'.

True, its residents were as rootless as gypsies, only, unlike gypsies, they have stopped wandering . . .

It was with relief that I boarded a 'streetcar' (tram) back to America. Half a day in a country which no longer existed was more than enough for me. To while away the journey, I leafed through a thick Russian rag that I had bought in Brighton Beach. My attention was captured by the following ad: 'Never!!! The Weiner Brothers' funeral parlour will **never** refuse service to Russian Jews!'

Joseph Heller—and Dr Bruce Gold, the protagonist of *Good as Gold* obsessed with uncovering the true meaning of 'Jewish experience' (whatever that is)—would have loved that, I was sure.

Heller's Coney Island, 'with its beaches, crowds, commotion and couple of hundred entertainments', to where 'people came from everywhere', would have been different of course—the neighbourhood of the Amusement Park, the 1920s Cyclone rollercoaster, the Parachute Jump from which Joseph had wanted to leap but never did—and now never will—and Nathan's Stand, the birthplace of the hot dog.

From Brighton Beach, the tram took me to Mermaid Avenue—the area where Joseph Heller lived.
Or 'had lived'—as I should have been writing from then on.

I found his school, still a school today.

At 'Major Prime Meats' butcher's shop, I had a brief chat with an elderly man called Stanley, who said he had been in the same class as Joseph, and I had to break the news of Heller's death to him.

After the rain, the area brightened up (bright-brighter-Brighton?) a bit. Muffled music could be heard from empty fun fair rides.

The Luna Park often mentioned in *Now and Then* was no longer there. Blocks of three-storied red-brick buildings, populated mostly by Soviet immigrants and still known as 'Luna Park', were in its place.

At Nathan's Hot Dogs, now a spacious emporium rather than a stand, I had a knish, a hot potato pie, reminiscent of '*karto-phelnik*'—a flat potato pancake of my Ukrainian childhood—both of my grannies made excellent ones. A black waitress who had never heard of Joseph Heller told me that it was Charles Feltman, a Jewish immigrant from Germany, who actually invented the hot dog in the 1870s and served it for the first time in his restaurant, where Nathan Handwerker was a waiter. In 1916, Nathan opened his own stand, lowered the price of a hot dog from ten to five cents and hired people dressed as doctors and nurses to promote his product . . .

I wandered into an empty circus tent and spoke with the owner, called Dick. He had never heard of Joseph Heller either.

Dick complained that his business was not doing very well. 'It is hard to find people who can do what we need, sword swallowers, for example,' he said.

That could have come straight from one of Joseph Heller's books.

Somehow I felt that by visiting Coney Island on the day after Joseph Heller's death and by adding my own memories to his, I had paid my last respects to the superb writer and satirist with whom could have become good friends. I suddenly understood where the amazing humour and the sense of the absurd of *Catch-22* and Heller's other novels might have come from. Growing up in America's largest (prior to the appearance of Disneyland) amusement park must have played a role . . .

When I returned to London several days later and was checking my phone messages, there was one that made me freeze.

Joseph Heller's feeble voice was apologising for not being able to see me tomorrow due to not feeling well. He knew I did not carry a mobile and was hoping I would check my London answer phone from New York.

It must have been one of the last (if not the very last) phone call he had made in his life.

As I am writing these lines, the world is mourning Alexander Solzhenitsyn.

All three of them: Ustinov, Heller and Solzhenitsyn—have now become ghosts. Only the 'ghost-chaser', i.e. I (or Vin, if you wish), is still alive.

How can I prove it?

Wikipedia has recently added one more 'category' (on top of 'British journalists', 'Soviet defectors', 'Russian journalists' and 'Ukranian journalists' where I had been listed for some time).

This new category reads simply: 'Living People'.

Dead phone ringing

I came to Dublin in early January to visit my son Mitya and to mark my fiftieth birthday with him.

The Dublin cottage where he lived (and where I was to join him nine months later) was called 'St Jude's'. (St Jude, by the way, is the patron saint of lost and hopeless causes—the saint you come to when all others have failed.)

On the eve of my first jubilee, we sat over a Russian meal of borscht, pickles and meat dumplings late into the night. When the clock was striking twelve, my son raised his glass to wish me a happy birthday.

It was right at that moment that the old black telephone on the mantelpiece gave out two short piercing rings.

Looking back now, I can see very clearly that the ancient apparatus was an exact copy—or possibly the twin—of our first telephone in Kharkov.

Or perhaps IT WAS THE SAME telephone magically teleported through space and time?

Now, the very fact of a telephone ringing at midnight wouldn't have been much of a story, had it not been for one simple fact: THERE WAS NO TELEPHONE LINE in the house of my son, who relied solely on his mobile. The disconnected antediluvian gadget itself was therefore but a useless piece of furniture—a leftover from some previous tenants of 'St. Jude's'. There was no cable, no number, no nothing.

And yet it did ring precisely at the moment when I turned fifty!

My son dropped his glass and grabbed the receiver. Of course, there was nothing but silence there. The phone was dead.

The next day we called (from my son's mobile, no doubt) a telephone exchange and were assured that there was no cable connection at my son's address and therefore the phone could not ring.

The problem was that it did!
A 'hopeless cause' indeed.

'You were contacted . . .' some of my metaphysics-prone friends suggested thoughtfully on hearing the story.

As if I didn't know it myself. The question was (and still is) by whom? By my Dad? My granddad? By my own childhood?

To me, there was nothing sinister about it at all.

Now, I am inclined to believe that it was simply a posthumous birthday greeting from my facetious friend, Piotr Ionovich Ustinov. It cured me of my age-long, almost innate, fear of phone calls. And of all sorts of funerals—*especially my own, ha ha*' . . .

Windows and views

You can change wallpaper and rearrange furniture in a house, but you can never alter the view from its window . . .

'If moving houses is a "cleansing experience", as one of my friends asserts, then by now—after five years of commuting between Britain and Australia—I should be transparent . . .' Thus started Vin's first *Guardian* column on his return to London from Australia.

As we know already, 'one of his friends' was his blue notebook, where the opening sentences originated from. He always regarded notebooks as his closest travelling companions, talked to them on his solitary voyages, sharing his impressions and observations—and not just on the voyages themselves. At times, a notebook would indeed assume the role of a trusted friend or even a partner (see below).

His old notebooks were the very last things he was likely to dispose of when moving houses/cities/countries/continents/ social systems.
Not because he entertained delusions of greatness but due to his reluctance in saying good-bye to his mates and confidants who had helped him survive through difficult times.

One of the two suitcases he was able to take with him (first to London and then to Australia), when defecting from the USSR with his wife and son, contained nothing but his old books and notebooks, full of his scribbles—unintelligible not just to an outsider but, in most parts, to himself as well. During his years and decades in investigative journalism, when the subjects and the names he was dealing with were at times more than 'sensitive' and could have cost the people involved not just lots of money, but their lives too, if exposed to the 'wrong' eyes—Vin had developed his own peculiar shorthand that took a while even for himself to decipher. While 'decoding' his own hasty scribbles, he had to recall all the accompanying circumstances, thus restoring in his memory a number of small and seemingly insignificant details which, on closer scrutiny, often turned out to be essential.

In short, his notebook scribbles were deliberately incomprehensible, as if slurred . . .

A notebook had always been one of the essential components of the LITERARY DEVICE that was his life.

Incidentally, much of *The Land of Plastic Fossils*, his unwritten book on the USA, as well as other unwritten books that comprise *Life as a Literary Device*, have been (and will be) reconstructed from his/Vin's/Victor R.'s/VV's/my old NOTEBOOKS.

The need for an interlocutor was particularly strong during his several days in New Orleans, a couple of years before Hurricane Katrina nearly wiped that incredible city off the face of the earth.

'New Orleans is a Sazerac of cultures,' he scribbled hastily in his notebook while elbowing his way along bustling Bourbon Street—the hub of New Orleans' never-ending fun.

It was the first of the many metaphors that kept haunting him in Big Easy (one of the city's numerous nicknames). Never before had his uncomplaining memo pad registered so many comparisons and similes—his largely futile attempts to catch the evasive spirit of New Orleans. Never before had they come off the tip of his pen so easily. Never before had his shaky scribbles been so hard to decipher the following morning, as if they had somehow recorded the erratic cardiogram of New Orleans—the city's jumpy heartbeat.

'A depot of metaphors,' was how Andrei Voznesensky, one of Vin's favourite Russian poets of the 1960s—70s, once referred to himself.
'I am Goya! Swooping down on a bare field, a foe pecked craters in my eyes. I am grief. I am the groan of war, the charred guts of cities in the snow of 'forty-one'. I am hunger. I am the gasp of a hanged woman, whose body clanged like a bell above the naked square . . .'

And so on . . .

'A cornucopia of metaphors,' was what Victor R. became in New Orleans . . . (and that is why it is time for my poetic alter ego—'Victor R.'—to take over).

In his subsequent days there he would compare the city to:
- a joyful scream;
- a gentle shock; a sophisticated mess—like a Cajun dish or an Arnaud's cocktail;
- a cup of strong black coffee (with chicory) that cheers you up and keeps you awake throughout the night;
- a friendly blow in the solar plexus that leaves you bent over and gasping for breath, yet with a blissful smile on your face;
- a glass of wine to go. New Orleans was the only American city outside Las Vegas with no closing law, which meant that alcohol was on sale twenty-four hours a day; it was the city where you could ask for a 'to-go' plastic cup of wine at a bar and drink it behind the wheel of your car. It was the city where one often bumped into pedestrians with glasses of champagne in their hands.

In a broader sense therefore, New Orleans was:
- a 'moveable feast', a flask of good wine that you carry
  with you wherever you are . . .

. . . He ended his first night in New Orleans dancing in the plywood shed of Preservation Hall, home of one of the city's best-known jazz bands. For lack of a dancing partner, he was pressing my faithful notebook closely to my chest.

On his last night in Big Easy, as he was lying wide awake in his bed listening to the muffled sounds of street jazz, mixed with the distant nostalgic whistles of South Pacific trains behind the windows of his Monteleone Hotel in the heart of the French Quarter, Victor R. thought of New Orleans as of a deviant vintage rail car that had come uncoupled from the gleaming express train of modern America. Derailed and rudderless, it kept rolling ahead on its own—jingling, clattering and opening its squeaky doors only to those who board it with open hearts.

That last metaphor was duly recorded in his notebook first thing the following morning.

Incidentally, as I am writing these lines, another hurricane, Gustav, is trying to wipe out New Orleans. Like Katrina, it is going to fail.

New Orleans will bounce back again for there is no force powerful enough to stop it from rolling.

A 'sophisticated mess' or a 'sophisticated chaos' . . . That's how mauvism has been described too. So if there's such a thing as a 'mauvistic city', New Orleans is one.

And another one is London, of course!

I will try to explain why.

London planners of the last century—starting with Patrick Abercrombie—were invariably subjected to sharp criticism. Walter George Bell, the author of *Unknown London*, even claimed in 1951—in the aftermath of the ill-fated Abercrombie Plan—that 'developers' (read planners) had inflicted more damage upon London than German bombs.

The Abercrombie plan was released in 1943 as a blueprint for London's development after the war. Patrick Abercrombie believed that London's problems could be solved through objective scientific analysis and proposed rational and logical (from HIS point of view) solutions which often depended on the separation of different activities within the city.

Roads were 'categorised' to ensure that different types of traffic used different types of roads; pedestrians were segregated, and areas of London were 'zoned' according to their function and proximity to the City.

He advanced the idea of 'pedestrian precincts'—'free from noise, dirt and the dangers of traffic'—a notion seized on by the next generation of planners.

As a result, London's traditional street pattern was overlaid with bleak 'pedestrianised zones'.

Abercrombie also recommended relocating London's distinctive street markets away from main roads.

Similar to the disastrous experiment of Celebration, Florida—Walt Disney's totally pedestrianised 'model town' that proved utterly unworkable in reality—the Abercrombie plan resulted in a spectacular fiasco. According to the Soho Society, the loss of traffic diminished the area's character, made deliveries impossible for local businesses, and fostered antisocial behaviour, particularly after dark. The Pedestrianisation of London proved to be not simply anti-car, but also anti-life and therefore 'anti-London'.

A similar fate awaited the Greater London Development Plan of 1969: its vision of London as a road network of high-speed urban motorways, orbital routes and ringways collapsed in the face of public opposition.

So, does London need planning?

In the year 2000, an 'anti-planning' exhibition was held in the Museum of London. It started with the following message from the Museum to the newly elected Mayor of London, as well as 'all would-be Mayors':

'DON'T STERILISE OUR CITY

Since the Second World War London has been transformed by the imposition of state-sponsored central planning. The Abercrombie Plan of 1943 and the Greater London Development Plan of 1969 promised Londoners a better future but didn't deliver. Today these clean-sweep, mega plans are gone but some of their thinking lives on. We say: "Attempts to impose neatness on our exuberant city are alien to London's past and unhelpful to London's future. We urge the new Mayor to think deeply about the character of London and the lessons of history."'

The main person behind the exhibition was Dr Cathy Ross, a historian and Head of the Museum of London's Later London History and Collections Department. 'That exhibition was a clever provocation,' she told me. 'Planners should be provoked . . . Our main argument was that London is an organic city that grows higgledy-piggledy and doesn't require planning . . .'

'But some planning IS necessary,' objected I and shared with her my sad experiences of Dublin—the city that for centuries was (and still is!) allowed to grow 'higgledy-piggledy': If architecture is indeed 'frozen music' (a metaphor attributed by different sources to Goethe, Schelling and Le Corbusier), the panoramic view from the top of the chimney of Dublin's former Jameson Distillery could be compared to an ear-grating cacophony, played by a madman. Dublin's cityscape is reminiscent of a huge sack of potatoes that has burst at the seams and carelessly dropped onto the ground. In recent years, lack of central planning and the 'Celtic Tiger' mentality of greed have led to the chaotic, so-called in-fill 'developments', i.e. cramming every vacant space with as many hideous, yet profit-making, concrete apartment blocks as possible.

'First we shape buildings, and then—buildings shape us,' Winston Churchill once famously remarked. And wasn't it the architectural turmoil of Dublin that has eventually 'shaped' it into a depressive and largely dysfunctional metropolis, with a high crime rate, all-permeating corruption, an unworkable transport system and one of Europe's worst dressed street crowds—in short, Dublin as a city is much less attractive than its pains-takingly created 'Celtic Tiger' image?

'Well, London is a messy city, therefore planning, if any, should not be monolithic and has to be strictly controlled,' said Dr Ross.

Symptomatically, the Museum of London, where our conversation took place, is itself a symbol of London's 'messy' character: a non-descript 1970s building, it is surrounded by the remains of the old Roman city wall and the post-modernistic skyscrapers of the Barbican Centre, and stands next to the graceful twelfth century St Botolph-without-Aldersgate church, off Little Britain Lane!

I asked Dr Ross about the connection between planning and a city's identity.

'Identity is of course tied up with what the place looks like, although planning on its own can't create a city identity. Nor can it be a driving force behind it. The identity is driven by people, economy and life-style. One of the most important factors of London identity is Londoners' individualism. Just look at the way Londoners cross the road—there's no single pattern there . . . London's chaotic nature is part of its character,' she concluded

So, just like New Orleans, London is a mess. Yet again—a beautiful and sophisticated one! In short, London is mauvistic—an urbanised representation of mauvism itself.

If mauvism were not a literary device but a city, it would have been called London!

That is probably why I love it so much.

Now, to a different set of windows and views. And to another set of metaphors, too.

. . . Looking out of my window and feeling jet-lagged and groggy after a twenty-four-hour excruciatingly non-smoking flight from Melbourne (a long-haul non-smoking flight for a heavy smoker of my ilk is like a long-haul non-urinating flight for a non-smoker) I see a slightly blurred (or is it Blair-ed?) view of London, my favourite city in the whole world. I can see the same endless row of sloping roofs with chimneys sticking out of them like stalagmites, or like phallic obelisks on the mass grave of unknown chimney sweeps. I see blooming chestnut trees, the trees of my Ukrainian childhood, looking like the frozen fountains of some bizarre my-time fireworks and lighting up the street. After dark, when it stops raining, I can see the hook-like crescent of the new moon, so close to my window that I feel like stretching out my hand and hanging my rain-soaked umbrella on to it to dry overnight—before realising it was left behind at Heathrow airport the other day . . .

That repetitive 'my window' was an obvious untruth, a touch of fabrication (self-fiction?), or, maybe, even a bit of wishful thinking on his part: he didn't have anything 'his' in London then.

Except perhaps for the hundreds of his books and old notebooks removed from Ona's house in his absence by his close friend Paul and stacked in his (Paul's) capacious loft in Balham.

The books—his only worldly possession—were normally regarded as a ballast (or millstone) by most Onas, yet for him they constituted a real treasure. And not just because, alongside the ever-growing library of his favourite Russian books in English, he could boast one of the UK's finest collections of antiquarian Baedekers—as well as first editions of many great travel books, including Robert Byron's magnificent and extremely rare *The Station* (in his opinion, the best book on Mount Athos, one of his favourite places in the world, ever written): he squandered several hundred pounds on it at a Charing Cross Road antiquarian bookshop after receiving a nice lump sum for a Channel 4 documentary he had filmed in Ukraine in 1994.

Nor because some of them had been acquired in the good-book-starved Soviet Union where not just honest writing but honest reading too was carefully rationed by the system. He could remember clearly where, when and under what circumstances (i.e. on which flea market and from which spiv or speculator) he acquired each of them, having often had to cough up an equivalent of his monthly salary for a book he needed, or thought that he needed.

And not even because some of them carried old dedications in faded ink of the type: 'To my dear little boy from his granddad, with love'; 'From Dad on your birthday'; 'To Vitali in memory of his successful completion of his first year at school'.

No, the real relative value of his books was **enormous** due to the fact that most of them had criss-crossed the globe on the way to Australia and back four or five times—the result of his inability to settle either here or there and being permanently torn between the two remotest big cities of the world: London, his spiritual home, and Melbourne, where his Mum and son had lived.

He often cursed himself for turning down a job offer from *The Yorkshire Post* he had received shortly after his defection from the USSR, before moving down under.

Commuting between London and Leeds is still preferable to a fractured intercontinental existence.

His first big purchase in the West was a complete set of the *Encyclopaedia Britannica* (thirty-odd volumes) supplemented with additional fifty-two volumes of *The World's Great Ideas* series thrown in for just a couple of hundred Aussie dollars by a glib Polish salesman—one of the very first visitors to their rented flat in the Melbourne suburb of East St Kilda. He could have bought a furniture set or a new car instead (the latter would have been unnecessary though, for at that time he didn't have a driving licence). But it had been his dream since childhood to own a complete set of the *Encyclopaedia Britannica*—a treasure trove of unlimited information so cruelly rationed in his unfortunate motherland, the USSR.

His last spell in Australia lasted only five months—just long enough for his books to reach him by sea from London. By the time they were unloaded in his Melbourne backyard, he already knew he was returning to London, so he simply called another removal van and sent the boxes (including a good dozen of those holding the *Encyclopaedia Britannica* and *The World's Great Ideas*) back—without unpacking them!

No wonder, 'My Books' by Henry Longfellow was one of his all-time favourite poems:

Sadly as some old medieval knight gazed at the arms he could
no longer wield, the sword two-handed and the shining shield,
suspended in the hall, and full in sight, while secret longings for
the lost delight of tourney or adventure in the field came over him,
and tears but half concealed trembled and fell upon his beard of
white, so I behold these books upon their shelf, my ornaments and
arms of other days; not wholly useless, though no longer used, for
they remind me of my other self, younger and stronger, and the
pleasant ways in which I walked, now clouded and confused.

This beautiful one-sentence sonnet was quite a challenge to translate into Russian. Victor R. did it while a student of Kharkov University. By then he was already a published poet and an armchair buccaneer of many years' sitting.

Yuri Olesha, a brilliant Russian writer and a close friend of Kataev's has the following observation on the power of books (and reading) in his posthumously published *The Book of Farewells*. He says that when he was young he was reading **forwards** meaning that most of the literary heroes were older than him and therefore devouring the books about them was like dreaming about his own future, whereas as he grew older, he started reading **backwards**, for he had become older than most of the protagonists and was subconsciously comparing their experiences with his own. This observation corresponds to my own perception of books as the simplest, the best and the most readily available means of travelling through time.

Time traveller

As a romantic travel-hungry boy in the dusty Ukrainian city of Kharkov, I often dreamt of a trip to Britain.

I imagined that I would start in some God-forsaken Ukrainian hamlet with a silly Soviet name (like Red Excavator, say—there was such a village on the outskirts of Kharkov). First, I would travel on a cart, dragged by a tired horse, then—no more speedily—on a fast *elektrichka:* a squeaky electric shuttle train.
'Where are you going to, boy?' the red-nosed residents of Red Excavator would ask. 'To London,' I would answer matter-of-factly . . . No, to puzzle them even more, I would indeed say: 'To Shrewsbury', or, better, 'To Bourton-on-the-Water' . . .

I wanted my imaginary journey to Britain, whose language, literature and history I had been studying assiduously since the age of eight as an antidote to the all-permeating Soviet dogma, to be long and unhurried. Planes were immediately discarded as too fast and impersonal: they wouldn't give me enough time to savour the sweetness of moving towards the place I was so longing for.

In my heart of hearts, I was dead sure that this journey would never really take place, for travels to the decadent and crumbling West were taboo for ordinary Soviet people . . .

If with the Soviet bit of my imaginary pilgrimage everything was more or less clear, the British part of it was clouded in mystery. The problem was that my arm-chair traveller's impressions of Britain were mostly captured from the books of Dickens, Thackeray and Conan Doyle (more modern authors were too politically explosive to be published in the Soviet Union), so the only pictures of London I was able to drum up in my fevered imagination was that of moustached Victorian gentlemen in bowler hats feeding pigeons in St. James's Park. As for the countryside, one of the few sources I could rely upon was Conan Doyle's *The Hound of the Baskervilles*, which described a turn-of-the-century train ride from Paddington to Devonshire once undertaken by Dr Watson and Sir Henry Baskerville.

I knew the passage almost by heart: 'The journey was a swift and pleasant one . . . In a very few hours the brown earth had become ruddy, the brick had changed to granite, and red cows grazed in well-hedged fields where the lush grasses and more luxuriant vegetation spoke of a richer, if damper climate . . .'

In my day dreams, I could easily visualise myself in a bowler hat, next to an equally bowler-hatted Dr Watson, smoking a pipe and looking at the civilised and well cultivated pastoral unrolling behind the window.

'The train pulled up at a small wayside station, and we all descended. Outside, beyond the low, white fence, a wagonette with a pair of cobs was waiting. Our coming was evidently a great event, for station master and porters clustered round us to carry out our luggage . . .'

At this point I, too, had to descend from cloud-cuckoo land to look up the word 'cob' in my dog-eared English-Russian

Dictionary, released in Moscow by the unpronounceable Uchpedgiz publishers in 1948. According to Uchpedgiz (I nicknamed it 'Uchpedgiz Khan' to echo Genghis Khan—an atrocious thirteenth century Tartar warrior), the word's only meaning was 'male swan'. A wagonette drawn by swans—it seemed to come straight out of Grimm's Fairy Tales, which perfectly matched my perception of Britain as a dream like fairyland.

When, with the advent of glasnost, I was finally—against all my expectations—magnanimously allowed to travel to Britain in 1988 (I was already thirty-four and a journalist in Moscow), I did not know what to expect. I had to rely on the advice of my omniscient friends who had either been to Britain themselves or, more likely, knew someone who had.

They told me never to declare my Russian-ness—let alone 'Ukraine-ness'—in public ('They don't like Russians and have probably never heard of Ukrainians in Britain'); always to check the billboard with today's menu and prices before venturing into a café or a snack bar ('They will rip you off otherwise'); under no circumstances to use taxis ('They will take you for a ride around the block'); to do all my shopping either on street markets or in second-hand charity shops ('They sell the same things as they do in the plushest boutiques, only much cheaper'); to have matri-oshka dolls and other cheap Russian souvenirs handy to be given away as bribes to co-operative shop assistants who in turn would agree to give me a discount (they assured me that a customer was always meant to bargain), and lots of similar expert tips which I dutifully recorded in my notebook.

The reality of my first-ever trip to the West, however, proved much more puzzling. I remember popping into one of the toilets on-board the *Queen Beatrix* cross-channel ferry, which took me from the Hook of Holland to Harwich, and, overwhelmed by mirrors and smells of deodorants, rushing promptly out, convinced I had wandered into a hairdressing salon by mistake. I stood speechless and dumbfounded at the entrance to the ship's small and poorly stocked (as I realise now) duty-free shop, not daring to step inside. It had many more goods on display than all of Moscow's stores together.

In Harwich, it took me a good half-hour to drag my abnormally heavy bags, full of tins of preserves (to minimise food expenditure) and souvenirs-cum-bribes, to the immigration area near the railway station. To my considerable disappointment, there was no station master, or anyone else, to greet me by tipping his bowler hat, and porters were not in a hurry to help me with the luggage. Sweating like a marathon runner at the end of the distance, I probably looked as if I had just robbed a brick factory. That was no doubt why I was led aside by a buxom female customs inspector, who was not wearing any hat, but wore a nasty sadistic grin instead. She asked me to open my suitcases, and when I failed (out of embarrassment) to find the keys, she simply hara-kiri-ed them with a pen knife—the last thing I expected to happen during my long-awaited first moments in the free Western world.

Despite the initial customs shock, I thoroughly enjoyed my first trip to Britain and soon learnt to ignore a ubiquitous and seemingly threatening sign 'Take Courage' which I came to realise was not a warning and did not imply anything dangerous, although it did imply something bitter. I grasped that a thunderous 'Mind the gap!' announcement at some Tube stations was not about banning commuters from rubbing against each other on overcrowded rush-hour trains, as I initially thought it was.

I took a surprisingly slow (as if indeed drawn by a couple of elderly swans) and dirty train to Rye in East Sussex—my first 'internal' trip in Britain. During the trip, I heard a new phrase 'leaves slippage', of which my trusted 'Genghis Khan' feigned complete ignorance.

I was overwhelmed with all the comforts of my first ever *British* hotel where I was put up by a London newspaper: a spare TV set in the sterile bathroom, snow-white bathrobes, a vast double bed, although I was on my own, and not a sign of previous tenants' pubic hair on the bathroom floor—a constant feature of an average Soviet hotel, of which I have seen hundreds. The well-stocked mini-bar was a special attraction, for I firmly believed that the price of all drinks in it was included in the price of the room (I knew that breakfast was). So, when it was time to go, I thought it would be a shame to leave behind all those nice-looking compact mini-bottles and, after some hesitation, relocated all of them into my suitcase.

'Have you used anything from your mini-bar, sir?' a reception clerk asked me when I was checking out.

'Yes,' I answered trying to hide my surprise at another blatant intrusion of my privacy.

'What did you use?'

'Er . . . everything actually . . .'

He gave me the special sort of 'stuff you' look that, as I learnt later, British hotel receptionists and waiters are so good at (you can get a similar look from a Harrods shop-assistant if you ask for a kilo of used nails), but didn't say anything.

I suddenly realised that I had done something wrong and could feel my face acquiring the colour of the cherry brandy in one of the mini-bottles in my suitcase.

Many stereotypes, illusions and delusions were shattered during that trip. Wherever I went I kept—subconsciously— looking for my fairy-tale late nineteenth century Britain, with its 'swift and pleasant' trains, helpful porters, respectable station masters, carriages, wagonettes and early stream trains, drawn by the white swans of my childhood dreams. At times, I could see it behind modern facades, at times I couldn't, but this constant quest for bygone days made my eyes sharper and my perception of the confusing late-20th –early-21st-century reality much more acute.

So strong are my childhood images of Britain, that even now, having criss-crossed the country (and the globe) many times over, I still like travelling with one eye on the past which enables me to move not only through space, but also through time. I think I know exactly how to do it.

In his book *Status Anxiety*, Alain de Botton advises those preoccupied with their position in society to visit old cemeteries to put things into a proper perspective, and to see how trifling all our anxieties are in the merciless flow of time. I would rather recommend old guidebooks—much more fascinating and alive than moss-covered gravestones.

Travelling back in time has always been one of humankind's most cherished dreams.

This explains the preoccupation of science-fiction writers with time machines or any other devices which allow us to peep behind the curtain of our own past.

Valentin Kataev's mauvism—the style that deliberately dislocates and totally destroys the chronological concept of time—is a writer's time machine of sorts.

I am proud to have discovered my own way of time travelling —Baedekers, Murrays, Bradshaws, Cooks—of all of which I am a passionate collector.

To me, these pocket-size tattered volumes are full of time travel magic, especially when I find an old London Tube map (with a curtailed pink 'Northern Line' ending at Highgate), a faded landing card, or just a dried-out hundred-year-old flower in between their tattered pages. Touching such books is like touching eternity itself, for bygone realities and small practicalities of a distant past come to life in their estranged, meticulous and matter-of-fact style. In this respect, old guidebooks are preferable to fiction: they provide me with an ossified time carcass, which I am free to fill with the contents of today's reality, or with that of my own imagination.

A casual pencil mark left by a long-deceased anonymous traveller of yesteryear in the margin of an 1873 edition of

Murray's *Handbook for Travellers in France*, opposite one particular ferry route from Dover to Calais; or a tick next to the cheapest horse carriage rate from the railway station to the city centre in my native Kharkov (*Baedeker's Russia*, 1914); or the exact departure time, of a train from Sienna to Milan in a nineteenth-century Bradshaw's *Railway Guide* for Europe, do more for my imagination (and, therefore, for my time travels) than heaps of post-Victorian novels. At that point, the only thing that separates me from completing my leap back in time (and therefore from making my experience—or rather experiment—fully relative) is the corresponding Victorian travel space.

Let us come back to H.G. Wells's ground-breaking 'scientific' approach to time travel which, in many ways, pre-dated by ten years the similar notions of Einstein's theory of relativity.

'There are really four dimensions . . . the three planes of Space, and a fourth, Time,' Wells wrote in *The Time Machine*.

Following this theory, an imaginative traveller who has equipped himself with old guide books and has limited his travel space to that of old books alone, can theoretically find himself in a peculiar time-warp, where almost nothing will remind him of the present. Transformation into a last-century traveller can also be helped by old phrase books (like Baedeker's *Traveller's Manual of Conversation*), with their unique insight into nineteenth-century speech patterns and mentality ('The mice prevent me from sleeping—pray let me have a mouse-trap'— from *The Traveller's Companion* by Madame de Gentils); by old shopping catalogues (like Sears Roebuck), meticulously listing details of costume, consumer items and household objects of the distant epoch; and by Victorian 'travellers survival guides' (of which there were many). Several other components come in extremely helpful, too: imagination, knowledge, and humour (or better, irony).

Talking about 'the three planes of space', H.G. Wells obviously meant length, height and width. Old travel books can easily provide us with all three.

Let us look at three nineteenth-century descriptions of the harbour at Calais, a starting point for a cross-channel traveller, which—together—give us a full three-dimensional picture:

'The (Calais) Harbour, which is accessible at all states of the tide, has been more than doubled in size by extensive new works, recently completed . . . The Old Harbour, with the former railway station, lies nearest to the Place d'Armes; the imposing New Harbour farther to the East. The new Gare Maritime, or Maritime Station, where passengers from England find the train for Paris waiting, is situated on the N.E. side of the Avant-Port and is connected by a short branch-line skirting the new harbour with the Gare Centrale . . . Calais contains 1500 English residents, chiefly engaged in its tulle-manufactories.' *Baedeker's Northern France* (1899)

'Terminus at Calais is on the Quay, close to the landing-place. It includes the Customs-house and Passport-offices, Refreshment-room (Buffet), and Hotel (where good beds may be had), all under one roof. Luggage is taken from the steamer to the Customs-house, and may be cleared at once . . . There is generally ample time between the arrival of the steamer and the departure of the train, for refreshment, &c. . . . An English traveller of the time of James I described Calais as 'a beggardly, extorting town; monstrous dear and sluttish.' In the opinion of many, this description will hold good at the present time . . . Except to an Englishman setting his foot for the first time on the Continent, to whom everything is novel, Calais has little that is remarkable, and all that there is of interest may be seen in an hour or two.' *Murray's Handbook for Travellers in France* (1879)

'I envy the young traveller to whom all is novelty in the foreign country. What a delightful epoch in his existence is the first saunter, after landing from the steam boat, through the streets and market place of a foreign town, even of a poor decaying one like Calais! He threads his way in ecstasy through the crowd of hucksters, and country women sitting in their brown wool cloaks beside their baskets of eggs, butter and vegetables.' *Observations of the European People* by Samuel Laying, Esq. (1850)

Whereas Karl Baedeker was famous for his impartiality and precision of detail, which remain unsurpassed even now, John Murray was a bit of a philosopher and a wit, who could get away not only with plenty of ads but also with such charming generalisations as:

'. . . the inns of the provincial towns of France are inferior to those of Germany and to those of Switzerland, in the want of general comfort, and above all cleanliness. . . Some of the most important essentials to personal comfort and decency . . . are utterly disregarded, and evince a state of degradation not to be expected in a civilised country . . .', or: 'Our countrymen [the English VV] have a reputation for pugnacity in France: let them therefore be especially cautious not to make use of their fists, however great the provocation, otherwise they will rue it.'

As for the prolific nineteenth century wanderer, Samuel Laying, he—while remaining a serious and insightful observer of European ways and manners—was prone to frequent emotional outbursts and overreactions of the type:

'What a world of passengers in our steamer! Princes, dukes, gentlemen, ladies, tailors, milliners, people of every rank and calling, all jumbled together. The power of steam is not confined to material objects. Its influences extend over the social and moral arrangements of mankind. Steam is the great democratic power of our age, annihilating the conventional distinctions, differences and social distance between man and man, as well as natural distances between place and place.'

As we see, dry and meticulous Baedeker, combined with witty and vitriolic Murray, and substantiated by sharp-eyed and emotional Laying, add up to an almost complete real-life impression of the nineteenth-century travel space. They also provide numerous bridges to the present. Don't the 'pugnacious' Englishmen in 1879 France evoke associations with the twenty-first century British soccer fans? And the landing site in Calais remains pretty much the same as it was in 1850, except that the market places are now called *hypermarchés* and the roles of both 'hucksters' and 'country women' are played by British one-day 'beer-tourists', sitting in their jeans beside their crates of Stella Artois and Gitanes.

No matter how busy I am, I make sure I open an old guidebook every day thus (literally) staying in touch not only with eternity, but also—with reality.

Baedeker Handbooks, or 'Baedekers', are the most famous guidebooks in the world. Started by the Essen-born and Heidelberg-educated publisher Karl Baedeker in 1829, they remain unsurpassed in their authority and precision of detail. Unlike the half-baked tips of my omniscient Moscow friends, Baedeker's advice was always based on first-hand experience. Even when saying—somewhat peremptorily—that 'Europeans as a rule should never inquire after the wives of a Muslim' (I like this overcautious 'as a rule') in the early editions of his Egypt Handbook, he sounded as if he knew exactly what he was talking about, and the reader was led to believe that Baedeker himself had made numerous 'inquiries' after Muslims' wives before coming to the conclusion that they should be best avoided.

It was very seldom that Baedeker allowed his personality (having travelled so much, he should have been a clandestine romantic) to come through. In the words of Alan Wykes, the compiler of *Abroad*, a comprehensive anthology of English travel writing, Baedeker 'was Schubert to the life, though without the glasses, and he had music in him which emerged through a clarinet; but nothing like as much as the information he and his successors have compiled over the years for the benefit of the practically-minded tourist'.

Baedeker never minced his words: 'The Sweizerhaus . . . is an inn built ten years ago, which, however, provokes complaints because of the landlord's lack of politeness,' he wrote in the first (1846) edition of *Handbook for Travellers in Germany and the Austrian Empire*. Or take the following tip from his 1904 *Central Italy*: 'Iron bedsteads should, if possible, be selected as being less likely to harbour the enemies of repose.' He was also a master of different styles, often combined in one and the same sentence: 'Over all the movements of the walker the weather holds despotic sway [reflective]: the blowing down of the wind in the valleys in the evening, the melting away of the clouds [poetic]; West winds also usually bring rain [scientific]'. He could also be dryly and reservedly facetious: 'Landlords sometimes make exorbitant demands on the death of one of their guests, in which case the aid of the authorities should be invoked.'

Baedeker himself used to travel under an assumed name, checking on hotels and restaurants, so that the information which he gave could be relied upon utterly. After his death in 1859 his sons continued his work. The first English translation appeared in 1861, the first French one fifteen years earlier. The English translation of *Baedeker's Russia* (1914) is one of the rarest: it was never reprinted. 1914 was clearly not a good year to publish a guidebook, not even a Baedeker.

Baedeker was the first writer to add stars after hotels to pinpoint the best and most luxurious; he also used this system for especially beautiful views. The popularity of his guidebooks was such that the following paragraph had to be added to the Introduction of some of them:

'To hotel-keepers, tradesmen, and others the Editor
begs to intimate that a character for fair dealing and
courtesy towards travellers forms the sole passport to his
commendation, and that no advertisements of any kind

are admitted to his Handbooks. Persons calling themselves agents for *Baedeker's Handbooks* are impostors.'

'Impostors' were clearly one of Baedeker's main concerns, and he always kept his eyes open for them. 'We need hardly caution newcomers against the artifices of pickpockets and the wiles of impostors, two fraternities which are very numerous in London. It is even prudent to avoid speaking to strangers in the street.' (*Baedeker's London*, 1900).

The name Baedeker became a dictionary word, not only for the excellence of its guides, but also for a sadder reason.

In World War II, British aircraft made raids on Cologne and Lübeck. In reprisal, the Germans staged a series of raids on Britain which were called 'Baedeker Raids'. They were trying to stamp out famous historic cities mentioned in Baedeker such as Bath, Exeter, Canterbury, Norwich and so on. The phrase was first used in 1942. Ironically, it was in Germany under the Nazis that Baedeker guides—for the first and the last time—were subjected to censorship: strategic areas, such as railways and bridges, were removed from the 1936 edition of *Baedeker's Berlin and Potsdam*, published for the Berlin Olympic Games.

The best Baedeker guidebooks came out between 1897 and 1909—the years known as the Golden Age of Baedeker. Among them were annual editions of *Baedeker's Great Britain* and *Baedeker's London and Its Environs*—the pride of my ever-growing collection.

My passion for Baedeker was such that several years ago I visited the offices of Verlag Karl Baedeker GmbH—a modern compound surrounded by cabbage fields where they grow what later becomes the famous Swabian *sauerkraut*—in the outskirts of Stuttgart. In the substantial office archives, I came across the correspondence between Karl Baedeker and John Murray of London, the latter being the undisputed pioneer of modern guidebook writing.

When Murray's first handbook—*Travellers on the Continent: Being a guide through Holland, Belgium, Prussia and Northern Germany*—appeared in 1836, Karl Baedeker was 35, and had been running his bookshop and publishing company in Coblenz for nine years. The first ever Baedeker guidebooks: a three volume *Rheinreise* and the first edition of *Belgium* and *Holland* (in German, of course) were issued three years later—in 1839. It has to be said that in his 'little books' Baedeker openly imitated Murray's format, cover design and substantial bits of the structure—a fact that he himself readily acknowledged in his letters. As time went by, the reverse was also happening. i.e. Murray started drawing upon Baedeker's works.

In the beginning, their collaboration went well, yet it was not destined to last: after all, Murray and Baedeker were competitors, rivals in the same innovative field. Friction began to show when Ernst Baedeker took over the firm in 1859, after which correspondence between the two publishing houses, while remaining formally polite, got rather acrimonious, with mutual accusations of inaccuracies and plagiarism:

My dear Mr. Murray,

. . . I must take this opportunity to tell you that there are loud complaints and expressions of regret from many quarters, that Mr Murray does not himself work at the new editions of his excellent books. I believe that these complaints are not entirely untrue. The books contain too much that is out of date, and much that takes up unnecessary space. I know of course from my own experience that it is much easier to add new things than to delete old ones, that it is less toilsome to write a fat book than a good , handy, slim one . . . It now seems to me that it would be greatly to the advantage of those who use your books, if you could find the time and enthusiasm, amongst your other numerous tasks, to cut as much text as possible with a critical and merciful pen . . .

I commend myself to you as,

Your grateful and devoted K. Baedeker [06.01.1852]

My dear sir,

... I do not wish to deprive you of any merit of your work—but merely ask you to state the extent of your obligations to my book—pointing out the routes and number of pages which you incorporated—when you first commenced the enterprise of publishing a Swiss guide for the Germans. I beg you to answer this by return of post ...

I am, my dear sir,

Yours very faithfully

John Murray (15.12.1852)

And so on.

Which of them was right or wrong in that 157-year-old dispute does not matter any more. One thing is certain: despite all their differences (Murray accepted hospitality and some advertising, whereas Baedeker didn't; Baedeker used between one and three commending 'stars', whereas Murray was happy with just one; Baedeker was fond of walking, whereas Murray had a thing about old churches, and so on), they both were and still are the greatest guidebook writers of all time.

Old guidebooks and directories, particularly the bulky (and thoroughly irreverent!) two-volume *Imperial Gazetteer*, published in 1855 and edited by W. G. Blackie, helped me stay sane during my life's longest and most devastating crisis.

ST: When it seems like there's no way forward, pause and look back. Open a hundred-year-old guidebook or a Gazetteer. Reading the outdated and seemingly irrelevant facts and figures will calm you down and will put everything into perspective better than any fiction.

The Hay Formula

'Can someone bring in the heater?!' the king shouted to no one in particular from his wobbly wooden 'throne' in the 'state rooms' of the grim and semi-ruined Hay castle. The king's brass crown was lying on the table next to him. His moth-eaten cotton-wool mantle was hanging on the back of a chair. His desperate, almost Shakespearean, scream echoed in the vaults of the chilly and unkempt hall that felt like the insides of an antediluvian, yet somehow still perfectly functioning, giant fridge.

I first met King Richard the Book-Hearted, the self-proclaimed monarch of Hay-on-Wye, a once unremarkable little town on the border of England and Wales, in January 1990, when he was still better known under his real name of Richard Booth. Having abandoned his futile royal pleas for a heater, the shivering king unveiled to the shivering me his plans for a global book empire with its centre in Hay. He wanted to create book towns all over the planet, including Eastern Europe and Australia. 'France alone will have at least two hundred of them to supplement their goat cheeses,' he cackled.

'According to the will of the people of Hay, I shall reconstitute the House of Lords in Hay-on-Wye,' he went on. I wanted to ask him where he was going to get the lords from, but couldn't: my tongue was frozen stiff . . . The answer, however, was fairly obvious. I knew that Mr Booth had appointed his horse, Caligula, prime minister after proclaiming himself the king of independent Hay on April 1, 1977 and couldn't see why the staid and appropriately 'tailed' Hay-on-Wye cats should not pass for a bunch of senile life peers.

The whole coronation and independence affair was obviously nothing but a jokey publicity gimmick consummating Booth's almost twenty years of struggle to put his rapidly declining town back on the map. When he opened his first bookshop in 1961, there were no hotels and just a couple of B&Bs in Hay. Determined to turn the place into the capital of his would-be book empire, he started bringing in truckloads of discarded volumes from American university libraries, buying them for an average price of ten pounds per truck. More and more bookshops appeared in Hay, but, lacking proper temperature conditions and cataloguing systems, they failed to attract customers. Thousands of folios, piled in cardboard boxes, were rotting in humid cellars and disintegrating outside— exposed to the elements. Booth became the laughing stock of the town, where second-hand bookshops pushed out almost all local businesses, including the only little cinema.

The 1976 'Home Rule for Hay' campaign was Booth's last chance. The media noticed the campaign's slogans 'God save us from the Development Board for Rural Wales' and 'Balls to Wall's, Eat Hay National Ice Cream.' The town's popularity grew. A number of top antiquarian booksellers moved in, and tourists began trickling in too. Soon, Hay was chosen as the venue for a major annual literary festival. By the late 1990s, the number of bookshops had reached forty and the number of visitors 500,000 a year. Pubs, hotels and all 108(!) B&B's were thriving, and the locals were eulogising their wise King Richard. Thus Booth and books saved the face of the town.

But King Richard's success did not stop there. Eighteen years after my historic royal audience in the frozen Hay Castle, there are over thirty places on five continents describing themselves as book towns modelled on Hay-on-Wye.

The geography of book towns spans five continents of the globe. They can be found in Scotland (two) and France (three), in Belgium (two) and Holland (one), in Germany (two) and Japan (two), in Switzerland, the USA, Canada, Malaysia, South Korea and Australia. Behind each of them is an eccentric book-enthusiast and a moving (and often ironic) story. Each of them proves that, in our age of space exploration, microcomputers and the Internet, people are still hungry for old books, these frozen fragments of by-gone times, that can—literally—transform the face of any average modern village or town.

One of the success stories was the East German village of Mühlbeck, halfway between Berlin and Dresden—a sleepy rural settlement of nine hundred people that, until recently, could not even be found on the map. It would probably have remained like that forever, had it not been for Heide Dehne, a fifty-five-year-old local resident and a divorced mother of six. Having spent a working week in Hay-on-Wye, she embarked on her project of converting Mühlbeck into Germany's first book village. To start with, she persuaded the local bar owner to make his back room into a small treasure-trove of antiquarian books. A year later, the stock of books has reached 150,000, and Heide was hoping to turn a trickle of visitors into a steady flow.

Wolfgang Metz, the Mayor of another East German town, Wunsdorf, which used to house the headquarters of the Soviet Army garrison until 1994, has turned it into a giant second-hand bookshop in an attempt to change the town's gruesome totalitarian image. What could be a better counterweight to totalitarianism than free and unlimited access to all the gems of human thought?

In the tiny picturesque Ardennes village of Redu, in Belgium, there are now as many bookshops—twenty-four—as there are children, and the trade is drawing 350,000 visitors every year. Interestingly, before bookshops appeared in its centre, the village was experiencing the same economic woes as Hay-on-Wye. Bredevort in the Netherlands also copied the magic 'Hay formula' and now boasts 300,000 visitors a year.

One of the latest converts was Wigtown in Galloway (Scotland), described by a mid-last-century guidebook as 'a sleepy little town with a ruined old Church'. By the late 1980s, however, the town's 'sleepiness' had come to resemble an irreversible coma. Having lost its status of county centre, its railway station and all its little 'industries': two creameries and a whisky distillery—Wigtown was dying.

'The place looked awful,' Don King, the former postmaster, told me. 'Houses were falling apart, and trees grew on chimneys.'

Our conversation took place in the very centre of the town—in its strikingly elegant medieval Main Street, now resplendent with all sorts of businesses—old and new, but mostly with bookshops, of course.

Walter Fitzsimmons, a corner store owner, soon joined us. 'We would have been finished without the book town,' he said meaning his little retail business, which had extended since Wigtown was officially (and with King Richard's blessing, no doubt) 'anointed' as a book town in May 1998.

If at one point in 1997, fourty-seven houses were on sale in tiny Wigtown (1,500 people), in January 2003 there were none. Properties were snapped up immediately after hitting the market, and the busiest professionals in town were . . . no, not the booksellers, of whom there were twenty, but builders, plumbers and electricians—all booked for weeks ahead. Suddenly, the formerly unremarkable Galloway settlement became a very 'cool' place to live. Two 'alternative therapy' outlets and several modern cafés (one doubling as a bookshop)—all within yards of each other—were among the sure signs of this new 'coolness'. Don and Walker told me that even the town's first and only cash-dispenser had appeared there courtesy of the book town office.

In less than five years, Wigtown had been transformed into what looked (to me, at least) like Scotland's happiest community.

Having spoken to most of Wigtown's book dealers, many of whom were relative newcomers, I noticed an interesting similarity: the majority of them ended up there as the result of a personal crisis—death of a partner, family break-up, illness, or loss of general direction in life. Old books tend to attract sensitive and emotional characters, prone to a sudden change of course, as well as those whose ultimate goal in life is not to make a fortune—an almost impossible thing for a modern book-trader—but to achieve spiritual balance.

They were all unanimous in saying: 'Moving to Wigtown was the best thing we ever did.'

Old books also attract eccentrics—that precious and endangered British breed, of which Richard Booth himself was a brilliant representative.

I was delighted to visit the unique house-cum-bookshop, owned and run by Marion and Robin Richmond, where books, animals (one dog, seven cats and five kittens, not including numerous chickens in the garden) and people mingled together in every corner, creating a happy 'organised chaos'. A domestic mauvism of sorts!

'Ming Books' was the name of their business—after one of their deceased pussycats.

Unlike the Richmonds, Carol Weaver—a diminutive lady with tragic eyes—an artist, a mathematician and an aspiring linguist—lived and traded alone in a tiny Victorian cottage in Bladnoch—Wigtown's sister-village. In her own words, her 'stock overflowed into her living quarters' to create the atmosphere of 'anti-minimalism'.

Bumping my head against bookshelves and climbing over neat stacks of books on the floor, I reached a case of Russian books, including several by Alexander Pushkin—Russia's greatest poet, whose life was cruelly cut short at thirty-eight. Leaving her live-in 'Transformer' bookshop, I thought that solitude among old books could never grow into loneliness.

The magic power of an old book, capable not just of salvaging one separate human being, but of changing whole communities even in our button-pressing (as opposed to page-turning) epoch of digital TV and the Internet.

'The Hay Formula' was the title of yet another unwritten book of mine.

In Balham

Now you will understand why Vin simply could not abandon his books and was carrying them with him—indeed, like a millstone (yet a blissful, life-saving one!), wherever he went.

This time, however, he had returned to London too soon. He realised he was still unwell the moment he landed in Heathrow. Having said good-bye to the miniature Chinese air hostesses who had successfully talked him out of having a cigarette during the flight, he got stuck in the Arrivals lounge not knowing where to go next, and hoping vainly that Ona would still turn up to meet him.

Seeing that peculiar I'm-lost-and-helpless expression fleetingly on the faces of the emerging passengers, to be replaced by the relief of recognition and followed by long hugs and even longer kisses, was unbearable.

It is the endearing uncertainty bordering on vulnerability on the face of your loved one waiting for you in the Arrivals lounge (before she/he can actually see you) that makes her/him look anxious and somewhat alien, yet still unbelievably and uncommonly **precious**.

He kept hallucinating he could see Ona in the crowd (she would normally meet him on his return from assignments, and for several days after a reunion they would be very very happy) and felt physically unable to leave the airport. His hands were shaking, his forehead was covered with beads of cold sweat, and the countless cigarettes and cups of coffee he was having in breach of the doctor's ban were only making it worse.

It took him over two hours to gain enough strength to drag his suitcase to the taxi rank and to give Paul's address to the driver.

He slept (having pumped himself full of sleeping pills) in the narrow children's bed of Paul's estranged young son, who stayed with his Mum during the week.

In daylight—propelled by Prosac—he mooched about Balham, trying not to come close to the Tube station, for Ona was on the other end of the Northern Line and he wanted to take that forbidden journey more than anything else in the world.

In the evenings, when Paul and his girlfriend were out, he sat in the kitchen correcting the proofs of *Dreams on Hitler's Couch*:

. . . I couldn't tear my gaze off Hitler's freshly upholstered couch standing there, in the lounge of Crabtree House in Tasmania, as if it had never been anywhere else (furniture pieces are like pets—very adaptable). How many amazing stories it must have heard. How many human (and sub-human) bums it must have accommodated during 170 years of its life. If only the couch could talk . . .

Mind you, there was nothing dictatorial or cannibalistic about it either. It was obviously innocent of any crimes against humanity. But its one-time owner had somehow left an invisible, yet ineffaceable, imprint—an indelible stigma, if not on its seat, then definitely on its reputation . . .

So engrossed was he in proof-reading which seemed to somewhat dull down his constant spiritual pain, that for several evenings he did not notice the strange happenings behind the window of the house opposite—straight across the road.

Several months later, when he was firmly on the mend, he wrote a column about it:

. . . I received a standard typed letter from the London Metropolitan Police. 'Dear Sir,' it began. 'I am sorry to hear that you have been a victim of crime. This has been recorded at this station under the reference as above . . .'

And so on.

It was my second letter of this kind in the last couple of years. The first one (exactly the same as the above-quoted, as if written by one and the same person—and it probably was the same person) arrived shortly after my personal computer was stolen from my flat in broad daylight. The incident was followed by a visit of a couple of tired and extremely polite CID officers who shook their heads and clicked their tongues in sympathy while drinking gallons of tea and reassuring me that the chances of arresting the thief were, unfortunately, close to zero.

A newcomer to the West, I tried then to treat the incident philosophically, thinking that Western freedom of choice must spread to burglars as well: they simply took a liking to my computer (I don't blame them) and chose to steal it. Or maybe, on the contrary, they were trying to teach me a lesson in primitive communism implying that everything is common property, and my computer belonged to them as much as it did to me?

The last incident, however, was different: not only was nothing stolen from me, but something was actually offered (or rather demonstrated) to me from the window of a Balham house, directly opposite to the one where I was staying with a friend last March.

How shall I describe this something without embarrassing my readers (and myself)?

The best way, I think, is to quote from my own police statement: 'On the night of 3 March I first spotted a rhythmically gyrating man in the bay window of the house opposite to our kitchen. Wearing nothing but a red G-string, he was doing something that I couldn't initially figure out (it looked like he was playing with a tightly-folded umbrella). Next night I could clearly see that he was actually masturbating near the window while holding an electric torch close to his groin. The moment I entered the kitchen he would switch on his torch and carry on. The moment I left he would switch the light off. He was obviously targeting me . . .'

When I shared my observations with my host (who has a young son, by the way), he initially dismissed them as my loneliness-induced Freudian hallucinations.

Next night, however, he was able to see for himself . . .

Outraged, he dialled the police and barked into the phone: 'Look, if you don't come soon—he will!' (He has a rather dry sense of humour).

The policemen arrived in two cars with flashing lights.

As soon as they entered our kitchen, the exhibitionist spotted them, switched off the torch and pulled down the blinds on his window. The inspectors rushed out, jumped into their cars and— with sirens wailing—screeched to a thunderous halt twenty metres down the road, at the entrance to the masturbator's den, which by that time had been firmly locked from inside and immersed in darkness.

'Sorry, folks, but we have no right to break in,' they told us on their return. 'The problem is that this particular offence is only arrestable at the moment it is committed. Also, by the existing legislation, a man cannot be indecently exposed to another man . . .'

Having said that, the detectives shrugged their uniformed shoulders, clicked their forensic tongues and left.

Some time later the 'Dear Sir' letter arrived. The end of the matter.

Since then, the blinds on the masturbator's window remained shut day and night. Soon we discovered that he had moved out. But, for some reason, we were not relieved (not half as much as he obviously was). We couldn't help thinking about the sheer impotence of this country's laws, unable to provide protection against such a hideous crime.

So if you happen to become the next target of this particular exhibitionist (or of one of his numerous brothers in arms) and want him arrested, bring your wife or girlfriend around to watch—that is if you are male: as we know, a man's indecent exposure to another man doesn't count. Also, irrespective of your gender, ask the police to try and arrest him in a way that will enable the offender to unlock the door, let the police in (maybe even offer them a cup of tea) and keep masturbating—all at the same time.

This so-called 'legislation' reminded me of a bizarre and archaic procedure for starting a murder investigation which is still in force in Andorra, a tiny pimple of a state in the heart of the Pyrenees.

On the discovery of a corpse believed to be that of a murdered man, a bailiff and a court usher, accompanied by a doctor, proceed to the scene of the crime. The usher then cries out three times addressing the corpse: 'Dead man arise, as justice demands of thee!' If the dead man fails to do so, the usher now cries; 'Dead man, who killed thee? Say who killed thee!' If there is no response to this too, the bailiff then announces: 'This dead man is indeed dead, since he neither arises nor replies. '

The only practical difference is that, unlike indecent exposures in this country, murders in Andorra are as rare as snowstorms in the Sahara desert.

That episode was a sure sign he had to move out.

Paul agreed to keep his books in the loft for a bit longer and gave VV a lift to his new abode in the Borough—a room in a flat that belonged to his friend and former editor.

The room would have been fine, had it not been for two factors: a) it was even closer to Ona on the Northern Line; b) the other room was occupied by an alcoholic woman whose daily menu consisted of a bottle of vodka mixed with milk(!)

and nothing else. Every evening, having reached her coveted drunken stupor, she would fall asleep in a sitting-room armchair in front of a TV set, then would gradually slide down onto the floor.

One day she simply disappeared—failed to return from work—and VV had to answer dozens of phone calls from her worried relatives and colleagues before going to the police several days later to declare his milk-loving neighbour missing.

Of course, she reappeared the same evening and gave VV hell for having stirred up all the fuss. 'I just spent a week with a friend!' she insisted, uncorking a fresh vodka bottle.

No wonder his psychological health was not improving.

Many years later he found a surprisingly precise description of how he felt in Robert Harris's book *The Ghost* (the protagonist, also a writer, has just experienced a deep psychological shock. On top of it, his girlfriend has walked out on him):

'And yet, paradoxically, at the same time as being sunk in a stupor I was also permanently agitated. Nothing was in proportion. I fretted absurdly about trivialities—where I'd put a pair of shoes, for instance . . . The nerviness made me feel physically shaky, often breathless . . .'

Vin suffered panic attacks and was unable to sleep.

In the morning, he couldn't wait for the dose of his anti-anxiety drugs that brought an almost immediate relief, as if his brain and heart were sprayed with a warm coating that was forming itself into a soft, yet strangely impregnable and comforting armour plate over his body and soul; when all his anxieties, cravings and irritations would bounce off it for a couple of hours and he would be able to do some writing . . .

He realised he was getting seriously addicted to the drug and went to see a local GP.

'What have you been taking?' asked the swarthy-looking doctor, of either Greek or Cypriot extraction.

'Xanax,' said he.

'Who prescribed it to you?' further questioned the doctor, having consulted some thick and heavy, almost Bible-like, directory.

'My GP in Melbourne, Australia . . .'

'He should be prosecuted for having made you a drug addict!' the doctor shouted. 'Look at yourself: you are pale, your hands are shaking . . . You are never going to get off this medicine!'

It was not the right thing to say to someone recovering from PTSD and still suffering from anxiety-cum-depression. Or perhaps, on the contrary: it was the ONLY right thing to be said?

As he was walking back to his milk-and-vodka abode, he could feel his hands shaking uncontrollably. 'This has to stop, this has to stop . . .' he was repeating like a mantra.

Without much logical connection, he recalled standing in an endless queue for butter as a little boy in the Soviet Ukraine of the early 1960s—with his granny and granddad.

The precious product was rationed per capita, that was why his grandparents, having wrapped him up in several layers of warm togs, took him to the queue with them. They were standing in the snow for over five hours before their turn came.

They were let inside the Tempo food store where a fat artificial blonde of a saleswoman in once-white overalls dispensed their three carefully weighed butter slices: two larger and one smaller. He remembered burying his little 'capita'—mouth first—into the cold moon-like slice he was entrusted to carry the moment he was back in the street, in full view of the still endless queue snaking along the snow.

'Look at this boy—he likes his butter so much,' the people who were themselves about to enter the shop were saying amicably, whereas those farther away from the entrance only tut-tutted.

An aspiring little glutton, he couldn't care less about gluten. To be honest, he had no idea it existed then.

Scratches left by his sharp little teeth on the yellow surface of the butter slice—like faint outlines of the craters on the face of the Moon he was able to spot in his toy plastic telescope—a birthday present from his Dad.

'I am alone on the earth. You are alone in the skies—and your crater-eyes are empty,' he wrote about the Moon in one of his first youthful poems.

St. John's Wort

Looking back at his childhood often helped him calm down by putting things into a proper perspective.

Another survival tip (ST): when everything else fails, look back at the lowest point in your life and the situation you are in now will appear less hopeless. If it feels as if you are actually going through that lowest point at the moment, think of other people—in Sudan, in Rwanda, in prisons all over the world, being starved and tortured.

He popped into a pharmacy near the Borough Tube station and spent over an hour looking for a herbal substitute for Xanax. St John's Wort—then a virtually unknown homeopathic remedy— sounded like the one that came closest—at least, according to the leaflet inserted in the box.

On that very evening, his dose of Xanax was a tiny bit smaller than usual, the missing grain-size piece substituted with the same amount of St John's Wort. Every day, the replacement crumb grew a fraction bigger, and the violet Xanax pill—smaller.

He was off the drug in one month. After that, giving up St John's Wort was easy.

Had he been a believer, he would have lit up a candle for St John, with all his magic Worts. . .

He felt much better: strong enough to consider relocating to his favourite North London suburb of Muswell Hill—very much inside the Ona zone.

He was no longer afraid of bumping into Ona in the street . . .

His much-travelled books and notebooks were liberated from Paul's loft and moved to Vin's new abode. The middle-aged removals man nearly had a heart attack carrying them (with Vin's help) up the steep stairs to the third level of a Muswell Hill maisonette. 'Next time when you move call a truck with a team, not a man with a van, to carry all these bloody books of yours,' he said bitterly.

But VV was not planning to move anywhere else in the foreseeable future.

He soon reacquired a London window of his own, through which he could again watch people and trees and sunsets, and conduct his endless observations of the world.

Autumn in London

A bright-yellow autumn leaf was stuck to the windscreen of my neighbour's old Volvo. It was like a parking ticket, issued by the meticulous and transparent traffic warden of late autumn, whose long droopy trousers make a soft rustling noise as he saunters around London in the middle of the night.

I read somewhere that the exact mechanism of the riot of colours displayed by nature every autumn is still unknown to the scientists. Just like the exact mechanism of a human smile.

A London autumn is a wry smile in itself, a farewell grin of nature soon to be replaced with the cold impassiveness of winter. It is the time of early darkness, when lonely pedestrians hurriedly make their way home. The pale evasive moon is mooching about in the whisky-coloured sky, like a pot-bellied drunk trudging unsteadily home after a long evening in the pub. It is the season of crisp foggy mornings, when moving around London is like travelling inside a huge chilled wine-glass, and of fragile mica-like sunlight, which shrinks, crumbles and crunches under your boots . . .

Emily Dickinson once beautifully called November 'the Norway of the Year'. By the same token, seasons can be compared to great cities, Paris is spring. Moscow is winter. Rome is summer. And London? Autumn, of course!

Londoners are known to take perverse pride in the all-permeating drabness of their winters. Every year newspapers report with triumph that London is experiencing is dullest (darkest, coldest, lousiest) winter on record.

How do they measure dullness? In 'glums'? Or maybe in 'spleens'?

Autumn, however, is different. It cleanses thoughts and emotions. It helps trees and humans to shed the leafy baggage of their past.

By mid-November, London starts looking light and slightly barren, like the interior of a familiar house from which the excessive furniture has been removed.

Trying to uncover the secrets of London's autumn, I go for long walks in Highgate Wood, touched with a brownish seasonal rash, as if the trees are all suffering from some botanical form of measles. I trudge through piles of fallen leaves, these fading flashes of summer sunshine. I stare at well-behaved Highgate squirrels (I wouldn't be surprised to learn that they regularly pay taxes to forest authorities). I pick up round—polished and gleaming (like the handlebars of an electric chair)—chestnuts and mumble to myself some half-forgotten autumn rhymes:

> 'O dear and cheerless time, you charm the eye and tender contentment to the heart. How wondrous to behold your dying beauty is, the lush and sumptuous splendour of nature's farewell bloom; the forests clad in gold . . .'[6]

Yes, on top of everything else, a London autumn is breathtakingly poetic. Its poetry affects everyone, even those who think that a trochee is a moss-like plant that grows in the desert, and a hexameter is an instrument used by joiners to measure crooked wooden surfaces.

That is why I wrote this autumn elegy—in the hope that Autumn will issue me, too, with its bright-yellow parking ticket, of which there is only a handful left on a branchy maple tree behind my window.

After the 'elegy' was published in the *Guardian*, he was inundated with letters from readers, who, contrary to the old stereotype of the English as cold and emotionless pragmatists, were genuinely touched by the poetry of autumn.

One reader gave him a highly confidential ('don't tell anyone, please!') piece of advice as to where in Highgate Wood one could find some 'proper' mushrooms ('near that ramshackle fence off Archway Road . . .').

As always, autumn—his favourite season—had a therapeutic effect on his health and soon he was ready to go on his first trip outside the UK since arriving from Australia. He travelled to Paris to meet a fellow Russian émigré who also viewed his life very much as a literary device.

6   Alexander Pushkin

Andrei

Andrei Makine snubs word processors. He writes his novels in longhand, agonising over every word, every metaphor.

'Can you really write poetry on a computer screen?' he asks rhetorically, squinting at me through his small Chekhovian spectacles. And without waiting for a reply he shakes his head: 'No, you can't. Poetic novels must be handwritten too. It is only thrillers that you can type!'

Andrei loves writing. Literature and France are his main— his only—passions. 'My perception of France is literary,' he says. 'While in Russia, I learned France like a subject from a school curriculum.'

Just like I had learned London. And Londonology, too . . .

We are sitting in a small bistro in Boulevard St-Germain; outside, Paris lies resplendent in soft wintry sunshine. We speak Russian, but I can't help noticing the genuine delight with which Andrei addresses a waiter in his flawless French.

What happened to Andrei Makine is a miracle, a real-life fairy tale. He had lived in Paris in poverty and despair for seven years, since his defection from the Soviet Union (he came to France on a teacher exchange scheme and simply did not return). Then one evening the phone rang in his tiny attic flat in Montmartre. Simone Gallimard, one of the top French publishers, was on the line.

'I have read your novel,' she said. 'C'est très bien!'

A phone call can sometimes, albeit extremely rarely, be a purveyor of good news too. Remember: we are talking about a miracle here!

By the time of that phone call, the novel, Le Testament Français, had been rejected by dozens of publishers. Like all his previous

175

novels, Andrei had written it in French, 'my grandmother tongue', as he calls it. Why a 'grandmother tongue'? Read on.

His previous three books had come out, but only after he pretended that they were translations from Russian (he invented a non-existent Russian writer whose works he, allegedly, had been translating into French). His tiny attic was brimming with piles of rejected manuscripts on which, unable to afford a bed, he slept fitfully during the night. His days were devoted to writing, to posting his manuscripts ('French publishers have a nasty habit of putting cups of coffee on the manuscripts, leaving brown circles on their pages which make it impossible to send them to anyone else'), and to trying to survive on one baguette a day. The attic was still an improvement on the first couple of years in Paris, when he had to sleep in a cemetery vault and write on park benches.

Or did the miracle happen much earlier, in the 1960s, when Andrei, a romantic Soviet boy from the smoky Siberian town of Krasnoyarsk, was sitting on the balcony with his displaced French granny, Charlotte Lemonier? She taught him to speak fluent French (hence the 'grandmother tongue') and fed him real-life fairy tales about France in her tiny flat in the outskirts of Penza, where Andrei and his sister used to spend their summer holidays.

'That evening we joined our grandmother on the little
balcony of her apartment; covered in flowers, it seemed
suspended above the hot blaze of the steppes. A copper sun
nudged the horizon, remained undecided for a moment,
then plunged rapidly. The first stars trembled in the sky.
Powerful, penetrating scents rose up to us with the evening
breeze.'

Andrei Makine made history in France by snapping up the country's three biggest literary awards—the Prix Goncourt, Prix Medici and Prix Goncourt de Lyceéns—all in a single year, 1995.

It took Andrei 28 years (he was born in 1959) to reach the country of his dreams, this mysterious and remote 'Atlantis' called France, where presidents die '*in the arms of their mistresses*', the land whose melodious language 'throbbed within us, like a magical graft implanted in our hearts.'

With a couple of hours to spare before our meeting, I was wandering around St-Germain-des-Prés until I found a Russian bookshop. It was there that I suddenly spotted Andrei—a tall bespectacled man in a short-sleeved blue shirt. I recognised him from the photo on the cover of *Le Testament Francais*, which had been translated into 27 languages, had sold a million copies in France alone, and had just been published in Britain (under the same French title— *Le Testament Francais*).

Despite his height and his resolute behaviour (he snapped several Russian newspapers from the shelf in one brisk movement—just like his literary awards), there was something deeply vulnerable about him. Was it the burden of his sudden wealth and fame? As he told me later, he was buying these newspapers for his Russian friend who couldn't afford them.

Now—after his 'self-fiction' novel's unimaginable success, after thousands of readers' letters ('I am about to lose my eyesight, but I am so happy that your book is the last one that I have read'), after a long lunch with President Chirac, after a phone call from the dying François Mitterand—Andrei could afford more than just the newspapers.

'My financial life hasn't changed,' he says, sipping his coffee. 'All my money is kept by the publisher, and I take only as much as is absolutely necessary. I don't need a country cottage or a car. Just like before, I never use public transport, but walk everywhere. I have walked all over France. My main luxury is to enter an unknown French town in the early hours of the morning. The only difference is that now I've got a bed.'

The most amazing writer's manifesto I had ever heard. (I thought that, with some reservations, I could put my name under it too: only 'French town' would have to be replaced with 'English', or—better—'European' one).

An archetypal member of the Russian intelligentsiya (who, by Chekhov's definition, feels his own personal guilt for every single injustice in the world), Andrei seems to agree with Tolstoy that 'a writer must suffer' (he even takes it further asserting that a writer has no right to have a family or children and keeps quoting his favourite Proust: 'Happy days are lost days for a writer'). And there is no pretence here: his ten years in France had been a continuous, if subconscious, attempt to translate this masochistic Tolstovian principle into reality.

'I've been cheated and humiliated many times,' he says. 'No one wanted to know me, let alone publish me. I would sit in my attic at 4 a.m. thinking: what am I doing to myself? It was only my belief in having something important to say that kept me struggling on. It was probably insane, but isn't the logic of writing insane in itself? And you know what? I look at these years with nostalgia.'

I will remember these words for as long as I live. They will keep reassuring me in the most hopeless situations in the future.

ST: When you feel down, juxtapose your plight to a gruesome experience endured by someone you know and respect or have simply heard or read of (there will be plenty of examples)—someone who has gone through a much worse crisis and not just survived, but came out of it as a winner.

Andrei's other persisting dream was to bring his grandmother Charlotte back to France. To invite her he needed French citizenship, which was being denied to him. Charlotte died in her dusty Russian Saranza (a fictitious town, invented by Andrei) without ever seeing her grandson, or her native France, again. The last pages of *Le Testament Francais*, where he describes his emotions on learning about her death, are the most poignant in the book:

'When I thought of Charlotte, her presence in these drowsy [Paris] streets had the reality, quiet and spontaneous, of life itself; what I still had to find were the words to tell it with.'

Andrei did find words, and his long-suffering granny could be proud of him. Yet he stops short of labelling *Le Testament Francais* autobiography, preferring to call it a legend. 'A legend is often more truthful than life itself. It is only today that we can really understand what happened yesterday. We all live in a mythical environment, and we tend to mythologise our past.'

'To write a good book about one's native country, one has to leave it first,' said a Russian literary critic.

Andrei takes this notion even further. 'Yes, to look back you need a distance. You even need death. And emigration is partial death . . .'

If emigration is partial death, defection can sometimes be a second birth . . . Andrei is reluctant to talk about the circumstances of his defection from Russia in 1987. (In Soviet legalese, it was—just like in my case—a 'failure to return' punishable by many years in prison or execution.)

'I was never a dissident. I simply could not cope with the new mafia-run Russia. I wouldn't have survived there. My country is the land of literature, my romanticism is living in-between two worlds. No, I don't feel like going back to Russia. They don't understand me there. They think I am showing off by writing in French.'

Do they understand him in his adopted France? Not always, it appears.

Bestowing the highest literary award upon a 'foreigner' was quite a blow to the arrogant and conservative French literary establishment. The Prix Medici, as Andrei asserts, was but an attempt to stop him from receiving the more prestigious Prix Goncourt. 'Some people still refer to me as 'this Russian writing in French, a sort of a clown. But I am a French writer, whether they want it or not . . .'

'My nationality is the language I write in,' Joseph Conrad once noted.

We part in a quaint fifteenth century courtyard near Place St Sulpice which Andrei volunteered to show me. 'Very few people, even Parisians, know about this courtyard, which is one of my favourites,' he says with pride, the same sort of pride I feel when showing my friends my favourite little known nook of central London that is geographically part of Cambridgeshire—Ely Place.

I look at his receding lanky figure standing out in the boisterous Paris crowd. He walks turning his head right and left constantly—as if still finding it hard to believe that he is indeed in Paris.

And I suddenly realise that in his heart of hearts he will always remain a little Siberian dreamer-boy floating on his granny's balcony above the steppe . . .

Andrei Makine, a French writer, is walking to his next appointment at the opposite end of Paris.

He has a long way to go.

When my second son was born some time later, I called him Andrei—in honour of his talented and courageous Russian/French namesake.

Clive

'Have a good trip, Vitali!' Clive James said to me in London. 'You will like Australia, and Australia will like you!'

These are the opening lines of my second book *Dateline Freedom* written in Australia

Clive James did play a huge role in my life—by having me on his popular TV show 'Saturday Night Clive' in the late 1980s and then by providing references for our move to Australia. He turned up at the ceremony granting us (Natasha, Mitya and me) Australian visas at the Australian High Commission in the Strand and made a warm valedictory speech. Clive wanted me to succeed there and I did. I think, in his heart of hearts, he always knew that I—like him—would never settle there for good.

We used to see each other regularly at the hospitable Cambridge house of our mutual friend Russell Davies, whom I had met in his capacity of last but one editor of the old Punch magazine I had been lucky enough to contribute to.

It was normally on a Sunday. I would arrive from London in the morning and by lunch time Clive would come over with his wife Prue, or with his daughter Lucinda. We would often go for a walk in some suburban fields from where stunning views of the colleges could be seen.

I recently found Clive's poetic description of one such walk:

Sunday Morning Walk

Frost on the green. The ducks cold-footing it across the grass Beside the college moat Meet a clutch of matrons Collared-up in Barbours Walking their collies Freshly brushed by Gainsborough. Buoyed by the world's supply Of rosemary sprigs Packed under glass, The moorcock emerging from the reeds Does a hesitation step As though dancing to Piazzolla. Cool shoes, if I may say so. In front of the

boathouses The rowers rigging fulcrums to the shells. Bite off their
gloves To push in pins, And the metal shines. Just short of a glitter
Because the light, though Croesus-rich, Is kiss-soft. Under the
bridge, the iron ribs Form a pigeon loft, A pit lane of sports saloons
Testing their engines. The final year Of the finishing school for
swans Passes in review . . .

In summer we would sit in the garden until it got dark talking about everything: from the future of Russia to poetry and oriental philosophy.

Out of all Clive's literary and artistic incarnations, poetry, in my opinion, was the strongest.

One Sunday, he arrived somewhat later than usual. His eyes were tinted red.

'I've been drinking with Joseph Brodsky until 2 a.m.,' he said. 'It's a shame you weren't with us, Vitali: you've missed Joseph by just a few hours.'

Joseph Brodsky—Russia's 20th century Pushkin, Nobel Prize winner, émigré, maverick, wanderer, sorcerer of Russian poetry . . . I've just finished reading his magnificent Venetian poem in prose called *Watermark*. Brodsky wrote it in English:

'Many months ago the dollar was 870 lire and I was thirty-two . . .'—was its opening sentence. What a start!

'Water equals time and provides beauty with its double. . .' Only a great poet could put it like that.

Brodsky is buried in Venice (he died about a year after that drinking session with Clive).

'. . . and when 'the future' is uttered, swarms of mice rush out of
the Russian language and gnaw a piece of ripened memory which
is twice as hole-ridden as real cheese. After all these years it hardly
matters who or what stands in the corner, hidden by heavy drapes,

and your mind resounds not with a seraphic 'doh', only their
rustle. Life, that no one dares to appraise, like that gift horse's
mouth, bares its teeth in a grin at each encounter. What gets left of
a man amounts to a part. To his spoken part. To a part of speech.'

Which 'part of speech, was left of Joseph Brodsky?

An adjective of beauty?
A verb of achievement?
A noun of recognition?
An exclamation mark of pain or admiration?

Whatever the 'part of speech', my link to Joseph Brodsky
whom I had never met and will never meet, will always go
through Clive.

Which 'part of speech' would I want to leave behind? Or does
it have to be a 'part of speech'? Would a 'Literary Device' do?

I was thrilled when approached by the *Independent* newspaper
to be interviewed with Clive for their 'How We Met' feature.

We were interviewed separately by one and the same
journalist, Isabel Wolfe, who later became a famous writer in her
own right. (Another strange correlation of my life: most women
journalists who interview me proceed to become acclaimed
authors in the long term.)

It was more like a live dialogue in which the participants were
not supposed to interrupt each other under any circumstances:

VV: I met Clive for the first time in 1988, on air; or rather he
met me because he could see me and I couldn't see him. It was
in Moscow and one day I got a call inviting me to appear on a
serious political talk show, introduced by Clive James. I had no
idea who Clive James was, but I put on my suit and my sombre
Soviet look and I went to the Ostankino studios in Moscow.

I was led to a little room where I was completely on my own, just facing the muzzle of the camera. Behind me there was a weather-beaten photo of Red Square just to show the viewers I was in Moscow. Then there was this crackling voice in my earphones, sounding very cheerful and saying: 'Can you hear me, Vitali Vitaliev?' I smelt a rat from the very first minute because if you look at the tape you can see I looked very serious, expecting to be interviewed in a serious way by the BBC. But the questions were not exactly serious, and for the first two or three minutes I looked quite ridiculous because there was this funny man in London and this man in Russia taking him very seriously. But then I saw it was a game and I started tentatively making some little jokes and getting into the spirit of it all. And the producer phoned me afterwards and said that they were sorry, they were pulling my leg, it wasn't a serious show and they did this sometimes with people who didn't know the programme. And they said that next time they wanted me to appear as I was, and that's how it started. What I didn't know then was that appearing on this show and meeting Clive James was going to play an enormous part in my life.

My impression of him when I talked to him by satellite that first time was good, because his voice was pleasant and friendly, and I could tell that he was trying to help me out. And his sense of humour was lovely and sardonic, and his questions were very tongue-in-cheek. I did several programmes and became their Moscow correspondent.

When I went to Britain it was a complete shock. Everyone knew me, even customs officers at the airport. Then I started being perceived as the Russian-Clive James, something I'm getting a bit fed up with, not because I don't like Clive James—I adore him, he's a wonderful man—but because it's a cliché. I defected in January 1990 and we came here. Because I wanted to get as far away as possible from the Soviet Union, Clive said: 'Why don't you go to Australia?'

So I went to the High Commission and the moment I entered

the building they all said: 'Oh, we know you, mate. You're Clive James's Moscow man,' and within a month I had an Australian resident's permit and off I went. I spend a lot of time in Britain now, so Clive and I see more of each other. I've always admired his versatility so much, his TV shows and his books. I feel his presence and I've always relied on his advice because I think he is a very wise man and he really cares about me, and I care about him.

We are both defectors. I left Russia and he left Australia, though for different reasons. We are both exiles. I think that destiny drew us together. We used to drink quite a lot of vodka together—I taught him how to do it properly. We have lunches that grow into dinners, we go for walks in the fields around Cambridge and we talk a lot. Clive's range of interests is very broad, he knows a lot about Russian literature and Russian culture, he can speak Russian too. I think we go well together on an intellectual level because we have lots of things to discuss. And he's had this enormous influence on my life. Funnily enough, we are both pursuing more or less the same range in writing and journalism, and I think that his sense of humour is very similar to mine. He is very ironic, and I love irony.

Our backgrounds are very different but we laugh at each other's jokes, not because we want to please each other, but because we find them funny. I think he's a very generous person and I don't just mean with money—though he is. I think he is generous in his attitude to people. He is extremely busy, but he is still very interested in people, and gives them his time. And he's very, very clever. I would call him one of the intelligentsiya, which is a very Russian word which has no real equivalent in English. It's something much more than someone who is just a knowledgeable person. It also involves compassion, and a sense of guilt for every injustice in the world.

Sometimes in his television appearances I think he goes a bit over the top—there is a very fine line between irony and ridicule and sometimes his jokes border on ridicule, but maybe this is just a requirement of the genre. As a person he is sometimes too sad, but people who have to be funny, are often quite serious people in their normal life. When we talk, lots of things we discuss are very serious, and, yes, sometimes he is a bit too sad.

I think he is a wonderful writer and poet, and although television is a good medium and very addictive, I think writing should come first. When I'm in Australia I often re-read his Unreliable Memoirs and the sequels. I have a tape of them and I put them on in the car and it's as though Clive is talking to me. I think his autobiographical trilogy is beautifully written, it's classic, and his poems are really fine, so I wish he could do more writing. If I didn't see him I would miss him so much. I think I would miss this light-hearted wisdom that he has, which isn't found very often. He is one of these people who can say something wise and profound in a very light-hearted manner. I think that's a very great skill, and that's where I would like to follow in his footsteps.

Clive James: I first met Vitali in 1988 on a satellite link to Moscow. I was doing my weekly television show and Vitali was a correspondent that our researchers had discovered. We learnt that he was famous, or notorious, for saying things that the government didn't like, and which the KGB didn't like, so he was obviously a very brave guy.

Vitali agreed to do a satellite transmission for us from television studios outside Moscow, in one of those huge concrete buildings. I could see him, but he couldn't see me, because I was communicating with him by audio. He did this terrific piece for us about Soviet TV, and he had this stunning command of English for someone who had never been outside the Soviet Union. He went far beyond the limit of what he could say and still be safe, and I learnt that he was in great danger. I knew other things he was saying in Soviet newspapers and journals which got him into trouble, and we heard the KGB were after him.

Vitali came on my programme a few times, and he was a big star. He attracted a lot of attention here and in Australia, where the programme was also broadcast. So when he left the Soviet Union, he went to Australia, because he was having problems getting a UK resident's permit, and because his family were keen to go there.

What I remember most about when I met Vitali was just this charming guy, bursting out of his suit with energy and sheer goodwill. I don't know how he got like that. It's like Gorbachev—where do these men and women who changed everything come from? It turned out that the Russian mafia were getting heavy with him, too. He wanted to go to Australia and the Australian High Com-mission wanted some referees for him, and so I was very happy to oblige. He got his papers and his family went off there, and we stayed in touch as he and his family shuttled back and forth to Europe. Then Vitali decided to make his base here in Britain because he felt too cut off from Europe. He made his own television documentary in the Soviet Union and he did insanely brave things like walking into Chernobyl without any protective clothing. He was the first émigré Russian journalist ever to go on television in this country and talk about the Russian mafia. Of course, nobody believed him.

Vitali was on a BBC programme here discussing the situation in the Soviet Union after Gorbachev, and he said that not only were things not going to change in the direction of democracy as everyone blithely assumed they would, but there was a new danger and that was from gangsterism. He was almost cut off the air on the BBC for saying this—nobody believed that it was relevant.

Vitali and I are drinking friends. I don't drink any more, unless I'm with him—when for some reason, the vodka bottle comes out, the top flies off and there we are drinking Smirnoff. He taught me how to drink vodka properly. He takes me out of myself. He's had a very adventurous life, he's taken real chances and I admire his writing, which gets better and better. He's getting to the point where he can express himself in English almost as well as in Russian.

I've had a very lucky life but Vitali and his generation didn't. It took great individuality and courage for him to become what he is. I admire that. He's an example of what can be done.

I admire the way Vitali operates between two languages with complete confidence; to me it shows that journalism and writing aren't just a question of the language you write in—it's what's underneath; it's what you're about as a person. There's nothing much that annoys me about him except that he's too happy—he gets a big, big bang out of life, and I'm enough of a puritan to wonder why he smiles so much. I wish I could be as merry as he is. I'm a bit of a sad bastard, and with less reason. We're both interested in the history of the twentieth century, but he's lived it, and I've been a spectator.

I feel that Vitali plugs me into history. In the West we live our media lives and don't affect what happens, we just report on it. To people like Vitali, what they said and did really mattered, and there were consequences for saying it—some of them very perilous. I often wonder what I would have done in the same circumstances, and I've a suspicion I wouldn't have been as brave, that I'd have shut up. A lot of people in the Soviet Union were trying to close Vitali down and I think they would have found it easy to close me down. It would only take one guy in a tightly-fitted suit to look at me sideways through his dark glasses to make me take up a different profession, so in a way Vitali is my conscience. We're both exiles, but there's a big difference between leaving your country because your life is in danger and switching location to find a job, as I did when I left Australia.

We both enjoy talking—when we're at the dinner table it's a riot—but on the whole he's a different character from me. You end up saying more than you expected because he gets everybody into conversation, which is ideal for his journalism. He's kind of adorable. No man likes to have that said about him – most of us would like to be thought of as dangerous and brooding. I don't know if Vitali would take kindly to being told he's adorable, but he is . . .

Despite all the similarities, there was one substantial difference between us at the time. It was hammered home rather cruelly (from my point of view) in the feature's standfirst:

'*Clive is married with two daughters and lives in Cambridge.*

'*Vitali is divorced, with one son, and lives alone in London.*'

Galina

Several months after Vin's trip to Paris, something happened that nearly threw him back nto blackness .

My friend Galina Starovoitova, a leading Russian MP and the soul of Russia, was gurned down in a dark doorway in St Petersburg.

How well I know these Leningrad/St Petersburg graffiti-ridden doorways, inundated with the smell of cats' urine and cabbage soup and treacherously lit with a single, naked bulb. They epitomise the hopelessness and despair of modern Russia—something Galina had so courageously and persistently tried to change.

It is unspeakably awful that she had to die like that. But it is also tragically symbolic: darkness and hopelessness overcame her in the end. Galina, the last example of decency in Russian politics, could no longer exist in a country where political murder has become the norm, where everything—from a human life to a government—can be bought and sold.

I first met Galina in London in August 1991, on the day the communist putsch was defeated in Moscow. We were invited to the flat of a mutual friend to celebrate. 'How nice it is to have something real to celebrate in Russia at long last,' Galina said. There was an aura of warmth emanating from her kind, round face. She told me that both our names were on the junta's hit list, and that somehow brought us closer together.

Perhaps the same hitmen caught up with her seven years later.

Our next meeting was in 1993, in Venice, when Galina, already known all over the world, was invited to address the general assembly of the International Press Institute. Her speech was supposed to be in English, a language she could hardly speak then. Of course, she could have asked for an interpreter, but it was not her style. I helped her render her speech into English and she delivered it brilliantly.

After that, our meetings became more frequent. She would turn up on my doorstep in London, which she visited often (her only son, Platon, lived here). When I was going through a personal crisis, Galina helped me with her wise guidance and advice.

Her ability to find time for everyone never ceased to amaze me. Though she was working flat out on her lectures, interviews and political commitments, she was always there to help the refugees from Nagorno-Karabakh or some poor Russian old ladies who came to her with their grievances in her capacity as the Duma's deputy. Democracy for her was not just a political platform, it meant her own constant accessibility and availability for anyone who might need her. Even her decision to run for the Russian presidency in 1996 (which many of her less idealistic friends tried to talk her out of) was dictated not by political ambition but by her wish to make a statement on behalf of all the underprivileged and domestically enslaved Russian women. And although she failed to get her candidacy registered, her statement was heard by many.

Over her last couple of years, Galina was becoming increasingly busy, as if she somehow felt that she did not have much time left. She was criss-crossing Russia by plane and train, and I never knew where I was going to find her when I dialled the number of her mobile telephone. Despite such a workload, her conversations were never snappy, and she never refused to write an article (which she would often do on the plane) or to give an interview.

I last met her less than two months before her murder, at the end of September 1998 in Istanbul, where we were both invited to take part in a World Press Council conference. We were not sure Galina would participate until the last moment. To see her so unexpectedly was a real gift of fate for me. She was happy and relaxed. 'I just decided to give myself a short break from politics,' she said.

We spent many hours walking around Istanbul and relaxing near our hotel's swimming pool. She had just got married for the second time and was full of plans. She wanted to write a book about the former Soviet republics. She told me about her intention to run for the governorship of Leningrad region—the very ambition that might have eventually cost her her life.

I couldn't help noticing a couple of worrying signs, however. For the first time since the collapse of communism, Galina did not feel optimistic about Russia's immediate future. One day, we noticed a group of young, heavily-tattooed Russian men near the pool. They were boorish and loud-mouthed. 'Hey, Starovoitova, would you like to be photographed with us?' one asked her. He brandished a camera. 'Let's go, Vitali,' Galina said to me quietly. 'They are the type of new Russians I do not have anything in common with.' We were not talking much about politics, but mostly about life, about our children and loved ones. Once, when we were walking in the park near an old mosque, she said: 'I am now fifty-two, and I think I know what the best thing in life is. It is when you know that you are loved . . .'

Just like her fellow idealist, my Mum, eight years later, Galina knew that she was loved when she died.

He learned about Galina's murder while on air, on the panel of a popular BBC TV programme where he was a regular.

The floor manager gave him a sheet paper with the

news—fresh from the wires.

He was asked to comment.

He said he was unable to. Not before he called her son.

Having done that, he rushed out of the studio at the TV Centre in White City and, having told the driver of the waiting BBC car that he wouldn't need him, walked home to Muswell Hill.

He reached his maisonette five hours later, at about 3 a.m. Some crazy London birds were screaming their little lungs out outside his flat which—for the first time since moving there from the Borough—he was reluctant to enter.

In Moscow, they said on the radio, hardliners were demonstrating near the Russian parliament building that very evening. 'We killed the snake!' ran one of the posters they were carrying.

His last warm feelings for Russia were murdered on that dark London night .

My perfect day

At sunrise, I would be on Mount Athos, self-governing republic of Orthodox monks in Northern Greece, where I once had an unforgettable sun-worshipping experience.

To say that my Greek guide, who accompanied me on that particular pilgrimage to the Holy Mountain, was a snorer would have been a gross understatement. Had Oscars been awarded for snoring, he would have definitely snatched up the one for the best and loudest soundtrack. Since the accommodation for visitors on Mount Athos is no more than basic, we had to share one and the same cell in the monastery of Philotheu.

After several hours of gentle whistling and diplomatic coughing, I had to resort to far less gentle pushes and far less diplomatic Russian swear words which I shouted at the top of my voice. The magnificent, Oscar-winning snores continued unaffected. I got dressed, picked up my cigarettes and went out on to the monastery's balcony hanging precariously above the cliff.

It was still pitch dark, and the lonely light of a detached mountain *skites*—a hermit's dwelling—was blinking in the distance, like an unknown star. Soon I heard the rhythmic and monotonous sounds of semantrons, the wooden drums calling monks to the morning liturgy.

I looked down: the black-hooded monks were sliding across the monastery yard towards the church in treacherous semi-darkness, like white-shrouded ghosts in a slow-motion picture, shown in the negative by the erroneous cinema operator of dawn.

An invisible multi-voiced choir inside the church was chanting psalms with amazing synchrony and grace.

The red-robed monk of the rising sun was descending slowly from his heavenly *skites* above the sea and covering the world with his pink see-through cassock.

Suddenly, everything around me was full of light, harmony and meaning. And although out of the three main virtues of a Mount Athos monk, chastity, obedience and lack of personal possessions, I could only boast the third one, for a fleeting moment I felt like taking a monastic vow, and spending the rest of my days in that truly divine part of the world.

'Thank you for snoring last night!' I said to my guide at breakfast.

For breakfast, I would go across the globe, to Melbourne.

One can easily put on a couple of kilos by simply staring at the mind-boggling displays of cakes and biscuits in the windows of countless cafes in Acklard Street in its cosmopolitan seaside suburb of St Kilda. No other city in the world comes close to Melbourne in quantity (if not always in quality) of food: I once saw a burger stall doing brisk trade in the lobby of a local cardiology hospital.

As a four double-espresso-per-day person, I like having breakfast in one of the Ackland Street coffee shops, most of which are either Jewish or Italian. Trying to watch my weight, I sip my coffee breathing salty sea air and gaping at the cream-capped culinary Everests in the shop windows. The view in itself is so hedonistic and so filling that it often helps me forsake my regulation morning croissant.

At lunchtime, I would be back in Europe, in Malta.

The Oleander restaurant in the village of Xaghra on Gozo, the second largest island of the Maltese archipelago, overlooks the Nativity of the Virgin church with a marvellous *trompe l'oeil* of a painted clock on its ornate facade. The clock is designed to confuse the devil when he starts dealing with the souls of the dead—an old Maltese tradition.

I am not sure about the devil, but these painted clocks all over the country must be very effective in confusing unwary tourists, of whom there are many—too many in Malta, if not yet in Xaghra, into missing their flights back home . . .

It is probably due to the painted clock that lunch at the Oleander is normally long and unhurried.

I would start with stuffed squid; the world's best squid can be found on Gozo, followed by bean soup and *fenek*—rabbit casseroled in red wine and garlic. The restaurant is usually buzzing with locals gobbling their beloved *gbejniet*, Gozo's homemade goat cheese, and washing it down with plenty of beer. Watching them, one comes to understand a popular Maltese joke. (The Gozitans are the butt of jokes in Malta, like Newfoundlanders in Canada, Tasmanians in Australia, Georgians in Russia, and the Irish all over the English-speaking world.) This goes to the effect that the Gozitans are 'cheese-headed' and should incorporate *gbejniet* into their coat of arms.

There is no better place for my dream afternoon than Hay-on-Wye, a small town in the county of Powys on the border of England and Wales. As a passionate bookworm, I absolutely adore browsing through the stocks of the town's thirty-odd second-hand bookshops.

Books in Hay are literally strewn all over the town. Apart from the bookshops, they can be found on numerous unattended open-air bookstalls, exposed to the elements: sun-beaten and often soaked with rainwater. Looking for a book you need is similar to digging for gold bullion in the sand: you never know what you might come across or whether you are going to find anything at all. It is precisely this uncertainty that makes the search so exciting and so similar to a treasure hunt. I remember ferreting out a thick Victorian monograph *Social History of British Sea-Weeds* one day and agonising for half an hour whether to buy it or not. In the end, I decided against it: seaweeds, no matter how socially active, were not exactly within the sphere of my interests.

And you know what: I have been regretting it ever since.

Come dinnertime—and my imagination transfers me to Vaduz, the tiny capital of the pocket-handkerchief alpine principality of Liechtenstein.

I remember how Felix Real, an acclaimed Liechtenstein hotelier and restaurateur, got upset one evening when I, being a teetotaller, refused the offer of Vaduse Rose from his cellars.

'But it is so good, so good—um-m-m . . .' he was saying kissing his own fingers as proof. The old man was so distraught that I became seriously worried about his health, and, possibly, even his life. Grief-stricken, he stumbled out of his 'Real' restaurant in Vaduz to continue suffering in the privacy of his house (or so I thought), and I was left in the hands of three buxom blonde waitresses who immediately brought me a menu the size of the Gutenberg Bible. The names of the dishes sounded like a French prayer—'*Homard, langoustines et coquille St Jaques grilles a l'estragon*' . . . Amen!

As soon as I had coped with the starter of wonderfully delicate smoked eel, they brought me a set of six knives and forks (plus a special little spoon for the sauce) and threateningly placed them on a wooden board on my table. My main course of lamb fillet was delivered on a gleaming trolley, which resembled a gun carriage carrying the body of a Soviet General Secretary of the eighties to be buried near the Kremlin Wall. Stainless steel lids covering the plates looked like brass cymbals, and I could almost hear the sounds of Chopin's Funeral March (was it mourning the contents of my wallet?), when the waitresses synchronically lifted them.

The trolley was then solemnly driven back to its kitchen stable. It didn't want to go and was kicking the waitresses with its obnoxious wheels.

At this point, Felix Real reappeared in the restaurant. He was smiling. My mounting appetite must have cured his distress.

Approaching night would find me in Venice, the city that I will never stop loving. I know it is banal to fall in love with Venice, but isn't it more banal not to fall in love with it?

At sunset, when the water in its canals gleams with a magic translucent light of its own, as if slowly, almost reluctantly, discharging the sunlight it has accumulated during the day; when blinds fall like thick black eyelids on the gaping eye-sockets of tired old houses; when the gentle tolling of distant church bells mingles with the soft smacking sound of lovers' kisses—there suddenly comes a whiff of fresh sea breeze, a reminder of the days when Venice meant ships, spices and trade routes to be explored.

At dusk, I like sitting on the bank of the Grand Canal listening to the soft splashes of water against the ancient Venetian stones. It is then that I start seeing Venice as an ageing but still graceful woman suffering from insomnia and shuffling restlessly around the house in her loose-fitting slippers in the night.

After a full and tiring globe-trotting day, I would have little problem falling asleep in my bed in the North London suburb of Muswell Hill—the place where I belong and where my home is.

It will always be there, even if I don't live there any longer.

The Falklands

I am often asked at public talks and parties what my favourite place in the world is. The answer to that is obvious—London.

No, they say: we mean what place you enjoyed most of all during your travels.

Answering that is not easy. I love all mini-states of Europe, Tasmania, the Channel Islands, the Faroes, Norway, Amsterdam, Perth, Alaska, Salzburg, the Hebrides—both Outer and Inner— and so on and so on . . . Yet, my most memorable journey was probably that to the Falklands.

It started with a peculiar RAF flight to Port Stanley.

A civilian to the core, I have always been puzzled by the military. The only bad mark I got at my Soviet University was in Military Tactics—a compulsory discipline for every high-school student in the jingoistic and paranoid USSR. I remember that among the things we studied were the composition and equipment of NATO armies—our potential enemies, the British Army, being one of them. Not even in my wildest dreams could I imagine that twenty-odd years later I would be given a chance not only to mix with British servicemen—and women, as political correctness requires us to say these days—better known as squaddies, but also to fly on board a real RAF jet.

It was the most curious journey in my entire, highly peripatetic, life.

The adventure started in Swindon, Wiltshire, where I was waiting for a bus to take me to RAF Brize Norton airport for a TriStar military flight to Mount Pleasant—the quickest, the cheapest and the only (after the scrapping—or, should I say 'Pinocheting'?—of the sole commercial flight from London via Chile) way to get to the Falklands. The bus was late, and I realised with horror that I would be unable to 'report for check-in' by 'the latest reporting time', specified in the strict 'Reporting Instructions JSTC/R2/30', attached to my ticket. Shifting from one foot to the other, I was nervously—for an umpteenth time—checking the availability of an overnight bag in my cabin luggage: the same Reporting Instructions demanded that every passenger had an overnight bag handy—in case our TriStar suddenly gets diverted to bomb Iraq, or so I thought.

The overnighter was there, but the bus wasn't.

The delay did not seem to worry my fellow travellers: a large group of vociferous crew-cut youngsters communicating with each other with the help of one f-word only– probably the servicemen (sorry, but there were no women among them), and a handful of confused and dishevelled civilians like myself.

Having finally received my RAF boarding pass: 'rank—none', I wandered aimlessly around the airport lounge, where only two outlets were open—a tiny newsagent, with an impressive choice of soft-porn magazines, and a note-exchange machine—'Insert £20 Queen's face up and last.' They were calling out passengers by names in alphabetical order, and for the first time in my life I rejoiced at having a name starting with 'V', which allowed me to have three additional fags before a strictly non-smoking flight.

Twenty minutes after take-off, plastic cups of 'RAF Fruit Juice' were served, or rather 'distributed', by muscular stone-faced stewards, who all seemed to stick assiduously to some mysterious, no-smiling-under-any-circumstances, military regulation. Just like the stewards' faces, the drink was frozen stiff. It melted and became drinkable by next morning, when, to my great relief,

I discovered in a seat-pocket in front of me an indispensable 'NATO Stock Number 8105-99-130-2180' air-sickness bag. Next to this thoroughly encoded bag, there was a copy of the RAF inflight monthly journal, ingeniously entitled 'Inflight'. Compared to it, a glossy safety leaflet in the same seat-pocket read—and looked—like *Hello* magazine.

Soon, we started our descent on Ascension Island, a barren volcanic rock in the middle of the Atlantic, for a refuelling stop and were duly instructed on 'de-planing procedures' over the intercom.

On RAF Ascension, I hesitated in front of a plywood shed with the scary sign 'Terminal Drinks Kiosk' before plunging into Tom Clancy's *Executive Orders*, a 1,374-page-thick brick of a paperback, which could itself easily prove terminal, if dropped onto your head from a ground-floor window, or in a more unlikely case of being read to the end.

The second leg of the flight was not that different from the first one. Same juice, chips and stale rolls with on unidentifiable (probably classified) filling were served—sorry, 'distributed'— by a different, yet equally unsmiling, crew members. Same peremptory announcements forbidding any movement around the cabin during meal times were made at regular intervals. Same choice of four old videos camouflaged as 'flight entertainment' was offered. It was hard to believe that the cost of an average ticket to the Falklands was almost twice as high as that of a Qantas flight from London to Melbourne.

'Didn't you know that in their flight documents, the military refer to civilian passengers as SLF—self-loading freight?' the facetious Falkland Islands official who met me at Mount Pleasant said as we were waiting for my luggage to arrive.

'You must be joking,' I wanted to say, but choked on my words as I looked at the moving conveyer and spotted my long-awaited weather-beaten backpack. The word 'Civilian' was printed in large letters on a cardboard tag tied to its handle.

At RAF Mount Pleasant, the Falkland Islands' 'international airport', the passengers of our Ministry of Defence flight RR3200 were welcomed by blazing summer sunlight and two unemotional bomb-disposal experts, a Sergeant and a Corporal. In the arrivals lounge, they showed us the dummies of Argentine land-mines, the sad relics of the 1982 conflict, of which 26,000 still sit unexploded in the Falklands' scarred terrain, and warned that venturing onto a minefield constituted an offence punishable by a thousand-pound fine.

I thought that to collect this fine, they would have to collect and put back together all one thousand pieces of the trespasser first.

The minefields, clearly marked with 'Danger:Mines' and 'Slow: Minefield' signs, lay on both sides of the road to Stanley, the Islands' tiny capital of two-thousand people. In the many years since the conflict the locals have learnt to live with the mines. On the island of West Falkland, I saw a golf course next to a minefield, and one of the houses in Stanley was adorned with a mock skull-and-crossbones sign: 'Danger: Karl'.

Despite, or maybe because of, the minefields surrounding it, there was an immediate charm about Stanley, with its multi coloured roofs, its quiet streets running down the hill towards the harbour, and its several little pubs, where some ancient ABBA hits were still played and all conversation stopped the moment you walked in.

Complete strangers said 'Good morning!' to you in the streets, and soon you started greeting them too. If you forgot about the newly opened Internet Café, this was what a typical British village of yesteryear must have been like. Only this wayward 'village' had split from its motherland and ended up eight thousand miles away, near the South Pole.

The smallest capital city in the world, Stanley had a life of its own. Shortly before my arrival the Islands' first zebra crossing appeared in Ross Road, Stanley's main street, outside the Post Office. *Penguin News*, a lively local newsletter, wrote that: 'police are now looking at ways to educate the public in how to use it.'

The residents of Stanley might still be unsure of how to cross the roads, but they did love driving their Land Rovers. Or, maybe, they simply did not like walking. I was constantly offered lifts from Upland Goose Hotel opposite the Post Office, where I stayed, to Malvina House Hotel opposite the Post Office, where I went for lunches and dinners, despite the fact that the hotels were no more than a hundred metres apart.

This puzzling reluctance to walk might lie behind a sudden proliferation of taxis in Stanley, where several years earlier the only cab had been the Governor's car, which doubled as a taxi when His Excellency was away or asleep in his stately residence.

Taxis and cars as well as houses were routinely left unlocked in Stanley. 'Familiarity makes crime difficult,' Ken Greenland, the Falkland Islands' police chief, told me in his headquarters, opposite the Post Office. Murder is practically unknown here. When the corpses of two Chinese fishermen were fished out of the sea in the Falklands' territorial waters, several months before my arrival, a forensic pathologist had to be flown in from London.

The local Community School was the pride of Stanley, and its oblong modernistic building on top of a hill opposit the post office was the loudest architectural statement in town. Its state-of-the art classrooms and laboratories were among the best I had ever seen. But the school's main assets were its 150 pupils—all neat, polite and well behaved. Probably because there were few distractions for them in the Falklands.

'Kids are such a joy here: out of 150, I haven't met a single nasty one. They are such a pleasure to teach,' one of the teachers confided in me.

By 9 p.m. Stanley goes dead. At this time, it is nice to walk along its deserted sea front, under strange unknown stars, breathing in the amazingly clean and crisp air, listening to splashes of water in the bay and to the gentle rustling of the fern and Diddle-Dee—an indigenous plant similar to heather. During one such walk, when I was ready to believe that I was in Zurbagan, a fictitious town of poets and seafarers created by Russian romantic writer Alexander Grin, I suddenly heard the theme tune of 'The Archers' from a house nearby.

After a couple of days in Stanley, I set out to explore the Camp. A derivative of the Spanish word 'Campo' meaning 'countryside', the Camp denoted 'everything outside Stanley'. Its area 4,700 square miles, was roughly equal to that of Northern Ireland. These vast expenses of windswept and treeless land, comprising hundreds of big and small islands, were populated by 800,000 sheep and less than two hundred people. With the near absence of roads, the only effective means of communication between the settlements was a small fleet of miniature Islander aircraft, whose pilots also acted as couriers carrying food, letters, money and gossip from one settlement to another.

The Islander that took me from Stanley to Port Howard was also carrying beer, ice cream, burger-buns and a teenage schoolgirl travelling to her settlement for the holidays. Embarrassingly, not only my backpack, but also its owner, had to be weighed up before boarding, and naturally I had to pay for the excess baggage, which was myself, no doubt. I suddenly felt indeed like 'a self-loading cargo', probably even ballast.

Our four-seater was hovering low above the ground, narrowly avoiding hilltops and sharp toothbrush-like rocks. I was rummaging through my pockets in search of air-sickness pills and looking down at the barren brownish plain, only occasionally dissected with dirt tracks. Wherever there was a hut, it meant settlement.

The pilot would then pull the joystick towards his chest, as if trying to bear-hug it, and the Islander would promptly land on a bumpy turf-covered air strip to be met by two locals in a dusty Land Rover, to which a car with regulation fire-extinguisher would be dutifully and rather unnecessarily attached. The Islanders were safe, and the only recorded accident happened several years ago, when the plane's chassis got stuck in a penguin burrow on an airstrip during a take-off. Luckily, the penguin was not at home.

'Port Howard is pretty large,' I was told in Stanley.

What can I say? Einstein was right: everything is relative. In the Camp, where most settlements have a population of between two and ten, Port Howard, which numbered over thirty and boasted a store, a school with three pupils and even a tiny War Museum, could be regarded as a huge metropolis and a cultural centre, on a par with Birmingham in Britain, perhaps.

My host was Robin Lee, a farmer and a fifth-generation Falklander, whose great grandfather came to the Islands as a shepherd in the 1870s. His farm had an area of 200,000 acres— enough to accommodate several European mini-states.

Well-mannered and softly spoken, Robin toiled non-stop from morning till night. His farm's main produce was wool, but with world wool prices going down, he was desperate to expand and to diversify his sphere of activities. He also helped his partner Hattie, a sophisticated cook from Cumbria, to run the Lodge—a warm and cosy B&B, with by far the best food in the Falklands.

'The most unpopular person here is the one who is not prepared to help others,' he said from behind the wheel of his Land Rover at the start of our quick—only half-a-day-long— drive around his farm.

To illustrate his point, he showed me an abandoned hut that used to belong to Mrs McCuskie, who lived there on her own in the 1980s. Coincidentally, it was straight above her house—the only dwelling for miles around—that the antediluvian telephone wires used to—literally—cross, and Mrs McCuskie volunteered to act as a telephone exchange operator, answering phone calls at any hour of the day and night and putting the callers through to their destinations. Only God knows how many lives she helped save, and how many problems solve. Mrs McCuskie had been dead for several years, and with the Cable & Wireless now operating in the Falklands, people could communicate without intermediaries, but the selfless lady was still fondly remembered in the Islands, and the bay of the Charters River, where Robin and I went fishing, was named after her.

And what wonderful fishing it was! Having hardly learnt to cast, I was able to catch five large spangled sea trout within just forty minutes. The fish could not wait to swallow my Silver Toby spoon-bait.

'Time you spend fishing is not included in your life span,' Chekhov once wrote. Indeed . . .

On the way back to the lodge, Robin showed me the wreck of an Argentine Mirage plane, with the paint on its twisted fuselage still untainted—a reminder of how relatively recent the Conflict was. A small crater near by was filled with rainwater, and two silvery Steamer ducks were floating happily on the surface of this man-made mini-pond—a triumph of Nature's common sense over the cruel irrationality of war.

Having spent some time on Sea Lion Island, I started having difficulty with the term 'wildlife'. The abundance of birds and animals on this tiny—five miles long and one-and-a-half miles wide—islet was such that after a while you started perceiving them as the main—indeed only—legitimate form of life, and a handful of visiting humans as asuperfluous and largely unnecessary link in the chain of evolution.

It was our hectic life in overcrowded smoky cities that suddenly seemed wild to me.

Wandering on my own along the beaches, I did not feel alone for a second, for I was rubbing shoulders with thousands of red-nosed Gentoo penguins, walking to and fro past me in their black-and white business outfits like leisurely lunchtime shoppers in Oxford Street, bumping into each other and into myself and moving on without apologies. They were demon-stratively ignoring me, and I was ignoring them until I inadvertently stepped into a puddle of their droppings—the stinkiest stuff I have ever come across, let alone stepped in. It took me a good half-hour of rubbing my trainers with 'Travelwash' back at Sea Lion Lodge to get rid of the all-permeating stench.

And the elephant seals—those huge (up to four tons each) tubs of fat with smallish, by comparison, feline faces—lying supine on the sand and snoring like drunken octogenarians in a nursing home. They were all males—enjoying themselves while the females (each male had up to 120 in his harem) were busy procuring food and bringing up pups. What a life!

The seals did seem clumsy, lethargic and too heavy to move—a cross between a garden slug and a cow.

One feels tempted to pat a seal on his oily belly or even to carve some graffiti on his uncomplaining back. But this impression is deceiving. The seals can be extremely agile, when in danger or hurt. Some time ago, a man from Stanley stumbled accidentally across one and had a buttock bitten off as a result. I heard he had had problems maintaining his balance when sitting ever since.

While on Sea Lion Island, I seriously wished I were a birdwatcher. But even the absence of a spy glass, a silly Panama hat and other essential birdwatcher's equipment could not stop me from actually **watching** all these Rock Cormorants, Black-necked Swans, Red-beaked Oystercatchers, Striated Caracaras, Turkey Vultures, whom I came to call Cookie Monsters—they did look pretty monstrous: the head of a turkey and the body of an eagle—their names alone could make any aspiring British birdwatcher cringe. As for a spyglass, one actually didn't need it, for most of the birds were totally unafraid of humans and were easily approachable. I got quite used to tiny black Tussock birds pecking matter-of-factly at my shoes.

But the bird that I truly fell in love with was the famous Upland Goose. There are only about three hundred of them left in South America, but in the Falklands they are still present in their thousands. You can see them everywhere: crossing the main street in Stanley, mingling with sheep in the Camp, or bravely waddling across a minefield.

The thing that attracted me in these birds was not just their natural grace and beauty—they have long necks, shapely bodies and lovely striped feathers—but their devotion to their families. Upland Geese mate for life and always walk and fly either in couples, or in extended families of four or five. They are very protective of each other, and males always hurry to the rescue of their partners when the latter are in danger—what a difference to the blatant male chauvinism of elephant seals (and of some humans)!

I couldn't help admiring these wonderful birds and thinking that by creating them Nature was trying to teach us humans a lesson.

In the Falklands' Government Archives in Stanley, I was shown a bulky folder of hand-written dispatches to London from Richard Moody, the Islands' first British Governor. In Dispatch 13 of 1842, he writes: 'The settlers best adapted to colonise these Islands would be from among the industrious population of the Orkneys and the Shetlands, accustomed to a hardy life and as much seamen as landmen . . .'

This observation stood true over a century-and-a-half later: the Falklanders remained a special breed. Torn away from their historic motherland, they were tirelessly clinging to their roots, defying the notorious 'tyranny of distance'. They were flexible, hard-working, extremely adaptable and always happy to help each other.

Just like in the days of Governor Moody, when people in

isolated settlements did not see any fellow humans for months on end, they still greeted their guests with a substantial 'smoko'—tea with mountains of home made cookies. Just like in the past, they were always happy to provide shelter for their fellow outcasts from all over the world—that was probably why I felt almost at home in the Falklands.

And the country itself had the hardy, resilient character of its first settlers: in a matter of years, despite the war and the continuing intimidation, it has travelled a long way—from a semi-forgotten impoverished outpost of the dwindling British Empire to a prosperous and self-sufficient state, with one of the world's highest gross domestic products.

Interestingly, among 250 or so 'land-based' visitors coming to the Islands each year there were a number of escapists. Travelling in the Camp, I came across recent divorcees, who had come to the Islands 'to recover'; the bereaved, grieving over the loss of a loved one; and simply dreamers fleeing the suffocating reality of modern Europe and America.

Remember Oscar Wilde: Society can forgive a murderer, but never a dreamer'?
The Falklands forgive dreamers. This distant country, whose soil is stuffed with unexploded landmines, gives them a warm welcome, a hearty smoko and coveted peace of mind.
Is it because, in their heart of hearts, the hardy Falklanders are themselves all dreamers'

One has to be one to be playing golf next to a minefield.

Closer to home

My other favourite spots lie very much closer to home. One of them is the island of Sark.

'*Haro, Haro, Haro! À mon aide, mon Prince, on me fait tort.*'

With my eyes closed, I am muttering this medieval mantra in Patois, or bastardised French, standing on the old stone pier. The sea is rough, and the boat is late. I hope it never comes.

Haro! Haro! Haro!

Is my desperate, whispered call capable of delaying the boat? It should be, according to the acting Constitution, which assures me that 'under Norman custom, a person can obtain immediate cessation of any action he thinks is an infringement of his rights. At the scene, he must, in front of witnesses, recite the Lord's Prayer in French and cry out '*Haro, Haro, Haro! A mon aide, mon Prince, on me fait tort!*'

All actions must cease until the matter is heard by the Court.

My only concern is the absence of witnesses, if I don't count the seagulls hovering above my head and giving out piercing, almost human, shrieks: 'S-a-a-r-k! S-a-a-r-k! S-a-a-r-k!'
On the hazy horizon, I can discern the outlines of the French coast, about ten miles away, with waves galloping towards it like droves of horses with white foamy manes.

I regard having to go as an infringement of my rights, for I do not want to leave the Isle of Sark, probably the happiest community on earth.

Not part of Britain, Sark is the Commonwealth's smallest semi independent state. It makes its own laws and manages its own money. Administered by the Seigneur, a hereditary ruler who holds the island for the British Crown, Sark is the last remaining feudal community in the Western world (or was until 2008 when the islanders voted for democracy). The Seigneur still pays an inflation-free tax to the Queen of £1.79 a year—obviously a fortune five hundred years ago when it first came into force and constituted 'one twentieth part of a knight's fee'.

Cars are banned from Sark, and planes are not allowed to land there, or to fly over the Island under 2,000 feet. The place is engulfed by a strange quiet, broken only by the wailing of the wind.

I have noticed that all Sark's permanent residents have a peculiar twinkle in their eyes. 'What is it?' I asked Jennifer Cochrane, a local writer. 'It is contentment,' she replied. 'We Sarkese are a fairly fortunate lot . . .'

The island still abides by ancient laws, one of which says that 'unspayed bitches are not allowed to be kept on the Island, except by the Seigneur'. This law was adopted in the seventeenth century, when Chief Pleas (the island's parliament) decided that too many dogs could cause problems with sheep farming.

'Yes, our island is bitch-free,' Michael Beaumont, the facetious incumbent Seigneur, who inherited his estate from the Dame of Sark, told me with a smile.

Another law states that forty local family heads, including the Seigneur, are obliged to keep muskets to protect the island from invaders.

A modest brochure, *Constitution of Sark*, written by Michael Beaumont himself, was destined to become one of the gems of my esoteric and ever-expanding—like a glutton's girth—book collection.

The defence of the island is not just an abstraction. During the Second World War, it was occupied by a garrison of three-hundred Germans. The forty muskets of Sark, however, remained silent. Not a single shot was fired from either side, and the locals still refer to that period as a 'model occupation'. One of them told me how the German commandant of Sark refused to take any action against those local residents who defied the occupation authorities by keeping short-wave radios at their houses—an offence punishable by death anywhere else in occupied Europe.

In 1989, the island experienced another foreign invasion, albeit on a much smaller scale. It was taken over—single-handedly—by a drunken Frenchman, André Gards, who landed on Sark with a rifle and a small load of explosives. In a 'manifesto', written in broken English and pinned on the village noticeboard, he announced that he was taking control of the island. Having stated his intentions, he retired for a refill to a village pub, where he was apprehended and disarmed by the part-time constable (head of Sark's part-time police force) and frog-marched to the island's miniature prison, consisting of one small windowless cell.

The Constable soon came to regret his bravery, for another island law made him responsible for feeding prison inmates, and the Frenchman proved to be extremely voracious. Luckily, two days is the maximum jail term in Sark, and in due course the gluttonous invader was deported to his motherland.

Exempt from Britain's ailing social security and health schemes, the island takes good care of itself. Special community funds help young people through schools and universities, pay medical bills for the sick, and provide pensions for the old. This makes the island into a unique welfare mini-state.

Sark is not a member of the EU. It remains unperturbed by the 'global village' and 'unified Europe' rhetoric. It stays clear of pacts, leagues and alliances, simply because it is quite happy to be on its own in our conflict- ridden chaotic world—striving for integration, and yet increasingly divided.

That is why I am so reluctant to leave this real-life idyll. *'Haro! Haro! Haro!'*

Private Jet

My travels were not always as idyllic as that.

. . . It was autumn and I was all set to go to the Island of St Helena—one of the world's remotest and most obscure places.

The reason for the trip was the recent arrival of television on the island—for the first time in its history. I wanted to establish whether the fact that St Helena boasted the world's most cultured and well-behaved children (according to numerous sociological surveys) had anything to do with the islanders' total lack of exposure to the 'small screen'.

The answer was fairly obvious even without going to the island, but, to be perfectly honest, I simply wanted to get there and to add St Helena to the already impressive list of obscure destinations I had visited.

Getting to St Helena was not easy.

The island was one of the few remaining places in the world that didn't have an airport, and the only way of reaching it from the UK was first flying to Cape Town and then taking the Royal Mail Ship *St Helena* - the island's only link with the outside world. The sailing time from Cape Town was five days. On the morning of the sixth day, if you were lucky, the RMS would drop the mail (and yourself) on St Helena.

The whole journey, including an even lengthier return journey, was supposed to take me just over a month. My trip had been booked throughout, including a cabin on board RMS *St Helena*. I had even exchanged emails with the man whom I was to share that cabin with—a UK government official travelling to the island to resolve some minor taxation issues.

On the afternoon before my departure day, when I was busy packing my suitcase with books and video cassettes (the latter, I thought, could prove nice souvenirs for the TV-deprived islanders), the *Daily Telegraph*'s Travel Editor phoned asking me to cancel the trip.

'We've got something else in mind for you,' he said. 'Something no less exciting. . .'

'But I have everything ready for St Helena,' I tried to object. 'Why don't you ask someone else to do the mysterious 'something'?'

'Because you are the only one of us who can do it,' he replied.

From the explanation that followed, it transpired that The *Telegraph* had been approached by Abercrombie & Kent, one of London's poshest travel agencies, who wanted to invite a writer to join for eight days what was officially the world's most expensive package tour. With an average cost of $70,000 US per person for twenty-eight days (drinks were not included!), it was called 'Around the World by Private Jet'—a fairly self-explanatory name.

The editor's point was that whereas a 'native' British journalist, when confronted with such a generous invite, would feel instinctively obliged to write something positive about the tour, I, as the only 'un-English' writer in the Section, wouldn't feel such a moral obligation and would actually be able to bring back an impartial piece of journalism. Besides, coming (as I did) from a hardship-ridden Soviet background was bound to invite some revealing comparisons and flashbacks.

His logic didn't strike me as particularly sound, but having weighed up all pros and cons (among the pros were visits—even if extremely brief—to India and Thailand, plus a natural curiosity as to what the world's most expensive package tour might involve), I called him back and accepted the offer.

The TV-starved islanders of St Helena were not destined to get hold of my carefully selected set of video cassettes that included such all-time favourites of mine as 'Once Upon a Time in America', Andrei Tarkovsky's 'Solaris' and 'Battleship Potemkin', too . . .

'For Monks Only' ran a peremptory sign above the only row of empty seats in the Domestic Terminal of Bangkok airport, where I was waiting for a connecting flight to Chiang Mai.

I had to beat the temptation to lower my aching jet-lagged frame onto a seat: for all my debts and bank overdrafts, I could hardly pass for an impoverished over-ascetic Buddhist monk. To begin with, I was wearing shoes. Also, I was on the way to joining in one of the world's ultimate hedonistic experiences—a twenty-eight-day-long Abercrombie & Kent 'Around the World by Private Jet' tour.

The 'Private jet' was originally meant to be Concorde, but after all Concordes were grounded the previous August, it had to be replaced with a Boeing 747, specially refitted to provide the clients with 'ultra-First Class luxury unavailable from any commercial source', according to an A&K brochure. There were stopovers, each of two to three days' duration, in this round-the-globe hop, starting and finishing in New York: Hawaii, Shanghai, Chiang Mai (Thailand), Jaipur (India), Dubai, Florence, Tunisia and Lisbon. I was supposed to join the group of forty-nine tourists, mostly Americans, in Chiang Mai and to fly back to London from Dubai a week later.

Yet so far the experience was far from hedonistic. My back was sore after being repeatedly stabbed by the sharp knees of some long-legged and fidgety British teenager, who sat behind me on the economy-class flight from Heathrow.

I bought a copy of *The Nation*, a Thai daily. 'Artificial legs are presented to disabled people at a public charity event to mark the hundreth birthday of the late Princess mother,' read the caption underneath the front-page cover photo. With my legs feeling numb and almost artificial, I trudged to Departures . . .

On the plane to Chiang Mai, I had another read of the A&K glossy brochure with promises of 'six-star tours', which made me wonder what kind of 'six-star' hotels they were going to put me up at.

I would probably be at a loss if asked to name the best hotel

I have stayed in. But, after many years as a travelling journalist in the former Soviet Union, I knew for sure where the world's worst hotel was—in the Turkmenistan town of Mari on the Afghan border.

I remember a bearded Turkmen woman solemnly giving me the key to the hotel's only 'luxury suite'. The room was full of flies and smelt like a mortuary. It was forty-two degrees of heat, but the air-conditioner did not work. Nor did the shower. The biggest surprise, however, was that I was supposed to share my room and the only medium-sized bed with a male Communist party official from Ashkhabad. He was snoring and fretting on his side of the bed all night, and when I finally managed to nod off, I dreamt of an earthquake. Also, I got severely poisoned at the hotel's restaurant (it only had eggs and cucumbers on offer, but this was enough) and nearly died.

Regent Resort, my Chiang Mai hotel, was built in the style of a traditional peaked-roof northern Thai village. It was a cluster of luxury villas, blending effortlessly into the surrounding landscape of rice fields and tropical forest.

The moment I approached the Reception desk, a stunning-looking and constantly bowing Thai girl put an orchid wreath around my stiffened neck. Another girl, also a stunner, was trying (in vain) to relieve me of my shoulder bag, while a third smiling beauty was filling in my registration form kneeling in front of me in what I thought was a rather suggestive manner.

My villa was a mere hundred yards away, but they didn't allow me to walk: a buggy truck with a smiling and bowing male driver materialised from nowhere, and I was politely, yet firmly, offered a lift.

Shedding orchid petals with every move, I climbed into the buggy.

Inside my teakwood-fitted villa, goldfish swam in circles in round water-filled flowerpots. To my relief, there was no Party apparatchik snoring on my enormous bed, the size of a medieval European town square. But the biggest surprise in the form of a thick A&K portfolio, awaited me on the desk. Apart from welcoming letters and useful tips, the folder contained an envelope with some pocket money in local currency and half-a-dozen picture postcards with my home address scribbled on them in round childish letters by one of the reception girls and with stamps lovingly affixed!

They didn't allow me to walk to the restaurant: I was picked up halfway by a buggy truck. While ordering an exquisite four-course Thai meal I had to remind myself not to worry about the prices: all food was included in the package.

It was at the dinner that I had the first glimpse of my travel companions from the Abercrombie & Kent round-the-world tour. They looked ordinary and were engaged in the usual touristy babble of the what-are-we-going-to-see-tomorrow type. It was hard to imagine that each of them had paid the equivalent of my two-year earnings for the trip.

Having firmly decided to walk back, I sneaked out of the restaurant unnoticed and had to hide behind the trees to avoid the ubiquitous buggies. Of course, I got lost and had to be escorted back to my villa by a white-clad security guard, who lighted my path with a torch. On depositing me at my door, he saluted with what sounded like a New Zealand rugby team war-cry, turned about-face and goose-stepped back to his booth. Looking at his receding back from the porch, I felt like a military ruler of a small banana republic watching his troops on parade.

Next morning, I met the members of the Abercrombie & Kent staff travelling with our group: a tour director, two tour managers and a luggage master—a soft-spoken Peruvian man—who went with us everywhere. They were all helpful, efficient and seemed to be enjoying what they did.

For the sightseeing, our group was split between two air-conditioned buses—'red' and 'blue'. 'What do you do?' I asked my blue-bus neighbour, a stocky, ruddy-faced man in a baseball cap. 'I manage money,' he said. In the following days, I noticed that most of my companions were fairly evasive when it came to their occupations. 'I own a business', or 'I am a retired financier,' were the most common replies.

Each bus had its own 'bus-boy', obsessively plying us with cold drinks and distributing special A&K refresher towels. I thought it would be nice to have one back in London on my erratic 100 bus route from Wapping to Liverpool Street (I lived in Tower Hamlets then).

First, we went on a bicycle rickshaw ride across Chiang Mai. My rickshaw was pulled by a dried-out sinewy old man, so thin that he was almost transparent. Pressing the pedals of his rusty antediluvian bike for all he was worth, he was constantly lagging behind the rest of the procession. Members of the Thai royal family were grinning at us condescendingly from the ubiquitous street posters. Few things make you look so silly as luxuriating in a cart pulled by an elderly cyclist in torn, worn-down slippers.

A boat ride on the Ping River was next. Snacks and fresh fruit were waiting for us on the deck. 'This is your lunch, ha-ha!' joked our facetious Thai guide. She knew only too well that it wasn't. And so did we (which didn't stop us from emptying our plates, by the way).

We chugged along the river, its banks lined with shabby wooden huts. 'Surely, in the rainy season these houses would be flooded and all the poor people's valuables washed away,' an omniscient woman from our group commented loudly, with her mouth full.

'What valuables?!' our tour manager interjected angrily, but cut himself short.

After a huge lunch, we drove out of Chiang Mai to visit a hill-tribe village, where we were quickly led through dimly lit shacks, past knitting women and playing kids, none of whom acknowledged our presence. They must have been used to such flying visits by foreigners.

The much-publicised Stone-Age nature of the village was somewhat undermined by satellite dishes on some of the roofs.

'Up to fourteen people live in each little house here,' our guide commented.

'Did she say people or chickens?' asked the same American woman. Everyone in the group laughed. The guide bit her lip.

It was scorching hot. 'Three showers a day wouldn't be enough here, especially if you only have five a year,' another American mumbled. And everyone, including the guide, had to laugh again.

My first evening with the tour was truly spectacular.

Halfway through a sumptuous open-air dinner, somewhere between the live Thai dancing and the fireworks, servants started launching *Kom Loy*—small hot-air balloons, made of *Sa* (Mulberry) paper. The air inside the Kom Loy was heated from underneath by candles installed in their baskets. As the balloons climbed higher and higher, the candles kept burning until their tiny flickering lights and the multiple pimple-like stars in the velvety tropical sky became indistinguishable from each other, and it was no longer possible to tell which stars were real and which weren't.

'We are fulfillers of dreams!' Roger Stephenson, Managing Director of Abercrombie & Kent's Thai office, who had come from Bangkok for the occasion, shouted into the night sky, where the coloured rockets suddenly took the shape of two huge fire-spitting letters—'A' and 'K'.

At that moment, I was ready to believe him, although he forgot to mention that the price of a single-supplement dream was just under $70,000, whereas a twin-share dream was worth a meagre $62,000.

Prices aside, can one live in a fantasy world for more than a day or two, after which even your wildest desires tend to shrink and lose their sparkle, like a cluster of charred burnt-out fireworks?

I asked myself this question next morning, when the very thought of breakfast was unbearable after the previous day's sophisticated gluttony. There was no time to answer it, though, for we had to go for more Thai meals, briefly interrupted by shopping, bamboo-rafting and elephant-riding.

One thing was certain: from day two I started slowly but surely losing the plot. And the mind-boggling luxury of the chartered Boeing 747, which we boarded the following day for a flight to Delhi, only added to my confusion.

My name was embroidered on a starched white napkin covering the headrest on one of my First Class seats.

Yes, I had four seats at my disposal with enough combined legroom to accommodate a couple of basketball teams. My fifth—smoking—seat was at the back of the plane, where I would often retreat to have my dessert followed by an after-meal cigarette.

Between leisurely puffs, I would get a glimpse of two youngish American women from our group jogging around the cabin's perimeter. They calculated that one full circle constituted approximately 0.2 mile.

Strict 'Do not throw foreign articles into the toilet' signs were hardly visible behind bunches of fresh flowers and piles of French perfumes, with which all the plane's bathrooms were stuffed almost to the ceiling. On board this jet, I felt very much like a foreign article in constant peril of being flushed down the loo.

We had a huge 'Hot Lunch' on the way to Delhi. My name was duly printed on the cover of a glossy five-page menu (I was getting fed up with seeing my name everywhere, as if A&K were worried that I would somehow forget it, so kept reminding me of it every two minutes).

When, halfway through the feast, the captain announced that

we were approaching Everest, I was tempted to ask whether it came with rice, vegetables or French fries.

The on-board 'wine of the day' was Chateaux Beaux, 1996. I asked one of the fourteen cabin crew members for Errazuriz—my favourite Chilean Chardonnay. His face fell, as if he had just learnt of a sudden failure of all the plane's engines. They didn't have it in stock! How outrageous! As a consolation I was given a leather-bound A&K notepad, with a silver Parker pen thrown in, and a glass of Dom Perignon.

A survivor of hundreds of super-austere Aeroflot flights, where the only drink (and food) they served was tepid mineral water in plastic cups with fossilised imprints of previous users' teeth, I felt like asking for political asylum in this flying first-class restaurant.

In Jaipur (India), we stayed at Rajvillas, built to resemble a Rajastani fort. The level of luxury there was pretty much the same as at Regent Resort, only the welcome wreaths were made of marigolds.

My villa was again full of flowers, but unlike in Thailand, it had a four-poster bed (sleeping in it alone felt like a minor offence) and a white marble bath, the size of a swimming pool. And, of course, the magic A&K portfolio, with money and stamped postcards, was also there, only this time I took it almost for granted. Again, was half expecting to find some hasty 'Love from India' messages scribbled for me on the postcards.

Unlike Regent Resort, discreetly hidden among the hills, the stone-walled complex of Rajvillas was across the road from a poverty-ridden Jaipur neighbourhood. The contrast was striking: the cost of an overnight stay in Rajvillas was much higher than the average annual salary in India (three hundred dollars).

Most of my travel companions didn't like the country, whose penury they found irritating.

Their animosity could not be quite shaken off by the beauties of the Pink City and Taj Mahal, nor by yet another elephant ride—the second one within three days.

They remained seemingly unimpressed by the opulent reception at the palace of the Maharajah of Jaipur, where we were met by dancing elephants with A&K banners on their backs.

I thought it wouldn't be long before, similar to a madness-faking (in an attempt to avoid a purge) accountant Berlaga from Ilf and Petrov's 'Little Golden Calf', I started shouting at the top of my voice: 'I am the Viceroy of India! Where are my trusty nabobs, my maharajahs, my abreks, my kunaks, my elephants?!'

The Americans squealed with delight when we boarded our faithful snow-white A&K jet in Delhi for a three-hour hop to the U.A.E. Suffering from Delhi belly (countless bottles of A&K-supplied mineral water for washing our faces and cleaning our teeth hadn't saved us from catching the bug), I could remember very little of Dubai, except for the gleaming marble-fitted bathroom of my Ritz Carlton Hotel room.

Back in London, I was finding it hard to recall the details of the trip. I could evoke what we had for lunches and dinners, but was unable—for love or money—to recollect where exactly we had been served this or that yummy soup or curry—in Agra? In Jaipur? Or was it on the plane?

And I wasn't alone in suffering from amnesia after that journey. 'We feel as if we are in the movies,' my stoic travel companions often commented while yet another foreign scene was unrolling behind the windows of our air-conditioned bus.

According to my calculations, the proportion of sightseeing to eating and moving from place to place was roughly one to ten. It was seldom that we had a chance to walk more than two or three hundred yards a day. To repeat Hemingway's famous description of Paris as a 'moveable feast', our trip was a 'moveable feast' in its own right, only 'feast' in this context meant not a 'celebration of the soul', but a huge hedonistic meal.

One good thing is that I now know the difference between travelling the world and 'doing the world' in a luxury jet. It is like the difference between the real stars and the lit-up hot-air balloons.

Hedonism is the enemy of a traveller. It makes his eyes oily and unable to see things for what they are.

Our Chiang Mai guide told us about Thai boxing—a local sport where you are allowed to use any part of your body, except for your teeth. It sounded like the antithesis of our tour, during which we were not allowed to exercise any parts of our bodies, apart from our teeth. No wonder my thirty-year-old stainless-steel dental bridge, a memento of my Soviet past (one London dentist used to call it 'Lenin Bridge'), broke in two and fell out of my mouth during one of the lunches. I brought it back to London in my pocket as a souvenir of all the wonderful food I had eaten on this trip.

The amazing finale of that journey, however, was the fact that Abercrombie & Kent absolutely loved my story, claiming it was precisely what they wanted. They even suggested I joined another package tour of theirs at a later stage. To me that proved the old 'capitalist' dictum that there is no such thing as bad publicity.

As for the offer to join them again, I wasn't desperate to accept it: 'Around the World by Private Jet' was by far the worst travel experience of my life.

It was actually useful in one sense: from then on when confronted with the question of what my best ever trip was, I could answer: 'Well, I am not so sure about the best one, but the worst was definitely . . .'

Private Love

A dried poppy flower fell out of my dog-eared memo pad as I was perusing my notes.

Once scarlet and now crimson—the colour of curdled blood—it marked the page describing the Bailleul Road East Cemetery at St Laurent-Blancy, one of a thousand British memorial cemeteries in France. It is there that a regulation stone obelisk with the Star of David marks the last resting spot of 'Private I. Rosenberg, Royal Lancaster Regiment, 1st April, 1918, aged 27'.

Isaac Rosenberg was a pale Jewish boy from East London, a soldier of the Great War and one of Britain's most sophisticated and promising poets, whose life was cruelly cut short on April Fool's Day in 1918. He lies there, under vast Normandy skies, between 'Lance Corporal L.F. Donovan' on his left and 'Private T.N. Bancroft' on his right—the gruesome 'multiculturalism'of death.

Bending down for a pebble to be left on Rosenberg's grave in accordance with an ancient Jewish tradition, I picked up a red poppy and put it between the pages of my notebook. And, having straightened up, I noticed the epitaph on a twin obelisk nearby:

'Private A.A. Love, age 20, 23 April 1917'.

There came an urge to write a poem about Private Love, who died so young that he had no time to experience what his beautiful family name really meant; about Love that always carries the rank of a Private, not of a General; about the sheer absurdity of wars.

I did write a poem in the end, but not about Private Love. The complete poem about him was already there—engraved on his tombstone. There was no need to add anything to it.

Having started my literary life as a poet, I was always of the opinion that the best examples of poetry were triggered by hardship. That was probably why Russia's twentieth century poetic palette was so rich and colourful: suffering was the only commodity of which the Russian people had never been short.

A detailed account of my four-day tour in the footsteps of World War I poets defies the powers of the pen. How can one describe High Poetry, made even more poignant by the fact that most of its creators had been killed in their twenties?

Poetry itself was my main travel companion on this trip. And my guides were World War I poets: Wilfred Owen and Siegfried Sassoon, Edmund Blunden and Isaac Rosenberg, Edward Thomas (the author of the most beautiful verses on the plight of a writer—or a poet—I had ever come across: *'Must I be content with discontent/ As larks and swallows are perhaps with wings?'*) and A.P. Herbert, David Jones and W.N. Hodgson— twenty altogether. I learnt about their lives and deaths, I read their poems aloud on buses and at their graves, I wandered with them across grassy fields and weed-covered old trenches, retracing their final footsteps towards eternity. They were of diverse backgrounds and social standing, of different physique and psyche (from athletic Sassoon to flaxen Rosenberg and emotionally disturbed Owen), of miscellaneous poetic styles. It was World War I, the bloodiest military conflict in human history, that had brought them together, having unleashed the 'hurricane of poetry' whose powerful gusts kept stirring my hair ninety years later as I trudged uneasily through the forests and dirt tracks of Normandy.

There are no stereotypical World War I poets—they come in all shapes and sizes. But they were all particularly sensitive people . . . It was probably their extreme 'sensitivity' that prompted many of them to write prophetic heart-rending verses hours before they were killed. I don't quote them here, because poetry is not a treatise. It is rather a deep sigh, an intimate whisper into the reader's ear. Most poems should either be reproduced in full, or left alone, for a sigh and a whisper cannot be cut into pieces.

One thing I learnt was that a poem makes much more sense than an air-raid or a battle.

The poem written by VV during the tour:

Wild Poppies

Above the trenches, grass and mud, wild poppies grow—like drops of blood, squeezed from the scarred body of the Earth, they smell of death, they scream of birth. But washed by the rain during the night, they start looking like clots of condensed sunlight, like belated smiles of the dead —these wild poppies—bright and red.

Poetry—particularly in its 'old-fashioned' rhymed variety—has always had a therapeutic effect on me. Repeating familiar rhymes in my mind I used to bring myself into a semi-hypnotic state when gruesome reality would first fade away and then disappear completely.

ST. When under stress, mentally recite familiar rhymes, even if the latter are irrelevant and meaningless. They will never fail to calm you down by providing a distraction, even if a momentary one.

The rhymes could be anything—from Monthy Python's *'always look on the bright side of life'*, to Yevtushenko's *'I'm like a train that's been shuttling for years between the city of 'No' and the city of 'Yes'*; or Henry Wadsworth Longfellow's incredibly powerful and melodious:

The day is cold, and dark, and dreary; it rains, and the wind is never weary; The vine still clings to the mouldering wall, but at every gust the dead leaves fall, and the day is dark and dreary.

My life is cold, and dark, and dreary; it rains, and the wind is never weary; my thoughts still cling to the mouldering past, but the hopes of youth fall thick in the blast, and the days are dark and dreary. Be still, sad heart, and cease repining; behind the clouds is the sun still shining; thy fate is the common fate of all, into each life some rain must fall, some days must be dark and dreary—

a poetic **Survival Tip** in itself!

Rhymes can be a powerful survival tool, as proved by Alexander Dolgun, a young American of Polish extraction who was picked up in the streets of Moscow by Stalin's MGB (forerunner of the KGB) and spent nearly twenty-five years in the GULAG, having been guilty of nothing at all. He recounted his extraordinary experiences in the eponymous book *Dolgun*—another volume from my 'golden shelf', to use the expression of Yuri Olesha, Kataev's friend and fellow Odessan, whose own autobiography *No Day Without a Line* (which should be every writer's motto and is another **survival tip** of mine!) stands on that imaginary 'golden shelf' too . . .

Incarcerated alone in Moscow's Lefortovo prison, deprived of sleep and subjected to beatings and interrogations every night, Alex Dolgun came up with two tricks to keep himself sane. One was 'walking home'—pacing up and down his tiny cell while counting the steps and measuring the distance covered: 'leaving Moscow', 'approaching Russia's state border', 'crossing France'—and so on. The other one was chanting and shouting the rhymes of his American childhood in defiance of a strict ban on prisoners in solitary confinement singing or talking to themselves. Luckily, some roadworks were under way behind the prison walls. The moment an invisible pneumatic drill started roaring and the guard walked away from the cell's peephole, to return several minutes later, Alex sang at the top of his lungs:

'Mairzy doats and dozy doats and liddle lamzy divey . . . A kiddley divey too, wouldn't you?'

'The effect was fantastic! I mean the effect on me. I was grinning to myself. I have discovered another instrument for my survival. It sounds crazy talking about this childish song as an instrument of survival. But this was a song from America. It was a song they were singing in New York somewhere . . .

If the words sound queer and funny to your ear, a little bit jumbled and jivery, sing mares eat oats and does eat oats and little lambs eat ivy
. . .

I immediately felt less tired. In about an hour I knew I had to go back to the interrogation room . . .'

Having read the Gulag-inspired books by Solzhenitsyn, Shalamov and lots of other Soviet ex-prisoner writers, having visited a number of real-life Soviet labour camps (including the infamous PERM 35 for political prisoners: in 1989, shortly before my defection, I became the first ever Soviet journalist to write about it), I was nevertheless profoundly shaken by Alexander Dolgun's Gulag memoirs. Probably because they were written by an American, a true 'Westerner' whose innate internal freedom made his experience more poignant than that of his Soviet fellow-sufferers . . . There's no doubt about it: songs, chants and even seemingly meaningless childhood rhymes (all of which constitute poetry), stored in the very depth of a tormented human soul and coming up to the surface at moments of extreme suffering and despair, can save lives.

I have written hundreds of poems in Russian. They all rhymed of course.

. . . What is creativity? It is an intoxication; It is loneliness without solitude . . .

. . . Translators are like carriers of the knowledge bacteria among nations;/Translators are like ferrymen across the rivers of misunderstanding . . .

By the age of eighteen, I had published enough poems for a collection that never happened, for it lacked a 'steam engine' which, in the peculiar jargon of Soviet censors and poets alike, meant a eulogy to the communist party, Lenin, Brezhnev or any other 'great leader' who hadn't fallen out of favour yet.

> . . . Railway stations at night . . .You are dear to all wanderers, you attract them with your lights, you are the sentries of my separation from the loved one. Anyone can enter here to find the smell of the road, sacks and suitcases, but when in the morning he lifts himself from the wooden bench—he will feel warm and hopeful. No matter how dark the night, no matter how much soot and dirt is around you—just look: the express train of dawn is already piercing the darkness, carrying the sun on its tail like a signal lamp . . .

As with the other poetry in this book, I've reproduced the above youthful poem of mine as prose—in full accordance with the (non-existent) 'rules' of mauvism elaborated by Kataev, who recorded his own youthful poems like that in his mauvistic books:

> 'We came and, musing, sat alone together on a grave, while dreamily a choir of crickets chanted crystal clear, and in the wind the sere everlastings waved mid tomb and cross of stone'. . .'

Keen as I was on real-life trains and steam engines, I had always had problems with metaphorical ones, and my suggested collection had been rejected by a number of Moscow publishers just for that reason—'lack of a steam engine', as a number of tame publishing house editors shamelessly and shamefully pointed out in their rejection letters.

No matter how hard my poetry tutor (I was attending a poetry studio from the age of fourteen) pleaded with me to write such a 'steam engine', I had found it impossible. Not that I hadn't tried, but whatever came off my pen as a result sounded more like an anti-Soviet lampoon than a eulogy . . .

Like everything else in the USSR, poetry was politics too.

The closest Victor R came to a 'steam engine' was perhaps his poem *The Man who Plays War.*

. . . Children are playing war games in the courtyard laughing piercingly. Among them—wearing a old forage Cup and an artillery board—is the Man who Plays War. He was severely shell-shocked at the front in 1943. Since then, as they say, he became a bit touched. And now he likes playing with little boys who don't care that he is old . . . He is running with a toy gun made of plywood, and his grey hair is gleaming in the sun. For him, the war will probably never end . . . The clock will be ticking rhythmically, and the boys will grow up fast. Yet for him, the game will probably never end . . . In the heat of the toy battle, he takes aim at sparrows . . . The sun is firing over open sights at the deep trenches . . . on his face . . .

He spotted the confused old man playing war games with the boys in the courtyard of a nearby block of flats. In the late 1960s, there were still plenty of World War II veterans in the streets of Kharkov. With one of them—a legless cobbler called Uncle Styopa—Victor R. was friendly. Uncle Styopa moved around on a crude wooden trolley, pushing himself forward with two small iron-like props. He ran his tiny cobbler's 'business' from a decrepit stall in the middle of Culture Street where Victor R. was then living.

Another one—Uncle Igor—had all his limbs in place. He lived one floor above Victor's flat.

'What? A crazy veteran of the Great Patriotic War?!' his kindly tutor exclaimed in disbelief and added: 'You must be mad yourself, Victor, to entertain any hope of a poem like this ever being published in the USSR!'

She wished Victor well of course, and—as if his war-time

confusion was not enough—*he Man who Plays War* was promptly blacklisted.

On another occasion, I nearly got expelled from the studio after my innocent poem called *Nonsense*, penned at the tender age of fifteen and intended as an imitation of the early twentieth-century humorist poet Sasha Chiorny, was published in a Kharkov literary almanac:

> . . . *I'd like to become a cow, to drive away the seconds with my tail, to gape sternly at people and to moo, to moo, to moo. I'd like to become a bird, to look down at the world below, and then, floating in the clouds, to eat up a dragonfly. I'd like to become an elk, to play on the grass in the forest, and to come back home with horns on my poor head. Well, to dream is not harmful at all, provided you have something to dream about. Human life is at times miserable: just a bed and four stone walls . . .*

The city's 'pink-cheeked' Komsomol official[7] responsible for 'Culture' wrote a whole fiery speech denouncing 'political decadence' among some young poets, based on *Nonsense*, *Railway Stations at Night* (he particularly couldn't get over 'soot and dirt' bit) and *A Man Goes Away*, the latter being a response to the death of my granddad Misha, whom I had adored.

> . . . *A man goes away to get dissolved in the pre-dawn haze, in the twinkling lights of a city. A man goes away to frequently feature in the dreams of those to whom he was dear. A man goes away, his heart remains; it rattles in the wheels of fast trains; it beats on the hand of his son as part of the lively mechanism of the wrist watch . . .*

7 As in one of Yevtushenko's Samizdat (officially banned) poems: 'When the pink-cheeked leader of Komsomol thumps with his first against us poets, and tries to knead our thoughts like wax, and wants to mold us in his image . . .'

I saw that last poem in a dream from the first line to the last and put it to paper - in one single go - the following morning.

It took Marina Gavrilova, the tutor of our poetry studio at Kharkov's Construction Workers Palace, a huge effort to persuade the Komsomol official that all three poems were written 'in jest'—as parodies of some pre-revolutionary decadents. Otherwise, my future life and career could have been in jeopardy.

My fellow poetry studio members were a curious lot.

Most of them were deprived, even tragic characters: Boris—a middle-aged man who had just lost a young son to leukemia and was now writing horrendous doggerel for children; Svetlana—a mannish woman of an indefinite age who always wore the same pair of rumpled black trousers; Ivchenko—a rather talented Ukrainian youth who wrote poetry in Ukrainian and insisted on speaking Ukrainian at all times, which in the end led him to being branded (by the same 'rosy-cheeked' Komsomol boss) a 'Ukrainian bourgeois nationalist', expelled from the studio and imprisoned! What was so 'bourgeois' and 'nationalist' about speaking Ukrainian in Ukraine still escapes me.

Among other Kharkov poets of distinction, there were:

- Alik Braginsky, who published one short collection of promising poems and was shortly afterwards run over by a tram while drunk;
- a pimpled young Jewish man nicknamed Ziama who attended all poetry readings in town, always sat in the back of the audience and after each recited poem would exclaim loudly either: 'NEVER!'—if he thought the poem was bad, or 'THIS IS POETRY!' if it appealed to him;
- Boris Chichibabin who later (particularly after his death) became very famous all over Russia and Ukraine— mostly for exposing the Soviet literary 'scoundrels', including—totally undeservedly—Valentin Kataev, only

because 'Kataev' in Russian rhymes with 'negodiayev' ('scoundrels'), I presume . . . In actual fact, Chichibabin himself was an alcoholic, an active member of the Union of Soviet Writers (a fact that spoke for itself) and had no moral right to judge others for having complied with the system;

– Lev Boleslavsky—a small man with a typically Jewish appearance who had somehow managed to become a member of the Writers' Union (which was twice as difficult for a Jew as for an ethnic Russian or Ukrainian). He once referred to me (or rather to Victor R., my 'roaringly poetic' *alter ego*) as a 'thoroughly literary' (whatever he meant by that) lad before publicly (at some officially sponsored poetry seminar) lambasting one of my lyrical poems, 'Pskov Pictures', for its lack of an ideologically sound 'steam engine' (he was right of course):

. . . Church bells are ringing above the ancient Pskov. A fisherman is distraught: no catch today. The only thing to bring back home from the vast and playful Velikaya River will be a bagful of bell-ringing . . .

I can still recall one of Lev's own four-liners that he condescendingly—in the manner of a true master addressing his disciples—read to us at one of our poetry studio sessions. It was called *Vodichka*—'Little Water':

'Little water is flowing freely into a vessel taking its shape submissively. But at night, when it gets frosty, it breaks the vessel apart!'

I remember him looking up at us triumphantly as he finished reading it (he was actually reading his poems from a sheet of paper rather than reciting them from memory as we were encouraged to do by our tutor).

We were all humbled by such a powerful allegory and by the poet's courage too.

Lev was clearly proud of his own bravery—having penned and read aloud such a seemingly political, iconoclastic and possibly even hiddenly anti-Soviet (extremely well 'hiddenly', it has to be said) four-liner.

Looking back at it now, I can't help concluding it was a piece of pseudo-philosophical pretentious trash.

He later moved to Moscow and vanished from my life.

I remember a boozy 'lunch' in an open air café in Kharkov's own Gorky Park (we too had a Gorky Park—as they did in Moscow) after some officially sponsored gathering of young poets. At some point, Chichibabin rose from his chair and holding a glass of vodka in a trembling hand pronounced the following toast:

'Let us drink to poetry—the bane of our lives which is simultaneously our lives' greatest fortune!'

Yet the poet who had the biggest influence on me (and he was a true poet!) was Volodya Grishpun—a permanently unshaven and stooping young Jewish man who worked as a turner at a large Kharkov factory. As such—albeit not a construction worker—he was our studio's biggest asset, for the city's ever vigilant Party bosses watched us with eagle eye and constantly checked our ranks for the presence of 'proletarians' (read workers) rather than some 'members of the rotten intelligentsia', as they themselves would put it.

Volodya was the only worker in our midst, a fact that gave us some legitimacy in the eyes of the officialdom and stopped the studio from being dispersed. He was also one of the brightest, best read and most talented people I had ever met.

On top of all this, he was extremely independent, the first truly free person I had met.

As a worker, he could do the unthinkable—like, say, tell his factory party boss to fuck off when the latter tried to recruit him to take part in the compulsory First Of May demonstration or to work overtime during a so-called 'communist *subbotnik*' (when 'patriotic and socially conscious' workers were supposed to toil for free during a weekend). 'Pay me double daily rates for that or fuck off,' would be Volodya's response.

He was also an accomplished poet.

'Only he can appreciate silence who is familiar with the din of battle.'
'Everything disappears from the face of the earth. Only poems and houses remain . . .'

I particularly liked the following:

'We poets are sunflowers of the world: we know for sure what we are looking at . . .'

I remember reciting the latter to a reluctant and sheepish young nurse from the hospital where I had been laid up for a month with the first symptoms of stomach ulcer. She had agreed to have a date with me at the Gorky Park. We were riding a cable car above the trees, and I was reciting Volodya's poem trying to snog her simultaneously: *'We poets are sunflowers of the world: we know for sure what we are looking at . . .'*

I certainly knew what I was looking at—her plump pink thighs showing from under the mini-skirt.

Reading poetry to the girls I was dating was my substitute for playing a guitar—that ultimate time-tested instrument of seduction. More often than not, poetry would promptly put them off going out with me ever again.

It was different with Volodya who—as a true poet—also

led a very bohemian (by our provincial standards that is) life. Married to a tired-faced and constantly laundering woman, he openly boasted of having lots of gorgeous mistresses which was (at least partially) true, as I had a chance to see one day.

I bumped into Volodya near the Kharkov Opera Theatre one evening. We sat on a bench and read poems to each other. Then Volodya said: 'Let's go. I want you to meet someone.'

He took me to an attic in an old house nearby where we were greeted by the most beautiful and intelligent young lady I had ever seen, who started passionately kissing Volodya the moment we entered—one of his 'mistresses', no doubt. It was clear she adored Volodya and was happy to wait for him indefinitely in her dark romantic loft.

He was the first real poet I had met in my life who not only wrote but also LIVED like one (*pace* John Mortimer), and the latter of course was 'much, much harder'.

Many years later, I was lucky (or perhaps unlucky, who knows) enough to meet another real poet—my poetic idol Yevgeny Yevtushenko.
Looking back, I wish it had never happened.
There's no better way of deconstructing an idol than spending an hour interviewing him while he is getting drunk on Irish Cream.
It was with a good deal of trepidation that I went to interview Yevtushenko in Cheltenham where he was promoting his novel *Don't Die Before You're Dead*.

With his increasingly nervous British publisher, we had been waiting in the lobby of Yevtushenko's hotel. The poet was running two hours late for the interview.

When at last he stumbled in, I noted that, well into his sixties he still had the face of an eternal teenager. His style of dress remained eccentric (green trousers and a red shirt with yellow vertical stripes that made him look like an oversized tropical parrot), and his public behaviour boisterous and erratic.

The poet was trailed by a young Englishman carrying half a dozen coat hangers, with items of Yevtushenko's colourful wardrobe on them. 'Sasha, please watch my trousers,' the poet would exclaim in Russian from time to time, pointing at a pair of bright-orange pants falling off one of the hangers and already sweeping the ground.

As it turned out later, Sasha was the product of Yevtushenko's latest (fifth) marriage to an English lady. He introduced his son to me by saying: 'This is Sasha. He will be reading my poems at a concert tonight!'

'I won't stay at this horrible place for one moment!' Yevtushenko shouted to no one in particular and dashed out of the hotel, having first acknowledged our presence with a quick nod. Followed by his son with coat hangers in both hands, he squeezed himself into a waiting car, sat behind the wheel and started circling around the Green at neck-breaking speed. Repeatedly, he would screech the car to a halt near the hotel's entrance, run inside followed by his faithful trouser-carrying Sasha, only to yell at the top of his lungs that he was leaving 'this moment' before storming out and getting into the car again.

Finally, during his fourth or fifth in- and-out-burst, the publisher managed to block Yevtushenko's way and reminded him that I had been waiting for over two hours.

The poet suddenly calmed down. We shook hands and were led to a side room of the hotel's restaurant. 'Please look after my trousers,' he said to Sasha peremptorily before sending him upstairs to his room. He then turned to me and I realised that he was not very sober (it was 11 a.m.)

'Listen, Vitali, can you order me some Irish Cream—it is very good for my throat,' he asked me in Russian and added: 'Come on, don't be greedy: I know you can put it all on expenses . . .'

I called a waiter who poured him a shot of thick brown liquid.

'That's not enough!' exclaimed Yevtushenko. 'I need a full glass! Don't be miserly!'

I translated his demand to the waiter who shrugged and placed a full bottle of Irish Cream in front of him.

'I am not comparing myself with Tolstoy,' he said downing his glass, 'but this novel of mine is much more topical than *War And Peace*, which was written almost a hundred years after the events it described—the war with Napoleon. It was easier for Tolstoy, since none of his heroes could sue him for libel, whereas in my case it is quite possible . . .'

I could not believe my ears. Was this increasingly drunk and totally self-absorbed ageing buffoon in green trousers the same Yevtushenko who wrote the brilliant anti-racist poem Babiy Yar,[8] commemorating the victims of the massacre of many thousands of Jews in Kiev in 1941, the poem that was banned by Soviet censors yet circulated in Samizdat:

'*No monument stands over Babiy Yar. A drop sheer as a crude gravestone. I am afraid. Today I am as old in years as all the Jewish people . . .*'?

The poem ended with a courageous manifesto:

'*There's no Jewish blood in my veins, yet anti-Semites of all sorts hate my guts, as if I were a Jew, and this is what makes me a true Russian!*'

Inspired by it, Victor R. wrote his own 'Babiy Yar' at the tender

---

8   Babiy Yar means 'women's ditch' in Ukrainian.

age of 16 (it was at a school lesson in Ukrainian Literature that he did it). The poem ended with the following no-nonsense stanza:

'. . . *Residents of Kiev, be afraid of that place. Don't go there, don't rumple the grass. Don't disturb Death. And let Revenge rest in the ditch until its time comes.*'

'Hide it well and don't ever show it to anyone,' his poetry tutor advised him in a whisper when he showed the poem to her. She looked around herself stealthily, then rolled her eyes up towards the ceiling (a typical Soviet gesture meaning 'walls have ears') and pronounced loudly (this time, for the 'wall's ears' only): 'It is a very good patriotic poem, well done, Victor!'

And Volodya Grishpun simply said: 'Good poem. The ending would make Yevtushenko green with envy.'

As a child Victor R. had a dark fascination with yars (ditches) which had nothing to do with the Babiy Yar war-time horrors.

Uncle Igor

. . . As a child, I used to live in a ditch.

Well, it was really a crater, made by an erroneous air bomb that hit the centre of my native Ukrainian city of Kharkov during the 1918-1921 civil war. Rain and snowfalls kept extending the hole, and by the time of my birth in 1954 it had turned into a long and deep ravine, overgrown with weeds and wild grass. At the bottom of the ravine there was a puddle of rainwater which gradually grew into a pond, fed by natural underground springs.

We boys spent hours in the ditch (Yar in Ukrainian) which served as a rubbish dump throughout the 1950s and 1960s until some local aquarium buffs jokingly released the fry of tropical fish into the 'pond'. Mysteriously, the fish started breeding happily in the yar, and soon we were able to catch some strange aquatic mutants with our primitive bamboo fishing rods there. The fish were small, prickly and utterly inedible, but we enjoyed the sheer fun of catching a fish in the middle of a big industrial city—much to the contempt of Uncle Igor, a Second World War veteran and an inveterate fisherman who lived in our block of flats.

Uncle Igor had the character of a child. A brilliant fabricator, he'd spend hours in the courtyard entertaining children with stories of his wartime feats and his fishing achievements. He would go to fish in the country once a week and would come back reeking of vodka and carrying a string bag full of freshly caught fish that he proudly displayed to us.

We all adored Uncle Igor, although my parents suspected that his plentiful catches had been secretly bought by him at the Tempo food shop round the corner. Of course, we kept asking him to come and fish with us in the yar, but he dismissed our pleadings with a wave of his rough fisherman's hand: 'What do you take Uncle Igor for? Uncle Igor will never deign to fish in that dirty bog of yours where only small fry can be caught!' He had a habit of referring to himself in the third person—as 'Uncle Igor'—like toddlers, robots and martinets do.

One day, however, being more tipsy than usual, he succumbed, and grudgingly went down to the yar with all his sophisticated fishing gear: spinners, flies, home-made spoon-baits and whatnots. We were most impressed by his folding fisherman's chair with a tarpaulin seat.

Having unfolded his magic chair, Uncle Igor sat down and solemnly threw three spoon-baited lines into the yar's opaque, urine-coloured water. We all flocked around him, watching his performance with our mouths agape as if it was a religious rite. The fish started biting immediately, and all Uncle Igor's three floats, made of wine corks, were diving and jumping like crazy.

Uncle Igor reluctantly raised his world-weary bottom from the chair, hooked and started pulling. The fish was obviously heavy and didn't want to give in. The silk Czechoslovakian line drew like a bowstring.

'See? It only took Uncle Igor two minutes to hook the biggest fish in this bog!' Uncle Igor, ruddy-faced and puffing, announced triumphantly.

We held our breath.

Soon, the top of a rusty funnel emerged from the water.

'What's that?? A bloody steam engine??' Uncle Igor cried out in disbelief.

It was not a steam engine he eventually ferreted out. It was an old and rust-eaten Tula samovar—a huge coal-heated metal urn for making tea—which had probably been dumped into the yar by its owners when electric samovars came into existence.

We didn't see Uncle Igor back at the yar ever again . . .

When I came back to Kharkov from London many, many years later, the yar was no longer there. I was told it had been filled up after some drunk drowned there. A small park was laid out in its place. And suddenly I felt a sharp pang of nostalgic pain for all those joyful days in the ditch, filled up by time, the days that could never be repeated.

I was standing on the grave of my childhood.

Don't Die Before You're Dead. Indeed. The title of the book that Yevtushenko came to promote in Cheltenham was in itself like a one-line poem—the poetic self-epitaph of a master.

'The Fire has something to say'

Interestingly, that Cheltenham meeting of Yevtushenko and VV had been precluded by their imaginary encounter several years earlier on the pages of *The Canberra Times* newspaper, or, to be more exact, in the 'Litbits' column authored by Robert Hefner—an American writer residing down under—who came to interview VV in Melbourne at the peak of his (Vin's) Australian fame.

It was one of his life's most amazing reviews:

'Now I've met two Russian poets. The first, the great Yevgeny Yevtushenko, I met in the early 1970s when I was still an under-graduate in North Carolina and poetry was my principal passion. I was both awed and disillusioned by meeting in the flesh a man whose poetic voice had seemed to sound such depths in my soul. He was one of my heroes, but . . . it's sometimes best not to meet your heroes (sic:VV).

At the time I was appalled when Yevtushenko stood up after a few drinks (sic:-VV) and started waving $500 in cash in front of a group of bewildered guests and suggesting that we all fly to Cincinatti . . .

You probably won't think of the second Russian poet I recently met as a poet even, as he certainly wasn't a hero of mine before I met him (though I feel he could become one). But as soon as I had read the first few pages of Vitali Vitaliev's new book, *Vitali's Australia*, I knew that somewhere beneath the surface of this hard-nosed award-winning Soviet journalist—and probably not that far beneath—dwelled a poet. It was as evident in his language and the way he made the words work together on the page as if the by-line on the cover of the book had read, 'Vitali Vitaliev, Poet' . . .

I was a bit nervous. Remembering how tongue-tied I had become when I first met Yevtushenko, and how, when the great poet had asked me what I had to say, I had uttered something banal and embarrassing like 'What does anyone really have to say'. He had looked into the fireplace and relied quietly, in one of those penetratingly sober moments that are occasionally imbedded in even the drunkest of evenings, 'The Fire has something to say.'

Well, there's no doubt that Vitali Vitaliev has something to say, and I immediately felt the same personal warmth in his personality that he conveys so fluently in his writing. His essays vary from whimsical . . . to sweetly nostalgic. Quite often I wish I'd written them myself . . . "You are the first interviewer in my life who has called me a poet . . . I've never been a political creature—right-wing or left wing, or anything. I just write what I feel . . ." he said.'

My impression after meeting Yevtushenko was very similar to Robert Hefner's. Yet, in my heart of hearts, I feel that a poet who can look into the fireplace and utter drunkenly: 'Fire has something to say', can be forgiven for almost anything . . .

'A cluster of dreams'

Several years after *Wild Poppies* I wrote another little poem in English. It formed in my head spontaneously as I stood on board the ferry taking me to the mainland from the island of Skye.

'Everybody who speaks Gaelic is a poet,' said Rob MacilleChiar, writer-in-residence at the Gaelic College in Skye and a poet himself. Brought up by English-speaking parents in Argyll, he turned to poetry as soon as he started learning Gaelic, and I thought I could understand why.

How could one not be a poet speaking that tongue, with consonants often 'aspirated', so that the words are not pronounced, but actually breathed out? How could one's soul not be poeticised by words like 'corra-ghritheach', denoting grey heron, but literally meaning pointed shriek? Or 'fork of wind'— for swallow; 'God's fire'—for butterfly; 'curtain of water'—for rain, and so on?

How could one stay unmoved by the fact that each of the eighteen letters in the Gaelic alphabet is associated with a tree name: Ailm (elm) stands for A, Beith (birch)—for B, Coll or Calltuinn (hazel)—for C, etc?

As Rob himself wrote in one of his poems:

Were I to send a love letter to you, I would send every tree in the wood . . .

Rob's portakabin on the college's old campus served not only as his writing den, but also as a literary hub of this unique educational establishment, where every other teacher, irrespective of what subject he or she taught, was a published Gaelic poet.

The college's residential quarters, equipped—among other gadgets—with the world's only Gaelic-speaking lift, became my home for three nights during my search for the Gaelic language, officially recognised as Scotland's national tongue.

It took me many hours by trains and ferry to reach this 'protected Gaelic enclave' (in the words of Roy Wentworth, a college lecturer) on Sleat peninsula in south Skye, although my first exposure to Gaelic occurred while still in Glasgow: it was a 'Welcome to Queen Street' Gaelic sign at the station, where I boarded a train to Mallaig.

I was tempted to assume that the train conductor was asking for my tickets in Gaelic (I couldn't understand a word of what he was saying), but it turned out that he spoke Glaswegian.

Disappointingly, a group of Fort William-bound Scottish labourers, sitting opposite me, kept communicating among themselves with the help of one short English word (and its derivatives) alone. One could be forgiven for thinking that, if Gaelic was indeed Scottish national tongue, then Glasgow and even the Highlands, to say nothing of Edinburgh, were miles away from Scotland itself.

'He who loses his language loses his land,' runs an old Cornish proverb. If so, Scotland must be in real danger of shrinking to the size of Monaco or San Marino in the near future. According to the recent census, the number of Gaelic speakers fell by 7000 during the past ten years and has reached the critical mark of 58,652.

Why critical? Because all Scottish newspapers in their coverage of the census quoted (with no source revealed) the figure of 50,000 language speakers, below which, allegedly, the tongue was considered 'officially dead'. As a multi-linguist, who wrote a lot about so-called minority languages, I had reasons to doubt it.

One piece of evidence was the Faroe Islands, which I visited some time ago. With just 40,000 people in total, this small semi-independent nation boasted eight daily newspapers and 150 books a year published in Faroese—its much-treasured indigenous language.

The purity of Faroese was fiercely defended by the committee for the protection of the language—a government-supported watchdog, making sure that every child born on the islands was given a Faroese name and that as few foreign borrowings as possible could sneak into the mother tongue. This might sound too harsh, but the Faroese had to resort to extreme measures to revive their language after five centuries of Danish domination.

Likewise, the history of Gaelic is, to a large degree, the story of its suppression, the first (successful) attempt at which was undertaken by the Romans. It was outlawed by the Crown in 1616. In the eighteenth century, Gaelic books were publicly burned in the streets of Edinburgh.

The 1872 Education Act made English compulsory in all schools, and Highland children were beaten into speaking it. This centuries-long chronicle of repression stretches as far as November 2002, when the Scottish Executive voted down the bill that would give Gaelic equal status with English in certain areas of the Highlands and Islands. It looked almost as if it had been done deliberately—to force the number of Gaelic speakers down under the 'magical' 50,000 mark, after which it would be pronounced 'officially dead'' and hence not worth bothering about.

How about the occasional Gaelic signs, you might ask? How about twenty million pounds (allegedly) spent on promoting Gaelic every year? How about the regulation photos of schoolchildren happily learning Gaelic, carried by many a Scottish newspaper? How about the college itself, after all?

I got the answer while crossing from Mallaig to Skye on a Caledonian MacBrayne ferry, whose skipper welcomed the passengers in Gaelic, only to switch over to English for the rest of his lengthy announcement concerning the ship's rules and safety procedures. I thought it was symbolic of the executive's general attitude to Gaelic: while supporting it on a purely superficial 'window-dressing' level (signs, greetings, some public broadcasting, the 'national tongue' rhetoric, etc,) very little is being done in the areas where funding is essential to stop the language from dying.

For years, the staff of the Gaelic College have been denied money for compiling and publishing a comprehensive Gaelic-English dictionary (the most recent dates from the 1880s).

Compared to the eight Faroese dailies for a 40,000 population, there is not a single Gaelic daily or weekly newspaper left in Scotland, with its 'official' 58,652 fluent Gaelic speakers. The only literary magazine in Gaelic—the acclaimed Glasgow-based 'Germ' quarterly—had to fold due to lack of funds. Many teachers and students at the college lamented what they called 'the death of Gaelic publishing'. One of the latter told me bitterly: 'Gaelic has become a marketing gimmick for Scottish tourism officials promoting it as if it were a tartan. '

Outside the college, there were not many Gaelic speakers left in Sleat. Even the pupils at the local Gaelic medium school were likely to 'play in English' during the breaks. A native of

Sleat, himself a Gaelic speaker (yet not a reader or a writer), told me of his shock on spotting two toddler girls 'playing in Gaelic' not far from his house. 'I haven't seen anything like this since childhood,' he said.

Those two little girls were probably the daughters of Lindsey Campbell, a local sculptor. She and her husband spoke the girls exclusively in Gaelic. They also had to chuck out their TV set. 'I hate it when tourists take photos of my Gaelic-speaking children, as if they were monkeys. They are like all other kids and simply play in their native language.' Lindsey said.

Sir Iain Noble, the founder of the Gaelic College and a Gaelic patriot himself, shared with me his conviction that to prevent the number of Gaelic speakers from dwindling even further, special pockets of language-enforcement should be created on the Islands. 'In such areas, only Gaelic should be taught at schools, and all public servants should be Gaelic-speaking.'

Sadly, such enforcements unless properly weighed up and legislated, like they were in the Faroes, seldom work in real life. Language is a living body and as such it cannot be imposed from above. But it can be helped from above to develop naturally—by carefully targeted funding and legislation.

As it is, the state of Gaelic in Scotland can be compared to an old croft, with a restored and freshly painted facade, but a neglected and crumbling interior. A language dies every week somewhere in the world. Is Gaelic destined to become one of them?

'Death is outside the language. The end of language is beyond language,' wrote Iain Crichton Smith. He was right of course. Forget about the mythical 50,000 viability mark. Even if only two people speak a language between themselves, it cannot be pronounced 'officially dead'. And Gaelic, this undisputed linguistic gem, should not be allowed to disappear in the years and centuries to come. For losing it would be like losing the very soul of Scotland.

How do people come to Gaelic?

I addressed this question to many students and teachers of the Gaelic College. Only very few of them were brought up as Gaelic speakers. Some, like Rob MacilleChiar, got interested in Gaelic through its peculiar place names. Others, like Simone Dietrich from Germany (the college has a number of students from abroad), were inspired by Celtic music. Scott MacDonald, another student, took up Gaelic after living in Holland— encouraged by the linguistic prowess of the Dutch.

'People turn to Gaelic to find a soul, a root, a ground under their feet,' Rob told me in his portakabin, where his weekly Gaelic writing class was about to begin. Angus Macleod, a shy first-year student and a native of Skye, read his poems—in Gaelic and in English (for my sake, I presume). His verse was dynamic and full of imagery. I liked two metaphors from one of his poems: his head being 'a cluster of dreams' as he wakes up in the morning, with 'dawn scratching at the door'.

Gaelic verse was alive and well. And as long as the poetry lives, the language can never die.

Dawn was 'scratching at the door', or rather at the window, of my room overlooking the Sound of Sleat—no more than fifty yards away. A bright piercing light, its source still invisible, was blending the sky and the sea into a pinkish whisky of sunrise. I opened the window and heard the surf whispering something in Gaelic. It was probably saying good-bye: *'Tiaraidh an drasda!'*

As the ferry was chugging further and further away from Skye, the following four-liner formed itself in my head:

> . . . *Every letter—a tree, Every sound—a sigh.*
> *I'll be missing the sea, Speaking Gaelic to Skye . . .*

Vin was living in Scotland by then—exposed simultaneously to the darkest prose and the highest poetry of life: in an unhappy marriage, with three beautiful little children . . .

Pegasus cottage

These are the very first lines I am writing in a new garden office that the Loved One has built for me.

It is a small rustic house, made of wood. Inside, there's one room still smelling of varnish and paint. It is warm and cosy, and behind the window large red apples keep falling from the selfless and hard-working apple tree every now and then— thump, thump, thump.

On the shelves along the wall are my peripatetic, long-suffering books.

I have spent the whole day taking them out of the loft and the garden shed where they had been stored after I liberated them from their three-year-long prison term in the former laundry room of Folkestone's Edwardian Metropole Hotel basement. Many of them must have forgotten what a proper book shelf feels like after years of being squashed in clumsy cardboard boxes, their pages glued together by the all-permeating moisture.

A small but powerful electric heater inside the hut is now winking at the books with its cheeky red eye. Slowly but surely they are warming up, their bent covers, rheumatic spines and arthritic concertina-ed pages stretching up, straightening and strengthening by the minute.

To me it appears as if the books are smiling.

Through the ornate glass door one can see a rusty horseshoe nailed to the wall above the entrance. I found this horseshoe by accident on the roof of the garden shed that used to stand on the same spot.

The shed's roof was leaking, and one morning I climbed up the ladder to mend it.

A large rusty horse shoe lay straight in the middle of the roof.

Horseshoes don't end up on roofs by accident.

As Woland—the satanic protagonist of Mikhail Bulgakov's novel *The Master and Margarita* once noted,

'*A brick never falls on anyone's head.*'

There was only one way a horseshoe could end up on the roof: if it had been dropped by Pegasus.

Or so we wanted to think . . .

It was a sign that my writing place was to be there—at the Pegasus Cottage, as we aptly monikered the house.

And here I am—having survived again (this time, a cardiological operation), having just published two new books and feeling happier than ever before—to the extent that it almost makes me feel . . . jealous of myself.

It is from here that I am looking back at an autumn evening precisely six years ago. A much colder and darker evening in Edinburgh.

. . . They were trudging down the Royal Mile hand in hand. He was smoking and munching a fried Mars bar in between puffs. His female companion—taller and much more mature than he—was swigging from a can of beer and smoking, too. In the treacherous light of a solitary street lamp, he looked no older than eight and his sister (I wanted to hope she was his sister, not a girlfriend)—about eleven.

Nightly walks up the Royal Mile to replenish the supplies of milk, duly decimated by my three young kids, were part of my daily routine during our first month in Edinburgh. 'You can never buy enough vodka,' we used to say in Russia. By the same token, you can never stock up enough milk to satisfy the burgeoning appetites of three little children.

Puffing up the High Street towards the area's only open corner shop, I couldn't help thinking of how different the real

Edinburgh appeared from its 'cool' Festival-inspired stereotype. Irvine Welsh has claimed on BBC Radio 4 that the Scottish capital was 'a cultural desert outside the Festival', with one of the biggest drugs and child-poverty problems in Europe. On the eve of our move from London, I chose to dismiss his words as a literary hyperbole. But the flesh-and-blood 'child-poverty problem', multiplied by two, was now stumbling towards me—smoking, drinking beer and chewing a battered Mars bar.

Packed solid with daytime traffic, so slow that it created the impression of crawling backwards, the Royal Mile would routinely go dead after 7 p.m. At least, its Canongate stretch did. The Festival had just ended with a big fireworks bang into the muted Edinburgh skies.

It rained twenty-five hours a day, and the evening air was thick and sticky like Haggis. Rare pedestrians looked sullen and flat like crude mannequins in the dusty windows of a charity shop.

On a night like that, I was wary of bumping into Deacon Brodie, the prototype of Stevenson's Dr Jekyll (alias Mr. Hyde), or other ghosts from the city's eerie past.

On one occasion, I thought I could discern in the distance the cocked-hatted silhouettes of Samuel Johnson and his reluctantly Scottish (like many other self-flagellating Scottish intellectuals, he 'couldn't help it', you see) companion James Boswell emerging from Jenny Ha's Tavern to start their historic walk through the 'effluvia' of the 'odoriferous' Royal Mile. I could almost hear Dr Johnson's sardonic remark to his escort: 'I can smell you in the dark.'

'Emigration is a dress rehearsal of one's own funeral,' a Moscow friend of mine used to say. What about the second emigration then? A quick reburial after exhumation?

I ask forgiveness for this moribund metaphor: too many night-time walks in the Royal Mile, I presume (and I hadn't even ventured yet on one of Edinburgh's famous City of the Dead tours!). I actually argued with that pessimism-prone friend of mine—also a writer, saying that emigration was more likely to herald a rebirth than a funeral.

Whatever the metaphor, coming to live in Scotland after twelve years in London (not to count a three-year-long spell in Australia) did make me feel a double expatriate, or an ex-expatriate (XX-patriate?), if you wish. Perhaps it would have been easier to end up somewhere entirely diverse—in Equatorial Africa, say—with all your internal resources mobilised to cope with the culture shock.

Here, in Edinburgh, many things were deceptively similar: Sainsbury's and Marks & Sparks, double-deckers and fluffy old ladies—these 'God's dandelions' (a good Russian expression) and Queen Mum look-alikes, speaking to shop-attendants in a posh London accent.

The street crowd, however, was different: it was considerably duller, probably due to the near-absence of African and Asian faces in it. Also, compared to London, Edinburgh felt very small. Much smaller than its thoroughly cultivated image.

As part of a cleverly engineered PR campaign, Edinburgh was promoted as the seat of the new—devolved—Scottish parliament and the site of its new—delayed—grand headquarters.

Jan Morris once called Heathrow airport 'a permanently unfinished city'.

The new Scottish Executive under construction struck me as a 'permanently unfinished' building.

Unlike Heathrow, with its four terminals, there was nothing terminal about it. In this respect, its constant semi-presence at Holyrood was reassuring: it was good to be reminded that not everything in this life was finite, after all.

I was amused to learn that the non-existent parliament edifice had to be 'bomb-proofed' against a terrorist attack—hence the delays and the skyrocketing costs. Allegedly, a small-scale copy of every single part of the complex had to be built and bomb-tested somewhere on the Yorkshire Moors, prior to putting together a life-size equivalent. Having examined a computer-generated image of the whole ensemble, I came to the conclusion that the new parliament's intended design was in itself the best deterrent against a terrorist attack. With its slanting, as if tipsy, roof tops, made to resemble 'upturned boats' (don't boats turn turtle before sinking?), and its irregular-shaped windows, as if bricks had been tossed through each of them, the complex gave the impression of having been bombed already.

And even the most daring terrorists are unlikely to attack the same place twice.

The simple truth is that the grandness and the bomb-proofing standards of a parliament house are of no relevance to the quality of debate within its walls. If architecture is indeed music in stone, it doesn't mean that a parliament building has to be a noisy military march.

With the devolved (I nearly wrote 'devalued'—a Freudian slip) Scottish parliament controlling a meagre 10 per cent of the nation's budget, no matter where they sit—in a palace or in a bomb-proofed pub, the MSPs will only be able to carry on legislating on such important matters as how to disrupt Scotland's enduring love affair with junk food. 'I intend to do everything I can to effect that change,' promised First Minister Jack McConnel.

Frankly, I couldn't see how he could effectively 'effect' it, apart from occasionally opting for a fruit salad instead of a black bun for pudding. He could perhaps introduce a bill banning sales of battered Mars bars to put them on a par with hard drugs, but even that is unlikely to persuade Edinburghers to give up their burgers, so to speak.

One thing I learnt after thirty-six years in a totalitarian state is that one's life style—healthy or unhealthy, honest or fraudulent—cannot be imposed from above or regulated by decree. It starts and finishes solely inside one's head. And one's heart. Just like independence, or lack of it.

I walk back home with two Pavarotti-size milk bottles weighing down my shoulder-bag. Tomorrow is a new day.

And although the December daylight is bound to be as bleak and as brief as the final flash of a dying electric light bulb, I know there will be a moment when the recalcitrant Scottish sun peeps out fleetingly from behind the Castle, momentarily transforming the malt-whisky-coloured Edinburgh clouds into the sky-wide Saltire. And my scepticism will turn into hope.

From a side-lane leading to Waverley Station, I hear the whingeing whistle of a locomotive. It reminds me of the runaway engine that recently got uncoupled from its train and travelled several miles away from that very station—on its own, without a driver! The Flying Scotsman turned the Fleeing Scotsman. What, or who, was it fleeing from? And where was it heading for?

I'll have to try and find that out . . .

'Our new writer will uncover Scotland,' screamed the *Glasgow Herald's* blue masthead on the following day.

'The air is thick and sticky like haggis,' echoed another one, straight under Vin's puzzled face distorted by an enforced smile.

Three children? Edinburgh? Scotland? Did it really happen? Or was that evening walk up the Royal Mile in the ghostly footsteps of Johnson and Boswell but a figment of his inflated imagination? Surely, it couldn't have happened in reality.

It did.

The proof is a December issue of the *Herald* newspaper. On page 14: VV's large (much too large) photo next to an article by Lorna Martin, 'The Vitali spark in search of a storm'—a punchy headline. And a no-less-punchy standfirst: 'He has lived two lives, rejected the KGB, and travelled the world. Lorna Martin talks to the Herald's new writer at large'.

Writer at large . . . That explained (to an extent) VV's very large photo . . .

'When Vitali Vitaliev, a self-confessed manic traveller and Clive James's Moscow correspondent on Saturday Night Clive, moved to Edinburgh recently, it was only minutes before he witnessed Scotland's omnipresent inferiority complex that manifests itself in puerile bragging.
'Edinburgh is the greatest city in the world. It is the most cosmopolitan place in the world to live, and the Bank of Scotland is the biggest bank in the world,' the taxi driver told him, talking non-stop, with one hand on the wheel and the other gesticulating wildly, on the journey from the train station to Vitaliev's temporary home near the new parliament building.
Vitaliev, with his wife and three children, could have been forgiven for wanting to make a hasty return to London, or at least wanting to feign a loud, exaggerated yawn in the cab driver's ear. Instead, he sat back, a wry smile lit up his pale electric-blue eyes and smoothed his troubled brow. He knew he was going to love this place, with its wealth of material for carrying out the occasional character assassination.
Vitaliev, a multi award-winning satirical and investigative journalist and novelist, who has written perceptive books and articles about his travels through Eastern Europe and America, joins the Herald on Monday as a writer at large, providing a fresh, funny, and unique look at nationalism, cultural identity, and what it takes to create a country.
The virtue of all of his writing, which has appeared in the (Australian) Age, Punch, Guardian, Spectator, and the Daily and Sunday Telegraph, is that it comes from a mind well stored with knowledge. It is also honest, humane, and quick to seize the unexpected but appropriate image of the truth. Born in 1954 in the Ukraine, the only son of a nuclear

physicist and his wife, a chemical engineer, he was told at
the age of seven never to say what he thought if he wanted
to survive. Reaching adolescence, he found the advice
impossible to adhere to and, after graduating from Kharkov
University and initially working as an interpreter and
translator, he became a journalist with the Moscow-based
Krokodil magazine and a thorn in the side of the KGB.
After writing several investigative accounts about the
connections between the Soviet mafia and the secret police
of the former USSR, he was approached by the KGB to be
recruited and, after many refusals, was subjected to months
of harassment. He defected with his then wife and young
son in January 1990, moving first to London, and then taking
up residence and citizenship in Australia. After a few years,
he moved back to the UK before coming to Edinburgh a few
months ago.

When we meet at the flat in Morningside that he shares with
his second wife and his three children, he talks somewhat
solemnly about his life during the decade after his defection.
He describes himself as being like a tightly suppressed
spring that was suddenly released. 'I couldn't stop
travelling,' he says. 'It became like an illness. For 35 years I
had dreamed of being able to travel. But I sort of resigned
myself to the fact that I would never be able to leave the
Soviet Union. I was an encaged dreamer who had spent so
much time in the gigantic cage of the former Soviet Union.
When the spring popped, it couldn't stop. I couldn't stay in
one place and visited more than 60 countries in 10 years.'
He says the biggest mistake he made after spending 35 years
in a totalitarian state was to treat his newfound freedom in
the same manner as an Old Bolshevik would have treated
communism—a flexible dream that could be adjusted to a
gloomy, down-to-earth reality.

He understandably took for granted what he describes as
some western liberties, such as unrestricted travelling and
buying books.

'I couldn't get enough of them and, unknowingly, I was

suffering from freedom bulimia. During the first two years in Australia I subscribed to dozens of British and Australian newspapers and magazines which represented to me the coveted and repressed freedom of information. I also got hold of every credit card I could and went on shopping sprees buying ridiculous and unnecessary things.'

After three years in Australia and a life of consumerism and freedom, his marriage collapsed and he realised he was missing Europe. Not any European country in particular but just Europe, with its smells and sounds, its history and architecture, its wars, troubles, theatres, newspapers, and its never-ending excitement. He moved to London but was still running at an unsustainable speed and unsurprisingly, after a couple of years, he burned out and ended up broke, desperate, and unhappy.

He believes he was predestined for some sort of fractured life, possibly because the day of his birth—in January 1954—was stuck between two epochs—37 years after the Bolshevik revolution and 37 years before the collapse of the Soviet Union.

He says his second, western life was in many ways no easier than his first, though it is certainly proving to be much more eventful.

Today, as he prepares to visit the Shetland Islands, there are still signs of his insatiable need to be on the go. He moves around constantly, making endless cups of coffee, smoking rolled-up cigarettes, answering phone calls from his children at nursery. He is much thinner than the chubby correspondent who appeared on *Saturday Night Clive*—something he puts down to giving up his beloved vodka and taking up martial arts (he has a red belt in tae kwon-do). He says he feels incredibly lucky to have lived two different lives on both sides of the Iron Curtain, and appreciates the unique outlook it gives him on the countries he visits. He ended up in Scotland almost by accident when his wife was transferred in her job but is already fascinated, sometimes bemused, and occasionally saddened by his brief experience so far of Scottish life.

'It is a fascinating country, going through an exciting process, and being an outsider sometimes you can see things better,' he says.

He was disheartened when he read about Don Cruickshank, Scottish head of the London Stock Exchange, urging Scots to leave the country if they wanted to be successful. 'It struck me as being absolutely typically Australian,' he says. 'In Australia, there is this feeling that you have to go to Britain if you want to make it. What rubbish. It comes from within. Of course, your background and family play a part. But it's in the power of everyone to 'make it'.'

He says the main manifestation of the Scottish chip on the shoulder is what he describes as a sort of 'superficial megalomania'. His first experience of it was from the taxi driver in Edinburgh. Another example, he recalls, which left him speechless, was when he read the headline in a Scottish tabloid following the death of David McRae from Angus after he contracted rabies. 'Scot is first Brit to contract rabies for 100 years,' he says, wearily. 'That was the headline. I think perhaps it helps to feed a national ego.' He rather worryingly compares the Scotland of today with Gorbachev's glasnost of the late 1980s, of which he was a victim.

'We were told we were getting freedom of speech. But if it had been freedom of speech it would've been called that. Instead it was called glasnost. In a way, it was very clever, because it was a euphemism for lack of freedom of speech. Devolution reminds me a little of that. Devolution isn't independence. It isn't even semi-independence. It's a euphemism. You can either be free or you are a slave. I really believe that. I think the Scottish Executive is pretty impotent but pretends to be powerful. It can debate things like having too much junk food in your diet or the colour of the Saltire. But that's not enough.'

On the question of Scottish nationalism, he says he thinks Scots want to be independent but 'when it comes to serious matters, there's this real uncertainty about yourself. People are not sure'.

However, he is convinced Scotland has what it takes to go it alone. 'If Liechtenstein can do it Scotland certainly can. I don't really see much point in devolution. It's like prolonging an agony of something that's dying. Making it more painful. Sometimes it hurts less just to cut the cord and get on with it.'

It was Robert Burns who said that it is a great gift to see ourselves as others see us. Unfortunately, most of us haven't been blessed with that talent. But luckily we have people like Vitaliev, who belongs to a rare group of people who can write with brilliance, humour, and style in a second language, to point out our foibles and idiosyncrasies and even enable us to laugh at ourselves in the process . . .'

'Answering phone calls from his children?' They were too young to make phone calls then . . That was the only discordant bit in that rather lovely article reconstructing (or deconstructing?) his whole life without the multiple common errors normally made by 'Western' hacks trying to write his 'profile'.

He could now recall that dull and cloudy evening-like morning in late November (most days felt like dull and cloudy evenings in Edinburgh). Lorna Martin was running late. She did turn up eventually trailed by a photographer—a shortish young man specialising in extra-large photos.

They will make friends with VV soon, and the photographer will tell him a story of how he got into Sean Connery's pants. With another *Herald* journalist, they went to interview Connery in Africa. The photographer's bag failed to arrive and during the interview he complained to Connery that he had no change of the underwear. The famous actor then lent him a pair of his underpants . . .

Several years later, Lorna will get the job—Scotland Correspondent for the *Observer*—that he too had been shortlisted for. Shortly afterwards she will plunge into depression and will write a very successful book about it in due course—*Woman on the Verge of a Nervous Breakdown*. The first words of the book will be: 'I was going to be late. Again . . .'

In September 2008, their ways will cross again, at a book festival in Wigtown where she will promote her book and VV—his two newly published ones—*Vitali's Ireland* and *Passport to Enclavia*. Their respective events will take place at different times of the day and at different venues, so they will never come face to face with each other. Yet VV will feel that, in a funny way, they have met again.

Receding tram

My Diamond Crown, one of Kataev's mauvistic novels, tells us about his Moscow literary friends of the 1920s, to whom he refers by invented nicknames. His close mate and fellow Odessan Yuri Olesha, the author of *Envy*, *The Book of Farewells* and *No Day Without a Line*, is called 'Kliuchik'—a name that can imply three different notions in Russian and therefore can be translated into English in three different ways: 'little key', 'little clue' and/or 'little spring'. And although he never clarifies which of the three meanings he had in mind, it was, most likely, the third.

Closer to the end of *My Diamond Crown*, there's an extraordinary episode:

'At times, Kliuchik experienced fits of paranoia. He suspected public transport of conspiring against him and assured me that trams hated him: the number he needed never arrived.
One day we were standing with him at a tram stop waiting for tram number 23.
'You shouldn't have come with me,' he was saying with irritation. 'Number 23 will never come, I assure you. Trams hate me.'

At that very moment, a number 23 tram carriage appeared in the distance.

'All your predictions are worthless,' said I.

He looked at the approaching carriage sceptically and mumbled in a doomed fashion:

'We'll see, we'll see . . .'

At that very moment, the tram, which was a mere couple of dozen steps away from us, halted, stood stationary for a moment, then started crawling away slowly, as if drawn back by some kind of magnet, and soon disappeared from view.

It was entirely incredible, yet I swear I am telling the pure truth here.

'Well, what did I tell you?' said Kliuchik with a sad smile. 'Trams do hate me. I have a complicated relationship with the city transport. It is unfortunate. But it is so.'

Don't think I am joking. It all happened as described: the number 23 tram went backwards, to some unknown dimension. How that could happen, I don't know. And will probably never know. But I repeat, I give you my word of honour that I am telling you the sacred and genuine truth. It was probably the only case in all the history of Moscow's electric trams. An excess that is beyond analysis.'

'An excess that is beyond analysis' was something that happened to VV in the late 1990s: his life trams number 43, 44, 45, 46, 47 and 48 suddenly halted and started crawling backwards—to the nearly forgotten 'station stops' of misery and deprivation that he was sure he would never see again.

And the reason for it all was simple. In the words of Charles Maurice Talleyrand, it was worse than a crime—it was a mistake. His mistake.

My life's worst and most dysfunctional relationship.

I will probably never be able to write the full truth about it because of my children. I will leave it to them to find it out when they grow up, if they so wish.

This is all I can say. No guilt. No blame. Just another—the most gruesome—chapter of *A Shattered Life*. Or *A Mosaic of Life*, if you wish.

VV had had a warning of what was to come several years before.

In summer 1996, he came to Blackpool to record a programme for his Radio 4 series on Britain's decaying seaside resorts. Blackpool, with its kitschy souvenirs (turd-shaped Blackpool rock, kiss-me-quick hats etc.), noisy and tasteless tourist attractions and scruffy, almost Soviet-like, crowd of holidaymakers, was easy to satirise.

In one of the shopping arcades he spotted the tent of a fortune teller advertising herself as 'Silvia, a Real Gypsy from Wales'.

'I didn't realize that gypsies originated from Wales,' he noted to Kevin, his producer, sarcastically.

They decided to persuade Silvia to record her session, hoping it would help uncover Blackpool's tacky and money-grabbing 'entertainers'. Kevin handed VV a tenner from the programme's budget, and they solemnly entered the tent.

'Silvia' turned out to be a blue-eyed blonde in her late twenties—the most unlikely gypsy Vin had ever come across. She didn't mind being recorded, only asked Kevin to wait outside.

With just a tenner to spend, Vin opted for a palmistry session, which was the cheapest on the menu.

He stretched out his right hand, switched on his brand-new digital tape recorder and, with a sceptical expression on his face, prepared to listen. . .

What followed was one of his life's biggest shocks.

Of course, the 'gypsy' could have deduced he was a traveller (it was a characteristic not too hard to assume in someone who was in Blackpool recording a radio programme—they had to introduce themselves first, in accordance with the BBC's code of practice); she could have also guessed (from his tiredness and eyes that had all but lost their sparkle) that he was not too happy in his current relationship. . . But how could she possibly know that his father had passed away exactly fifteen years before (which he did!), that he was a scientist and had a hard life? How could she find out that his mother was 'very far away' (in Australia—as far as she could be) and was missing him terribly (that latest bit, to be honest, was but a logical continuation of being 'very far away') and was going to fall very ill soon?

How could she know about his then only child (son) who was 'as far away as your mother'? About Mitya, who was living in Melbourne then. Just like Vin's Mum . . .

'You are now with a woman you are not happy with,' carried on the perceptive Welsh gypsy. 'You will leave her soon, but it will be a while until you find your true love . . .'

At this point, she got visibly frustrated (in an agitated sort of way): 'I can see a hospital. . A serious illness, but you will be OK in the long run . . . And prior to that, I can see . . . a birth . . . No, not one, but several births . . . Don't know where they come from, but definitely births . . More than one . . .'

'What baloney,' he thought then. Having more children was the last thing on his mind.

'What did she say?' Kevin asked eagerly when VV—pale and shaken—emerged from the tent.

'Never mind,' Vin said. 'It looks like we won't be able to use this bit in the programme, after all . . .' He took a small shiny disk out of the machine, broke it in two and tossed it into a rubbish bin.

'Never mind,' he repeated. 'She is barking . . . Totally bonkers . . .'

Five years later, every single prophecy of Silvia's—including the break-up with ONA, his mother's illness and multiple births—all had come true.

She also said to beware one date, 26th September. Until now, Vin doesn't know what she meant, for nothing spectacular—good or bad—has happened on that date. As yet.

Could it be that she had somehow foreseen the date of his death too? Out of all her forecasts that last one was not for Vin to verify.

Another of her predictions that hasn't come true (yet, or as they say, at the moment of writing) was that he was going to come back and see her again one day. She didn't say when. Vin hadn't been to Blackpool since then but kept thought of going there, often.

A letter from his mother in Australia:

'Vitiusha, dear, I've been meaning to tell you a lot, have been thinking long and hard about it, but the moment I put pen to paper I find it difficult to concentrate, to pull my thoughts together, so to speak . . .
Winter has just started here: short days; dark, damp and long evenings. When the rain and wind stop, it quickly gets stuffy, even scorching . . .
I am reading a voluminous book, *Vladimir Nabokov's World and Talent* by Boris Nosik—the first biography ever of the writer in Russian.[9] It has lots of photos, including those of Nabokov's extraordinary butterflies and herbaria . . .
Nosik had been collecting these photos for years, buying them from the people in many countries who had known

9 In the Soviet Union, the works by and about émigré writers had been banned.

Nabokov . . .

What I cannot get over are the numerous similarities
between you two. Like you, he wrote poetry, prose
(including satire), poetic translations, articles—all both in
Russian and in English. Like you, Nabokov had been an
Anglophile, albeit, having studied in Cambridge, he got a bit
disappointed with England and with the English character,
in particular. The book carries an extract from Nabokov's
essay about Cambridge which reminded me of your 'Little
Ben'[10] . . .

Well, it is not only your writing 'talents' that seem similar
to me. Like you, he enjoyed sleeping in of a morning and at
times also wrote in his sleep, or rather in semi-slumber—
like you used to compose some of your poems . . . The
similarities do not end here. He had two failed marriages,
yet his third one—to Vera Slonim who became his best
friend, helper and his first reader; who understood and
accepted him as he was—was a very happy one. He was
always short of money, despite the fact that he wrote a lot,
particularly after the move to America, so that he had to
do tutoring to keep the ends meet. Like you, he was fond
of cinema, tried to write film scripts. And also . . . he had
a very strong spiritual bond with his mother, particularly
after his father died. In his letters to her—always loving and
poetic—(she was in Prague with her other children, he—in
Berlin), he shared his writing ideas, described the places he
had visited. In one of his letters written after a visit to his
father's grave, he said he believed he was going to see his
father again—in some unexpected, yet natural, 'heaven'
where he will enjoy some radiant eternity . . . He wrote that
every little thing connected with his father was still alive in
him . . .

10 'Little Ben', or 'Malen'kiy Ben', was the title of VV's first book about
Britain written in Russian. And the title of his first BBC TV documentary
release in 1990 was 'My friend little bear'.

By the way, do you know that Nabokov's son was called Mitya?

I remember reading a review of one of your books where the similarities between you and Nabokov were mentioned. Whoever wrote that review was right . . .

And another thing . . . I believe in that 'third' woman who, I know, will come into your life one day . . .

That was what I wanted to tell you, Vitiusha. I've tried my best to share with you all the thoughts and feelings that I experienced while reading Nabokov's biography. I didn't do this very consistently, sorry, but I did speak out my heart . . .

It is summer in Europe now. I am rereading the letter you wrote to me last July from a small French café in East Finchley: it is so summery, so graphic—like an epistolary novella. And again I think about you and Nabokov . . .

You must be in Greece now doing your BBC programme. I pray for you.

Your Mum

'. . . at a small French café in East Finchley' . . .

How clearly I remember it. I came there one summer morning after another row with ONA, feeling drained and needing to share my feelings with my best friend, Mum, thousands of miles away.

Why did I come to East Finchley? Because I had been associating that area with Mum since her five-month-long stay in London with me several years before. I was writing *Little is the Light*, and she was looking after me—walking around my spacious rented flat on the fringes of Highgate and Muswell Hill noiselessly like a cat. At about midday, I'd go out for a walk and a cup of coffee, and she would trail behind me at a distance—not to disturb 'my writer's thoughts' by her 'mundane' conversation—with a shopping bag in her hand. We always had coffee at that very French café in East Finchley High Street.

After a while, however, she got bored staying at home all

day and applied for a position as a volunteer carer at a nursing home in Fortis Green Road She would feed the patients, many of whom were not too much older than she was (although she always looked much younger than her age—before her illness that is) and used to tell me how pleased they appeared to see her . . .

Little did she know that only a few years later she would become one of them and would have to be fed herself. A cruel symmetry of life . . .

It was to East Finchley that I came to remember Mum shortly after her death. The modest little grave under the scorching Melbourne sun had nothing to do with her. For me, she was there—in East Finchley, trudging across Cherry Tree Wood with her Moscow-style just-in-case 'avos'ka' string bag (an old Soviet habit) in her hand on the way to 'work' (as she proudly called it)—to the nursing home.

My big consolation was that she did see London and fell in love with it—just like I had done several years before.

One of her 'poems in prose' written after she read 'The Nights of London' by H.V. Morton—my birthday present to her—and published in Australia:

The writer (H.V. Morton: V?) stands alone, leaning over the parapet of the bridge, watching the hues of the dawn over the great city . . . The sun fights hard with the darkness . . . The clouds' colour changes, the pink clouds fade into the grey . . . The sun rises . . . London is standing clean and fresh like a strong boxer entering the ring . . . It is a surprising coincidence—when I stood on the bridge over the Thames and looked at the huge ancient buildings—the Parliament, Westminster Abbey—I, like Morton, felt that London was the most masculine city in the world. I felt his force and glory . . . It is probably obvious . . .

As before, Mum is helping me to write this book.

The House of Hope

Frequent travels were VV's salvation during those months in Edinburgh. Their geography was now limited to Scotland but it didn't matter: he was always of the opinion that the distance was unimportant. The important thing was what you discovered.

Yet initially—just like after his return to the UK from Australia when he was eager to go as far as possible and ended up in the Falklands—his first journey from his new shaky 'base' in Edinburgh was to Scotland's and UK's northernmost point—Shetland.

Similar to that his trip to the Falklands, the journey to the Shetland Islands became one of his coveted 'foreign home-comings' and could be included in the eponymous, if yet unwritten, book.

. . . The painfully familiar Cyrillic letters were crabbed and uneven—as if battered by gales.

A Russian sign was the last thing I had expected to see in Lerwick—the wind-swept 'capital' of the Shetland Islands. Yet there it was: '**DOM NADEZHDI**', and underneath—the English translation: 'The House of Hope'.

The house in Mounthooly Street used to belong to the Norwegian Seamen's Mission—a religious charity looking after the crews of Norwegian fishing vessels during their visits to Lerwick Port. In the late 1980s—early 1990s, flotillas of Soviet (then Russian) *klondykers*—floating fish-processing factories – came to Lerwick to buy mackerel from Shetland fishermen. This was when 'The House of Hope' became also '**DOM NADEZHDI**,' offering a cup of tea and a bible to every Russian who would venture inside.

Russian fishermen stopped coming to Lerwick in 1996, and the only Russian visitors to Shetland these days are migratory birds (I don't count myself among them) and the bitter northern wind, which, as the locals assured me more than once in a mildly accusatory sort of way, always blew from Russia—a fact that invariably (and for no clear reason) made me cringe a little.

The Russian house-sign was one of many unexpected discoveries I made in Shetland, UK's northernmost archipelago. They started long before I boarded a miniature two-engine plane to Sumburgh, the islands' main airport, with a breathtakingly short runway at the very edge of the North Sea surf.

On most maps, the Shetlands were plonked in a box somewhere near Aberdeen. Only after looking at my little son's globe did I get a proper perspective: the tiny specks of land were closer to Bergen than to Edinburgh, and, in proportion to the size of their Scottish mainland, a journey there was the equivalent of a trip from Moscow to Vladivostok in Russia, or from Melbourne to Darwin in Australia.

The fresh issue of the *Shetland Times*, the islands' weekly tabloid, which I had bought in Edinburgh, was gruesome reading. The Shetlands had just been hit by a succession of disasters: their two major industries, oil and fishing, were in deep trouble—the former due to massive job cuts at the Sullom Voe Oil Terminal, the latter because of the draconian cod and white fish catch quotas imposed by Brussels. Almost simultaneously, a major local construction firm collapsed with the loss of many jobs, and the islands' council was pressing ahead with its proposed school closures. This negative build-up brought to mind a joke about the Russian Pessimist, who said that life was so bad that it couldn't possibly get worse, to which the Russian Optimist retorted cheerfully that it could, it certainly could!!!

The stories on just one page of the paper were: 'Tanks stolen from boats', 'Light vandalised', 'Man arrested', 'Man injured', 'Laundry stolen'. Against this sombre background, the headline 'Driver swerved to avoid sheep' on the same page stood out like a beacon of positivity—if only for the sheep and not for the driver, who hit a fence.

The first thing I did on hitting the 25-mile-long stretch of road from Sumburgh airport to Lerwick was . . . Yes, you got it right: I swerved to avoid a sheep!

I couldn't wait to see the next issue of the *Shetland Times*, with that truly momentous event properly highlighted.

I drove through the grey rainy dusk of an early Sunday afternoon, with scanty daylight clinging desperately to hilltops before being swallowed by darkness. It was not yet 3 p.m. The landscape was barren, brown and totally treeless. It reminded me of the Faroe Islands, where, as they told me, 'flowers did not grow because of the wind, and trees because of the sheep'.

I didn't need to swerve to avoid the Shetland ponies—those vertically challenged endemic horses, whose faces, framed with long shaggy manes, had a shy 'girlish' look. Martin Martin, a seventeenth century Skye-based explorer and a Scottish namesake of Vitali Vitaliev (or so I wanted to think) described 'shelties' as 'hardy' and 'sprightly, though the least of their kind to be seen anywhere'. Conscious of their importance as part of the official Shetland Heritage, the ponies kept to the grass patches alongside the road and never played Anna Karenina with passing cars. Unlike the unruly sheep—those fluffy felons of the Shetlands pastures—they were so orderly and law-abiding that I wouldn't be particularly surprised if they duly paid council tax to the islands' authorities.

First impressions are often misleading.

Next morning, I noticed that the belated December dawn was emerging not from the sky but from the *voe* (the local Norse name for a sea-bay) in front of my hotel. The water was slowly oozing out a soft and transparent light it must have accumulated the day before (or, more likely, during the last summer).

For the first time in my life, I was watching an upside-down sunrise!

It was not long before the sun found its legitimate place up in the sky—and its first timid rays got entangled in the narrow winding lanes (*'closses'*) of Lerwick—like bright-yellow ribbons in a Victorian beauty's elaborate hairstyle, dishevelled by the wind.

The tiny 'capital' of Shetland turned out to be one of the loveliest towns I had ever seen. It resembled a cosy bedsit with sea-views and 'many Victorian period features', to use the peculiar jargon of real-estate agents.

My subsequent conversations with Brian Smith, a Lerwick archivist and historian, and several other locals, helped to deconstruct the following persisting stereotypes of the Shetlands:

'Shetlanders were more Scandinavian than British.'

Apart from place names, ruins and *Up Helly Aa* Fire Festival, there was not much Scandinavian culture left in Shetland, which ceased to be a province of Norway in 1472, when it was given to Scotland as the dowry for a Norwegian princess. In the run-up to the last World Football Cup England-Denmark game, a Scottish tabloid sent a pack of hacks to Lerwick in the hope of finding thousands of Denmark supporters. Not a single one could be identified: everybody in Shetland supported England. They should have tried Glasgow instead . . .

'Shetlanders were fiercely pro-independence.'

A small Movement for Independent Shetland, which ceased to exist in the late 1980s had never stood for complete independence—just for a greater autonomy within the UK. True, at times the islanders still called Shetland 'a country' and said 'I am going to Scotland next week', but there were no independence undertones in those statements, coined purely by the islands' geographic remoteness. At the same time, there was definitely such a thing as a 'Shetland identity' which—like any other cultural character—was fairly hard to define.

'Shetlanders speak a variation of Old Norse, like their Faroese or Icelandic neighbours.'

Norse, as spoken by the Vikings, died in Shetland in the eighteenth century. Modern Shetland dialect, taught at the islands' schools, was closer to Lowlands Scots, and the number of Scandinavian borrowings in it was constantly decreasing (Incidentally, I also noticed that the islanders spoke the best English I had heard anywhere in Scotland).

Brian Smith translated for me a randomly chosen passage from a story in *The New Shetlander* magazine: '*Noo bairns. My peerie kist is aa tied up. I'm ready to geng.*'—'Now, children. My little chest is all tied up. I am ready to go.' I liked both the sound and the message of these three short sentences in the living 'Shetlandic language'.

The only visible 'Scandinavian' feature of modern Lerwick was its extreme cleanliness. The ubiquitous rubbish bins had special (and very un-British) receptacles marked 'gum'. While Glasgow and Edinburgh were conducting propaganda wars against this sticky bane of city streets, little Lerwick had solved the problem by simply providing a sufficient quantity of clearly marked 'specialised' bins. As a good Russian writer once noted, rather than struggling for cleanliness, it is much better to sweep the floor.

'*Dunna chuck bruck!*' as they say in Shetland.

Another telltale detail was that the black rubbish bags left for collection in Lerwick's streets were covered with . . . pieces of disused fishing nets. It was tempting to conclude that, in view of the looming collapse of the islands' fishing industry, it was the only remaining use for them. But the truth was much more prosaic: the nets, provided by the council, offered the best possible protection from seagulls, those flying pests of Lerwick, who used to rummage through the contents of unprotected rubbish bags with the zest of Her Majesty's Customs inspectors ransacking the luggage of a suspected Colombian drug baron.

In a BBC Radio Shetland evening programme, I heard the islanders coming up with possible solutions to the seagull problem—from destroying the birds' eggs to persuading them to fly over Lerwick upside down! What could I say? Thank God, Shetland ponies cannot fly!

Lerwick, bustling with traffic and agitated Christmas shoppers, showed few signs of gloom and doom. 'Times are changing and we must change with them,' Tavish Scott, a youngish local MSP, told me in his Lerwick office. 'Fishing and oil industries are indeed in crisis, but we are trying to find alternatives.'

I saw what he meant when I went to the island of Unst, Shetland's (and Scotland's; and the UK's) most northerly point, connected to Mainland (I mean the Shetlands' largest island, where Lerwick is located) by excellent roads and frequent ferries. In Haroldswick, its northernmost settlement, I was saddened to learn that its 'UK's most northerly post office' had closed down a couple of years before, and its coveted franking stamp was now used by the post office in Baltasound, the island's 'capital'.

Driving back to Baltasound, past a cluster of historic ruins resembling some obscure Cyrillic letter, I nearly missed the world's most amazing bus shelter—complete with a sofa, a microwave oven, a floor rug, an old Amstrad computer and a telephone with a 'hot line to the Palace'. A local schoolboy, Bobby Macaulay, started this charming joke several years earlier, when he got fed up waiting for a school bus in the old shabby and leaking bus shelter. With the help of his family and friends, he transformed it into the island's most popular tourist attraction. The quirky bus shelter now attracts thousands of tourists. It even has its own website, designed and maintained by Bobby himself.

I thought that London, Edinburgh and Glasgow bus stops would never look the same to me again, and, waiting for a bus, I would always be on the lookout, if not for an in-shelter PC, then definitely for a sofa!

Initiative must run in the Macaulay family. I met Bobby's father, Sandy, Manager of Unst Regeneration Project—a position that spoke for itself. Wind turbines rotated merrily behind the window of his little office.

'This is part of our renewable energy project,' he said, pointing at them. 'We have to think strategically. The power of the wind is never going to run out—not in Shetland.'

Unst, this remotest bit of Britain, was also home to an IT and training company, a learning centre, a modern brewery and a number of other 'un-traditional' modern businesses. It even had a film-making unit—Unst Animation Studio, into which I popped only to note that, with its state-of-the art equipment and hairy (Shetland-pony-like?) film makers, it looked like a twin of its many counterparts in London's Soho.

It took me just one step outside to be confronted with piercing wind and the black hostile waves of the North Sea a mere hundred yards away. Lighting up a cigarette was like stopping a low-flying skua with bare hands.

Before leaving, I went to have a last look at 'The House of Hope'. Hope was what I found on this trip to the Shetlands, with all their voes and woes.

It was Hope not just for the islands, but also—for the whole of Scotland—and possibly even for myself—my new country-sized 'DOM NADEZHDI'?

'Now, children. My little chest is all tied up. I am ready to go.'

The longer Vin stayed in Scotland, however, the more it appeared to him as the House of No Hope At All.

November days in Edinburgh were bleak. Domestic torture continued, and again—as had happened so many times in the past—travelling was his only comfort zone where he could function and write properly. In the absence of a proper home, his weekly assignments for the *Herald* became part of a continuing search for his imaginary 'foreign homecomings'.

Moscow in Ayrshire

'Notwithstanding the utmost efforts of the police, no trace whatever has been found of the perpetrator of the diabolical murder and robbery at Moscow . . .'

Thirteen years after defecting from the Soviet Union, I was finally returning to Moscow. My brand-new British passport, however, had not been stamped with a hard-to-obtain Russian visa, for the Moscow I was heading for was in Ayrshire, Scotland—halfway between Kilmarnock and Galston.

In my breast pocket, I had an unsent Christmas card to my ailing Mum in Australia. She was in the first stages of rapidly progressing dementia and was often finding it hard to remember where she actually was: in Kharkov, in Australia or in Moscow, where she had moved in 1982 after the death of my father. By sending her a card with a Moscow stamp (even if in English: in her childish state, she wouldn't have grasped the difference) I was—perhaps naively—hoping to help her exclude at least that one point from her increasingly confused reality.

Doing my homework for this particular trip was easy: there was only one mention of Moscow, Ayrshire that I was able to find in library books: the 1992 *Illustrated Architectural Guide to Ayrshire & Arran* described it as an 'oddly named village and telephone exchange beside the Volga Burn, for the motorist on the main road no more than two unnecessarily large signs drawing attention to the name, and a sprawling untidy garage'. My thinking was that if the village had a telephone exchange, it was bound to have a post office with a franking stamp, too.

In a separate box, the *Guide* explained the origins of the village's name, which, allegedly, had no connection with Russia, but derived from the Old Scots '*Moss haw*' meaning a marshy ravine. As for the Volga Burn, it was but 'a facetious nomenclature coined to strengthen the putative link', as explained by the omniscient *Guide* or, in plain English, it was simply a joke.

I also browsed through newspaper archives.

In two faded 1884 issues of the *Kilmarnock Standard* I came across a description of the mysterious Moscow murder—obviously the first, last and only village event of any distinction during the last 150 years. And I immersed myself in its photocopied account:

'Mr. Robert Rankin, a well-known Kilmarnock gentleman, who had lived for some years in retirement at the hamlet, had been found dead in circumstances which demanded enquiry. The body of Mr. Rankin was found lying in a pool of blood, and even a casual glance was suggestive of foul play . . . In the right hand, was an ordinary nail hammer which at first was suggestive of suicide, but a closer examination showed that the hammer was not at all grasped by the hand, having evidently been placed in it after death . . .'

I was contemplating the sheer inconvenience of committing suicide by hitting one's own head with a hammer, when Eddie, my driver, drew my attention to a road sign 'Waterside 13, Moscow 3'—the first proof that the Scottish Moscow actually existed. It was not long before the view in our windscreen was blocked with another enormous sign, looking more like a memorable 'Lenin is Always with Us' billboard—the only sort of road advertising one was likely to see in the Soviet Union.

'Moscow. Please Do Not Stop,' it ran.

I am pulling your leg, of course, for in reality the sign said: 'Please Drive Carefully', but it could have just as well been the former, for the passing cars did not drive carefully and made sure they roared through Moscow without slowing down. In a way, I could not blame them: 'You blink—and you've missed it,' as one Ayrshire Muscovite put it to me later.

At a first glance, modern Moscow did not differ greatly from the 1884 crime-scene description in the *Kilmarnock Standard*:

'Moscow, lying quite apart of any main road, consists of only a single row of small houses extending for rather less than a hundred yards. On the other side of the road . . . is Volga Bank Cottage, in which Mr. Rankin resided . . . Such is the scene of the tragedy. A novelist could not choose one more fitted to excite the imagination with a sense of loneliness and awe . . .'

One didn't have to be a novelist to deduce that 'loneliness' was still there. The village was entirely deserted, except for a flock of sheep, grazing dispassionately next to what could indeed pass for 'an untidy garage'.

As the sheep seemed to be the only living Muscovites around, I was about to try and chat them up, when a florist's van pulled over next to me.

'Do you come from Moscow?' the driver asked me. 'Yes, I do,' I replied honestly.

'Where is Dykescroft Cottage?' he then enquired to my understandable bewilderment.

Yet the very fact that flowers were to be delivered to someone in Moscow was reassuring: unless it was a funeral wreath, someone alive could still be found in the village, which I decided to keep exploring by locating first a public toilet and then a post office—in that nature-dictated order.

Both my attempts were fiascos. Total absence of public 'facilities' of any kind was probably the only feature shared by the Scottish Moscow with its Soviet namesake, as I remembered it.

My other negative discovery was that not only did the village have no phone exchange any longer, it had never had a post office of its own, the nearest one being in Galston—a stamp that I didn't need on my long-belated Christmas card for it would have only confused my poor Mum even further.

One positive sign though was that, unlike in Soviet Moscow, there were no queues, which could be explained by the absence of such essential queue-forming components as shops and people. The last queue in Moscow's uneventful history occurred shortly after the mysterious 1884 murder and originated from the fact that the unfortunate Mr Rankin was last seen alive at the village inn (another victim of Moscow's time-related decline), where he asked for 'a half-mutchkin of whisky, 'stating that a young man had come in to his house, who 'thought he would be the better of a hauf-ane'.

This is how this historic event was recorded by the *Kilmarnock Standard*:

'On Sunday last Moscow was visited by large crowds of people from the town, attracted thither by morbid curiosity and the fineness of the weather. The village inn was literally besieged by thirsty travellers, who were admitted in relays until the entire stock of liquor was exhausted.'

Driven by the fairly benign, if pressing, curiosity of a traveller whose state could be best described as opposite to being 'thirsty', I simply had to find at least one living Muscovite to talk to. And fast!

I was lucky, for in the end I met and befriended not one but three: the delightful Mrs Caldwell—widow of a local farmer; her no-less-delightful daughter Ann, and their dog—a Jack Russell called Scampi, whose bark was much better than both his bite (which I didn't have a chance to experience) and his height (which I did). All three lived in a Victorian croft on the bank of the vociferous—like a Russian peasant woman telling off her husband for being drunk—Volga Burn (creek).

Mrs. Caldwell, a real patriot of her little Moscow, assured me she wouldn't swap it for any other place in the world. Her daughter didn't have immediate plans to move out either. The ladies lamented the gradual degradation of the village, which had recently lost its much-loved community centre. They also deplored the plight of local dairy farmers, driven out of business by supermarket chains, making sure they bulk-bought milk at ridiculously low prices.

Ann told me how as a kid in the 1980s she used to play in a . . . nuclear bomb-shelter, built by an overcautious local farmer for his own family needs. The farmer must have been afraid that Americans would nuke the Scottish Moscow, instead of the Russian one, by mistake (I thought that had Dubya Bush been the President then, the farmer's fears could have been more than justified).

This brought back memories of my own childhood on the opposite side of the Cold War fence. We had compulsory Civil Defence classes at school and state-run concrete bomb-shelters in every courtyard. Of course, as a little boy, I used to play inside them too. The Cold War paranoia accounted for similar children's games in two Moscows on different sides of the Berlin Wall!

When I was leaving, Mrs. Caldwell showed me the envelope of a letter, addressed to her, but 'missent to Russia' by the Royal Mail several years ago. With a stamp of *Moskva*'s Central Post-

Sorting Office, it had finally found its addressee in Ayrshire. For once, the beleaguered Russian post proved more efficient than the Royal Mail.

This reminded me of my unsent Christmas card to Mum which I posted immediately (better late than never) at Moscow's compact 'post-sorting office' in the shape of the village's only red mail box, thus putting an end to the whole Christmas card saga.

The stamp failed to impress her: by the time she received the card, her vision had deteriorated so much that she was unable to read—even with a powerful magnifying glass. It could have been a Russian Moscow stamp, or the stamp of one of the USA's several dozen Moscows, or even a plain Edinburgh or Hemel Hempstead one—it wouldn't have made any difference. I started buying her books on tape, but, with her dementia progressing fast, within a few months she lost the ability to comprehend them...

But how about the Moscow murder, you might ask? Who on earth was it that killed and burgled Mr. Robert Rankin—a quiet recluse from Volga Bank Cottage?

Alas, until now 'no trace whatever has been found of the perpetrator'. For all I know, it could have been a 'big cat', similar to the one, spotted in Ayrshire the week before my visit. The only problem with this version was that a whisky-guzzling 'big cat' had yet to be identified by zoologists.

To help solve the mystery, I appealed from the pages of the *Herald* to anyone who might have been in the vicinity of Moscow and noticed anything suspicious on 13 March, 1884, to come forward and phone Captain McHardy, Chief of the Ayrshire County Constabulary, on 'Moscow 232'...

It was his second 'Moscow homecoming'. The first had

occurred a couple of years earlier in the USA.

There are about a dozen little Moscows all over America, and Moscow, Pennsylvania, was no different from many other small American towns. Cars were passing through it without slowing down. It didn't even have a 'motion-picture theatre'. A short town profile, kindly emailed to me by Lackawanna County CVB, mentioned three playgrounds offering recreation for children of all ages' and the annual Moscow Country Fair.

I failed to locate a single playground, but spotted a row of rusty tracks and a half-ruined wooden shed of a long-deserted railway station, with the word 'Moscow' still clearly visible on its battered facade. I also ticked off a 'China Delight' take-away, a 'Synergy' hair salon, a 'Moscow Vol. Fire & Hose Company' and, encouragingly, a 'Vital Link Chiropractic Center'. It was good to know that I still had some sort of a link to Moscow.

The only building of note was a colonial-revival mansion on the hill. 'This building was given by Joseph Loveland to the men of Moscow to be used as a YMCA,' ran a memorial plate above the porch. Well, Joseph Loveland would have been upset to learn that, contrary to his wishes, the mansion now housed Moscow Borough Police Department and—aptly—'Women's Self-Defence Courses', too.

'Ask Why We Are Successful' invited a poster above a dingy car-wash outlet. I wanted to ask but there was no one inside. Behind the car wash, the town ended.

I sat down on the grass, opened a copy of *Moscow Villager*, which I had picked up in the general store, and read the lead story: 'On the first day of this fine month, Moscow's Borough Council conducted the first of its two regular monthly meetings . . . Council offered its congratulations to fellow Council member, solicitor Zero (*sic* : VV), who recently became the father of a bouncing baby boy . . . Zero now has enough members in his household to warrant two recyclable (*sic*: VV) bins . . .'

Having looked up from the paper, I noticed a 'Moscow Borough Police' van cruising near by. A patrolman inside was staring at me suspiciously. Reading a newspaper on the grass was probably an offence in this town.

I walked back to my car, started the engine and, for the second time in my life, defected from Moscow—never to return.

And he never did. A brief two-hour-long sojourn in Moscow, Ayrshire, didn't count.

More ghosts

Working in Scotland was a good opportunity to track down two of his all-time literary icons. Not the writers themselves, both of whom had been dead for many years—but, indeed, their ghosts.

Listen to this:

'Briefly, what I think is that it (Scotland : VV) has suffered in the past, and is suffering now, from too much England. The choice before Scotland today is whether in the future to suffer from less England, or from still more . . . I am now convinced that Scotsmen must decide . . . whether they wish to be citizens of a free country or citizens of a rather stale music-hall joke . . . Fundamentally, there is no half-way between freedom and slavery. In the end, there is no such thing as a free and enlightened provincialism . . . It is all very well for the ostrich to hide its head in the sand, but we Scots must remember what happens to the ostrich. He ends up in a farm where his owner plucks out his feathers and makes money by selling them . . .'
My Scotland (1937)

Or this:

'Edinburgh has been called the New Athens. It cannot be allowed to be a very happy description. The framework is there, the city, the education, the history, all is there, except the divine spark. Edinburgh is the greatest dead thing in the world. Athens was the greatest alive thing in the world.'
Ibid.

Or how about this:

'It is one of the peculiarities of the Grand Central Station in New York City that whereas it is possible to buy hats, oysters, diamonds, umbrellas, shoes, flowers, silk stockings, caviar and toys under its hospitable roof, and probably, for all I know, artificial teeth, battle cruisers, and parrots, nevertheless it is almost impossible to find any trains.'
A Visit to America (1935).

I could quote endlessly from the works of A. G. Macdonell, almost totally forgotten both in England and in his native Scotland.

I first learned about him by accident, having rescued *A Visit to America* from an unassailed dust-ridden bookshelf in Hay-on-Wye in 1999. It was only because I was then researching my own book on the USA that I picked up the tattered pale-blue volume with such an unpretentious, even boring, title. I opened the book at random and . .

Three hours later, when the shop was about to close, I was still standing there, glued to the floor and unable to stop reading the sharpest, the wittiest, the clearest and the most evocative (as well as provocative) prose I had ever come across (this book is now standing happily on the 'golden shelf' of my favourite volumes in the Pegasus Cottage).

On returning to London, I started questioning my literary-world contacts about Macdonell. No one had ever heard his name, conspicuous by its absence from reference sources—as if the man had never actually existed. As a last resort, I went to the British Library, where—finally—I had a stroke of luck.

In an obscure late 1940s Writers Directory, I found a short biographical note, according to which Archibald Gordon Macdonell was born in Aberdeen in 1895, 'the son of William Robert Macdonell, LLD, and Alice Elizabeth (White) Macdonell; the name is accented on the final syllable (sic :VV).' After childhood in Aberdeen, he studied at Winchester, was a lieutenant in the Royal Field Artillery during World War I, then worked for the League of Nations and was a Liberal candidate for Parliament in 1923-24.

Macdonell's short literary career was amazingly prolific and versatile, particularly during the last several years of his life, when he would publish two or three books annually, as if consciously running against his final God-set deadline. He wrote novels, award-winning thrillers (under the pseudonyms 'John Cameron' and 'Neil Gordon'), travel books, plays, journalism, reviews, short stories, historical studies. According to the Directory, he was killed in an air raid in Oxford in January 1941, 'two months after his forty-fifth birthday.'

One thing led to another. Soon I managed to dig up 'the Glasgow Herald' obituary, dated 18 January, 1941, which claimed that Macdonell was born . . . at Poona, India and died not in an air raid, but . . . in the bath in his Oxford flat, where his body was discovered by a maid.

By the end of the year, I was in possession of half-a-dozen short biographical articles, half of which asserted that the writer was born in India and died during the Blitz, the other half—that he was born in Aberdeen and died peacefully in his flat, except for one source claiming that he actually committed suicide.

I had also managed to get hold of several of his other books:

England, their England—a scathing heartfelt satire of warfare and the English upper classes; *My Scotland*, where Macdonell comes through as ardent Scottish nationalist, believing (somewhat naively) that it is the Lowland Scottish writers and—especially—poets, who represent the country's main driving force in its struggle for independence; and *How Like an Angel*—a brilliant satirical exposé of budding Hollywood culture describing the escapades of an American filmstar in London (among other things, she insists on being driven to a station in a carriage drawn by members of European royalty).

I was particularly taken by *The Autobiography of a Cad*—a spoof political memoir of Edward Fox-Ingleby, a Tory MP, an aristocrat and a vile hypocrite of a politician. Written in a deliberately highbrow style, the book, published in 1939, sounded extremely topical and modern. When I read, for example, how Fox-Ingleby's 'Buy British' campaign was undermined by the fact that all his three cars were foreign, it immediately brought to mind parallels with the two Jaguars of John Prescott, portraying himself as a champion of public transport.

One thing all the scanty biographical sources were in agreement on was that Macdonell had spent his formative years (childhood and early teens) in Aberdeen. Being familiar with the peculiar Aberdonian humour, I thought that the writer's incisive and punchy wit had been clearly influenced by it.

Aberdeen looked as grey and uninviting as only Aberdeen could look on a dull January afternoon: grey granite houses, grey satin skies, grey seagulls. There seemed to be three shades of grey in the spectrum: light-grey, dark-grey and Aberdeen-grey.

Despite all clichés, the 'sparkling city' staunchly refused to sparkle during short spells of sunshine. The only sparkling bits were the eyes of two Professors of Scottish Literature—David Hewitt and Derek McLure—whom I met on the medieval campus of Aberdeen University.

No, they had never heard of A.G. Macdonell either, but were kind enough to give me an insight into the literary Aberdeen of the early 1900s, dominated by locally bred poets writing in Scots. Wasn't this a reason for Macdonell's life-long fascination with Scottish poetry?

Prof. Hewitt took me on a tour of Old Aberdeen and showed me the spectacular St. Marchar's Cathedral. None of us knew that, once inside the Cathedral, we had come as close to Macdonell's childhood and his family as we could be: the following day I learned that the Macdonells, who had lived nearby, in Brig o' Balgownie, used to pray there; that Archibald's sister Margaret Rachel, who died at seventeen, had been buried in the Cathedral's graveyard; that Daniel Cottier, a Glasgow-born nineteenth-century artist, who decorated Macdonell's family home, was also a creator of the Cathedral's stained-glass windows, which we admired.

Aberdeen City Archives and the Registrar's Office had no records of A.G. Macdonell's birth, but at least I now knew that Archibald was born not in Aberdeen, but, most likely, indeed in India, where his father was a one-time president of the Bombay Merchant Company.

With my search looking more and more like chasing another ghost, I had a sudden breakthrough in Aberdeen's Central Library.

Having found nothing, I was about to leave, when a helpful librarian suggested I looked through back issues of *Aberdeen Leopard* magazine. There, in the 1987 April/May issue, was a large article on A.G. Macdonell, calling him 'a star of most individual brightness'. It also had a photo of Bridgefield—a Georgian house in Bridge of Don—where he grew up.

An omniscient local joiner pointed out Bridgefield to me from his street shed next morning. To my great relief, not only was the house still there, but it was now inhabited by a highly artistic lady, whose multi-sided talents were on a par with those of A.G. Macdonell himself.

Sculptor, artist, interior decorator and maker of unique 'designer cakes', Seona Mason-Chadburn had moved into Bridgefield ten years ago. Since then, she had been single-handedly restoring the damp and disintegrating 'C-listed' house, of which she felt an integral part. Under layers of plaster and paint, she was able to uncover elements of the original Cottier decor and other Georgian and Victorian features. She conducted guided tours of Bridgefield and wanted to have it classified as a 'B-listed' structure.

The view of the sea from Bridgefield's grand drawing room was now somewhat blocked by new trees, but otherwise it was the same as seen by little Archie. It is impossible to fully understand a writer (or any other person, for that matter) without visiting the house of his childhood and looking out at the world through HIS eyes.

'Manuscripts do not burn,' wrote Mikhail Bulgakov. Likewise, no real talent disappears without a trace. The trees of oblivion will eventually wither away.

Seona showed me another amazing find of hers. On one of the walls, there was a faded Indian-ink cartoon of a long-nosed and arrogant early twentieth-century 'aristocrat' in flannels. The 'naughty' childish drawing was on a twelve-or-thirteen year-old eye-level. We were both quite sure that it was done by young Archie Macdonell.

Born into a family of prominent Scottish aristocrats, who wanted to be more English than the English and even made sure their purely Scottish names were anglicised by being 'accented on the final syllable', he came to rebel against that very aristo-cracy and spent a large part of his literary career satirising it. A lifelong quest that had started with a simple childish drawing on the wall.

After my visit to Bridgefield, Macdonell no longer felt like a ghost. I now saw him as a flesh-and-blood Aberdonian—superficially grim and blunt, yet sardonic and sentimental beneath the surface.

One surviving description of A.G. Macdonell's appearance comes from the USA, where, strangely enough, he is better known than in Scotland. In 1934, they saw him as 'a tall, athletic, energetic young Scot, with a close-cropped moustache'. Several years later, in his obituary, they called him 'the most picturesque, dashing and talented figure' that had ever graced 'Fleet Street and literary London'.

But I would rather remember him simply as an 'energetic young Scot', who had lived a short life of talent, laughter and controversy. . .

VV's other Scottish literary hero was Gavin Maxwell, whose abridged stories about otters were introduced to him by Grigoriy Alexandrovich Polonsky—his first English teacher. Even then, VV was able to notice that there was much more to the stories than just otters: they were like small masterpieces of a writer's vision, humour and humanity.

VV knew that some of Maxwell's books were set in Sandaig Bay and some on the small Hebridean island of Soay off the coast of Skye which the writer owned in the 1940s, and he couldn't believe his eyes when he read in a Scottish newspaper that the island had been put up for sale—a brilliant excuse for an assignment, with VV posing as a potential buyer.

. . . My feet got soaked the moment I stepped on board the moored powerboat, tossed about by the waves as if we were already at sea. Through the thick curtain of unceasing rain, I could discern the dark, forbidding presence of the Cuillins across the bay.

I was about to join the cheerful crowd of twelve-hundred or so Scottish lairds, who jointly owned two-thirds of the country's territory. True, I could not afford the Cuillin mountains, put up for sale for (£) ten million, and even if I could—what would I do with them? They were a bit too bulky for a paper press on my desk . . . I was after something more affordable—an island, to which I was about to cross.

It all started several days earlier with a short newspaper report announcing the sale of 'the three-mile-long island of Soay off the coast of Skye' with 'no roads or shops', but with a nineteenth century two-bedroom 'mission house' and several other buildings thrown in. As a writer, I had always dreamed of having an island of my own, where I could pen the most important book of my life.

I contacted Inverness-based Macleod & MacCallum estate agents for an advertising brochure. To my surprise, it referred to 'Soay House & the Owner/Occupancy of South Soay Croft & Common Grazings' rather than to a straightforward romantic island.

'Common Grazings' did not sound very romantic, yet even my rudimentary knowledge of farming was sufficient to deduce a direct link between 'grazings', which featured in the brochure, and 'droppings', which, for obvious reasons, didn't.   The encouraging thing, however, was that, between 1945 and 1951, Soay was owned by Gavin Maxwell—one of the last century's most interesting Scottish writers, who used it as a base for his ill-fated shark-fishing enterprise, described in one of his books, *Harpoon at a Venture*.

Gavin Maxwell always struck me as an underrated genius. Best remembered for *Ring of Bright Water*—an internationally acclaimed book about otters—he was not just a naturalist turned writer, but also an artist, a racing driver, an army officer, a secret agent, a fisherman, a traveller and a poet.

Maxwell once complained that he could not write a novel, because he was unable to structure it properly. His own life, resplendent with dramas—financial and personal—was itself like a badly structured, yet gripping, work of fiction.

'Rabbits, have two habits, breeding, and feeding (the purpose of the second, is just to keep them fecund),'

he wrote several hours before his agonising death from lung cancer (he was a chain-smoker, too) in 1969 at the age of 55. What an iron-cast spirit he must have had to crack jokes from the very 'jaws of death'!

Whatever the dramas, Maxwell had lived his short life to the full, and Soay, to which he often referred as 'my Island Valley of Avalon', played a huge role in it.

The writer bought it in 1945 for £900, borrowed from his mother, and sold it in 1951—two years before all thirty islanders were evacuated to Mull, except for one family—that of Joseph 'Tex' Geddes, Maxwell's wartime friend and his shark-fishery's harpooner. It was Tex Geddes's Orkney-based son Duncan, who was now selling the vacant island croft for 'over £280,000'—the price of an average two—or three-bedroom flat in London or Edinburgh.

My crossing to Soay could be best compared to a roller-coaster ride under a cold shower. In my borrowed wetsuit, I felt like a U-boat captain who had given an order to submerge and only then realised that he had left his submarine at home.

The weather forecast for once proved right: 'gale-force wind', mixed with rain, was targeting me with what felt like handfuls of prickly deep-frozen shrimps, some of which would stick (and then thaw reluctantly) in my ears and nostrils. Grabbing my seat handle with both hands, I was sinking and flying up in the air - all at the same time...

'I had not dared to cross to Soay myself, lest I might be stuck there for an indefinite time,' Gavin Maxwell once wrote. I realised what he meant by the end of the crossing. The powerboat could not approach the shore, and we (Chris, a photog-rapher, and myself) had to be 'evacuated' from it by a fisherman, Oliver Davies, one of Soay's two remaining permanent residents (his wife Donita was the second) in his multi-purpose inflatable dinghy.

Despite wind and rain, the island felt beautiful, although, with my eyes full of water, I could not be quite sure what it looked like and kept conjuring up photos from the real-estate brochure and lines from Maxwell's poems about Soay ('. . . *and the waves crept over the lonely beach* . . . ' and so on) in my rain-soaked imagination. I thought that Maxwell's quick decision to buy the island could largely be explained by the fact that he first visited it on a hot summer day in 1944.

We 'inspected' the mission house, which was blissfully dry and felt very much alive—as if the residents had just popped out for a . . . whatever one could pop out for in Soay. Books were everywhere. In one room, I saw a faded complete set of *National Geographic* magazine for 1984.

We peeped inside Soay's one-room primary school, now serving as a 'community centre' (rather bizarre, with no community left), with a brand-new and seemingly untouched pool table and a box of library books under a not-too-promising handwritten note: 'Next delivery date 10 October 2002'.

Oliver told me how all the current and former islanders got together to protect the school building from being sold as a holiday cottage several years ago.
'If this house is kept as a school, there is a chance that one day the island community can be revived,' he said.
'Do you seriously believe in this revival?' I asked him.
'Why not? It's a great place to live and to bring up children. Here you don't have to put up a show—you can be yourself, and

life itself becomes your only challenge.'

I asked him how he saw a potential buyer.

'We need an active person. Preferably, a writer. He will also have to be a fisherman, for fishing is the only way of making some money here.'

I wanted to tell him that they had found such a person: I was a writer, still fairly active (as proved by the crossing) and once managed to ferret out a couple of perches from a pond at the tender age of six. But at that very moment, Donita, Oliver's wife, ran into the room and said that we had to dash back to the shore: the weather was getting worse (could it?), and the skipper of our boat radioed her to say that we had to sail off immediately.

'Life is precious, and there are enough beds in my house,' said Oliver somewhat mysteriously. I thought he simply didn't want us to go.

Although vetted (well, almost) as a potential new laird by half of Soay's population (I mean Oliver), I still wanted to clarify the crofting and (particularly) the 'grazing' issues. In Inverness, I was lucky enough to get an appointment with Derek Flyn, one of Scotland's leading experts in crofting law.

Can I buy Soay?' I asked.

'First, you'll be advised to finalise your plans as to residency on the island,' Mr Flyn replied in legal-speak.

In plain words, it meant that I had to decide whether I was going to live there or not. That came as a shock, for like many present-day Scottish lairds, I would have been quite happy to spend a couple of weeks on my croft and to cruise the globe for the rest of the year (using the change left from my would-be National Lottery jackpot).

Mr Flyn proceeded to tell me that the main purpose of crofting legislation was to protect the land against such absentee landlords. 'You will either have to live on the island, or to find a tenant,' he said sounding as weighty and authoritative as the three-volume Encyclopaedia of Value Added Tax on a bookshelf above his head (I thought that compulsory reading of all three could be a good punishment for absentee landlords—like me).

He explained that not only would such a tenant have to be approved by the Crofters' Commission, but, in accordance with Scotland's new Land Reform Act, he (or they) would have an immediate right to buy the croft from me, whether I wanted it or not.

'Buying a croft involves responsibilities, and you'll have to demonstrate your commitment to the land.' he concluded gravely and added: 'Soay is a special place for a special person.'

I was obviously not special enough. Besides, I always had a problem with commitments. But I could now understand Gavin Maxwell, who wrote on leaving Soay:

'I remember it on those glorious summer days when a
smooth blue sea lapped the red rock of the island shore
and the cuckoos called continuously from the birch-woods;
or on bright winter mornings when the Cuillins were
snow-covered, hard, intricate and brittle as carved ivory;
I remember it with nostalgia for something beautiful and
lost, the Island Valley of Avalon.'

The Hebridean Avalon—Soay—was still waiting for its new King Arthur.

The Net

. . . The fish, joined at the fins, stood upright—balancing on their tails, as if trying to form a live shield to protect the town. But their desperate links were running loose and were about to be severed.

Through the gaps between their wriggling bodies, one could see boarded-up shop windows and scruffily dressed rare pedestrians, scouring the streets in search of post-Christmas bargains.

'The Net'—a surrealistic bronze sculpture in Saltoun Square in the centre of Fraserburgh—a dying fishing community in the extreme North East of Scotland—was one of the most evocative works of art I had ever come across. Created by David Annand, it represented a swirling school of fish, but, in the sculptor's own words, was designed to produce a three-dimensional sensation of sea depth as viewed from the surface. With the town's ever-growing decline, triggered by drugs and the EU fishing quotas, 'The Net' has acquired a special meaning, for Fraserburgh itself was slowly sinking into the quagmire of poverty and decay, from which the fish were no longer able to protect it.

A town's demise is similar to that of a man sliding down into depression—the state of mind and body which was all too familiar for VV.

Having lost motivation, he stops looking after himself, grows stubble and shuns sunlight. His eyes and spirit fade by the hour; he loses hope and the desire to carry on.

Likewise, the depressed town's streets get covered with the stubble of refuse, and the boarded windows of insolvent businesses look like patches on the eyes of a perfectly-sighted person, unwilling to face the light of the day.

Winston Churchill compared depression to a black dog, whereas the continuing waning of Fraserburgh is more readily associated with white fish—cod and haddock, whose catch quotas were drastically cut by the thoughtless EU directives. With over half of the town's jobs dependent on white fishing—that meant the loss of its whole raison d'être. 'Each fisherman at sea supports 67 jobs on land,' Alex Shand, editor of the *Fraserburgh Herald,* told me. 'The latest EU quotas will be the last straw for our community when they come into effect. They will mean more drug abuse, more unemployment, more family break-ups.'

Reams have been written about the causes of the Scottish fishing industry crisis, with heated and seemingly persuasive arguments from all sides involved. The fishermen blamed the EU bureaucrats, the British and Scottish governments and the 'bogus' scientists for letting them down. They argued that Scotland had been victimised again, despite doing more for stock conservation than any other European country. They called Franz Fischler, the embattled European Fisheries Commissioner, 'Ayatollah Fischler' and publicly compared him to Adolf Hitler. The environmentalists, in their turn, were saying that the fishermen themselves were at fault, that only a complete ban on white fishing could save the North Sea wildlife from extinction, and therefore the 45% reduction of fishing quotas, with the maximum fifteen days at sea per boat per month, was the very least that could be done to prevent the disaster.

For someone like myself, whose fishing experience was largely limited to ferreting out a couple of perches from a pond at the tender age of six and who—until fairly recently—was convinced that an artichoke, an unseen delicacy in the Soviet Union of my youth, was a leafy tropical plant, taking sides in this dispute would hardly have been appropriate.

Yet one would have had to be both blind and heartless not to notice the immediate implications of the crisis for thousands of human beings, whose entire livelihood had been taken away. Whatever the arguments, this should have never been allowed to happen.

Plywood seemed the only building material still in demand in Fraserburgh. In the High Street, I walked past the locked and boarded 'Fraserburgh Football Social Club'; past Murray McKie' Hi-Fi Shop, its windows firmly shuttered; past Tech Hide Computers—the only shop where the windows were covered not with plywood, but, in accordance with its once high-tech profile, with iron sheets; past 'Jesters Joke Factory'—a party accessories shop, boarded and 'for sale'.

True, there were not many jokes (or parties) left in Fraserburgh, and the only remaining humour was rather black:

'**Question**: What is the similarity between the Scottish Fishing Industry and a Christmas turkey? **Answer**: 'They both get stuffed.' (*The Fraserburgh Herald*).

I moved on to Saltoun Square, once the hub of the bustling royal burgh, with its own coveted Market Cross. Three quarters of its businesses were now closed for good. An attractive Victorian Saltoun Arms Hotel, 'commended by the Scottish Tourist Board', stood locked and abandoned; the nearby Insports and 'Sweetie' shops were shut down, and the 'Furniture & Accessories' store, although still going, had had a brick (or some other heavy object) thrown through its window, in which a large spider-web hole was gaping.

The only outlets that seemed relatively busy were video rentals; numerous charity shops and a '99 Pence' store, doing a brisk trade in cut-price children's toys, toiletries and packets of crisps.

With sadness, I noted that the average value of a Fraserburgh house—as advertised in the still intact windows of real estate agents—was £25,000, whereas flats went (if they did at all) for as little as £12,000. The town was obviously not taking part in Britain's continuing housing boom.

I stopped at the (closed) Tourist Information Bureau to read a plaque commemorating 'Thomas Blake—'The Scottish Samurai' and a native of Fraserburgh, famed for 'his work in the development of Japan', when I was approached by an unshaven and whisky-reeking, yet not unfriendly, character offering to find me a 'nice and cheap' B&B. I refused and questioned him about Thomas Blake, whom he claimed to have known personally ('the Scottish Samurai' died in 1911).

'It looks like Fraserburgh could do with a modern Thomas Blake,' I said to my new acquaintance.

He shook his dishevelled head resolutely: 'Nah... He was only good for Japan, but did absolutely nothing here. Nothing at all!' He had mermaids tattooed on both wrists, and when he gesticulated, the mermaids winked and wiggled their tails playfully.

Instead of a Thomas Blake figure, I ended up finding a Joan of Arc.

And not one, but three! I mean the three wives of Fraserburgh fishermen calling themselves The Cod Crusaders: Caroline Bruce, Carol MacDonald and Morag Ritchie. These ordinary down-to-earth ladies, sharing thirteen children (and one grandchild—Carol Macdonald had just become a granny at thirty-five years of age!) among them, had decided to take the future of their community in their own hands.

I met them at a coffee shop in the outskirts of Fraserburgh. Only two—Carol and Morag—were able to make it: Caroline was busy with her kids. Their husbands were at sea, and I could not imagine how they coped with all the house chores (Morag being the mother of seven!) on top of running a high-profile international campaign.

'We are used to hard work,' smiled Carol. 'With our husbands constantly away, we have to be mums and dads simultaneously. We are cooks, taxi-drivers, DIY experts and decision-makers— all at the same time. In this case, we are fighting for the future of our children, and although we feel angry and let down, nothing will stop us.'

The ladies had achieved a lot. They brought seven-hundred demonstrators to Edinburgh, where Jack Macdonell, Scotland's First Minister, refused to join their protest, saying it was 'too wet outside'. In London, they handed over their Petition, with 45,000 signatures they had collected, to the MPs at Westminster and at 10, Downing Street. But the highlight of their campaign was on 9 December, when they flew to Brussels to confront Franz Fischler himself.

'He went straight past us, pretending we weren't there,' recalled Morag.'But we accosted him in the lift and didn't let him out until we'd voiced all our demands.'

The Commission nevertheless decided to go ahead with the quotas. Yet Fraserburgh's Joans of Arc, with perseverance and spirit reminiscent of the 'hope against hope' approach of Soviet political dissenters, kept fighting 'to save what little is left of our community', as Carol poignantly put it.

In their battered four-wheel-drive, the Cod Crusaders took me to the Harbour, incongruously empty for the end of December, when most fishermen would normally be home celebrating the New Year with their families. Now, many were out at sea to take advantage of the last weeks before the quotas came into effect, and the remaining few boats were rocking gently, moored to the pier. They rubbed boards, as if trying to reassure each other, or simply to warm themselves up.

There, in the seagull-filled Fraserburgh Harbour, the women told me about an old local tradition, according to which fishermen's wives would carry their husbands to the boats to make sure they didn't get wet before stepping on board.

This echoed a legend I once heard in Turkmenistan. When a medieval fortress was captured after a long and bloody siege, the invaders' commander magnanimously decided to let all the defenders' wives walk away in peace. He declared they could take with them whatever valuables they could carry. Without hesitation, the women picked up their bearded armour-suited husbands and dragged them out of the fortress on their shoulders.

The fishermen's wives of Fraserburgh no longer practised their ancient husband-carrying ritual. Yet, having met the Cod Crusaders, who—unlike most local males I had spoken to—had not succumbed to gloom and doom, I thought that, metaphorically speaking, this was still pretty much the case.

Looking into the women's determined eyes, I wanted to believe that their shoulders were strong enough for the burden. And also—that there was still an escape route from their common 'besieged fortress'.

The assignment in Scotland's beleaguered North East was significant for VV at that point in time. Like the impoverished town of Fraserburgh, he was plunging deeper and deeper into despair, yet like the tenacious Cod Crusaders, he was finding it hard to give up hope completely.

His 'hope against hope' was largely triggered by the flow of readers' letters in response to his Monday feature/column:

'Dear Sir,
I used to greatly enjoy your programmes on BBC Radio 4. To my
great pleasure you turned up as a writer on my daily newspaper
telling me things I didn't know about my native Scotland . . . My
usual reading of the paper starts with the 'small crossword', and
Mondays were rather dull—not now!
May I thank you for your articles—long may they keep coming.'
Jean M. Cameron, Glasgow

'Dear Mr Vitaliev,
Just a note to congratulate you on the Scotland series in Monday's
Herald. I particularly enjoyed the Sighthill story—interesting
& high standards of composition. We in Scotland could be doing
much more of 'as others see us'.
More inspiration to your pen!'
Betty Millar, Isle of Arran

The Sighthill story

'Nas ne ponimayut,'—they don't understand us—Edik Veronidi repeats in Russian.

We are in his neat tiny flat in Sighthill, a North Glasgow housing estate and home of 2,500 asylum seekers. Stooping and abnormally thin, Edik, who was referred to me as a 'Russian', is actually an ethnic Greek from Tajikistan—a war-torn former Soviet Republic on the border with Afghanistan.

When he smiles, he does so with his lips and protruding cheekbones only: his velvety brown eyes do not seem to take part, but stay tragic and alert, as if reflecting all the pain and fears of his not-so-distant past.

Born in Dushanbe, the capital of Soviet Tajikistan, he grew up among Tajiks and Russians and attended a Russian school. After the collapse of the Soviet Union, the republic found itself being sucked into the quagmire of civil war, with Afghanistan-supported Islamists, pro-Russian government forces, troops from the neighbouring Uzbekistan and local warlords all fighting each other. Violence, chaos and lawlessness reigned supreme in that ongoing conflict, totally ignored by the West.

Edik, trained as a male nurse, was trying to help the wounded from all warring camps and therefore came to be regarded as traitor by everyone. Tortures, beatings and imprisonment followed until he could take no more.

'I didn't want to kill or to be killed,' he says, staring blankly at the wall in front of him.

Having buried many of his relatives and friends—all victims of the conflict, in which over 40,000 people had lost their lives, he fled to Russia, then to Ukraine, from where—via Turkey—he eventually arrived in Holyhead several years ago. His stomach swollen with malnutrition, he looked like a living corpse. After a stretch at a detention centre, he was 'dispersed' (an official Home Office term, more readily associated with germs and poisonous gases, yet routinely applied to asylum seekers) to Sighthill. It was there that he learned about the death of his younger sister.

At Sighthill, he started recovering and was able to pursue wireology—a sophisticated artistic technique to create colourful three-dimensional images on wood with the help of hot wires. He mastered this unusual art during a 13-day-long recovery after an unwarranted arrest by the Tajik police, who had beaten him up so badly that it took him thirteen days to recuperate. Unable to move, he lay in his bed watching butterflies flutter behind the window. Fascinated by their shapes and by the unmitigated freedom of their movements, he decided to make one for himself.

Edik is now an acclaimed award-winning artist, and recently had an exhibition at Glasgow Hilton Hotel. Waiting for his asylum application to be approved (or rejected), he spends time teaching his skills to Scottish children. He was one of the very few asylum seekers in Sighthill who was not afraid to give me his name. 'Scotland is a free country, it is not the Soviet Union,' he said.

Nevertheless, he had been staunchly refusing to be photographed until I said that he would really help us (me and Chris, a Herald photographer), if he agreed. He then nodded, and Chris took his photo inside a battered graffiti-ridden Sighthill bus shelter.

He sat there obediently, his lean frame bent forward—like an old slanting tombstone in an abandoned church cemetery overlooking Sighthill.

Life had bent him, but didn't manage to break him.

On the day of my first visit to Sighthill, the Scottish Sun, on its front page, urged its readers to sign a petition against what it called 'Asylum Madness' On the same page, it invited them to 'get into Kylie's knickers'—not into the worn-out shoes of the 'illegal asylum seekers', against whom the paper had launched a crusade.

Let me tell you straight away that I have never worn those shoes myself. Nor have I ever been a refugee or lived off a social support system of any kind—not for a single day.

But as someone who was forced to defect from a totalitarian state, I know what running for your life, with your family in tow, feels like. The simple truth is that immigration, no matter how successful, is never bliss—it is, rather grief bordering on misery. Unless a convinced 'rootless cosmopolitan' (like me), one cannot be totally happy outside the country where one grew up, and normally people will not leave their homeland just for fun or because they have nothing better to do.

I am not talking about fraudsters and/or terrorists, who will sneak into any country of their choice no matter what.

During my travels in Eastern Europe, I saw on sale numerous badly printed brochures, full of advice on how to dupe the immigration systems of every single Western state. I know of (Western) lawyers specialising in concocting plausible 'legends' for bogus asylum seekers.

In London, I heard of a man from Ukraine who had his asylum claim approved on the grounds that he had endangered himself by voting 'for a wrong party', although supporting any party in post-Communist Ukraine is no more dangerous than shouting either for Celtic or for the Rangers in Scotland (probably even less so).

The roots of the ongoing crisis of the UK's immigration system lie in its sheer inability to distinguish between the genuine cases and the bogus ones.

'They don't understand us', indeed.

I was stunned to discover that over forty different organisations deal (or claim to deal) solely with the issue of refugees and asylum seekers in Scotland. Some are genuine: they do not rely on government (read public) funding and try to help the outcasts. Others—simply sponge off the problem. The latter have nice spacious offices—with faxes, computers and coffee machines, but their staff are unlikely to have ever encountered a single flesh-and-blood asylum seeker.

Meanwhile, the issue itself increasingly resembles a house fire that has got out of control during a firefighters' strike. The burning house is surrounded by a crowd of onlookers. Pro and anti-immigration activists, pure racists and whatnots flock around the fire warming up their social fervour. Political parties force their way through the crowd to try and cook their election platforms on it. The media add coals. And in the meantime, thousands of human souls are being slowly roasted inside the burning house—the souls of those for whom coming to this country was the question of life and death—no less.

Covered with graffiti—like the body of a hardened criminal with tattoos—Sighthill was far from a pretty sight. What struck me most, however, was neither dust and litter flying in my face, nor frozen spittle in the lifts or putrid puddles of dubious origin under my feet, but the behaviour of some of its Scottish residents. Whereas 'foreigners' were invariably civil, neatly dressed and polite, the 'locals', particularly teenagers, were—with very few exceptions—foul-mouthed, aggressive, uncouth and either tipsy or dead drunk (or stoned). Putting aside race and religion, they corresponded to the image of would-be terrorists better than any of the asylum seekers in Sighthill.

It seemed unfair that such unlikely bedfellows as human suffering and (largely) self-imposed degradation, as genuine aspirations and outright cynicism were forced to cohabit—literally—under one roof.

Stephen Cochrane, a community safety officer from the nearby Baird Street police station and one of the organisers of the annual North Glasgow International Festival, agreed that Sighthill's main problem had always been not refugees, whose behaviour was on the whole a 'model,' but 'young Scottish offenders'.

'It used to be much worse,' he said referring to the murder of Kurdish asylum seeker Firsat Dag and the stabbing of Masood Gomroki, an Iranian some time before—both of which were like cold showers for the Sighthill community.

I could feel the cleansing effects of those 'showers' of innocently shed human blood in Sighthill's One Stop Shop— the headquarters of a small organisation, trying to bring the community closer together by looking after the interests of all residents—without dividing them into refugees and locals. Probably Scotland's last office where smoking seemed compulsory, it was run by young and energetic Billy Singh.

It was in that Sighthill office-cum-flat that I met an Iranian woman, who had been imprisoned and forced to leave the country for having a drink with a friend in her own flat (she was denounced to the police by her neighbours); an elderly Kurdish man, who was too frightened to tell me his name; and lots of other refugees mixing-freely and amicably with the Scottish visitors to One Stop Shop: the first 'stop' in the right direction— towards peace and tolerance—in Sighthill.

The value of 'genuine' refugees—those honest, brave and desperate people willing to put their skills and energy at the service of the nation that harbours them—is unquestionable.

The overnight queue to Lunar House—the Home Office Immigration Directorate in Croydon—is perhaps the most educated crowd to congregate anywhere in Britain (I couldn't remember seeing so many people reading serious books in any other queue).

It was migrants who built the industrial might of modern America. It was they who—within the last several decades— managed to change the face of Australia. Or take prosperous Luxembourg, where 40 percent of the population are foreign nationals. Or Norway, with its little-known recent success story of integrating many thousands of Vietnamese refugees into its once forbidding Nordic community.

I remember asking some Vietnamese schoolkids in Bergen what freedom was. The answers ranged from 'Freedom is being able to express yourself and do whatever you like' to 'Freedom is not being spied upon by your neighbours.' But one little Vietnamese girl in a ski jacket (she had just come back from a skiing lesson) simply muttered: 'Freedom is Norway'.

Edik dives under the sofa and reappears with a 3D picture of a bagpipe player in a kilt. 'Scottish man,' he says and smiles broadly—still without his eyes taking part.

I want him to be able to say 'Freedom is Scotland' one day. I want his eyes to learn to smile again.

Perhaps Benjamin Franklin was right when he wrote to his son: 'Wherever liberty dwells, there is my country.'

Edik's story reminded VV of his own past and helped put things in proper perspective. At least, for some time. The proverbial 'scale of comparison' he had used many times before to stop himself from sliding down into depression proved helpful again . . .

Despite all the 'enemies within', he was still a free person by definition, albeit to keep reminding himself of that required a conscious effort.

He was trying hard to shut out his Edinburgh 'family' routine—with frequent travels, with wine, with trying to fill every spare moment with writing. Apart from the sheer joy of being with his kids, his memory of those grim Edinburgh days is very sketchy, almost non-existent.

And here's another ST: try never to focus too much on the

moments of your past misery and humiliation, erase them from memory, shut them out—that will make you much less prone to going through them all over again.

'How come you write in your second language and you are the best writer on the paper?' one of the Herald's executives asked rhetorically when she came to Edinburgh and took Vin out for a coffee.

'Are you sure you are not going to leave us and return to London?' she kept prying.

Vin had no intention of leaving Scotland at that point. Not yet. Not when he had just started developing a bond with his readers. Such a bond would from inevitably all through his career, no matter where he was working—in Moscow, where he would receive thousands of letters after his investigative pieces in *Krokodil*; in Melbourne where the overwhelming readers' response to his column was, according to his own Editor and to *Time* magazine, an unprecedented phenomenon in Australian journalism; in London, and now—in Scotland. Leaving Edinburgh at that moment would have been very much like a betrayal, or so he thought.

A regular newspaper column is like a flower bed: it takes a lot of watering and cultivating before it starts flourishing and becomes pleasing to the eye.

When not travelling, he was trying to find solace in red wine. His nightly trips to the nearest off-licence along the dark and unfriendly streets of Marchmont (a posh Edinburgh suburb and—ironically—a former 'temperance area', which still had just one pub) became as routine as his milk-procuring walks up the Royal Mile several months earlier.

He had managed to get some unexpected consolation (or was it just a distraction, a temporary outlet for his unhappiness?) in . . . football, after he was asked to write about a match between two Glasgow teams: Celtic and Rangers—the so-called 'Old Firm'.

. . . In my lifetime, I have stood in all sorts of queues: as a child, for butter and white bread in the Soviet Union of the early 1960s (5-6 hours); as a youngster, to a visiting USA Today exhibition (about half a day of waiting before you could get a coveted American plastic bag and leave—the exhibition itself did not matter). Then as an adult for a bottle of vodka during Gorby's futile anti-drinking campaign of the late 1980s (that could take up to three days, with family members relieving each other every ten hours or so).

But, unlike Gerhard Messerklinger from Salzburg, I never had to wait for nine years to get a ticket to a football match.

I met Gerhard in a Parkhead lounge after the Celtic-Rangers derby. It took him nine years to receive a ticket. His friend, Klaus Waha, a young Salzburg lawyer, was somewhat luckier—he 'only' had to wait for four years to attend the game of his dreams.

They were both in seventh heaven, drinking Guinness and reliving the details of the match. Multiple TV screens in the lounge were showing endless repeats of Hartson's winning goal, and the thinning crowd would cheer at each, as if trying to recreate the exciting moment.

What made these two Salzburgers fly to Glasgow, instead of staying at home and watching the game on TV?

'It is the atmosphere,' Klaus muttered through a white bushy moustache of beer foam. 'It is unique. I have been to lots of stadiums all over Europe but none of them can compare.'

For me, meeting the Austrians was one of the highlights of this extraordinary day. It was my ultimate Glasgow experience, despite the fact that my knowledge of football in general and Scottish football in particular was worse than Gerhard's English—rudimentary, bordering on non-existent.

. . . In the Soviet Union, as in any totalitarian state, a football stadium was the only place where one could (temporarily) get rid of the unbearable pressure of political dogma. Watching a football match was the closest thing to freedom, for it allowed one—at least for a couple of hours—to think and behave like an uninhibited human being. Like a glass of vodka, it provided you with momentary oblivion and a short-term obliteration of oppressive reality. The very unpredictability of the game's result, in a country where almost everything else was predictable ad nauseam, was inspiring.

Afterwards, we discussed the games that we had seen and the fact that we could openly express contradictory opinions about them, that at least something was not affected by the iron grip of the Party line; it never failed to give us kicks, making us all into human footballs of our own Soviet existence.

A devoted soccer fan in the USSR, where football and weather were life's only variables, unaffected by the Party line, and the football stadium, therefore, was the closest venue to freedom, I lost interest in it the moment I came to the West. Also, living in London, I was rather put off by the peculiar human (semi-human?) breed of English football hooligans. Pugnacious and foul-mouthed, they had turned the game into a scuffle, an act of aggression, a collective neurosis.

In London streets and on the Tube on their way to (or from) a match, they were easily identifiable, as if bending over backwards to correspond to the soccer-hooligan stereotype they had themselves created. They had clean-shaven heads and unshaven cheeks, which gave the upper parts of their bodies the *look of dried cacti. They had regulation beer-bellies, as if each* of them had swallowed a football. They were tirelessly pumping up their intestinal 'football s' through their mouths from cans of lager. Their red hairy hands were covered with pale tattoos of unclear message and origins . . .

Football was one of Scotland's self-confessed obsessions.

Significantly, if William Shakespeare asserted that life was theatre and people actors, Sir Walter Scott regarded it as 'but a game of football', with people if not all players, then definitely all football fans (or so one could assume).

Just like the BBC and Coca-Cola are the Western world's most recognisable—and hence unavoidable—brand-names, Celtic and Rangers are among Scotland's best known realities, which no-one residing in the country can either ignore or stay away from.

A week before my first Old Firm game, I started reading the sports pages of newspapers—for the first time in thirteen years. I discovered that initially both Celtic and Rangers had strong religious backing, and whereas both squads were now fairly international in their composition and it was no longer unusual for a Catholic to play for Rangers and a Protestant for Celtic, divisions still ran rampant among the fans.

I learned that all Old Firm games were both 'passion and badness', which could explain the unusually early (12.30 p.m.) Saturday kick-off, aimed at reducing drunkenness among the fans. I worried that the latter measure could backfire by encouraging some to start drinking the night before.

On the eve of the derby, a Glaswegian friend (let's call him Dennis) gave me an extensive pub briefing on dos and don'ts of the day.

'If they ask you on the terraces which team you support, say 'Partick Thistle',' he said.

'Why not Moscow Spartak or Dynamo?' I wondered

'Because they could connect Spartak with Rome, even if ancient, and decide that you are a Catholic. As for Moscow Dynamo, it will tell them that you are a Russian, meaning possibly a Russian Orthodox, meaning an anti-Catholic, meaning a Protestant.'

In vain, I tried to spot a hint of irony in Dennis's voice. He was dead serious.

'They will look for the slightest sign of what you are and who you support,' he went on, and told me that many Glasgow taxi-drivers were wary of working on the Old Firm game days, not willing to be confronted with the same sacramental question: 'Which team do you support?'

At this point I had to fight down the urge to run back to Queen Street Station and catch the first train back to Edinburgh. I was also wondering how on earth I would be able to achieve a balance in my story without offending anyone's sensitivities— not because of a bias towards any side, for I had none, but out of pure ignorance.

I decided that rather than calling the teams by their real names in my 'coverage' of the match, I would stick to their lexical fusions, 'Rantic' and 'Celgers', which would guarantee me against any accusations of prejudice. After all, I was not a sports reporter, and what mattered most to me was the general feel of the game—not which team was better or worse. As for the persisting religious divisions, I thought that, for my own purposes, it wouldn't be too blasphemous to describe both as basically 'Christian'.

We were lucky to find one courageous taxi-driver who ventured to take us as close to the stadium as possible (about a mile away). Brave as he was, he was not foolhardy enough to display his name tag above the dashboard. 'Partick Thistle, *Partick Thistle,*' I was mumbling to myself, trying to memorise the tongue-breaking team name.

Empty whisky flasks clanked under our feet like broken wind chimes, as we progressed towards the stadium. The ground was covered with them—like with some slippery loose cobbles.

'Communism versus alcoholism' was the banner waved by Scottish fans at the Soviet Union versus Scotland World Cup game in 1982. Judging by the number of empty bottles, the forthcoming game was in real danger of becoming an alcoholism versus alcoholism one.

Two differently coloured and seemingly endless processions were snaking through the gates from two different directions. The great divide started long before the game. Apart from a handful of types with bleary unseeing eyes (they must have started drinking the night before), the crowd was unexpectedly orderly and gentle. The fans held doors open for each other and called each other 'pal'.

This all changed the moment the game started. With Celgers and Rantic supporters carefully segregated, it felt as if they were still rubbing shoulders on the terraces.

There had been attempts to compare a football stadium to one multi-headed human being. If Celtic Park was one, he (or she) would have been suffering from a severe split-personality disorder. Whenever a Rantic player was hurt and left lying on the grass, the Celgers supporters would burst into applause, whereas Rantic fans would go berserk with uncompromising rage. And the other way around. When a Rantic defender casually returned the ball to his goalkeeper, the Celgers supporters would boo. When their team's defender did the same, they would cheer.

The correlation between the opposing camps was roughly as follows: singing—booing; applause—wild gestures; cheering - swearing, and so on. I was clasping my notebook with both hands as a lame excuse for not applauding and/or gesticulating with the crowd.

In Russia, it was OK to criticise one's own team for a bad performance. Here, any criticism seemed out of the question. Whatever your team did was absolutely perfect—a complete and unquestioning loyalty.

To my relief, no-one had questioned me about the team I supported as yet.

After the only goal, twelve minutes into the second half, emotions at the stadium heated up considerably. The fans in front of me would jump up every two seconds to point their outstretched hands, not towards the field, but towards the opposing terraces, spitting out threats and profanities, which I hoped they did not mean.

They would also block my vision with their backs, and to keep following the game, I had to start jumping up too—very much against my will. Soon, almost without noticing, I began applauding, waving my hands like a windmill and whispering instructions to the players: 'Stay on the corner! Watch your back! Shoot!!!'

The peculiar electricity of Celtic Park was having its effect.

'Which team do you support, pal?' a bespectacled ruddy-faced man sitting (or rather bouncing on his seat) next to me, enquired.

'Here it comes,' I thought, and blurted out without thinking: 'Spartick!' Luckily, my confused reply was drowned in the powerful roar of the terraces.

The most amazing thing was how quickly all passions died away after the final whistle. Well, to be fair, they did not die down completely, but relocated from the stadium to Glasgow pubs.

An hour later, with Dennis and my new Austrian friends, we were inside a well-known Rantic (or was it Celgers?) pub, filled to such an extent that it only took one more newcomer for it to explode with a bang. Propped up on all sides by fellow-drinkers, I had finally reached a balance—the only sort of balance one could hope for in the aftermath of an Old Firm game.

We squeezed ourselves out. It was raining. Glasses in hand, we stood there watching the crowd. The atmosphere was noisy, but not nasty.

Without realising it, the people in (and out of) the pub were celebrating neither victory nor defeat. They were celebrating Scottish football. Beleaguered and humiliated, it remained their favourite game, rising above class, religion, politics and all other imaginable divides.

'You know why we have no armed confrontation in Scotland, like they have in Northern Ireland?' Dennis asked me. 'Because here we spend all our passions on the Old Firm.'

He could be right, for during the previous several hours I hadn't thought once about the war in Iraq . . .

The wine in my glass tasted of rain water.

It was time to move on to another pub.

Life as a football match

One of Vin's first published short stories was about football.

It was inspired by his devoted and largely thankless support for 'Metallist'—a rather mediocre team from his native Kharkov—scornfully and yet lovingly (these too adverbs often go hand-in-hand in descriptions of football, or any other passion, read obsession) nicknamed 'Metallolom' ('scrap metal') by its fans for its chronically poor performance.

Why 'Metallist'? Because formally the team belonged to

a huge steel-making factory, the same one where Volodya Grishpun, Vin's poetical idol, worked as a turner.

There was a moment, however, in the mid 1980s, when the most stubborn 'Metallist' supporters were finally rewarded: the team—then not even in the Soviet Premier League—unexpectedly won the USSR Football Cup.

By then, VV was already living in Moscow. He came to watch the final game at a Moscow stadium with his son Mitya, who was then six or seven and as someone born and bred in the capital was supporting 'Metallist' rivals: Moscow's Torpedo team.

'Metallist' won 2:0, Mitya was in tears, whereas VV was beaming and humming to himself all the way home.

His first (and last) serious disagreement with his son.

The short story he wrote some time later was published in a prestigious Moscow weekly with a circulation of more than ten million. It was in Russian of course.

I don't have a copy of that story but remember it well enough to retell it.

It was called 'The Ball is my Heart'—a cliché coined by Sir Stanley Matthews, whose book VV had read in a Russian translation. As far as I know, what Stanley Matthews actually said was 'Football is my life and the ball is my heart,' but I cannot be sure. . .

The protagonist, Adam Grigor'yevich Nadin, an old-age pensioner from the fictitious provincial Soviet city of Krupinsk, liked to silently apply those words to himself. He had never been a footballer and even in his teens, being a sallow and pale youngster, had hardly ever *kicked a ball himself, but football* was everything to him. It had come to replace his wife who had left him ages ago, unable to cope with his all-consuming soccer obsession; and his son Zhenia who was living thousands of miles away—in Eastern Siberia; and now also his job as an accountant at the local zoo, which he had to quit on reaching sixty.

Adam Grigor'yevich was a 'professional' football fan—fervent and knowledgeable in equal measure, a true connoisseur of the game.

His whole life was there, on the emerald-green carpet of the pitch when the stadium would suddenly freeze in complete silence and then explode with one all-permeating powerful roar, and the fans would spring up from their seats—drunk with largely self-inflicted joy or anger and totally oblivious of the outside world.

It was like being a tiny cell of a huge multi-headed and multi-mouthed human Hydra—an intoxicating and strangely calming sensation.

As for his own heart, it could no longer be compared to the stiff, resounding and bouncy ball used in the Premier League games. Instead, it had come to resemble a pear-like half-blown freak kicked about by kids in a primary schoolyard. At times, it suddenly froze inside his chest—like a ball kicked off by a goalkeeper which, having reached the highest point of its trajectory, hangs motionless for a split second over the heads of the players.

Meteor, the team he supported, had been doing badly for years, but having nothing else to occupy himself with, Adam Grigor'yevich kept stubbornly attending every game. When Meteor finally made it to the first division, his positive stress was such that it had led to severe arrhythmia and morning chest pains.

He started taking nitroglycerine pills to the terraces . . .

. . . Why hadn't VV described in his short story what Adam Grigor'yevich looked like? He had done it (or rather hadn't done it) deliberately: lack of physical description was supposed to underline his character's ordinariness: there was nothing about him that was worth noticing or describing. Nothing, apart from football . . .

That year Meteor—as often happens after a brief revival—was doing particularly badly. At the end of the season, it was second from the bottom of the table. There was just one game left for the team to play—against the Moscow squad that was one place ahead of it. Victory meant Meteor would retain its place in the first division. A loss or even a draw would see it relegated to the sticky bog of the second division for many years, possibly forever. . .

The last game was to be played in Moscow. Three days before the match the Meteor fan club, the so-called 'Brekhalovka' (from the rude slang Russian word '*brekhat*'—to yap-yap) gathered in the dilapidated city park—its usual place of unofficial congregation: any mass gatherings, except for the officially approved ones, were frowned upon in the Soviet Union, and 'Brekhalovka' was only tolerated because of the several KGB stooges planted in its midst to keep a record of the 'popular mood'.

After a long and heated (despite the freezing weather) debate, it was decided to send a team of supporters to Moscow.

The club's unelected leader—a short podgy man nicknamed *Peniok* (Tree Stump) took off his cheap *ushanka* (winter hat with ear flaps), made of cheap rabbit's fur, and invited everyone present to chip in for the tickets. Adam Grigor'yevich surprised himself by volunteering to go. He tossed a rumpled ten-rouble note, his weekly pension, into Peniok's smelly hat.

'Are you crazy, Dad, or what?' Zhenia, his son, was screaming at him from Siberia during his weekly phone call the following day, his voice hardly audible through the crackles of the chronically bad phone ine. 'Have you forgotten about your heart? You are simply too old and too infirm for this trip!'

He was probably right, for Adam Grigor'yevich had not left Krupinsk for many years.

It was an overnight train journey.

Adam Grigor'yevich could not sleep. 'Why am I doing this?' he kept asking himself while tossing and turning on his stiff lower sleeping berth. For the first time in his life, his passion for football appeared worthless and immature. On the other hand, it wasn't his fault that he had always been shy, feeble and unremarkable and his love of football—just like this insane trip to Moscow—was his strongest ever attempt to prove to himself, to his estranged son—and to the world, in case it cared—that he wasn't an empty space, that he was capable of real deeds and not immune to passions .

He thought he could hear the muffled rumble of the stadium terraces in the rattling of the train's wheels.

It was late autumn, and the game was to be played under the roof of a large new sporting complex. Adam Grigor'yevich felt claustrophobic in there: it reminded him of his pokey pensioner's bed-sit in Krupinsk.

At the start of the game, the Meteor players were finding it hard to get used to the enclosed limited space under the dome: after their initial kicks, the ball struck the ceiling repeatedly. But soon they adapted and their playing improved a lot.

At the end of the first half, Sultanov, the halfback, scored 1:0.

The Krupinsk fans were jumping with joy during the interval. One of them gave Adam Grigor'yevich a bottle of tepid Pepsi, still a novelty in the Soviet Union.

Adam Grigor'yevich didn't like the drink: much too sweet. He suddenly felt hot and stuffy and started fanning himself with a copy of *Sovietsky Sport*, the only newspaper he ever read.

In the second half, Meteor staked it all on defence: its defenders had always been better than its forwards. The Muscovites were pressing, but one could see they were getting tired.

Minutes before the final whistle, the Muscovites launched a desperate attack: they didn't want to leave the first division either.

Drops of sweat appeared on Adam Grigor'yevich's forehead. 'Please, please, dear boys, hold on for a little longer. Please, please,' he was whispering with his dried up lips.

A sharp pricking pain started in his left side, under the ribs. Adam Grigor'yevich produced a pill nitroglycerine and put it under his tongue.

Two minutes before the end, Tarakanov—Moscow and the Soviet national team forward—dashed towards the goal. At the very last moment, when it seemed nothing could stop him from scoring, a Meteor defender tripped him up. Tarakanov collapsed on the green carpet.

'Penalty,' thought Adam Grigor'yevich, amazed by his own calm. With strange detachment he was watching Tarakanov place the ball on the eleven-metre penalty mark and adjust it by pushing it forward slightly with his right foot. He could see Tarakanov going back for the kick almost to the centre of the pitch and Konarev, the Meteor goalkeeper, bending down in waiting . . .

It suddenly appeared to Adam Grigor'yevich that he was still young and was watching a game at his native Krupinsk stadium, with little Zhenia beside him.

'What is this man going to do?' Zhenia was asking his Dad—as he often did during the match. 'This man is preparing to throw the ball in,' Adam Grigor'yevich would answer feeling very proud of himself: at least, there was something he could explain to his son with knowledge and authority.

But this time it all felt different . . . 'This man . . . this man . . . ,' Adam Grigor'yevich was whispering semi-audibly. Through the veil of cold sweat dripping from his forehead and blocking his vision, he could see Tarakanov running—faster and faster—towards the ball resting on the penalty mark, getting closer and closer . . .

'This man is preparing to kill me,'—unwillingly, he uttered that out loud, and the last word he screamed at the top of his lungs: 'Me-e-e-!!!' And in the watchful silence of the stadium it sounded like a piercing shriek, and Tarakanov slowed down for a split second.

Then he kicked, and the ceiling seemed to collapse onto the pitch, and the ball—instead of flying in between the goalposts—hit Adam Grigor'yevich's side, but didn't ricochet and kept screwing itself into his chest, forcing his heart from under the ribs, and then exploded with a loud bang wheezing out its air, and the pain became unbearable, and darkness fell . . .

The scream from the terrace may have prevented Tarakanov from delivering a precise kick.

Or it could have been the Meteor goalkeeper who had found the right spot in the goalmouth . . . Whatever it was, Tarakanov did not score.

And in a moment or two, all the Meteor supporters jumped off their seats and started chanting in chorus: 'Mo—lod-tsi!!! Well done, lads! We have won!!!'

Having exhausted their lungs, the fans started for the exit.

Soon the stadium was empty.

And only one supporter, a grey-haired man in a rumpled old-fashioned suit and with his head lowered onto his chest, was still sitting on the terrace as if he wanted to stay there for good.

Next to an empty seat

The best possible travel companion on a twenty-eight-hour-long Melbourne—London flight is an empty seat next to you.

VV was lucky enough to have one on the last leg from Singapore to Heathrow. At least, he was able to stretch a little and to quietly contemplate the gruesome personal journey he was about to complete.

It was his eighth trip from Europe to Australia (and vice versa) within less than two years—since his mother had been hospitalised with progressive dementia. With every fresh visit, her condition deteriorated.

While in Melbourne, VV went to her 'specialised psycho-geriatric ward', with an unlikely aboriginal name 'Namarra', as if to work. He stayed there all day among the screams and wails of Mum's fellow sufferers.

After several days, he would get used to them and would no longer be put off by the elderly woman called Rosa who spent her days walking around the ward, bumping into walls, furniture and other patients and—in a very loud and low, almost masculine, voice—conducting a 'dictation' for her invisible pupils in several languages—English, Polish, Russian: 'Tram-vai . . . Tram . . . vai. . . Yevrei . . . Yevrei . . . Doc-tor . . . Doc-tor . . .' And so on. All day long . . . A haunting, almost hypnotic, repetition.

The head nurse told VV that as a child Rosa had spent time in Auschwitz and then worked all her life as a primary school teacher.

Unlike VV's Mum, physically Rosa was still healthy and was a hazard for frailer patients during her all-day dictation rounds when she would sweep everything and everyone out of her way. (She ended up throwing VV's Mum out of her wheelchair one day.)

VV witnessed the very fast decline of an elderly Korean lady, who looked almost 'normal' when she was first admitted to Namarra and was saying something vaguely endearing in Korean (she spoke no English whatsoever) to a visiting child. Yet during his next visit six months later, she was reduced to a constantly screaming ball of pain wriggling in convulsions on the floor.

VV tried to take his Mum out of the ward as often as he could. Pushing the heavy and clumsy wheelchair in front of him, he took her on long walks in the permanently sleepy and ever deserted Melbourne suburb of South Caulfield. She was getting more and more wayward—like a child—asking him to take her back to Namarra (she was afraid of missing a meal). Yet the moment he wheeled her back inside, she would start demanding to be taken out again . . .

At times, VV couldn't cope. He would run out of the ward and head for the nearest 'hotel' (pub), trying to calm himself down with a glass or two of wine. Sitting outside a dodgy Turkish restaurant under a typically Australian chip-on-the-shoulder advertising banner 'European Women in the Kitchen', he would gulp his wine and drag on one cigarette after another before he felt ready to go back.

At times during these brief escapes, he would start having pangs of terrible guilt for not being there. He would then run back to Namarra only to realise that Mum had not noticed his absence at all and was in the same mood and posture as when he left her.

'Don't blame yourself!' the angelic Namarra nurses were telling him. 'Rimma's illness has nothing to do with you . . . And it's OK not to cope occasionally. We are professionally trained and still find it hard to cope sometimes.'

To calm down VV, they started inviting him out in the evenings.

He came to know them all rather well. It was shocking for him to learn that almost all of the psychiatric nurses—male and female—had shattered personal lives and were either already divorced (some of them more than once) or heading towards separation from their partners.

These superhumans were probably spending all their warmth and love on the patients (who often physically attacked them!) and had little left for themselves. They all adored their job and couldn't imagine doing anything else for a living.

They soon convinced VV (and he could see it himself) that the amount of time he spent with his Mum was not proportional to her feeling better. She was very much in her own world and was likely to feel even more agitated or distressed after a long spell with her son. They advised him to spend no more than three or four hours a day with her—better in the afternoon.

In the mornings, he was writing his book on European enclaves and after a quick lunch at the hospital canteen would go to see his Mum. She did seem calmer during these shorter visits—a fact that in its turn made VV feel guilty again.

Boarding a plane at Melbourne airport on the way back to Europe was therefore something of a relief, and VV was ashamed of himself for being unable not to feel it.

This time, however, the relief was mixed with fear and uncertainty about his own future.

Flying back 'home,' he did have a nasty premonition which proved right: on arrival in Edinburgh he realised he had no place he could come back to any more.

The real estate agent was glib and matter-of-fact. 'I'll need the address and phone of your next of kin,' he said, having shown VV around the quirkiest flat the latter had ever seen (that was probably why he decided to go for it): it had three (!) large bathrooms and only one pokey bedroom-cum-lounge-cum-living room.

'What for? To inform them in case I die?' VV asked with a cheerless cackle.
'Aye. You can laugh as much as you like, but someone of your age can keel over any time. We've just had a man even younger than you kicking the bucket in a flat of ours.'

VV shrugged and gave him the details of his eldest son, then living in Dublin.

Despite (or maybe because of) the three bathrooms to choose from, the flat was depressing, and VV tried to spend as little time in it as possible.
He also hated the thought of a darkly satisfied and omniscient I-told-you-so grin on the face of the estate agent on discovery of Vin's lifeless body on the lounge's linoleum-covered floor or, more likely, in one of the bathrooms.

Luckily, staying away from that triple-toileted diarrhoea sufferer's heaven was not hard, due to the nature of his job.

In between the assignments, he spent most of the time with the kids or typing away his copy in the Herald's small Edinburgh offices in George Street.

VV had always wanted to do a piece on Dounreay, a former nuclear power station in the north of Scotland whose continuing decommissioning had become a serious issue in Scottish life and politics.

His train to Thurso was to leave Waverley station in about an hour and he was tossing some last bits and bobs in his backpack ready to leave the flat when the phone rang.

He had a phobia of phone calls from childhood, and his first instinct was not to answer, but the thought that it could be something about the kids made him lift the receiver.

It was the Herald's senior executive, the same woman who had recently praised him as the paper's best writer and had questioned him on whether or not he was secretly planning to leave Scotland.
'We've just been taken over by an American conglomerate,' she said. 'The new owners demand major cost-cuttings. Your column is expensive, and we'll have to stop it as of next month.'

She was obviously expecting some reaction from VV: shouts of protest, even threats perhaps. But he stayed silent.
'It is nothing to do with you, believe me,' she added. 'But let me be honest with you: if we keep freelancers on contracts like yours, we'd have to cut our own jobs instead, and we don't want to do it!'
'Look, I can't talk now: my train to Thurso leaves from Waverley in half an hour. I still have a couple of columns to write and research.'

He had plenty of time to digest the shock. The seemingly endless journey from Edinburgh to Thurso took over nine hours. The train was dragging its wheels through a drab brown landscape that looked almost Martian. Grey satin daylight was lingering outside the train window until late.

It was May. It was drizzling.

At some point during the journey, VV realised with sudden clarity that he had lost everything again—a thought that was scary and strangely titillating both.

He was familiar with this ticklish standing-on-the-brink feeling from his previous crises, only this time the abyss in front of him appeared darker and deeper than ever before, for he had lost not just his job and his home, but his children too.
Or had he?

'I am going to show them that I am strong and will make these two last columns my best ones yet.' he thought and remembered the title of Yevtushenko's novel—*Don't Die Before You're Dead*.

The their journey was coming to an end, but he was still on the move, and that was all that mattered at the moment.

For as long as the journey went on, there was always hope.

. . . If columns could take dedications like books, I would have dedicated this one to my father—a nuclear physicist who died of the long-term effects of radiation in 1982 aged fifty-six.

Or, maybe, to both of my parents, who started their careers in a 'closed town' near Moscow in the early 1950s. Newly-married graduates of Kharkov University, they were dispatched to a secret facility, developing nuclear bombs (my mother was a chemical engineer there) in an unmapped and unnamed town of 40,000 people behind a concrete fence which no one could enter or leave without a special pass. The town was where I spent the first three years of my life.

During my visit to Dounreay—the site of decommissioning of what had been Scotland's nuclear power research and development station—I had frequent memory flashbacks to

Zagorsk, near which the 'secret town' of my early childhood was located (I knew it mostly from my mother's stories and notes), and to Chernobyl, which I visited with a Channel 4 TV crew in 1994.

Let me tell you straight away: Dounreay had very little in common with either of them, and any direct comparisons would be totally far-fetched and irrelevant.

On the other hand, as the son of a Doctor of Science, who died of radiation, and as someone who—most likely—got his wee share of it, too, I thought I could be excused such purely associative recollections, a chain reaction of memory, so to speak.

Caithness

'This is the end of the fifty-year-long experiment,' Colin Punler, communications manager of UKAEA Dounreay, told me from behind the wheel, when the site we were heading for first came into view. In the distance, I could see the golf-ball-shaped DFR (Dounreay Fast Reactor, also known as the Dome), constructed between 1955 and 1958 and closed down in 1977.

Colin said that the 'golf ball' would be the only structure left standing on the site after the end of decommissioning (about another fifty years—and four billion pounds): Historic Scotland was thinking of making it a listed building.

A computer-generated image of the fully decommissioned site, which I saw at the visitor centre, showed a giant one-hole 'golf course', with the white Dome ('golf ball') in the middle of an empty field.

We arrived at the check-point, where I was given a chance to flash my new British passport. A policeman was called to inspect my shoulder bag.

'Security state of vigilance Black Special' ran a sign at the site entrance. Colin assured me that, despite the sinister wording, it implied a pretty low level of security.

The barbed-wire fence around the site's perimeter was lined with heavy boulders ('to prevent trucks from crashing through' in Colin's words). From within, the plant resembled a huge construction site—ironic if we remembered that in reality it was the spot of Scotland's biggest ever **deconstruction**. 'What you see is in fact a large chemical works, complicated by radioactivity,' said my escort. And I suddenly realised why it all looked (or rather felt) somewhat disturbing to me.

Chernobyl (nine years earlier)

We were unable to obtain cover for that particular day of the shoot from any UK insurance broker.

At the entrance to the 10 km 'interior' (heavily contaminated) zone, we were offered sets of baggy 'protective' clothing, which were merely used battle fatigues. We were given face masks to protect our lungs.

Our guide cheerfully informed us that, within the exclusion zone, the level of radiation was thousands of times higher than the accepted safe maximum. We exchanged black jokes and nervous cackles, made even more uneasy by the knowledge that there had been an even bigger radioactive leak the day before our visit.

Chernobyl, we were given to understand, leaked all the time, yet Sasha, a young local dosimetrist (a specialist in radiation measuring) assigned to our film crew, was not wearing a mask—in a gesture of youthful bravado. With our every step towards the leaking reactor, his bulky antediluvian Geiger counter showed great jumps in the levels of background radiation.

I couldn't tear my eyes from the faded slogan crowning the building next to it: 'Communism Will Win!' Several times they had tried to paint that tragically ironic slogan over, but the stubborn white letters were still clearly visible through layers of paint.

Caithness

I came to like Colin for his openness and constant readiness to be confronted with 'difficult' questions.

He was willing to acknowledge that the background radiation levels around Dounreay were slightly higher than elsewhere in Scotland, yet not high enough to cause any health concerns.

He was prepared to talk at length about the 1977 explosion in the notorious radioactive waste shaft, about the increased incidence of childhood leukaemia around the site (allegedly not connected with radiation), about the recent suspected contamination of several workers with uranium waste, about the radioactive particles that were still being found (at an increasing rate) on the rocks and beaches around Dounreay, calling it all 'a sad legacy for many years to come'.

'We don't take part in all these pro—and anti-nuclear energy debates,' he told me earlier. 'We simply have to do our job—to sweep the place clean.'

Unlike Colin, an ex-journalist who came to Dounreay several years ago, Alistair Fraser, who had worked at the plant since 1956, had every reason to feel bitter.

'The first workers and scientists who came here in 1955 were a special lot—full of energy and pioneering spirit. They had to design and build everything themselves, they created the basics of nuclear technology, which was then perceived in a positive light. When the government decided to close the station, we felt demoralised and bitterly disappointed.'

This disappointment could be well understood: Dounreay

had totally transformed—one could even say 'ennobled'—the area.

The population of nearby Thurso, a once godforsaken outpost, had trebled within several years, and its cultural and employment potential had grown a hundredfold thanks to the 'atomics' (the locals soon stopped referring to the newcomers as 'dirty atomics' as they initially had).

I could also understand the 'pioneering spirit', so familiar to me from my parents' stories. They were all young scientists, and the job was so new, so challenging, and so absorbing—they couldn't quite acknowledge the danger, even when their comrades were literally dying before their eyes from overdoses (none of my father's colleagues had lived to see his or her sixtieth birthday).

Yet people like Geoffrey Minter, a local landowner, would probably wish the station had never come to Dounreay in the first place. The golden beaches of Sandside Bay near the village of Reay were part of his 11,000-acre estate. They were also the places where radioactive particles had been found consistently since 1984. Mr Minter told me that his two dogs, who liked to run on the sand, 'died of tumours'.

'The beach is indeed monitored for twelve days a month, but what we need is not occasional scanning, but thorough and consistent cleaning.'

He was now seeking a court order to urge UKAEA to—literally—clean up its act. Colin Punler, on the other hand, assured me that the facility did not have enough resources to provide for constant monitoring and cleaning.

Issues and controversies, mixed with radioactive particles, were piled up high on that pristine-looking beach, where the owners did not walk their dogs any longer.

Chernobyl (nine years earlier)

Pripyat, the nearest town to Chernobyl, which housed 50,000 people in 1986, was dead and empty. It was evacuated in one day, thirty-six hours after the explosion at reactor number four, though for most evacuees it was already too late.

The town was eerie.

The motor of our camera whirred in utter silence. Flowerbeds had vanished beneath thick, eight-year-old vegetation.

In the town funfair, nestling between abandoned high-rise apartment blocks, the wind slowly propelled a rusty merry-go-round. Here was an overturned go-kart; there a broken LP with 1986 Soviet musical hits trampled in the ground.

Walking around this dead town one could almost feel the radiation lingering in the still, jelly-like air.

Silence and death. It was like trudging through the ruins of my childhood.

Scotland

'It is only by good fortune that we didn't have an accident like Chernobyl in Dounreay,' Lorraine Mann, Scotland's leading anti-nuclear campaigner, told me.

I knew, of course, that the types of reactors in Dounreay and Chernobyl were totally different, the former being many, many times safer. 'We all live here ourselves, so it is quite obvious that we are trying to decommission Dounreay as safely as possible,' I was assured more than once while in Caithness.

And yet even the tiniest possibility of Thurso—a friendly windswept town in the middle of great northern nothingness, the town that I had come to enjoy—being turned into a Scottish

Pripyat gave me shivers. As well as the already existing reality, when 40 per cent of the UK's nuclear waste was being routinely dumped on Scotland's territory.

I was ready to agree with Lorraine, who asserted that nuclear energy as such, being at first hailed as progressive, had proved hugely expensive, contaminating and leading up a blind alley.

Call me a retrograde, but I would have happily written this column in candlelight if only my Dad—still 'just' 77—were peeping lovingly over my shoulder.

'Geometry of losses'

On return to Edinburgh, he realised that he wouldn't be able to afford his three-bathroom kitchenette for much longer.

He had no savings or assets of his own (except for books) and had only just paid off the last of his debts incurred during the previous crisis. With some money still owed to him by the *Herald*, he could get by for another month or so.

Passing by a small office under the sign 'Edinburgh City Council Advice Shop' one day, he decided that advice was exactly what he needed in the given situation.

His book *Dreams on Hitler's Couch* was prominently displayed in the window of a Blackwell's bookshop next door. VV thought it was a good sign and ventured inside the Advice Shop.

He had to wait in a queue. Still in denial, he took out a notebook and began scribbling down in it—his favourite, time-tested ruse of turning life into research:

'Advice Shop. The titillating self-destructive temptation to reach an absolute brink and to see what happens. Am close to it (the brink) now.

Like at a school exam: knowing the answer to the question but—driven by the spirit of contradiction—or whatever else that internal little devil may be called—staying mum to see what happens . . .

Destitute, sullen faced people in the queue leafing through dog-eared back copies of 'Hello' magazine: posh celebs, plush interiors . . . I used to be there too. Am I now on the other side of the fence?

How is it all going to end? . . . Interesting . . .

I can overhear some ear-grating, as if prickly, words: 'homeless assessment', 'sequestration' . . .

'Sequestration'—what a disgusting, nasty-sounding term. Like a cockroach stirring its antennae . . .'

An agreeable woman behind the counter happened to have his books and columns.

'Do you realise that you are effectively homeless, Vitali?' she said, having listened to Vin's story.

'Well, not quite . . .' he tried to object.

She showed him a stack of drab, badly printed pamphlets with fuzzy photos of grey council estate towers in the Edinburgh suburbs he had never heard about: Duddington, Craiglockart.

He looked up and noticed a pink poster on the wall above the agreeable woman's desk:

'TEMPORARY ACCOMMODATION
FOR HOMELESS PEOPLE.
**Due to the high level of demand we are finding it very difficult to provide temporary accommodation for everyone who needs it. As a result we are having to use B&B accommodation outside Edinburgh. We apologise for the inconvenience and problems that this may cause.
Homelessness services'**

He felt as if he was standing on the threshold of a totally new world that was entirely alien to him.

He had had a similar feeling when trying to absorb his first house in Australia, with an indoor swimming pool, a state-of-

330

the-art 'barbie' and a lemon tree in the back yard, that he was able to acquire after just a year of very hard work in Melbourne: writing books, columns for the Melbourne Age, regularly appearing on radio and TV (and publishing, his first book *Special Correspondent* sold to a number of foreign countries).

He couldn't remember how much he had earned during that first year, but the tax he had to pay at the end of it amounted to nearly 40,000 Australian dollars.

That Melbourne bungalow had also felt alien, not part of his world, albeit for entirely different reasons: he felt uncomfortable about the prosperity that had come much too soon, as if it was someone else's life he had nicked inadvertently and had to be living from then on.

It was someone else's life too that was staring at him from the pink poster on the Advice Shop wall.

'Apply now! When your lease expires in a couple of weeks, we'll put you up at a B&B first and then move you to a flat for the homeless,' the woman pointed at the stack of brochures on her desk. 'You can ask for a two-bedroom flat which would allow the children to come and visit you.'

He never gained enough courage (or was it cheek?) to apply and started a new notebook instead.

The first entry in it was a four-liner poem by Joseph Brodsky:

The square of my rented room. The duvet made of canvas
Geometry of losses is simple to the point of madness.

In Russian the poem rhymed beautifully and sounded like one melodious musical movement.

The next entry was: 'The bland, as if extinguished, faces of train commuters . . .'

It was probably made on a train to Glasgow . . .

And on the next page: 'Feeling is the main thing'—a logo on top of a condom-vending machine in a pub'.

Life was offering him another unique opportunity of in-depth research into the human condition. He was saying to himself how lucky he was to have got such a chance.

What does it feel like to be homeless? You have to experience it yourself to understand and to be able to write about it . . .

At times though, a rather treacherous thought occurred to him: wasn't he subconsciously trying to undermine himself to generate material for his future books? He certainly wasn't doing that deliberately, but could it be that he was in fact driven by the power of his subconscious writer's mind?

He soon had a chance to share his deliberations about that with the whole nation: he was invited to appear on Radio 4's *Reporters' Notes*—a summertime version of *Desert Island Discs*.

It was perhaps the most prestigious thing he had ever done. What worried him a little was a touch of finality attached to it: you were supposed to tell your whole (!) life story summing it up with seven pieces of music of your choice.

They bought him a first-class Caledonian Sleeper return ticket to his beloved home town—London—where the recording was to take place.

He specifically asked for a sleeper ticket, for he had always felt very much at home on an overnight train. He adored sleeper trains—part and parcel of his Soviet childhood and youth.

Being back in London was like true homecoming. The train arrived at Euston very early. With several hours to spare before the recording, he went to Highgate Wood.

There he lay down on the grass behind the Old Cricket Pavilion and closed his eyes. He suddenly felt very tired.

Trees were rustling above his head as if whispering something comforting and soothing, maybe even humming softly the seven melodies he had chosen to 'illustrate' his life:

Beethoven's Moonlight Sonata

He first heard it at the age of six. One morning, he woke up to its beautiful haunting sounds. The Sonata was played by an old piano tuner sitting behind an old Blüthner grand piano brought from World War II as a trophy by Little Vitya's granddad. That behemoth of a musical instrument took up half of the room where Vitya slept (the room also doubled as the lounge room at his grandparents' flat).

Apart from Vitya's mum, who tickled the ivories as a girl, no one in the family could play it. But his grandparents had a secret (from Little Vitya) plan to cajole him into learning to play it. That was why the piano tuner was called in that morning and that was why he was playing the Moonlight Sonata as a test. The sound was far from perfect, and certain keys got stuck from time to time, but for Little Vitya it was the most heavenly piece of music he had ever heard. The harmony of the Moonlight Sonata impressed him so much that nine years later, when already a published young poet, he wrote lyrics (in Russian of course) for it.

> . . . You are alone. Only the moon is crying silently with starry tears. And the Milky Way glistens and rustles in the dark like a night-time stream . . . The piano is playing . . . oozing sadness. . . and the sombre melody is lighting up the sky. . .

The Sonata's every single movement was rhythmically matched with Russian words.

Several listeners to the programme wrote to him later that they were shedding tears while listening to his Russian lyrics to the accompaniment of the music and followed by their rendition in English.

It would be fair to say that it was the Moonlight Sonata

that—for better or worse—had made VV a poet, having eventually turned Little Vitya into Victor R.

His own music lessons that he started taking at the age of seven lasted for two weeks only: his teacher, Nadezhda Adolfovna, an old Jewish woman from their block of flats, had a nasty habit of hitting him on his fingertips with a wooden ruler whenever he pressed a wrong key. Vitya was secretly sure she was a clandestine daughter of Adolf Hitler (that explained her rather rare in Ukraine patronymic—'Adolfovna', literally daughter of Adolf). After the third or fourth lesson, he would simply run away and hide in the Yar. The truth was revealed very soon, of course. But contrary to his expectations, grandma and granddad did not tell him off and never sent him back to Nadezhda Adolfovna's one-bedroom flat where she kept torturing other kids.

The power of that childhood experience was such that even now the tips of VV's fingers would start aching occasionally at the sound of a piano.

Verdi's March from 'Aida'

This piece of music was, curiously, a reminder of the late 1980s in Moscow, when suddenly, as a result of *glasnost*, some previously banned books were published. One of them was Mikhail Bulgakov's *Heart of a Dog*, a satirical novel about an agreeable stray dog, Sharik, who undergoes an operation and gets transformed into a horrible little man, Sharikov—a drunk, a womaniser and a Bolshevik (communist). The novel's protagonist, Professor Preobrazhensky, was a huge fan of Verdi and would often attend performances of *Aida* at the Bolshoi.

The novel appeared for the first time in an obscure magazine, *Literary Kirghizstan*, (in the same issue where several of VV's own short stories and poems were published too!) and was then adapted for stage by *Moscow Young Spectator's Theatre*. VV went to see the adaptation with Natasha, his wife, and felt like pinching himself all through the hilarious and thoroughly anti-Soviet performance accompanied by musical themes from 'Aida', the very sounds of which—both reassuring and disturbing—became a symbol both of changing times and bitter disappointments to follow: it was only a couple of years before the sheer emptiness behind Gorbachev's rhetoric would become apparent and he would have to defect from the still oppressive USSR after a clash with the still omnipotent KGB.

One of the most famous bits of *Heart of a Dog* picked up and repeated by intellectuals all over the country was an extract from a dinner conversation between Preobrazhensky (or 'Philipp Phillippovich' as he is often referred to in the novel) and his assistant—Dr Ivan Arnolcovich Bormental. The latter tries to justify certain negative goings on in the old Moscow block of flats where they live, like disappearance of flowers from the landings and galoshes from the downstairs stand, by the general 'collapse ' of the country as a result of the recent Bolshevik revolution':

> 'No,' objected Philipp Philippovich . . . 'What is this collapse of yours? An old woman with a stick? A witch who has knocked out all the window panes and put out all the lamps? It just doesn't exist at all. What are you implying with that word?' Philipp Philippovich enquired furiously of an unfortunate cardboard duck hanging upside down next to the sideboard and answered on its behalf himself: 'This is what: if I, instead of operating every evening, begin singing in a choir in my apartment, I'll start to suffer a collapse. If I, going into the lavatory, begin—forgive the expression— urinating outside the toilet bowl, and Zina [his servant: VV] and Darya Petrovna [his cook: VV] do the same, a collapse will start in the lavatory. Therefore the collapse is not in WCs, but in heads . . .'

Mikhail Bulgakov was one of VV's two most favourite authors of all time (alongside George Orwell). 'Manuscripts don't burn,' he claimed famously in his epic novel *The Master and Margarita*. The protagonist, 'the Master' is a struggling author, who—in a fit of despair—burns the manuscript of his novel in a stove, only to have it returned to him later by 'Woland'—a kindly Satan-like figure—with the pronouncement: '**Manuscripts don't burn.**'

Had Bulgakov not written anything else but just this three-word sentence, he would have still been a great writer.

'Manuscripts don't burn.' This phrase became a popular saying in the Soviet Union. It was used especially in reference to writers whose works were considered dangerous by the government. Many of these writers—like Solzhenitsyn and Bulgakov himself!—never wrote down some of their stories or poems. They memorised their works so that the police would not find copies. This method helped preserve their stories for years. As a result, 'manuscripts don't burn' because no matter what happens to the written version of the work, it will always exist in the mind of its author.

In a topsy-turvy world of Soviet reality, where one of the two main story lines of *The Master and Margarita* was set, Woland, the Satan, therefore came to represent a virtuous force opposed to the truly 'devilish' official regime.

Rereading *The Master and Margarita*—in Russian and in English, in an outstanding Michael Glenny's translation, had become of VV's survival gimmicks. The novel, which he knew almost by heart, had never failed to restore faith and hope in him.

'How sad, ye gods, how sad the world is at evening, how mysterious the mists over the swamps. You will know it when you have wandered astray in those mists, when you have suffered greatly before dying, when you have walked through the world carrying an unbearable burden. You know it too when you are weary and ready to leave this earth without regret; its mists, its swamps and its rivers; ready to give yourself into the arms of death with a light heart, knowing that death alone can comfort you.'

I seldom part with a tiny the size of a cigarette box, Russian-language copy that I was given at a special warehouse of books to be smuggled into the Soviet Union in New York in 1990.

Yes, miniature copies of *The Master and Margarita*, printed on semi-transparent tissue paper, were smuggled into the USSR together with the Bibles and were confiscated in their hundreds by the Soviet customs.

Bulgakov himself never saw *The Master and Margarita*, his life's main book (which he had been writing for over twenty years) published: it first came out in the USSR many years after his death in 1940. It would have been very gratifying for him to learn that his novel became such an anathema to the Soviet regime—together with the Bible.

One of VV's proudest moments was when he found out that his book *Special Correspondent*, a copy of which he gave a Moscow friend who visited him in London, was confiscated by the Soviet customs at Sheremet'yevo airport.

In the late 1980s, I was able to trace my own, even if flimsy, 'connection' with Bulgakov.

The Master and Margarita only saw the light due to the heroic efforts of the writer's third wife and then widow Yelena Sergeevna Shilovskaya—the prototype of Margarita in the novel (Bulgakov saw himself as the Master). After the writer's death in 1940, Yelena Sergeevna (who had outlived her husband by thirty-one years) had been tirelessly campaigning for publication of Bulgakov's works, particularly of his main novel, *The Master and Margarita*. She had finally managed to persuade Alexander Tvardovsky, the progressive editor of the 'thick' literary monthly '*Noviy Mir*' to publish the novel (in a heavily censored and shortened version) in the late 1960s.

My 1980s editor at *Krokodil* magazine, Eduard Ivanovich Poliansky (who told me this story), then worked as a courier boy at '*Noviy Mir*' and was asked by Tvardovsky to phone Yelena Sergeevna at home and tell her to come to the office to read the proofs.

'I'll be there in a jiffy,' she said being absolutely thrilled by the success of her twenty-eight-year-long struggle for the novel's publication.

'She lived at the other end of Moscow—at least an hour away by public transport, but somehow managed to get to '*Noviy Mir*' ten minutes after I spoke with her at home,' Eduard Ivanovich told me. 'We could not believe our eyes when we saw her on our doorstep.'

'How did you get here so fast, Yelena Sergeevna?' we asked her.

'I flew on a broomstick of course!' she replied. 'Have you forgotten that I am a witch?'

In the novel, Woland makes Margarita a witch and invites her to be the queen of his annual satanic ball.

Yelena Sergeevna was seventy-five years old then.

No wonder Bulgakov loved her so much.

When he was dying, he asked her to bring the manuscript of *The Master and Margarita* to his bed.

Bulgakov's last words addressed to Yelena Sergeevna, his Margarita, were: 'You are everything for me . . . You are my whole world . . . I love you, I adore you! My love, my wife, my life! I saw a dream yesterday: we were alone with you in the world . . .'

And then he said: 'Light!' It was his final word . . .

But our 'connection' doesn't end here.

The other day on a train to London I sat next to young Eduard Ivanovich Poliansky, my *Krokodil* editor!

The resemblance of the long-nosed young man (no older than twenty-five) sitting opposite me on the train and reading *Metro* to Poliansky (who should be in his late sixties now) was striking.

I was close to starting a conversation with the young man, but didn't . . . What could I say? 'Is it you who were my middle-aged *Krokodil* editor in Moscow twenty-odd years ago?'

For all forty minutes of the train journey from Letchworth Garden City to London Kings Cross I couldn't stop looking at the courier boy who had met and spoken to the love of Bulgakov's life—Moscow witch Yelena Sergeevna Shilovskaya!

Miracles did happen routinely in the surreal world of *The Master and Margarita* . . .

Abba's 'Money, Money, Money'

In Vin's mind, this uncomplicated and importunate ear-worm of a tune had become firmly associated with Australia. Why?

The explanation lies in a tacky 1970s Australian movie-musical *Abba*. The film, with no plot as such, was but a chronicle of Abba's tour of Oz. He watched it in the plywood shed of the 'Park' cinema in Kharkov's Gorky Park 'of Culture and Relaxation' next to which he used to live.

The picture was bleak and fuzzy. It was freezing and draughty inside the cinema. But VV did not notice any of those. Nor did he care about the music or breathtakingly short skirts of Abba's pretty female soloists. He was glued to the time-battered screen offering him his first ever glimpse of Australia—the land no less mysterious and remote than Lake Titikaka, the Brahmaputra River or indeed Venus or Mars . . .

A different planet.

Vin was unable to tear his gaze off the colourfully dressed Australian crowd. When the camera did close-ups of Abba's audiences and separate spectators—men, women or children, it became obvious they all had one thing in common—a relaxed and entirely carefree 'no worries' expression on their sun-tanned faces.

A seal of freedom as opposed to the seal of oppression, carried by VV and his compatriots.

The movie, or rather, the Australians in it, impressed him so much that he was unable to think of anything else but Australia—that sun-drenched land of peace and plenty—as it appeared to him from the screen for weeks to come.

That movie did play a role in his decision to emigrate to Australia after six months in London following his defection, the decision that later he came to regard as his life's biggest mistake.

'Lilliburlero'—the BBC World Service signature tune

VV had been an avid (and clandestine!) listener to the BBC World Service since the age of eleven or twelve.

The station's English language broadcasts were not as heavily jammed in the USSR as those of the BBC's Russian Service or Radio Liberty, and after midnight the reception could sometimes be almost perfect.

The World Service broadcasts were essential for polishing up his English, but they were much more than that: they had helped him mould an outlook of the world which was very different and in many ways totally opposite to the stale dogmas preached by Soviet officialdom.

In short, he was a BBC World Service self-confessed addict. The problem was he was unable to share this addiction with anyone, including his parents, except for his best friend and fellow anglophile Sasha Kas'yanov. They often listened in together and even tried to imitate their favourite BBC presenters.

To be interviewed by the BBC World Service flagship programme 'Outlook' during his first visit to Britain in 1988 was like a dream coming true.

'You won't believe, but I've been your fan since the age of twelve,' he told John Tidmarsh, the programme's veteran presenter.

'I didn't realise I was that old,' said John.

'You are not, it's I who is still fairly young,' retorted VV, who was then thirty-four.

Having settled in Australia in the early 1990s, Vin was finding it hard to get used to the insularity and narrow-mindedness of the country's mainstream media. Satellite TV was then banned down under, the Internet didn't exist, and tuning to overseas radio stations during the day was problematic: the reception was normally poor, and all one could hear clearly were the muffled crackles of space that sounded like shuffles of a distant surf against the sand.

Yet at night the reception would improve dramatically, and VV made sure he stayed awake well past midnight to tune to the BBC World Service.

. . . Until one day (or rather one night) he was struck by the sheer irony of what he was doing—as if he had never left the USSR! He realised that—if you overlooked his bungalow with an indoor swimming pool and well-stocked (normally even overstocked) shops and restaurants—he had simply swapped one Iron Curtain for another.

And if the first one, made of the loose and badly fitting old bricks of political dogmas, was at least theoretically negotiable (one could ram through it with a truck, fly over it in a balloon—like so many escapees from East Germany, or walk around it, i.e. defect—as he did himself), the one built of new and shiny Aussie dollar coins was equally (if not more) impregnable.

It was then—during one such stuffy Australian night, with possums pounding the roof of his house with their tiny feet—boom, boom, boom—that he decided to leave Australia and to return back to Europe.

Lilliburlero—the BBC World Service signature tune—was oozing from his transistor radio, lighting up the pitch dark Australian night.

Just like the Moonlight Sonata of his childhood many years before.

Chants of Mt Athos monks

Mount Athos—semi-independent republic of Orthodox monks in the North of Greece—was one of the most amazing places Vin had visited in his post-Australian journeys that took him to over sixty countries of the world.

Because VV had never been religious himself, Mount Athos could not count as one of his 'foreign homecomings', yet while there he definitely felt a touch of something almost divine, well, if not exactly divine then definitely spiritual.

That 'something' emanated not so much from the ancient monasteries and the azure Aegean Sea as from the monks themselves.

VV was able to share their frugal meals and to attend their liturgies. The monks spent at least eight hours a day in prayers which at times resembled a seemingly endless, yet surprisingly harmonious—to the point of becoming hypnotic—a cappella song. He liked being mildly hypnotised by these chants which allowed him to forget—at least for a while—that most of the beliefs of his childhood and youth had been mercilessly shattered by the system under which he had the misfortune to grow up and that his only faith since then had been 'the refusal to give up'.

Having visited Mount Athos twice, VV was both eager and somewhat reluctant to go there again, for according to a monastic legend, he who visited the Holy Mountain for the third time never came back and stayed there for good.

Preservation Hall jazz band, New Orleans

It was in the plywood shed (yes, just like that of the 'Park' cinema of his youth, only smaller) of the Preservation Hall jazz band that VV was dancing with his notebook while in pre-hurricane-Katrina New Orleans, his favourite place in the USA.

The musicians, all in their seventies and eighties, would routinely nod off inbetween the numbers, but would then wake up to produce a fiery celebration of music and *joie de vivre* reflecting the irrepressible spirit of New Orleans, which celebrates life even after death.

To VV therefore, the cemeteries of New Orleans were anything but dull. He was quite taken by the way a caretaker (or the 'director of operations'—her modern PC job title) at St Louis Cemetery No. 1 greeted a funeral procession at the cemetery gates—with a broad smile on her face. Like everything else, they seemed to take death easy in Big Easy, where it was not unusual to have jazz played or a cocktail party held among the double-decker tombs.

'New Orleans is a rough place, but my cemetery is safe,' the same caretaker told Vin with a pride which reminded VV of the dubious Soviet-style poster he once saw in the office of a Moscow graveyard—'Let Us Turn Our Cemetery into Muscovites' Favourite Resting Place'.

The plush Bultman's Funeral Home in the prestigious Garden District of New Orleans (later totally ravaged by the hurricane) was often hired out for fun gatherings, musical recitals and business functions. Having a company's board meeting at a funeral home would be bizarre anywhere else, but not in Big Easy. 'People come to us to have fun,' a black-clad Bultman's official assured VV with a professional sombre grin.

In 1980, a businessman from Houston, Texas, chose New Orleans' Lafayette Cemetery as the site for his wedding. The ceremony was held in one of the cemetery aisles, while a lone trumpet played 'Summertime'.

The bride and groom, both married previously, told the graveyard superintendent (executive director of operations?) that they had come to New Orleans to bury their past.

Indeed, there's no better place to re-charge yourself with hope and optimism. *'Laissez Les Bons Temps Rouler'* ('Let the good times roll') is an old Cajun expression which remains New Orleans' main (and only) rule of life.

No hurricane—real or metaphoric—is capable of destroying it.

'Little Brass Band of Hope' by Bulat Okudzhava

That was the only tune out of the seven chosen by VV to 'illustrate' his life that was not to be found in the extensive BBC sound archives.

Written and performed by a famous Russian/Soviet poet and bard of Georgian extraction, Bulat Okudzhava, 'The Little Military Band of Hope' was chosen to sum up his philosophy and his whole outlook on life. The choice couldn't have been better, even if VV had to translate a couple of melodious, beautifully sung stanzas for his listeners:

'At the times of storms, at the times of troubles, when raindrops made of lead were hitting our backs without mercy; and all commanders lost their voices, the Little Brass Band of Hope with Love as a Conductor took over from them . . .'

'In the middle of the battle, with all soldiers wounded or dead, the Little Military Brass Band of Hope conducted by Love keeps playing notwithstanding, because it is in an eternal collusion with humankind.'

'It is very hard to interpret poetry,' VV said to Emily, the presenter. The recording was almost over.

'Would you like to go back?' was her last question.
'I don't believe in great comebacks,' he replied. 'What's the point? One has to keep moving on . . .'

In one of the endless corridors of Broadcasting House, Vin bumped into an old acquaintance of his, a Radio 4 producer whom he hadn't seen for many years.

'Where is home now, Vitali?' he asked him with a grin.
'I don't know. It looks like I don't have a home any more,' VV replied and briefly explained his situation.

Why did he do that? Was it because he had just shared his whole life with the nation on the radio (or so it felt)?

'But this is horrible!' the other man exclaimed. 'We must do something about it and we will.'

VV never heard from him again of course.

In the months to come he would get used to a similar reaction from many people—friends (luckily, not all of them) and strangers. They recoiled from him as if he were the carrier of an infection that could affect their own life and well-being.

But he had drafted his course himself.

He had to keep moving on.

Back in Edinburgh, it was the annual festivals time. In one of the continuing ironies of his predicament, VV was asked to give a talk at the Book Festival. He accepted if only for the sake of the £150-pound fee: he had to count every penny from now on.

As a Book Festival participant, he was also invited to the Festival Garden Party and to a reception at the Consulate General of Norway, both of which he attended if only to have a free meal.

Inside the Festival's Writers' Tent, he bumped into his old friend, best-selling novelist Douglas Kennedy, whose books had always given VV support at the time of crisis, for they were all essentially about survival. Douglas signed his latest book for VV calling him 'a survivor and a friend' and that helped Vin to restore a bit of inner strength.

ST: Douglas Kennedy's novels—particularly, *The Dead Heart*, *The Big Picture* (my absolute favourite), *The Job* and *Temptation* (the hero is a writer) affirm—in Douglas's inimitable unputdownable manner—that there's no such thing as a totally hopeless situation, no matter how dire the state you are presently in may appear. I unreservedly recommend them to anyone who has found oneself in what seems like a terminal impasse.

That reassuring meeting with Douglas led to a couple of welcome developments.

His old friends Dea and Kevin—both writers—came to the Fringe Festival from London. Having learned of VV's situation, they invited him to stay in their empty cottage in Folkestone, Kent, for a nominal rent.

'You can stay there for as long as you like!' Kevin assured him.

That was precisely what VV needed to hear.

Being so far away from the kids was a downside, but for lack of better (or any other, to be honest) offers he accepted with gratitude.

He consoled himself with the thought that no matter how far Kent was from Edinburgh, it was still nothing compared to the distance between London and Melbourne which used to separate him from his eldest boy for a number of years and had still failed to affect their bond.

His tested 'scale of comparison' proved helpful again.

The next challenge was how to relocate himself and his precious books from Edinburgh to Kent—a seemingly irresolvable problem.

Yet, as often happens, one good thing triggers another.

By then VV was staying with a friend from the Herald who volunteered to put him up for a couple of weeks (his books were already in storage). It was next to the friend's house that he spotted an old, yet not too decrepit-looking, jalopy of a Honda station wagon, with 'B' number plates and a 'For Sale' sign on the windscreen. The owner, an old Italian lady, who for years had only used the car to do her weekly shopping, was happy to let him have it for three hundred quid.

It was VV's last bit of cash, albeit the Herald still owed him for his submitted and yet unpublished last column, but the bargain was too good to refuse. The Honda's speedometer showed that in all its twenty years of existence it had hardly covered 40,000 miles. Despite its tired looks, its heart (the engine) was still full of life.

Andrei, VV's five-year-old boy, fell in love with the car at first sight and christened it 'super jalopy'. 'Daddy, can't you park 'super jalopy' next to our house, put the back seats down and sleep in it?' he kept asking. 'Then I'd be able to see you whenever I want and we could still go for walks and do fun things together. I could also come to visit you in the car, and you could read to me there . . .'

It was physically painful to be leaving his little ones behind, even if for a short time, before he gained enough money to come back for a visit, but Vin had no choice: there was nothing left for him to do in Edinburgh.

Besides, Folkestone was not that far from his beloved, almost native, London where he still had lots of contacts who remembered him from his columns, books, radio and TV appearances (or so he thought). Being jobless and homeless in Edinburgh was not going to help either himself or his kids, who would hate to see him ruined and miserable.

On his last day in Edinburgh, he received a peculiar postcard from London—with a coloured view of pre-revolutionary Kiev. Sent by Wendy Bracewell, Professor of the School of Slavonic & East European Studies at UCL, it asked VV's permission to have his books—*Borders Up!* in particular—studied and put on the School's curriculum as part of UCL's 'East & West Through Travel Writing' Course.

It was raining on the day his massively overloaded (with books) 'super jalopy' crawed out of Edinburgh.

And just like in the famous poem by Paul Verlaine, *'il pleure dans mons coeur comme it pleut sur la ville . . .'*, it was raining inside VV's heart too.

Contrary to the *Herald's* front-page promises, VV *did not* have enough time to 'uncover Scotland', but he did manage to 'uncover' a bit of himself.

. . . Life is like one long train journey.

The train is chugging forward along the tracks, its wheels rattling—clickety-clack—on the points of days and weeks. It whooshes past the whistle-stops of childhood and youth. It slows down at the station of maturity, and there, on the hazy horizon, one can already discern the sad blinking lights of the terminal.

Every journey has its beginning and its end—a rule that applies in equal measure to my six-month exploration of Scotland. It was promised at the start that I was going to 'uncover Scotland' for the Herald readers. I am not sure if I have succeeded in the 'uncovering', but if you think that I have managed to lift the lid even slightly, it would make me feel more than happy.

I have criss-crossed Scotland many times over—by bus, car, boat, train and even plane. Yes, yours is a big, little country—a realisation that struck me after an hour-and-something flight from Edinburgh to Shetland, or—particularly—after an eight-hour train journey from Waverley to Thurso.

Trains were by far my main means of transport, and, looking back, I see my Scottish wanderings as largely a train journey.

In one of my first columns, I compared Scotland to a driverless locomotive. Six months and one Scottish Executive later, I feel like modifying this metaphor by using a true episode from my travels, when an Edinburgh—Glasgow shuttle got stuck at Falkirk High—and then backed all the way down to Waverley, the explanation being that the driver had made a 'wrong turn'.

This is how I see Scotland now: a train shuttle that went halfway towards the junction of independence, but then, due to uncertain and inexperienced driving, made a wrong turn and was forced to reverse to where it had started from.

The real-life—as opposed to metaphorical—Edinburgh-Glasgow shuttle was probably my most frequently used train. Connecting Scotland's two main cities, it too served as a moveable (as well as moving) bridge across the age-long 'great divide' between them.

To me, it was also a link between two different ways of life—friendliness and standoffishness, openness and obscurity, authenticity and pretence, soul and soullessness (I don't need to tell you which is which).

I used to particularly enjoy taking the last train from Glasgow leaving Queen Street at 11.30p.m. and arriving in Edinburgh fifty minutes later—at the very start of a new day. Its passengers, compared to those on earlier shuttles, were less stressed, less sober, and never in a rush, for where could one possibly hurry to at midnight?

They were travellers—not just commuters.

It so happened that the midnight Glasgow—Edinburgh shuttle took me on my column's very last research journey.

Glasgow Queen Street-Falkirk High

My carriage welcomes me with a strong smell of stale fish-and-chips (the stench itself probably contains more calories than a 'healthy' lunch of bread roll and tuna salad): almost everyone is indulging in the favourite Scottish pastime—stuffing oneself with fast food.

The good thing, however, is that, unlike daytime shuttle carriages, with their taciturn and businesslike 'mind-the-gap' attitude, this one is chatty and vociferous.

'Would you like a chip?' I am asked by a kindly, ruddy-faced man sitting opposite.

'Thank you, I have just had dinner,' I say.

I am coming back to Edinburgh after an evening at Glasgow's Cafe *Cossachok* ('Little Cossack')—Scotland's first and only Russian restaurant, doubling as an art gallery and a concert hall. I stumbled upon it in my six-month-long look-out for 'Scotland's best-kept secret'—a cliché that I had heard applied to dozens of sites and places—from the cold war 'secret bunker' near St Andrews to the Court of the Lord Lyon in Edinburgh.

I, myself, had reason to believe that Scotland's best-kept secret was the seemingly unremarkable Quids In discount shop in Edinburgh's Princes Street, where they sold excellent reading glasses without prescription and for a mere 99p a pair (I was tempted to buy dozens of them—enough to open a discount shop of my own): it saved me countless trips back to my flat, where I would routinely forget my 'main' £100 ones.

Cossachok was the most unusual Russian restaurant I had ever been to. And I have been to many. Matrioshka Receptions in Melbourne was an archetypal one. Run by Lialia, a roly-poly Chicken Kiev-shaped veteran of Soviet public catering, it offered a set meal of seventeen courses—a clever gimmick, for even the biggest of gluttons were never able to cope with more than seven, and therefore the remaining ten never needed to be served (or cooked), yet were duly included in the bill. It also offered fiery and soul-piercing 'go-and-get-yourself-into-trouble' live music and wild dancing—as if there were no tomorrow.

Cossachok was different in everything, except perhaps for the food—abundant and authentically Russian. Owned and run (on a non-profit basis) by Yulia and Lev Atlas—Russian-Jewish immigrants from Rostov—it was a 'catering establishment' all right, but it catered more for the customers' souls than for their stomachs.

Designed by Yulia herself in conjunction with Tim Stead, an acclaimed Scottish wood sculptor, the café's interior resembled a fairy-tale Russian marquee. Upstairs was an exhibition of Russian puppets, and downstairs—in the food-hall—a never-ending celebration of Russian cuisine, music and culture . . .

Falkirk High-Polmont

Why is it that drunks, madmen and football hooligans always choose to sit next to me on trains?

The man who enters (or rather stumbles into) the carriage at Falkirk seems to be a curious fusion of all those three species.

He starts by telling me—with a burp—that he supports the English BNP (Burping National Party?) and, mystified by my accent, no doubt, proceeds to ask where I am from—a difficult question, with which, for some reason, I am confronted in Scotland more often than anywhere else.

Initially, I tried to be honest. Contrary to the good English proverb, it was not always the best policy (not in Scotland), for almost inevitably the following dialogue then occurred:
   – I am from Edinburgh.
   – You don't sound Scottish.
   – Actually, I used to live in London until several months ago.
   – You don't sound English either.
   – You are right: I am Australian by passport . . . as well as
      British . . .
And so on.

I still wonder what it is that makes the Scots particularly interested in my elusive origins—a natural curiosity, xenophobia, or just some mysterious small-nation sensitivity?

In any case, I decide that, inebriated as he is, my new travel companion won't appreciate jokes or puns and the best thing would be to give him the shortest possible answer.

'What? From Ukraine? . . . We accept everyone here,' he

mutters with disdain and burps out sarcastically: 'Are you enjoying Scotland?'

'Yes. I do. How about you?' I reply, but the BNP supporter is already fast asleep, dripping saliva on to his hairy chest.

I shut my eyes and transfer myself back to *Cossachok*, where Lev, who combines his role as a café proprietor with that of principal viola of the Scottish Opera Orchestra, is playing 'Romance' by Sviridov.

The laments of his magic violin brought everything to a standstill. The patrons stopped eating. The waiters stopped serving. Even the coffee-machine in the corner stopped hissing.

Music was the only creature that spoke and moved inside the café.

I looked at the faces of the people, filling the smallish premises to the brim, and suddenly realised that—just as the passengers on the shuttle were not commuters but travellers—they were neither patrons, nor customers.

They were an audience

I thought I now knew what Scotland's 'best-kept secret' was.

Polmont-Linlithgow

Taste buds die last.

I open the bottle of 'Three Bears' Russian beer, given to me 'for the road' by Yulia. The label says it was produced by Ivan Taranov Brewery. At least, it is no longer a Lenin brewery (everything used to be named after Lenin in the Soviet Union): things must be really changing in Russia. Yet, the taste is still unmistakably Soviet—bitterish and medicine-like. It is much easier to change labels than to improve the contents.

I savour the half-forgotten taste of Russia in my mouth as the train keeps dashing ahead through thick Scottish darkness, making me feel strangely at home—more so than any place in the world that I have visited or lived in.

More even than the Cossachok café—that enclave of Russian culture in the heart of Glasgow, where no one would ever ask me where I was from.

Maybe, this is because—unlike all 'normal' trains—a shuttle never quite arrives at a destination. After a quick clean-up, it is bound to go straight back to where it came from.

A seemingly endless journey . . .

Linlithgow-Edinburgh

On the last leg of the shuttle just leaving Linlithgow for Edinburgh, the few remaining passengers in the carriage are all asleep.
A navy-and-red 'Route of Flying Scotsman' train, travelling in the opposite direction, flashes past, blinding me momentarily with the jumpy ECG-like garland of its window lights.
It is good to know that Scotland is still on the move.

It is here—on board the shuttle, permanently commuting between Edinburgh and Glasgow—that I am going to leave you.

It is two minutes past midnight. A new day has just begun.

'Dear Mr Vitaliev,

I want you to know that I am really, really sorry that you
have ended your series for the *Herald*. I have greatly enjoyed
them, cutting out quite a few to keep and sending some to
my eldest son—a homesick exile in Germany . . . Mondays
will not be the same!

I particularly appreciated your writing about Gaelic that
has no word for 'to own' or 'to possess' . . . I also loved your
articles on buying a Scottish island, on Celtic & Rangers
and your final one with its references to Scottish
independence . . .

Although you found fault with us Scots sometimes (and
quite rightly so), I hope you will have happy memories of
Scotland . . .'

Alison Cowey, Feddens, Cardness

Electronic cigarette

Meeting Simon Gray, a true British mauviste, two months after
his death (please bear with me, I haven't lost all my marbles yet)
was the last link in a chain of coincidences ('connections'?) with
which my own (and everyone else's) life is so resplendent.

It all started with my book *Passport to Enclavia* which I began
writing while still living in Edinburgh, or rather on trains,
planes and at hotels during my weekly newspaper assignments
that took me all over Scotland. I finished that book in agony
during my one-year-long exile in Folkestone, Kent (see below),
but—for all sorts of reasons—was unable to publish it until five
years later. The book was first picked up by a US publisher called
'Wild Child', but then I read in the *Bookseller* magazine about a
new London imprint, 'Reportage Press' specialising in fiction
and non-fiction with foreign connotations, and decided that
'Enclavia' was more suitable for them than for an obstreperous

(if only in name) American kid. I had to pay the Americans a kill fee before they reverted all the rights back to me and I, in my turn, granted them happily to Reportage Press.

The book was launched in October 2008 at Daunt Bookshop in Holland Park Avenue (where Reportage Press normally launch their books).

During that launch, I spotted an eye-catching yellow-green paperback, *The Smoking Diaries: The Last Cigarette* on one of the counters.

The title immediately grabbed my attention: after the operation to unblock my clogged arteries (angioplasty), an obvious result of thirty odd years of heavy smoking, which I had undergone several months earlier, it sounded more than topical.

'No cigarettes and lots of red wine,' my facetious surgeon, Dr Rodney Foale, told me when I was still on the operating table.

Seeing your own blocked arteries, with two tiny stents just installed inside them, on a TV monitor above the operating table (as I did) is the best—and the most effective—anti-smoking propaganda in existence.

I gave up smoking there and then, but was still addicted to thinking about cigarettes and to reading about them too.

The author's name, Simon Gray, was vaguely familiar, not so much from books, but from some semi-forgotten West End posters. The blurb confirmed that Simon Gray was indeed a rather well-known award-winning playwright.

I opened the book at random:

'How can one trust doctors? They seem to know more and more about their own specialities, less and less about their patients. If they are ear, nose and throat people, then they know the ear, nose and throat of you, but not what these are attached to, you're not present as a living and ailing organism, you're there in the bits and pieces he knows about, and he's unlikely? unwilling? unable? to speculate about alternative explanations for your illness, there's nothing wrong with your ear, nose and throat, so you'd better go to someone who specialises in something else and if you are lucky you might eventually hit on a man who happens to specialize in whatever is killing you.

I am not ready to give up smoking yet. Insufficiently settled. I tried yesterday, managed until dinner, but then sitting in a café, a coffee in front of me, the sea lapping softly a few yards away, and such a moon! It was the moon that did it, the moon's fault.'

I could almost hear the author's hoarse and wheezing voice of a life-long sixty-five-cigarettes-a-day smoker whispering conspiratorially in my ear. It was simultaneously literary and conversational, cynical and poetic, funny and sad . . . A bit like Kataev in English translation.

'A free-flowing stream of report and reminiscence' was how David Lodge characterised Simon's Diaries.
That could have been another definition of mauvism.

Leafing through the book, I noticed that not only were *The Smoking Diaries* thoroughly non-chronological, deeply solipsistic and 'significantly chaotic' (three main characteristics of mauvism) in their structure, they were unmistakably mauvistic in their tone too:

'The trouble with the dead is not that they are lost, and therefore might be found, but that they are beyond finding and are not therefore lost, they are absent to this world, in all the places that they were accustomed to be present in, and that you were accustomed to their being present in, the space at your side, the opposite seat at your usual table, the other half of the bed, the neighbouring pillow—nothing can be more finally absent than a dead person, and yet the dead persist in being almost present in traces and glimpses, whisking around the corner of your memory to drive you mad, like the incompletely forgotten name of a film star from many years ago—there was one I was trying to remember the other evening, a man in the restaurant reminded me of him, a slim middle-aged man eating by himself, not out in the open part of the restaurant, but in a cramped bit by the bar—he reminds me, I said to Victoria, of that actor, in that film—I could see the actor's face quite clearly, though in the film it was usually half in shadow, a neat little moustache, opaque eyes, and he had a cleft in his chin, more dimple than cleft, shiny black hair pasted back, and there was the voice, drawling but toneless, I knew him so well in my teens, but who was he?'

Yes, all one sentence, and by far not the longest in the book . . . At the first read, it felt as if it could do with some editing, yet if you actually tried to mentally edit the sentence, it became clear that you couldn't add or take out a single word without ruining the tone—slow, as if hesitant and constantly correcting itself, and yet deeply and thoroughly balanced—artistic in the true sense of this word.

The author was not 'almost present' on these tightly typed pages. He was present in all his larger-than-life entirety—self-adoring and self-hating in equal measure.

The same blurb asserted that Simon Gray died in August 2008, two months earlier, aged seventy-one.

Needless to say, I bought all three volumes of *The Smoking Diaries* plus Simon's first book of diaries *Enter the Fox*, plus his very last volume, aptly titled (by him!) *Coda*, in which he describes—in the same highly ironic and totally irreverent manner—the last months of his life when he was dying of lung cancer.

The final tragic irony of his book (life?), however, was that it was not lung cancer that he eventually died of. The cancer unexpectedly went into remission, yet several days after hearing this highly reassuring news from his doctor Simon Gray died suddenly of another smoking-related condition—rupture of an aneurysm.

Incidentally, the last words of 'Coda', i.e. effectively Simon Gray's last words (life is a literary device, remember?), written when he didn't know he was going to die within days, in fact he was given at least another eighteen months to live by his doctor, were (are) '. . . *to avoid disappointment*'.

In the book that I bought at Daunt, these words are followed by sixteen totally blank pages—a quietly powerful symbol of an interrupted life.

What struck me most about Simon Gray and his writing were not even his clearly mauvistic undertones and intonations (he would have probably hated to be branded a mauviste or anything else and would insist on being a 'Gray-ist', I am sure), but the fact that his whole existence was a brilliant illustration of the writer's life being but a literary device. He went even further having turned even his death into a **coda**, i.e. a literary device too! His last twenty years during which he had been writing his *Smoking Diaries* were a protracted build-up of the narrative towards the climax, or coda, of his own demise.

He needed to die to put a final full stop in that permanently unfinished book, and he knew it.

Death as a literary device?
Why not?

The plot that has become a life. The life turned into a plot, with its own denouement, climax (being diagnosed with terminal cancer) and coda (death).

'. . . to avoid disappointment.'

He has certainly managed to avoid it ('disappointment') big time. If prior to his death, reviews for his books of diaries were mildly positive, yet nothing special (I've checked), the posthumous ones were all but spectacular:

'The most perfect reading experience you can imagine.'
'One of Britain's greatest writers.'
'Remarkable achievement. A last word by a writer whose voice will be missed.'
'It is for this tragicomic chronicle of self-destruction that Gray will be best remembered.'
'Addictively readable, unsparingly honest journals . . . his greatest achievement.'

And so on.

A posthumous triumph of mauvism?

In a way, Simon duped the Grim Reaper. By dying, he has achieved something he was unable to achieve during his lifetime—Immortality. For what sort of death is that when the writer keeps talking to you in his own inimitable voice?

I would (most probably) never have met Simon, had my book not been launched at that particular Daunt bookshop. But coincidences and 'connections' do not end here.

Reading (or rather gloating over) Simon's diaries—one minute being moved (or irritated) almost to tears, next minute laughing out loud—I very soon learned that the last twenty years of his life had been firmly associated with Holland Park where he had lived and where I eventually—and accidentally—made his posthumous—at the Daunt Bookshop in Holland Park Avenue!

'It takes an act of will, now that we are back in London, to put on my shoes, my scarf and coat, and get down the stairs on to the pavement, where often I do a lumbering pirouette and within a few minutes find myself back where I started, taking off my coat and shoes—or I make it up Holland Park Avenue as far as the Renaissance, drink down two coffees at a table on the pavement, and then labour home, take off my coat. This is no life for a sentient man, or at least sentient enough to know that this is no life for him.'

Or:

'. . . So, still loaded down internally (physically, not gastrically) but with some small prospect of lightening up in sight, I trudged to the bus stop on Holland Park Avenue and waited for a bus to Notting Hill.'

Holland Park is an area of London that I don't know particularly well, and one bleak November afternoon, at the time when Simon was likely to be getting up having spent half of the night writing ('It's 4.30 in the afternoon . . . I've only been up a few hours . . .'), I return to Holland Park Avenue hoping against hope: *dum spiro spero*—my favourite mode in the Soviet Union, so I can easily be called an expert in that seemingly pointless occupation: hoping against hope—to bump into him.

I fail to find the Renaissance (hasn't Renaissance as an epoch ended with Simon's—the last Renaissance man's—demise? only joking), but install myself instead outside another café in Holland Park Avenue and keep staring at the passing crowd. In the treacherous early dusk ('I must change my sleep-waking pattern because at this time of the year there's so little light, and it diminishes, diminishes, beginning to darken as my day begins.'), each person in it looks like a shadow of himself (or herself), just like in Yevtushenko's poem about a park in March *'where there are no men or women, but only shadows of men and women . . .'.*

Simon must be here somewhere, his lanky stooping

361

frame, grey hair and smoking fag sticking out of his mouth, of course.

I myself drag on an 'electronic cigarette', a recent Chinese invention consisting of an atomiser and an oblong rechargeable battery and looking like a real cigarette, only somewhat longer.

The tip of it lights up (electronically) as I inhale. I can even belch out rings of totally harmless 'smoke', or rather vapour, produced by the above-mentioned atomiser (don't ask me how—I don't have a clue!)—literally—out of thin November air. There's no nicotine, no nothing in this cigarette, it is perfectly legal to smoke it anywhere (although I wouldn't try in on board a plane where a marshal is likely to shoot you first before making sure you were actually not breaking any laws). I have lit it up repeatedly in London pubs and restaurants (all fully non-smoking of course), but instead of being told off (or arrested, or shot) for breaching the smoking ban (for the illusion that I am smoking is complete), the most common reaction I get is indifference: the patrons, having caught sight of me, quickly turn away and start pretending I don't exist, their rationale being probably as follows: if this man is doing something as outrageous and inexcusable as smoking in a public place, he is either mad, which is dangerous, or a bully (gangster, murderer, child molester), which is also dangerous, so the best way to avoid trouble is to pretend he doesn't exist. And they do. I find this sort of reaction (or rather this total absence of any reaction) typically English: in any other country, even in Ireland, they normally tell you off or, at least, express some curiosity as to what it is you are doing, the moment you light up, albeit you actually don't light up, because nothing burns in the electronic cigarette—that's the whole point of it. In actual fact, it is just a dummy, or, as Americans say, a pacifier, to pacify an ex-chain-smoker like myself and to dupe his nicotine-soaked brain into believing that he continues to imbibe much-coveted nicotine together with all the yummy and genuinely carcinogenic by-products of burning . . .

I am mentally sharing all these thoughts and observations with Simon, having noticed that I am subconsciously imitating the style of his Diaries, which has a psychological explanation: we always—subconsciously, no doubt—tune to the style, manners and/or mannerisms (what's the difference between the two, I wonder, and why is it that having 'manners' or being a person of 'manners' is a good thing whereas 'mannerisms' have a negative connotation and are almost reproachable like most 'isms', it has to be said?) —of an interlocutor we want to impress?

I wonder whether Simon would have given up smoking with the help of this 'electronic cigarette' as I did (it would have probably been too late for him)? I had tried everything: acupuncture, hypnosis, you name it—nothing helped, but the 'electronic cigarette' did.

Acupuncture was the worst. Sitting in a hospital chair, with dozens of sharp needles stuck in my uncomplaining ear which made it resemble a small yet aggressive, porcupine crawling up my head, I couldn't wait for the torture to end which would allow me to light up in peace.

Or was it the sight of my own clogged arteries on a TV screen (monitor?) inside the operation theatre (as opposed to a movie theatre or a West End theatre, say) that made me give up smoking for good? I am not sure. But one thing is absolutely certain: this revolutionary Chinese invention (I would award a Nobel Prize in . . . not sure what branch of science—chemistry perhaps?—for it) is definitely my

LAST CIGARETTE.

I leave my freezing *al fresco* observation post and walk back to the Daunt Bookshop—the same place where I first met Simon while the tenth (or eleventh?) book of mine was being launched.

It is in there, of course that I see him again. On the photo in the album (or rather 'coffee-table book'—what a ridiculous definition for a creative endeavour) *Notting Hill* by Derry Moore shown to me by Tom, a young salesman (salesperson? bookseller? or perhaps the shop's manager or assistant manager—I forgot to ask him). The photo, taken inside that very bookshop, shows Simon standing in the middle of that very bookshop and the caption says (in Simon's own words and voice) that that very bookshop was (is) a dangerous place where people go in to buy one book and come out with five they hadn't realised they wanted (sounds so Simon!), and I completely agree with him on this occasion, for on my previous visit to that very bookshop I did not intend to buy any of Simon's books (for I had no idea who he was) and ended up buying all four (or five) of them!

Now, two of MY books are on sale at that very bookshop, and I wish Simon could pop in and buy them, or simply pop in without buying them, but this is now rather unlikely.

'He lived right across the road and used to pop in very often, the last time several days before he died,' explains Tom, looking so brazenly, I would even say insultingly, young.
He says that Simon's wife (now obviously his widow) Victoria, to whom all of his Diaries are dedicated –
'*Victoria—without whom, nothing*'
– still comes in fairly often.

'Yes, I've got it. *Beware of Pity*, by Stefan Zweig. Why this? Now let's think—yes, I picked it up at Daunt's partly because the cover caught my eye . . .' (*Coda*)

He explains that Simon's favourite haunt (where in Simon's own words, he dined almost every day), portrayed in his Diaries as '*Chez Moi*' restaurant ('almost opposite' his house) is, in actual fact, a small French bistro called 'Cyrano' next door to the shop. This doesn't surprise me, for I already know that Simon was *extremely careful not to offend anyone mentioned in his Diaries* and had changed most of his characters' names (including those of the horrendous three doctors who had led him—rather matter-of-factly—through the last year of his life). And although he never says a bad word about 'Chez Moi' (read 'Cyrano') restaurant, changing its name could have been justified by other considerations: like, for example, Simon's natural reluctance to allow his name and his Diaries (which, he must have known it, were bound to become hugely popular after his death) to be used for any sort of publicity.

I talk to the well-read and intelligent young Tom about Kataev (he has never heard about him—unsurprisingly), mauvism (he has never heard about that either) and the latter's similarities with the style of Simon's *Smoking Diaries*.

'You would probably like Fernando Pessoa, a Portuguese modernist writer of the first half of the twentieth century,' remarks knowledgeable Tom. An erudite and a bookworm, he is—first and foremost—a salesman. I've never heard of Fernando Pessoa before.

Tom briefly disappears to a mysterious 'store room', which I visualise as a treasure trove on a par with the vast storage cellars of the Hermitage Museum in Leningrad (now St Petersburg) where I spent countless hours in the late 1970s—early 1980s while working as an interpreter for foreign museum curators on exchange visits, and soon re-emerges with a weighty and pricy (£12.99!) paperback.

I rather like the title—*The Book of Disquiet*.

Having stepped away from the counter, I open the book at random. It comprises about five hundred numbered entries that do not seem to be connected with each other:

'21.   Whether or not they exist, we're slaves to the gods.

154.   Who am I to myself? Just one of my sensations. My heart drains out helplessly, like a broken bucket. Think? Feel? How everything wearies when it's

defined!

366. Useless landscapes like those that wind around Chinese teacups, starting out from the handle and abruptly ending at the handle. The cups are ever so small . . . Where would the landscape lead to . . . if it could continue past the teacup handle?'

I like the last teacup 'entry'—or shall I say 'entity'?—yet the book has nothing to do with mauvism (or 'Gray-ism') because there's no narrative in it. Just a collection of carefully numbered epigraphs.

A very modernist literary endeavour reading like an imitation (or a parody?) of itself.

I decide to buy the book nevertheless so as not to disappoint Tom. Besides, clever (if somewhat zany) epigraphs always come handy for a writer—like an extra couple of good lighters (which tend to disappear without a trace never to be found again) for a smoker—which brings me back to Simon Gray.

Sorry, Simon, I shouldn't have used that last lighters simile, for that was your permanent 'gentleman's set': two packets of cigarettes and two lighters. You never left home without them and were unable to write without having all four of these murderous little objects on your desk.

But I used to be exactly the same, albeit ONE cigarette box (I used to smoke rollies, the daily supply of which I self-manufactured every morning with the help of a Porta cigarette-making machine) and ONE lighter. Mind you, I had never been a sixty-five-cigarette-a-day person—thirty-thirty-five maximum. I used to jokingly call my daily ritual of cigarette making my fifteen minutes of 'meditation', or 'piano-playing', or even 'knitting', and had convinced myself that the process was 'calming'. Occasionally confronted with the sheer absurdity of wasting fifteen minutes a day to produce something that was killing you slowly, I had always tried to wave these thoughts away like importunate flies. But experiencing mild (at times, not so mild) panic attacks (complete with heart palpitations and drops of cold sweat on my forehead) every time I thought (mistakenly, for the most part) I had left the deadly kit behind or, God forbid, lost it (that only happened twice in many decades and in each case the lethal set was quickly recovered) was scary and humiliating, as if you were no longer in control of your own life. Simon described very similar sensations in the Diaries.

On top of *The Book of Disquiet*, I buy several other books in that very shop, including the unavoidable 'five I hadn't realised I wanted', plus a set of two CDs on which Simon himself reads his *Smoking Diaries* (I will soon find out that he has—had?—an unexpectedly soft and gentle voice that doesn't seem to be badly affected by all those years of heavy smoking) and, having said goodbye to Tom, start walking along Holland Park Avenue— now dark and near deserted—towards Notting Hill Tube station.

I walk on Simon's side of the road (opposite *'Chez Moi'*, aka 'Cyrano'), past the grey modernist monument to 'St Volodymyr', an ancient ruler of Ukraine, erected by London's Ukrainian community in 1988. Simon must have walked past it hundreds of times. How much did he know of my native Ukraine? Probably not a lot. Even the Queen, to whom I was once introduced at a press reception, on hearing the word 'Ukraine' in response to her regulation 'Where are you from?', corrected me by saying: 'I see: you were born in Russia.'

At least, unlike the Queen, he must have realised it was not Russia (someone who wrote: *'The state of terror is the state itself. And the state itself is the man himself. Hitler, Mao, Stalin were the state and the terror . . .'* must have known the difference.)

'Vladimir', or 'Volodymyr' in Ukrainian, was also the name of my father, and my patronymic therefore is 'Vladimirovich'.

Connections . . .

And here, on the opposite side of Holland Park Avenue, is the 'Gate' cinema, to which Simon was once denied entry because he was fifteen minutes late for a show. Crassly turned away by a young pseudo-Bohemian manager who claimed he didn't want to disturb 'his audience' by letting Simon in after the film had started.

Simon then left obediently but was badly hurt by the experience and even wrote a letter of complaint. Or thought of writing such a letter—I can't remember.

'Where have you been?' the Loved One asks when I enter our Letchworth abode a couple of hours later.

'To Holland Park to catch up with Simon,' I reply.

I walk across the garden to Pegasus Cottage and spend half of the night listening to Simon Gray talking to no one in particular from the CD and describing my on-going encounter with the person who, even after his death, remains a powerful proof of Life being nothing more—and nothing less—than a Literary Device.

Folkestone blues

I've just done something that Simon Gray never did (or claimed he never did): reread and rewritten the previous several pages.

He hated rereading and rewriting his 'copy' (please forgive my editor's jargon).

'*We are what we write, not what we re-write,*' he wrote in his Diaries. That remark strikes me as harsh and opinionated. Also, I suspect it is not entirely sincere: I simply won't believe that Simon never edited (or rewrote) his 'copy', i.e. his plays, books and Diaries.

Not everything, by far not everything he said am I ready to accept or to agree with—a fact that makes my passion for his writing even stronger: few things can be as off-putting as total and complete 'perfection. Like, for example, Simon hated the *Guardian*, *Guardian* readers and, most of all *Guardian* writers, particularly columnists, and I had been in each of those roles at different times and am still a *Guardian* reader, I am happy to say . . . Does this mean Simon would have hated me too? I don't think so. On the contrary, I somehow believe that we would have got on extremely well.

It was only the 'great leaders of the Soviet Union' who were always perfect and always right (up to the point when they were denounced and it turned out that they had always been wrong). Mistakes and delusions, on the other, hand, can be delightfully human. Even if they are your own mistakes. At least, some of them may appear as such when you look back at them many years later . . .

VV was still living through one of his life's biggest mistakes (the second biggest after emigrating to Australia) and was therefore unable to assess it objectively.

Ten hours after leaving Edinburgh, his newly acquired 'super jalopy' braked screechingly at the doors of his new abode—a small pink cottage in Folkestone, Kent, but it took him a while to gain enough moral strength to get out of the car and start unloading it.

Tired after a five hundred-mile drive, he was sitting inside his petrol-reeking 'super jalopy' with his eyes shut, unable to force himself to make this one final step—towards the porch of the pink cottage, towards the start of his long (he knew it would be long) self-imposed exile.

Big Folkestone seagulls were screaming above his head, in the voices of his abandoned little children.

Sunday

My first morning in Folkestone. Suicidal mood on waking up. Can't bear the silence and the seagulls' screams. Walk down to the harbour. Along the seafront—a tacky fun fair of the type you find in every decaying British seaside resort and a flea market selling tawdry knick-knacks and nothing much else.

A local rock band is performing outside an oblong wooden shed: a makeshift bar. The band consists of a bald, topless, beer-bellied and heavily tattooed middle-aged man and a stone-faced teenager in dirty jeans who looks like he may be the topless man's son. They both play electric guitars and yell out the lyrics from some old Beatles numbers. A couple of very old ladies with tearful eyes and shaking hands are trying to dance to the tunes. A gentle breeze is blowing from the sea. I order a pint, sit down on a wooden bench next to some frail local alcos and squint at the sea trying to discern the outlines of Boulogne on the other side of the Channel which, as one alco tells me, should be possible in fine weather. The day is fine, and the visibility is excellent, but France is nowhere to be seen. . .

I suddenly feel trapped and miserable. 'I wanna hold your h-a-and . . .' the topless man and his son are now shouting. The favourite song of little Andrei during our walks around 'Ebrandah' (this is what he calls Edinburgh, unable to pronounce the name properly) together.

Having dropped an unintended tear into my pint, I stand up and go back 'home'.

My cottage has a nice study, with a sturdy wooden desk and rows of bookshelves above it, in the attic. I need to unpack my computer and books (I have only brought half of them so far and will drive back to Edinburgh—Ebrandah?—to pick up the rest in a couple of weeks' time), but, for some reason, *being in the attic depresses me (probably because the seagulls' screams sound* extremely loud from there—as if amplified and ricocheting from the walls). Instead, I try to watch TV in the downstairs lounge, but there's no escape from 'music' for me today: at about 6 p.m. another aspiring rock star starts playing an electric guitar in the neighbouring cottage behind the wall. 'Playing' in his case is a huge overstatement, for unlike the tattooed family duet earlier on the beach, he doesn't know how to play his guitar: the cacophony of horrible screeching noises is unbearable. His singing skills are much worse than his guitar playing. Besides, he keeps rehearsing—over and over again—just one 'song' with the frequent (much too frequent) refrain 'I want to fuck you!' I bet he has written it himself . . . For obvious reasons, neither the non-existing 'melody', nor (particularly!) the 'lyrics' agree with my state of mind very well.

I pop out to get a Chinese takeaway and a bottle of wine, hoping the vociferous 'musician' will have shut up by the time I come back.

The area where I live is not particularly upmarket. Not even by pretty downmarket Folkestone standards. My cottage is almost at the end of a street that runs down the hill towards the harbour. Three more battered cottages on, a council estate begins. I read somewhere that Folkestone had one of the country's highest rates of teenage pregnancies (no wonder: with such sex-obsessed local rock stars as my neighbour), and my street is teeming with heavily pregnant teenagers of both sexes (the male ones all have beer bellies that make them look pregnant too).

I still don't know who my neighbours on the other, left-hand, side are, but judging by the outward appearance of their cottage: peeling stucco, broken window frames, backyard full of litter, I assume they are unlikely to be the family of an ageing Oxford don with whom I could talk literature and arts across the (non-existent, or rather, smashed) fence of an evening.

(I will soon find out that my neighbours on the left run Folkestone's largest drugs den. Yet, funnily enough, they will never bother me half as much as the roaring raunchy rock star on the right: outside drug-taking hours, they will normally be civil, even polite.)

I have seen lots of third-world poverty and deprivation in my life (in the Soviet Union, in India, in Romania etc.), yet for some reason, Britain's 'first-world poverty' has always struck me as much more aggressive and even amoral, if you wish. In most cases, let's be honest, it is poverty not by predicament but by choice, which does make it amoral in my eyes.

A Woman in red

Evening. Mollified by the wine and the tasteless, if filling, Chinese food, I smoke in my puny back garden overgrown with weeds. Having looked up at a brightly lit window in a large house behind the drugs den, I spot a woman in a red dress (or a dressing gown) typing away at her desk.

What is she writing? A novel? A romantic poem? A complaint to the Shepway District Council about the appalling state of her neighbours' (the drug addicts') garden that 'has become a source of filth and vermin for the whole street'? Her annual tax return?

I can see a man (husband? lover? father?—can't determine how young or old he is from the distance) coming up to her from behind, staring at the computer screen for a minute or so and patting her on the shoulder lovingly, or just reassuringly. Or perhaps impatiently: come on, darling, time to go to bed . . .

The scene behind the window makes me feel lonelier than before. It also makes me feel guilty—for not writing, for being tipsy, for smoking in the garden instead of sitting in my attic study and either finishing my book or doing some journalism to supplement my non-existent income lest I should end up on the dole and join the ranks of the genderless dwellers of the nearby council estate.

To assuage this burning feeling of guilt, I promise myself to start working tomorrow morning, no matter what . . .

The last sentence in that 'Sunday' entry of the notebook was scribbled on top of the next, otherwise empty, page:

'Nothing short of death can stop me from telling this story.'

What exactly did VV mean by that somewhat pathetic-sounding sentence, so uncharacteristic of his usual tongue-in-cheek style?
Was that a joke? Or a quote? A touch of self-pity?
Or simply talking to his notebook (as he would often do for lack of any other interlocutors) while not being entirely sober?
And which 'story' in particular did he have in mind? His first day in Folkestone? His whole life?
Or was it the very first line of his main book 'Life as a Literary Device' which he was already writing without putting anything on paper?

Who knows . . .

That 'woman in red' scene was destined to be replayed in front of his eyes every evening for over two months—before he was able to force himself to climb up two flights of stairs to the attic and start writing himself. He began referring to the woman in the window as his 'living reproach'. Strangely enough, he had never bumped into her in his street or anywhere else in Folkestone. Or maybe he did but was unable to recognise her from the blurred reddish shadow in the window above his head.

Silence and rain

The worst was silence. Not the deafening sort of complete and utter quiet, but the humanless silence of solitude filled with the heart-piercing screams of seagulls, with mercilessly synchronic and slowly murderous in their scary inevitability tic-tacs of the old clock in the lounge room, with persistent knock-knock-knocks of rain against the roof of the small kitchen conservatory (it would start pouring at precisely one p.m. every day and wouldn't stop until the morning).

Different types of rain in Folkestone (from VV's notebook):

1. Normal drizzle (seagulls keep screaming).
2. Shower (seagulls shut up or get outshouted by the noise of the streams of water falling down from the sky).
   (Victor R. once unwittingly (and rather precisely) described it in one of his youthful poems, 'Shower above the Sea':
   The air is full of a cocktail of smells. Seagulls are piercing dark-green clouds. From heavens—a fresh-water sea is falling down into a salt-water one!)
3. 'Mushroom rain' or 'blind rain'—both are Russian idioms describing rain with sunshine. Seagulls disappear from view.
4. Gale (can occur on any day of the year)—looks very much like a snowstorm, only the snow melts on touching the ground. Seagulls freeze in their flight.
5. 'Folkestone sleet'—gale plus shower (occasionally, plus thunderstorm). Seagulls get shredded to pieces.

The seagulls must have been driving him crazy.

To beat the silence, he kept his radios on at all times. He had radios in every room, including the bathroom. They were all tuned to BBC Radio 4, and often two or three were on simultaneously—blasting away at full volume as if trying to outshout each other.

Radio 4 voices (Vin was once one of them!) were flooding the cottage. He would switch them on first thing after waking up and would turn them off last before going to sleep. The subconscious aim was to create an illusion of human company, yet in actual fact the radio voices only highlighted the sheer artificiality of this 'company' and accentuated his loneliness.

That was how listening to Radio 4 became one of his life-time obsessions. He still starts and finishes his day with it.

Trying to put things in perspective, he often recalled his recent visit to one of the world's few remaining bastions of silence, the Hebridean island of Lewis

Stornoway

'Only he who is familiar with the din of battle can fully appreciate quiet,' said Volodya Grishpun, the favourite Russian poet of my youth.

There are different types of silence: A hush-hush conspiratorial whisper, a pause in a conversation, a lull before a storm, or a minute of silence in mourning or commemoration.

In Russia, all broadcasts would stop for three minutes at midnight to allow any SOS signals to be heard—three minutes of anxious, listening silence. Also, a silence à la my friend Bill Bryson: 'It was so quiet in the pub one could hear a fly fart.'

Compare any of those with: 'Wailing air raid sirens were drowned out as laser bombs homed in on military installations and Republican Guard strongholds'—a newspaper account of the first days of the second Gulf war.

What would you rather listen to? Silence is becoming an increasingly coveted and hard-to-get commodity in our noise-ridden war-torn world.

Sh-sh . . . Close your eyes, shut out all noises and listen to silence . . .

On Sunday morning, I awoke in my Stornoway hotel to the shattering, deafening stillness behind the window. All habitual noises that constitute part of a quiet Sunday morning in any small town—the sounds of passing cars and human footsteps— were missing. Even dogs did not bark.

The silence was such that it almost made my teeth ache. With awe, I remembered that had I indeed had a sore tooth, there would be no chance of buying a pain-killer: all pharmacies and shops (as well as pretty much everything else) on Lewis were firmly shut down for the sabbath.

The best description of this most silent of all silences ('the mother of all silences', as Saddam Hussein would put it) can be found in H. V. Morton's 'In Search of Scotland':

'It is the sabbath. I lie in bed for a time listening to it. You can feel the sabbath in the Highlands of Scotland just as in cities you can feel a fall of snow: the world is wrapped in a kind of soft hush; normal early morning noises are muffled or absent.'

Morton wrote this in 1929, when the sabbath was strictly observed in many rural areas of Scotland. Seventy-five years later, the Outer Hebrides were among its very last strongholds.

Thank God, water in my bathroom taps was not affected by the sabbath and kept running, as it must have done for H. V. Morton in 1929:

'I sing in my bath; then, remembering with shock that I am breaking the sabbath, stop, and feel criminal.'

I took the previous day's newspaper to breakfast. Until a couple of month earlier, when the first Sunday flight from Inverness landed in Stornoway to a fairly low-key protest at the airport, the only Sunday paper you could read there was a Saturday one.

Even now, after Jock Murray, the entrepreneurial landlord of the Whalers' Rest Hotel, has arranged for a stack of Sunday papers to be flown in (he has to pay for the freight out of his pocket), the earliest you can get them is at 2p.m.—if the plane is on time, that is.

This shunning of Sunday newspapers (the Sabbatarians are not supposed to use anything produced on Sundays) did not make a lot of sense, for they were all printed on a Saturday, whereas Monday newspapers were put together on a Sunday. Paradoxically, from what I knew, there was no stigma attached to reading Monday newspapers on Lewis—a pleasing realisation for a writer of a Monday column.

At breakfast, the rising air-bubbles in the glass of mineral water on my table were the only things that moved in the whole of Stornoway.

I made sure my car had a full tank of petrol: all filling stations on the islands were closed (well, except for one pump, as it turned out later). Unlike the hapless visitor of several years ago who didn't bother to stock up with basics, I was not in danger of starving: a small handful of pubs, restaurants, and takeaways were now open for Sunday custom.

After a couple of days on Lewis and Harris, I was pleased to discover that the general situation around the sabbath was much more peaceful and relaxed than its portrayals in the mainland media and the gossip.

After a generous dose of both, I had expected a mini-Belfast scenario, with sabbatarians and anti-sabbatarians at each other's throats. Nothing could be further from the truth. The issue did split the island community down the middle, but this split was largely in people's minds and not at all bellicose or aggressive. 'It is the clash between the head and the heart,' a local journalist told me.

Having spoken to a number of islanders, I came up with the following spectrum of opinions (most of my interlocutors asked not to be named—not out of fear, but purely out of reluctance 'to upset the neighbours'):

Radical supporters of the strict sabbath observance (among them, significantly, Western Islands Council and the local tourism board) would argue that the fourth commandment left no space for middle ground and/or compromise and were therefore strongly opposed to Sunday flights and ferries as well as any commercial activity on 'God's day'.

They maintained that they didn't need to prove anything to anyone, for 'God knew best what was good for us', and snubbed the latest opinion polls—heavily in favour of livelier Sundays. 'When in Rome, do as the Romans do' was their favourite mantra. (What if some Romans did certain things differently, I was wondering.)

They feared that even slight deviations from God's rule (like three existing Sunday flights and a couple of open pubs) would open the floodgates for total secularisation of the islands. Yet even they stopped short of any sort of violence and/or force to make themselves heard and restricted themselves to 'praying and writing letters'.

Moderate sabbath supporters, like the Rev. Dr Iain Campbell, believed they had to accept the changing reality, but should keep making their point and 'showing a different example'. They thought that, rather than putting would-be visitors off, the islands' Sundays could be turned into a tourist attraction for those who wanted to get away from it all and indulge in quiet contemplation.

Radical supporters of the change, like Donald MacSween, a local councillor, stood for a referendum that would give a green light to Sunday ferry services and referred to the day of the first

Sunday flight as 'the day of liberation'.

They argued that increased industrial activity on Sundays was the only way to reverse the islands' stagnating economy and declining population.

'Tourism and jobs will come to an end, and the Free Church will be the last one out,' an angry Stornoway youngster told me. They recounted horror stories of unsuspecting Sunday visitors trapped on Lewis and Harris without food or petrol.

Moderate supporters of change, like Eileen Macdonald, the proprietor of Doune Braes Hotel—the first fully licensed hotel on the islands, thought that the changes, although welcome, should not go too far the other way and that some 'mysticism' of the sabbath should be preserved and kept intact.

Out of countless local opinion poll results, shown to me by Mr MacSween, I was most impressed by one: 59 per cent of all islanders 'did not feel restricted' by the beliefs and attitudes of others. Unbeknownst to most, the residents of Scotland's last truly sabbatarian islands taught the country—and the rest of our conflict-ridden world—a quiet lesson of tolerance and democracy.

I enjoyed walking the empty streets of Stornoway on Sunday, between 11a.m. and midday, when 99 per cent of the locals were attending their Sunday services. Being the only pedestrian in town at this hour of prayer did feel, if not exactly 'criminal', then definitely like a minor breach of public order.

Muffled, yet strangely synchronised, singing could be heard from numerous churches. Dozens of cars, parked bumper-to-bumper near the islands' largest Free Church in Kenneth Street, were patiently waiting for their owners. It was another sign of change: even the strictest of sabbatarians thought it was now acceptable to drive to church on Sundays.

If one so wished, one could have a pint or three at The Whalers' Rest or at HS 1—a 'cool' modern bar with a Sunday 'table licence'. Sundays were getting unstoppably 'normal' on

Lewis, and I was not sure whether to rejoice at this or to grieve.

I drove twenty-five miles west to see two of the island's landmarks: the 5,000-year-old standing stones of Callanish and a couple-of-years-old 'historic' petrol pump at Doune Braes Hotel—the first and only one open on Sundays.

The stones' visitor centre was closed, but the mysterious phallic rocks, thoroughly arranged by hard-working Neolithic farmers, stood there silently as they did on any weekday. Unbreakable and refusing to budge, yet gradually and inevitably worn out by time and elements, they were the living metaphor of the enduring sabbath tradition.

One day—many years from now—it will crumble away completely, and petrol pumps will spring up all over the place, like obelisks on the mass grave of some of the islands' unique ways and beliefs.

I did fill up my already nearly full tank in the end: how could I beat the temptation of using the islands' only sabbath-less petrol pump? It was only a five-minute drive from the equally sabbath-less standing stones of Callanish.

All the way back to Stornoway, the road was empty.

Going out

In Folkestone, his delusionary 'human company' of the BBC Radio 4 full-volume voices continued until they (the voices) too became part of the all-permeating, all-embracing and all-enveloping silence better known as loneliness.

Other symbols of loneliness (and homelessness too) were the naked light bulbs in the kitchen, bathroom and a small second bedroom. They reminded him of a prison cell, albeit he had never been incarcerated in one, and of a horrible hospital in the God forsaken Ukrainian town of Apostolovo, into which he was once admitted with severe pneumonia.

He was coughing out blood.

The ward he was in accommodated over fifty male patients of all ages—some on the verge of dying (two-three patients would normally pass away overnight), others—seemingly robust and healthy enough to keep drinking vodka and playing dominoes all day long—at times throwing pieces at the dying patients when they would start moaning too loudly . . . There was no ventilation (it was summer) or water of any kind, and the toilet (just two holes in the ground) was outside.

At night, the ward was lit up with one single naked bulb, straight above his bed. He had to stare at it for hours on end.

VV was sure he was going to die there. Another near-death experience of his . . .

His almost physical hatred of naked light bulbs stemmed from those gruesome hospital days when only elephantine doses of penicillin administered by a duty nurse, generously bribed by his friends, saved VV from dying.

His first purchase in Folkestone was therefore a set of three cheap rice-paper Chinese lampshades, or rather lantern shades for they were in the shape of Chinese festive lanterns, to cover up the disturbingly shameless nudity of the light bulbs inside the cottage.

One rainy November night, he was unable to take it all any longer. Having spent almost two months as a near-recluse inside the cottage, only leaving it for an hour or so of a morning to buy newspapers and food, he was desperate for an evening out.

It was 7.30 p.m. The whole evening was ahead of him.

With an umbrella in his hand, he briskly walked down to the dark and empty harbour and from there—climbed up the hill to the Bayle, Folkestone's oldest area with the town's most famous pub, The British Lion, which (allegedly) used to be frequented by Dickens himself.

He hadn't met a single living being on his way.

The semi-dark lounge of The British Lion was empty, except for a fat and visibly tipsy barmaid and one male patron at the bar.

They didn't acknowledge VV's appearance when he—water dripping from his clothes—approached the bar and asked for a glass of house red wine.

They didn't even turn their heads towards him.

They were busy staring at the TV screen above the bar.

A teletext page of a football game—with a clock, names of the two competing sides and the score: 0:0—occupied the whole screen, at which they were staring unblinkingly.

For a minute or so VV could not grasp what they were doing.

Then it dawned on him: they were watching a football game on teletext and were waiting for the score on the screen to change.

The realisation was so frighteningly depressing that he dashed out of the pub and—not bothering to open his umbrella—ran back home.

Only when safely inside his cottage, he did swear outshouting the 'I want to fuck you' rock musician behind the wall.

He then swore again—this time not to ever venture outside the house after dark.

After that 'going out' in Folkestone came to denote having a solitary meal, abundantly washed down with wine, in his tiny back garden while watching the never-ending chain of impatient 'clients' jumping over the neighbour's fence on their way to the drugs den.

They were invariably polite (if somewhat worn out at the edges) and always said 'Good evening' to VV.

One morning he woke up to the sounds of a scandal behind his bedroom window. It transpired that the owners of the 'drugs den' cottage had suddenly arrived from Cornwall. To say that they were shocked by the state of their property would have been a gross understatement. It also turned out that their tenants hadn't paid a penny of their rent for many months . . .

Police were called and the humbled drug addicts were frogmarched out of the cottage to the waiting black van.

After their departure, Vin's solitude became complete—not counting the roaring rock musician behind the wall and the screaming seagulls, of course.

There was nothing else left to do but start writing.

. . . While in Folkestone, Charles Dickens was suffering writer's block—a highly unusual occurrence for such a prolific author.

He came here in the summer of 1855 to work on the opening chapters of *Little Dorrit*, but . . . 'I walk downstairs once in every five minutes, look out of the window once in every two, and do nothing else,' he complained in a letter. The view from the window of his house at 3 Albion Villas was the main distracting factor: 'You can sit at your open window on the cliff overhanging the sea beach and have the sky and the ocean, as it were, framed before you like a beautiful picture,' he noted in another letter.

Another irresistible distraction lay in long walks across the town and along the sea-front: 'Our [Folkestone's: VV] situation is delightful, our air is delicious, and our breezy hills and downs, carpeted with wild thyme, and decorated with millions of wild flowers, are, on the faith of a pedestrian, perfect . . .'

In the intervals between walks and staring out the window, the great writer would pop in for a pint at 'British Lion in the Bayle[11]' and would use every opportunity to give public readings of his earlier works. No wonder he had little time left for writing in this 'world of wealth, privilege, servants, carriages and bath-chairs'—as the nineteenth century Folkestone was described by an old guide-book.

I came to Folkestone in 2003. Remembering Dickens' experience, I was initially wary of being hit with writer's block too, but my worries were superfluous, for these days 'distractions' in Folkestone are few and far between. To begin with, the view from my window, 'overhanging' not the beach and 'the ocean', but a nearby council estate, is of piles of black rubbish bags.

Torn newspapers and junk-food wrappings are flying in the wind before landing on my porch, from where I dutifully pick them up every morning.

Folkestone is still strikingly beautiful, mainly due to its unique situation among the cliffs 'overhanging' the English Channel, so vast and open that it indeed looks more like 'the ocean'.

I enjoy the town's nostalgia for its former glory, its battered Victorian beauty, its cobbled winding lanes running down the hill towards the Harbour.

On the other hand, one has to be blind not to notice the ever-growing decay. The famous harbour, which had been bustling with ships, visitors and foreign dignitaries since 1843, is now incongruously empty. After almost 150 years of operation, the passenger ferry link with France was stopped. For good. And shortly after that, all cargo traffic from the harbour was termi-nated too. 'Folkestone will never again have a sea link with the

11 I bet there weren't many patrons there watching football on teletext then.

384

Continent,' the executives of Falcon Distribution, the port's owners, reassured the town's residents.

The only vessels to be found in the Folkestone Harbour today are small fishing boats and the huge rusty bulk of the Black Widow U475 Soviet-made Submarine. Bought from the hard-currency-starved Russian Navy several years ago, it was brought to Folkestone and turned into a floating museum under the kitschy motto '**Red Alert. Look What Has Surfaced Now That Communism Is Sunk**'.

I walk along the wind-swept Marine Parade towards the Leas, 'one of the finest marine promenades in the world', according to the 1934 *Ward Lock's Red Guide*. These days bumping into a holidaymaker under sixty years old on the promenade is as unlikely as spotting an Aleut in the streets of Abu Dhabi.

Of an evening, Folkestone's streets are populated almost exclusively by seagulls and flocks of idle youngsters. Businesses in the town's main streets are closing down and the owners are moving out. The most prospering establishment in the architecturally unique Old High Street is now 'Tattoo Studio. The Only Honest, Experienced and Professional Studio in the Area.'

Even the once thriving fishing industry has come to a halt (allegedly, due to the draconian EU regulations), and most of the seafood on offer at several seafront kiosks is 'not real' and 'made of minced fish'—as described by an honest saleswoman, from whom I tried to buy a fake lobster tail the other day.

The signs of decay are ubiquitous. The *Folkestone Herald* newspaper, with provincially judgmental headlines of the type 'Nasty Baker Kicks Sheep', runs a regular photo column 'Dumped Car of the Week'. In the 'Lidl' supermarket, where I do my shopping, all portable shopping baskets have been stolen. The Leas Lift is closed down 'until further notice', (the tiny funicular train vanished into thin air one fine night—I wouldn't be surprised to learn that it was nicked too), and the rare strollers, including myself, have to puff their way up the hill.

In a funny way, 158 years after Charles Dickens' visit, Folkestone itself has become thoroughly 'Dickensian'. I don't think the classic author would have had any problems writing there these days.

True, Folkestone still has beautiful (if not very clean) beaches. Yet it is only on it's few warm days a year that one can safely plunge into the freezing waters of the Channel. Another challenge is not to be blown away by the unceasing icy wind, while you trudge reluctantly towards the water—in full accordance with Lenin's famous dictum 'one step forward, two steps back'.
Masochistic by nature, I ventured to swim in the sea once or twice to the locals' open mouthed consternation, and am now expecting my name to pop up in the next Royal Honours List.
A good old bathing machine would come in handy (at least, it had walls to protect you from the wind, and an attendant was always there with a towel ready), but, alas, that is now a thing of the past.

Folkestone needs help. It desperately needs investment and government funding, and these are, sadly, not forthcoming. It also needs lots of holidaymakers willing to spend money. But crowds of 'quality' tourists are unlikely to turn up at a place which boasts one of Britain's highest per capita rate of pubs (I once saw a funeral held in a pub up my street!), but only one classy restaurant, 'Tavernetta', whose elderly Italian owner characterised his Folkestone experience as 'twenty-five years of madness'. For me, eating out in Folkestone, means a solitary dinner in my little back garden on occasional rainless evenings.

Living in Folkestone these days is as challenging, at times as uninviting, yet always as genuine as the open sea, or, indeed, 'the ocean', on whose steep white-cliffed shores it is so stunningly located.

A small Victorian cottage next to my house is now empty. Its former tenants—a bunch of young unemployed men—were evicted the other day for not paying their rent, and all the furniture was taken away. With its doors wide ajar, there it stands—tattered on the outside and mutilated from inside yet still graceful.

Like Folkestone itself, it is waiting for new—CARING—tenants to move in.

I look away from the window and carry on writing . . .

Several years later, they will tell VV that his feature (it appeared in the *Daily Telegraph* and generated considerable response) was the first trigger for Folkestone's revival. But then, in 2003, the town's decline—just like that of VV—seemed terminal.

Despite the fact that he did start writing every day, Vin felt increasingly like the rusty Russian submarine moored forever in the empty Folkestone harbour.

He was then finishing an amusing book which brought to mind an expression coined by Russian émigré satirist Vladimir Voinovich (another VV!): 'it is difficult to write amusingly while lying under the wheels of a truck' which referred to the latter's last years in the Soviet Union when all his books were banned and he was deprived of the means of existence.

On the surface of it, Vin was now living in the West, in a free and democratic society—yet at closer inspection, Folkestone, with its ubiquitous despair and total lack of opportunity and hope, didn't appear a part of the free world.

He had a similar sensation in Belfast which he visited on an assignment for *The European* in winter 1994, when the Troubles were still in full swing. He noticed that the people of Belfast carried on their faces the same 'seal of oppression' which characterised his former compatriots in the USSR: a mixture of fear, stress and discomfort as if they were constantly expecting a blow from behind their backs, a typically Soviet 'I-am-waiting-to-be-hurt' facial expression that no Western freedoms were capable of altering.

Fear for one's life outweighs all human freedoms. Corpses— and there was a real chance of being murdered every minute (a man was shot dead paramilitary style in the pub next to Vin's hotel)—have no use for freedom of expression.

Folkestone was of course much safer than the Troubles-torn Belfast, yet the level of despair was comparable.

He drove to Edinburgh to see the kids every month until he could no longer afford the petrol. Articles he was writing alongside the book allowed him to keep his head above water. But only just. He had to shop in Lidl and switched over to casks of wine, which were cheaper than bottles.

His rule was no booze before 6 p.m. Heaven knows why. Probably because he had always found it impossible to write after even a minuscule dose of alcohol—very much unlike many of his former Fleet Street colleagues who were unable to put a single word on paper without an alcohol intake. He looked forward to the 6 p.m. watershed ('wineshed'?), to the wave of warmth enveloping him from inside after the first couple of glasses, as if to a romantic tryst. Thank God, he had given up spirits many years before. The illusion of warmth provided by vodka was stronger yet very brief, whereas with wine he could spread it over a couple of hours—as long as he kept drinking of course.

It was a dangerous pastime, and he realised it very well, but told himself that without his only friend, the wine, his solitary evenings to the accompaniment of 'I-want-to-fuck-you' roaring sounds behind the wall, would have been unbearable.

His biggest nightmare was overdoing his one-bottle-a-day dose (which was easy when pouring wine out of a cask), to fall asleep at 10 –11 p.m. on the sofa in front of the TV and then wake up at midnight—bleary-eyed and heavy-headed, with no hope of falling asleep again until morning.

Writing commissions were petering out—slowly but surely. He knew only too well that to freelance successfully one had to do lots of networking: attend launches and events, rub shoulders with editors and the London literati, but he was simply not up to that any more. He had done years of active networking and knew personally 90 per cent of the people he saw on the BBC 10'clock News every night. Yet being a hopeless self-promoter, he would rather die of hunger or (more willingly) of booze than phone Jeremy Paxman, Alan Rusbridger or, say, Clive James asking for help.

His Folkestone friend Nick, a bookseller, told him that *Saga* magazine's head office had moved to Sandgate, Folkestone's Victorian suburb. VV knew he should have tried to get a commission or two from that magazine, which had the highest circulation in the UK and allegedly, paid its contributors the astronomical (by UK standards) rate of one pound per word. Moreover, his old acquaintance Katy Bravery was then *Saga's* deputy editor.

In his wine-warmed mind, he was playing with the idea of writing in his would-be email's 'subject' space something like 'To Ms Bravery from Mr Crisis'.

Not-yetism

You always miss your 'estranged' (I hate this word) children more in the run up to Christmas when your longing for them turns—from a dull and bearable constant ache which one can get used to—into an acute and almost physical pain.

Late December 2008. The shortest day of the year. I am writing inside Pegasus Cottage having taken three days of my annual leave to press on with *Life as a Literary Device*.

Andrei calls on my mobile and starts telling me about the beautiful Christmas tree they have in Edinburgh this year. 'Anya has made an angel for it . . .'

Pre-Christmas fuss . . .

Last week I was in London to attend a journalists' Christmas lunch at Ye Olde Cheshire Cheese, London's oldest pub.

Having withstood several weeks of rain and drabness, the city was basking in water-colour-ish December sunlight.

The lunch itself was a noisy affair in one of the pub's vaulted basements. I was giving out my business card right and left: as features editor of a large magazine I was responsible for commissioning over a hundred articles a year and needed lots of freelance contacts.

'Are you a journalist?' I asked an elderly man who came to sit next to me at a massive oak table.

'Not yet,' he replied nursing his steak-and-kidney pie.

He explained that he was a mathematician, lived off an inheritance and had never worked in his life.

'I only did four days of work in 1967, and I am now seventy-one.'

Thin and sprightly, he didn't look his age.

'Have you achieved a mathematical breakthrough?' I asked him.

'Not yet,' was the reply.

From then on, whichever question I asked the Mathematician, 'Not yet' was his only response:

'Do you have a family?'—'Not yet' (a rather optimistic stance for a seventy-one-year-old).

'Are you happy with your life?'—'Not yet'.

He was not teasing me but was genuinely and reassuringly unsure of himself.

'What a wonderful, therapeutic attitude to life,' I thought then.

A perennially young hero of one of John Cheever's novels said that the secret of his unfading youth lay in reading children's books and nothing else. The confused and somewhat nutty 'mathematician' from Ye Old Cheshire Cheese was a living proof of yet another secret of longevity—'not-yetism'—the attitude that makes one's life permanently unfinished and ever full of promise.

As it turned out, the Mathematician had invited himself to that party: he did it routinely by browsing the Internet in search of numerous PR agencies' functions where he could get a free meal and a drink, and putting his name on the guest list. The chances of being caught were small: most of the attendees did not know each other.

'Are you going home now?' I asked him when he finished his dessert.

You may have guessed what he replied:

'Not yet . . . I am off now to another party.'

That accidental encounter reminded me of an earlier one, but before I recount it here, let me say this:

. . . 'A writer must write,' a pre-war Soviet satirist (incidentally, Ilya Ilf) noted succinctly. He was not serious, of course. These days, apart from writing, an author is expected to appear at parties, book launches and literary festivals. He or she has to go on wearisome publicity tours (one American writer died of exhaustion while promoting his book last year) and to have, or 'to do' as London literati like to say, countless lunches (dinners, suppers and breakfasts) with an agent, a publisher, a publicist, an accountant, a solicitor and God knows who else. Meanwhile, the writer's unfinished manuscript gradually gets buried under tons of glossy invitations.

I am often told that attending these functions is essential if one is to remain in the limelight. But in reality they are of very little use: the wine is sour, the food is mediocre, there is no place to sit down, and the talk is very small indeed ('How did you get here?', 'What a lovely/beautiful/beastly/ghastly day!' and 'Lovely to meet you'—meaning, 'How boring you are').

To cut a long story short, several years prior to my self-imposed Folkestone exile, when my career was at its peak, I was invited to a writers' gathering. 'Relax and enjoy a lovely talk with your sisters and brothers-in-trade,' ran the invitation. As my mother's only child, I had always wanted to have brothers or sisters, so I decided to go. To my great surprise, most of my promised relatives-in-waiting were little old ladies who had never written anything, apart, perhaps, from annual tax returns. They all came to the gathering in the vain hope of meeting a 'real writer'.

As the only man of letters at the party, I became the centre of attention. Later on, to my considerable relief, I was joined by another 'real writer'—a thickset elderly gentleman with a hearing aid sticking out of his massive funnel-shaped ear like a nosy shrimp out of its shell. He was wearing a yarmulke and an open-necked shirt to underline his broad writer's soul, or so I thought.

When I asked him (in a very loud voice) what sort of books he wrote, he hesitated for a second and said: 'All my books are about the liver . . .' Thinking that I misheard him, I repeated my question. 'Yes, I write novels, ballads and short stories about the human liver,' he confirmed and explained. 'I am seventy-one, you see. Prior to my retirement, I used to be a doctor . . .' 'And does your liver-writing sell?' I asked tentatively (here I for some reason recalled a well-known metaphor coined by Ilf and Petrov—'a jolly liver of an alcoholic'). 'It certainly does!' he replied. 'Whereas most writers try to describe places and events of which they have little knowledge, my subject is close to everyone's heart.' And rectum, I was tempted to say.

'Most modern literary heroes are not very trustworthy,' he continued, 'and few writers have enough honesty to look inside themselves, inside their own bodies. What could be more realistic and trustworthy than a human liver—this modest sentry of our abdomen, this indefatigable internal labourer, purifying our bodies of garbage?' 'How about a love-line?' I asked, having choked on a stale canapé. How about a brief and tempestuous romance between your honest labourer, Mr Liver, and a light-minded promiscuous Ms Spleen?' The writer-liverist turned his deaf (shrimpless) ear to my suggestion. Having mumbled the traditional mantra of 'Lovely to meet you,' and 'Let's do lunch one day', he drifted away.

I was relieved, for talking with him made me feel, if not exactly livid, then definitely liverish.

On the way home, I bought myself a pound of chicken liver for supper.

The totally unexpected end to this story is that the other day (we are talking late 2008 here) I heard on the radio that a well-known London-based novelist (not the man in the yarmulke) is finishing a novel on . . . the human liver.

A classic case of great minds—or rather great livers—thinking alike? Or just a triumph of **liverism as a literary device**?

I suddenly thought that both the Mathematician and the Liverist were exactly as old as Simon Gray at the moment of his death—seventy-one. I bet Simon would have been very interested to learn about 'not-yetism' as a philosophy and

liverism as a writing trend. And who knows, 'not-yetism' (if not
liverism) might have even prolonged his own life:

'Are you dying?'—'Not yet'—whereas in his last book he was
always answering this question in the affirmative.

The very title of it—*Coda*—was tantamount to 250 pages
(plus sixteen blank ones) of a continuous 'yes' answer, i.e.
capitulation.

One should never underestimate the sheer power of
persuasion.

Not yet . . . And long live the liver!

The irony of fate

VV learned about it on returning to Folkestone from Edinburgh
two days after the Christmas he had spent with the kids . . .

He had to write about it of course.

. . . The other day, when I was doing my routine banking at
a building society branch in Folkestone, there suddenly came a
sharp buzz from under the counter. Before I could say 'Halifax',
a bullet-proof security curtain sprang up between me and the
cashier.

'Security alarm. Staff can't communicate. Police will arrive
shortly' was written on it in big letters.

The customers (me included) were looking around worriedly,
expecting to spot an armed robber—but instead a smiling
manager emerged from a side door. 'Don't worry, I've just
pressed a wrong button by mistake,' he announced cheerfully.
'The partition will come down in a few minutes.'

Standing at the counter and facing a wall, I felt claustrophobic
and uneasy. Not that it was the first impenetrable barrier I have
been confronted with in my life. But those previous walls were
largely metaphorical, whereas this one was real. 'Staff can't

communicate . . .' But who can? How often we feel trapped in what looks like a dark stuffy room with no windows and no exit.

For many, this claustrophobia intensifies greatly during the so-called festive season. Feelings of loneliness and despair become highlighted amid the boisterous celebrations, which anyway have largely lost their meaning, becoming a massive hedonistic exercise in gluttony, hard drinking, debilitating hangovers and frantic exchanges of tacky Christmas cards.

A London landlord told me once that every year he looked forward to Christmas and made sure his offices stayed open, for this was the time when families and relationships broke up at a record rate. 'Suddenly they find themselves alone in the street. Everything is shut down. Their friends and relatives are all cut of reach—celebrating. What do they do? They come to me in search of a roof over their heads and, bingo, my business is booming.'

Somewhere in the middle of the Christmas rush the moment comes when your whole life starts looking shrunk, lacking, empty as a Boxing Day broadsheet. It is not just consumer goods that go at throw-away prices during the post-Christmas sales. Lives and relationships also get cheapened and devalued by the all-permeating commercialism, which makes the festive season the year's biggest sale of human suffering.

A neighbour of mine committed suicide on Christmas Day, at the very time when I was having a nice Christmas meal with my kids in a Pizza Hut restaurant in Edinburgh, hundreds of miles away. He lived across the road and I had never spoken to him, but from my windows I could often see him cooking something in his kitchen, talking to his wife, arriving from somewhere in his new car . . . He was in his early thirties, tall and muscular, and had an open smile.

Apparently, his wife left him shortly before Christmas. Or he left her. Whatever it was, on that fatal Christmas Day he was in the house alone. His wife was an actress and a local celebrity of sorts. This is why on the day when his body was discovered, our street swarmed with journalists pestering his neighbours with questions. Like a pack of hungry wolves in a barren wintry forest, they were sniffing around tirelessly in search of prey. They misled the neighbours, claiming that they were 'putting together a tribute to the deceased'.

The stories which appeared in the local papers next morning were intrusive, tactless and sensationalist (to say nothing if being very badly written). They wrote a lot about the actress and almost nothing about her late husband. Even his father was referred to as 'the actress's father-in-law', as if the poor fellow himself had never existed. Such was their 'tribute'.

From my office window, I can now see a bunch of red roses pinned up to his door. Raindrops sparkle among the fading petals, stirred gently by the wind. Kids are running past on their way to school. Cars are speeding by. The world doesn't seem to grieve over the loss of one of its young souls.

Had I been aware of his misery, I could have crossed the road and knocked on his door. We could have had a drink and a chat. I know what it feels like to be alone on Christmas Day and maybe, just maybe, I could have persuaded him to change his mind.

Something is wrong with a society where people—be they smart landlords or tabloid journalists—are happy to make money out of someone else's grief. Something vitally important is amiss if we can't hear each other's screams from behind the soundproof walls of indifference. Our communications are reduced to: 'How are you today?' and we seldom bother to wait for an answer. We are frightened that the reply might be: 'Actually, I am not so well. I think I need help . . .'

'Staff can't communicate.' But who can? And is anybody willing to?

. . . The New Year was approaching.

Remembering the prescient Russian saying 'the way you meet the New Year is how you are going to spend it', Vin was dreading meeting it alone.

Once, about ten years earlier, he neglected the proverb's authenticity by marking the New Year while on a newspaper assignment on board a ferry in the middle of the English Channel and ended up stuck behind a bar in Dover in the company of a whingeing fresh divorcee.

As a result, he had spent the following year on his own, getting divorced and surrounded by strangers.

With Christmas celebrations banned, New Year was the only de-politicised public holiday in the Soviet Union. As such it came to incorporate the family element of the former combined it with the friends-get-together spirit of the latter. On the first night of a new year, the whole country was drinking itself into oblivion and stuffing itself stupid with the hard-to-get foods specially saved for the occasion.

Vin remembered thinking as a child that if the devilish 'imperialists' had indeed wanted to attack his 'glorious country', there could'nt have been a better time than New Year's Eve, when all 200 million Soviet adults, scattered over eleven time zones, were drunk out of their minds.

It was on a New Year's Eve that he would be allowed to stay up late, at times until midnight, and had his first timid sips of some nauseatingly sweet port.

'Happy New Year, Happy New Happiness' was a nice Russian New Year wish.

VV couldn't therefore bear the thought of meeting the New Year on his own—in the company of screaming seagulls behind the window and the roaring rock musician behind the wall.

'Fuck-you rock' . . . Was that what they meant by 'Folkestone

Rock' displayed in the windows of the Old High Street sweet shops? If so, 'Fuckstone Rock' would have been a better name for it.

On 30th December, he bought a hugely discounted Christmas tree (which was known as New Year Tree in the Soviet Union, of course) in Lidl, installed it in his attic office and decorated it with bits of cotton wool (to imitate snow) and pieces of kitchen foil.

He spent the whole of the next morning cooking Russian salad—a habitual Soviet New Year treat—and preparing 'zakuski': beetroots, stuffed eggs 'à la Russe', salami, pickled herrings.

Little Andrei was an admirer of VV's cooking and even suggested once that he should open a Russian restaurant in his Folkestone cottage and call it 'Papa's Café.'

Vin then ventured outside and headed for the Folkestone English Language School which, as he knew, had a handful of students from Russia and Ukraine.

It was not long before he heard Russian (with a thick Ukrainian accent) spoken by a couple of girls as they came out of the building.

Blushing with the fear of being misunderstood or—worse— mistaken for a middle-aged sex predator, he introduced himself and invited the girls—with as many friends as they wanted—to come to his place for an impromptu New Year party.

'There's plenty of food and booze, and we can all watch The Irony of Fate afterwards . . .'

The Irony of Fate was a 1970s cult Soviet TV melodrama: charming and sentimental in equal measure. It was always repeated on a New Year's Eve and had become part and parcel of every New Year celebration.

It must have been The Irony of Fate (a rather appropriate title) that tipped the balance of suspicion in his favour.

Also, he knew that his Russian was literary and cultured, with a good Moscow accent, and the girls from the provinces (which the students very obviously were) were bound to be positively impressed and reassured by it.

They all came shortly after 10 p.m.—the two girls and several friends of theirs. After a couple of minutes of shyness, they attacked the food. And the booze too. They were all very nice, and VV learned a lot about their lives in small provincial towns of post-Communist Russia and Ukraine (not that he was particularly interested).

As tradition dictated, they saw off the old year with shots of vodka at about ten to twelve. And at midnight, they all drank champagne (according to another old Russian ritual, religiously observed by VV, one had to open the bottle, fill the glasses and toss them down—bottoms up—while making a secret wish for the New Year—all during the twelve midnight chimes) and wished each other 'New Happiness' (something that VV was desperately in need of).

Then each of the guests wanted to call home to wish a Happy New Year to their families, and VV magnanimously encouraged them to use his telephone (several weeks later, it will be that particular phone bill that will make him—for the first time in his life—go to the local DSS office).

Then they watched *The Irony of Fate*, but after half an hour or so Vin could see that his guests were getting edgy. Soon, having made various excuses, they all went down to the Harbour where the town's only disco was under way. In fact, VV had encouraged them to do so: he was past the critical moment (midnight) and now had reasons to believe that, although he could still end up spending his new year surrounded by strangers, there was some hope it was going to be less lonely than the old one.

Next morning, he had his first attack of chest pain in several years.

Oscar

Ten days later, I was in Dublin. My eldest son Mitya, who lived there, invited me and little Andrei to celebrate my fiftieth birthday with him in Ireland and bought return tickets for both of us (I had to pick up Andrei from Edinburgh first).

It was a dream birthday.

On the night before it, after a hearty Russian-style dinner (Russian salad, borscht, pork cutlets with buckwheat) cooked by Mitya, we were sitting in the lounge of St Jude's cottage. With little Andrei fast asleep upstairs, Mitya and I were having a nightcap of vodka.

'You know, Dad, I am telling everyone about you, and I dream of you often too,' said Mitya. He was not prone to sentimentality which made his words even more precious. I was only hoping he was not saying them deliberately—to pacify me in the middle of a crisis.

'We are so much alike, Dad,' he continued. 'We walk and even laugh like each other.'

Trains were rattling behind the windows of the cottage of St Jude's, the patron saint of hopeless causes.

Then, at precisely midnight, when I 'officially' turned fifty, a disconnected old black phone gave out two piercing rings. I've described that spooky episode earlier in the book (see 'Fear of phone calls').

Mitya's birthday present was a thick Eason Book Shop Desk Diary in a green imitation-leather binding. Its introductory pages listed a variety of Ireland's memorable dates and events—pretty useless in my situation, as I thought then.

In actual fact, the gift turned out to be prophetic for it was Ireland where I ended up living by the end of that very year!

Next morning, Mitya took me and Andrei to Merrion Square, just round the corner from St Jude's.

In a small leafy park opposite the childhood home of Oscar Wilde, was one of the world's most amazing monuments. On its pediment, Oscar—a self-absorbed and decadent aesthete, clad in his favourite velvet smoking jacket with floating tie was reclining comfortably against the rock. In this exceptionally brilliant sculpture by Danny Osborne (the eccentric charm of which was strangely enhanced by the fact that it had been commissioned by the 'Guinness Ireland Group'), Oscar appeared extremely relaxed. So natural in fact that I am tempted to write—and remember: 'I can resist anything but temptation'?—that he looked as if he was about to step off the pedestal and dash off for a pint of 'Guinness' (if only out of gratitude to his 'sponsors') to a nearest pub—just 'to keep body and soul apart', no doubt. On the other hand, in reality he was probably not that relaxed, for 'being natural is simply a pose'.

He sat there, under a branchy rowan-tree (in winter, the berries on it got deep purple, the colour of freshly spilled human blood) inside 'little tent of blue which prisoners call the sky'. Oscar had earned the right to coin such a seemingly 'sentimental' metaphor after two years in Reading gaol.

For me Wilde was not just a literary classic and a wit but more like a close personal friend. 'How come? On the surface it, Oscar Wild, who died in 1900, couldn't possibly be a friend of mine, for even an ancient 50-year-old wreck like me was not antiquated enough for that!'

Well, let me explain.

Firstly, I am an experienced time-traveller.

Secondly, what is a friend? He is someone to whom you address your joys and sorrows; who stands by you in grief and trouble; who is always there to reassure and to cheer up. If so (and it is so!), I can earnestly count long-deceased Oscar as one of my closest soulmates and confidants.

I am sure I wouldn't have survived my latest (the last of many) personal crisis, had it not been for a postcard, pinned to the wall above my writing desk (next to 'My faith is the refusal to give up' by Britain's Chief Rabbi Jonathan Sachs), with just one sentence on it:

'We are all in the gutter, but some of us are looking at the stars.'

One of the most beautiful things ever written (or said), this sentence is worth volumes of insipid modern prose and poetry.

And about seven years earlier—recovering from yet another massive setback—I was eventually able to replace Prozac and Xanax with St John's Wort and the following hourly mantra:
'A Society can forgive a murderer, but never a dreamer.'

God knows how many times—facing a pile of unpaid bills, feeling cornered or suffering writer's block—I was taken out of limbo and forced to smile by recalling my friend's sardonic pronouncements of the type: 'I was working on the proof of one of my poems all the morning, and took out a comma. In the afternoon I put it back again.'
Or: 'History is an account of events that did not happen written by the people who weren't there.'

I was ever so grateful to Mitya for having arranged this coveted rendezvous on the morning of my fiftieth birthday.

The house in Merrion Square where Oscar spent his so-called 'formative years' accommodated *Dublin's 'American College'*— an irony, if we remembered Oscar's tongue-in-cheek comment from *The Picture of Dorian Gray*: 'Perhaps, after all, America never has been discovered. I myself would say that it had merely been detected'.

From Merrion Square we moved to 21, Westland Row—the house where baby Oscar was born 150 odd years earlier.

If the deceased have any permanent 'address' at all, it should not be the graveyard or the place where they died, but the house where they were born. For it is there that we materialise out of 'nothingness' (I am an agnostic), so it is only logical that it is also there that we eventually rejoin that very 'nothingness'.

What was the first work by Oscar that I had read? It was probably *The Canterville Ghost*. Later—at school—we studied (as a 'scathing satire of capitalist society', of course) *The Importance of Being Earnest*. Interestingly, in the Soviet Union, the play's title was translated as *The Importance of Being SERIOUS*.

The word 'earnest' (read 'honest') in the title of a popular play that was constantly performed in many a theatre and hence featured prominently on posters all over the country was deemed too subversive by the ever-vigilant (and ever-so-dumb) Soviet censorship.

Having died seventeen years before the Bolshevik coup d'état, Oscar was privileged enough to be censored by the 'socialist' state he had himself so craved. He would have loved the irony of that too . . .

We then visited yet another 'home' of Oscar's in North Dublin, although he had never lived in it: the small and cosy Dublin Writers Museum in Parnell Square.

Unlike his two other Dublin abodes, this was not a mansion but rather a Soviet-style communal flat, where one had to share bathroom and kitchen with several other tenants. For Oscar, at least, it was. The space allocated to him in the Museum was tiny—and not just in proportion to his own ego. He did have to share—not a bathroom, thankfully, but one and the same glass case with Bernard Shaw.

Why? A possible explanation could be found on the 'interpretation plate' above the exhibits:

'He (Oscar: VV) never took Ireland as his subject and for that reason is usually classed as an English writer.'

What a load of nonsense!

Firstly, geniuses are by and large stateless: they belong everywhere and nowhere—all at the same time. And Oscar, like no one else, would have hated the idea of being labelled, or 'classed'. Secondly, he was born in Ireland and therefore could be safely regarded as Irish by definition.

And lastly, he did write a lot about Ireland and Irishness and could easily enter into a dialogue on these subjects with his glass-case neighbour Bernard Shaw.

I wouldn't have been surprised if this was precisely what they did during the Museum's closing hours:

Oscar: 'Don't you think, my dear Bernard, that **there are some who will welcome with delight the idea of solving the Irish question by doing away with the Irish people**—just like they tried to do with the Jews?'

Bernard: 'I am not sure, dear boy. **I may be a tolerably good European in the Nietzschean sense, but a very bad Irishman in the Sinn Fein or Chosen People sense** . . .'

Oscar: 'Nevertheless, even you can't deny that **what captivity was to the Jews, exile has been to the Irish** . . .'

And so on . . .

At first glance, Bernard Shaw appears a suitable 'neighbour': a fellow playwright and a wit, he was born just two years after Oscar, in 1856, yet outlived him by fifty years and died at the 'venerable' age of ninety-four in 1950.

'He whom the gods love dies young.'

Can you imagine Oscar living into his nineties? You can't? And neither can I. Unlike, it has to be said, Malcolm Muggeridge: 'I have little doubt that if Oscar Wilde had lived into his nineties . . . he would have been considered a benign, distinguished figure suitable to preside at a school prize-giving or to instruct and exhort scoutmasters at their jamborees. He might even have been knighted.'

'Sir Oscar Wilde, OBE . . . How incongruous! One thing I am sure of, however, is that, unlike the elderly Bernard Shaw, Oscar would have never been duped by Stalin into believing that communism was the best thing after sliced bread.

Or, maybe, he would, who knows . . .

It is another writer, playwright and wit who strikes me as being the closest to Oscar—in life, in literature and even in death: Anton Chekhov. The two never met of course, but the coincidences are striking. They lived at almost exactly the same time, albeit in different countries. Chekhov was born six years later and died at forty-four in 1904—four years later than Oscar.

Chekhov was a practising physician, and Oscar, although not a doctor himself, was the son of Ireland's best-known ophthalmologist.

They both worked in the same genres, although Chekhov never wrote poetry.

Even their sexual preferences were, allegedly, not that dissimilar.

Like Oscar in English, Chekhov is by far the most quoted writer in the Russian language. 'I dreamt that what I had thought was reality was a dream, and what I had thought was a dream was reality,'—this entry from Chekhov's 'Diaries' could easily be nominated for an Oscar, i.e. pass for something Oscar Wilde wrote or said.

Their tragically parallel lives ended on largely the same note—a joke.

Looking at the particularly naff and faded wallpaper in need of replacement in the Paris hotel room where he was dying, Oscar said: 'One of us will have to go . . .'

Chekhov on his deathbed asked for a glass of champagne. He was dying in Germany, in the rather posh spa town of Badenweiler, and was being looked after by a German doctor called Swerer. It was the latter whom he asked for a glass of champagne.

According to an old German tradition, a doctor who had given a lethal diagnosis for a colleague (Chekhov, of course, was a practicing physician too) was to treat the dying man to a glass of champagne.

He injected Chekhov with camphor and asked a servant to bring champagne.

'I haven't had champagne for ages,' said Chekhov in Russian and smiled.

Then he turned over to his left side and added in German:

'Champagner ich sterbe[12] . . .' These were his last words.

Both Wilde and Chekhov wrote through their lives and lived through their writing. I am sure they would have enjoyed each other's company.

---

12 I am dying (German).

'Dear venerable table'

Once in Australia, the editor of the large daily newspaper where I worked asked me to write an article about Chekhov. Its publication was to coincide with the first night of Melbourne Theatre Company's new production of Uncle Vanya.

Chekhov is one of my favourite writers of all time and I keep rereading (in Russian and in English!) his novels, short stories, plays and letters.

Alongside Chekhov's works, I had gone through a lot of the 'Chekhoviana', i.e. memoirs of Chekhov written by his artist brother Mikhail, his actress wife Olga Knipper, his mistress Lika Mizinova etc. Surely I could not say anything new about Chekhov and that was why I eventually decided to write a feature not about Chekhov himself, but about his co-author, with whose unflinching solid assistance Anton Pavlovich wrote some of his best plays, novels and short stories.

Wait a moment . . . Did Chekhov really have a co-author? This sounds like a small revolution in the Chekhoviana.

Yes, he did! Moreover, one of my last assignments in Russia was to secure an interview with this little-known co-author of Chekhov's who, despite being well over a hundred years old, was still alive and amazingly well.

CURRICULUM VITAE

FAMILY NAME: Table
GIVEN NAME: Writing
SOCIAL ORIGIN: Piece of furniture
PLACES OF RESIDENCE: 1889–1892, Moscow; 1892–1899, Melikhovo; 1899–1957 Yalta; 1957—present time, permanently registered in Melikhovo
OCCUPATION: Exhibit
PRINTED WORKS: *Uncle Vanya, The Seagull, Ionich, The*

Man in a Shell, The Darling, Gooseberry, Ward Number 6
etc.—all written in collaboration with A.P. Chekhov
DISTINCTIVE FEATURES: Since 1897—covered with
  green cloth

This was not an attempt at eccentricity on my part, albeit I own
up to having penned an amazingly peripatetic 'life story' of an
antique Biedermeier couch that used to belong to Hitler in the
book called *Dreams on Hitler's Couch*.

Chekhov himself liked breathing life into furniture. In the
Chekhovs' Taganrog house, where he was born and spent his
childhood, there stood a cupboard where Evgenia Yakovlevna,
the future writer's mother, used to keep sweets. Walking past
this cupboard, young Anton would stop, bow and exclaim
with reverence: 'Dear venerable cupboard!' Later he used this
mocking address form in *The Cherry Orchard*.

Alone in Chekhov's modest study in the village of Melikhovo
(about fifty miles away from Moscow), I was touching with
trepidation the gleaming door handles that Chekhov used to
touch and polished with his hands.

'A good memorial museum starts with authentic door
handles,' Yuri Avdeev, the museum's director, told me.

Behind the window, I could see the kitchen garden the
Chekhovs loved and called 'The South of France' . . .

And here it was—Chekhov's authentic writing desk still
upholstered with the original green leather (not dissimilar to the
one I am now writing at inside Pegasus Cottage).

There's nothing more intimate for a writer, nothing that can
evoke his (or her) spirit better than the writing desk, behind
which hours, days, weeks and years of struggle, elation, hard
work, inspiration, tedium and whatnot are spent.

If pieces of furniture had personalities, then a writing table should
be the most engrossing of them all. And by far the best interlocutor .
. . Streets ahead of a couch, a cupboard or even a bed.

To breathe life into the legendary table I repeated Chekhov's own magic mantra: 'I dreamt that what I thought was reality was a dream, and what I thought a dream was reality' before whispering reverently:

'How do you do, my dear venerable table?'

A floorboard creaked, the table stirred slightly, as if acknowledging my greeting, and started its unhurried narrative:

'We were inseparable with Anton Pavlovich—in woes and in feasts, and my master recognised only one sort of feast and one sort of woe—they were both called 'writing'. Here my participation was indispensable.

'I can't help thinking every moment that I must write . . . Write, write and write,' he confessed in one of his letters to Lika written with my help, i.e. on top of me, of course.

'Before me, he didn't have a permanent table. The Chekhovs were poor, they kept roaming from flat to flat and using landlords' furniture. True, Anton Pavlovich's brother, Nikolai, who was an artist, once got a writing table as a royalty (or rather instead of a royalty) from the publisher Utkin. That table now lives in Moscow, at Chekhov's Museum, but Anton Pavlovich worked at it only sporadically . . .

'I will never forget how happy Chekhov was when he bought me. 'I am writing another short story now. I am totally engrossed and practically do not leave my writing table. By the way, I have bought myself a new one' he wrote proudly to his publisher Suvorin in March 1889.

In three years' time, together with other members of Chekhov's family, I moved to Melikhovo, our country retreat.

'In Melikhovo, the Chekhovs used to get up early—very much in a peasant way. Peasantry was in Chekhov's blood: his grand-father was a serf of landowner Chertkov.

At 5 a.m. Anton Pavlovich would already be sitting at me, unless he was to receive his patients that morning. Yes, he was a doctor, too, and was treating local peasants in this very study where we are now.

'The daily routine was meticulously observed by the Chekhovs. Anton Pavlovich bought a discarded church bell, hung it in the courtyard, and precisely at noon one of the servants would strike it twelve times. This was the signal not only for the Chekhovs, but for the whole neighbourhood to go for lunch . . .

'During lunch, Anton Pavlovich would leave the dining table from time to time and would run up to me to jot down a couple of lines. He then returned to his favourite seat in the dining room, next to the door of his study—as close to me as he could be. After lunch, the Chekhovs rested, and in the evening they had music, guests and lively discussions . . .

'But even then Chekhov did not forget about me and did some writing. That was not easy for it was a democratic household and the visitors were allowed to move around the rooms freely; they could also enter Chekhov's study whenever they wished, and Anton Pavlovich never told them off for having disturbed him

'It was very easy to be his guest,' V. Giliarovsky, a well-known Moscow writer and journalist, recalled. True, it was easy indeed for the guests but not necessarily for the host!

'Chekhov, however, never expressed his irritation aloud; only on paper did he sometimes let go. . . I remember clearly him writing on me to Suvorin in December 1892: 'Oh, if you could only know how tired I am! Exhausted to bursting point. Guests, guests, guests. . . My estate stands on Kashirsky High Road, and every passing intellectual thinks it is OK to stop at my place and warm up, and sometimes even stay overnight. The whole legion of doctors alone has visited me of late! Yes, it's pleasing to be hospitable, but there must be a limit. It was because of the guests that I fled from Moscow after all!'

'Such bitterness was rare for Chekhov. More often he tried to be ironic about his home's popularity. 'They play and sing romances in the living room next to my study all day long, that's why I am constantly in elegiac mood,' he joked in his letter to L. Avilova in March 1893.

'In 1884, however, fleeing the incessant stream of visitors, Chekhov moved his study to the newly built outhouse.[13] I moved with him—for the summer only. Here Chekhov and I wrote *The Seagull*.

'On the balcony of this garden office there was a flagpole. When Anton Pavlovich was at home, a red flag was hoisted on it to let the entire neighbourhood know that Doctor Chekhov was available to receive patients!

'Now let's look at the objects on my green cloth top: an inkpot with a lid, a pen, a candle in a candlestick, a bottle with glue, envelopes for letters. These are all fairly uninteresting, yet some other things resting on my surface do deserve separate descriptions:

'**French seed catalogue** The Chekhovs loved to work in their garden. They ordered seeds from the South of Russia, from St Petersburg and from abroad. Having returned from his trip to Sakhalin Island where he had conducted the first ever census, Chekhov brought back the rhizomes of Sakhalin buckwheat and planted them in his Melikhovo garden, whence this plant has gradually spread all over Central Russia.

'In the garden, you can now see Chekhov-planted Berlin poplars, cherry trees and lilac. They all start blooming in spring. The Chekhovs also grew artichokes, asparagus, aubergines, watermelons, which, when they ripened, were given to guests and to the Melikhovo peasant kids. During the last years of his

13   Chekhov's equivalent of my Pegasus Cottage! VV

life, Chekhov would often say: 'I think that if it were not for literature, I would have been a gardener.'

'**Pince-nez**. It is hard to imagine Chekhov without a pince-nez. In actual fact, however, he started wearing glasses only in 1897, when eye-surgeon P. Radzvitsky visited Melikhovo, diagnosed Chekhov with astigmatism and selected a pince-nez for him.

'**Medicine chest**. This is one of the most interesting of Chekhov's possessions. If you open the chest and sniff it, you will feel that a weak odour of medicines still lingers in it . . . The longevity of smells is impressive . . . Stories still circulate in Melikhovo district about experienced and unselfish Doctor Chekhov. He could be contacted for help any time of the day or night and he had never refused anyone—not once.

'I could also tell you about a village school for Melikhovo kids Anton Pavlovich built with his own money, albeit he was far from rich. Chekhov himself acquired wooden desks for that school, and they are still there—my junior brothers and sisters. Ask them—and they may tell you much more about my famous owner and co-author . . .'

When it came out, my 'interview' with Chekhov's writing table was sent to the Melikhovo Museum and became one of its exhibits. I am extremely proud of this, of course.

As for 'Uncle Vanya', its Melbourne production was appalling. The actors shouted a lot on stage, as if they thought that the louder they yelled, the better their acting was, and—encouraged by the director, no doubt—had turned this rather tragic play into a farce. The audience was laughing their pants off (according to my observations, many Australians went to the theatre primarily to have a good laugh). As a result, Chekhov's characters on stage talked, moved and behaved artificially—like pre-programmed robots, not living people.

During the interval, I was approached by my newspaper's theatre critic—a tall elderly man of Serbian extraction.

'What do you think of it all, Vitali?' he asked me.

I honestly told the critic that the company had fallen into a trap by trying to act a Chekhov play 'as it was written', by concentrating on its uppermost superficial layer, whereas Chekhov's plays existed not on one, but on several—at times, four or five—different levels that had to be kept firmly in mind and reflected in the acting.

Having opened the paper the following morning, I saw the review signed by the critic: 'The company had fallen into a trap by trying to act a Chekhov play "as it was written", by concentrating on its uppermost superficial layer, whereas Chekhov's plays existed not on one, but on several—at times, four or five—different levels that had to be kept firmly in mind and reflected in the acting, it ran.

It was my first (and, hopefully, last) piece of writing neither in the first, nor in the third, but in (or rather by) the SECOND PERSON.

Writers' tools

Here it is relevant to say that the most amazing change experienced by my generation of writers has been in the field of technology.

At my Soviet primary school, we had to use only wooden pens with metallic tips that had to be dipped into a personal inkpot every pupil had to bring in from home in a special Mum—(or Gran-) manufactured bag. The real bane of my existence was the subject called *Chistopisaniye*—'Clean Writing'. No matter how far I extended my ink-smeared blue tongue, my pen kept leaving horrible navy-blue spots all over the paper. The spots kept spreading and growing, like cancerous tumours, until I mopped them up with a fluffy 'blotter' which would stop their malignant growth and turn them into smears.

The advantage of the metal-tipped pens was that they could be easily transformed into darts during the interval. One of my fellow pupils nearly lost an eye as a result.

We were first allowed to use fountain pens only in the fifth form.

I wrote my first poems and stories in longhand of course—first a 'black' copy, then a 'clean' one. Typewriters were prohibitively expensive and required a special permission to own.

My university diploma paper was also written in longhand (I then asked a girl with a nice calligraphic handwriting with whom I was friends to copy it for me—for a fee of course).

At Moscow newspapers and magazines of the late 1970s—early 1980s, they had typewriters, but most of the hacks (including yours truly) were slow with them and would rather write their copy in longhand and then carry it to a 'typists' bureau' staffed with noisy (and normally single) women, prone to gossip and affairs. One had to be on friendly terms with the typists for fear of having to spend long hours banging out your own copy on some antediluvian East German-made electric 'Erica' which, despite its nice-sounding foreign name, was likely to be rusty, semi-broken, and make a clatter comparable to that of a platoon of Soviet soldiers goose-stepping on the Red Square cobbles. Or else—give you a nasty electric shock via your fingertips, as happened to me more than once.

When my father gave me my first typewriter as a birthday present I—by then an established Moscow journalist—was speechless. It was bright-red, portable and made in Yugoslavia. What else could one dream of? *Konstantin Paustovsky's pronouncement to the effect that writing was a mysterious* interaction of the author's brain, a pen in his hand and a clean sheet of paper was quickly forgotten.

I saw my first computer in London while on a short attachment to the *Guardian* in 1988.

No, actually much much earlier . . .

It was 1961 and I was six—approaching seven—when Dad took me to his Institute's *Novogodniaya Yolka* (literally, New Year Fir-Tree)—a special New Year party for kids of the Institute's staff (as I have said already, Christmas and Christmas parties were taboo in the atheistic USSR). Dad's place of work was known officially as Physico-Technical Institute of the Academy of Sciences of the Ukrainian Soviet Socialist Republic. It was a pioneering establishment in the field of physics, where the nucleus was split for the first time in Europe in the 1930s. The party was at the Institute's Kharkov offices in Yumovskaya Street, whereas its main offices that housed one of Europe's largest and most powerful accelerators (at which Dad, incidentally, worked) were in the outskirts of the city, in the village called Piatikhatki (Five Huts). Everyone in Kharkov knew that Piatikhatki had a very high level of background radiation . . .

Having greeted Grandfather Frost (I remember he carried an impressive cane with a blinking electric knob at the top) and *Sniegurochka* (the Snow Maiden), having jumped (sheepishly) with other children around the New Year tree (not the Christmas tree, mind you!), having received a plain-looking goodie bag with several sticky lollipops inside, I got tired and wanted to go home.

'Before we go, I want to show you something.' said my Dad with a mischievous smile.

He took me to his laboratory—a spacious brightly lit room now totally deserted. Half of that room as well as half of the next one and half of the corridor were all taken by a bulky brownish installation which looked like a long row of multi-tiered gym lockers.

'What is it?' I asked him.

'It is called a computer,' Dad replied.

'And what can this ka . . . poo . . . ter do?'

'Almost anything . . . For example, it can count . . .'

Dad pressed some buttons—and the enormous machine came to life: red and yellow lamps began to blink frantically to the accompaniment of the loud even noise like that of a giant car getting started. The floor was shaking slightly under my feet.

'Give it a task!' Dad kept encouraging me and I couldn't think of anything better than asking the machine to add two and two. Dad shrugged and typed the 'task' in on a large and clumsy keyboard.

The noise increased dramatically; it was no longer a car getting started but rather an airplane's engine revving up. The lights were blinking faster and faster, like some demented winking octogenarians. I shut my eyes and covered my ears with my hands.

It all lasted for a couple of minutes after which the noise suddenly stopped. I opened my eyes.

'Here's your answer,' my father said. In his hand he was holding a piece of yellow perforated paper on which a bleak and hardly visible little 'four' was sloppily printed.

I will never forget that 'meeting' with my first ever computer.

When I joined *the Age* newspaper in July 1990, I had to master a computer very fast. But it was easier said than done. I kept losing my columns and whole chapters of my second book *Dateline Freedom* which I was then writing. Curiously, both columns and chapters tended to disappear never to be found again at the point when I was about to put a final full stop. Not a moment earlier! One *Dateline Freedom* chapter of fifty-two pages I managed to lose twice! Floppy discs onto which you could save the text did not exist then.

I could put my name under P.J. O'Rourke's remark that a computer was but a machine that let us make mistakes faster than any other invention in human history, with the possible exception of handguns and tequila and ended up writing an open letter to my computer as one of my weekly columns. Entitled 'Unrequited love turns to terminal nightmare', at a first glance the column indeed looked like a letter to a mysterious Taiwanese woman-lover (the machine was made in Taiwan) who spoke with an American accent (the machine's spell-checker only accepted American spelling).

. . . I love you . . . It's only a month since we met, but I can't live without you now. . . I was afraid even to touch you in the beginning, but then, when I took you to my place, my fear was gone . . . You were so engaging, encouraging and clever. You seemed much cleverer than I, to be frank, and that was a bit unsettling . . . But you were also friendly and never paraded your innate intelligence and erudition unless I asked you to do so . . . Since we started living together, my writing had grown so much faster . . . You were giving me inspiration and loads of advice too. We were also playing games and I couldn't help admiring your playfulness, despite the fact that I always lost . . . I was spending days on end just looking at your face and you didn't mind my staring at you in the least. Probably I loved you too much. The more we are in love, the less we are loved ourselves—that's the sad law of human existence. You were becoming whimsical—interrupting my writing and demanding attention. You took some of my written pieces away and never gave them back. You were making ridiculous faces and teasing me with some nasty guttural sounds. I thought you must have fallen ill and called my mate David who is experienced in dealing with creatures like you. David examined you carefully and pronounced his diagnosis: you have gone mad! Two blokes in uniforms grabbed you rudely by the sides and took you away.

And so on.

The fact that it was a computer, not a mistress, I was writing the letter to was revealed in the only penultimate sentence.

'I log for you!' ended the column.

I remember the bulky first-generation Toshiba laptops, with a set of rubber caps to transmit a story to the office via the telephone—an early 1990s precursor of the World Wide Web. The caps were supposed to fit the shapes of telephone speakers and receivers: if the grip was not tight enough, the copy would get corrupted to the point of complete abracadabra. Well, they seldom did fit, and, having wasted the precious minutes (at times, hours) in the run-up to the deadline trying to send a story via the telephone (with some fancy square-shaped receiver that—no matter how hard I tried—simply couldn't be gripped tightly enough by the stiff and round rubber cap) in my hotel room, I would end up dialing the office and dictating the text to a dispassionate copytaker.

And just eighteen years later . . . Please read on.

'There's nothing else here but the bloody sea and the bloody rocks . . . And it is in such a drab place that I am going to kill you,' the woman muttered.'

Not a bad start for a thriller novel. How about an end? Here it is:

'After that, he sat on the wet sand, so close to the water that the waves—heavy and clumsy like pregnant seals—were almost touching his feet. The setting sun was painting pink the under-bellies of the clouds hanging low above the grey sea. White caps could be seen here and there, but it was obvious that the storm he had been expecting all day was not going to happen.'
A fairly fluent and lively description, I would say. If you discount the 'pregnant seals' . . .

Whose literary style do the extracts (which, incidentally, I have translated from Russian) remind you of? Ian Fleming? Stephen King? Harold Robbins? Vitali Vitaliev? (thank you, but no).

No need to phone a friend. The name of the author is PC Writer 1.0, and the above quotes are taken from a 285-page book, with the intriguing title *True Love.wrt* (for brevity, let's call it simply *True Love* from now on) and the subtitle 'An impeccable novel', he (or rather 'it') has penned.

'The first ever book written by a computer,' says the blurb (in Russian, no doubt).

And that reminder is helpful, for opening *True Love* at random and leafing through it, one can be forgiven for thinking that this is an average (possibly even above average) modern novel whose heroes (both goodies and baddies) happen to have the same names as the characters of Leo Tolstoy's *Anna Karenina*: Levin, Vronsky, Kitty (at times, referred to in a familiar Russian fashion as 'Katen'ka') and Anna, of course. The only Tolstoy's protagonist that is missing is the fatal Steam Engine (or 'Parovoz' in Russian)—definitely a baddy.

The development of the software program for the book took about eight months, but it took the computer only three days to write it!

The style of *True Love* is truly 'impeccable', if at times a bit clichéd:

'Kitty couldn't fall asleep for a long time. Her nerves were strained like two tight strings, and even a glass of hot wine that Vronsky made her drink, did not help her. Lying in bed she kept going over and over that monstrous scene at the meadow.'

The book's razor-sharp and very colloquial dialogue is totally devoid of any peculiar speech patterns, i.e. all the characters sound precisely like one and the same early twenty-first century young urban professional.

And the vocabulary, the turn of phrase and the sheer length of sentences (succinct), as you might have noticed from the above samples, are definitely not Tolstoy's. If so, you are absolutely right, for the authors of the computer program, a St Petersburg-based company Astrel-SPb, have uploaded (on top of *Anna Karenina*) seventeen modern works of Russian literature into it. A Russian translation of a novel by Japanese author Haruki Murakami was (to make PC Writer 1.0 more PC, so to speak?) used as the main style matrix. The result is a grammatically correct and free-flowing 'Russian-ese' mongrel of a modern novel, populated by Tolstoy's characters.

But how about the plot?

The computer-devised denouement of *True Love* is of course significantly different from that of *Anna Karenina*.
Compare.

Anna Karenina by **Leo Tolstoy**: Anna meets and falls in love with Andrei Vronsky, a handsome young officer. She abandons her child and husband to be with him. When Vronsky tires of her and leaves her to go to war, she kills herself by leaping under a train.

True Love.wrt by **PC Writer 1.0**: The characters find themselves on an uninhabited island. All of them have amnesia. They know who they are, but don't remember if they are married or have children, and what relationship they have with each other. They are given a chance to build their relationships anew.

Would the latter plot make Leo Tolstoy's ghost even paler (with envy) than he is already? I don't think so. But outwriting Tolstoy was not the aim of the program's creators. As Alexander Prokopovich, chief editor of Astrel-SPb, explained modestly in his interview for *The St Petersburg Times,* 'the program can never become an author, like PhotoShop can never be Raphael.'

His opinion, however, was not shared by the ebullient post-Communist Russian media.

'The new author is indeed promising. He doesn't require royalties, won't go on leave and will always deliver on time,' enthused NTV, Russia's main TV channel. Their 5th Channel colleagues took the concept even further, having russified it a bit: 'A cyber author won't get pregnant or go on a drinking binge!'

I am happy to agree with the last statement: making PC Writer pregnant would require a coup of audacious science fiction. Yet it cannot be stopped from creating other pregnant creatures, like the 'heavy'-going (crawling?) and rather naff 'pregnant seals' (see above). Metaphorically speaking, a 'cyber-writer' can still be made pregnant with clichés and give birth to a piece of unadulterated trash.

Whatever the scary (for real flesh-and-blood writers) predictions may be, I myself am not in a hurry to change my battered author's toga (an imitation one, bought for a fiver at London's Leather Lane Street market) for the expensively casual jeans-and-trainers outfit of a computer geek.

Contrary to some Russian newspapers' prognosis, *True Love* has not become 'a literary bomb'. While being an undisputed achievement of the country's IT professionals and linguists, it still has a long way to go to be even distantly comparable in literary merit to the hasty black-ink scribbles of the bearded and shortish Russian Count.

As the serious *Izvestiya* newspaper hurried to conclude, 'Leo Tolstoy would have had enough sense of humour to laugh off the whole PC Writer idea. . .'

So, in the foreseeable future there's little chance of a computer producing a new *Anna Karenina*, *War and Peace* or even a *Harry Potter and JK Rowling's Fortune*.

The only possible blockbuster we can expect is most likely to be called *PC Writer and the Pregnant Seals.*

As the modernised, computerised and Haruki Murakami-sed Levin mumbles prophetically on page 61 of *True Love*:
'You know what: I would have been very scared of what's to come had I not been so drunk.'

A talking writing table, after all, is not such a huge incongruity compared to a computer-generated pregnant seal.

Doris Lessing

I met Doris Lessing at a literary do several years ago. After a long conversation and several glasses of champagne, we decided to exchange contact details, and I asked her for an email address.

'I don't do Internet or emails,' she told me proudly, scribbling down her postal address and landline telephone number instead. I didn't know then that Britain's greatest lady of letters was also a convinced technophobe and Internet-hater. That, incidentally, did not in any way reflect on her writing, and I was thrilled when she was awarded the Nobel Prize for Literature at the end of 2007.

In her highly publicised acceptance speech, Lessing raged against modern 'young men and women' who 'know nothing of the world' and 'read nothing knowing only some speciality, for instance, computers'. One can almost hear disdain in her voice at the very mention of computers.

She went on to pour scorn at the Internet, 'which has seduced a whole generation with its inanities so that even quite reasonable people will confess that, once they are hooked, it is hard to cut free, and they may find a whole day has passed in blogging . . .'.

Paradoxically enough, only a couple of years earlier I would have been happy to agree with her.

True, I was ready to recognise the convenience of sending an article to a newspaper by email rather than dictating it over the phone to a copytaker or scribbling it down in longhand and handing it over to a typist (as I had done for so many years). On the other hand, I used to be a staunch opponent of mobile phones and was the world's last (and possibly only) mobile refusenik.

That was until 2007, when the Loved One gave me a nice little phone as a gift. To cut a long story short, now I can hardly imagine my life without that tiny gadget. It helps me stay in constant touch not just with her, but also with my children, who live several hundred miles away.

True, technology can at times be intimidating and intrusive. But it can also be profoundly HUMAN. For example, Skype allows me not only to talk to my three small kids on a regular basis, but also to see their beautiful faces, their smiles, their new haircuts. Miles apart, we spend whole evenings playing chess, dominos and bowling (also on Skype), and the distance between us all but disappears.

Can one think of a more human application of technology than helping children and their 'estranged', yet loving, Daddy to maintain their bond?

The 'Irish' diary

14 January. Folkestone

The day of great change. I am at the brink . . . £75 left in my account—all the money I've got in the world (not to count mounting debts). Mess in the cottage on return from Dublin. Panic attack.

After hours of internal struggle, I get into 'super jalopy' and drive to Folkestone's DSS office.

Rain. Fog. Even the weather spells out despair. Am I part of it all now?

I drive past the local police station feeling like a criminal about to give himself in . . .

Several dozen battered cars (of the unemployed?) are parked outside the 'Job Centre' (should it rather be 'Jobless Centre', I wonder?).

My B-plated jalopy which had just had its windscreen wipers bent and twisted (for no reason) by some vandals overnight, doesn't look out of place here.

Inside, there's a queue of bedraggled unshaven people, mostly men, with blank, as if extinguished, eyes. They are all holding their 'unemployment books' looking like dog-eared white memo pads.

In a desperate attempt to detach myself from reality, I take out my notebook and start making notes of the snippets of conversation reaching me from behind the counters:

'Your case is with our special decision unit . . .'

'Happy retirement, Mr. Baker . . .'

'What shall I do if my payment doesn't arrive?'

'Give us a ring. Or throw yourself down the loo!' (the last remark is made by a fat ruddy-faced man from behind the counter).

I then turn my attention to the fellow queuers:

– An unshaven man without an eye. Drink-sodden face. 'The last job I did was washing up at the college,' he says to a woman behind the counter.

– A man with multiple scars on his head. Dirty trainers and no socks.

The staff address the 'clients' patronisingly as 'mate' and even 'matie'.

I try to make myself feel like I am on an assignment. For whom or what? Life? Destiny? Investigating into my own survival skills? If so, the research is getting truly life-threatening—as it should be.

My turn comes. I am being interviewed by a tired-looking Indian woman.

'Your savings?'

'Exactly £75 . . .'

She asks where I had worked before. I say The *Guardian*. She asks what it is. I explain that it is a newspaper. 'How do you spell it?' she asks.

I can't help feeling that we must have swapped roles with her by mistake and remember reading somewhere recently that clerks in Britain's benefit offices 'sit behind anger-proof screens'.

The interview is suddenly interrupted by one of the Job Centre senior officials. I can see he is more senior than my interviewer from his bossy manner and a large 'Job Centre' badge, the size of a sheriff's star, on his chest.

'Excuse me a moment,' he says to the woman. 'I need to have a word with this gentleman.'

He takes me aside.

'Please correct me if I am wrong, but have I seen you on TV?' he asks.

'Well, yes, it is quite possible,' I reply and mention several programmes I was on, including Saturday Night Clive and Have I Got News for You.

He turns away from me and shouts to no one in particular: 'I was right! I was right!'

At this point, several of his colleagues, including the woman who interviewed me, leave their counters and join us in the corner paying no attention to the grumbles they are causing in the queue.

'We thought we had a celebrity here,' another man enthuses.
'If I am a celebrity, then an F-list one, where 'F' stands for Folkestone,' I try to joke.

'I was once on TV myself,' butts in the ruddy fat man whom I heard advising a client to jump down the loo if the payment didn't arrive. 'I was at a Tube station in London and they were filming something there. The same evening I could see my face on the ten o'clock news, can you believe it?'
Someone then remembers hearing me on the radio . . .

I've become a Job Centre celebrity!

It's obvious I've made their day, but I dread the inevitable question. And here it comes:

'And what are you doing HERE, Vitali?'

My response is quick, almost automatic: 'To be absolutely honest with you, I was just doing some research on the state of Britain's social services for a possible future book.'
I take out the green notebook and demonstrate my undecipherable scribbles.

I realise that I have just told them a lie that was a hundred percent true.

They all escort me to the exit telling me in chorus that I am welcome to pop in at any time or give them a ring if I need any more information.

15 January

A default notice from my bank arrives with the morning post.

After the failure of my yesterday's DSS attempt, I am now

doing survival full-time. It is now my main and only job.

Home, family, love . . . All those words have largely lost their meaning. Future? The least meaningful of all.

Actions. I need money. Took more books to my friend Nick's second-hand bookshop in Old High Street. Its interior now feels pretty much like my no-longer-existing home: half of the books on the shelves are mine (or rather formerly mine). I part with them without regret, but will never sacrifice my favourite ones of which I still have about five hundred. If I lose them, I'll lose a huge chunk of my soul.

A new small magazine is being launched in Folkestone this afternoon and I was asked to give a talk at the launch party. Am I becoming part of Folkestone's (non—existent) cultural scene? Scary . . .

Evening. Spoke at the party. Said something about cherishing hope that one day the phrase 'Folkestone intellectual' would stop being an oxymoron. Everyone laughed, albeit I suspect most didn't know what 'oxymoron' meant and have simply reacted to the 'moron' bit.

It is funny how easy it normally is to make an average crowd laugh. You come on stage and say 'fuck' or 'bum'—and paroxysms of laughter are guaranteed.

A surprise encounter at the party was with David, the former chief designer at the *European* and now head of design at *The Times*. He happens to be living nearby. It was nice to remember our ex-colleagues. And again something stopped me from asking him to introduce me to his bosses at *The Times*. What is it? A fear of self-humiliation? Of appearing less successful than people perceive you to be?

From tomorrow I am starting a concentrated email attack on editorial offices all over the country and, if necessary, overseas too. After all, my skills and experience are still there, even if my age is now a disadvantage . . . And if I have to work for a small local rag, no matter—I need the money to survive.

Have forsaken my daily bottle of wine and been rereading *Manuscripts Don't Burn*—a collection of Mikhail Bulgakov's letters—instead. Bulgakov, as it appears, also couldn't stand loneliness and suffered 'attacks of terror' when left on his own.

Is the professional success of a writer necessarily a result of his personal life failure? I don't believe it, for the profession (writing) eventually starts suffering from a messy personal life too.

It is important to keep reminding myself how very lucky I am being able to put all my innermost thoughts on paper.

The Master

. . . Bulgakov himself was a survivor par excellence. When all his plays and novels were banned by Stalin's censors in the late 1930s, he wrote a letter to Stalin in which he insisted on his right to be published and carried on to say that if he—for one reason or another—could not be granted that right, he should be allowed to emigrate.

Bulgakov added that he had no means of subsistence left, that he was seriously unwell (it was true: he had progressive TB that would finally kill him in March 1940) and that all his creative skills and imagination were running to waste.

Now, that was a crazily brave thing to do at the height of the Great Purge when thousands of innocent Soviet people—writers and non-writers alike—were disappearing without a trace every single day. Yet Bulgakov thought he had nothing to lose.

He received no reply, of course.

Here it has to be said that Stalin was very much aware of Bulgakov's existence. Moreover, he could even be called a fan, if not of all of the writer's works then definitely of one of his plays, *The Days of the Turbins*, which the dictator had seen on stage dozens of times. That was why Bulgakov's life—unlike that of Daniil Kharms, Isaac Babel, Nikolai Gumilev and hundreds of other writers—was temporarily spared.

Several months after the letter to Stalin was sent, a phone rang blaringly in Bulgakov's basement flat. The dictator was on the line.

'So, you don't like us, Mikhail Afanas'yevich?'
'I just want to live normally and to be able to work,' Bulgakov replied.
'All right,' said Stalin. 'We'll find you a job. Have you tried the Bolshoi Theatre?'
'Yes, I have. They said they had no vacancies . . .'
'Do try again. I have a feeling they will find something for you this time round . . . And let's get together and talk properly soon.'

The meeting never took place, but Bulgakov did get a job (for a short while) as a librettist at the Bolshoi.

In a truly sadistic fashion, Stalin kept playing this sinister cat-and-mouse game with terminally ill Bulgakov: by applying whip and carrot alternatively, he had been trying to subdue the latter's creative spirit until the writer's untimely death.

Yet, unlike Bulgakov's mortal body, the spirit of the Master was indestructible.

Konstantin Paustovsky, another literary mentor of mine, who went to school with Bulgakov and knew him very well, recalls in his epic autobiography *Story of a Life* how the dying master entertained his friends with stories of his imaginary encounters with Stalin. One of those stories went like this:

Bulgakov is supposed to be writing long and enigmatic letters to Stalin every day, signing them 'Tarzan'. Stalin is surprised and even somewhat frightened every time he gets them. He gets curious and demands that Beria, his secret police chief, should immediately bring the author of the letters for him to see. Bulgakov is found and brought into the Kremlin. Stalin smokes his pipe and asks him in a leisurely, even cordial, way:

'Is it you who writes these letters to me?'
'Yes, Yosiph Vissarionovich.'
'So, it's you—Bulgakov, the famous writer?'
'It is me . . .'
'Why then these patched trousers, broken shoes?..'
'Oh, it's just that . . . my earnings are a bit on the low side at present . . .'

Stalin summons the Commissar for Supplies.
'What are you doing here, eh? Can't you clothe one writer? Clothe him at once. In gabardine. And look at your boots! Take them off at once and give them to this man! Why so pale? Frightened? Do as I say!'

He then does the same with his Commissar for Food.

So now, with Bulgakov being well dressed and having plenty to eat, he strikes up a friendship with Stalin and starts visiting the Kremlin frequently. Stalin trusts him unreservedly and even complains occasionally:

'You see, they all keep screaming: genius, genius! And yet there's no one I could have a glass of brandy with . . .'

One day Bulgakov is tired and depressed.

'What's the matter, Misha?'
'Well, I've just written a play, but the theatres won't produce it.'
'Theatres are getting out of hand! Don't you worry. I'll fix it.'
Stalin takes up the telephone.

'Miss, get me the Moscow Art Theatre. The MAT? Who is this? Listen, this is Stalin speaking. I'd like to have a word with the Director . . . Where is the Director? . . . pause . . . What? Died? Just this minute? Well, really! People are so nervous these days!'

I go to sleep with a smile on my face . . .[14]

16 January

This morning my friend Nick, the bookseller, popped in without warning.

He often does that to check up on me, in his own semi-jocular words, to make sure that I haven't committed suicide yet.

Yet this time he is excited.

'You know who I have in my shop? Your old friend—a senior editor of Penguin Publishers who met you a long time ago, but is still a fan. He came in lured by the display of your books in my shop window and couldn't believe it when I said that you are actually living here in Folkestone . . . I left him in the shop on his own as a hostage . . . ha . . . ha . . . and came to fetch you . . . Get dressed quickly and let's go! He is dying to see you!'

The editor from Penguin?

Yes, I remembered him—a knowledgeable and gentle middle-

14 According to some sources the very moment Bulgakov died in 1940, the telephone rang in his Moscow flat. 'We are calling from Comrade Stalin's Secretariat,' a stern male voice said. 'Is it true that Comrade Bulgakov has just died?—'Yes, it is true.' And the caller hung up . . . Not that Stalin had the last laugh in the story which, as I tend to believe, could have been made up by Bulgakov himself!

aged man who wanted to see me during my first—or was it second?—visit to London, for he was interested in publishing my first—or was it second?—book.

He invited me to the Penguin London office, and I was shocked by the tight security in and around it: only several months ago the Ayatollah Khomeini had announced a fatwa against Salman Rushdie, one of Penguin's celebrity authors.

I didn't know Salman Rushdie then, but his first wife Clarissa was already my literary agent. She encouraged me to write my first book *Special Correspondent*, and quickly sold the proposal to Hutchinson, who out-bargained Bloomsbury in the bid to publish the book.

We became friends with Clarissa and I visited her several times at her house in Highbury. Mitya played with her and Salman's son Zaffar (they were almost the same age, about nine or ten years old then). They once had a fight and Zaffar ended up with a bleeding nose. I remember telling Mitya off severely: 'Zaffar and his Mum have enough on their plates –with the fatwa and all the dangers involved. They don't need an injury to worry about on top of it all . . . !'

Clarissa's behaviour was extraordinarily brave. Her ex-husband's would-be executioners were likely to try and harm his only son (Zaffar) too, yet she staunchly refused to go into hiding or even to change her name.

'We are not afraid of those fanatics,' she told me once. 'Our name is Rushdie and we are not going to change it!'

In the mid 1990s, Clarissa fell ill with breast cancer. She temporarily left her job at A.P. Watt literary agency and had chemotherapy. Her hair fell out and she was wearing a wig.

She was determined to beat the illness by strict regime and strenuous exercise and several years later—she did! At least that was how it appeared then.

Last time I saw her alive was at her fiftieth birthday party. It was there that I met Salman too. The fatwa had not been rescinded but had somewhat 'eased up' by then . . . He still had Scotland Yard protection officers escorting him everywhere, and I ended up having a drink with one of them at the party.

Clarissa was in a great shape: she danced a lot and was full of joy.

Shortly after the party the cancer suddenly came back.

A couple of months later, I came to Golders Green Crematorium to say my last farewell to my good friend and my first literary agent. I shook hands with Zaffar and Salman.

'Clarissa loved and valued you very much and often spoke about you,' Salman said.

He spoke very movingly at the ceremony remembering how he and Clarissa met and started living together. The hall was full to the brim. Clarissa's beautiful face was smiling at us from a large photo.

Before the cremation, they played a lullaby Clarissa's dad used to sing to her when putting her to sleep as a child . . .

I told Nick to go back to his shop and tell the editor that I was not feeling well.

I had nothing to offer him and was not in the mood for reminiscences.

Nick later assured me that in his absence the editor had looked after the shop very well and even sold a book.

17 January

A letter from Club Direct Travel Insurance is in the post this morning. I had to stop paying my contributions to the Club— alongside so many other non-essential expenses.

'We've missed you over the past year,' said the letter.

I knew it was an ordinary PR turn of phrase targeting over-sentimental ex-customers who could be brought back to the stable by the mere 'fact' of being 'missed', yet it nearly brought tears to my eyes: at least someone was missing me.

And immediately—a stronger (survivor's?) inner voice: 'Don't be soppy, you have things to do.'

It's Saturday. Weekends are the hardest. I wish they didn't exist.

Did some writing in the afternoon. With the onset of darkness, panic came: started looking up insolvency practitioners on the Internet and leafed through the brochure 'How to Cope When the Money Runs Out' which I found in the cottage.

What can they do to me, after all? The KGB couldn't get me and neither will they. 'They' who? I don't know. It feels like an onset of paranoia.

Went outside to fix the bent windscreen wipers. Why did the vandals do that to me, of all people? Was it their angst over my stubborn continuing survival?

The last thought made me feel a bit better. If I have any know-how in this life, it is how to survive in seemingly hopeless situations. I've proved it more than once.

I'll be OK this time too!

18 January

Spent the whole day putting my CV in order. It does look impressive. Took out the date of my birth, just in case—it's no one's business how old I am, after all.

In the evening, watched the 'living reproach woman' in the window of a neighbouring house typing away on her computer. The sight made me feel less guilty than usual: I've done a lot of work myself today.

19 January

It is Monday. Pop out in the morning to buy *the Guardian*, with its comprehensive 'Media Jobs' section.

Back at the cottage, I send out twenty-three job applications by email, having applied for anything even distantly compatible with my skills. Will now have to wait for replies.

6 February

Watching 'Question Time', where I happen to know all the panelists personally, and feeling back-stage in drizzly, dark Folkestone.

In a pharmacy earlier this morning saw a hard-written toothpaste price tag saying 'SEHSATIVE'.

That's what I've become here—SENSATIVE; possibly even OVER-SENSATIVE.

The first replies to my job applications have started to arrive. They are all formal and negative I think people are put off by the discrepancy between my CV and my present state of affairs. Or can it be that I sound desperate in the covering letter? Must edit it and make it more self-confident . . .

Got royalties for a couple of *Telegraph* articles. Enough to survive for another ten days. Just in time, for my rent is due tomorrow, and I've made it a rule never to be late with it, not for a single day, no matter what . . . To do otherwise wouldn't be fair to my friends, thanks to whom I have a roof over my head.

7 February

Nick rings me up in the morning to say that my complete set of *Encyclopedia Britannica*, my first big purchase in the west, sold for a hundred quid. He sounded very proud: it is next to impossible

435

to sell multi-volume reference editions these days when they are all available on CDs. The people who buy them normally use books for decorative purposes—to liven up their lounge rooms, so to speak. Disgusting . . .

Well, on the positive side, the hundred pounds in my situation comes in extremely handy.

The sale, however, upsets me considerably, as if with *Britannica* a part of my long-lasting childhood dream has been sold—and this is indeed so: I had been dreaming of owning it since the age of eleven or twelve . . .

To beat the spleen, I resort to my yet another time-tested cure: collected works by Konstantin Paustovsky, whom I regard as my literary teacher despite the fact that we never met and that he died in 1968, aged seventy-six—a shortish chain-smoking old man with an intense and prominent, as if stone-carved, face, as it appeared in his lengthy *Pravda* obituary— when I was fourteen and had just had my very first poem published.

These two volumes have travelled to Folkestone all way from Kharkov (via Moscow, London, Edinburgh and Australia). They were 'procured' by a student of mine (I did a lot of English tutoring while in Kharkov) who worked at a bookshop (I think that was largely why I agreed to teach her in the first place).

The sun's little giggles

I call Paustovsky a writer who never raised his voice.

A school-mate of Bulgakov, a life-long admirer and a vicarious disciple of Ivan Bunin, who was in turn the literary mentor of the founder of mauvism, Valentin Kataev (connections, again!), Paustovsky managed to stay truthful to himself and to his readers all through the horrible epoch he had to live in.

His survival during Stalin's purges is one of Soviet literature's big mysteries, for his writing had little, if anything, to do with 'socialist realism', the official Soviet literary doctrine.

A brilliant lyricist and an unsurpassed stylist, Paustovsky had two big passions: the sea and the nature of Central Russia. He was also the author of what I think is the best (and possibly the longest: about 2000 pages) autobiography ever—the six volumes of the Nobel Prize-nominated 'Story of a Life'—one of my favourite 'therapeutic' books of all time which I often reread (in Russian and in English—lovingly translated by Manya Harari and Michael Duncan and published by Harvill Press in the 1960s) when feeling down or distressed It is in a way a story of one man's (one romantic nature-loving writer's, to be more exact) survival of the twentieth century's most calamitous events: wars, revolutions, purges.

Rereading *Story of a Life* by Konstantin Paustovsky is one of my trusted survival techniques.

It was Paustovsky who famously advised young writers to always write about themselves, no matter what they wrote about.
By that he meant that one should only write about things which one knows as well as he knows himself and should look at everything through the prism of one's own unique personality and perception.

A very Russian, or 'East European', literary principle, some would argue . . . Indeed, in Russian literature and even journalism, a strong author's 'I' (having little to do with ego!) has always been welcome. Eduard Poliansky, my editor at *Krokodil* magazine, would often return my (or other writers') articles with only one criticism: 'there's not enough of the author in the copy.' Paustovsky was the first to formulate this highly personal approach to writing and to make it into a literary device in its own right.

'I' (as a writer's alter ego) was so important in Russian/ Soviet literature because individuality as such was mercilessly suppressed in the USSR. Very few Westerners know, for example, that learning or teaching oriental martial arts was a criminal offence there. The respective article of the Soviet Criminal Code justified the punishment (several years in prison) on the grounds that martial arts nourished the 'cult of individualism'—the totalitarian system's biggest bugbear. No wonder: 'individualism' implies freedom of thought (and hence questioning of the official dogmas) almost by definition.

When I was clandestinely studying karate in the late 1980s Moscow, we (the students and our young instructor) knew only too well the possible implications of what we were doing.

Our classes were therefore conducted in a suburban forest, and one of us was always on the lookout for militia patrols (we had a rota whereby every student was to act as an 'observer' instead of taking part in the class every so often). When such a patrol would appear, the 'observer' would give out a coded signal (a whistle or a cough) at which point we'd produce a ball from under a bush, form a circle and pretend we were playing volleyball. The policemen knew what we were up to of course, but to prove we were practicing karate would have been tricky, so, having wagged their law-enforcing nicotine-stained fingers at us, they would leave us alone.

When they had receded to a safe distance, we'd resume our class.

Another unlikely connection—between Paustovsky and karate . . . The writer himself would have been surprised by it, and yet by publicly calling for the 'cult of individualism' (or individuality) in literature ('always write about yourself'), my mentor was treading a very dangerous ground.

When Ivan Bunin, academician and Nobel Prize winner, read Paustovsky's first short story 'The Inn on the Braginka' while already in exile in France, he sent the young author a congratulatory letter that started with

'My dear brother-in-writing . . .'

I was first introduced to Paustovsky by my mother who gave me 'The Black Sea', one of his early romantic novels. One sentence from it was destined to stay with me forever:

'If you are given the doubtful happiness of being born, you must at least see the world . . .'

This beautiful sentence alone could have turned me first into a restless 'armchair buccaneer' and then—after my defection from the giant cage of the USSR (partially triggered by that very sentence too, it can be said—into a tireless globetrotter who had managed to travel to over sixty countries of the world during his first ten years in the West.

One of my (or Victor R's) youthful poems—'The Vertushinka Rivulet'—was inspired by the following paragraph from Paustovsky's *The Restless Years*, the last volume of his *Story of a Life*:

'In Russia, rivers, lakes, villages and towns have wonderful names that excite our admiration. One of the most apt and romantic names belongs to the little river Vertushinka[15] which twists its way through wood-clad gullies in the Moscow Province, not far from the town of Ruza. Vertushinka whirls, fidgets, murmurs, mumbles, rings and foams round every stone or birch trunk that has fallen into it, hums softly and talks to itself, whispers and carries very clear water over its gravelly bed . . .'

That description alone was so graphic and picturesque that

15 A diminutive of vertushka; a whirligig.

it only took closing one's eyes to visualise the bubbly little rivulet making its way among the stones and to hear its joyful babbling.

My short poem in Russian was full of alliterations. It compared the Vertushinka rivulet (which I had never seen with my own eyes but only 'observed' with the eyes of Paustovsky) to 'a girl's wavy plait, tucked under a pink kerchief of dawn'. It said the stream carried in itself 'the sun's little giggles' and called it 'a daughter of the sun's first morning ray'.

It was 'the sun's little giggles' that stopped it from being published!

'It's a great poem, Vitali, but we simply cannot publish something like that—'the sun's little giggles'—I can't really explain why, but we can't,' an experienced Kharkov newspaper editor who had run many poems of mine in the past told me.

He called me the next day and said he would publish the poem if I changed 'giggles' to 'sparkles', but I refused . . .

I still cannot quite understand what exactly he meant and why 'the sun's little giggles' were deemed taboo by Soviet censorship.

The rationale of Glavlit[16] (if any) was an enigma wrapped in a mystery. In Kharkov, I was friendly with Ernst Marinin (his *nom de plume*, no doubt: his wife was called Marina and he himself had an unpublishable typically Jewish last name—a very common occurrence in the profoundly anti-Semitic Soviet Union), an aspiring science fiction writer, who once wrote a story about a group of super-intelligent aliens arriving on Earth from a distant planet and finding themselves in a toy shop. Having spotted toy pistols, tanks and missiles on the counters, they fly back to their star, having decided that the dwellers of the Earth are

16 An abbreviated merger of 'Glavnoye Upravleniye Literaturi'—Chief Directorate of Literature—the term that came to denote Soviet censorship as a whole.

not advanced enough for interplanetary contacts of any kind. A nice pacifist story. Ernst even managed to have it published in a Moscow magazine. All of it but one sentence: 'The helicopter landed on water several cable lengths away from the aircraft carrier.'

'The censor told me they couldn't publish such sensitive technological details,' he explained.

Paustovsky's most important (from my point of view) book, his writer's manifesto, is, without a doubt, *The Golden Rose: Literature in the Making*. It is a series of beautifully written stories on different aspects of creative writing.

The book's chapter titles speak for themselves: 'Precious Dust; Inscription on a Rock; Artificial Flowers; My First Short Story; Lightning; Characters Revolt', and so on . . .

My English-language edition of *The Golden Rose* is rather cosmopolitan in itself. Bought in a second-hand bookshop in Edinburgh and published in Moscow by Foreign Languages Publishing House (no date, but I assume some time in the late 1950s), it also has the stamp of a Shilpa Niketan Super Market in Dacca, East Pakistan. Paustovsky would have been pleased to see it, I am sure.

If there's such a thing as a bedside table book, *The Golden Rose* is mine. I would have called it my writing manual, had Paustovsky himself not stated in the Introduction: 'This book is not a theoretical investigation into the subject of creative writing, nor it is in any way a guide to literary craftsmanship. It contains merely some of my own personal experiences and desultory thoughts on the making of literature.'

The Golden Rose begins with the legend of Jean Erneste Chamette, an ex-private of the 27th Colonial Regiment and a Paris dustman. When his military commander was killed in action, Chamette was entrusted to look after the former's daughter, Susie, for whom in time he developed a powerful (and totally platonic!) fatherly affection. Susie's biggest dream was to be given a golden rose which she believed was going to bring her everlasting happiness. In Paris, Chamette earned his bread by sweeping the small shops of artisans. At the end of the working day, he threw out all the refuse he had collected, except the sweepings from the jewellers'. These he sifted carefully, for he knew that they contained gold dust from the jeweller's file. After many years, he found himself in possession of a sufficient amount of this gold dust to make a mould of it and to shape it into a golden rose to be given to his beloved Susie. He didn't have time to deliver his gift though. When he passed away quietly in his Paris slum, the golden rose, 'wrapped up in a crinkled blue ribbon' (which Susie gave him many years before) was found under his soiled pillow. 'The ribbon smelt of mice.'

Paustovsky presents the golden rose put together by the old soldier out of specks of gold dust as a powerful metaphor for the writer's craft and literature itself:

'Every minute, every chance word and glance, every
thought—profound or flippant—the imperceptible beat
of the human heart and, by the same token, the fluff
dropping from the poplar, the starlight gleaming in a
pool—all are grains of gold dust. Over the years, we writers
subconsciously collect millions of these little grains and
keep them stored away until they form into a mould out of
which we shape our own particular golden rose—a story,
a novel, a poem. And from these precious little particles a
stream of literature is born.'

Some of the most beautiful words ever written or said.

When it looked as if the whole world had turned away from me, my favourite writers and their books were always with me: in London, Melbourne, Edinburgh or Folkestone—helping me to survive. They are my strongest and weightiest (in more than one sense) **SURVIVAL TIP**.

Mel's emails

A friend in need is a friend indeed . . . Most languages seem to have a proverb to this effect.

'Only in trouble can a true friend be seen,' is a Russian equivalent. The message is so familiar that it is almost banal. Yet VV had a chance to check its validity on himself during that long Folkestone winter.

Not that most of his numerous friends had turned away from him—it was rather his own initiative to temporarily sever contacts—not to burden them with his plight and to avoid difficult and ever-so-painful explanations of 'how come you ended up like that, mate?'

Besides, from Douglas Kennedy's books and from his own experience, he knew that people tended to recoil from those they perceived as losers, as if afraid of contracting the virus of bad luck.

He had a visit from his university friend Yuri, now based in Washington DC and working as a senior interpreter for the USA State Department.

Yuri emigrated to the West ten years prior to VV's own defection and they had lost touch for a long time until VV, already in Australia, placed an ad in 'Novoye Russkoye Slovo', America's Russian-language daily, looking for Yuri, who spotted it and got back in touch. Since then, they had seen each other several times—in Melbourne (Yuri was one of the very few old friends who had a chance to dip into VV's indoor swimming pool), London and the USA. A translator's assignment had brought Yuri to Brussels from where he took the Eurostar to

Ashford. VV met him in his mutilated 'super jalopy' and took him to his Folkestone abode.

That very evening, having consumed several bottles of wine, they were smoking in the tiny conservatory overlooking the garden to the muffled sounds of the Fuckstone Rock behind the wall.

'It is a difficult situation, Vitya,' said Yuri, having listened to VV's lamentations ('Vitya'—the address used only by VV's parents and closest friends—was like music for VV's rock-and-seagulls-tormented ears).

'Well, you've lost your Australian prosperity and the indoor swimming pool—too bad. But, on the other hand, try to look at it from a purely Soviet perspective: if someone had told you twenty years ago that you would be living in the West, in England, in a three-bedroom house and would have a car of your own, you would have dismissed it as a wild fantasy.'

Yuri was right of course.

Vitya's childhood dream had always been to live surrounded by 'foreigners', or rather 'Westerners'—that peculiar human species which could at times be spotted near and inside Intourist hotels and whose main distinctive features were: total absence of a 'seal of oppression' (so common to all VV's compatriots) on their self-satisfied rosy faces; assertive and self-confident manners and body language resulting in all of them behaving as if they were true masters of the world, which they probably were.

In moments of crisis while in the West, Vin often called back that old dream of his and tried to look around himself with the eyes of a Soviet teenager/youngster: normally he did register a number of 'Westerners' in close proximity to himself and that would calm him down.

In the streets of Folkestone, however, it was difficult: the vision of carefree 'foreigners' kept escaping him. The local crowd looked deceptively—often unmistakably—Soviet.

Putting things in perspective was VV's own favourite old trick (albeit calling his defaced 'super jalopy' a car, as opposed to a motorised squeaky cart, was a gross overstatement). It normally worked, even if the relativist approach was bound to be less effective for any former owner of an Australian bungalow with a lemon tree and a state-of-the-art barbie in the backyard. Yes, and that of the blasted useless indoor swimming pool too!

Yuri himself had a nice house in a leafy DC suburb where a lovely wife and a daughter were waiting for him.

VV told him of a treacherous, yet strangely titillating, thought of giving up his struggle and returning to Kharkov thus closing the thirty-year-long circle of his movements around the globe, starting with his move from Kharkov to Moscow after the uni-versity. As a native Kharkovite himself, Yuri was likely to support it. But he didn't.

'You must be mad, Vitya, even to think about that,' he said. 'The return of the prodigal son . . . That never works in real life. Only in the Bible . . . You know what's going to happen? For the first couple of weeks, you'll be the town's biggest news and everyone will be eager to buy you a drink. But then they will get fed up and will be telling you to fuck off . . . They are different people now, Vitya: too preoccupied with their own survival to be interested in anyone else, even you . . .'

Unlike VV, Yuri often travelled to the former USSR for work and obviously knew what he was talking about.

He felt a bit better after Yuri's short visit. And then Mel, another friend of his, not even a friend but a recent USA-based acquaintance, an academic who had written a glowing review of VV's book 'Borders Up!' for an American magazine, did something unbelievable . . .

A couple of years earlier Mel had found VV via the latter's web page and they met briefly in London. VV showed Mel his favourite bits of the city, they had a nice lunch and after that simply exchanged occasional emails. It was in one of his emails that VV wrote to Mel about his Folkestone exile, mentioning in passing that he was struggling financially and was looking for work. Mel asked for a copy of his CV which VV emailed to him a couple of weeks before.

One Folkestone morning, VV's computer nearly crashed after over three hundred emails cluttered his email box. They were all from Mel—copies of his missives to his contacts all over the world: academics, politicians (several foreign ministers and prime ministers among them)—telling them about VV's plight and asking them to 'save' him by assisting in finding a suitable job anywhere in the world, CV attached!

A busy man himself, Mel had spent nearly two weeks writing these letters full-time . . . The good will and the selflessness of the man he hardly knew nearly made VV cry.

Replies started coming in soon, and Mel duly copied each of them to VV. There was one word that characterised them all—disbelief. Mel's addressees (some of whom VV knew and many of whom knew VV) simply refused to believe that someone of VV's stature, 'an internationalist with a CV that read like a thriller, or an adventure novel' (a quote from one of them), could find himself in such a mess. They all advised VV to 'pull himself together' while promising to keep his CV 'on record'.

He received several puzzled phone calls from places like Baku and Tallinn, but that was it.

In short, Mel's attempt failed, yet the very fact that someone could get so concerned about him was a powerful stimulant that had made VV redouble his own job-hunting efforts. After all, he had been able to find a job—not one but several at a time—in the corrupt and anti-Semitic Moscow of the late 1970s where he ended up after university, he was saying to himself while trying to silence the fact that he had been in his early 20s then . . .

John Ross Scott
Editor
Orkney Today

Dear John

<u>Re: Reporter—or other editorial position</u>

You might be surprised by this letter.

Let me explain.

I am an experienced award-winning editor, reporter, writer and broadcaster. Like you, I've had a great career in journalism spanning over 20 years and a number of countries and continents. You might be familiar with my recent hugely successful column for The (Glasgow) Herald 'Vitaliev's Scotland'—1700 words every Monday, which—to a considerable chagrin of the readers and the paper's executives (you are welcome to check with them and/or to read the columns on the *Herald* website) had to stop last June due to a sudden corporate takeover of the paper—not uncommon in modern media business. I have criss-crossed all of Scotland and visited a number of islands, including Shetland which fascinated me. My intention was to do a piece on Orkney—the place that I had always dreamt of visiting, but, due to the above-mentioned circumstances, have yet been unable to do so.

Here I have to tell you that I have visited (and written about in my books and columns) various islands of the world, including the Falklands, the Faroes, St Helena, Inner and Outer Hebrides, Tasmania, all Channel Islands, islands off the coast of Australia and so on and have an ongoing fascination with them.

Unfortunately, the stoppage of my *Herald* column coincided with the break-up of my marriage and I had to hastily relocate to Folkestone, Kent (I was offered a rented cottage by my good friends), from where I regularly commute to Edinburgh to see my three little children (all under 6 years of age).

One more thing: I turned 50 last Sunday (still fit, healthy and full of ideas), and—having more than satisfied my ambitions (see my CV) and being somewhat tired of the never-ending turmoil of international journalism, would love to settle down in a quiet place, where I could work while continuing to write my books. Orkney sounds ideal for that (and is closer to Edinburgh). The example of George Orwell, one of my two favourite authors of all time, who loved Orkney, is encouraging.

Now—to my profile . . .

I'll be looking forward to your reply, which can change my life.

With warmest regards

Vitali Vitaliev 'signed'

To that, he received a very warm reply, but the position had been already filled.

Or, maybe, despite trying his best not to appear desperate, he had been unable to avoid some anxious and despondent undertones?

At that point in time, Orkney sounded like a good solution.

There were some positive responses though.

VV was asked to meet an executive from Endemol, a giant

Amsterdam-based TV production company responsible for (among other things) 'Big Brother' and other reality TV shows of which VV had never been a fan. He couldn't even recall applying for a position in the company's PR department, but went to the meeting nevertheless.

The Endemol envoy told VV that he was shortlisted for the job and was in fact one of the two remaining applicants, out of nearly four hundred . . He explained the whole procedure of relocation to Amsterdam with the help of a company called 'The Dutch Way of Life': You won't have to do anything—they will move all your stuff and will find a flat in Amsterdam for you too.'

Amsterdam was one of VV's favourite cities in Europe. He wouldn't have minded moving there (or almost anywhere, for that matter) from Folkestone, even if he had to transport 'all his stuff' and look for a place to live himself. Another advantage of Amsterdam was that it was closer to Edinburgh than London.

It sounded too good to be true . . . And as such it was not meant to happen.

A couple of weeks later, the same executive emailed him from Holland to say that the job had gone to the other applicant who 'had more experience in TV' and was also much younger (he didn't voice the last bit of course).

There was another weird phone call—from . . . Bethlehem. Yes, from the birthplace of Jesus Christ!

The divine aspect of the call ended there and then. A young woman, who spoke almost unaccented Russian and introduced herself as half-Palestinian, half-Ukrainian (!), said she worked for Bethlehem's PR department, for which they needed a new head (moi?) to promote the besieged city in an attempt to attract more tourists there.

'It is a great job,' she said in Russian. 'The only inconvenience is that you can't really leave the place without passing through several Israeli cordons, and they are notoriously difficult to us.'

The idea of being stuck in a blockaded ancient city, even if Christ himself was born there, was unappealing, to say the least, and VV was frantically looking for an excuse to cut the conversation short. As often happens, his cosmopolitan interlocutor supplied it herself.

'There's one condition though,' she said authoritatively as if they were already working together and she was his boss (not the other way round). 'You have to be a supporter of the Palestinian people in their struggle against Israeli occupation.'
'Look,' he said. 'It all sounds great, but the problem is I am really not into politics. Besides, I am actually Jewish.'
She mumbled a quick excuse of a 'have to go now, will call you back tomorrow' type and put the phone down.

He never heard from her again, of course.

Whenever he hears the word 'Bethlehem' in Christmas carols (for where else can you hear it these days?), he remembers that spooky phone call which allowed him—for the first time—to see a comic (even if darkly so) side to the situation he was in.

Whether there was indeed a divine touch attached to that call, very shortly after it he did get an offer of another job, albeit it was not necessarily a welcome development . . .

Green notebook

16 March

Having returned from London last night, I find my B-plated

'super jalopy' vandalised again: this time they threw a brick through the windscreen. The fragments of thick windscreen glass crunch under my boots like heavily consolidated snow. But this time I am not upset. Why? Because I've just returned from a successful job interview. Moreover, in my breast pocket I carry a freshly printed copy of my new contract. The salary is not great, but they promised to increase it soon!

I had to do a translation test which was not hard at all. Yes, the job has a lot (everything in fact) to do with translation. The new company, Britafra TV Ltd, with offices in Tottenham Court Road, will be translating the whole output of the BBC World Service Television into Russian and beaming it to Russia and all over the globe via satellite. My duties will be not just to translate but also to voice my own and other people's translations of the BBC programme . . . Well, it is of course not quite as creative as writing, but still challenging. After all, I am a translator/interpreter by education, a graduate of a special males-only interpreters' department of Kharkov University. As such, I could do synchronic interpretation too. Prior to becoming a professional journalist I used to work as a translator and interpreter in Kharkov and then in Moscow. It would be fun to galvanise my old skills. But the main thing is that at last I'll be able to leave the horrible 'alienation zone' of council estates and 'job centres', that I won't have to save every penny to get the cheapest ten-quid return coach ticket to Edinburgh to see my kids which means travelling for two nights in a row perched on the edge of a stiff seat, next to some snoring and smelly drunk . . . . I'll be able to leave Folkestone (in due course), to rent a decent flat in London and to start living again!

The brick that smashed the jalopy's windscreen is probably my last farewell from 'the lower depths' of Folkestone, my 'smashing' (in more than one sense) little reward for having escaped them again—this time for good. Not such a high price to pay for the escape, moreover the car is insured (I paid the premium while still in Edinburgh). Just the small inconvenience of replacing the windscreen . . .

I have already met some of my new colleagues—a bunch of rather pleasant and intelligent Russians of different ages. The boss, Sandor, is Hungarian with Russian connections, and the woman who runs the show—a bouncy middle-aged brunette—is a London-born Romanian called Ada. 'We are going to have an affair with you,' she told me jokingly (or so I hope) and winked before giving me the contract. She didn't have to give it to me straight away but I asked her to, and she was nice enough to have it typed out there and then!

One thing I don't like is that the whole operation, as I was told, is being financed from Yekaterinburg, an industrial Russian city in the Urals notorious—as I knew from my own investigations into the Soviet mafia of the late 1980s—for its high levels of organised crime. But maybe I am just being overcautious? And what choice do I have anyway?

The company's offices are light and clean, with the latest computers and state-of-the art recording equipment, in a new high-rise office block housing dozens of media companies—just a two-minute walk from the Tube station.

One problem: I won't be able to afford—either materially or time-wise—the daily commute from Folkestone, so will probably have to rent a room in a cheap B&B for four nights of the week and go back 'home' on weekends. The salary should cover it, but before I get the first one, I'd have to borrow some money from a friend perhaps . . .

Farewell to the 'lower depths'!

The boy with a bucket

In the course of several subsequent months, Vin often recalled one particular passage from the satirical novel *The Golden Calf* by his beloved tandem of 1930s writers, Ilya Ilf and Evgeny Petrov (the latter, as you may remember, was Kataev's younger brother).

The extract in question dealt with the more than shadowy past of Alexander Koreiko, the underground Soviet millionaire and one of the novel's two main protagonists (the second one was, of course, Ostap Bender, the smooth operator), and described one of the many scams that had helped him (Koreiko) to accumulate his fortune.

Vin knew *The Golden Calf*—as well as its predecessor *The Twelve Chairs* almost by heart:

'The back room (of the token Revenge Chemical Plant started by Koreiko : VV) was the workshop. It contained two oak barrels with manometers and hydrometers, one on the floor and the other on a raised platform. The barrels were joined by a thin enema tube through which a liquid flowed, gurgling busily. As soon as the liquid had passed from the top to the bottom barrel, a boy in felt boots entered the workroom. Sighing in an unchildlike way, the boy scooped the liquid out of the bottom barrel with a bucket, dragged it up to the platform, and poured it into the second barrel. Having completed this complicated operation, the boy went off to the office to get warm, while the enema tube again began emitting a gurgling noise: the liquid was making a routine journey from the top container to the bottom one. . .'

It later turned out that the gurgling liquid in the 'enema tube' was pure water.

What Ilf and Petrov portrayed in the above extract was a classic money-laundering operation—a totally useless cycle that nevertheless allowed for considerable sums of dirty money to be cleaned (or 'laundered') through it.

The nature of money laundering had not changed a lot since the 1930s, and in the early years of the twenty-first century London, due to the UK's rather lenient regulations in relation to limited companies (anybody could open one having paid one pound in tax—no questions asked), became one of its global centres.

It didn't take VV long to establish without a shadow of doubt that his new employer, Britafra TV Ltd, was one of such international scams.

It was like his recent marriage: he knew from the start it was wrong, but had no choice (or thought he had no choice) other than to go along with it . . .

For the first couple of weeks everything went smoothly, if you didn't count the company's truly draconian rules maintained by the ever-vigilant Ada who looked down at the employees and referred to them as 'my monkeys'.

During office hours (and being five minutes late was punishable by immediate sacking), the translators were not allowed to talk, to walk, to eat or to drink except for the lunch interval that lasted precisely thirty minutes. Any jewellery was banned. A young Jewish woman who once came to work with a Star of David pennant and refused Ada's demand to remove it was sacked on the spot.

'I am in a foul mood and feel like sacking a couple of monkeys today,' Ada would mumble to VV (for some obscure reason, she chose him as her closest confidant) during a lunch-time smoking break.

It has to be said that her prison-style ways went down well with VV's Russian-speaking colleagues whose English was not good enough to be hoping for a better job than that. Or for any other job, for that matter. Most of them, particularly those in their fifties and sixties, were thanking their lucky stars for having been hired.

'Yes, I am a slave and proud of it,' Igor, a London-based Russian writer in his early sixties kept saying, adding that he was ever so grateful to Sandor for having given him his 'life's last opportunity of proper full-time employment'.

The 'employment' was full-time indeed (yet far from 'proper' as will transpire soon).

The translators worked in two shifts every day of the week, including Sundays (with no extra pay). They first had to watch the latest BBC World Service programme on their monitors, then translate it into Russian, timing every single word. At the end of the day, they were expected to voice the programs in the basement studio, so that by the following morning the whole previous-day output of the BBC World Service TV was available in Russian. The quotas for both translation and voicing were extremely tough, even for VV who had to spend a considerable amount of time helping his less experienced colleagues comprehend what this or that BBC presenter (be it Liz Doucet or Nik Gowing) was saying—a practice that was frowned upon, yet grudgingly tolerated, by Ada.

The tough schedule was justified by Sandor's repeated assurances that the would-be Russian BBC World Service TV satellite channel was about to be launched soon (in two months? By the end of the year? No one knew). The satellite was allegedly ready and waiting and the only hitch was us, the lazy translators, who had so far failed (in Sandor's and Ada's words) to achieve the required quality and speed of output and therefore had to keep practising day and night . . .

In retrospect, it is hard to believe that VV, with his investigative journalism background, did not smell a rat straight away. One quick call to the BBC, with whom as it was established later, Britafra didn't even have a contract, would have made everything clear.

Yet it has to be remembered that Vin was still reeling from his five months in Folkestone and was therefore inclined to close his eyes to certain 'discrepancies', like Britafra's total disregard for Britain's employment legislation, say . . . He was happily commuting to work from his clean and cosy North London B&B, hired rather cheaply with the help of a rentals company whose manager happened to be VV's reader and fan—'Are you *the* Vitali Vitaliev?'. . . He was rediscovering his beloved London, and whenever he worked second shift, would get up early and revisit his favourite spots before going to the office . . .

The blow came about a month into his employment (so far unpaid).

VV stayed at the office longer than usual, having to translate and then voice a David Beckham interview (he particularly enjoyed imitating—in Russian—Beckham's characteristic high-pitched voice). Having left the studio well after 9 p.m., he had to come back ten minutes later to pick up his M&S ready-made dinner he had left behind in the office fridge. As he was approaching the building's back entrance (the front doors were normally closed at night), he saw Pete, Britafra's sound technician, disposing of a stack of video cassettes (there was a hand-written label on each of them which left little doubt these were the cassettes so painstakingly recorded by VV and his colleagues during the day) by putting them—one by one—inside a huge black wheelie bin.

His immediate impulse was to confront Pete there and then. Or go to the police. That would of course mean the end of his short-lasting 'job' even before the first payment due the following week. And that, in turn, would imply a return to Folkestone, with all its misery, its seagulls, its Fuckstone rocker behind the wall . . .

'What if Pete was simply getting rid of defective cassettes?' he was thinking rocking inside the Tube train taking him back to North London. He had no real proofs. No proofs except for being a hundred per cent sure Britafra was a scam.

It was then that he remembered the boy with the bucket from

The Golden Calf and realised with a mixture and disbelief that he and all his fellow 'monkeys'—irrespective of age and gender—had assumed the role of that exploited 'unchildlike' boy . . .

Vin's first salary was ten days late. The cheque given to him (and to each of the 'monkeys') by Ada and sloppily signed by Sandor, bounced, having invoked a £30 fine from his bank.

Ada hurried to assure everyone that Sandor 'was going to bring some money from Russia soon' and it would all be OK. Indeed, the second payment cheque did clear, albeit Vin's payslip showed a suspicious 50 per cent income tax deduction.

And although he didn't know it then, it was also the very last bit of money he was to receive from Britafra TV Ltd.

The sight of Pete conscientiously disposing of the fruits of the day's hard work meant that VV's days at Britafra and those of Britafra itself were numbered. He had to keep looking for something else, and when one day he received an email from the editor of a 'new international magazine' who claimed to be a fan and suggested a meeting, he responded immediately.

Prawn crackers

They agreed to meet one evening (after VV's second shift) in Piccadilly Circus.

VV had waited for over an hour, but the editor failed to turn up. He then called the editor's home number from a public phone. To Vin's astonishment, the latter picked up the phone straight away and claimed to have no recollection of the meeting arrangements. He sounded drunk and spoke with a slur. Berating himself (and the editor) for the wasted evening, VV was about to slam down the phone, when the editor suddenly . . . burst into tears (or at least he sounded as if he was crying) begging forgiveness and proclaiming his 'unlimited respect' for VV.

He implored VV to take the Tube to Wimbledon (!) where he lived, promising he would meet him at the Tube station and take him out for a 'huge restaurant meal with lots of wine'. From the shaky sound of his voice, 'lots of wine' was the last thing the editor needed.

'What the hell,' thought VV. The evening had been wasted anyway. He took the Tube to Wimbledon.

When he arrived an hour later, the editor was not there. Cursing himself for being so gullible, VV dialled the same number. The editor had been asleep of course, yet, having been woken up by the phone call, said he was on his way.

He did turn up twenty minutes later—a shortish podgy man of Mediterranean appearance, his clothes and face rumpled heavily—as if he had been snoozing inside a washing-machine dryer.

All the restaurants in Wimbledon were either already closed or closing, and they headed for the nearest pub where the last orders were being taken.

The editor asked for a bottle of wine and a plateful of prawn crackers, then claimed to have 'no change', so VV had to cough up.

By then, it was entirely obvious that the editor was mad and all VV wanted was to get away.

Having downed two glasses of wine, the editor chased them noisily with prawn crackers. He then tried to chat up the obviously Australian barmaid asking her what part of the United States she was from.

'You are m-my b-brother,' he burbled drunkenly, wet fragments of prawn crackers flying out of his mouth shrapnel-like. 'I w-want to write "we are b-brothers" on the top of this t-table—in blood!'

From his pocket, he produced a penknife and tried (or pretended he was trying) to cut a vein.

That was too much for VV to take. He dashed out of the pub

and, having shaken sticky prawn-cracker bits off his shirt, ran towards the Tube station to catch the last train back to North London.

If he were ever to write a story about that evening, he would call it 'Prawn Crackers', he decided.

It was a bizarre Tube journey.

The whole 'population' of Vin's carriage was in different stages of inebriation—an animated, yet strangely subdued, night-time Tube crowd.

He was sitting next to a young man whose once white shirt was covered with blood-stains, as if the mad editor himself had tried to pledge his brotherly allegiance on it. After a couple of stops, the young man took his shirt off and continued the journey topless . . .

'Thank you, London!' ran a poster at Camden Town station where Vin was changing trains. Under the poster, a drunken blonde woman was whistling loudly. As VV was pondering whether to thank London or not, he was approached by another young man who seemed sober for a change.

'Can I ask you a question?' he asked VV making that very question quite pointless.

'I am genuine,' he continued and, having opened up the collar of his shirt, demonstrated a fresh stab wound across his neck.

The 'question' as such never followed, so VV had to ask it himself on the last stretch of this journey.

'What next? Am I going to lose London, the city that I so love, again?' he scribbled in his notebook. 'What a miserable, ridiculous failure that whole meeting with the 'editor' was! And that had to happen after the day of abuse at the office with Ada teasing him during a smoking break: 'I won't pay you at all, monkey! Why? Because you have no respect for Sandor who is such a nice person. Just think about it he feeds thirty families!' Does he really? For how much longer can this humiliation continue?'

He looked up from his notes, having realised he was wallowing in self-pity. Most of his fellow passengers were dozing, a slim black girl next him was snoring loudly.

He turned over the page and wrote in large letters:

'WHY DO I KEEP BUMPING INTO GOOD STORIES, NOT GOOD PEOPLE? THERE HAS TO BE AN END TO THIS!'

He got off at Brent Cross station. A full orange moon was hanging above the small station square, and underneath the moon half a dozen night-time Tube workers were squatting. They were waiting for the last train to leave the station so that they could start mending the track or whatever they were meant to do during the night.

They were eating sunflower seeds spitting out the shells onto the ground.
They were speaking Ukrainian.
Their yellow overalls were reflecting the moonlight and appeared orange.
The empty sunflower seed shells were reflecting the moon too and looked like droplets of orange moonlight spilled out onto the ground.

VV froze in his step and was imbibing the view breathlessly. Suddenly, it all started making sense: his job at the dodgy Britafra, his meeting with the mad editor, his crazy Tube journey.
That silent moonlit scene on the station square was a gift of fate, one powerful justification of his unfading passion for London. And of his messy writer's life too.

He opened his notebook and—for the first time—wrote:

'LIFE AS A LITERARY DEVICE'.

Back to Square One

What happened at Britafra Ltd. during the following three months had been easily predictable. Below is the summary:

1. No more payments to the staff. Each time the salary was due, Sandor would buy a stale cake or a bagful of croissants 'to cheer up the monkeys'. We were growing increasingly wary of these increasingly frequent signs of Sandor's miserly 'generosity'.
2. Ada banned speaking English (!) in the office after Sandor bizarrely hired several more employees—all native Brits. 'They don't have to know what's going on here!' persisted Ada.
3. Eventually, even the meekest of the 'monkeys' had had enough. A Scotland Yard financial fraud unit was notified, and Britafra stopped 'trading' (even before it had started!).
4. It turned out that in the course of the six months of its existence the company did not pay a penny in tax or in office rent. All the equipment (computers, faxes, telephones etc.) was bought on (non-existing) credit and had to be confiscated. Altogether, the company owed the state, its creditors and employees over ten million pounds.
5. We (the 'monkeys') went to an employment tribunal and were promptly awarded several thousand pounds each in compensation, but it took many more months of appeals to the numerous bankruptcy and insolvency bodies to actually receive the money.

And what happened to Sandor and Ada, you may ask? Nothing at all! They got away scot-free and—from what I heard—were soon masterminding yet another scam in the UK.

Having claimed a failed—for no fault of theirs, no doubt—business venture, they didn't have to pay any fees or fines and couldn't care less about thirty or so ruined (or semi-ruined) lives of the 'monkeys' they had so mercilessly duped.

Despite the extremely gruesome situation he found himself in, VV could not help further analogies with 'the boy with the bucket' story from Ilf and Petrov's 'The Golden Calf':

'. . . the chairman of the committee (of inspectors: VV) said 'Hmm' and looked at the committee members, who also said 'Hmm.' Then the chairman looked at the boy with a ghastly smile and asked:
'And how old are you, young man?'
'Just twelve,' the boy replied.
And he burst into such sobs that the committee members, pushing and jostling, fled into the street and getting into their carriages, left in complete confusion. As for the Revenge plant, all transactions with it were entered in the bank and trust ledgers under Profit and Loss, or, to be more exact, under Loss.'

Again, literature was able to provide a better explanation of the events than life itself . . .

Seriously defeated and feeling mugged and beaten up, VV—now totally broke and despondent—had to return to Folkestone.

The news of his friend Peter Ustinov's death made his mood even gloomier.

It was then that his Folkestone friend Nick uttered his sacramental: 'In your shoes, I'd just lie on the floor and scream!'
Well, VV didn't. Severely bent, yet not broken, if he did scream—it was only in his dreams:

— He is trying to get inside a number of Russian restaurants in different countries but gets turned away everywhere, with the staff pointing at him and laughing . . .

- He meets his Dad at the entrance to Kharkov's Gorky Park. Dad, who looks haggard, very thin and extremely young—almost a teenager—keeps staring at him intently with his grey piercing eyes without saying a word . . .

- Peter Ustinov is on the phone. 'I am calling to ask you, Vitali, to interview me about my death—ha, ha, ha . . .'

— Failing an entrance exam at a university (which, in Soviet terms, would mean being drafted into the army the same year) and being cruelly teased and humiliated by his would-be teachers . . .

The last dream was so realistic and so black that he had to take a Xanax (yes, again!) to stop shivering.

The following morning—a near-death experience: his super jalopy's engine suddenly switched off in the middle of the A1 motorway. A lot of honking and screeching sounds followed, but feeling 'pickled' (the effects of Xanax?), he experienced no fear. Just sat there turning the key in the ignition until the engine came back to life again.

He wished he had a key like that to restart his life.

Green notebook

'Let's face it: I have no more energy left to keep fighting, to keep coming back to the same place where I started—only with fewer emotional and other resources . . . Back to Square One . . .

I feel like a beggar sitting at the road curb and begging for alms. A heavy truck is going past, its driver slows down at the sight of me sitting on the ground with my hand outstretched. My first thought is that he will give me some money, but instead he runs me over and speeds away . . .'

He would often experience chest pains first thing in the morning . . .

With no more money left for wine and/or (luckily) for psychiatric drugs, Vin had only two things he could rely upon: his roll-up cigarettes and his books.

Ilf and Petrov

'There were so many hairdressing establishments and funeral homes in the regional centre of N. that the inhabitants seemed to be born merely in order to have a shave, get their hair cut, freshen up their heads with toilet water and then die. In actual fact, people came into the world, shaved, and died rather rarely in the regional centre of N. The spring evenings were delightful, the mud glistened like coal in the light of the moon, and all the young men of the town were so much in love with the secretary of the communal-service workers' committee that she found difficulty in collecting their subscriptions.'

This opening paragraph of *The Twelve Chairs*, my favourite satirical book of all time, is another great example of taking a plunge into a narrative, or *in medias res*.

The Twelve Chairs and its sequel *The Golden Calf* were both penned by the brilliant tandem of Odessa-born Russian writers—Ilya Ilf and Evgeny Petrov in the late 1920s—early 1930s. Hilarious, vitriolic and deeply anti-Soviet, the novels became cult reading for the embattled Soviet intelligentsia. They were like a breath of fresh air in the stuffy communal flat of Soviet reality, replete with stale smells of cabbage soup, human sweat and rotten political dogma.

By the age of sixteen, I had read the novels dozens of times and knew them almost by heart.

In 1966, when I was twelve, we were asked at school to write an essay on our favourite literary hero. Instead of extolling the tailor-made virtues of Pavel Korchagin, the clichéd proletarian protagonist of Nikolai Ostrovsky's politically correct drivel *How Steel was Tamed* (as we were all expected to do), I chose to write about Ostap Bender, the 'smooth operator' and the 'great schemer' from *The Twelve Chairs* and *The Golden Calf*, whose famous pronouncements included: 'No, this is not Rio de Janeiro, this is much worse . . .' and 'The building of socialism bores me. What am I—a stone mason in a white apron? . . .'

In *The Twelve Chairs*, Ostap Bender travels about the Soviet Union trying to find which one of a dozen dining room chairs contained the jewels hidden in its upholstery by a provincial aristocratic family during the revolution (the plot idea was prompted by Kataev!), whereas in *The Golden Calf* he becomes a 'captain' of a ramshackle 'Lauren Dietrich' jalopy who ventures to fleece an underground Soviet millionaire.

'Things are moving, ladies and gentlemen of the jury! Things are moving!' Ostap Bender liked to say when his schemes were developing according to his scenario. In my school essay case, however, 'things' were certainly not 'moving' the way I expected them to.

As a result of my timid literary deviation, my grandfather, an old Bolshevik and a revolutionary in his youth who became profoundly disillusioned with communism by the end of his life, was summoned to the school headmistress, a blue stocking and virago, and was reprimanded for his grandson's 'dangerous literary tastes'.

He came back home very upset. But instead of telling me off, he said:

'I am ashamed. Not for you but for your teachers. They want you all to like the same books. They want you to have the same tastes and thoughts. If this is what we fought for in the revolution, then I am ashamed for myself, too.'

I will remember this first real lesson of literary integrity, taught by my granddad and by Ilf and Petrov, for as long as I live.

Apart from saving me and many of my ilk from going crazy under the impact of the unyielding and all-permeating Soviet propaganda, Ilf and Petrov opened my eyes on . . . America and played a huge role in my ongoing fascination with it.

In 1935–36, in the company of 'Mr. Adams', their eccentric American guide, and his young wife 'Becky' who was the driver, they made a six-month automobile trip across the United States which they described in 'One-Storied America' ('Little Golden America' in the US translation). As the writers themselves concluded in the end of their remarkable travelogue, '. . . we had been in twenty-five states and several hundred towns, we had breathed the dry air of deserts and prairies, had crossed the Rocky Mountains, had seen Indians, had talked with the young unemployed, with the old capitalists, with radical intellectuals, with revolutionary workers, with poets, with writers, with engineers. We had examined factories and parks, had admired roads and bridges, had climbed up the Sierra Nevadas and descended into the Carlsbad Caves. We had travelled ten thousand miles.'

Unlike their novels, where each sentence was a product of joint creative effort, Ilf and Petrov wrote *One-Storied America* separately—twenty three chapters each. By that time, their literary partnership had reached such sophistication that even the nosiest of their critics were unable to say which chapters were written by Ilf and which by Petrov.

'It is very difficult to write together,' they noted in their facetious 'autobiography'. 'It was easier for the Goncourts, we suppose. After all, they were brothers, while we are not even related to each other. We are not even of the same age. And even of different nationalities while one is a Russian (the enigmatic Russian soul), the other is a Jew (the enigmatic Jewish soul) . . .'

One-Storied America was almost impossible to find in the Soviet Union (my own copy originated from some god-forsaken town in the Soviet Far East). Probably because it was favourably disposed towards many aspects of American life. It was also extremely witty. Having first read the book in my late teens, I dreamt of repeating the writers' journey one day—a totally Utopian dream.

In my inflamed imagination, I was often approaching the shores of New York on board the *Normandie* (as Ilf and Petrov did) after a six-day-long transatlantic crossing and could even discern Manhattan skyscrapers 'rising out of the water like calm pillars of smoke'.

To this day, I don't quite understand how the writers were able to get away with their positive portrayal of America in the atmosphere of Stalinist terror and mounting purges. I am sure that had Ilya Ilf not died of tuberculosis in 1937 (aged forty), and had Evgeny Petrov not been killed in the siege of Sevastopol in 1942 (aged thirty-nine), their arrest and subsequent execution would have simply been a question of time.

Even the Bolsheviks were unable to arrest and execute someone who was already dead.

In a sadly ironic twist, the fact that both writers had somehow managed to avoid the purges made them targets of the ebullient Russian press of the mid-1990s which—unjustly and without adducing any proof—accused Ilf and Petrov of collaborating with Stalin's secret police, satirising 'Russian intellectuals' and being generally 'anti-Russian'.

Their American guide, the opinionated, absent-minded

and adorable 'Mr Adams', whose real last name was Tron, was ridiculed as a 'useless and pathetic left-winger' (Mr Tron was indeed a left-winger in reality).

The mercenary new Russia's literary critics' views had very quickly (within several years) travelled the whole way: from staunchly and 'uncompromisingly' pro-Soviet to ardently anti-Communist.

The law of a pendulum—from one extreme to another.

A short extract from Chapter 6 ('Papa and Mamma') of *Little Golden America*:

'The door of the Adams's apartment was opened to us by a Negress to whose skirts clung a two-year-old girl. The little girl had a firmly moulded little body. She was a little Adams without spectacles.
She looked at her parents, and said in her thin little voice: 'Papa and Mamma'.
Papa and Mamma groaned from sheer satisfaction and happiness.'

Why did I reproduce that seemingly random and irrelevant extract?

Because it is with that 'little girl' with 'a firmly moulded body' that my delicate and fragile 'connection' with Ilf and Petrov rests.

Before starting my American journey in 1999, I found out from a visiting Russian literary critic that Mr Adams's wife 'Becky' was still alive and living in London (!) with her daughter. That was all she knew, and my first reaction was disbelief: even if 'Becky' the driver was a lot younger than 'Mr. Adams' (in his fifties in the book) in 1935, she should be well into her nineties now.

I consulted a London phone directory. There was only one entry under the name of 'Tron'. I dialled the number—and 'the little girl' answered the phone.

Her voice was no longer 'thin' and 'little' but rather 'thick' and husky, with a slight American accent. I did some fast calculations: if she was 2 in 1935, then 64 years later . . .

I introduced myself and explained that I was about to start my journey across America in the footsteps of Ilf and Petrov.

On hearing my Russian name, 'the little girl' immediately hung up.

I re-dialled thinking we had been disconnected.

'If you are from Russia, don't call us ever again!' she said sternly.

I explained that I was actually a British writer and journalist and a defector from the former USSR.

She softened up a bit.

'If you only knew how much grief those Russian journalists inflicted on my Mom . . . They came in droves a couple of years ago, interviewed Mom and myself only to call us and my late father, whom Mom still adores—decades after he died, all sorts of horrible names in their articles . . . Having read them, Mom got very upset, and her health deteriorated—don't forget she is almost ninety. She said she would never talk to another Russian . . .'

I suddenly heard in the receiver a muffled and rather feeble ('thin'?) old woman's voice enquiring from the distance: 'Who is that calling?'

'I have to go now,' said 'the little girl' and promised to convey my request for a quick meeting and a chat to her Mom, yet—as she said—she was almost sure of the response.

And she was right.

When I called back several days later, she said that the very mention of 'another Russian' willing to speak to 'Becky the driver' made her very upset. A meeting—no matter how brief—or even a phone conversation were absolutely out of the question.

'Tell me please,' I said to the daughter before hanging up. 'Does she ever talk to you about the two Russian writers whom she drove across America in 1935—36?'

'Very seldom. It is all rather disturbing to her and not good for her health. She did mention the two Russian gentlemen a couple of times lately and said that they were both very nice— unlike those horrible modern journalists . . .'

She asked me not to call them ever again. And I didn't.

But at least I was lucky enough to have heard the voice of 'Mrs Rebecca Adams', the 'young lady who wore the same kind of protruding spectacles as did Mr. Adams'—Ilf and Petrov's knowledgeable, witty and courageous driver and one of the main protagonists of *Little Golden America*.

And of 'the little girl' too.

I also knew that 'Becky' was remembering Ilf and Petrov with genuine fondness.

And that—to me—was very, very important.

I am now lucky enough to be able to compare the Russian original of *One-Storied America* with *Little Golden America*—the book's 1937 American translation. The fascinating thing is that whereas the most openly pro-American bits were removed from the Soviet 'original', the parts most critical of America were skillfully 'downplayed' in the translation.

The book's title itself can serve as an example: *One-Storied America* was obviously deemed not hooray-patriotic enough for American readers in the times of the Great Depression.

Whenever I come to the land of Uncle Sam these days, it evokes in me the sparkling humour and the brilliant insights of Ilf and Petrov—the writers who discovered America for me.

470

My KVN America

Not that I was totally unaware of America before reading Ilf and Petrov, although my knowledge of it was only marginally better than that of the early twentieth-century Russian peasant from Stephen Graham's *With Poor Immigrants to America* who was convinced that the Statue of Liberty was the tombstone of Columbus.

I remember having breakfast with my parents in our flat in Kharkov (or the 'regional centre' of K., as Ilf and Petrov would have put it) in October 1962. We were listening to our antediluvian radio-transmitter, mounted on top of the fridge. Like the all-seeing Orwellian TV set from '1984', the radio could not be completely turned off at any time.

'American imperialism .. Missiles . . . Cuba . . . Aggression,' crackled its sea shell-shaped loudspeaker, made of black cardboard. The news was read by Yuri Levitan, the famous Soviet presenter, with a voice so deep and velvety that, combined with the crackles, it tended to envelop listeners like a rough army blanket.

Levitan's hypnotic baritone was revered as a Soviet national treasure and as such was saved for special occasions only.

I did not understand the meaning of all the words, but from the grave faces of the adults I deduced that something serious was brewing.

'Is there going to be a war?' I asked, secretly hoping for an affirmative answer: wars sounded so exciting for an ebullient eight-year-old. 'We don't know yet,' my parents replied diplomatically.

I looked out of the window: a habitual endless queue was snaking along our drab Culture Street and turning the corner towards the 'Tempo' food-store, where I was occasionally allowed to buy myself an ice cream. This time, however, the queue consisted almost entirely of distraught elderly women, clad in black cotton wool jackets. Still remembering the grievances of the last big war, they were stocking up on candles, salt and soap.

I didn't have to ask my parents who was threatening us with war.

From weekly political information lessons at my school, to which we were subjected from the age of seven, I knew there was one hostile country, bent on destroying our glorious and peaceful Soviet Union—the country, which, to quote our politically mature history teacher, 'had brazenly appropriated the name of the whole continent'—the United States of America. From what we were told, America was a horrible place, where they exploited workers, lynched negroes and constantly chewed some disgusting gum (the latter sounded intriguing: at least they had something to chew on a permanent basis). It was in the throes of an unstoppable decline, and Comrade Khrushchev had promised in his recent speech that we were going to overtake it soon, although I didn't quite understand how we could overtake America, when it, as Comrade Khrushchev himself assured us, was balancing on the brink of an abyss . . .

A year or so later, on our first-generation KVN TV set (a popular witticism deciphered KVN as 'kupil, vkliuchil—nie rabotayet'—bought, switched on—doesn't work), whose match-box-size screen had to be enlarged by a special water-filled lens, I watched the funeral of John F. Kennedy. I couldn't comprehend why everyone was so upset by the murder of our number-one enemy's leader. Was it because he was so relatively young and handsome, even if viewed through the distorting lens of our old KVN TV set?

'Force breeds counterforce' is Newton's third law of motion, which can also be applied to societies. By my late teens, I, like most Soviet kids of my generation, had become so fed up with blunt anti-USA propaganda that I started taking a genuine interest in all things American In our 'regional centre of K.', however, there was little to feed this interest: 'contacts with foreigners', particularly with Americans, were actively discouraged, and we, students of the Foreign Languages Department of the local university, were strictly forbidden to come close to the run-down Intourist Hotel in Lenin Avenue.

As an undergraduate, I chose the works of Henry Longfellow, the great American poet of the nineteenth-century, as the subject of my diploma paper:

In vain we look, in vain uplift our eyes to heaven, if we are blind.
We see only what we have the gift of seeing; what we bring—we
find.

Indeed, we were forcibly blinded by the system, which had deprived us of the precious 'gift of seeing' the world.

Well, not all of us, to be fair. Some of my most politically correct (proficiency in English was the least important criterion) fellow-students were sent to work on board the Black Sea Shipping Company cruise liners taking American tourists from New Orleans to the Caribbean.

As someone who was not too PC and had already had unpleasant confrontations with the KGB (one of the accusations was 'unhealthy interest in American literature'), I was not even considered for the job, for which I should thank my lucky stars. Otherwise, I would have almost certainly shared the fate of one of my mates, Kolya Barisnev, a congenitally tongue-tied and hence taciturn guy from the poorest part of K., who had lived all his life with his mother in a semi-ruined wooden shed, with no running water and/or toilet.

Having never been outside the Soviet Union before, one fine day Kolya suddenly found himself in New Orleans.

Utterly unprepared for the experience, Kolya went mad. On day two, he tried to defect, but was apprehended and brought back to the ship by his vigilant 'comrades' (for reasons of 'security', the Soviet seamen were only allowed to walk around the town in groups of no fewer than three). He was promptly sent back to his native 'regional centre of K.', where he was not arrested only because he had—literally—lost all his marbles.

From morning till night, he roamed the dusty streets of K.— gesticulating and mumbling to himself.

One day he accidentally stumbled upon me. 'In the beginning, I thought they had set it all up deliberately—to impress us,' he muttered, grabbing me by the sleeve. 'But later I realised that it was all for real—all these shops bursting with goods, and the beautiful houses, and the people . . . They were all smiling, can you believe it? As if the whole world belonged to them. Suddenly I wanted to run, run, run . . .'

He let go of me and drifted away—a stooping and solitary figure, reeking of cheap plonk, yet still proudly sporting a soiled 'New Orleans' baseball cap—the only American 'souvenir' he was allowed to keep.

He had nowhere else to run to.

Coincidentally, I also felt like running during my first visit to the USA in July, 1990, shortly after my own defection to the West. Only, unlike poor Kolya, who wanted to run towards America, I was desperate to run away from it.

A thick impenetrable haze hung over New York City, wallowing in wet, suffocating heat. The countless homeless slept on soft littered pavements, which felt as if they were about to melt. Aggressive beggars accosted passengers on the subway with their sacramental 'Can you help me out?' A dishevelled man was dashing through the Broadway crowd brandishing a knife. Police sirens wailed piercingly, like a bunch of Russian country women at a funeral.

Far from smiling and relaxed, New Yorkers looked as nervous and bedraggled as my Soviet ex-compatriots. The only visible difference from the Soviet hell was that it was a hell with well-stocked shops, and, although I had never been to Brazil, I was almost ready to repeat after unforgettable Ostap Bender (who, incidentally, had never been to Brazil either): 'No, this is not Rio de Janeiro. This is much worse . . .'

First impressions are often misleading. Nineteen years later, I was no longer disgusted by New York, which had become much cleaner and safer. It was also the only place in the world (apart from the former USSR, of course), where the locals did not recoil on hearing my name and did not get surprised when I introduced myself as a Ukrainian-born Russian with Australian and British passports. 'There are lots of people like you in this city,' a New York friend of mine told me during my last visit to the Big Apple, where I now feel perfectly at ease.

It has to be said that I still find it hard to cope with some aspects of America, particularly with its unlimited, unending and mind-boggling choice of everything: from bagels and hot dogs to religious sects and cable TV channels, from hamburgers and coffees to cars and fitness clubs. The whole country is like one large spoilt child—never quite sure of what new toys to choose for he already has too many.

My attitude to choice, moulded by thirty-five years in the Soviet Union, has always been simple: when you see something nice, grab it while it's available and think what to do with it later. This is why I dread unlimited choices, which to me can be almost as baffling as no choice at all.

I find it bewildering when American waiters bombard me with choices of muffins ('blueberry, strawberry, Shrewsbury, plain, vain, drain . . .'), salad dressings ('Italian, Rotarian, Barbarian . . .') or mustards ('French, English, Danish, Amish, Rubbish . . .').

Doing this, they stare at you blankly, and their voices sound threatening and hypnotic—almost Yuri Levitan-like.

Occasionally though, I came across some striking similarities with my poor motherland.

In the 'Strand' second-hand bookstore in Broadway, boasting of having 'eight miles of books' (never before had I heard of books measured in miles), I once bought a mere dog-eared inch of Jay Franklin's 1937 biography of Fiorello H. La Guardia, who was the Mayor of New York in 1935. On the book's front flap, there was a miraculously preserved sticker:

'The publishers call to your attention that, owing to objections made by Mayor La Guardia, a portion of the text on pages 58 and 74 has been excised'.

I opened the book and saw that several offending paragraphs on the indicated pages were neatly **cut out with scissors**!

No wonder *One-Storied America* became the innocuous *Little Golden America* in the 1937 USA translation.

The difference from Stalin's Soviet Union, however, was that the Soviets wouldn't bother attaching an explanatory sticker to a shredded book. Also, the biographer himself would stand a good chance of being 'excised', i.e. arrested and shot . . .

And yet, nothing can beat the sheer excitement of arriving in the US and being confronted by a grinning immigration officer, with a huge brass badge on his chest gleaming under the lamps, as if grinning, too. America is the last country in the world where immigration officers still smile, or wish you 'a nice day', or even say: 'Take it easy, guy!', while stamping your passport.

In the book *The Land of Plastic Fossils* that, due to the tragedy of 9/11, was never completed I tried to stick to the main principle of Ilf and Petrov, who, according to the 1937 New York Times review of *Little Golden America*, were 'never guilty of sacrificing the facts as they saw them for the sake of a quip'—a huge compliment for the writers who had managed to retain their wit and integrity against all odds.

Like all my other books—written and unwritten—I regard it as an integral part of *Life as a Literary Device.*

Fall foliage

At the end of their first month in the USA, Ilf and Petrov were invited to address the prestigious Dutch Treat Club at the New York Hotel Ambassador. They prepared a brief speech, which was translated into English, and one of them, 'in no way embarrassed by the fact that he found himself in such a large gathering of experts of the English language, read it from a sheet of paper:

'Mr. Chairman, Gentlemen:

We have come on a great journey from Moscow to see America. Besides New York we have had time to be in Washington and in Hartford. After living a month in New York we felt the pangs of love for your great and purely American city. Suddenly we were doused with cold water. 'New York is not America,' we were told by our New York friends. 'New York is only the bridge between Europe and America. You are still on the bridge.' Then we went to Washington, District of Columbia, the capital of the United States, assuming thoughtlessly that surely this city was America. By the evening of the second day we felt with satisfaction that we were beginning to discriminate a little in matters American. 'Washington is not America,' we were told. 'It is a city of government officials. If you really want to see America, you are wasting your time here.' We dutifully put our scratched suitcases into an automobile and went to Hartford, in the state of Connecticut, where the great

American writer, Mark Twain, spent his mature years. Here we were again honestly warned: 'Bear in mind that Hartford is not yet America.' When we began to ask about the location of America, the Hartfordites pointed vaguely to the side. Now we have come to you, Mr. Chairman and gentlemen, and ask you to show us where America really is located, because we have come here in order to learn as much as we can about it.'

'The speech was a great success. The members of the Dutch Treat Club applauded it a long time,' Ilf and Petrov remark in *Little Golden America*. 'Only much later we learned that most of the members of the club did not understand a single word of this speech, because the strange Russo-English accent of the orator drowned out completely the profound thoughts concealed in it.'

I kept recalling the writers' 'speech' while travelling around New England during the so-called Fall Foliage season, normally occurring between mid-September and mid-October. On a bus from Boston airport to Concord, New Hampshire, I was glued to the window. With my mouth agape, I was trying to absorb the wild riot of colour displayed by the trees lining the highway. It was simply beyond description: I never knew so many shades of purple, red and brown existed in nature. I felt myself dissolved and drowning in this incredible natural palette.

The moment I arrived in Concord, however, I was 'doused with cold water'. 'You have come too late,' a young woman from the local Chamber of Commerce who met me at the bus station commented. 'The leaves are just behind peak. Not half as good as ten days ago.'

I tried to object meekly that they were still good enough for me, but she didn't listen. 'Leaf-peeping is a big business here,' she said while driving me to my hotel, and explained that the season is 'officially' divided into four 'official' stages: 1. Just beginning

2. Well-established 3. Peak and 4. Just behind peak. With my Jewish luck, I obviously hit the last—and the least interesting ('officially', no doubt) stage.

The Notting Hill Carnival of maples, aspens and birches was whooshing past the windows of our car. Having suppressed a sudden yawn, I had the impression that the screaming brightness of their leaves had indeed faded in the past several minutes.

In his *United States, 1893* guidebook, Karl Baedeker remarked that 'the colour of autumn leaves is an additional attraction' of New England. 107 years later it has become the main attraction and a 'big business' indeed. True, one can still admire autumn leaves for free, but, as I was told in Vermont (after they dutifully assured me that my arrival was 'belated': what I saw was not the 'real fall' and the leaves were not as good as the week before), the visiting leaf-peepers add over a billion dollars to the state coffers each autumn. No wonder leaf-peeping is often referred to as 'a cornerstone of the New England tourist industry'.

Like every big (and small) business, the New England autumn has to be properly managed. In New Hampshire, they designate twenty 'official leaf-peepers' whose no-less 'official' duties include observing the leaves, compiling twice-weekly reports and suggesting the best 'leaf-peeping routes'.

There were not many of those on offer by the time I arrived in Connecticut, where I was immediately informed that 'the oaks had turned' (meaning become brown and no longer gold) and the prime fall-foliage was over. They nevertheless kindly offered to take me to a 'primary foliage viewing area', where, allegedly, I could still catch some last 'truly golden' leaves, but I refused.

I couldn't, however, refuse a copy of the *Leaf-Peeper's Guide* which I studied in the quiet of my hotel room. I had read somewhere that the exact mechanism of the spectacular displays of autumn leaves' colours was a mystery to scientists. Whether it was true or not, I preferred it to remain a fairy tale—like that of

Santa Claus. But the 'big business' that New England's autumn had become in America had no place for fairy tales.

My brand-new *Leaf-Peeper's Guide* left no stone (or leaf) unturned in shattering the mystery to smithereens: 'In fall, partly because of shorter periods of daylight and the cooler temperatures, the leaves stop making food. The chlorophyll breaks down and the green color disappears. Yellow and orange, previously masked by the green (?—VV), appear. The vibrant reds, purples and bronzes come from other chemical processes . . .' Nice and clear.

A brilliant book, *Vinyl Leaves: Walt Disney World and America* by Stephen M. Fjellman, a leading American anthropologist, starts with the following description:

'There is a tree in Central Florida. It is maybe ninety feet high and huge around the base and has a crown that stretches across almost as many yards as the tree is tall. From the top of this tree, when the wind is still, you can see almost to the Caribbean. The trunk looks about as much like that of a live oak as one might wish. The bark is deeply grained and covered with that pea-soup green colored stuff you see on the trees in hot, wet places. It's a big nice tree, a good place for the treehouse that adorns it. But it's not made of wood. The trunk and the branches are formed out of pressed concrete wrapped around a steel-mesh frame. The bark and green stuff that cover much of it are painted on. *The leaves, all 800,000 of them are made of vinyl.* [Italics are mine:VV.]'

Stephen Fjellman proceeds to explain that the tree, 'Disneyodendron eximus ('out-of-ordinary Disney tree')', is in the Adventureland part of Walt Disney's World Magic Kingdom. For him, it became a symbol of 'commodification' (just another word for 'plasticising', I presume) of modern American culture.

The Land of Plastic Fossils . . . And of plastic leaves too.

The window of my hotel room in Concord, NH, overlooked the vast courtyard of a Victorian lunatic asylum, now—a 'psychiatric hospital'. In the treacherous semi-light of the early dusk, the 'past-peak' autumn leaves in it were aglow and blending with the headlights of the cars behind the hospital fence. What 'chemical processes' had made them look so desperately gorgeous? Or was it simply because they preferred burning alive to being plasticised?.

'Authentic replica'

'Classifieds' and 'Personals' are by far the best reads in Alaskan newspapers. Where else in the world can you see hundreds of ads offering to buy (or to sell) second-hand snowmobiles and hydroplanes and/or spare parts to them? Alaskans are a prosperous lot (they are exempt from federal taxes, but receive a thousand dollars per person per year from the US government as a special allowance): there are thousands of hydroplane owners in Anchorage alone and parking spots for the planes are as common there as supermarkets and fast-food outlets. There is also a growing problem of night-time drink-flying, when tipsy plane-owner locals whiz back home after a rowdy evening in the bar.

As for 'Personals' (or 'Lonely Hearts') ads, they beat anything of the kind in their sheer desperation. I mean the ones coming from men seeking women. The reason for that is that men outnumber women five—sevenfold in Alaska.

Here are a couple of examples from 'Pressonals'—the 'Personals' section of 'Anchorage Press': 'Need a F right now! Let's have hot monkey love in public places!'; 'Need a woman! Age and race open. You will not be disappointed!' The last 'cry in the womenless Alaskan wilderness' might be just a bit too optimistic, for Alaskan women do get 'disappointed' fairly often. They have even come up with a saying to describe their chances of finding a 'quality' partner: 'The odds are good, but the goods are odd.'

The only other regular features of Alaskan newspapers that can compete with the ads in their idiosyncrasy are stories of encounters with wildlife. The headlines of such reports are usually self-explanatory: 'Bears Sighted in Town' (*Homer News*) 'Bear Attacks 2nd Dog in Sitka' (*South East Empire*), 'Jogger Chased by Bear' (*Anchorage Daily News*), and so on. They show that Alaskan wildlife is generally alive and well, with the exception perhaps of some unfortunate Sitka dogs who do not count as wildlife anyway. Every resident of Alaska has his (or her) own wildlife encounter story to tell. A woman from an Anchorage suburb assured me that elks routinely wandered into her back garden of an evening. She also told me how she was pursued by a brown bear while jogging (jogging seems to be a risky occupation in Alaska unless you can run faster than a bear). But the story that I read in '*Homer News*' one day was so utterly incredible that I could be forgiven for taking it not with a grain, but with a good handful of salt. Here it is:

'Orca Takes the Hali-Bait' ('Orca' is another name for killer-whale: VV)

'Clients aboard a Flat Fun Charters boat last week got their money's worth when an unexpected guest paid a visit. A deckhand on the Sea Hawk was pulling in what he thought was a fair-sized halibut when a bull Orca surfaced with the fish in his mouth. The crew and the passengers spotted the killer whale about 50 feet from the boat, which was in open water near the Kachemak Bay. 'He rolled and looked at us and chomped it then kind of spat it out,' said Martin Reid, the skipper. The Orca crushed some bones in the halibut but didn't eat it . . . Then it came for a closer look, dodging under the boat and swimming next to it. 'You could have stepped off the boat onto his back,' said Reid. 'It was kind of freaking everyone out.'

The story was substantiated by photos (made by the skipper) on which one could clearly see a hapless angler trying to pull out a torpedo-shaped submarine-sized whale, or at least pretending to do so.

I ran to the harbour and promptly booked myself on a halibut fishing charter the following morning. 'Remember, all the fish you caught can be packaged and sent anywhere in the world,' a 'fish controller' girl told me from the window of her shabby wooden booth on the pier. I said that I didn't want my whale to be sent 'anywhere in the world': I wanted it to go straight to London, even if they had to charter a special cargo flight for that.

'Sure!' the girl replied with a smile and proceeded to compliment me on my 'lovely British accent' (it is only in Alaska and, possibly, also in Tasmania that I can occasionally pass for a Brit).

But instead of hooking a whale, or even a halibut, I caught a severe bout of seasickness and spent all my time on board the Sea Witch lying supine in the boat's tiny cabin. My only consolation was that, with my environmentally friendly fishing (i.e. fishing with no catch), I played no part in packaging any of Alaska's burgeoning wildlife.

The boat's owners were called 'Sorry Charlie Charters', by the way. I wish I'd known that before embarking.

'This claw is an authentic replica from a grizzly bear,' ran a price tag, which I spotted, in the gift shop of a museum in Kodiak. The 'authentic replica' (what an oxymoron!) was, naturally, made of plastic.

The replica claw, no matter how 'authentic', was not good enough for me. To make up for my fishing and whale-glimpsing (to say nothing of whale-catching) failure, I was heading for the wilderness of the Kodiak Island, famous for its 'watchable wildlife'—as a local tourist brochure put it, particularly its brown Kodiak bears. The same brochure contained some 'Common Sense in Bear Country' tips which included:

- Avoid surprising bears and make plenty of noise
- Avoid crowding bears; respect their personal space
- Plan ahead, stay calm, identify yourself, don't run

I was quite happy not to 'crowd' the bears, albeit not quite sure how that could be combined with 'identifying myself' and not running away immediately afterwards. Should I just say: 'Hi, my name is Vitali, and I came here just to watch you!'? But what if the bear mistakes this tirade for an intrusion into his 'personal space'?

With all these questions on my mind, I boarded a four-seat Cessna 206 hydroplane for a 40-minute flight to the shores of Fraser Lake in the depth of the Alaskan wilderness. Apart from Dan, the pilot, there were two more passengers on board: a young honey-mooning couple from Philadelphia.

'Can your hydroplane land on the ground?' the husband asked Dan shortly after we took off.
'Yes, it can. But only once,' the taciturn pilot replied.

We landed ('watered'?) on the lake and, having put on anti-mosquito nets, kindly provided by Dan, walked through the dense forest for about ten minutes until we saw a happy family of brown bears trout-fishing in a stream. I was about to identify myself, but Dan pressed a finger to his lips. So preoccupied were the bears that they paid no attention to us for the whole duration of our hour-and-a-half watch. I was particularly taken by a fluffy bear cub, being taught how to fish by his daddy (or was it mummy—I couldn't be sure). The cub was a quick learner, and soon he started ferreting out a wriggling fish each time he dipped his little paws into the water.

He was a much better fisherman than I.

When we were hiking back to the plane, I felt an urge to go to the loo. 'Can I quickly hide behind the bushes?' I asked Dan. 'There's no need to,' he said. 'There's a nice rest room on your right.' He pointed to a little clearing in the forest. There, half hidden by lush foliage, stood a gleaming stainless-steel hut. Inside, it was spotless—with hot water, hand-drier, generous supply of paper towels and paper toilet seats. In the corner, there was a special tap for washing one's feet!

If you asked me what impressed me most in America, I would probably say: 'A state-of-the-art public toilet in the midst of Alaska's Bear Country—a pristine and untouched wilderness, with no roads and no humans for hundreds of miles around.'

I must have looked ridiculous emerging from that air-conditioned loo into clouds of mosquitoes in the middle of nowhere. What's more, it made me feel ridiculous too. Suddenly my bear-watching experience was no longer an adventure, but just another 'authentic replica'—a virtual-reality 'presentation' in a museum auditorium, with soft comfy seats and 'Exit' signs glowing soothingly in the dark.

Messing with Texas

For over eleven months, with coaches as my main means of transport, I carried on searching for a genuine, not plastic, America.

Having crossed New Mexico, our hard-working bus rolled into Texas, America's second largest state after Alaska.

For the first hundred miles or so, the landscape remained indistinguishable from New Mexico: same arid, sun-burnt prairie; same brown mountains on the horizon; same ranch fences along the highway, which was getting more and more forlorn and deserted. As Ilf and Petrov observed driving through the area sixty-five years earlier, 'the gasoline stations became less and less frequent, but to make up for that, the hats of the rare residents became broader and broader.'

The 'gasoline stations', where we stopped, were selling only local newspapers, carrying little apart from school lunch menus and 'Lonely Hearts' ads, with head shots of people in different stages of obesity. They also offered fly-stained collections of bearded 'cowboy jokes', appalling machine cappuccino and cans of mysterious 'Meat Food Product'. The customers were beefy, ruddy-faced farmers in 'broad' Mexican hats and leather belts, with buckles so huge that they covered their groins.

We passed through several nondescript little towns—each with its own point of pride, announced by multiple road-signs: 'Pecos—the Home of the Rodeo'; 'City of Marfa—County Seat', etc. The town of Presidio smugly advertised its own 'International Airport'—a wooden shed, from where one little plane flew across the nearby border into Mexico twice a day. 'Each small [American] town wants to be like New York', noted Ilf and Petrov. 'We even found one New York consisting of nine hundred inhabitants, and it was a real city. Its inhabitants walked on their Broadway, their noses high up in the air. They weren't quite sure which Broadway was generally regarded as the more important, theirs or New York's.'

But New Yorks they were not.

The doors of the only café in Fort Davis were sealed with a Soviet-style 'Gone for Lunch' note above the massive lock. And in Fort Stockton, boasting of the 'world's largest' sculpture of the roadrunner, New Mexico's long-tailed state bird, the only other feature of distinction was that books in the town's smallish book-shop were sold in pre-packaged parcels of five (the choice was NOT the customer's!), each priced at $1.37.

'**Don't Mess With Texas**' warned a sticker on the windscreen of a passing farmer's truck, carrying a sad, cockroach-like (black and compact) longhorn cow in its back.

To be frank, there was nothing much to mess with, for after this brusque encounter other vehicles disappeared, and the only moving things in sight were oil pump-jacks, nodding tirelessly, like praying Orthodox Jews. We were in the Chihuahua Desert, whose sandy, cactus-thorned fingers reach into Texas from Mexico, across the Rio Grande, to blend with the southern extremes of the Rocky Mountains.

'One can hardly find anything more grandiose and more beautiful in the world than an American desert . . .' where 'the beauty created by nature is supplemented by the beauty created by the deft hands of men.' wrote Ilf and Petrov.

Coming from the hastily 'industrialised', yet still distinctly third-worldish, USSR of the 1930s, the writers could not help admiring 'the even highway with its silvery bridges, its neatly placed water mains, its mounds and dips'. They even concluded that 'the automobile in the desert seemed twice as beautiful than in the city'!

Could it be partly due to the fact that the speed limit in Texas was then just 45 miles per hour?

Riding along the semi-dried Rio Grande, marking the border with Mexico, sixty-five years later, I was ready to share the Russians' enthralment with the natural beauty of the desert—its piercing silence and quiet loneliness echoing the official logo of Texas: 'The Lone Star State'; its resilient Dead Man's Fingers—a breed of red-blossomed cacti, stubbornly sticking out of dry earth; its carpets of blue bonnets (tiny azure flowers), making parts of it aquamarine and almost sea-like; its 'dust devils'— gentle puffs of sand and dust lifting above its surface here and there, as if the desert itself was breathing them out, while mischievously indulging in the most subversive of all anti-

American activities—smoking.

As for the 'man-made beauty', I was not so sure. It was nice to see (and to feel) that the desert highway was indeed as smooth as the Beltway around Washington DC, that plumbing in the abundant and spotlessly clean roadside 'rest rooms' in the middle of nowhere was as perfect as at a Marriott Hotel in Manhattan. On the other hand, I was rather taken aback by the eyesore of a huge hothouse, which, in the permanently red-hot desert, looked as appropriate as a fridge on top of an iceberg; or by a handful of useless picnic gazebos, made of iron and offering no protection from the scorching desert sun. The only good thing about these gazebos was that burgers and sausages would fry spontaneously (together with the unlikely picnickers) inside them.

Unlike Ilf and Petrov, who stayed for several days in El Paso, I stopped in the little border town of Lajitas, claiming to be 'the remotest settlement in the USA'.

Local tourist brochures asserted that more people had spent the night at the bottom of the Grand Canyon than in Lajitas, boasting 'the most breathtaking sunrises and sunsets in Texas'—a fact that was probably meant to make the gullible Grand Canyon revellers green with envy. According to the brochures, Lajitas was also the home of the 'famous beer drinking goat' (one resident wit confided in me that he was actually the town's Mayor).

Built in 1915 as a cavalry post to protect the area from the Mexican 'hot-eyed bandit' Pancho Villa, Lajitas had gone into decay by 1977, when it was bought by the Mischer Corporation, with the aim of turning it into a popular health spa. A couple of hotels and a small touristy shopping mall were constructed, but potential holidaymakers were not in a hurry to visit this natural sauna, especially in summer, when the temperature in Lajitas seldom drops below 100 degrees Fahrenheit.

As for the three hundred local residents, their plight remained almost as pitiful as in the times of Pancho Villa, although much less exciting.

An ageless local woman—dried-out and sinewy, like a desert plant—told me that to buy basic groceries they still had to travel 160 miles, and that children had to be driven to school to the town of Terlingua—a two-hour-long daily journey.

'Parents of schoolkids get partly reimbursed by the state government, but, in actual fact, we spend this money—25 cents per mile—on other things,' the woman chuckled.

Listening to her, it was hard to believe that she was talking about the twenty-first century USA.

The breakthrough came recently—when the Mischer Corporation had all but given up on Lajitas and put the town up for auction.

The bids were lazy and half-hearted, like the biting of bream in April, until—one hour before the closure—the auctioneer heard the characteristic rattle of chopper blades above his head.

Like in a good ancient Greek tragedy (or in a bad Hollywood movie), the sound signified the arrival of the *deus ex machina* (a god routinely introduced into an ancient drama to resolve the intricacies of the plot), or, in this case, the highest bidder, who—quite literally—descended onto Lajitas from the heavens, in his personal French Astar 350 B3 helicopter. Having barely touched the ground, Steve Smith, an Austin property developer and a co-founder of Excel telephone company, snapped up Lajitas for $3, 950,000 ($4.2 million with the auctioneer's fees).

'The sale ends an era. Begins another,' commented the *Lajitas Sun*, the town's monthly rag, in its usual laconic fashion, imitating the locals' habit of speaking curtly and through clenched teeth to prevent ubiquitous flies from entering their mouths.

I was lucky: Steve Smith was in town and agreed to a quick

interview. A tall, thick-set man in a navy polo-shirt, he had a radiant smile and oozed the famous Texan can-do attitude.

'I came here, to the desert, to realise my dream and to express my creativity. The place was stale when I bought it, and I gonna change it,' he said.

He shared his plans to build a jet strip, a golf course and a swimming pool in Lajitas 'to attract families in winter'.

I asked about the locals, and he promised 'to improve utilities and to supply school buses and medical facilities'—a perfect rhyme, which, as I hoped, would not end up as just another abstract example of the never-ending poetry of the desert.

'The word 'desert' is frequently used as a symbol of monotony. The American desert, however, is unprecedentedly varied,' noted Ilf and Petrov.

Indeed, the last thing I expected to find in Lajitas, the remotest and the most 'un-American' place in the USA, was an archetypal 'American' story of the sale of a modern, even if god-forsaken, town—with all its long-suffering inhabitants.

The Russian writers were right: the American desert was anything but boring.

Across the bridge

'A Day in Mexico' is one of my favourite chapters in *Little Golden America*. As transpires from the chapter's title, Ilf and Petrov made a brief foray into Mexico while staying in the Texan city of El Paso. They only had to walk across 'a bridge over the Rio Grande . . . and there it was: Mexico—the city of Juarez.'

The seeming ease of their walk-about was complicated by the writers' fear of borders: they were wary of—literally—making a *faux pas*, which for them, citizens of the Stalinist USSR, could eventually prove—no less literally—fatal. 'We were afraid to go to Mexico,' they wrote and explained: 'On our passports was a one-year visa for staying in the United States . . . But every visa ends automatically as soon as you leave the country . . . Horror possessed us at the very thought that the remainder of our days we should have to pass in the city of Juarez, located in the Mexican state of Chihuahua. On the other hand, we wanted very much to be in Mexico.'

In the end, the Russians must have recalled one of the unwritten rules of Soviet life: 'If something is forbidden, but very much desired—then it is allowed'—and ventured onto the bridge.

A cigar-smoking (it was 1935, don't forget!) American immigration official, having carefully scrutinised their passports, kindly escorted them over to the Mexican 'border station'. 'There, true enough, near a booth stood a saffron-faced man with a dirtyish neck, dressed in a dazzling uniform of dark-coloured khaki, with gold pipings. But on the face of the Mexican border official was utter contempt for the duties imposed upon him. On his face was sketched: 'Yes, a sad fate has obliged me to wear this beautiful uniform, but I will not soil my graceful hands by looking over nasty scraps of paper. No! You will never live to see that done by the honourable Juan Ferdinand Cristobal Collbajos!' We . . . were very glad that we had come across such an honourable hidalgo, and quickly walked down the main street of Juarez.'

Ilf and Petrov had a full day in Juarez: they tasted Mexican food, visited a church, witnessed a street rally and attended a bullfight. On their way back to the States, they walked past 'Juan Ferdinand Cristobal Collbajos', who as before, paid no attention to them . . .

Although I tried to follow in Ilf and Petrov's footsteps as closely as possible in my trans-American journey 65 years on, certain deviations from their itinerary were inevitable. Unlike the Russians, who stopped in El Paso, I spent several days in Lajitas, a border town priding itself in being 'the remotest settlement in the USA'. A small Mexican hamlet of Paso Lajitas was a stone's throw away, across the Rio Grande. Similar to my predecessors, I was very keen on the idea of venturing across the border and adding Mexico to the list of 50 odd countries which I had visited in the last 10 years.

My indisputable advantage over Ilf and Petrov was that I had a multiple-entry US visa in my passport, and, with the Cold War firmly in the past, I did not expect any complications resulting from my distinctly Russian-sounding name in the unlikely, as I hoped, event of my detention by frontier-guards.

I knew that the 2,000 mile US-Mexican border was guarded, even if sporadically. On the way to Lajitas, our bus was stopped a couple of times by heavily armed (and heavily sweating) US border guards, dressed in dark-green battle fatigues and cowboy hats, for perfunctory checks. They were looking for drugs, which smugglers, as they explained, often hid inside *piñatas*, traditional Mexican toys. Having made sure that none of the passengers was carrying *piñatas*, they wished us a nice day and waved the bus through. Border-patrolling, like almost everything else in Texas, seemed to be taken easy. No wonder a leading American Mexico specialist recently compared the US-Mexico border to 'a sieve blasted by buckshot.'

The residents of Lajitas assured me that they routinely went to Paso Lajitas for a cheapish Mexican lunch—and thus encouraged, I eventually decided to follow their lead.

With a dog-eared Australian passport in my breast pocket (and with a good deal of trepidation underneath), I walked down to the Rio Grande one scorching afternoon. I nearly turned back, having spotted an empty 'Waco Christian School' van parked on the river bank, next to a strict 'Permits Required' sign-post: anything coming from Waco, Texas, could be safely regarded as a bad omen.

A battered leaking boat, paddled by a bearded Charon look-alike, materialised from nowhere. I jumped in without thinking. The dark-green waters of the Rio Grande (or was it indeed the Styx?) were opaque and uninviting. My grim Mexican ferryman didn't utter a word throughout the crossing. 'Permits' were obviously *not* required. Nor was conversation.

Having barely stepped onto the Mexican soil, I saw two Mexican soldiers, their tunics unbuttoned, having a siesta in the shade of a tree. 'Border guards . . .' I thought with awe, bracing myself for an unpleasant encounter. But, being probably the descendants of the honourable Juan Ferdinand Cristobal Collbajos, they didn't pay the slightest attention to me.

Another unshaven type appeared and offered me a lift to the village, only several hundred yards away, in his jalopy of a pick-up truck. Just like 'Charon', he was taciturn and seemingly altruistic (he adamantly rejected payment). I wondered whether they both received commissions from one of the village's restaurants.

The first thing that struck Ilf and Petrov in Juarez 'were smells of fried food, burned oil, garlic, red pepper', so different from 'the odour of gasoline, which reigns in the United States'.

When I got off the pick-up truck in the centre of Paso Lajitas, I was hardly able to smell (or to see) anything at all. A dust storm was raging above the village. Rags, empty plastic bags and torn newspapers were flying in the air. The wind, like a bored village bully, was tugging aimlessly at the permanently unlocked doors of lop-sided clay bungalows, trying to tear them off their rusty hinges.

When clouds of dust somewhat dispersed, I started along the unpaved main (and only) street of the village.

Escorted by a couple of sorry-looking dogs with dust-ridden tearful eyes, I went past skeletons of ruined cars, past an empty water tank, past an unexpectedly clean and freshly painted basketball pitch (the only bit of the village that seemed to be properly maintained). A lonely satellite dish on a holey house roof, hastily patched up with rubber-foam, looked alien and out-of-place—like a stranded UFO, which had landed here by mistake.

Further down the street, I stumbled over a toy-truck, abandoned in the dirt and no-less-decrepit than its full-size counterparts lining the road.

Everything in Paso Lajitas spoke poverty and despair of the proportions I had only seen in the most deprived parts of Romania and on some East London council estates.

A man in a greasy singlet sat on the steps of *Tienda Rural*, the village general store, swigging beer from a can.

Inside, a sad-faced and dark-eyed teenage girl of about 15 was rocking a baby behind the counter. The stock was limited to rolls of toilet paper, cans of chilies, several packets of cornflakes, one (!) bottle of *Kahlua*—a strong Mexican liquor, and a couple of crude wooden eagles.

'Where did he buy the beer?' I asked the girl pointing at the man outside, barely visible through a grimy shop window. 'In America,'—she replied with a clear-cut Texan accent. 'I went to school there,' she explained, having registered my surprise. 'All village children do, although it is kinda illegal . . .'

Her lips parted in a radiant half-smile that momentarily lit up the shop's gloomy interior.

She told me that she was born in America, since village women always preferred giving birth across the border.

'There's little choice: the nearest Mexican town is two hours away.'

'Why aren't you at school now?' I asked.

'I kinda dropped out,' she shrugged, squinting at the baby in her arms.

In the shop's tiny 'front garden', all plants were dead, except for one fading red rose, its few remaining petals covered with thick layer of dust. It was obvious that the miraculously surviving flower wouldn't last here for much longer . . .

I had late and solitary lunch of *Platillo Mexicano*—a plentiful Mexican food platter—at *Los Amigos*, the village's only functioning restaurant (which made the choice easy), and washed it down with a bottle of local *Carta Blanca* lager. The meal was prepared by a fat Mexican woman, who lived next door. When she saw me approaching, she waddled out of her hut and into the restaurant and, without saying a word, started cooking. The dining area was Spartan, yet clean, and the menu was in English. The place was obviously targeting clients from across the border. Behind the window, ostriches were grazing among rusty carcasses of smashed cars.

The woman's son, a little boy called Orlando, was running in and out of the kitchen munching a *burito*.

My return journey to the USA passed without incident, and soon I was back in my air-conditioned hotel room in Lajitas watching CNN. Larry King was grilling his guest, but, staring at the screen, I could only see the eyes of the Mexican girl from the store—the eyes full of quiet resignation to all the injustices of fate.

I switched off the TV, opened my copy of *Little Golden America* and reread the last paragraph of 'A Day in Mexico' chapter: 'Having travelled considerably in the United States, we had become so accustomed to good roads, to good service, to cleanliness and comfort that we stopped taking any note of it. But after one day in Mexico we began to appreciate once again . . . all the material achievements of the United States. It is useful at times, in order to know a country the better, to leave it for a day.'

With sadness, I had to conclude that the last 65 years did

little to bridge the gap between the First and the Third Worlds, still securely separated by the narrow and virtually unguarded stretch of the Rio Grande.

Old Believers

. . . She was sitting on the pavement (or, as they say in America, 'sidewalk'), next to a 'Paws for Coffee' coffee-shop for dogs, in a wind-swept suburb of Anchorage, Alaska's biggest city. Her slanting Inupiaq eyes stared straight in front of her, across the buzzing freeway and further—past a McDonald's outlet and a grey modernistic bungalow of an 'Alaska Cremation Center'—into nowhere.

She was drunk. Or stoned. Or, most likely, both—alcoholism and drug-addiction are still rife among Alaska's natives. A soiled Russian Orthodox cross, carved out of whale's bone, was dangling round her dried-out parchment-like neck.

I spotted her while trying to walk off my jet-lag on my first afternoon in Alaska, although my first encounter with what is known as 'Russian Alaska', or 'Russian America in Alaska', occurred several hours earlier, on the flight from Minneapolis to Anchorage, where I sat next to a taciturn Alaskan Indian dressed in the black robes of a Russian Orthodox priest.

Peaceful Russian Orthodox missionaries were eventually much more successful in Alaska than bellicose communist preachers in Russia itself: communism in Russia is no more, whereas Orthodoxy in Alaska (and in Russia, for that matter) is stronger than ever, and three-bar Russian Orthodox crosses are still scratching the vast, stormy and pinkish (as if chronically inflamed and itchy) Alaskan skies from the tops of missile-shaped church domes. They have become an inseparable part of Alaska's ever-dramatic landscape, so brilliantly conveyed in the paintings of Norman Lowell, an Alaskan artist who lives on the

Kenai Peninsula.

His canvas 'In the Stillness of the Night' features a solitary
Russian church in the shadow of a snow-capped mountain, with
Aurora Borealis ablaze above its roof. This artistic image is a
true reflection of modern Alaska, where ethnic Russians are few
and far between, but Russian Orthodoxy remains the dominant
religion.

When the first Russian colonists started arriving in Alaska
in the middle of the 18th century under the banner 'For God and
Tsar', they brought their religion with them. The locals, who
used to believe in supreme divine force, proved easy converts.
They eagerly took to Orthodoxy not only because of its kindness and its impressive rituals, but also because many Russian
priests were highly educated people, who shared their medical
knowledge with the Indians and helped them create their
own alphabets by translating psalms and gospels into local
languages. Soon, it became common practice for the natives to
adopt the names (first and last) of their Russian Godparents after
baptism.

Leafing through a bulky 1999 Anchorage White Pages, I
kept coming across Russian names: 'Olin', 'Oleksa', 'Oleksyk',
'Oskolkoff'. Among them, there were three 'Ivanovs' and six,
somewhat Westernised, 'Ivanoffs'.

After the sale of Alaska to America in 1867 (at $7, 2 million, it
was USA's ever-best bargain), many locals chose to keep their
Russian names, whereas others opted for easier-to-spell Anglo-
Saxon ones for secular purposes.

Camille Fergusson, a young Tlingit woman in Sitka, the ex-
capital of Russian Alaska told me that her real church name was
Yelizaveta. And although some aspects of the Orthodox mass are
becoming increasingly Americanised (I couldn't believe my eyes
when I saw pews in the Holy Resurrection Church in Kodiak,
for one is supposed to stand or to kneel on the floor during the
fairly Spartan Orthodox service), and most of the liturgies are

now conducted in English, some hymns and psalms are still sung in Old Church Slavonic.

Nowhere else in Alaska this peculiar fusion of cultures is so obvious as in Eklutna—a native Athabascan Indian village twenty-six miles north-east of Anchorage.

On entering the graveyard of the Old St. Nicholas Orthodox Church, I was momentarily blinded by a sudden riot of bright colours emanating from the graves—the last thing one would expect at a normally sombre Orthodox cemetery. Each burial was marked not only by a traditional three-bar cross, but also by a multi-coloured 'spirit house'—a transitional Wendy-house-like 'dwelling' for the deceased in accordance with an ancient Athabascan system of beliefs which has no concept of physical death. The colours of these toy-houses—complete with gabled roofs, doors and tiny window-frames—differed from clan to clan, and their size was in proportion to the age of the deceased, but each of them was radiant, cheerful and (indeed!) death-defying.

Any child would love to have one in a toy-box . . .

Travelling in Alaska, I often thought what it would have looked like, had it not been sold to 'the Boston Men' (a Russian nickname for the Americans) in 1867 and remained part of the Russian Empire—not a far-fetched historical alternative, if we remember that the sale was debated in the US Senate for over six months.

There would have certainly been many more Russian names in phone directories, but fewer churches, which would have been replaced by Stalinist wedding-cake skyscrapers, with stars—not crosses—on their cheeky spires. There wouldn't have been a lot of 'No Touch Laser Car Wash' stations, Aircraft Parts centres selling spare parts for privately owned hydro-planes, and ubiquitous 'drive-thru' Espresso coffee shops (Espresso is America's new consumerist idol), routinely offering forty odd types of coffee, including a 'half-caf'—a cross between a proper espresso and a de-caffeinated one.

One thing is certain, however: had Alaska stayed Russian (and then Soviet), it—paradoxically—would have never become home to the world's most obscure community of Russian outcasts confined to a handful of small villages (Nikolaevsk, Voznesenka, Razdolna, Kachemak-Selo, Port Graham and Nanwalek—no more than 2-3 thousand people altogether) in the south-west of the Kenai Peninsula. Visitors are not welcome there, but I was lucky (my name must have helped).

. . . The road to the village of Nikolaevsk was overgrown with fireweed, an endemic bright-red wild flower, and pushki, a cauliflower-like poisonous plant. The latter's name was distinctively un-English and must have originated from Alaska's Russian settlers ('*pushki*' means 'canons' in Russian).

In vain, I was trying to spot a road sign for Nikolaevsk: there were none. Finally, following the instructions given to me in Homer, the nearest town, I turned into an unpaved dirt-track. After a half-hour-long bumpy ride, I was overtaken by a battered old Rover with a bearded man behind the wheel. A woman in strange Mennonite-style headwear was sitting next to him. It was my first glimpse of Nikolaevsk residents, the Russian Old Believers—a much-persecuted and therefore extremely reclusive religious group, who first came to Alaska in 1960s.

The origins of the Old Believers' movement go back to the so-called 'Great Schism' of 1650s, when Nikon, a strong-minded Russian Orthodox Patriarch and a strict disciplinarian, decided to correct the Church-Slavonic holy texts and the method of worship practiced by the Russian masses. His reforms were opposed by a section of the Orthodox Church, who accused Nikon of heresy and vowed to stick to the old ways. Nikon's reforms were far from iconoclastic and concerned such seemingly insignificant issues as how many fingers (two or three) would be used to make the sign of the cross; whether 'Alleluia' should be sung two or three times; whether the priests should walk around the altar with or against the passage of the sun, and so on. But in the eyes of the more conservative believers this constituted a huge change in their faith. Organically opposed to any reform, the Old Believers (as they became to be known) suffered severe persecution under Peter the Great, whom they saw as the Antichrist. As a result, many had to flee to the outskirts of the vast Russian Empire. After the Communist coup d'état of 1917, a considerable number escaped over the border to China, where they stayed until the Chinese revolution of 1949 forced them even farther away from home—to South America and Australia.

The majority of Nikolaevsk residents came to Alaska (in 1968) from Brazil, via Oregon, where they survived by growing wheat and corn. In the words of Father Kondratiy Fefelov, with whom I spoke inside the village church of St. Nicholas, they left Brazil because of its poverty ('We couldn't sell our crops') and Oregon— in fear of the 'corruptive influence' the American media, mainly television, could have on their children, traditionally brought up in strict accordance with the Old Believers' religious values. 'We wanted to get away from Western civilisation, with all its drugs and sexes (sic), and to be on our own . . .'

'How come you allow this?' I asked him pointing at a satellite dish on the roof of a neighbouring house. The priest waved his hand nervously: 'We had to slacken up eventually. You ban television—and the kids run to our American neighbours, or go to the cinema, which is even more dissipating . . .' He pronounced 'cinema' with disgust—in precisely the same way the Old Believers of Peter the Great times must have uttered the hated word 'reform'.

With 11 children and 36 grandchildren, Father Kondratiy, to whom the villagers reverentially referred to as *Batiushka*, knew what he was talking about.

Children were everywhere in Nikolaevsk, where each family had 10-15 offspring (it is not unusual for a girl to get married at 14 or 15). They were all serious, quiet and too shy to talk to a stranger like myself—particularly the girls in their traditional long dresses ('talichkas') and coloured kerchiefs, which they were bound to change for a more sophisticated headwear ('shashmura')—a cap covered with a scarf—after getting married and becoming 'khoziaiki' ('house-hostesses'), preoccupied mainly with cooking and child-bearing. Marriages in Nikolaevsk had still to be approved and blessed by the 'Batiushka' ('little father').

And yet, the feared Western civilisation has crept its way into this closed anachronistic world.

'We have a problem with young Russian village guys who are in the habit of getting drunk and driving their pick-up trucks at breakneck speed across the town,' a tourism official in Homer confided in me. When I asked the 'Batiushka' about it, he pretended he didn't hear the question.

In a challenge to the age-long traditions of male domination, several Nikolaevsk women found themselves jobs in Homer, whereas a couple of others chose to leave the community altogether and moved into the 'real world', where, as one Nikolaevsk resident told me with horror, 'they wear shorts and even use make-up'. On the other hand, three American families came to live in Nikolaevsk and seem to be getting along well with the Russians.

Yet even the most conformist of the Old Believers cannot dismiss all the fruits of Western civilisation as harmful.

The 'Batiushka' himself was telling me with pride about the villagers' own small fleet of ultra-modern fishing vessels, with latest electronic equipment (fishing constitutes their main source of income). Nikolaevsk boasts an excellent secondary school, one of the best in Alaska, where all the subjects, except for Russian, are taught in English. No wonder, the village teenagers prefer communicating in English, although most of them retain a reasonably good command of their melodious old-fashioned Russian language. As for smaller kids, they hardly speak any Russian at all.

'They don't want to learn Russian,' complained Nina Fefelova, at whose house I was put up for the night. Nina, herself an Old Believer, came to Nikolaevsk from the Russian Far East seven years ago and married one of the 'Batiushka's' sons, a deacon called Denis. She taught Russian at the village school.

A bubbly and outgoing character, Nina was not devoid of a business streak and ran a tiny Russian gift-shop from her own back-yard. She made me wear a traditional Russian 'rubakha' (a collar-less silk shirt) and a 'kushak' (sash), both borrowed from her shop, and kept snapping pictures of me in this ridiculous (from my point of view) outfit, now only worn by dancers of Russian folk ensembles when on stage.

. . . In the evening, I was invited to watch fish-canning in the courtyard of Feopent Ivanovich Reutov, a thick-set elderly man, who was born in Russia ('My parents didn't tell me where') and grew up in Brazil. The canning was done in an antediluvian way: tins of pink salmon were placed into a capacious iron barrel with water and boiled for 4 hours on a powerful bonfire—'to kill all the microbes'. Two youngsters, Iona and Flegon, both duly bearded (the Old Believers' men are not allowed to cut their facial hair) and wearing baseball caps, came to help.

A neighbour, Father Deacon Josip, popped in, allegedly, to borrow a scythe and stayed.

I felt at ease in the company of my fellow outcasts, who seemed to accept my 'Western' attire, my 'modernised' Russian language, my shaven beard-less face, even my camera (the Old Believers are notoriously camera-shy).

There was only one thing about me that they could not come to grips with: smoking.

'In Voznesenka, they would attack you with an axe, if they saw you with a cigarette in your mouth,' Iona told me with a grimace of disapproval on his face. I made a mental note never to come close to the village of Voznesenka, which had a reputation of being even more reclusive and more conservative than Nikolaevsk.

They told me off, when I inadvertently dropped a cigarette end on the grass: 'Pick it up and hide it somewhere. If the *Batiushka* finds it, you are in trouble . . .'

'Don't you realise that smoking is a sin?' Josip, the Deacon, persisted. I mumbled something to the effect that we were all sinners in one way or another.

'This is true,' Josip said pensively, and the subject of smoking was dropped for the rest of the night, although the word 'sin' came up again, when Flegon mentioned his girlfriend, an American divorcee with a child.

'We must ask the *Batiushka* to marry you and to take you out of sin as soon as possible, in the name of Jesus Christ, our savior,' Iona, who himself was properly married to an Old Believer Russian girl, commented.

'He must be joking,' I thought, but Iona's face was dead serious, and his dark-brown eyes were full of sad reproach.

. . . A warm and velvety summer night fell upon Nikolaevsk fast, as if the smallish village was suddenly covered with an oversized black and fluffy *ushanka* (a traditional Russian fur-hat with ear-flaps) from Nina's gift-shop.

The fire was burning brightly in Feopent Ivanovich's courtyard tearing the darkness into shreds, dagger-like. Iona produced a bottle of raspberry-flavoured (we were in America, after all!) Smirnoff.

All the men, except for me, crossed themselves before every drank.

Deacon Josip was telling us about his childhood in Brazil.

And although he had never been to Russia, his Russian speech was amazing: it was the language of Tolstoy and Turgenev, free of foreign borrowings and clumsy modern abbreviations. Like their life-style and customs, the Old Believers' mother-tongue was frozen in the time-warp of 1917-1920, when their grandparents, with bags and baggage and under cover of darkness, crossed the Russian-Chinese border into Manchuria.

Merciless and insatiable Alaskan mosquitoes were buzzing above our heads, and some big dark shadows were moving in the bushes, behind the lawn. Could they be the moose?

I felt as though I was watching a perfectly directed (by Andrei Tarkovsky?) Russian movie set in the middle of the last century.

Only this Jurassic-Park-like 'movie' was for real, and I myself was among the cast.

It was already past midnight, when Josip and Iona burst into a heart-rending Russian folk-song which I had never heard before.

They sang about long farewells, dusty roads and a hard life in foreign land, which in Russian is called 'chuzhbina'—a word that doesn't have a direct equivalent in English. Contained in it are willows rustling soothingly above the winding creek, the wind whistling through a birch grove, and an endless snow-covered Russian steppe glistening like marble under the moon.

I suddenly understood why, after centuries of wanderings, these people chose to settle in Alaska, which looks so deceptively similar to their cruel, yet dear, homeland—the country that most of them have never been to and will never see.

Like Russia, Alaska has willows above creeks, snow-covered plains, and birch-groves. It used to be a part of Russia and, in a sense, it still is, for the genuine Russian spirit destroyed by the Bolsheviks and no longer found in Russia itself, has been smuggled out and kept intact here by the Old Believers.

Looking at their faces, lit by the last flashes of the dying bonfire, I knew: they had found their new home for many years to come.

I remembered a memorial plate which I had seen earlier at the Nikolaevsk School Assembly Hall:

'In Commemoration of the Old Believers Who Became United States Citizens,' it said.

Dozens of old-fashioned Russian names followed.

Among my literary and journalistic awards, there's one that I treasure most: Ilf and Fetrov Prize for Satirical Journalism for 1989. I picked up the award and the medal with profiles of both writers on my very last day in the USSR—the 31st of January 1990.

They would have loved the irony of it all.

Meditations

'Take a nice long and slow deep breath in and slowly breathe out . . . Take three of these breaths . . . Notice that on each one you feel more and more relaxed . . . You relax even deeper as the anesthetic is administered and allow yourself to go into dream time . . . Begin to descend now . . .'

TEN—floating down, deeper and deeper down . . .

Didn't I say earlier that I was going to LIVE through this book rather than just write it?

I am on an operation table, and the anaesthetic has indeed just been administered by a Jewish guy in a yarmulke. When they rolled me into the theatre, he was hastily and finishing his sandwich. He introduced himself, but because he was speaking with his mouth full, I couldn't discern the name.

'I am Carol, your operation nurse,'—a lovely head of a very

young girl appeared above me.

Why do they call it 'operation table'? It doesn't look or feel like a table at all—rather like a trolley or a narrow uncomfortable bench on wheels . . . Memorial bench, like they have in English public parks—'In memory of John who loved to sit here.'? No, I should stop thinking that, even as a joke; it is not the positive attitude to life I have mastered after two years of daily meditations and self-hypnosis.

I started meditating in Folkestone, carried on in Ireland, to where I temporarily moved, and continued in London, to where I finally—and inevitably—returned in early 2006.

After a year or so of daily practice, I was able to dream, relax, travel and fly in my imagination—a wonderful feeling. With time, my unconscious mind was able to absorb all the subliminal suggestions I had been feeding it while in a trance. That had gradually changed my behaviour, my pattern of thinking and my whole life—from hopelessness and despair to happiness and well-being.

'Unhappiness isn't simply a state of mind; it is also a habit,' says Jane Howard, the heroine of Douglas Kennedy's latest book, *Leaving the World*. How true!

The human mind is an extremely powerful tool for change, and as Glenn Harrold, one of my self-hypnosis mentors, asserts there's nothing you cannot achieve if you master the art of positive thinking.

I had reached the stage when I was able to put myself into a healing trance within minutes—on a bus, on a plane, on a park bench. How wrong I was to be dismissive of the power of self-hypnosis—to the extent that I had actually thrown out a meditation tape after my visit to the island of Tiree!

Even meeting the Loved One was largely an achievement of my new self—strong, confident and successful.

Two years after my first 'relaxation' session, I was able to stop meditating on a daily basis and just enjoy my new happy life.

I had to restart meditating after the first angina attacks and was doing so every day again in the run up to the operation—this time seeking courage and good health.

ST. This survival tip is short: learn to meditate.

NINE—falling deeper and deeper—like an autumn leaf pirouetting slowly towards the ground . . .

These ostentatiously casual introductions—'I am Carol'; 'Nice to meet you, Carol, I am Vitali'—while you are lying supine and inelegantly 'bottomless' (with your nether regions covered with a bed sheet) on the oblong, irregularly shaped bench claiming to be a table, as if it is some sort of a perverse party where the birthday boy (can't resist the 'deathday boy' pun, sorry, Glenn Harrold) has to stay horizontal at all times, and will take drugs—like morphine in this case—not orally (and voluntarily) but have them injected into his veins. Don't tables have moribund connotations too? In Russia, they used to always put a corpse on the table before taking it out for burial . . . Positive thinking, Vitali, no sombre thoughts! Didn't you hear Dr Foale saying he didn't believe in risks and would rather not perform the operation at all? The risk of dying, after all, is not that huge—five percent, as VV (he? I?) has read on the Internet.

EIGHT—floating down nearly weightless, letting go of all doubt and anxiety . . .

He could have walked to the theatre easily, but they didn't let him to.

Simon, an elderly black porter, with a deep and low throaty voice, came to pick him up with his heavy wheelchair. He could have passed for Charon, the mythological ferryman who carried the souls of the dead across the river Styx to Hades, had it not been for his absence of a beard . . . This moribund thinking has to stop! No, Simon was more like the Mexican boatman taking me across the Rio Grande from Lajitas . . . But didn't I compare the latter to Charon too? Enough of that! How do you know that Charon had a beard anyway? From a fuzzy, badly printed drawing in the book *Myths of Ancient Greece* given to me as a birthday present (can't remember how old I was) by my Dad. He always bought me books for my birthdays, and I didn't want anything else . . .

Being wheeled along a long hospital corridor, past some pretty young nurses, in a stupid hospital dressing gown made him feel even more awkward than he did while sitting in the dilapidated side car of an ancient, skeleton-like Chiang Mai rickshaw driver in torn sandals.

Being rolled into the lift . . . Floating down . . .

SEVEN—letting go, floating down—even deeper relaxed. . .

Jean and Alex Beaumont . . . His first meditation teachers . . . Or rather gurus . . . They ran a couple of 'alternative' new age shops in the centre of Folkestone. Not a believer in anything he regarded (for lack of knowledge and due to the atheistic Soviet upbringing whereby every tiniest sparkle of faith—other than the officially perpetrated one—had to be mercilessly extinguished) as 'paranormal', Vin used to look at their windows with disdain: all those angels, tarot cards, crystal balls and other rubbish.

Yet after the Britafra fiasco when he returned to Folkestone feeling as if he had been run over by a heavy truck, he couldn't help spotting a street sign advertising free meditation sessions ('learn to relax, go on a fascinating journey of the mind'—something like that) at the couple's flat on Wednesday evenings. He thought he had nothing to loose (which was true) and decided to try.

Half a dozen people were sitting in deep comfy armchairs. Candles were burning. Alex's low calming voice invited VV to close his eyes and to start breathing deeply. It taught him a diaphragmatic breathing technique which was at first uncomfortable and sounded illogical: he had to stick out his tummy when breathing in and to take it in when breathing out.

His last thought before getting into trance was: it's not going to work in my case. A moment later he was floating along a sparkly river in a light boat under the gentle soothing sunlight with no thoughts or feelings left in him apart from the sheer enjoyment of the journey and his own lightness, almost weightlessness—both physical and spiritual, the same sort of lightness one experiences having just recovered after a long and debilitating illness.

SIX—feeling safe and secure . . . safe and secure . . . floating down . . .

'Well done, Vitali,' said Alex. 'Very few people can experience the journey at the first session.'

He felt weightless and carefree while walking down the dead Old High Street towards the harbour and then up the hill to his pink cottage. The sensation, albeit short-lasting, was purifying and calming. Vin didn't need his daily intake of wine to go to sleep that night and soon he became a regular at the sessions experiencing the beautiful 'journey' every single time . . . Once Alex had a cold and asked VV to conduct the session instead of him. 'With your deep calming voice, you should be good at this, Vitali,' he said. And he was right: not only was VV able to send everyone present on a journey, he somehow managed to get into a trance himself while continuing to lead the others.

It was an amazing development: if not yet a solution, then definitely a salvation.

FIVE—Feeling calm and relaxed . . . Not a care in the world . . .

The angioplasty must have started already. From the corner of his eye, he can see the blurred silhouette of Dr. Foale bending over him and cutting a vein in his groin; he doesn't feel any pain, as if the body on the table/bench is no longer his own . . . He is eager to continue his journey which—as he knows—can take him not only to his past, but also to the future.

. . . Six months after the operation, I am writing (well, almost finishing, or so I hope) *Life as a Literary Device*.

It is the end of December and the garden behind the window appears empty. Yet, when observed from the rustic shelter of Pegasus Cottage, it soon fills with life, even with drama.

For about an hour already I've been watching a fluffy black squirrel trying to get to the bird feeder full of nuts that I have put up on the apple tree. Black squirrels (or 'super squirrels' as they are sometimes called)—peculiar and aggressive testosterone-loaded mutants that force out grey squirrels in the same manner the latter force out the red ones—are endemic to Letchworth Garden City, yet even here it is not easy to spot one.

I've never seen a black squirrel so close by, about a metre away from the window. He is extremely quick and agile, beautiful even, I would say. Every movement has a purpose. He takes a beeline to the apple tree, climbs onto the branch on which the bird feeder is suspended, moves the feeder's handle (with his tiny pitch-black paw with miniature sharp nails) forwards trying to push it off the branch. On the fourth go he succeeds: the feeder collapses, the lid falls off—and yummy brown nuts roll all over the ground. The little black 'hunter' runs away—just in case—for a minute or so and watches what's going on from a nearby fence. Having made sure it is all quiet, he returns, sticks his head into the feeder's netted basket and pulls some more nuts out. He then picks up a nut from the ground, peels it off quickly, holding it in his front paws—like a tiny human rubbing his little palms in glee (I begin to understand why in Soviet animated cartoons for children squirrels were often depicted playing cymbals) and takes it to his abode in the neighbouring garden. He soon returns for another nut, then another and doesn't stop until all the nuts from the feeder end up in his little (not that little, it seems) hole.

I pity the birds who are left without food by that agile black creature and fill the feeder with nuts again. This time he collapses it at the first attempt.

A super squirrel indeed!

During the next several days, I change the position of the feeder on the apple tree, yet the beastie still gets it every time. I am being defeated by a squirrel and feel the authority of humankind has to be restored.

I pop out to the shops, buy two metal hooks and suspend the feeder from the very edge of a rather thin branch.

In the following hour I witness Blackie's numerous futile attempts to get to the nuts: he is too heavy to be supported by the thin branch and invariably ends up on the ground. The feeder is now safely out of his reach, but he keeps trying. Like the proverbial and rather clichéd spider which allegedly inspired the defeated and imprisoned Robert de Bruce to keep on fighting, he simply refuses to give up

The squirrel does get the nuts in the end. I help him by moving the feeder up the branch a little. Perseverance and the refusal to give up must be rewarded.

FOUR—Nearly there . . A pleasant ticklish feeling in the tips of fingers and toes . . . A wave of heavy warmth spreading all over the body . . .

I've just returned from Folkestone where I spoke at the literary festival. Yes, Folkestone now hosts the annual literary festival as well as well as the Triennial—the international festival of arts under the logo 'Tales of Time and Space'.

It is not the same Folkestone, the drab neglected town of my exile of only four years earlier. Countless restaurants, cafes and coffee shops (coffee culture is a sure sign of gentrification), classy shops, art galleries, Sir Norman Foster's Academy, the arts faculty of a university—all new . . .

And also:
  - the demise of the tacky flea market and funfair in the harbour where sea food (real, not fake!) is now being sold from the stalls near the beach;
  - lovingly restored Victorian facades everywhere;
  - constantly running art exhibitions in the former Metropole Hotel where—courtesy of Nick—after my departure to Ireland my poor books had been stored for several years in the Edwardian laundry room basement.

And what about my old pink cottage? My friends sold it shortly after my departure and it now houses . . . a police safe house (sh . . . shh . . . don't tell anyone)!

This makes sense: it was in a way a safe house (albeit a sad one) for me too. And the whole regeneration of Folkestone that went alongside my own has its logic. After all, I was the first writer who had called for Folkestone's revival in my old *Daily Telegraph* feature:

'Folkestone needs help. It desperately needs investment and government funding, and these are, sadly, not forthcoming. It also needs lots of holidaymakers willing to spend money . . .'

Well, the government money never materialised, but private funding did. In the year when I finally left Folkestone, possibly even on the same day of the same month, a local businessman, philanthropist and connoisseur of arts, Roger de Haan, set up the Creative Foundation thus starting one of the largest regeneration projects in the whole of the UK's history.

A Creative Quarter was formed, and artists were invited to move in for token rents to the eighty odd thoroughly renovated buildings.

The face and the soul of the decaying seaside town have been rejuvenated by arts and books.

I make sure I return to Folkestone at least twice a year and each time I see numerous new additions to the Creative Quarter.

I need these visits for inspiration and no longer feel a massive relief on driving out of the town towards the M20 motorway— as I used to in the past.

I loved leaving Folkestone and hated returning to it.

In the USSR, they used to award the title of 'Hero City' to settlements that had distinguished themselves during the Second World War—like Stalingrad, Kursk, Moscow etc.
I am not sure about the pompous-sounding 'Hero City', but Folkestone—of all places in the UK—certainly deserves to be known as Survivor Town

There is another place in Europe that deserves this title—the German city of Dresden.

On my first visit there in October 1992, I was mistaken for a bodyguard to Princess Di. I came there to report on the Queen's first trip to the former East Germany for the now-defunct *European* newspaper. With a young lady from Her Majesty's press office (who vaguely resembled the Princess of Wales), I stepped off the Royal Train and got immediately separated from the rest of the 'rat pack'. To be in time for the next Royal function, we had to run across Dresden at random stopping every now and then to ask for directions. A pedestrian whom we questioned on how we could get to the *Rathaus* (Town Hall), squinted at my companion and said in English:

'I know who you are. You are Princess Diana.' Despite the lady's ardent denial, he didn't budge: 'Don't try to fool me,' he insisted. 'You are Diana!' 'And who do you think I am? Prince Charles?' I demanded impatiently. 'No,' he uttered firmly. 'You must be Diana's bodyguard!'

I shall never forget that first flying visit to Dresden.

The mutilated capital of Saxony, once known as the Florence of the Elbe and the realm of the glorious Saxon kings, had only just started recovering from the forty odd years of Communist rule.

The locals showed little enthusiasm for the Royal visit. The Queen was even booed briefly when attending the service of reconciliation at the Kreuzkirche. This came as no surprise to those remembering the horrors of the Anglo-American fire-bombing raids of 13th February, 1945, during which Dresden, an officially designated Red Cross City, with no significant industry, was raised to the ground, and thousands of innocent people (135,000 by German estimates, and 35,000 according to one modern British source!) lost their lives. The famous baroque Frauenkirche in Neumarkt got a direct hit and was literally erased from the face of the earth. The Communists, installed in power by the Soviets after World War II, chose not to restore it and turned it into a 'war memorial'. In 1992, the inspired creation of architect George Bahr remained what it became in 1945—a big pile of rubble.

Apart from the booing episode at the Kreuzkirche, the locals didn't show much hostility towards us. The long-suffering people of Dresden knew the dangers of being blatantly blamed for the crimes of previous generations.

'Go through my backside and then turn left!' the buxom blonde receptionist of my Dresden hotel said curtly when I asked her for directions to the Neumarkt.

That was how my second encounter with Dresden started a coulpe of years later: through the backside of the hotel receptionist (she meant the hotel's back door, of course).

It was like coming back to an entirely different, yet still recognisable, place. The huge statue of Lenin that used to dominate the cityscape had disappeared. I was told that the costs of its removal were so high that the city fathers had to appeal to the hard-up Dresden residents for donations.

The city tidied itself up by replacing a number of 'Communist' facades with new, 'Western' ones, although multiple scars of the past were still visible everywhere. Some of these 'scars' were mobile: clumsy GDR-made Trabants (or 'Trabbies', as they were affectionately called in East Germany), those much-ridiculed snuffboxes on wheels, were coughing defiantly amongst gleaming Western limos.

And 'the seal of oppression', enhanced by the inevitable pains of reunification, was still imprinted on people's faces. My guide, a sad-eyed middle-aged woman, complained of the trials of her daily life, spent in fear of losing her job and being replaced 'by a machine'. 'That's what they are going to do to all the guides soon,' she asserted.

My other contact, a local businessman, proudly wore a solar watch, totally useless in permanently overcast Saxony, and kept asking me the time every five minutes. He wouldn't part with this 'Western' toy of his for love or money.

Having successfully negotiated the receptionist's ample backside, which stretched for a good couple of miles, I finally reached the grassy Neumarkt Square and froze in disbelief: the foundation and some of the supports of the destroyed Frauenkirche were back in place! What's more, all its remaining fragments (about ten thousand) were dug out, numbered and neatly piled under canvas tents around it. Non-existent only a couple of years before, the magnificent church was now being reborn in front of my eyes, put back together bit by bit like a giant jigsaw puzzle, with truly German meticulousness and precision.

Sitting at the Espresso Café next to the Square, I was thinking about the phenomenal resilience of Dresden—twice destroyed, twice disfigured, but never dispirited—when my attention was drawn to an opening hours sign on the Café's door:

'*Samstag:* 10.01—02.02
Sonntag: 10.01—22.21
Montag—Dienstag: 10.01—00.31'

Reading this, convinced me even further that the Frauenkirche was going to be fully restored one day, with not a single fragment gone missing.

My chance of being taken for Di's bodyguard on my third visit to Dresden was mercifully, close to zero: Diana was still alive then, but the faces of real heroes and anti-heroes of the never-ending soap-opera of the British Royal Family had become too familiar in the former East Germany.

Despite high unemployment, the creeping economic recession and the rise of the Far Right, Dresden's 'westernisation' was going ahead full speed. Asthmatic 'Trabbies' had all but vanished, and the only 'Communist' car I could spot was an abandoned coffin-like Skoda. A new, state-of-the art Volkswagen factory was being built in the Neustadt area. Its main assembly line was being placed under a huge glass dome which would allow passers-by to observe the goings-on inside. The brand-new cars were to be stored in a special tower, also made of glass and visible from afar. The whole project was about space, openness and accessibility—a daring architectural decision for Dresden, the city that values its newly reacquired freedom.

The headquarters of the Stasi, the GDR's much-feared secret police, on the bank of the Elbe River (where future Russian president Putin had been based during his time as a KGB snitch in Dresden), have been turned—quite symbolically—into a disco. Almost all the city facades, even the old Soviet-style apartment blocks, have been repainted in bright 'Western' colours.

It is amazing how much difference a bright paint can make. It puts a smile on the city's face.

Nowhere else had I seen so many travel agencies as in Dresden. Their 'density' could only be compared with that of pubs and hairdressers in a small town somewhere in Kent. Residents of the former East Germany were making up for the years of enforced immobility by becoming the world's most adventurous travellers. You bumped into them anywhere, even as far as in the Falklands, where I had met a group of fishermen from Dresden!

This time, I was put up at a brand-new hotel in Radebeul, a leafy Dresden suburb. The staff were helpful, yet unsmiling and tense. It was with sadness that I had to admit: 'the seal of oppression' was still there and was probably going to be the last totalitarian trait to disappear, for painting houses and changing street names is much easier than altering human mentality.

Speaking of street names, I was pleased to observe that Dresden did not take part in the name-changing frenzy, which seized East Germany in the wake of reunification. In one city, they even re-named Spartacus Street, although, as far as I know, the ill-fated Thracian slave and gladiator never tarnished himself by collaborating with the Communists. A convinced opponent of Marxism (I have always been of the opinion that Marks & Spencer is the only sort of Marxism that works) and never a fan of 'the great proletarian writer' Maxim Gorky, I was nevertheless pleased to see that both Karl Marx Street and Maxim Gorky Street still existed in Dresden.

The latter, by the way, was next to my hotel, and it was in Maxim Gorky Street in Radebeul, Saxony, that I had one of the best Greek meals in my life ('Zorbas', an extremely successful Greek restaurant, had Greek staff, a manager named Staphis, and all products—from ouzo to yoghurt—daily flown in from Athens).

Street names are part of history, and Dresdeners had learnt (at long last) to treat history with care.

Eager to see how the restoration of the Frauenkirche was progressing, I took a tram from Radebeul to the city centre. I love trams, these moving wrinkles on the faces of modern cities. In Dresden, they had replaced the squeaky Czechoslovakian-made trams with much smoother German ones.

Despite the brand-new tram, my ride was slow and bumpy. According to the official statistics, six per cent of Dresden roads got 'upgraded' (read 'smoothed up' and 'westernised') every year, yet it felt as if our tram was deliberately avoiding them. Also, every couple of minutes it would grind to a long halt at one of the countless sets of traffic lights that seemed to display three variations of one and the same colour—red. During one such stop, the driver entered the salon to announce: 'Tram kaputt!', and everyone had to get off. I did it without regret, thanking Dresden's erratic electricity supply for interrupting my endless journey and giving me an excuse to get a cab.

My joy, however, was premature. The taxi was almost immediately stuck in the worst traffic jam I have ever experienced. Narrow and not-yet-'upgraded' streets of central Dresden were more suited for compact Trabants than for modern Western cars. Standing in a traffic jam, however, was much safer than moving. In the five minutes that it took us to reach Neumarkt, I witnessed two nasty collisions, both taken by the participating drivers with truly German sangfroid. What a striking contrast to the dull and nearly carless streets of the GDR!

The piles of numbered stones in the middle of Neumarkt had

melted away considerably since my previous visit, whereas the church itself, its regenerating carcass covered with scaffolding, had become several metres higher. I stood there for a while, mesmerised by the slow and painstaking process of restoration. Like the growth of a flower, it was invisible to the eye, and yet—continuous and unstoppable. It was like witnessing the rebuilding of democracy itself—a laborious task that cannot be completed overnight. Stone by stone, fragment by fragment—is the only way it can be done.

The restoration of the Frauenkirche was due to be completed by 2006 to coincide with the 800th anniversary of Dresden. Don't ask me why, but somehow I was sure that the moment the last piece of the church was fitted neatly into its niche, 'the seal of oppression' would be erased forever from the beautiful face of Dresden.

I wanted to come back again and see for myself.

And I did—in 2005, when the reconstruction was completed one year earlier than planned.

Just like there are born survivors among people, there are survivors among towns, cities and countries (e.g. Estonia and Latvia) too.

ST. Make sure you visit towns, cities and countries with a history of endurance, stamina and revival against all the odds, and learn from their past.

I couldn't help remembering Dresden while wandering the painfully familiar, yet hardly recognisable, streets of rejuvenated Folkestone in 2008.

The 2008 Folkestone Triennial was amazing.
I returned to the town of my gruesome and solitary exile with my three little kids in July. It rained non-stop for the whole

of our stay, but it was a different kind of downpour—a welcome addition to the five types of depressing Folkestone rain I've described earlier in this book.

I would call it a 'jolly rain'.

Indeed, it didn't stop the kids from enjoying Britain's best children's playground on the hill overlooking the Channel. A short (and painfully familiar) walk from there, on the famous Victorian promenade, was *The Whispers*—one of the Triennial conceptual art installations—by a Paris-based sculptor Christian Boltanski. It was in the shape of a large irregular boulder from inside which some muffled human voices, near whispers, could be heard.

This is how the artist himself explained its meaning:

'Folkestone is full of ghosts. Over time the shores have witnessed the arrival and departure of many people. It has been a place of transition and a site that has borne witness to much activity; from the departure of troops for the front line to the loss inflicted by war that was endured by those who remained. *The Whispers* is about love, longing and loss derived from the letters written during the First World War. *The Whispers* quietly speak the words written by those stationed in Folkestone and those who had already departed for the battlefields . . . Folkestone marks a point from which we can remember the love that was lost . . .'

I was mesmerised by the whispering stone which to me was all about the First World War and the 'hurricane of poetry' it unleashed. It was about Wilfred Owen and Siegfried Sassoon, Edmund Blunden and Isaac Rosenberg, Edward Thomas, A.P. Herbert, David Jones and W.N. Hodgson—all brilliant young English poets who sailed to the battlefields from then prospering Folkestone and never came back. It was about the forever twenty-year-old 'Private Love' whose modest grave I spotted at the Bailleul Road East Cemetery at St Laurent-Blancy several years ago.

But it was also about something else—a 'transition', a change, a perseverance, if you wish. And about 'the love lost'. But also about the love found.

As well as about loneliness—a detached stone whispering in solitude like I was four years earlier during my Folkestone exile.

Next to *The Whispers* was the *Kite Kiosk*—another Triennial 'installation' where one could hire kites which symbolized 'modernism, culture and regeneration'. Unfortunately, it was closed due to the incessant rain.

You cannot fly kites under rain, can you?

From *The Whispers* we proceeded to the *Mobile Gull Appreciation Unit* by Mark Dion—a small kiosk on wheels in the shape of a huge Folkestone sea-gull, inside which a young lady was comfortably installed. Her task was to provide passers-by with all the information about seagulls they (the passers-by) could require thus trying to change a negative stereotype of that noisy and intrusive bird . . . It was like my own reconciliation with the seagulls who had tortured me daily and nightly during my stay in Folkestone with their piercing, almost child-like, screams. My kids were now smiling staring at the cute and inventive *Mobile Gull Appreciation Unit*, and the screams of real seagulls dashing above our heads no longer sounded like children's cries to me.

And of course, with all of us being avid readers and lovers of books, we couldn't miss *Tales of Space and Time* by Ivan & Heather Morison—a converted old truck with a small library of science-fiction books inside.

'We wanted to build our own escape vehicle, a bit like the Time Machine, that equipped its occupants with the knowledge of every imaginable future and mankind's solutions to these problems,' explained the artists.

By the time we found the Time Machine of a truck (it was not stationary and was touring around Folkestone—an incongruous addition to the town's street scene), we were all soaked, and it was great to warm up near the cozy and warm truck-cum-library's fireplace while leafing through science fiction books. They even had *The Star Diaries* by Stanislaw Lem, an acclaimed Polish philosopher and science fiction writer whose witty and meaningful stories I adored since childhood.

Such was Lem's popularity in the Soviet Union that a couple of my university mates had specially learned Polish to be able to read some of the writer's books that were published in Poland, but had failed to pass the rigorous test of Soviet censorship.

My father, a nuclear physicist and an avid reader of science fiction, adored Lem's *Solaris*—a powerful futuristic tale of an intelligent ocean on the distant eponymous planet, an ocean capable of reading and recreating the astronauts' innermost desires and dreams. Andrei Tarkovsky, brilliant Russian film director and son of the Russian lyrical poet Arseniy Tarkovsky, has made *Solaris* into a distopian movie raising eternal human issues of love, loss and eternity.

Tarkovsky's intelligent ocean was sinister and totalitarian: it drove people insane by taking over their internal world and recreating their innermost dreams.

As for *The Star Diaries*, the book's hero, Ijon Tichy, was a fabricator adventurer of the future, a Baron Münchausen of the space era.

A cheerful and nonchalant space pilot fond of hanging his wet spacesuit out the porthole to dry, he was seemingly capable of surviving the most astounding ordeals, from being disintegrated into his constituent elements to flying through a series of 'gravitational storms' that twisted time and being endlessly reduplicated in a time loop, so that he ended up arguing on Friday with his previous self from Thursday about which one of them got the spacesuit that he needed to wear on Saturday, not to mention which day of the week's self stole the chocolate from the spaceship's dwindling supplies.

Like my writer's 'I' reduplicated by the 'gravitational storm' of mauvism into Vin, VV, Vitya, Victor R and he?

Once I came very close to interviewing Stanislaw Lem while in Krakow (the city where he had lived) making a Radio 4 documentary. Our Polish fixer got hold of his home telephone number. Lem's wife who answered the phone said: 'Mr Lem is not very well,' and added that 'he didn't speak any English' but 'would see me briefly and give me a short interview in German' which I didn't speak.

I had to refuse politely.

Several days later, already back in London, I suddenly remembered that Lem spoke fluent Russian (I had heard his interview given on a Moscow radio station while still in the USSR). I should have suggested that, of course! But it was too late. Due to my stupidity, I was destined never to meet Stanislaw Lem who died in 2006.

Like Lem, I always liked the idea of a time loop and once interviewed two famous ghosts from the past on board *The Pride of Kent*, a cross-Channel ferry from Dover to Calais from where I was to report for the *European* on the unveiling of the Single European Market on 1 January 1993 (which incidentally didn't happen then).

I was then able to meet the New Year twice—first in Calais and then in Dover which was an hour behind but only a 40-minute hop away by a fast ferry. It was on the way back to Dover that I found myself in the black hole of time. Indeed, it was past midnight in France, yet not quite midnight in Dover, and I was in-between!

'Ladies and gentlemen, this is your captain speaking. I'd like to remind you that we are now back in 1992!'

On her way back to Dover *The Pride of Kent* found herself in the no man's time zone—the one-hour time loop between Central European Time and GMT. This could not fail to attract a couple of ghosts from the past. I was looking for two in particular, without whom the Single Market celebrations guest list would not have been complete. Both tried to unify Europe by force in their own time and both failed.

After another glass of Chateau Tourbier, I spotted the first.

With a cocked hat on his disproportionately large (in comparison to his body) head, he was standing on the upper deck looking at the receding shore through an old-fashioned spyglass, his black mantle flying in the wind.

'What do you think of European Union?' I asked
'I've always said that this Channel is a mere ditch, and we'll be across as soon as someone has the courage to attempt it.'
'But aren't you pleased that England and France have become much closer?'
'Ha! L'Angleterre est une nation de boutiquiers! [England is a nation of shopkeepers!]' he chuckled.

I decided to change the subject.

'You look amazingly fit for your 223 years,' I said.
'The bullet to kill me has not yet been moulded,' he muttered.
'Shall we drink to that?'
'Not tonight, Josephine,' he replied turning away and pressing the spyglass back to his eye.

I found the second ghost in the Club Class lounge.

Throwing back the fringe of black hair from his forehead with twitchy jerks of his head every now and then, he was tossing coins into a slot machine. He was dressed in a grey semi-military service jacket and gleaming thighboots with jodhpurs. From the angry look on his face, with a dot of moustache under the nose, it was plain that he was losing.

'Sorry to interrupt you,' I said, 'but what do you think about the Single European Market?'

He turned back sharply.

'It's a big lie,' he barked, piercing me with his beady, fierce eyes. 'The great masses of people will more easily fall victims to a great lie than to a small one.'

'But didn't you try to unify Europe in your own way?'

'This is the last territorial claim that I have to make in Europe,' he answered sadly, pointing to the gambling machine. 'I go the way that providence dictates with the assurance of a sleep-walker!'

'But don't you agree that this is a historic night?' I asked.

'Jetzt ist die Nacht der langen Messer!' [This is the night of long knives] he screamed suddenly, and, snatching a long SS dagger from his pocket, chased me around the ship.

I was saved by the sound of Big Ben, We were back in 1993, and my persecutor vanished into the thin, wintry air . . .

Twisting time—isn't this what mauvism is also about?

A lonely truck full of books under rain . . . I thought that somehow it symbolised my gruesome months in Folkestone too.

We had a great time inside the library truck.

On the way back we spotted some life-size children's shoes and socks made of bronze and strewn around the town centre. That was Tracey Emin's *Baby Things* aimed at drawing attention to teenage pregnancies of which Folkestone still had one of the highest rates in the UK.

The part of Folkestone where I used to live hadn't changed much, since I described it as 'full of pregnant teenagers of both sexes'. Not yet. The time gap between us 'shaping the buildings' and the buildings (or art works) starting 'to shape us' (*pace* Winston Churchill) can be substantial But, as Gorbachev used to say in his habitual tongue-tied manner, 'the process has begun'.

I was grateful to Tracey Emin for not having displayed her *Baby Things* in Folkestone four years earlier, when I was still there. The sight of discarded children's shoes and socks (even if made of bronze) in the town's streets would have been too much for me to take then.

The whole Triennial was like one powerful metaphor aimed at me.

Each of the installations was like a monument to an Unknown Writer or Artist striving to be noticed and heard through loneliness, rain and despair.

The self-critical nature of most of the exhibits—objects and people—like a group of actors behaving awkwardly and unnaturally in Folkestone's streets and cafés (e.g. getting entangled in and nearly strangled with their own sweaters —a 'normal' drunken Folkestone behaviour)—symbolised the start of self-deprecation as a way of life and therefore the end of insecurity and provincialism, for self-directed humour and self-righteous provincialism were thoroughly incompatible—at least that was how I saw it all.

Sitting in the new 'Whole World' café in the Old High Street, I thought that the revived Folkestone was a little new whole world of its own.

As for me, I could no longer be compared to a rusty Russian submarine moored in the empty harbour (the decrepit U-boat itself was no longer there: she must have sunk). Coming back to the thriving and prosperous Folkestone as a winner—with three kids and two freshly installed stents in my arteries—was in itself a piece of science fiction that took four long years to create.

Had *Life as a Literary Device* been a 'normal' book, this would have been a good point to finish it, to type a final full stop and then 'The end'.

But since *Life as a Literary Device* can never be completed (not until I die), we'll carry on.

As my six-year old daughter Alina said as we were reluctantly leaving Folkestone on that rainy morning in July 2008, 'Put it in your book, Dad!'

And so I did.

THREE—letting go, going deeper . . . the world is fading away . . .

Like in my childhood, I wake up on this grey winter morning to the sounds of the Moonlight Sonata.

The Loved One is practising it on her electronic keyboard in the guest bedroom which we call 'hotel'. Other familiar childhood sounds are reaching me from behind the window: Letchworth Garden City street cleaners are peeling off the ice from the pavements with spades and crowbars—knock, knock, knock . . .

I grew up to this measured and echoing wintry rattle.

It is my fifty-fifth birthday today, and we drive to the near-by village of Wallington to say hi to George (aka Eric) Orwell (aka Blair) who used to live there in a small cottage called 'The Stores' (he also ran a grocery shop in the village) in Kits Lane in the late 1930s.

It is less than a ten-minute drive from Letchworth . . . The bushes, the fences, the haystacks in the field and the green holly leaves in George's front garden are all beautifully glazed with frost as if nature itself has baked me a giant snowy birthday cake.

The old village pond is frozen and a couple of puzzled ducks are waddling about on the ice.

A lonely fiery pheasant, looking so outrageously and dangerously ostentatious on the snow, is the only living creature (not counting the ducks) we come across.

A snow-covered landscape inevitably reminds me not just of my childhood, but also of Skane, a part of Sweden where I have never been but where most of Henning Mankell's Kurt Wallander novels are set.

I discovered that amazing Swedish writer (who is now based in Mozambique where he works as a theatre director) by accident many years ago. One day, as I was completing my research into the book on Europe's remaining enclaves, I got stuck at a tiny German railway station called Landau, or possibly Oberstdorf— can't remember.

I had two hours to kill before my train was due, and the only book in English at the station kiosk was *Faceless Killers*—a thriller by a certain Henning Mankell, translated from Swedish. Having run out of things to read, I bought it reluctantly.

From the very first pages, however, I was gripped by Mankell's lucid and economic style and the intricacy of the plot. It was a thriller all right (and a pretty unputdownable one at that), but it was also literature. The book's main character—police inspector Kurt Wallander from a small Swedish town of Ystad (an unlikely location for a detective novel) struck me as one of the most skilfully shaped heroes in modern European literature. A lonely (his wife had left him for another man) workaholic, Wallander had lots of self-destructive habits: overeating, addiction to coffee, working crazy hours, not looking after himself, and so on. Constantly unsure of himself, he had disastrous relationships not just with women, but with his own father and daughter, too.

The only people he was able to communicate with properly were his police colleagues—all with similar-sounding names: *Rydberg*, *Svedberg*, *Martinsson*. Brusque and snappy on the surface, yet warm and sentimental underneath, Wallander had a brilliant analytic brain, helping him to solve even the most heinous crimes. He also had a keen sense of morality, brooding a lot about the growing moral degradation (from his point of view) of Swedish society.

In short, Kurt Wallander (aka Henning Mankell) became my favourite travel companion for days to come. Mankell's easily flowing narrative never failed to have a soothing effect on me—like a meditation—as if I was indeed exposed to the severe, yet calming, beauty of the Swedish rural landscape, where most of the action was routinely set.

His books—among other things—had helped me to cope with loneliness and despair while in Edinburgh and in Folkestone.

The qualities that made Wallander's character so appealing were not limited to his well-pronounced self-destructive streak and/or his love of strong coffee. They also included his innate resistance to bureaucracy and his broadmindedness in the face of other cultures and beliefs, which he always tried to understand, even if at times he failed.

As I am writing these lines, Mankell is one of Europe's best known writers, a winner of the prestigious Gold Dagger Award. A BBC TV series 'Wallander' based on his novels has just had a successful run on Britain's small screens.
Yet I can't wait for his next Wallander book.

But today our thoughts are not about Wallander, but about Wallington, or George Orwell, to be more exact.

The village is tiny, pristine and perennially quiet. If we stare at the low and narrow front door of Orwell's cottage for long enough, we can almost discern a tall dishevelled man emerging from it (he has to bend down to fit through the door). He is holding a letter which he carries across the road to the village's only pillar box before disappearing inside the cottage again.

I first read *Nineteen Eighty-Four* in Moscow in the late 1980s. A tattered soiled paperback was lent to me for one night only, and next morning I was to pass it to the next person in line.

The book, like all other works by George Orwell, was strictly banned in the USSR. A huge scandal erupted when an American publisher tried to display it on his stand during the International Book Fair in Moscow in the early 1980s. I worked as an interpreter at the Mitchell Beazley stand and remember an irate Soviet official shouting at the hapless publisher: 'Take this book away from your stand this very moment! You can display anything—even bloody Golda Meir (*sic*), if you wish, but not Orwell—this anti-Soviet filth!'

The punishment for being caught in possession of *Nineteen Eighty-Four* could be a prison term. Curiously, that only added to the clandestine pleasure of reading.

In the Soviet Union of my childhood and youth, it was not just honest writing but **honest reading** too that was a risky, dangerous and hence a highly creative occupation, an art form of sorts . . .

I was savouring the book until dawn, and by the time the last page was turned, I was close to tears. How could someone who had never been in the Soviet Union and had never lived in a totalitarian state, describe our life with such poignant precision?

We had a real-life 'Ministry of Truth', the KGB. One of its departments was called Glavlit, the state censorship agency. The word in itself (an abbreviated merger of *Glavnoye Upravleniye Literaturi*—Chief Directorate of Literature') is Orwell's 'Newspeak' par excellence. From the moment of taking power, the Bolsheviks were meticulously destroying the Russian language by simplifying its grammar and littering it with thousands of meaningless neologisms.

Each week, Glavlit released a constantly updated thick instruction manual listing books to be confiscated from all libraries and bookshops of the USSR.

A student of mine who worked as a bookseller, used to show me these censorship bulletins regularly—at considerable risk to herself. Alongside the works of Orwell, Solzhenitsyn and other 'enemy' or émigré writers, they contained thousands of seemingly innocuous titles in physics, chemistry, engineering and technology. The whole 'danger' of those books lay in the fact that they contained mentions of Khrushchev, Stalin and/or other political figures who had by then fallen out of favour with the system and hence become unmentionable, in the introductions.

They constituted a huge part of the list, since every book, no matter how scholarly and esoteric, was supposed to begin with a quote from a 'great leader' in power.

On one of the shelves in my Pegasus Cottage in Letchworth stands a large light-brown folio of 'Kniga o vkusnoi I zdorovoi pishche'—The Book of Tasty and Wholesome Cuisine, published in Moscow in 1952. I remember leafing through its pages with their coloured pictures of alluring and not necessarily 'wholesome' Russian foods (never seen in reality and therefore exotic) at the age of five or six. The 'subversive' book of recipes (with all but imaginary ingredients) which had miraculously withstood all my life's wanderings (Kharkov-Moscow-Melbourne-London-Melbourne-Edinburgh-Folkestone-Dublin-London-Letchworth etc.) begins with a huge-lettered quote from Stalin on a special flap preceding the title page:

'One of the peculiarities of our revolution lay in the fact that it gave the Soviet people not just freedom but also material well-being and a possibility of a plentiful and cultured life.'

It would have certainly been banned in Brezhnev's times

when the names of Stalin or Khrushchev were not supposed to be mentioned in print in any context. My mother told me how, in the early 1950s when the head of the Soviet secret police and Stalin's henchman Beria was exposed as a 'British spy' and subsequently shot, all subscribers of the multi-volume *Great Soviet Encyclopedia* received in the post several printed sheets to be glued into the letter 'B' volume where the article on Beria was printed.

The enclosed instruction requested that all the Beria pages be cut out of the book and the new ones, with a disproportionately lengthy article on the Bering Strait (!), inserted instead. Special Glavlit inspectors would conduct random house checks to make sure everybody had complied.

Wasn't it precisely what Orwell's O'Brien meant when confiding in Winston Smith during the latter's Room 101 interrogation that if a single mention of person or event could not be found in print it was as if they had never existed or taken place?

The other indisputable reason for banning technical—as well as children's and all other—books in Brezhnev's times was emigration of the author.

No wonder *Nineteen Eighty-Four* was one of the Soviet system's biggest bugaboos: it explained the technology of totalitarian power.

Amazingly though, those who controlled the printed word found it quite proper to read the banned books themselves (remember 'All animals are equal but some animals are more equal than others'?).

Not too many people in the West know that, in a brilliant case of Orwellian doublethink, all major Soviet publishing houses had secret departments producing limited editions of prohibited books for the elite's exclusive consumption. I've seen such books (each individually numbered and with the word 'Classified' prominently stamped on the cover) a number of times thanks to a friend's mother-in-law who worked in the CPSU Central Committee library. One of them was *Nineteen Eighty-Four*—in impeccable Russian translation.

The number on the plain white cover was '59', and underneath it the word '*Sekretno*' ('classified') was printed.

Another 'special edition' that I saw was *Secrets of Eternal Life* by C. Northcote Parkinson (again, rather conscientiously translated into Russian). The senile octogenarians who ruled our poor country were naturally—and exclusively—curious about the secrets of 'eternal life'. since it was they—not the oppressed voiceless crowds they controlled—who were supposed to live forever.

By the year 1984, Orwell's dystopian *Nineteen Eighty-Four* had been all but translated into reality in the Soviet Union . . .

'We knocked on the door of a little cottage, and it was opened by a tall figure, face and clothes covered with coal smuts, who peered of us through the billowing cloud of smoke; Blair had been trying to light his first fire of the season, to find that the chimney was in some way defective . . .'

That was how writer Mark Benney (quoted by Bernard Crick in *George Orwell. A Life*) described his visit to Wallington in 1936. This is probably why whenever I try to visualise George emerging from 'The Stores' cottage in 2009, I see him 'with coal smuts' smudged all over his face.

Orwell was happy in Wallington clattering away on his typewriter (he was finishing *The Road to Wigan Pier*) when there were no customers in his cottage-cum-shop which was most of the time: for some reason, the shop was not very popular among the locals (were they somewhat put off by Orwell's refined and aristocratic—even if occasionally coal-stained—face, his posh Etonian accent and his 'classy' lanky frame?), not to mention the pilfering village children (to watch them Orwell had to drill four holes in the door!), and soon had to be closed down.

George/Eric went on long walks around the village, and the very few descriptions of nature in his books (he was hardly a lyricist) can be easily traced to Wallington, like this one from *Nineteen Eighty-Four* describing Winston's pastoral secret tryst with Julia:

'Winston picked his way up the lane through the dappled light and shade, stepping into pools of gold whenever the boughs parted. Under the trees to the left of him the ground was misty with bluebells . . . It was the second of May. From somewhere deeper in the heart of the wood came the droning of ring doves.'

Most rural landscapes hardly change with time.

It was probably during one of these walks that he spotted the dark wooden buildings of near-by Bury Farm that he used as his model for *Animal Farm* in the eponymous classic novel set, incidentally, near the fictitious village of Willingdon (where the farmer kept the pigs)!

The large black sheds and barns of Bury Farm are still there. Looking at them, I can't stop praising fortune for the mere fact that no enterprising developer has yet come up with the idea of digging up the uncomplaining Hertfordshire countryside and building an 'Animal Farm Theme Park' on that spot.

Such an oversight is surprising if we remember that *Animal Farm* is one of the best known, most loved and most prophetic books in human history.

It has to be said, however, that in many respects the Soviet reality outstripped even George Orwell's insightful fantasy.

To make a photocopy of anything, for example, a journalist like me had to collect three signatures from his bosses for each item he wanted to copy—be it a reader's letter or a sheet of his travel expenses. The last signature was to come from the so-called 'First Department', a virtual KGB office at every single Soviet office. Then, if you were lucky enough to collect all three signatures, you had to go down to the basement (at least, at my *Krokodil* magazine offices it was in the basement) and shove the letter or the article to be copied through a tiny barred window where three woman in dirty blue overalls were operating the only copying machine shared by a dozen large newspapers and magazines located in the building.

As a rule, the women would tell you to come back at the end of the day and collect the copy, but their working hours remained a mystery, possibly even a state secret. The window of their copying sanctuary was normally closed and through it you could hear the muffled angry hissing of the overexploited photocopier.

What were they copying there, behind the bars? A collection of Stalin's speeches? The Constitution of the USA brochures? Or a popular hard-to-get paperback *All You Should Know about Sex*, translated from Hungarian? No one knew.

It was not by chance that photocopiers and typewriters had always been treated as a threat to the USSR's very existence—comparable only to subversive plots by the CIA, FBI, ICI, Mossad and Mitsubishi combined.

In full accordance with Orwell's *Nineteen Eighty-Four*, communists never underestimated the importance of the printed word. That was also why on the ninth floor of our twelve-storey magazines building, they installed the modest office of Valeri Nikolayevich—a lanky rosy-cheeked fellow whom everyone was eager to greet in the corridors and in the canteen but no one offered a hand to shake.

He was the representative of the ominous and omnipotent Glavlit (see above), or in plain words, the censor. Everyone knew who he was (he didn't even try to conceal it), and, I have to say, I often pitied him.

I imagined him trying to chat up a woman, who at some point would be likely to ask: 'And what do you do, sweetie?' What would he say? 'I am a censor'? But that would be on a par with saying 'I am a murderer' (remember Bernard Shaw's 'Murder is but an extreme form of censorship'?), or 'I am a child molester.'

Pitiful as he was, Valeri Nikolayevich was in possession of a large and round rubber stamp—his main (and only) working tool. He had to sweat in his puny office stamping every single piece of paper duly delivered to him from all the editorial offices in the building. Not a sentence or even a word could be published without his stamped approval. He had to be very fit, that rosy-cheeked lad, to cope with all this stamping, whereas in actual fact his censoring role was quite superfluous, since every article before coming to him had to pass at least five other controlling points. And controlling pens too: the editor with his two deputies, heads of departments and the much feared editorial official—a sort of editorial commissar—called 'executive secretary' (and his deputy).

Those relatively insignificant (compared to the full-time, 'professional' and KGB-designated censor) officials constituted the main threat to freedom of speech both in totalitarian states and in the 'democratic' West, something that even Orwell was unable to foresee—the so-called self-censorship.

I remember how several years ago a book on Hong Kong by Chris Patten was dumped by the Murdoch-owned publishers HarperCollins. Murdoch himself emphatically denied he had anything to do with the ban, and as someone who had spent many years as a journalist in the old Soviet Union, I had no reason to doubt either Murdoch's unequivocal denial of his involvement in scrapping the book ('I did not tell people to try to censor the book . . .'), or the sincerity of his subsequent apology.

Of course, he 'did not tell people'. He didn't have to, for he knew that his 'people', would do it for him anyway.

And this is exactly how censorship—the corner-stone of any totalitarian regime—works: not from top to bottom, but the other way round—from the lowest to the very top.

The dreaded state-controlled media or a newspaper tycoon's metaphorical red pen are not half as dangerous as the little demon of self-censorship sitting inside the kowtowing editors and hacks, frightened of losing their precious jobs as well as company cars, expense accounts and other perks.

In 1980, a prestigious Moscow publication decided to change the first name of a fictitious personage in one of my fictional satirical stories from Leonid to Alexander, just because Brezhnev's first name was Leonid, too. My poor editor was summoned by the angry editor-in-chief, who told him that if one more Leonid—fictitious or not—ever appeared on his humourous pages again, he (my poor editor) would automatically disappear from the staff.

Did that mean that the fearsome Glavlit, the KGB-controlled state censorship agency, had banned the use of the name Leonid in print at the peril of imprisonment? Nothing of the kind. And Brezhnev himself, who by that time could hardly speak, let alone read, did not sign any decrees to the effect that he alone was allowed to be referred to as Leonid in the Soviet Union. Had my protagonist's name remained unchanged, the chance of it being spotted by Brezhnev was less than zero—it was minus ten.

So why all the fuss? The answer was simple: being on the staff of a leading (God knows where to) Soviet publication meant special food supplies, a nice dacha outside Moscow, frequent trips abroad and other perks, which neither my poor editor, nor the editor-in-chief wanted to lose ('some animals are more equal than . . .'). They were not prepared to take any risks, no matter how minuscule. As a Moscow friend of mine used to say: 'Risk is a noble thing, provided it is not I who has to take it.'

On another occasion, a colleague's seemingly innocent piece which dealt with chronic shortages of socks and electric-light bulbs in the shops of Dnepropetrovsk was dumped (or 'butted', in Russian journalistic jargon), because Dnepropetrovsk was Brezhnev's birthplace and, as such, was supposed to be a horn of plenty, stuffed with decadent consumerist luxuries—socks and electric-light bulbs among them. Like Caesar's wife was above suspicion, Dnepropetrovsk, 'the birthplace of Comrade Brezhnev', was beyond any criticism. It was on a par with Moscow, 'an exemplary communist city' which also suffered from shortages of socks and electric bulbs, by the way.

Again, I am positive that Brezhnev himself, who had never experienced any shortages, apart from severe brain deficiency, and couldn't even pronounce Dnepropetrovsk, would not have minded the article. It was his boot-licking underlings and factotums who did.

During my twenty-odd years as a journalist in Britain, Ireland and Australia, I had numerous encounters with the vivacious little demon of self-censorship which feels as comfortable in the West as it did in the former USSR.

Once, my tongue-in-cheek column on the Pope's visit to Australia was 'butted' by a Murdoch-owned newspaper. Unable to secure a real-life interview with the Pontiff, I wrote an imaginary interview, in which, among other things, I (allegedly) asked His Holiness what his biggest nightmare was, and His Holiness replied that it was a pregnant lesbian female priest willing to have an abortion.

I also (and no less allegedly) asked the multi-lingual Pontiff whether he could speak Strine (Australian English), and he replied that he had so far mastered only one sentence: 'God on yer, mate!' and so on . . .

Editors of my column knew that Murdoch was friendly with one high-ranking Australian cleric, who could not stand any Pope-directed jokes, and who was likely to complain directly to Murdoch whenever he spotted any. In short, my imaginary 'interview' was branded unimaginable for publication, although Murdoch himself would neither have minded nor noticed it, I am sure.

From a 'tongue-in-cheek' to a 'tongue-in-check' column.

I feel equally as positive that Murdoch wouldn't have bothered to ban a short story with the main baddy called Rupert, or an essay criticising chronic shortages of (say) snow in the streets of Melbourne, the city of his birth.

Whether the editors at Murdoch's newspapers and publishing houses in whom he pledged 'full confidence' would have accepted such stories for publication is a different matter.

How ironic it is that having come from history's cruellest real-life communist Dystopia, I ended up living in the world's first 'Utopian' Garden City, next to the former abode of the creator of the world literature's most powerful fictional Dystopia!

It was here, in Wallington, that Orwell married Eileen Shaughnessy in the old and eternally open parish church of St Mary.

With the Loved One we often come to the church which is permanently empty and freezing inside in winter. We read the new entries to the Visitors' Book that always surprise us with their geographic versatility.

When do all these people come here, we wonder? We have never bumped into anyone else inside the church.

On the table next to the Visitors' Book is a pencil holder with reading glasses which suit my slightly presbyopic eyes perfectly—as if left there specifically for me. There's also the first scary sign of a potential Animal Farm Theme Park—a stack of photocopies George and Eileen's marriage certificate—two pounds fifty each.

One of the most treasured books in my collection is *The Penguin Essays of George Orwell*.

And not just because Orwell's essays, to my mind, are unsurpassable in their originality, clarity of thought and lucidity of language. This book was given to me as a gift in Moscow by my first-ever British friend Martin Walker, then the *Guardian*'s Moscow correspondent.

'For Vitali. My favourite journalist of all time, Orwell, to the first Soviet investigative journalist,' reads a faded dedication.

It was 1988 and I had just been voted the Soviet Journalist of the Year for my investigations into the Soviet Mafia. I met Martin, who had just been voted the British Journalist of the Year for his emotional, at times poetic, and yet precise and instructive (Orwell-like?) reports from the USSR, at a British Embassy do, and we immediately clicked. It was Martin who—later that year—arranged for my first ever visit to the West and to Britain on a short journalistic attachment to the *Guardian* during which I wrote and published my first ever articles in English.

That visit had changed my life forever.

It was with extreme delight that I found several of Orwell's poems in the book. Until then I was unaware that Orwell was also an accomplished poet. The poems were part of some of the essays and I translated a couple of them, including the bitter, poignant and romantic *The Italian Soldier Shook My Hand* . . . from the essay 'Looking Back on the Spanish War', into Russian:

'The Italian soldier shook my hand beside the guard-room table; the strong hand and the subtle hand whose palms are only able . . .'

And so on.

It was from Wallington, by the way, that Orwell went off to Spain to report from the Civil War in 1937. In May he was hit in the neck by a sniper's bullet and while recovering in a field hospital developed an obsessive fear of rats which he later 'passed on' to Winston Smith, the *Nineteen Eighty-Four* protagonist.

Martin liked my translations very much and several years later I had them all published in a Russian-language literary magazine that used to come out in Australia.

It was that very collection of Orwell's essays that I took with me to my hospital ward in June 2008.

As I meditate on my bed after the operation, the book is resting on the small bedside table—next to a box of 'Soft Clinical Professional Tissues, NHS Code MJT058'.

I've read and reread the collection a number of times, and, like every great book, each time it reveals something new.
The latest such surprise happened yesterday, when I discovered a twenty-year-old Moscow bus, tram and trolley-bus ticket ('Valid for one trip. Price 5 kopecks; 89903 AY 21; Invalid without a stamp') hidden behind its spine which came unpeeled.

I touched the tiny piece of yellowish paper—and that very moment was miraculously transferred to the dark, dirty and crime-ridden Moscow of 1988 when I was reading Orwell's essays during an Underground journey from Voikovskaya (where my Mum then lived) to Babushkinskaya (where I resided) stations.

To get to Voikovskaya station from Mum's street, I had to take a tram—a normal Czech-made red-and-yellow Moscow tram— where the ticket had been bought. You would toss a five-kopeck coin into a metal box from which a ticket paper roll would be sticking out and tear one off. You could of course tear off the ticket without putting the coins into the box (no one was likely to check), but the sum was so ridiculously negligible that very few people were tempted to cheat.

By 1988, it was already quite safe to be reading Orwell

(particularly in English) in public (in Moscow, at least, it was). In 1984 . . . Well . . . I wouldn't have gone far with an Orwell book (in English or in Russian) in my hand.

Reading Orwell in the capital of a slowly disintegrating, yet still powerful, totalitarian state gave me an unparalleled sensation of symmetry—both literary and social.

Pencil notes on the margins . . . Dried flowers or old bus tickets between the pages . . . They are the gears, pedals and steering wheels of the world's best and only time machines—old books.

I remember once spending my very last tenner in a Folkestone antiques shop on a handwritten diary of an English young woman (a teenage girl judging by her handwriting) 'A Souvenir of my Visit to Switzerland and Belgium, July 1908)'. Signed only by two letters 'M.L.' (Mary Lowe? Margaret Little?), the album contained (alongside the calligraphic text) dozens of the early 20th century picture postcards. In the end, there were several pages with herbaria: dried flowers, leaves and weeds 'from the cemetery at Waterloo', a couple of wheat spikes 'picked from very near the place were (sic) the Duke of Wellington met Prince Blucher' (sic) and a page with 'A few mountain flowers' among which was an 'Edleweiss' (sic) 'from Audermatt'.

The dry flowers were (and still are) extremely well preserved, with every little detail of their stalks and blossoms clearly visible. Whereas M.L. herself, with all her neat handwriting and spelling mistakes, is gone forever.

I've said it earlier and want to say it again: to me, touching old books and whatever is kept between their pages (be it a dried leaf or an old tram ticket) is like touching eternity itself.

With the Loved One, who also loves Orwell, we once went to Wallington for a barn dance. Why? Perhaps we were hoping against hope to bump into George whose presence is always so strikingly real—almost palpable—in the village? Or at least to have a chat with the people who now live in 'The Stores'?

It was a cloudy autumn night. We left our car at an impromptu parking lot off Manor Farm and—in pitch darkness—made our way to the barn where the dance was to be held.

We saw ordinary country folk: men, women, children—all with the open, wind-beaten faces of country dwellers. The food was fresh and local, the wine . . . Australian.

George was nowhere to be seen.

Apart from him, we didn't know a single soul in Wallington.

One hour into the 'dance' we sneaked out of the barn and drove back home.

TWO—Floating down . . . I am now at peace . . . peace . . . peace . . .

The window of the hospital ward from which I was wheeled to the operating theatre and to which I was 're-wheeled' after it faced a brick wall.

The 'view' made me smile uneasily: it could have passed for a good metaphor of my life in the not-so-distant past, but not any more.

With my new meditation skills, a brick wall behind the window was no longer an obstacle. I could simply close my eyes, take a couple of deep diaphragmatic breaths—and within seconds end up anywhere I wanted.

My flying hospital bed

This time I choose to teleport myself to New York, simply

because the brick wall behind the hospital window brings back to memory a sentence from Ilya Ilf's letter to his wife from America:

'My room has a beautiful view of the wall of a neighbouring skyscraper . . .'

In one of the first chapters of *Little Golden America* (aka *One-Storied America*), Ilf and Petrov described the view from the windows of their respective New York hotel rooms beyond 'the wall of a neighbouring skyscraper', and I, while researching my own book on America, *The Land of Plastic Fossils*, was keen to discover how that view had changed in the course of sixty-five years.

The problem was that in their book the writers never mentioned their New York hotel's name, only wrote that it was 'not very old and not very new, not very expensive, and, to our regrets, not very cheap'; that it had 'thirty two brick stories'; 'the very ordinary marble vestibule', leading to 'spacious elevators with gilded doors' and 'the tobacco stand' on the left. The latter detail had been made totally irrelevant by the mounting American anti-smoking zeal. Indeed, in the modern USA it would probably be easier to find a hotel with a coffin store in the lobby (I knew of a hotel in Albania whose lobby actually doubled as a mortuary) than the one with a dreaded 'tobacco stand'.

With my head tilted up towards the elusive New York sky, I walked the length of Lexington Avenue counting the floors of numerous skyscraper hotels, many of which had turrets with windows on their roofs, and I was not sure whether they could count as 'stories'.

Two days later I found it. Having entered the wood-and-marble lobby of the red-brick thirty-two-storied Marriott East *Side Hotel* one evening, I was momentarily blinded by a set of shiny gilded elevator doors. On my left, where 'the tobacco stand' could have been, was now the wooden cubicle of the Concierge.

Christened the Shelton Towers, the Marriott East Side was built in 1924 by Arthur Loomis Harmon—the acclaimed architect of the Empire State Building. The world's largest hotel (at the time), originally conceived as a 'bachelor residence', it was renowned for more than just its size. In April 1924, the prestigious *Architecture* magazine called it 'the most notable architectural achievement of our time'. Georgia O'Keefe celebrated the Shelton in two of her paintings, and later Harry Houdini performed one of his great escapes from a locked and chained box, submerged in the hotel's swimming pool.

Explaining his project, Arthur Loomis Harmon wrote in the same issue of *Architecture* magazine:

'An English architect says that a building such as the Shelton would be almost impossible to erect in London . . . and that if erected it would not be successful, because the single male Londoner lives either in lodgings or in a club . . . Evidently the Englishman defends his individuality more strenuously than does the American. Perhaps he is less socially inclined, or perhaps he has not been forced to realise that in great communities freedom is more easily reached by mingling with a large mass than with a small closely woven unit . . .'

By 1935, when it became a temporary home to Ilf and Petrov, the Shelton—contrary to the architect's intentions—had started accepting female guests as well as married men—like both Russian writers.

So what did Ilf and Petrov see from their 'little rooms' on the twenty-seventh floor of the Shelton of an evening in 1935?

They saw 'several skyscrapers' which seemed 'so close that one could touch them with his hand'. And further away, behind a 'dark unlighted swath [the Hudson? Or was it the East River?]'—'a sheer gold dust of tiny lights. In that world of lights, which at first seemed stationary, one could note a certain movement. Now down the river slowly floated the red light of a cutter. A tiny automobile passed down the street. At times, suddenly, somewhere on the other shore of the river, a light as little as a tiny particle of dust would flash and go out. Surely one of the seven million denizens of New York has turned off the light and gone to bed. Who was he? A clerk? Am employee of the elevated railroad? Perhaps a lonely girl had gone to sleep—some salesgirl (there are so many of them in New York). And at this very moment, lying under two thin blankets, stirred by the steamer whistles of the Hudson, was she seeing in her dreams a million dollars?'

It could well have been, however, that the New York 'denizen' who turned off the light just then was not 'a lonely girl' but the very censor-clerk entrusted with 'excising' (with the help of scissors) Jay Franklin's biography of Fiorello H. La Guardia. Having not coped with the massive challenge of 'trimming' pages 58 and 74 of every single printed copy, he took some work home that evening.

'I am sorry, darling,' he said to his wife, 'but you'll have to dine alone tonight: I have an important government task to complete . . .'

He then withdrew to his tiny cubicle of a study where he kept mutilating the submissive pages until that late-night second registered by Ilf and Petrov!

A frozen moment of the past, immortalised by two Russian writers . . . Standing in the same room seventy years later, I could feel 'the wind of time gently ruffling my hair' (pace Petrov's elder brother Valentin Kataev).

Or was it just the flow of warm air from the room's modern temperature-control device?

The view itself was now all but blocked by the Lexington

Hotel, the City Bank Tower and other high-rise stalagmites.

In most places, seventy years are hardly enough to significantly alter a cityscape. But not in New York.

Ilf and Petrov spent several months in the Big Apple. They wandered the streets of Manhattan, saw a boxing match at the Madison Square Garden, ate at brand-new 'automated' cafeterias (the experience they described in their 'Appetite Departs While Eating' chapter), watched a burlesque show in the now-defunct Hollywood restaurant, had a drink with Ernest Hemingway.

It was in New York that they bought a 'sedate, mouse-coloured Ford' to take them across America and met the bubbly Mr. Adams, their would-be travel companion and guide. But the real starting point of their Trans-American journey was when they stood, transfixed by the blinking night lights of New York, at the window of their hotel room:

'New York was asleep, and a million Edison lamps were guarding its slumber Immigrants from Scotland, from Ireland, from Hamburg and Vienna, from Kovno and Bialystok, from Naples and Madrid, from Texas, Dakota and Arizona, were asleep Asleep were immigrants from Latin America, from Australia, from Africa and China. Black, white, and yellow people were asleep. Looking at the scarcely trembling lights, we wanted to find out as soon as possible how these people work, how they amuse themselves, what they dream of, what they hope for, what they eat . . .'

One-Storied America began on the twenty-seventh floor of the Shelton, the distinguished 1920s hotel overlooking the Hudson.
Or possibly the East River . . .

I was remembering the Russian writers' description of New York while looking out of the window of my room on the thirty-second floor of the Marriott Financial Center Hotel, part of the Twin Tower complex, where I stayed sixty-six years later—several months before the 9/11 attacks. . .

I was reluctant to fly back from New York to the confines of my London hospital ward, but Simon, the Charon-like (sorry, never again) porter was already waiting at the door with his bulky wheelchair/trolley to take me to the operating theatre.

Roof Garden

My most frequent meditation while in Ireland was that of a garden in the sky.

I enter a lift and press the 'Up' button. On a small electronic monitor above my head, I can see the floor numbers changing slowly: 1 . . . 2 . . . 3—and with each number I am feeling more and more relaxed.

The lift cabin finally stops and its doors slide apart noiselessly.

I come out and find myself in a beautiful and totally deserted garden.

This is a very large garden and I cannot see all of it at once. The bit that I can see is bathed in sunlight . . . It is a lovely summer day—not uncomfortably hot, just right. A warm gentle breeze is caressing my skin.

All my favourite plants are there, and I can see colourful butterflies fluttering above them. Bees are darting from flower to flower collecting the pollen and making a soothing buzzing sound as they do so.

I head for a small pond under a branchy willow tree and instal myself on a bench in the willow's shadow. This is my starting point from where I can fly wherever I choose. The garden, after all, is in the sky, it is a flying garden which makes it an ideal take-off point.

I spread out my hands as if they are wings, then levitate above the bench for a couple of minutes before dashing away—across the sea—to England.

Or to Australia (Tasmania, to be more exact). Or even much closer—to the beautiful Avoca Valley in the Wicklows—less than twenty miles away from my temporary abode in Sandycove, Co. Dublin.

After a year of living in the centre of Dublin, we (my eldest son Mitya and I) moved to Sandycove, a coastal village near Dalkey.

Mitya was hoping that my mood would improve near the sea, but it took longer than we both thought.

Although distance-wise my little ones were now a bit closer to me than when I was in Folkestone, we were in two different countries and between us was the sea. The job for a new Dublin magazine which had invited me to Ireland was no more, and the magazine itself was on its last legs. Mitya was seldom home, and I kept drinking at least a bottle of wine a day.

On the positive side, the contract for a book on Ireland (the publisher approached me after one of my weekly magazine features) was signed, the advance received and it was time to start my research.

My first research journey nearly became my life's last.

In a hired little car I was driving westwards, to County Cork, when near Wexford I suddenly felt dizzy. As they write in bad novels, everything in front of me went black . . . It did . . . And I nearly collided with a huge truck on my right. My side mirror came off with a loud crack . . . I veered left towards the kerb, pressed the brake and briefly fainted.

The truck driver himself took me to the nearest hospital where they tried to measure my blood pressure and were unable to. The upper level was higher than the highest mark on the monitor.

And several days later, a little old Sandycove lady of a GP (I had to pay 50 euros to see her; there's no such thing as free health care in Ireland), having taken her stethoscope off my chest, said:

'You are lucky not to have had a massive heart attack, sorr . . . Do you drink?'

'Yes, but only red wine which is supposed to be good for you,' I replied.

'Sorr, red wine in very small doses may indeed be good for some people, but let me tell you: you are not one of them.'

She added that I had a very clear-cut choice: to keep drinking, smoking and stuffing myself stupid to guarantee my premature demise ('very soon, sorr. . .') or to drastically change my lifestyle.

I was one of the last patients she had received in her long career of a GP: as the following morning she was due to retire.

It was perhaps the finality of her advice or, more likely, the fact that she did give me a choice that made me mobilise all my remaining willpower.

I stopped drinking the same day.

And on that same afternoon (I had seen the GP in the morning) for the first time in many years I did a short taekwondo workout in my bedroom. I'd lost all my form of course: when I was still training I could easily do a hundred press ups and eighty sit ups, now I could hardly manage twenty of each.

I was in the middle of the puffing and huffing session when Mitya popped into my room. Unbeknownst to myself, he had been watching me for some time.

'Are you crazy or what, Dad? Two days after the accident! You are going to kill yourself!'

'I certainly will, son and very soon, if I carry on living the way I did . . .' I muttered through clenched teeth, trying to conceal severe shortness of breath.

From that day on, exercise became my daily routine. Soon I was back to the 40-minute workout of my old taekwondo days.

It was then that I recalled the lessons of Jean and Alex Beaumont and their meditation sessions in Folkestone.

In the nearest Eason bookstore I bought several Glenn Harrold's CDs and added listening to them to my exercise routine: a workout first, then half an hour of meditation and self-hypnosis.

I was looking forward to that moment of the day when I could fly out of my bedroom's open window, whoosh above the promenade and head eastwards, towards London.

A month later, I was fit enough to continue my research .The main new challenge was to abstain from drinking and to keep exercising while on the road. In my luggage I carried a portable CD player, and Glenn Harrold (or rather his voice) became my faithful travel companion.

I frequented hotel gyms instead of hotel bars, and if a hotel had no gym, I did a full workout (stretches, kicks, punches, press ups etc.) in my room. (It was addictive, and Mary, my London taekwondo instructor, would soon start jokingly calling me 'adrenaline junkie').

I washed down my room service meals with tomato juice, not red wine. I was falling asleep to the calming, hypnotic sound of Glenn Harrold's voice.

After three weeks on the road, I collected my first reward.

It was in Belfast. I had spent a disturbing day in the Shankill Road area—talking to people on both sides of the divide which seemed as great as ever.

I left the area with relief and was walking towards my hotel near Queens University along a busy road when a young woman in the crowd looked me straight in the eye and smiled.

Nothing of the kind had happened to me for a long time. No wonder: I was depressed, overweight and looked ten years older than my age.

I can still remember her reassuring face. She had blonde curly hair and was wearing a brown parka.

What was her name? I will never know the answer. Deirdre? Aoiffe? I am inclined to think it was Oonagh.

Oonagh as opposed to ONA!

Her casual smile gave me back my confidence. More than that: it gave me back my life.

From that moment I knew I was ready to return to London.

The research for that particular chapter of *Life as a Literary Device* was nearly over.

Before relocating, I went to London on a recce trip with the aim of renting a flat, or a room, where I could bring my few earthly possession and my books—those that were not stored in Folkestone.

From the book *Secret London* which I was reading on the plane, I learned about the six-thousand square-metre Kensington Roof Gardens on top of the former Derry & Toms department store on Kensington High Street. Laid out by Ralph Hancock in the 1930s, they are divided into three themed parts: a Spanish Alhambra-like garden in a Moorish style, complete with palms, fountains and a chapel; a Tudor-style garden, with archways, secret corners and wisteria; and an English woodland garden, with a stream and pond with ducks and Chilean flamingos whose names are Bill, Ben, Splosh and Pecks.

And here I am in Derry Street, just twenty metres away from the hustle-and-bustle of High Street Kensington, facing an ordinary office entrance with no sign above the door.

I enter a lift and press the 'Up' button. On a small electronic monitor above my head, I can see the floor numbers changing slowly: 1 . . . 2 . . . 3—and with each number I am feeling more and more relaxed.

The lift cabin finally stops and its doors slide apart noiselessly.

I come out and find myself in a beautiful and totally deserted garden.

This is a very large garden and I cannot see all of it at once. The bit that I can see is bathed in sunlight . . . It is a lovely summer day—warm but not uncomfortably hot, just right—and there is a gentle breeze blowing.

All my favourite flowers are there, and I can see colourful butterflies fluttering above them. Bees are darting from one to another collecting the pollen and making a soothing buzzing sound as they do so.

I head for a small pond under a branchy willow tree and instal myself on a bench in the willow's shadow.

A graceful pink flamingo stands on one leg in the middle of the pond, its head buried in its feathers. I wonder whether it is Bill, Ben, Splosh or Pecks. Whatever the name, it looks like a question mark on the margins of my life's main book— *Life as a Literary Device*—the book that is never destined to be completed.

This bench is going to be my new starting point from where I can fly wherever I choose. The garden, after all, is in the sky, it is a flying garden which makes it an ideal take off pad.

The bench is on the same level as the spire of a nearby church. From it I can look down at the London sprawl underneath me without lowering my head.

I need to see this view telling me without a shadow of doubt that I am back in the place where I have always belonged.

I spread out my hands as if they are wings, then levitate above the bench for a couple of minutes before dashing away—across the sea—to Australia (Tasmania, to be more exact).

Or much closer—to Ireland, to Meeting of the Waters in the beautiful Avoca Valley, where two small rivers: the Avonmore and the Avonbeg—merge just twenty miles away from my former coastal abode in Sandycove, Co. Dublin, which I can now begin to miss as the place where my final recovery started.

Meditation becoming Life?

Or is it the other way round?

ONE—I am calm and relaxed . . . calm and relaxed . . . completely relaxed . . . more relaxed than I have ever been . . . Doing fine . . . Going to be alright . . . Going to sleep now . . . Into a deep and dreamy sleep . . .

It is 5 a.m. A crispy summer morning in Letchworth Garden City. I have just left our cottage and—notebook in hand—am walking slowly towards the station to catch the first train to London.

I am carrying my David Lloyd's gym backpack, but on this occasion, instead of towels and swimming trunks, it contains my overnight hospital kit and a book by George Orwell.

I am off on an assignment which involves an operation on my heart, a so-called angioplasty. With a special catheter, Doctor

Foale is going to reach as far as my heart (well, nearly), to unblock a couple of clogged arteries and, if necessary, install a stent or two to keep them (arteries) open.

An unexpected and somewhat risky (a five per cent chance of dying) piece of research that came to replace my pre-planned trip to the Baltics.

Twenty to one . . . The odds are not bad by any standards.

My beautiful town is deserted. Not a living soul is around if you don't count some invisible wood pigeons cooing from the trees—another childhood sound: my native Ukrainian city swarmed with wood pigeons in summer, and half of my so-called 'formative years' passed to the accompaniment of their pitiful monotonous cooing.

We found a badly wounded wood pigeon (its wing was broken—probably by a cat) limping around our garden the other day, while its mate was hovering above desperately, not knowing how to react.

Wood pigeons—just like Upland Geese in the Falklands and many other bird species, yet very much unlike humans—mate for life, or so we are told.

It takes less than five minutes to walk to the station. In fact, it takes under five minutes to walk almost anywhere in Letchworth, with its grid system which keeps shopping, residential and industrial areas in close proximity to each other and yet totally separate. Six leafy streets radiate towards the spacious central square with fountains which I am now crossing.

Lined with Arts & Crafts-style buildings, it always reminds me of Paris, or, more precisely, of the green stretch of Avenue Des Champs Élysées leading to Place de la Concorde.

It is also reminiscent of many other urban spaces in Europe—in Belgium, Holland, Germany and even in my native Kharkov, which boasted Europe's second largest square, unfortunately named after Felix Dzerzhinsky, Lenin's chief executioner, founder of the Gulag and the secret police.

Yet, at the same time, the town centre of Letchworth feels unmistakably countryside-ish, not to say rustic: green lawns, lots of trees, slow pace of life . . . Behind it is the 'Utopian' concept of Ebenezer Howard, a flamboyant revolutionary, a dreamer and a visionary, whose aim was to build an ideal settlement, a so-called Garden City, with the comforts of a town and a countryside lifestyle, as a positive alternative to the slums of post-Victorian London and other major European capitals.

'There are in reality not only, as is so constantly assumed, two alternatives—town life and country life—but a third alternative, in which all the advantages of the most energetic and active town life, with all the beauty and delight of the country may be secured in perfect combination; and the certainty of being able to live this life will be the magnet which will produce the effect for which we are all striving— the spontaneous movement of the people from our crowded cities to the bosom of our kindly mother earth, at once the source of life, of happiness, of wealth, and of power,'

he wrote poetically and prophetically in his ground-breaking book *To-morrow: A Peaceful Path to Real Reform*, first published in 1898 and reprinted four years later—one year before the world's first garden city, Letchworth, came into existence—as *Garden Cities of To-Morrow*.

It is a mystery to me why Ebenezer Howard's ideas were— and still are—branded 'Utopian', for Letchworth remains not only a real but also a fairly 'ideal' place to live.

I do see a meaningful symmetry in the fact that, having spent thirty-five years of my life in the negative Utopia (or Dystopia) of the former Soviet Union, I ended up (accidentally) living in Ebenezer Howard's positive and real Utopia—the world's first and only Garden City that works.

I want to write a book about it one day—an intention which was strengthened recently when I learned that Lenin visited Letchworth in 1907 thus bridging my life's two 'Utopias' into one.

And George Orwell, the creator of world literature's most powerful Dystopia, *Nineteen Eighty-Four*, lived several miles away whereas George Bernard Shaw, the writer famously duped by the Soviet Dystopia's main guardian (Stalin) into believing that it was in fact a Utopia turned reality, spent the last years of his life at a country estate near Welwyn, where Howard's second Garden City which didn't quite work, is now located.

What a wealth of material for a book! And it all rests on the success or failure of the medical procedure I am about to undergo.

I walk past Broadway Hotel, one of the first Arts & Crafts buildings in Letchworth. Its front doors are decorated with a poster advertising 'Elvis Commemorative Night' and featuring an impersonator called (rather wittily and self-deprecatingly) 'Elvis-Shmelvis'.

Squirrels—grey, not black—are crossing empty roads. I am making notes as I walk to the station ready to embark on one of my life's riskiest bits of 'research'.

On the train—among a handful of sleepy red-eyed commuters—I open a letter from a friend which I received only yesterday and didn't have time to read:

'Good luck for tomorrow!! You won't need it, it'll be a
breeze. But don't let too many people know just how easy it
was—they'll all want one and your share of the available
sympathy will be seriously diluted! . . . Remember, string out
the convalescence for as long as you can. Be sincere and above
all, be 'brave'. A little dignified stoicism works wonders. Oh
and yes, some practical advice: for the time being it's probably

best to avoid high-flying unpressurised aircraft and scuba diving below thirty meters. Your doctor probably didn't tell you about that but I'm sure you'd prefer to be fully informed.

So, my dear Vitali, welcome to the community of the fit and the well but please, don't give up all your 'bad' habits. With a little determination and the right attitude, you can still manage to disappoint most of those with 'your best interests at heart'. After all, who wants to live for ever?

Just keep having the checkups, make sure the health insurance is kept up to date and enjoy the hell out of life! If you need some help, my neighbour makes an excellent 60% rakia which he assures me is proof against almost all the diseases known to man so why don't we share a bottle—soon . . .

And many congratulations on your arteriosclerosis! You've worked hard for it and I'm sure you've earned all the benefits it'll bring you. Just imagine, all that time to indulge only yourself. All that attention from concerned friends and relations, not to mention fragrant nurses. All that time to do something self-indulgent and relaxing without having to justify it to yourself or to anyone else! Wow, you lucky man. But of course, Vitali, I know there are risks. Although the angioplasty will be a breeze—all my friends tell me it is, I do hope you'll not have to suffer the post-operative indignity of a 'Cardiac Rehabilitation Programme'. I'm sure you'll soon be approached by someone who'll try to convince you that your heart disease is all your own fault, the product of a dissolute lifestyle but actually, that's bollocks. There's lots of genetics in there too, so if you have to blame anyone, blame Watson and Crick! You'll probably be told that your only hope of salvation (aka, an undignified descent into even more awful diseases of old age) is to devote yourself to their programme of regular exercise, a healthy diet and a stress-free lifestyle. Please, take my advice. Resist them with all the determination and bloody-mindedness you can summon up. Just have the operation, make sure you have regular checkups in the future and enjoy the hell out of life. Trust me, it's the best option.'

Good old Matthew.

The train gets delayed at Potters Bar where I nearly bought a house ten years ago. The survey showed that it had considerable subsidence, and the purchase didn't go ahead as a result.

My new mobile phone, a present from the Loved One, suddenly comes to life with a jerk. It's a text message from my American friend Tom who has been going through a hard patch of late:

'Dear Vitali, thank you for your support and friendship—I continue to learn from you, recall the bravery and perserverance you showed and often reference this to myself . . .'

Timely, even if somewhat obituary-like.

I get a glimpse of Ally Pally (as the locals refer to Alexandra Palace), with a TV mast on top like a large crucifix without Christ, as the train rattles along the 'Alexandra Palace' platform.

When we lived in Muswell Hill, I used to bring little Andrei, Anya and Alina there to watch the trains. They were sitting in pushchairs, their soft hair ruffled by the wind of the passing trains.

We used to particularly look forward to a navy-blue 'Flying Scotsman' express to Edinburgh or Glasgow: it was the fastest and it stirred up the strongest wind which made me grab the pushchair handle tightly lest it should be blown onto the track. Little did we know that soon we were all going to end up there— to where the 'Flying Scotsman' was 'flying' so fast: I—for a couple of miserable years, my kids—for much, much longer.

A sudden disturbing thought: am I trying to construct this train journey as the last flashback to my past?

The closer the train comes to London, the slower its progress. I am worried about being late, although in this case, I probably shouldn't be.

I know that London will help me again—as it always has done.

Before entering the hospital I smoke my life's very last cigarette.

In my room with the view of a brick wall I change into a hospital dressing gown which makes you look submissive, vulnerable and slightly ridiculous.

A nurse says I have to wait.

I lie down on my hospital bed and close my eyes.

I still have time for at least one quick meditation—a flight towards the past or, possibly, the future . . .

One late November evening I drive the Loved One to the tiny Hertfordshire village of Clothall where we are hoping to attend 'Lighting the Path—a Candlelit Service for Advent' according to a brochure we picked up at Wallington parish church. I've never attended a 'candlelit service' before, nor has she.

We leave Letchworth an hour before the service scheduled to start for 6 p.m. It is already dark and extremely foggy. As we leave Baldock and hit a country road, the mist becomes truly impenetrable: I cannot even discern my own screen wipers. The beam lights do not help, on the contrary: they make the surroundings look like a thick milky porridge.

We progress at a snail's pace. The small road sign for Clothall that we had spotted the other day is nowhere to be seen. I am thinking of aborting our journey (like my American book?) and going back to Letchworth—a task no less difficult than that of finding Clothall.

We end up in a different village and realise we have driven through Clothall without noticing it.

I put the car into reverse and we crawl back along the same road until we hear the muffled sound of church bells. It is nearly six o'clock. We climb out of the car and nearly bump into another couple who have just materialised out of the mist.

'How do we find St Mary's Church?' I ask them.

'Follow the church bells,' they reply before getting dissolved in the mist without a trace—like two sugar lumps in the cup of boiling-hot porridge.

We follow their advice and walk towards the sound of the bells hand in hand.

The sound is getting slightly louder, yet neither the church nor even the road (or path) we are treading can be made out in the fog. We cannot even see our own boots and are moving forward purely on instinct.

'Let's go back,' says the Loved One.

But the notions of 'back' and 'front' as well as those of 'backwards' and 'forwards' have largely lost their meaning.

We bypass a tall shadow of something that looks like a tree, although it could just as well be a bush, a hedge or even a house, and . . . suddenly we freeze.

In front of us is a wide path going upwards and lined on both sides with burning candles.

At the end of the path—on top of a small invisible hill—we see the brightly lit facade of an old country church.

With darkness underneath, it appears that the church is hanging in the air—between the sky and the earth.

It is the most breathtaking, the most divine sight I have ever feasted my eyes upon.

For a minute or so we stand there, mesmerised, staring at the two rows of candles, making the path they light up so inviting, and at the flying old church above our heads.

Then, with our hands joined together—like two small rivers at Meeting of the Waters in the beautiful Avoca Valley—we start slowly walking up the candle-lit path, towards the sky . . .

'"Let's go back," my wife managed to say, having become completely transparent, diffuse and motionless, like a dream or rather like the memory of a dream. Melting and losing substance before my eyes, she pressed up against my shoulder and I realised that we would not be going back anywhere, because I could not remember the name of that evergreen plant which was covered in the middle of winter with very bright rosy flowers. Only that name could save us. Beyond the grey shroud of the sky, flying into the vastness of the world, silently raging and licking the universe on all sides, was an eerie flame of decaying matter, invisible, intangible, cold and at the same time spreading the sharp unpleasant fresh smell of rust, the smell of oxygen which, it turns out, I had been breathing for some time through rubber tubes inserted deep into my nostrils. I could hear the oxygen bubbles whispering through the gauze over my lips, and I realised fairly clearly that I was no longer asleep but that I was lying in a high surgical bed in my ward, that the black blood dripping into the bottle was my own blood, that outside, under the window, the garden of my heart was in flower, that the slit-eyed anesthetist had not forgotten to wake me up, that man cannot die until he had been born, nor be born without having died . . .'[17]

Thanks, Valentin Petrovich Kataev, for talking to me from wherever you are. And long live mauvism!

17 from The Holy Well.

. . . I open my eyes. It feels as if only seconds have passed since I was shown two little stents inside my arteries on a monitor above the operating table.

My first thought is whether I am now going to beep each time I am subjected to airport security checks.

Somewhere from above, I hear Doctor Foale's voice.

'Finished,' he says. 'You are a very lucky boy . . .'

1996-2009

Melbourne—London—New York—Edinburgh—Folkestone—Dublin—Sandycove—London—Letchworth Garden City

A Note of Thanks

Vitali Vitaliev and Beautiful Books Ltd. are grateful to *the Guardian, the European, the Herald, the Daily/Sunday Telegraph, the Canberra Times, the Age, the Independent, Village Weekly,* and *E&T magazine.*

**Beautiful
Books**